THE EPIC OF
MARINDEL

Book I

CHOSEN

Nathan Keys

The Epic of Marindel: Chosen
By Nathan Keys
Second Edition
Copyright © 2020

Printed in the USA
All rights reserved

ISBN (softcover): 978-1-7331164-0-4
ISBN (hardcover): 978-1-7331164-1-1
ISBN (ebook): 978-1-7331164-2-8
Library of Congress Control Number: 2020923795

Editor: Zannie Carlson
Cover Designer: Sharon Marta
Turtle&Crown Designer: Michelle Keyser
Map Designer: Michelle Keyser

Table of Contents

Pronunciation Guide

Abdeel: AB-deel
Abysso: uh-BISS-oh
Antoine: AN-twon
Armavir: AR-muh-veer
Armaviran: AR-muh-VEER-in
Auben: AH-ben
Bothnia: BOTH-nee-uh
Bothnian: BOTH-nee-in
Château Pierre: SHAH-tow-pee-YEHR
Dantoneia: DAN-tuh-NAY-uh
Eisenstadt: AI-zen-stat
Galyyr: guh-LEER
Galyyrim: guh-LEER-im
Heiban: HAY-ban
Ibadan: AI-buh-dan
Ibadanian: AI-buh-DAY-nee-in
Ibara: ai-BAR-uh
Izendor: IH-zen-dor
Izendoran: ih-ZEN-dor-in
Jaedis: JAY-diss
Jinshi: JIN-shee
Khai: KAI
Kaya: KAI-uh
Kaze: KAH-zay
Kharduman: KAR-doo-mahn
Kindar: KIHN-dar
Kirdaq: KER-dak
Königheim: KOH-nig-haim
Kurai: ker-RAI
Lukúba: loo-KOO-buh
Nebioth: NEH-bee-oth
Manas'ruh: MAN-us-RUH

Marindel: MEHR-in-del
Marindelian: MEHR-in-DEL-ee-in
Meiling: may-LEENG
Meiro: MAY-row
Misham: MEE-sham
Murumbwé: moo-room-BWAY
Murumbwéan: moo-room-BWAY-in
Nox Abyssae: NOX-uh-BISS-ay
Pythoria: pie-THOR-ee-uh
Pythorian: pie-THOR-ee-in
Qodesh: KOH-desh
Rhema: RAY-muh
Rheman: RAY-min
Shaama: SHAH-muh
Solvys: SAHL-viss
Sunophsian: soo-NOFF-shin
Sunophsis: soo-NOFF-siss
Tarento: tuh-REN-toh
Tethys: TETH-iss
Tethysian: teh-THEE-zhin, or teh-THISS-yin
Tyrizah: TEER-ih-zuh (second syllable almost silent)
Verdanelle: VER-duh-nell
Verdyth: VER-dith
Zetsumei: ZET-soo-may
Zhemushi: JEH-moo-shee

Timeline

TIME WITHIN THE realm of Tyrizah is measured using the Imperial Calendar. It was set as the realm standard by the first emperor of the Tethysian Empire in the year 0 IE, the start of the Imperial Era. All years prior were labelled BIE (Before the Imperial Era), counting backward. The Imperial Era lasted for 234 years. After the fall of the Tethysian Empire, the calendar was reset to 0 AIE (After the Imperial Era), counting forward.

The Imperial Calendar is seasonal, with the spring equinox marking the first day of the year. Each year has four "months," marked by a solstice or equinox. The season and year is indicated in every chapter heading and at every time-skipping scene change.

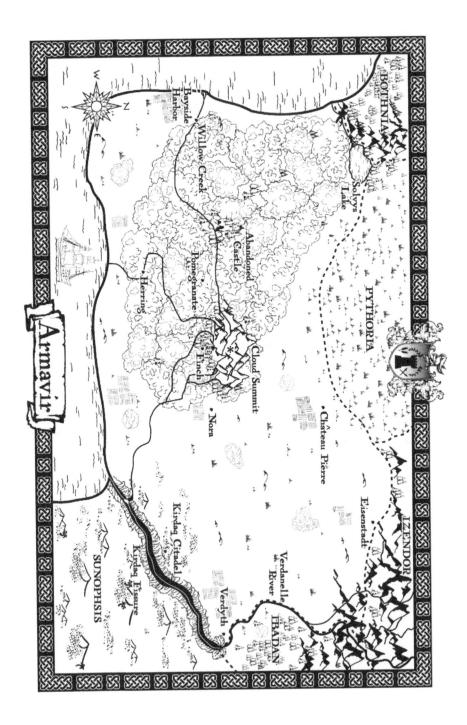

Magic

ELEMENTAL MAGIC WITHIN the realm of Tyrizah is made possible by an ethereal substance called L'Esenzi, which naturally occurs in varying amounts within the earth, seas, and living creatures of the realm. It adheres to natural laws and boundaries that can be considered a form of science. Elemental magic can be used for good or evil. Some kingdoms are accepting of the use of magic in daily life, while others are not.

Marindelian magic, from the realm of Qodesh, is "good" or "light" magic. Only Galyyrim and followers of the Great King (after the Great Story) are able to use it. Marindelian magic sometimes adheres to the laws governing elemental magic, but not always. It is the most unpredictable form of magic—but those who commit themselves to knowing the Great King are permitted to discover its secrets.

Bygone magic, from the realm of Tyrizah before the coming of Marindel, is "evil" or "dark" magic. It is superior in strength to elemental magic, but *always* inferior to Marindelian magic. Bygone magic users thrive on deception, counterfeit, and intimidation to appear more powerful than they really are.

The use of magic in The Epic of Marindel is not meant in any way to endorse or encourage the use of magic in the real world.

0
The Hunted

Summary, 1419 AIE

A BLAST OF THUNDER resounds overhead.

The woman awakes with a jolt.

The thick boughs of the tree beneath her sway in the strengthening wind. The leaves of the canopy rustle above, whispering of the terrors to come.

She sits up, and the sound of distant howling catches her attention. "Not again," she moans with a sigh.

For almost a year, she had lived with relative peace and isolation in the wilderness of western Armavir. But she knew all too well it was only a matter of time before someone found her again.

It looks like that day has come.

The woman scrambles down the tree with nimble expertise. Landing with a thump on the leaf-laden turf, she races toward a sheltered thicket, where a chestnut horse awaits.

The animal snorts at her arrival, pawing the ground and flicking its ears as a thunderclap shakes the air.

"They're coming for us," the woman says as she tightens the horse's saddle. "It's time to move on."

The horse responds with an anxious whinny, tossing its head about and tugging on a rope that tethers it to a gnarled stump in the thicket.

"Easy, there." She undoes the rope from the horse's bridle and slings herself upon its back. She slides a hood over her head to conceal her golden curls and facial features. Then she urges her steed forward with a shout, "H'ya!"

The horse takes off in a flurry of hooves, leaves, and dirt. It navigates the storming forest with masterful confidence.

Rain begins to fall in torrents, and lightning flickers across the sky. The howling is heard, coming closer, above the din of the storm.

The woman looks back and sees an eerie, green glow far behind in the woods. They're in pursuit. With a frown and an extra kick she goads the horse, "Quickly, to the countryside! I know a place where they won't be able to get us."

1
Storm
Summer, 1419 AIE

~Connor~

I REMEMBER WHEN I used to visit the old countryside tavern. It was an exciting place, especially during the summer. Fishermen, local farmers, and travelers from kingdoms near and far would pass through on their way to do business with the inland cities of Armavir, and they'd bring a myriad of stories to tell. When I wasn't busy helping my father on the farm or getting into mischief with my friends, I was at the tavern talking to strangers and hearing their stories. Some were ordinary; and others, not so much. I liked the latter much better.

I was only a child then. Now, at the age of twenty, I have a few stories of my own to share. Not mine personally, of course—I've never been further than Bayside Harbor, a port town three miles west of the homestead—but mine in that I remember them from my childhood. I remember all of my favorite stories, most of which tell of legendary quests, noble kingdoms, and thrilling struggles between good and evil, all with dynamic plot twists.

I wouldn't mind visiting the tavern again to share some of those stories. I smile at the thought. Things are getting *extremely* boring around here. What better way is there to spice up a bland summer than by engaging the imagination with some good storytelling? If only I weren't—

"Connor! Quit standin' around!" my father barks from across the field.

"Sorry!" I reply, sighing deeply as I take up the shovel I'd been leaning on and resume digging.

I'm a full-time worker on my father's homestead now. I don't get paid, but at least I have a place to stay and three good-enough meals every day. We aren't usually too busy during the summer, but this time it's different. My father wants to build a stone wall along the side of our field that borders the main road to prevent foraging animals and shady characters from trespassing and trampling the grain.

Yup, that's all the action we get around here.

Within the next few days, we'll finish digging a trench along the border where we can lay a firm foundation. From there, my father and I will have to work extra hard to complete the project by harvest. If we don't, higher-priority farming obligations and moons of unfavorable weather will require us to postpone it until late spring of next year.

In that case, we'll be stuck for half a year with an unfinished stone wall, and everyone who passes the homestead will shake their heads with disappointment, thinking us to be lazy oafs.

I shake the negative thoughts out of my head. My father and I are *not* going to be thought of as lazy oafs, because we're going to conquer this project and conquer it well!

After taking a pause to wipe the sweat off my brow, I plunge my shovel into the ground, scoop up the moist dirt, and toss it to the side.

I do it again, and again, and again.

Once we're finish digging, we'll need stone for the wall. That means my father'll send me to Bayside Harbor to find a stonemason.

I perk with excitement at the idea.

Tethysian stonemasons often pass through coastal cities, selling their services and wares. Even if we can't afford their stone, I'll still have an opportunity to glean a few stories. The Tethys Region is much more interesting than Armavir, the kingdom my father and I live in. It's a vast collection of islands west of Bayside Harbor, the closest of which is a five-day nautical journey. Almost every Tethysian I've talked to has a story about some kind of dragon or giant squid or pirate battle.

Even more interesting are stories from the kingdom of Felidae, a distant island known for might in battle and technological ingenuity. The people of Felidae are fierce and disciplined in their martial arts because the land is dangerous; crawling with monsters and horrible creatures.

Chapter 1: Storm

Twice, maybe three times in my life, I've met an adventurer from Murumbwé, a mysterious kingdom south of the Tethys Region and very far from here. The dark-skinned adventurers from Murumbwé are some of the most impressive people I've ever met.

I notice that, in my daydreaming, I've stopped digging. I glance anxiously at my father to see he hasn't yet noticed, and with a sigh of relief, I resume my work. I can't let my thoughts wander; when my mind is in the clouds, I lose touch with reality. That's what my father always says.

Just then, at the sound of distant thunder, I pause again. Looking east down the road, I see billowing thunderheads looming over the woods, obscuring the wilderness beyond. They're approaching fast.

"Storm's coming," my father says. "A big one, by the looks of it. No sense in digging anymore. Those rains will destroy the progress we've made so far, and then some."

I frown, pondering my father's words. I wish I could dismiss his comment as mere cynicism, but I know he's telling the truth.

I've always been able to tell when my father is lying, or even just exaggerating. It drives him crazy! It would take a ridiculous amount of rain to destroy our trench, so I could try to be optimistic. But today, the inner voice that catches my old man's fibs is silent. That storm is something else, and both of us know it.

I throw my arms up and groan, "Well, isn't this just great? Now our hard work has gone to waste, and we'll have to start all over again next year!"

"Don't worry about it, son," my father says, barely masking his own disappointment. "The titans of the realm will have their way with us no matter what we have to say about it."

"If only it wasn't so," I mutter as I take up my shovel and walk toward my father.

A rolling thunderclap shakes the countryside. The air grows heavier by the second, and my hair stands on end with increasing anticipation. I watch the advancing clouds as pricks of lightning dance about within the looming abyss.

"Odd storm, this one is," my father says as I come alongside him. "Quick, let's get inside."

We walk down a small dirt path between vast swaths of growing barley on our way to the modest farmhouse in the center of the property.

A moment passes before my father puts his arm around my shoulders and says, "Connor, will you do me a favor?"

"Sure. What is it?"

He looks both ways as if he's about to tell me a secret. My interest is piqued, and I lean in closer. After another booming thunderclap he says, "I just remembered we've run out of beer. I need you to run to the tavern and get me a bottle for tonight."

Are you kidding me?

I feint a cough to prevent the scathing words from escaping my mouth. "Sure, but why *now*?"

He pulls out a few bronze kappes and hands them to me. "Because I'm thirsty. Go on! Get!" He begins shooing me off.

"Whoa, hang on! Let me grab a coat first, and I'll be on my way."

My father's reply is obscured by the loudest thunderclap yet, but I don't stick around for a repeat. I run into the house and take a brown leather coat from the rack by the door. It has a voluminous hood and covers down to the knees; perfect for getting caught in a downpour. As I exit the house and run back to my father, I ask, "Anything in particular?"

My father looks at me with a sparkle in his russet-brown eyes. "Ginger Tethysian brew! No exceptions!"

"Got it." Of course, I should have known. "Say, you don't think Brono has any Tethysian brew, do you?" If our neighbor across the road has my father's favorite beer, I can satisfy him without running all the way to the tavern and back.

My father's face wrinkles with displeasure. "Not a chance. That man only drinks soft lager! You know how I feel about soft lager! Off with you!"

"All right, all right!" I take off running without further argument. As ridiculous as my father's request seems, I'm relieved to be doing something more interesting than shoveling dirt.

I reach the main road and turn westward. I have my back to the approaching storm as it blots out the sun and blankets the countryside in darkness.

I can't help but smirk. Racing a thunderstorm to the tavern and back *could* make for an interesting story. I'd have to exaggerate a few details to keep the audience captivated, but that's not a problem. I could say the thunderstorm was sent by an evil sorcerer to destroy Bayside Harbor, and I was in a race against time to find the only thing that could possibly save the day. A bottle of beer? No, that'll never do. I'll say it was an elixir made of blue elderflower and mermaid tears. Then, when I finally defeated the evil bartender... or ogre...yes, I'll make him an ogre. When I finally defeated the evil ogre, I took the elixir as my prize, went outside to face the storm

6

of the sorcerer, and I saved the day! ...Eh, forget it. No one would believe that.

A gust of wind buffets me from behind, and I stumble. Still keeping my pace, I notice how much the storm has picked up since I left the homestead. Dark clouds cover the sky. The winds are kicking up dust from the road and sending ripples across the tall grass on either side. The blasting thunder and searing bolts of lightning have become more frequent; they rage overhead like celestial beings locked in an epic struggle for the fate of the realm.

I see the familiar shape of the tavern in the distance. It sits on the crossroads of two major trade routes, bringing in business from all kinds of crazy places. Not to mention the stories. Oh, the stories...

Snap out of it, Connor. Focus. You're almost there.

Other travelers are arriving at the tavern as well, no doubt to find shelter from the storm. Some are clinging to their belongings as the wind threatens to carry them away, while others are struggling to secure their skittish horses in the stable nearby. My mind throbs with curiosity. Where do these people come from? What are their stories? If only I had time to stick around and ask! I clear my mind as I approach the tavern and enter the old stone building.

The place is packed. The smell slaps me in the face as I step through the doorway: a blend of spilt beer and wet dog. As I navigate through the bustling seating area, I realize I can hardly hear any one conversation because the din of the tavern is so chaotic.

Arriving at the bar, I flag down the bartender. "I'll have a bottle of ginger Tethysian brew."

The bartender shrugs. "I'm sorry, brother. We ran out of bottled brews earlier this afternoon. We have a few kegs in the back if you'd like that instead. We're expecting a shipment to come this evening, but it might be delayed by the storm."

The plot thickens!

For anyone else, I'd simply order a different kind of beer, but my father said "no exceptions." That means he won't settle for any other drink I bring him. Wincing at the idea of enduring his disappointment, I ask, "How much for a keg?"

"Two blics."

"Blimey," I mutter. My father only gave me a few bronze kappes; not nearly enough to equal even one silver blic.

The sound of heavy rain on the tavern roof catches my attention. I look out the nearest window with a frown as the deluge pelts against the panes of glass in wind-blown spurts. So much for beating the storm; I suppose I ought to head home now. I tell the bartender, "I'll come back tomorrow morning."

As I head for the exit, the bartender calls, "Brother, wait! You're not going out there *now*, are you?"

"I brought a coat for a reason," I reply, slipping the hood over my head.

"What's the rush? It's raining skunks and rabbits out there. Why don't you wait out the storm here?"

I turn to argue with him, but a thought causes me to pause. If I stay at the tavern during the storm, I can talk to people. If I can talk to people, I can ask them about their stories. If I get even one good story, it'll be well worth waiting out the storm. Maybe it'll keep me here long enough to catch the new shipment of ginger Tethysian brew, and when I get home I'll tell my father I waited patiently for his beer to arrive and that's why I took so long to return. It's ingenious. A smile spreads across my face as I think about it.

"Why are you looking at me like that?"

I realize I had been staring at the bartender while the ingenious plan hatched in my head. "Oh, sorry. Yes, I'll stay here. Thanks for the advice."

"No problem, brother. Let me know if I can get you anything else."

"Thank you," I nod before turning away from the bar. There are people and conversations everywhere, and it's mildly overwhelming. As I navigate through the seating area, my ears are alert for any interesting conversation. My eyes are on the lookout too; I know what travelers with interesting stories look like. Usually, the stranger-looking the better. If they're foreign or shady, they probably have something decent. If they carry exotic weapons, even more so. But the real targets are the old geezers. Not only do they have a treasure trove of stories to tell, but they're also the easiest to convince to talk about them. In fact, it's hard to get them to stop.

Across the room, I arrive at a two-seater table. Wanting to claim the spot before someone else does, I take a seat and continue to observe my surroundings. A conversation behind me catches my attention: two burly men wearing leather and chain mail outfits. Local market guards, perhaps. They *might* have interesting stories.

A man with a thick mustache is speaking. "...And then, when there was only one goblin left, I cornered it against a crop of boulders."

"Whoa! And then?" the other man asks.

"I pointed my weapon at it and said, 'Surrender, goblin fiend! You and your scavenging vermin have been defeated!'"

"Yeah? What'd it do?"

"It pointed its chin at me with a scowl, and it called me a fool!"

I listen to the story with increasing intrigue. If I find it exciting enough, I'll turn and join the conversation.

The mustachioed man continues, "After I kicked it down, it began cursing and saying its master was a fire witch, and she would seek vengeance on me for attacking his tribe!"

"Hoho, that's some big talk for a little goblin!"

"Aye, it is, and that's why I tied it to a tree and said, 'If your master is a fire witch, call for her to come to your aid!'"

"Whoa! And then?"

"It screamed and *screamed*, and nothing happened!"

While the men roar with laughter, someone tugs on my coat. I look aside to see a little boy. He says, "Sir, you look lonely."

"Huh? I'm not lonely," I scoff. The men's conversation was just getting interesting. I've heard very captivating stories about fire witches before. Their magic is *so* powerful, it's on par with dragonfire! But now I won't ever find out if a fire witch showed up to protect the goblin because this boy is asking if I'm lonely.

And he's still standing there.

I sigh, setting aside my own impatience, and say, "If *you're* lonely, you can sit at the table with me."

"Hmm, yeah." The boy hobbles into the chair at the opposite end of the table.

"Are you here by yourself?" I ask.

"Nope. I have my friends with me."

Another boy and a girl emerge from the packed seating area to stand near the boy. All three look to be around ten years of age. Huh. What are three children doing in a tavern on a stormy late afternoon like this? Tilting my head, I ask, "Is there something you're after?"

"You look a little shady," the first boy says.

"What? *Shady?*" I'm taken aback. My brown hair is of moderate length and decently kept, and my facial stubble is far from imposing. As far as size goes, I'm on the leaner side compared to most others in the tavern.

"You're wearing a hood," the girl says.

"And you're in a corner by yourself," the second boy adds.

"Yes, that's right," I nod. "But that doesn't mean—"

"And you were listening to those guys behind you," the first boy says.

"Er, no I wasn't," I lie.

The girl pouts and says to the first boy. "You know, I don't think he's got any."

"Got any what?" I ask suspiciously. Are they looking for money? Treats of some sort? Why would I give them anything of mine?

"Stories," the girl replies. "Devin said you look like you have some really cool stories. But I think you're a phony."

I gasp. These kids are looking for stories, just like I used to when I was young! I can't pass up this opportunity! "Hey, hold on! I have plenty of stories!"

"You do?" the first boy, Devin, cracks a jovial smile. "I knew it all along! See, Carmi? I told you! Shady people always have the *best* stories!"

"Prove it." Carmi sticks her tongue out at Devin.

Oh, they want a *good* story, do they? Challenge accepted. I search my memory bank for a story to fit their requests, and sure enough, I think I know just the thing. "All right, kids. I'll give you a *really* good story. But first, let's get you two a couple of chairs."

It takes a few minutes to help the kids get settled, but soon we're all gathered around the small table. I straighten my posture and clear my throat before introducing myself. "My name is Connor, your storyteller for the night. Your names are Devin, Carmi, and...?" I had nodded at each of the kids upon mention, and now I wait for the second boy whose name I haven't heard.

"Peter," he says.

"Peter, yes. Now," I lean in and speak expressively, "The story I have for you today is one of my all-time favorites. I was only a little older than you three when I heard it told in this very tavern."

"Oh, boy!" Devin wriggles in his seat.

With my audience already captivated, I smile and jump right in.

2
The Princess of the Sea
~1700 BIE

L ONG AGO DURING the Era of Peace, there was a great city unlike any other. Unmatched in splendor and power, it truly was the crown jewel of the realm. It belonged not to any kingdom, for it was never on land. It appeared here, it appeared there; no one knew where it would be next. How is that possible, you might ask? Many find it hard to believe, but this majestic city rode on the back of a giant sea turtle!

The city was called Marindel, and it was home to a thriving race of elves who lived under the governance of the Galyyrim of the Sea. Each of the Galyyrim elves possessed tremendous wisdom and magical abilities, enabling them to command the very seas they dwelled in, along with every living thing in the depths.

The sovereign ruler of Marindel, the head of the Galyyrim, and the oldest, wisest, and most powerful of them all, was called the Great King of the Sea. Together with the citizens of Marindel, he sought to ensure peace, justice, and harmony for the entire realm of Tyrizah—not only for elves and sea creatures, but for every living thing. The Era of Peace was established as the fruit of their efforts. Not a single monster or any creature of darkness was found in any kingdom of the realm at that time.

But one day, everything changed.

The Great King frequently traveled to other kingdoms to settle important political matters. A very patient man, he always traveled on foot to enjoy the fresh air and scenery. He was never in a hurry, and it was his joyful habit to stop in the villages along the way. Royal and powerful though he was, he never considered himself too lofty to spend time with the common people. He truly cared about them and sought to promote their welfare.

As the Great King was returning from an errand one fateful day, he and his entourage passed an abandoned shed on the roadside. As they drew near, they could hear a muffled infant's cry coming from within.

The Great King stopped and listened for a moment before ordering the captain of the guard, "Search the shed and bring me what you find."

"Right away, sire." The captain opened the door of the shed and disappeared inside. A moment later, he emerged holding a small baby, which he presented to the King.

The baby was human, a little girl no older than a moon. Her feeble cries and thin frame betrayed her weak and malnourished state. She was covered in dirt and had no swaddling clothes of any kind.

When the Great King took the baby and realized her terrible condition, he had compassion on her. Taking a white towel out of his bag, he wrapped her snugly in it and held her close to his chest. He rocked her slowly while gently stroking her head, and she began to calm down.

"Shall I search for the baby's parents, Your Majesty? Perhaps they are still somewhere nearby."

"No one who leaves their child in a shed has any intention of coming back for her," the Great King replied. "This little one has been abandoned for hours, or perhaps longer. She is in need of immediate care."

"Understood. Shall we press on to the next village, then?"

The Great King was silent. He smiled lovingly at the baby, who had stopped crying and was now looking up at him with curious brown eyes.

"From now on," the King whispered to her, "You will be called Melody, the daughter of the Great King of the Sea. An heir to the throne of Marindel."

Those in the King's entourage were shocked beyond words. How could the King pick up a newborn baby on the road—a human one, at that—and adopt her into the Galyyrim? A human had never stepped foot in Marindel before, let alone ruled it. They didn't understand the King's motives, so they tried to convince him to drop her off at the nearest village to be cared for by a human mother. However, the Great King insisted this girl was no ordinary human. He saw something special in her, something no one else had seen. For that reason alone, he gave her a name and adopted her into his family.

"The times are changing," the Great King said. "There will come a day when humans, elves, and sentient creatures from every kingdom in Tyrizah will live in Marindel side-by-side. I have chosen this little one to be the first."

"But what of your son, Prince Eli?" the captain asked. "Will he not succeed you as the King of Marindel?"

"He will indeed." The King's gaze was firm. "And she will rule beside him as the Princess of the Sea."

No one among the elves understood what the Great King had in mind, but they marveled at his words and returned to Marindel without any further quarrel.

Now, the Galyyrim were able to breathe underwater using their magic, but the other elves could not. Whenever the giant turtle traveled underwater, the Galyyrim created an air bubble around the city. Aside from special occasions, Marindel remained dry whether the turtle was deep beneath the sea or floating on the surface. Because of this, it wasn't hard to bring Melody into the life of the semi-aquatic kingdom.

Melody lived in the royal palace, where she grew to be an inquisitive, adventurous, and spirited girl whose beauty was noticed by all. The Galyyrim loved her and treated her as one of their own, and though the citizens of Marindel took some time to get used to the presence of a human girl in the city, they also came to love and accept her. She fit in so well that, in most cases, it was easy to forget Melody was human.

The biggest exception, however, was the physical aging difference between Melody and the elves. While the human lifespan was around eighty years, the elven lifespan was closer to two thousand, and the Galyyrim lived even longer than that. As time passed, Melody grew just like all human children do, but the elves hardly aged at all.

As part of his promise to adopt her into his family, the Great King voiced his intention to one day grant Melody the authority and inheritance of a Princess of the Sea, which included the magical powers wielded by the Galyyrim. Melody eagerly anticipated the day she would be deemed ready to receive her inheritance. The big event finally arrived when she was twelve years of age.

"Hold still, dear, I'm still fixing your hair!" A nursemaid fumbled anxiously with Melody's thick blond curls.

Melody stood in front of a mirror, vibrating with excitement. She was wearing a white dress that shimmered like sunlit marble. Her hair was tied in a neat bun with few small curls hanging down in front of her ears. She shifted her feet impatiently. "It looks fine to me. Come on, I don't want to be late!"

"Ah, there!" The nursemaid stepped back. "Look how beautiful you are."

Melody had run away before the nursemaid said, "Look." She scampered down the palace halls toward the throne room of the Great King. Marindel was underwater, so the sunlight cast deep blue rays through the vaulted windows, accompanied by the shimmering patterns of reflected water. The palace interior was dazzling on its own, but the dancing hues of blue cast by water overhead amplified its beauty beyond comparison. There was nothing else like it in any kingdom above the sea.

Melody arrived at the throne room, panting for breath. The Great King was seated on a grand central throne atop a wide flight of steps, and Prince Eli was seated at his right hand. Although Eli appeared to be the same age as Melody, he was actually much older. Despite their age difference, Melody considered Eli to be her brother and closest friend. At her arrival, the Prince smiled warmly.

Glancing around the enormous room, Melody noticed none of her other family members were present. She approached the King and said, "Here I am. I didn't miss it, did I?"

"Of course not, little one. There would be no ceremony without you."

"No one else is coming?" Melody frowned. She wanted all her friends and family to see her on her special day.

The King smiled.

Suddenly, the Galyyrim appeared in a brilliant flash all around her, dancing and blowing horns and throwing confetti. They shouted in unison, "Surprise! Hail Melody, Princess of Marindel!"

After the initial shock, Melody shrieked gleefully and joined her family in the merriment. Melody was almost as spirited a dancer as they were.

The celebration continued until the Great King stood. The company of magical elves fell silent, and Melody held her breath.

The King grinned proudly as he descended the steps toward the assembly. "Let us begin, shall we?"

Eli, beaming, followed closely behind his father.

The King said, "This is a very special day, both for my daughter, Melody, and for the Kingdom of Marindel. Never before has a human been grafted into the Galyyrim, nor has our magic been given to any creature, except through the royal bloodline. Today, both of these things will take place." At the foot of the steps, he knelt on one knee. "Melody, come to me."

Melody ran to the Great King and gave him a flying hug. "I love you, Daddy!"

"I love you too, little one." The King smiled and held Melody for a moment. He put his strong, gentle hands on her shoulders and looked into her eyes. "Are you prepared to serve Marindel to the best of your ability, no matter the cost?"

"Yes!" Melody's eyes glowed.

"Are you willing to endure the time and training required to master your magical abilities, and use them to bring forth life for the common good?"

"Yes!"

"Are you willing to take up your position within the Galyyrim with honor and respect?"

"Yes!"

"Lastly, Melody...when you come of age, will you take your place as the Princess of the Sea in marriage to my son Eli, the Prince of the Sea?"

The final question caught Melody off guard. She glanced for a second at Eli, whose excitement could be felt, but she avoided eye contact. Eli was nice, but Melody had no desire to be married to anyone yet, least of all someone she thought of as a brother. But she really wanted her powers and to become a princess, so she decided to say 'yes' and think about the consequences later.

"Yes!"

The King's face glowed with a father's pride as he reached inside his coat pocket and pulled out a plain silver amulet. "Hold this tightly and close your eyes."

Melody squealed as she took it with both hands and squeezed her eyes shut.

The Great King moved his hands around hers, close but never touching, fluid like the ocean waves. As he drew his hands apart, tendrils of silver energy swirled around Melody's hands, causing the amulet to glow. It became brighter and brighter, until a brilliant burst of blue light was emitted, and the amulet absorbed all of the silver energy strands that had been moving around it.

"Open your eyes," the Great King said, "and look at the amulet."

Melody gasped. A beautiful glowing gemstone now adorned the amulet. It must have contained every known color in the realm. "It's beautiful!"

"It was formed using your signature energy," the Great King explained. "As long as you wear the amulet, you will be able to use magic. No one can take it from you and use its power unless you surrender it to them. It's all yours."

Melody put the amulet around her neck. She expected to feel a surge of energy or an electrical sensation, but she didn't feel any different. "Now what?"

The Great King pulled out a small pot containing a dead plant. The leaves were brittle and the stem was darkened and hard. "Reach out your hand and touch the plant. Imagine you can feel energy flowing from the center of your being, down your arm, and into the plant."

Melody took a deep breath and did so. She felt a slight buzzing in her fingers as the plant returned to life from the roots up. Her eyes widened. "Daddy, look! I'm doing it!"

The Great King chuckled. "Of course, you are! Now, use your hand to guide the growth of the plant. Imagine you're sculpting clay. See in your mind how you want the plant to grow, and let it follow the flow of your hand."

Melody thought for a moment, and then she brought her hand up in a spiral. The plant regained the rest of its life and continued to grow, following the path Melody set for it. The Galyyrim whooped and cheered at the sight.

"Wow!" Melody beamed. "This is great! I *love* making plants grow. Can I do another? Please, please, please!?"

"You can beautify the halls of the palace, if you'd like," the King said. "The pots out there haven't been cared for in quite a while. One might say we were saving the task for a creative little princess like you." He gave her a wink.

"Yes! Thank you, Daddy!" Melody turned to exit the room, but the King called, "Hold on, little one. There's one more thing I'd like to ask."

"Yes?" Melody looked back at her father. She was so excited about bringing plants to life and helping them grow, that she couldn't imagine anything more wonderful.

"Since the day I brought you here, we've been unable to flood the palace like we used to. It was a necessary sacrifice, because you couldn't breathe underwater before." He paused. The twinkle in his eye said it all before he even spoke. "Now that you have the amulet, you can enjoy the flooded palace with us. What do you say?"

Melody's eyes sparkled. Eli had told her many stories about the flooded palace.

Whenever the Galyyrim wanted a change of pace in an otherwise average day, or when they desired to exercise and play with their aquatic magic, they would manipulate the air bubble around the city to exclude the palace. Water would fill every corridor, room, nook, and cranny until the whole structure was submerged. The windows would open to invite fish and other sea creatures inside, and they made for great fun—or great meals, depending on whom you asked.

Before Melody's arrival, the palace was often flooded because the Galyyrim enjoyed the feeling of unity with the ocean. Their powers were stronger and their hearts lighter as they conducted their business in the flooded palace. Melody had never experienced it for herself, but now was her chance. She responded to the King, "Yes! Oh, yes!"

"Did you hear that, everyone?" The Great King stood as he addressed the Galyyrim. "It's time to flood the palace! Let's celebrate!"

The elves cheered as they left the room. It had been twelve years since the last time the palace was flooded, so everyone was ecstatic to hear the Great King's decree that day.

3
Compromise
Summer, 1419 AIE

~Connor~

I PAUSE THE STORY. "Devin, you don't look so good. Is something wrong?"

Devin's elbows are on the table and his bored face rests on his fists. "You didn't tell us this was a *girl* story."

"Girl story?"

"Yeah. About princesses who use magic to make plants grow."

I frown. As someone who works year-round to grow plants the old-fashioned way, I would *love* to have magic plant powers. "What's so girly about magic plant powers?"

"Only girls grow plants. Men kill the plants and fight!" Devin pounds his fist into his palm.

"Hmph," I furrow my brow. Clearly, Devin believes growing plants even *without* magic is girly, which implies he believes farming is girly. How absurd! Where does he *think* his food comes from: wheat, corn, tomatoes, beets, and cabbage, just to name a few? Farming is a *very* important trade! This little brat has no idea how hard I've worked just to—Oh, never mind. He's just a kid. I take a breath to calm my nerves. "Listen Dev, there's more to a good story than killing and fighting."

"Yeah, Devin, grow up!" Carmi interjects before turning to me, eyes sparkling with innocence. "I *love* your story. Please continue."

"Can you at least skip to the good part?" Devin asks.

18

"Stories lose their power if we start leaving things out. It's just about to get good; I promise you'll think differently when it's over."

"Oh, all right," Devin sighs and pouts.

"Ye're quite the storyteller, young lad."

I jump at the unexpected voice, belonging to a frail old man who stands nearby. We were so busy bickering, we hadn't noticed him approach us. He's dressed in an old sailor's outfit and leans on a cane of polished bone. His face is weathered with age and his sea-blue eyes look filled with stories—er, I mean wisdom. "Thank you, sir."

The old man smiles. "Do ye mind if I join and listen? I promise I won't be a bother."

"Oh no, please do," I say, standing up. "Take my chair. I'll find another."

"Thank ye, lad." The man sits down with the kids, who are timid and awestruck at his appearance.

I survey the seating area. The tavern has lost a few people since I last looked up. Glancing out the window, I see it's past nightfall and the storm is still in full swing. Bayside Harbor isn't far, so I suppose some people must have gone there to find an inn for the night. With their departure, I quickly spot a few vacant seats.

I claim the nearest chair, pull it up, and sit down. The children and the old man wait for me to continue, eyes sparkling with suspense—though Devin's not so much. I wonder how much of the story the old man heard before coming over, but I dismiss the thought. I clear my throat and lean in to continue.

~1700 BIE

AFTER EXITING THE throne room, Melody wasn't sure where to go or what to expect. She tried to imagine the palace being flooded. Would water just appear inside? Would it trickle in slowly, or come crashing through the halls? Her excitement became mixed with nervous anticipation.

"Feeling all right, Mel?" Eli's voice called behind her.

Melody whirled around, hiding her premonition with a huge smile. "Of course, I've *never* been so excited!"

"I'm sure," Eli smiled. "I'm so glad you can use magic now. How about we play a game once the palace is flooded?"

Melody's eyes glowed. She loved playing with Eli, but it would be much more fun now that she too could use magic. "Sure!"

A distant roar echoed down the hall, and the floor trembled. Melody looked out the window to see the bubble that encapsulated Marindel coming down on the towers of the palace, exposing them to the open ocean. Melody imagined torrents of water rushing down the halls, sweeping her up and throwing her around. She cringed.

"Don't be afraid," Eli said, placing a hand on her shoulder. "I know this'll be your first time underwater. Stay close and watch me. I'll show you how it's done."

The roaring of the waters intensified until, just as Melody imagined, a foaming swell came rushing down the hall toward them. At the same time, the windows opened to dump torrents of water inside. Melody shrieked and cowered behind Eli.

"Here we go!" Eli took a wide stance with one palm facing forward at the incoming flood, and another above, where a window was about to dump water. When the surge was nearly upon them, Eli moved his arms in wide, circling motions to redirect the waters and cause them to swirl around them. It was very similar, Melody noted, to how the plant had grown in the path left by her hand. As the waters in the hall rose, Eli kept the two of them dry by keeping a cylindrical wall of swirling water around them.

As the flood level neared the top of the hall and the momentum of the current slowed, Eli said, "I'm going to release the air pocket, nice and easy. We'll be in still waters before you know it. Ready?"

Melody, though still uncertain, trusted Eli and summoned as much determination as she could. "I'm ready!"

Eli stilled his hands, causing the swirling of the cylinder to stop. Then he brought his hands in close and lifted them slowly. As he did, water came from underneath to fill the cylinder. Melody stood still as the waters covered her feet first, then her knees, and then her belly.

"Don't hold your breath." Eli cracked a smile and lifted his hands the rest of the way. The remaining air in the cylinder went up and escaped with the last bits of air in the hallway. Everything was now completely submerged.

Melody, against her instinct, took a deep breath. And then another. And another. Breathing water instead of air was strange, but she was doing it. The current down the hall had slowed enough that it felt like a gentle breeze. Even so, it lifted Melody off the ground and moved her slowly.

"Well? How does it feel?" Eli asked, floating off the ground and reclining in midair—or mid-water, rather.

Melody was surprised to hear Eli's voice so clearly. Not even that—she heard him *more* clearly. She saw him clearly, too. But she didn't know how to move. "It feels funny. How do I walk? The current is taking me away."

"You don't *walk* underwater. You swim, using magic! Like this!" Eli oriented his body straight and parallel to the ground before darting down the hall. He moved incredibly fast, as if he were flying, with minimal movements from his arms or legs. On his return he performed several corkscrews and flips, before coming to a stop near a wide-eyed Melody in the same reclining position he started in. "Now, you try."

"O-okay," Melody nodded. She tried to orient herself in the position she had seen Eli swimming in, but she flailed about and went nowhere.

"You won't go far if you keep flopping around like that," Eli laughed. "You have to use magic. Focus on moving the water around you. That's what's going to propel you forward, not your own strength."

Melody nodded and took a deep breath. She held her hands forward, like when she resurrected the plant earlier. She focused on the internal energy flowing from her heart to the tips of her fingers. Then she moved her arms around experimentally. She felt the water flowing around her, following the paths set by her hands. Once she got the hang of it, she used the currents to position herself in the same way Eli had.

"Well done! You're a quick learner. Now, point your hands behind you and imagine you're releasing streams of water from your palms and feet."

Melody did so and began moving forward. A radiant smile spread across her face. "Look, I'm doing it! I'm swimming!"

"Very good! Focus on the amount of energy you're releasing to control your speed. Change the angle of your hands to guide yourself in the direction you want to go."

Melody swam back and forth down the hallway, experimenting with different turns and flips. She loved how her white dress flowed with the water around her. When she remembered her hair was still in a bun, she immediately pulled out the pins. Her hair was straight underwater, which made it appear very long. She shook her head and caused it to fan out in every direction.

Eli laughed. "Having fun, anemone-head?"

"Lots of fun!" She swam toward him, hair trailing behind like a gold ribbon, and tapped him on the head as she passed. "Tag, you're it!"

"Hey!" Eli took off after her.

Melody and Eli chased each other throughout the palace, whooping and laughing all the while. They weaved in and out of the windows and skirted the palace towers and spires like playful otters. Melody had never had this much fun playing tag before. The flooded palace was more thrilling than she could've ever imagined.

After a while, Melody entered a room decorated with large pots containing dead or dying plants. At the sight of them, she remembered what the Great King had told her about beautifying the inside of the palace. She stopped and turned. "Hey, Eli!"

Eli caught up with Melody and tapped her on the head. "You're it. What's up?"

Melody tapped him on the head. "Do plant-growing powers work underwater?"

Eli tapped Melody on the head. "Yep, they sure do."

Melody tapped Eli on the head. "But I thought plants needed air to breathe."

Eli tapped Melody on the head. "Most do, but the plants we have here can survive both on land and under the sea."

Without tapping Eli on the head, Melody said, "Oh, that's neat. Do you mind if I help a few of these plants? I really want to practice."

"Sure, go for it," Eli grinned. "Gives me plenty of time to get away!"

"Hey, wait!" Melody grabbed Eli's arm. "Let's play a different game. How about you count to, uh...a thousand while I hide, and then you have to come find me. But I'll leave a trail of beautiful plants for you to follow as hints. Sound like fun?"

"Great idea, Mel. I'll go to that corner up there and get started." He pointed at a corner by the ceiling. Of *course* he'd choose a place he could only count in while the palace was flooded. He swam up to the corner, hid his face, and began counting. "One, two, three, four..."

Melody giggled. She gave him so long to count because she wanted to make every plant as beautiful as it could be, with time to spare to find a good hiding spot.

She approached the pot closest to her. There was a pillar nearby that looked rather bare. Nodding confidently, she extended her hand toward the plant and caused it to grow up in several vines. She made the vines weave around the pillar like braids of hair, as thick with foliage as she could manage. Soon the entire pillar looked like a bush, but something was still missing. Melody thought for a moment, and then imagined beautiful pink flowers as she maneuvered around the pillar with her palms pointed toward it. The vines broke out with tiny pink flowers in her wake. *"There,"* Melody thought, admiring the pillar with a proud grin. *"Now it's the most beautiful pillar I've ever seen."*

Melody moved on to the next pot, which she made into a large bush shaped like a mushroom. She even gave it big red roses to look like polka-dots. In the next pot, she made a grass-like plant that stood tall and bushy, with a single yellow hibiscus perched at the top. There wasn't a single plant Melody grew the same as another. She experimented with every idea she could think of.

As she went, Melody grew more accustomed to her powers. She had simply to imagine what she wanted, point her hands at the plant, and move them about in proper form. Soon, schools of colorful fish were drawn to her use of magic and followed her around. She enjoyed their company, and pretended she was putting on a show for them. She even took ideas from her audience, creating some plants that looked like vibrant coral reefs, and others with flowers resembling various fish.

Melody had long since left the room where Eli was counting, and even forgot she was supposed to find a hiding spot. She was captivated with her task of making every plant in the palace as wonderful as it could be. She wholeheartedly enjoyed using her magic to create beauty and life.

Soon, Melody came across a pot that was different from the rest. It was dilapidated and cracked, as if it hadn't been replaced in a while. Melody thought that odd, since the Galyyrim put great effort into making interior design repairs when needed. Despite this, she smiled as she imagined a gorgeous flowering vine cascading over the sides of the pot to mask its imperfection.

As she approached it, the fish following her turned and swam away, but she failed to notice. Melody pointed her palms at the plant and threw her arms wide to make her image a reality.

The plant stirred with the current, but it didn't regain life.

"Huh?" Melody tilted her head. She tried again, but to no avail. She leaned in closer to inspect the plant. There didn't seem to be anything different about it. Concentrating hard, she slowly extended her hands toward the plant. She could feel magic buzzing in her fingers. She lifted her hands, expecting the plant to resurrect and grow.

The Epic of Marindel: Chosen

A leaf dislodged from the stem and sunk slowly to the ground.

Melody pouted. She pointed at the plant. "You *will* grow when I tell you to!" She tried again, but nothing happened. "What's wrong with you!? Grow, stupid plant!" She tried two more times, and then finally, with a grunt of annoyance, she sat cross-legged in mid-water and pouted some more.

Only when she stopped chastising the plant did she notice her surroundings. First, she realized the fish had left. Then she realized where in the palace she was.

Melody had been allowed to explore the palace as freely as she wanted, with the exception of one room. Guarded by massive dark brown double-doors and sealed shut by an inconspicuous lock infused with magical energy, it was the only room in the palace the Great King declared to be off limits. Melody didn't know what was inside, but she trusted the Great King well enough that she'd never stopped to wonder.

Now, Melody realized she was twenty feet down the hall from that very door.

It stood, looming and foreboding, at the dead end of the hall. There were no windows or lamps nearby, so it was cast in shadow. The way the door was carved made Melody feel like it was glaring down at her.

She tore her eyes from the forbidden door and looked at the pot. Then she scanned up the hallway in the opposite direction. There were no pots in the hallway besides that one. She looked at the plant again and frowned. "If only I could make you grow. This hallway could use a little cheering up."

"*Do you really want to make the plant grow?*" a smooth voice asked in Melody's thoughts.

Melody flinched and looked around. She thought she was alone. "Hello? Eli?"

"*You will not see me, for I am speaking to your mind.*"

"*How are you doing that?*" Melody thought.

"*Telepathy.*"

"*Oh, nice. Can I do that too?*"

"*You may learn someday. After all, you are a much stronger magician than I am.*"

"*Thanks, but...*" Melody frowned at the plant. "*I couldn't make this plant grow.*"

"*Not to worry. I know how to make it grow, and if you'd like, I can show you.*"

"*Really?*" Melody's eyes lit up. "*But...I don't know who you are.*"

"Yes, and neither do I know you, but I'm eager to meet one as strong and beautiful as you. Will you do me a favor?"

"Sure."

"I've been trapped for quite some time on the other side of the door that stands to your left. I am very sad, hungry, and lonely in here. Would you please let me out?"

Melody looked at the forbidden door, eyes wide. *"N-no! I can't do that! The Great King has forbidden anyone from opening that door."*

"Did he, now? What a cruel man he is. What is he keeping in there all to himself? Come now, you must wonder."

"M-my daddy doesn't keep anything to himself. He shares with everyone. He's the most generous, kind-hearted person in the realm."

"There are many things you do not know, child. Many things your daddy will not tell you."

For the first time, Melody's mind was filled with doubts about her father and curiosity as to what lay behind the forbidden door.

"Tell me, why didn't the Great King give you the ability to grow this plant?"

Melody frowned. *"I don't know."*

"He is most unfair. The Great King only gave you the powers he wanted you to have, and kept many others to himself. But I know how much you really want that plant to live again."

Melody looked at the ground. She had never doubted the Great King before, and it made her queasy. Nevertheless, the voice seemed to be very wise, and a small part of her wanted to share in that wisdom.

"I will give you the power to resurrect the plant," the voice said, *"but first, you must help me."*

Melody remained thoughtful, wrestling with the new ideas posed by the voice in her head.

"Mel! Where are you?" Eli called, his voice distant.

"You haven't much time," the voice said. *"Use your magic to unlock the door. Then come inside and I will give you the power you seek."*

Melody looked in the direction she knew Eli was coming from, and then at the forbidden door. She swallowed her fear and stilled the doubts swirling in her head. *"All right. Here I come."*

She swam toward the door. In the dim light she could just make out the lock built into the door. She placed her hand on it and willed for something to happen. Magical energy flowed out of her fingers and onto the lock, causing it to glow. It clicked and whirred as the internal pieces spun and shifted. The clamp bolting the two doors came undone with a *clunk*.

"Melody? Melody!?" Eli was close.

"Hurry, inside!" the voice instructed.

Without thinking, she opened one of the massive doors and slipped inside, shutting it and hoping Eli wouldn't notice the lock was undone. The room was pitch dark; Melody couldn't see a thing. Regret came crashing over her like a wave. She sunk to the ground, curled up into a ball, and said aloud, "What in the realm of Tyrizah am I doing?"

"Why are you sniveling on the floor?" the voice asked. *"Get up. I have another task for you.*

"But it's dark, and I already opened the door for you. Isn't that enough disobedience for one day?"

"You are a powerful magician; there is no reason to fear the dark. Create a light and carry it in your palm."

Melody stood and held out her palm. She imagined a light appearing there, and a bright blue orb flickered to life. It floated just above her hand and even provided a bit of warmth.

Now that she could see, Melody looked around the forbidden room, squinting through the clouded, murky water. Large and circular, the walls stretched up farther than Melody's light could shine. The room was empty except for a black treasure chest in the center.

"Come to the chest and open it," the voice instructed.

Melody swam cautiously toward it. There was a lock on it similar to the one that had sealed the door. She used her magic to undo it, and with bated breath, she slowly opened the chest. She expected to see some kind of treasure, like gold, jewels, or pearls. But when she peered inside, shining the light to get a better look, all she found was an elongated, twisted piece of stone. The mere sight of it filled her heart with foreboding.

"Pick up the stone," the voice commanded.

Melody did as she was told. It was slimy and gross.

"Focus your power into it."

Melody did so. Tiny cracks appeared, casting rays of dim yellow light. When the stone was covered in cracks, it flashed once, and the outer layer fell away in tiny flakes. What remained of the stone was mushy and limp. When it began to wriggle on its own, Melody shrieked and let go.

The thing writhed a bit more as it grew in size and adopted eel-like features. It turned to face Melody, and as it did, the voice spoke to her. *"Thank you, kind one. It feels good to move around again."*

Melody grimaced. *"You're...just an eel?"* She had seen many eels in her twelve years of life, but she'd never seen an eel half as ugly as this one. She couldn't imagine why the Great King would go to such great lengths to hide such a pathetic creature.

"Indeed, I am just an eel," it nodded. *"Now that you've freed me, I will keep my promise and give you the power to bring your plant back to life."*

"How are you going to do that?"

"Let me see your amulet," the eel replied. *"Place it around my neck, and I will enchant it with the power to resurrect every plant in the realm."*

"Every plant in the realm?" Melody gaped. She fumbled with the amulet on her neck and pulled it over her head, careful not to let it snag on her free-floating hair. She admired the multicolored gemstone embedded within it as she placed it around the eel's neck. *"It's a little big for you, isn't it?"*

The eel's haughty gaze caught Melody off guard. *"I wouldn't say that, dear. I'm afraid I'm a little too big for it."*

Before she could question the eel's response, the light in her palm fizzled out. She opened her mouth to gasp, but she choked on water and quickly held her breath. *"Wait! Why can't I breathe anymore!?"*

Her answer came in the form of a flashback, when the Great King said, "As long as you wear the amulet, you will be able to use magic. No one can take it from you and use its power unless you surrender it to them. It's all yours."

Melody felt sick. She'd been tricked into giving her amulet to the eel, and now she had no powers. Though blinded by the darkness, she lunged forward to grab the amulet. *"Give it back!*

"It's not yours anymore," the eel chuckled. *"Your foolishness is my reward!"*

Panic welled up in Melody's heart as she flailed about. She couldn't hold her breath for much longer. *"I'm going to drown! Help me!"*

"Yes, that would be unfortunate, wouldn't it? Watching you die here would be no fun at all. There are many ways we could have fun together, if I save you now."

Melody felt something touch her forehead and jolt her with electricity. She ran out of breath and inhaled deeply, expecting to choke on water, but to her relief she was able to breathe again. She reached forward and waved her arms to find the amulet.

The eel's sinister laugh seemed to come from everywhere at once.

Melody kept searching until she hit her fingers on something solid. Surprised, she touched it again. Whatever she hit was taut and rough, like the skin of a shark. She immediately let go. "*You're not an eel anymore, are you?*"

"*Why don't you see for yourself?*"

Bright light flooded Melody's vision. She covered her face at first, and then peered through her fingers to look. Her vision was blurry, but she could just make out a large, dark shape in front of her. She rubbed her eyes and blinked for clearer vision. When she finally saw the creature poised in front of her, she almost wished it had left her to drown instead.

4
Seer's Gift
~1700 BIE

THE MONSTER HAD a long, serpentine body, a dragon-like head, sharp spines like a crown around its neck, a membranous dorsal fin and tail fluke, long, sharp teeth, and even sharper green eyes. Its colors were dark blue and black with thin yellow markings, and its face was like a hideous skeletal mask. The Serpent, illuminated by a magic orb many times brighter than Melody's had been, was so massive that it nearly took up the entire room.

Melody was horrified, her face as white as a ghost. She could barely find the strength to move, let alone pull her eyes away from the monster.

"What's the matter—scared?" the Serpent jeered, baring his teeth in a threatening smirk. *"You're not afraid of sea serpents, are you?"*

Melody knew about sea serpents, and had even seen a few. But in her twelve years of life, she'd never seen a sea serpent half as terrifying as this one. Summoning what little strength she had, Melody did the only thing she could think to do.

"DADDY!" She turned and tried to swim for the door, but because she no longer had magic, she flailed about uselessly.

"Ha! Pathetic girl!" With an amused growl, the Serpent bowed his head and clamped his jaws on Melody's hair. With a flick of his powerful neck, he threw her against the wall. *"The Great King won't come to your rescue after you so blatantly disobeyed him!"*

Melody gasped upon impact and sunk to the ground. She began to sob. "D-daddy...help!"

"*No one will save you!*" The Serpent faced Melody, his body moving fluidly in the tight space of the room. "*But don't worry, I will take care of you. We'll have so much fun together!*"

Melody couldn't resist. The Serpent picked her up by the hem of her dress and tossed her upward before swatting her with his tail fluke into the wall. With a dark chuckle, the Serpent flexed his body to pin Melody to the wall and scrape her along the stone surface. He continued to toss and abuse Melody as she accumulated open wounds, bruises, and broken bones. Portions of her hair were ripped out, and her dress was marred and torn beyond recognition. She was completely helpless. For the entirety of the beating, these thoughts passed through her mind: "*I did this. It's my fault. I'm a horrible daughter.*"

Before long, the Serpent stopped his cruel torture and let Melody sink to the floor like a soiled rag-doll. He purred with delight, "*It's been far too long since I've had the pleasure of entertaining myself at some hapless creature's expense. Still, I cannot do much with you because you're pathetic and weak. You deserve to die.*"

Melody was nearly unconscious. Pain like nothing she had ever felt crippled her body and soul. "I...deserve...to die," she mouthed silently.

"*Yet, I will have mercy on you,*" he said. "*I must repay you for freeing me.*"

A black cable-like tendril emerged from among the Serpent's neck spines. The tip touched her forehead, jolting her with electricity, like when she regained the ability to breathe. Her severe wounds closed up and healed, strength was restored to her body, and she could feel magic buzzing in the tips of her fingers. Yet her heart was still in great pain.

"*Get up,*" the Serpent commanded. "*I have restored you.*"

Melody wouldn't have moved if it weren't for the buzzing in her fingers. She didn't stop to wonder how the Serpent restored her powers without losing his own. "*The monster gave my powers back. Maybe now it will let me escape.*" Using magic, Melody pushed off the ground and oriented herself upright. She backed away toward the door, keeping eye contact with the beast.

The Serpent lunged toward her, jaws wide. Melody darted upward, narrowly dodging his attack. He laughed. "*This will be much more exciting, now that you think you can defend yourself!*"

Melody stiffened, horrified by the thought of another beating. *"You said you'd repay me for freeing you. Please, let me go!"*

"Yes, the Serpent purred. *"This room is a bit cramped for our game, isn't it? Let's go outside, you and I, to be free at last!"*

Before Melody could react, the Serpent lunged and shut his jaws over Melody, trapping her in his mouth. A massive forked tongue pinned her in place. Though she struggled, she was unable to escape.

The Serpent spiraled upward along the walls of the room, gaining speed, until he crashed through the ceiling like a battering ram. Shards of polished stone and roof tiles scattered about as the Serpent emerged from the tower and escaped into the open ocean. After creating some distance between himself and the city of Marindel, the Serpent spat Melody out like an unwanted piece of meat.

Melody tumbled through the water, completely helpless. When she finally slowed enough to orient herself, she was dizzy and could hardly see.

"Oh, I've missed this! It feels wonderful to stretch out the open sea. Now, with the whole realm as our playground, we will have such great fun together!"

When Melody regained her balance, she looked behind her to face the Serpent, but he wasn't there. Instead, she saw the massive sea turtle, patrolling the ocean depths, carrying Marindel away from her. Melody knew that if she lost sight of Marindel, it'd be nearly impossible to find her way home ever again.

"Hey! Wait!" Melody darted after the turtle. She hoped with all her might that a Galyyr would see her and signal the turtle to stop.

The Serpent's voice intruded on what little hope she had. *"Why are you so desperately trying to return? You've disobeyed the Great King. He will never let you set foot in that city ever again."*

Against the pain in her heart, Melody asserted, *"My daddy loves me, and so do the Galyyrim. I may get in trouble for this, but soon they'll forget all about it, and everything will be back to..."*

Melody's thoughts trailed off when she saw the Serpent's massive silhouette, circling her from a distance. He had grown much larger since she last saw him. His body was as thick around as the largest tower of the palace, and he was as long as the sea turtle itself. His jaws were large enough to swallow a dozen whales all at once. With a fearful shriek, Melody channeled as much power as she could into her palms and feet as she swam after Marindel.

The Serpent laughed. *"You know not who you're dealing with, little girl! Do you see how I've grown? I am the most indomitable being under the sea, stronger than any of the Galyyrim—and I will become even more powerful than this! Because you've given me your royal authority, I have the power to bring destruction upon Tyrizah, the likes of which have never been seen. Surely you have placed a death sentence on your own head and on every living thing in the realm. Not even the Great King will forgive you for such a crime. He will surely hate you!"*

The Serpent's accusation crippled Melody's soul so badly that she lost the will to pursue Marindel. She watched as the turtle-borne city grew smaller and smaller before fading away into the ocean blue.

As Marindel disappeared, the Serpent said, *"They will all hate you. Not just them, but those above as well. No one will welcome you into their city. They will chase you and try to kill you for no reason at all, except for pure hatred. You will live out the years of the long life the Great King has given you in great misery."*

Melody closed her eyes. *"It's all my fault. I'm so naive, so stupid and worthless. No one will ever love a horrible person like me. You're right, I can't return to Marindel. My father will disown me. I deserve to die!"* The last thought caused her to sob.

"Finally, you have come to your senses. You're nothing but a runaway and a criminal. Begone from the sea, and embrace the suffering you've brought upon yourself."

Melody didn't resist as the Serpent came near and coiled a black tendril around her. He carried her up to the surface of the deep and leapt into the air. At the pinnacle of his flight, the Serpent hurled Melody with all his might, sending her tumbling over the horizon and out of sight. With a victorious roar, the Serpent plummeted back into the ocean and disappeared into the darkness.

ELI OPENED THE forbidden door and stood at the entrance. He'd felt the palace tremble when the Serpent escaped, and he desperately hoped Melody wasn't the cause of it. "Mel!? Melody, where are you!?"

The Great King entered, passing Eli to stop at the center of the room, where he saw the black chest broken to pieces. The water was tainted with blood, and bits of Melody's dress and hair were scattered along the floor. A ray of light from the gaping hole in the ceiling illuminated the pitiful sight.

The King fell to his knees and wept. "Oh, no! Melody, my beautiful daughter! This can't be!"

Eli frowned as he approached. "Father? What happened? Is Melody...?"

The Great King, consumed with anguish, could say nothing but his beloved child's name.

Eli had never seen his father so distraught. Fearing the worst, he began to weep as well. The two of them wept until they were spent, unable to say a word.

Hours later, the Great King mustered his strength and said, "My son, you must understand—Melody has done a very terrible thing by surrendering her inheritance to the Great Serpent."

Eli looked up at the King with wide eyes.

"Tyrizah will not be the same. It will be filled with chaos, perversion, destruction, and death. There is no easy solution, for as long as the Serpent has Melody's inheritance, none of us can stop him. Moreover, only she can reclaim what is rightfully hers."

"Will she?" Eli asked.

"No," the Great King's eyes welled up. "Not without help."

Eli picked up a blood-stained fragment of Melody's dress. He was flooded with memories of playing with her when she was little. He taught her about life in Marindel and showed her around the city. He was with her when she learned to play the piano, and they even created songs together. They would often play tag in the palace halls and gardens, though Eli never used his powers and almost always let her win. He remembered how his heart burned with excitement when the Great King told him they would be married if she agreed to it. But that could never happen now. Unless...

"I will help her!" Eli declared. He stood and looked at the King, a zealous fire kindling in his gaze. "Send me, Father! I'll do whatever it takes to save Melody and help her reclaim her inheritance."

The Great King looked at his son with mixed compassion and determination. "Very well, my son. When the time is right, I will send you to the realm above to find her. In the meantime, prepare yourself and wait patiently."

Summer, 1419 AIE

~Connor~

"AND THAT IS how the Era of Peace ended. The dynamic struggle between good and evil now rages on all around us, and in our hearts."

The kids stare at me silently. They'd been captivated since my last intermission, allowing me to tell the rest of the story uninterrupted.

The old man, leaning back comfortably in his chair, nods with satisfaction. "Well told, lad."

"Well told!?" Carmi blurts. "That was the *saddest* story I've ever heard! Couldn't you at least give it a happy ending?"

"There may be a second part to the story with a happier ending, but I haven't heard it yet. Believe me, I'm as interested as you are to hear what happens next." I ask Devin and Peter, "What did you guys think?"

"It was totally *wizard*!" Devin shouts, pounding the table with one fist.

I laugh. "I'm glad to see you came to enjoy it after all!"

"I thought it was good," Peter says.

"Just 'good,' huh?"

Peter nods. "It's good for a legend, but I want to hear *real* stories. Can you tell us about something you've done, or a place you've been?"

"Yeah!" Devin agrees. "Have you fought any monsters? Done anything dangerous? Been to other kingdoms? You're so shady, you must have *something*!"

I chuckle to hide my embarrassment. I'm not inclined to tell the kids about my uneventful life as a farmer. If they thought magical plant powers were boring, hearing about last year's barley harvest would put them to sleep.

Just then, someone barges into the tavern. He quickly shuts the door against the elements and leans back against it. His face is mostly hidden in the hood of his coat, which I can't help but notice is similar to mine. He stays there breathing heavily for a few seconds before composing himself and walking to an empty table in the middle of the seating area. The bartender asks him if he'd like anything to drink, and the newcomer gives him the cold shoulder. The bartender leaves and returns a moment later with a glass of wine and a lily growing in a small vase. As he sets them down, I hear him say, "Cheer up. It's on the house."

"That guy's weird," Peter says, observing the stranger.

"And scary," Carmi adds.

"You know what I bet?" Devin whispers, "I bet he has some really good monster stories!"

I chuckle and whisper, "You may be on to something there. Did you see how he came in and held the door back like that? There might have been some monsters chasing him down the road. As he came near the tavern, they wounded his horse, so he left it for dead and ran inside for safety. Now the monsters are surrounding the tavern, lurking in the shadows, waiting for him to come out...!"

Devin gasps. "That's horrible! We have to help! Come on, let's go kill 'em!"

He moves to get up, but I grab his arm. "Hold on Dev, it's not a *true* story!"

"Is it not?" the old man asks.

I cast a questioning glance at him. "No, it's not. I made it up."

"Are ye sure?"

"Yes," I nod. "Why do you ask?"

The old man smiles. "I see a gift restin' powerfully upon ye."

Devin pipes up before I can respond, "What gift?"

"You brought us gifts?" Carmi asks, wide-eyed with excitement.

The old man chuckles and says, "Why don't ye three run along and listen to someone else's stories for a wee bit?"

"Okay!" they all say, tumbling off their chairs and heading elsewhere in the tavern.

"See you later!" Devin calls over his shoulder.

I watch the kids go for a moment before the old man says, "We've met before. Do ye not recognize me?"

Not that I remember. I look at him to be sure, meeting his blue-eyed gaze. His expression is as profound and mysterious as the setting of the story he told me long ago. It clicks, and my eyes widen. "You're...that man...!"

He smiles, leaning back into his chair. "That's right. I am he who first told ye the tale of *The Princess of the Sea* years ago. Ye can call me Jed."

Everything comes back to me like a gust of wind. I distinctly remember hearing *The Princess of the Sea* told with his thick northern-Tethysian accent. "Is that why you came over here to listen?"

"Aye. Ye tell it even better than I do, and for a good reason. Ye have the gift of a very powerful Seer!"

I raise an eyebrow. "A powerful what-now?"

"A Seer. One who can discern details about events that are

hidden to others. I too am a Seer. When I first saw ye in the tavern eight years ago, I saw the gift restin' so *clearly* upon ye! It was no coincidence that I shared *The Princess of the Sea* that day."

I furrow my brow. "I still don't understand. How can I be a Seer? I've never discerned or predicted anything in my life. Don't get me wrong, it'd be a great trick, but...that can't be me."

Jed's eyes wander to the nearest window. "Do ye know how long this storm has been goin' lad?"

I follow his gaze. It's as dark and stormy as ever. "A few hours, I suppose."

"How long do summer thunderstorms last?"

"Thirty minutes to an hour," I reply. That's common knowledge here in the Armaviran countryside, where summer storms blow in every now and then to disrupt an otherwise great day's work. However, the more I think about it, the more I realize what the old man is suggesting. "This isn't a normal thunderstorm, is it?"

Jed shakes his head.

"Hurricane?" They rarely make it this far north, but it's not impossible.

The man shakes his head again. "From which direction did the storm come?"

"Inland, from the east," I sigh. Why does it matter what kind of storm this is? I wish Jed would cut to the chase already; his cryptic manner is annoying. I ask him straight, "Do *you* know what kind of storm this is?"

"Ye discerned it yerself on the way here."

An idea hits me.

But, it *can't* be! Not in Armavir.

Or...can it?

"A sorcerer," I whisper. "A sorcerer sent this storm."

"Aye."

"And that means..." my eyes widen as I remember the rest of the story I thought I had fabricated on my way to the tavern. "A sorcerer sent this storm to destroy Bayside Harbor, and an elixir of blue elderflower and mermaid tears is the only thing that can stop it! And the worst part of it is..." I peer over my shoulder at the bartender. "He's an *ogre*!"

Jed laughs. "What a load of goblin dung! Ye're only right about the sorcerer bit."

"Oh, thank goodness."

"Ye must learn to tell the difference between yer Seer's gift and yer imagination," Jed says.

"Apparently. How do I do that?"

"Begin by acknowledgin' ye have the Seer's gift. Believe that some of the thoughts comin' to yer mind on a whim are more than pure fantasy. Cherish them as they are, and refrain from addin' to them. With practice, ye'll learn to foresee and overcome the schemes of yer enemies."

Something within me lights up as he speaks, but I'm hesitant to believe. At his last statement, I throw up my hands. "How is that possible? I'm no fighter. I can't do anything about a storm-brewing sorcerer even if I know what he writes in his diary at night!"

"Aye. A Seer does not use his gift for his own good, but for the good of others. If ye develop this gift and use it well in service of the Great King, many lives will be spared. In time, ye'll become a mighty leader of armies."

"Leader of armies?" I scoff. "I don't know what you're talking about! I have no desire to join the Paladin Order or the local village guard, let alone command an army. I'm just a simple farmer!"

"Ye will not be so simple a farmer for much longer."

I narrow my eyes. "How do you know that?"

"It will become clear to ye very soon."

Blimey! Who does this guy think he is? I can't take any more of his crazy ideas! I've got to abandon this conversation and head home. Besides, it's getting late and my father is probably wondering why I've been gone for so long.

I fake an exhausted yawn. "Well, Seer or no Seer, I should get going. It's late, I'm tired, and I have work to do tomorrow. Thank you for your wisdom, kind sir. I'll see you around." I stand up, pat him on the shoulder, and take my leave.

Jed calls out behind me, "Beware the monsters lurkin' in the shadows!"

"Yeah, got it," I say with a dismissive wave. On the way out, I pass the table where the stranger sits, as still as a statue with his head down. The wine glass is empty and the lily in the vase is dead. Not thinking much of it, I continue on my way out the door.

5

On my Honor

Summer, 1419 AIE

~Connor~

I'M BUFFETED BY the wind and rain as I close the tavern door behind me. I pull the hood over my face and shelter my bare hands in the coat pockets as I walk toward the crossroads in front of the tavern. Lightning flashes frequently enough that I don't need a lantern to see where I'm going. After all, home's only a mile away.

When I reach the crossroads, I notice a bulky object slumped on the road a short distance ahead. I stop in my tracks.

It's a dead horse, with huge chunks of flesh ripped out of its body.

"Ugh," I mutter, disgusted.

As I stand on the crossroads with my eyes on the carcass, I begin to think. I had told Devin that the stranger hid in the tavern from monsters that killed his horse. That's when Jed started pestering me about being a Seer. As I got up to leave, Jed warned me about monsters lurking in the shadows.

My muscles tense. Wind-blown tall grass surrounds me on every side. If there *were* monsters lurking in the shadows, they'd have to be small enough to hide in the grass. Unless of course they're flying monsters, the idea of which is absolutely terrifying. With that thought, I decide to run the rest of the way home.

Just as I'm about to sprint past the dead horse, I see a wiry animal creeping out from behind the body. A cougar-like creature with hairless black skin as slick as rubber, it has curled black claws, and gleaming teeth protruding from the sides of its mouth. Its tail is short and blade-shaped, perking straight up like a dog's tail. Finally, it has a crown of twelve luminescent green tendrils framing its face like a lion's mane.

My blood runs cold. It's too late to hide; it already sees me. I begin backing away, pulling my hands out of my coat and holding them up to show I have no weapons. "Easy there, I mean you no harm..."

The monster advances with narrowed eyes and a low hiss.

Terrified beyond all reason, I turn and sprint back to the tavern. I hear the monster howl and give chase behind me. And now there's another one coming at me from the left!

I run screaming toward the door and throw myself inside. Then I slam the door shut and hold my body against it to keep the monsters from breaking in. I feel the door thud as one of them crashes into the other side.

My mind reels at a pace that matches my frantic breath. Why are there monsters prowling around outside a peaceful countryside tavern!? This is unheard of!

I stay with my back against the door for a few seconds before I realize everyone is staring at me. The stranger is the sole exception.

"Welcome back, lad!" Jed winks at me.

I shoot him an angry glare. My first instinct is to march over there and interrogate him about the monsters, but I think better of it when I remember he was the reason I decided to leave the tavern in the first place.

A better idea comes to mind.

As people return to their business, I walk up to the table where the stranger sits. He doesn't move as I pull up a chair. After waiting in vain for him to acknowledge my presence, I move the flower vase aside and lean across the table. "Who are you, what is your business here, and what in the land of Armavir is outside waiting for you?"

The stranger doesn't respond.

After a few seconds, I continue. "Why did you lead them here? No one can leave the tavern now, thanks to you. What are you going to do, wait until they give up? *Will* they give up? Huh? What do you have to say for yourself?"

"Leave me alone," the stranger murmurs, her voice feminine.

A *girl* stranger, huh? There's no way I'm letting her off the hook just because she's a girl. I press the attack. "'Leave you alone?' No way! You brought your troubles to the door of this tavern, and now you must answer for them!"

The stranger lifts her head, peering at me from under her hood with hardened brown eyes. "I said, 'leave me alone!'"

"I will, once you tell me what's out there."

"I don't know."

"Where did they come from? Why are they chasing you?"

"I don't know!" She folds her arms on the table and puts her head down. "Just leave me alone."

I glare at her. I don't believe her for one second. For all I know, she could be a sorceress—perhaps the very one who caused this storm. I look at the vase with the dead lily. I remember it *wasn't* dead when the bartender placed it on the table. Plants don't die in a matter of minutes. This stranger *must* be a sorceress! And perhaps she wore a coat similar to mine on purpose, to trick the monsters into thinking I was her, so they'd kill me and go on their way. Then she'd be as free as a bird! It's so crazy, it might just be true!

With that thought, I find myself staring at the stranger with unbridled hatred. The feeling in my gut is both thrilling and terrifying. I don't believe I've ever been this angry before, but it feels so *right*. She's not going to get away with this, and someone ought to tell her so!

I open my mouth to accuse her, but on impulse I glance at Jed. He's watching intently, and when we make eye contact, he smiles.

Why is he looking at me like that?

The glimmer in his gaze causes me to pause and think. As I swallow the urge to verbally assault the girl, my mind begins making connections.

I'm reminded of the Great Serpent's words, *"They will all hate you. Not just them, but those above as well. No one will welcome you into their city. They will chase you and try to kill you for no reason at all, save for pure hatred. You will live out all the years of the long life the Great King has given you in great misery."* Next, I'm reminded of the story I told Devin about the stranger's arrival, which was already proven true by my experience outside the tavern. Finally, I think about how Jed had shared *The Princess of the Sea* with me because he believed I was a Seer.

My eyes lock on the stranger as I vocalize my thoughts. "Those monsters chasing you were sent by a sorcerer. The sorcerer sent the storm because of you, too. He's after you for no good reason at all, except for pure hatred. Just now, I almost gave in to the same curse of hatred that likely befell the sorcerer. And that is because..." I pause. The concluding thought is completely ludicrous, but something deep inside me is certain about the identity of this stranger.

She looks at me bitterly.

"Your name is Melody, isn't it?"

Something stirs in her eyes, but her gaze hardens quickly. "No. Where'd you get that stupid idea?"

"Oh, nowhere," I sigh. It was worth a shot. "Well, what is your name, then?"

"Mara."

I have a feeling she's lying. It's the same feeling I get when my father lies; I know it well. After glancing at Jed for permission, I go ahead and tell her so. "You're lying."

"Hmph," she grunts, straightening her posture and lifting her head. Now I can see her face clearly: dirt-smudged and scarred, devoid of any happiness. She looks nothing like the joyful girl I imagine she once was, if indeed she is who I think she is. She asks, "What does it matter if I'm lying or not? Why don't you run along and mind your own business, you impudent, useless peasant?"

I pause to think, careful not to lash out in response to her outburst.

Truthfully, deep down, I feel a connection to this woman, as if I've known her for a long time. It's so much more than sensing whether or not she's lying. A moment ago I was motivated to despise her, but something in Jed's gaze snapped me out of it. Now that I realize who she is, I feel like it's my duty to help her. I believe she *is* Melody, even though she denies it. There's a significance about her I don't entirely understand, and even now it's moving my soul with courage and determination.

Is this what it means to be a Seer?

Is this what the Great King felt when he found Melody on the roadside?

Is this what Jed felt when he first saw me in the tavern?

Does Jed feel this way all the time?

I silence the tide of questions in my heart. This is all very strange, but somehow, I know what I need to do. After another glance at Jed for permission, I say to the stranger, "I believe there's something special about you, and that's why the sorcerer's monsters are chasing you. If I can, I'd like to help you escape."

The stranger rolls her eyes. "You're a Seer, aren't you? Only a Seer would say something so ridiculous."

"I, uh..." She seems to think I'm a Seer, too. First Jed, and now this woman. I'm still only half convinced myself, but the more I press in, the more certain I become. I think I'll keep playing along. "I'm sorry; do you have something against Seers?"

The stranger speaks resentfully, "All my life, Seers have been chasing me around, telling me shit I don't want to hear. I swear, you're worse than the monsters!"

Whoa. If this stranger really is Melody, then 'all my life' must be a *very* long time. Given I could hardly endure five minutes of Jed telling me things I didn't want to hear, I can't help but empathize with her. "I understand, Melody. I just—"

"Don't call me that!"

"Sorry, sorry," I raise my hands. "I just want to help you, that's all."

She grumbles. "All you Seers are alike. You say you want to help, but in the end, you'll turn on me like everyone else."

I frown. "Why would I turn on you?"

"Look at me!" She erupts, becoming very animated. "I am the most miserable woman in the realm. Can any suffering be compared with *my* suffering, which the Great King himself has inflicted upon me? Don't you *dare* say you're out to help me. I know your kind! You'll turn on me just like the rest! *Everyone* turns on me eventually. *Everyone!*"

"Whoa, whoa," I say, taken aback. I can see why most people wouldn't have the patience to deal with this woman for long; her ability to trust has been completely shattered. I wonder what caused her to feel this way? What event in her story traumatized her so badly that she won't even allow someone to help her escape from monsters? Was it the Serpent's release, or...something else?

No matter. I can't bear the thought of giving up on her so easily. The longer I speak with her, the stronger this heart connection becomes—and the more I can't stand simply 'playing along.' I *must* help her. There is one act I can think of that will prove my words to her, and my rational mind begs me not to do it. A swear of honor is nothing to be taken lightly. Nevertheless, I know it's the right thing to do.

I straighten my posture and look her in the eye. "All right. I know we just met, and you've been through more hardship than I can imagine. But I want to convince you that I'm sincere when I say I'm going to help you."

"I've heard that *so* many times," she mutters.

I put my hand on my heart and say, "On my honor as a citizen of Armavir, the Land of Peace, I swear to do whatever it takes to help you escape from the monsters, and I will *never* turn on you for any reason. If I do, you have every right to...hmm." What's a suitable punishment for me going back on my word? As I think through the options, my eyes wander to the dead lily on the table.

"Every right to what?" she presses.

"You...may do to me what you did to that plant."

She glares at me. "I didn't do anything to the plant!"

"You're lying again."

She is visibly frustrated, but says nothing.

I extend my hand toward her. "Will you shake on it?"

"No."

Blimey, why won't she just cooperate already? I bite my tongue before the retort becomes vocal, and instead I say, "I won't force you, but *please*. Would it hurt to allow me to help you just this once?"

"Probably."

"You can trust me," I urge. "I swore on my honor. That's a big deal here in Armavir. If I go against it, you can turn me into a dead plant. No questions asked."

She glances at my hand for a few seconds, and with a reluctant sigh, she reaches out to shake it.

"Very well," I smile at her.

She avoids my gaze.

"Now, even though I'm certain your name is—well, you know—I'll call you Mara if it makes you happier."

She nods, still not looking at me.

"My name is Connor. I'm a simple farmer from just down the road. Apparently, I'm also a Seer, though I don't know much about that yet. Anyway, I'm going to try my best to help you escape from those monsters."

She looks at me for a second, then looks away. "If you want."

"All right." I take a deep breath to clear my mind. If I'm going to get any bit of information out of this tormented soul, I have to do it very carefully. "Mara, I need you to tell me everything you know about the monsters chasing you. What would I need to know if I were to fight one?"

She shudders at the memory of them. "They're like a smaller breed of Abysso, with a venomous bite. They run faster and for longer than horses, and they love to kill."

Abysso. I've heard stories about them. Native to Felidae, Abysso are enormous cat-like creatures notoriously immune to magic. Their eyesight is their strongest sense, followed by their sense of smell. They have no 'ears,' strictly speaking, but they use the glowing tendrils around their heads to detect sound vibrations in the air. I realize the monsters outside *did* look like tiny Abysso. But venomous? That's something I've never heard. I ask, "Venomous, huh?"

She nods. "One bite was enough to down my horse in moments. I assume a person would die even faster."

"Ouch," I frown. "How many are out there?"

"Four."

"Where did they chase you from?"

"The woods, a few miles east from here."

"How'd they find you there?"

"I don't know. Really, I don't. Trouble always has a way of finding me."

"They just showed up and started chasing you?"

She nods and sighs. "I'm used to it, though. It's not a big deal."

'Not a big deal?' Every fiber of my being cringes under the weight of this injustice. Mara might believe this is all just an everyday coincidence, but I have a strong feeling the sorcerer deliberately sent the monsters after her. And there's no way he's the first to do it! How many times have people tried to kill this woman? I *can't* let this continue! There must be something I can do to help.

I stand up and declare, "Mara, I'm going to find someone to defeat the monsters. From what you've said so far, I think archery is our best bet against them. There has to be *someone* in this tavern with a bow who's willing to help."

She looks at me scornfully. "Don't waste your time! It's futile! Even if those monsters are killed, more will come to take their place. It never ends."

"It's going to work," I insist. "You stay here. I'll have the monsters killed soon enough, and then you can go on your way."

She leans back and crosses her arms. "Fine then. Go. I'll watch you fail from here."

I force a polite smile in reply, and then I look out at the people remaining in the tavern. I need to find someone who looks strong and brave. My eyes fall on the two burly men I was eavesdropping on earlier. I remember with a grin how one was telling the other about threatening a goblin. Surely they would be up to the task.

But wait.

They'll need a bow and arrows.

I survey the tavern again. They're not weapons you can hide in your pocket or under your cloak, and I can't seem to spot any.

Chapter 5: On my Honor

Just then the bartender, carrying a tray laden with drinks, stops near me. "You looking for something, brother?"

"Yes, yes I am. You wouldn't happen to have a bow and some arrows, would you?"

"None. You're not hoping to go hunting in the storm, are you? If you're hungry, you can order one of our late-night specials, and I'll have it out for you as quick as a fox."

"No, I'm not hungry," I wave my hand, then I lean in close to whisper, "There are four venomous monsters outside, and archery is needed to kill them. Forget the storm; anyone who leaves the tavern now will be in grave danger."

"Blimey," the bartender frowns. "Are you certain?"

I nod. "I saw them myself. They're after this woman here," I flick my chin at Mara, who's gone back to hiding her face in her crossed arms on the table.

"You don't say?" the bartender's eyes widen. "You know, she comes by every now and then, and just sulks around without talking to anyone. I've tried to cheer her up, but no luck. Now I get it: she's hiding from monsters."

I nod. "I've sworn on my honor to help her escape, but perhaps I've spoken too soon. Without a bow and arrows, I don't think I'll find anyone willing to fight them."

A fierce glimmer lights up the bartender's eyes. He looks this way and that, and says, "Hold on, brother. Stay right here." He goes throughout the tavern to distribute the drinks. Upon returning, he says, "You can't just tell a lady you'll help her defeat some monsters—with a swear of honor, no less—and then turn around and find someone else to do it!"

I'm taken aback. "Hey! I never said anything about defeating them *myself!*"

The bartender shakes his head. "If that's not what you meant, you shouldn't have said 'on my honor.'"

"But I'm just a farmer! What do you expect me to do, beat them with a shovel? I'll be dead in less than a minute! For all our sakes, I think *they* should be the ones to do the job," I point with my thumb back at the goblin-teasing men.

The bartender looks at me with sad disappointment. "It's because of situations like this that Armavir is no longer the respectable kingdom it used to be."

I have no words. I agree with him, but I *do not* want to be the one risking my life out there! I can't fight to save my own skin!

45

Perhaps with a bow I'd give it a shot, but with no weapons? No way! I can't do it!

Suddenly, I'm overwhelmed by a wave of anguish. I hear a voice as clear as day speaking in my mind: *"Who will go? Who will I send? Who will bring justice to this land and proclaim the end of all evil? Who will fight in the final days?"*

The anguish and the voice are so powerful, I have to lean on a nearby table for balance. What's happening? Who's speaking to me? Images of child-Melody's innocent face flash across my mind, along with the scene of the Great King and Eli weeping over her loss. The sensation grips my heart so strongly, I can't help but respond, *"If no one else does, I will."*

At that moment, the anguish morphs into a smoldering passion. It's like the zealous courage I felt upon deciding to help Mara, but now many times stronger.

The voice replies, *"You are the one I have sent."*

I double over with awe, gripping the table with both hands to stay standing. What in the land of Armavir is happening to me? What am I being sent to do?

The monsters.

I have to fight the monsters.

"You feeling all right, brother?"

Oh, I almost forgot he was there. Slowly, with trembling breath, I straighten my posture and face the bartender. "Okay, I'll do it. But I still need a weapon."

"Hmm," the bartender glances the bar. "There's an old spear collecting dust behind the counter; we only use it to clean cobwebs off the ceiling. You can use that if you want."

I think about it. A spear might be similar in shape and weight to a pitchfork, which I've used frequently. I may not be a fighter, but I *do* know how to thrust a pitchfork. As long as I'm agile enough to stay out of biting range, it just might work. It's definitely better than nothing. "Bring me the spear," I say finally.

"Right away, brother."

Meanwhile, I gaze at the people in the tavern. I see Jed, who smiles proudly when we make eye contact. I see the back of Mara's head, since she's still face-down on the table. I see Devin, Carmi, and Peter on the far side of the tavern, captivated by a story told by an old couple. I'm glad the kids have no idea what I've set out to do.

"Here it is," the bartender says, toting a spear.

I take the weapon and move it around to get a feel for it. The wooden shaft is seven feet long, with a spearhead made of iron. It's not much heavier than any given farm tool. It may not be the spear of champions, but it'll do the job.

I hope.

"Good luck brother," he says, patting me on the shoulder.

"Thanks," I pat him on the back in return before walking toward the exit.

Everything seems surreal as I approach the door. I'm about to challenge four venomous Abysso-monsters to a fight to the death, and all I have is a spear. I know I should be afraid for my life, but I don't feel much of anything. Even the boldness I experienced a moment ago has subsided into a dull state of shock. In all my childhood years of imagining myself to be a hero, I never thought becoming a real hero would feel this way. What have I gotten myself into? I came to the tavern to buy a beer for my father, and now I find myself taking part in the type of quest I've only ever heard about. How do I know I didn't fall asleep at some point? Maybe I was so into *The Princess of the Sea* that now I'm dreaming about it. The whole Seer business could be a dream, too.

No. Something within me knows this definitely isn't a dream.

The thought breeds nervous anticipation in my heart as I reach the door. I look back at everyone in the tavern one last time. Only the bartender and Jed are watching me go, and they give me encouraging nods. I nod back at them before opening the door with a trembling hand and stepping into the stormy fray.

6
Nox Abyssae
Summary, 1419 AIE

~Connor~

I WALK FORWARD A few steps before standing still. I take in my surroundings: the crossroads in front of me, the tall grass stretching into the darkness, the dead horse on the road leading to my house, the tavern behind me, and the horse stables adjacent to the tavern. No sign of the monsters yet.

I begin to strategize. Abysso primarily use their sight and smell to track prey. The rain renders the latter useless. Therefore, it would be in my best interest to stay out of the monsters' line of sight.

First, I need to figure out where they're hiding. They probably see me already. Since I'm wearing a coat similar to Mara's and their sense of smell won't clue them into the difference, they will likely attack me with all the vicious hatred meant for her.

Still standing in the same spot, I scrutinize the movements of the tall grass and frequently look toward the dead horse. There's no sign of them. I don't want to walk too far from the tavern in case I need to run for cover.

Suddenly, I get the urge to look up and behind me at the thatched tavern roof.

There, crouched on the edge and leering down at me, is one of the monsters. Lightning flashes the instant I spot it.

At first I'm paralyzed with fear, but then I stand ready, pointing my spear at it. "You want some of this, you hideous cat? Of course not. Why don't you go back where you came from before somebody gets hurt?"

An amused glimmer appears in the monster's eyes, but it remains still. I wonder if I should attack it while it's on the roof? I almost decide to do it, but a sharp hiss prompts me to turn around.

A second monster slithers out of the tall grass a dozen feet away. Its glowing tendrils fan out around its face like the petals of a flower.

I point my trembling spear at it, glancing back at the first one every so often, and I back away from both of them.

The third monster reveals itself from behind the horse stable and prowls toward me from the side. And finally, the fourth monster comes out of the tall grass on the far side of the crossroads and advances from my other side.

I'm surrounded.

The first monster alights in front of the door, blocking all hope of escape.

This is it. A fight to the death.

"You are the one I have sent," the mysterious voice echoes in my mind, charging me with strength and purpose.

No sense in standing around waiting. I swore on my honor, and I'm going to help Mara escape, even if it kills me.

I yell a battle cry against the rain and thunder, charging toward the monster immediately in front of me. I hold my spear above my head, ready to plunge it into the flesh of that hideous beast.

There's a flicker of surprise in the monster's eyes as I come, but it doesn't last long. Just as I bring my spear down, the monster leaps nimbly to the side and my weapon meets the muddy ground. Then the monster jumps at me with claws extended.

I have just enough time to kick and send it sprawling backward.

I haul my spear out of the ground in time to meet the next monster, coming at me from behind with a furious yowl. I prepare to thrust the leaping creature head-on, but another one jumps me from the side and takes the butt of the spear in its jaws. My balance is offset by the unexpected weight at the end of my weapon, causing me to twist and fall to my knees. The leaping monster soars over my head after I fall. I hang onto my spear as the monster on the other end tries to take it from me.

Another monster comes from the side, preparing to snap its jaws on my arm, but I roll to the side and narrowly escape its poisoned fangs.

My rolling action twists the spear out of the other monster's mouth. I spring to my feet and swing the spear to thwack that monster across the face. The iron spearhead cleaves off a portion of two of its tendrils, causing it to hiss with mixed surprise and anger.

A hit.

I got a hit!

The minor victory causes me to lose focus for a half-second too long.

One of the monsters lunges toward my leg with its jaws wide open. I notice it in time to avoid being bitten, but the monster snags my pant leg and pulls hard, causing me to fall onto my back. The monster lets go of my pant leg and tries to bite again, but I quickly kick it hard in the face.

Not giving me time to recover, another one comes straight for my neck. I take the spear and lodge it horizontally in the beast's mouth as it comes.

The monster tries to yank the spear away from me, but I hold on tight. Seeing another one coming at me from the side, I roll forward, still holding the spear, and swing the monster biting the spear into the one approaching. They collide in a tangle of limbs and claws, saving me from immediate death, but the force of the impact causes my spear to splinter in half.

Terrific.

I wield half of the spear in either hand just in time to meet the monster that had grabbed my pant leg earlier. Its claws slice through my cloak and into my shoulder, drawing blood.

With a wince I stagger back from the monster, which yips with excitement before coming in for another attack. I throw the blunt half of the spear to stop its advance, but it catches the rod in its mouth and casts it aside without breaking stride.

In terror I turn around to run, but I slip in the mud and fall on my back.

The next few seconds seem to happen in slow motion. I have fallen, and a monster is upon me. It leaps, claws outstretched and jaws wide open, eyes hungry for bloodshed. I have no time to evade.

A figure steps between me and the monster. Wielding a sledge-hammer, the figure bludgeons the monster on the side of the head and sends it flying back with a broken yowl.

The figure turns to me and extends his hand. "Get up, son! Quick!"

It's my father.

Breathless, I take his hand and he pulls me up. "Father, what are you doing here!?"

"Saving your life," he says with a gruff snort. "I should've known you'd get into trouble when I sent you to the tavern. Beer's all I wanted, not an animal skin!"

"I'll explain later," I say, looking toward the monsters. The one my father hit is getting back up. Its jaw hangs crooked; probably dislocated. Another monster approaches and sniffs its injured companion before glaring at us with seething hatred. The other two are prowling in a circle around us.

"Stand with your back to mine," my father instructs. "Keep your guard up. Never let them out of your sight!"

I obey him without a word. Has my father fought monsters before?

He answers my unspoken question immediately. "This is just like time I fought off a pack of wolves when I was your age. Your uncle and I scared off the whole lot of them with nothing but a shovel and an axe!"

"Do you think we can beat these monsters with nothing but a broken spear and a sledgehammer?"

My father pounds his palm with the hammer. "Of course, we can! We're farmers of Armavir, aren't we?"

"Yes. Yes, we are!" I stand with my back to my father, holding the spear ready.

Just then, one of the monsters that had been circling us comes in for the kill. Feeling in my gut the precise moment to do so, I swing my weapon at the monster's face and score a direct hit across the eyes. It yowls and whines as blood obscures its vision.

Meanwhile, my father takes on a charging monster with his sledgehammer. With a mighty swing, he sends it tumbling across the mud.

Another one comes toward me, evading my attack and knocking me down. Before its jaws clamp down upon my throat, my father turns and kicks it off me with an angry grunt.

The distraction offered by my father is just long enough for me to fumble with my weapon and plunge it into the kicked monster's belly. It shrieks and writhes, gnashing its teeth and scrambling to get away. I stand and give it space, not willing to risk being bitten by the frantic creature.

My father doesn't think like I do. He follows the monster, taunting, "You pathetic, hellish creature! Go back to the dark pit where you came from!" He brings his foot down, crushing the monster's skull. After one last twitch of its tail, the monster lies still.

My jaw hangs open. That was *wizard*!

He turns toward me with a smug grin. "I won't let any evil beast from this realm or the next touch my son."

I smile back at him, fumbling for words to say, but a desperate howl from one of the monsters brings me back to the battle at hand.

There is only one monster left that hasn't been injured. It stands in front of its companions, one with a dislocated jaw and the other blinded by a slash across the eyes. It paws the ground like an angry bull with tendrils flared, eyes narrowed, and jaws parted.

"Angry, are ye?" my father taunts. "I'll do to you what I did to your friend here. That'll teach you to mess with men of Armavir!"

My father is fearless. I can only hope to someday be as bold as he is.

Without a word I stand beside him, ready to fight.

The monster howls and sprints toward us.

My father stands his ground, lifting his hammer and preparing to bludgeon the monster when it arrives.

The monster skids to a stop. Its tendrils search the air as if sensing a disturbance, and then it slinks back to its original position. All three of the monsters crouch low and bow their heads.

"Ha! What's this? Ye scared, little kittens?" My father laughs.

I don't share my father's haughty attitude. I have a bad feeling about this. "Something's not right."

My father looks at me with a chuckle. "Of course, something's not right. For them! We're giving them the beating of their lives!"

"No, no, something else..." I trail off and my eyes widen.

Water begins to gather in the center of the triangle formed by the monsters. It swirls like a waterspout and grows, accumulating volume from the rain and the mud, until it stands about six feet tall. Then it takes the shape of a person, spawns a magic staff, and materializes into a man.

He looks to be old, but his eyes are fierce. His robe is decorated with elegant patterns of white and blue. His silver staff is crowned with a radiant sapphire. His bald head glistens with the flashes of lightning; it's a remarkable sight. Most remarkably of all, he is completely dry. Every drop of rain falling toward him just happens to miss.

Lastly, though lightning continues to flash with regularity, the thunder has all but fallen silent.

It's him. It must be.

"The sorcerer," I breathe.

"Sorcerer?" my father echoes, followed by a mocking guffaw. "A circus freak, I say. What's he doing bringing his magic tricks all the way out here?"

"Shh!" I nudge my dad with my elbow.

The sorcerer smiles and extends his arms. "Greetings, gentlemen. What a pleasant night for a stroll through the countryside, wouldn't you say?"

"I'll stroll all over your countryside!" My father steps forward.

I grab his arm. "Father, stop! He's a *sorcerer!*"

My father grumbles, standing beside me with an angry glare at the sorcerer.

"Unruly fellow, isn't he?" The sorcerer rests his hands on the top of his staff as he looks at me. "It's a pleasure to meet you at last, Connor."

My entire body tenses up. How does he know my name?

My father casts a bewildered look at me. "You know this nutcase?"

I shake my head in response.

"I've waited a long time for this night," the sorcerer continues, reaching down to stroke the heads of his injured monsters. "Here we are, at the crossroads of fate. The realm as we know it is about to change. What road shall we take? The choices are many, but I for one will do what is necessary to travel the path I see fit."

I don't know what he's talking about, but the sinister gleam in his eye leads me to believe it isn't good.

"My name is Jaedis, the Sorcerer of the Northern Bluffs," he says, with a small bow, before gesturing toward the monsters, "These are my pets, the Nox Abyssae. I created them myself. Marvelous, aren't they?"

That's when I notice the monsters are no longer injured. Jaedis must have healed them with his touch.

"Terrifying," I reply with a gulp. "You already know who I am, and this is my father. We're farmers. Harmless, hardworking, Armaviran country folk."

Jaedis narrows his eyes. "Harmless indeed. I know that you know whom it is I seek. And I know, young Seer, that your heart wills to defend her."

So far, I'd say Jaedis has more Seer points than I do. He seems to know everything.

The sorcerer continues. "However, it's not too late to change your path. If you step aside now and forget about this encounter, no harm will come to you. But if you choose to stand in my way, death will come upon you swiftly and without mercy."

At first, I'm too afraid to speak, but I know deep down that something must be done.

My father scowls. "How dare you threaten my son!"

"Mind your temper, old man."

"Who are *you* calling old, you rusty codger!?" My father retorts, hefting his hammer.

Jaedis looks at my father sternly.

I put a hand on my father's shoulder, and he looks at me. I force a confident smile and say, "Leave it to me. This is my fight."

He looks stubbornly at me for a second, but finally concedes with a nod and lowers his hammer.

With a deep trembling breath, I take a step forward and speak. "Jaedis, you've come here all the way from the Northern Bluffs, wherever that is, seeking to kill a woman who has done you no harm. I won't let you hurt her. The injustice against Melody has to stop, and I'll do everything I can to help her live in peace."

Jaedis frowns. "Consider your words carefully, young Seer. You naively assume I'm the villain for pursuing this woman. How do you know it was not *she* who wronged *me*? You would be wise to avoid dabbling in matters you do not understand. Now, I will graciously extend my offer a second time. Step aside now and live, or continue your insolence and die."

My father pats me on the back and says, "Let it go, son. Let's get out of here."

I ignore him. Straightening my posture to appear more confident than I feel, I say to Jaedis, "Melody is a danger to nobody. I ask you kindly to forget this grudge of yours and return to your home."

My father face-palms with a groan.

Jaedis stands still, his expression dark and foreboding.

The Nox Abyssae curl their lips in a snarl.

Even the storm seems to hold its breath.

Finally, Jaedis looks at me with eyes as venomous as his monsters' bite. "So, you have made your decision, Connor the Seer. May the blood of all who die from this day forward be on your head!"

The sorcerer raises his staff.

A cluster of ice spikes extends out of the mud in front of my father and impales him, lifting him up in the air. His surprised shout ends with a terrible gurgle as the sledgehammer slips out of his hand and falls to the ground with a muddy splash.

"*NO!*" I scream.

He is suspended in mid-air by one spike through his abdomen and another through his right shoulder. Blood trickles down the spikes in tiny rivulets, and the rain makes it run all the more. He is breathing with small rapid gasps.

As soon as I find the will to move again, I take up my father's hammer and strike the ice. It only dents in response, but I *will* break it down. I *must* save my father!

Jaedis, with a smug grin, orders his pets, "Finish them."

I hardly notice. My sight is set on my father, as I continue to swing at the ice. "Hang on! I'll get you down! Hang in there, you *have* to!"

With a few more strikes of the hammer, the main spike buckles and gives way. The weight of my father causes the rest to break along with it, and he falls to the ground. I rush over to him and pull the icy protrusions out of his body.

A monster jumps me from the side, bowling me over and locking its jaws on my forearm. I scream, but not for my own sake. I scream for my father, who is now being further mutilated by the remaining Nox Abyssae.

Suddenly, a powerful light envelops the area. Brighter than any bolt of lightning, it consumes the darkness and renders sight useless.

The Nox Abyssae screech and recoil, letting go of me and my father and scrambling off in separate directions.

I hear Jaedis scream, "Agh! What is the meaning of this!?"

Then I hear a female voice, more powerful than thunder, "Leave them alone!"

Jaedis yells again, but his words are jumbled. I feel like I'm floating off the ground. The sounds of the sorcerer's storm fade into the background. I'm surrounded by light. That's all I know. My thoughts have become fuzzy. What's happening? Am I so disoriented by grief for my father that I'm going insane? Oh, I remember.

A monster bit me.

I've been poisoned.

I notice an acute pain spreading up the length of my arm and into my chest. I feel my consciousness slipping away like autumn leaves in the wind.

Or like a mighty sea turtle disappearing into the cold blue of the deep sea.

7
My Own Adventure
Summary, 1419 AIE

~Connor~

"CONNOR," A GENTLE voice calls.

I open my eyes. My vision is blurred, but I can tell I'm looking up at the sky. It's a wondrous, beautiful blue sky. Puffy clouds like swaths of cotton seem to float just out of reach. A flock of birds flutters through my field of vision with carefree twittering. I take a deep breath. With the exhale, I feel tension leaving my body. I enjoy the simplicity of mere existence for a few seconds before my memory returns.

The storm.

The sorcerer.

My father.

I sit up and look around, but when I do, I'm rendered breathless by what I see. I'm not at the crossroads by the tavern anymore. For all I know, I'm not even in Armavir anymore.

I'm sitting in the middle of a lush green meadow dotted with small yellow flowers. The grass billows in the breeze, which carries the fragrance of honey. Several dozen feet behind me the meadow ends with a cliff, below which is a grand expanse of ocean. Bordering the meadow on every other side is a forest, shimmering in the sunlight. The tree trunks are strong and their canopies dense with foliage.

Where am I?

I blink several times and rub the dullness out of my eyes to make sure I see everything right.

"Connor," the voice calls again.

I stand up. My body is strong and filled with vitality. I turn to face the sea, and there I see a white figure overlooking the cliff.

He is tall and stately, with a coat and pants like those of a nobleman or a king. A white cape billows gently behind him. His dark hair and earthen skin contrast greatly with the outfit, and on his head is perched a white cavalier with a silvery plume.

As I study him from afar, he turns to face me and beckons. "Don't be afraid. Come closer."

I hestate briefly before walking toward the figure. As I go, I'm comforted by his friendly amber eyes.

I stop about seven feet away from him.

"Are you rested?" He asks.

"I feel...great." I inspect my arm to search for the monster bite, but I see it's no longer there. I also discover the scratch wound I received earlier is nowhere to be found.

I must be dreaming.

The man says, "There is a reason you've been spared, Connor. The Great King's favor rests strongly upon you."

"The Great King? Didn't he exist a long time ago, if ever at all?"

He smiles. "Though the Era of Peace has been all but forgotten, the Great King is still alive and active, seeking to restore all that was lost when the Serpent was released."

I stiffen. "The Serpent is real, too?"

He nods. "And he resists the Great King to this very day."

I let his words sink in. Although I've always considered *The Princess of the Sea* to be one of my favorite stories, I never thought it to be more than a legend. The recent happenings at the tavern have convinced me otherwise.

"If that's the case," I say, "What do I have to do with any of this?"

The figure smiles. "The Great King has given you the Seer's gift. You must cherish it, develop it, and use it. From the end of the Era of Peace until now, the Great King has sought after Melody, whom he loves with all his heart. He has raised up many Seers and gifted individuals to remind her of her royal inheritance and call her back to Marindel, but to this day she has not listened. The Serpent's tormenting lies run deep in her soul and are no easy matter to deal with."

I nod as he speaks. I remember how stubborn and hardened

Melody had been when I spoke with her, and how she had even rejected the name given to her by the King himself.

A feeling of dread suddenly comes over me. "You're not telling me it's my destiny to follow a stubborn woman around to convince her to renounce lies she's believed for countless centuries, are you?"

"Not quite. The times are changing, and tension builds between the forces of good and evil in this realm. A time is soon coming when all the kingdoms of Tyrizah will be deceived by the Serpent, and they will try to destroy Melody once and for all. Even then, out of every kingdom, a remnant will remain steadfast to resist the will of the Serpent. Against all odds, they must unite as one to defend her in her darkest hour. Only through their courageous love and sacrifice will Melody remember the love of the Great King. Only then will she call for the Great Prince of the Sea, and only *then* can there be everlasting peace in the realm of Tyrizah."

Whoa. How does he know all this? How can he be certain? My head spins as I try to make sense of it all.

The figure continues, "Connor, you are the Final Seer. It is your word, your devotion to truth, your courage, and your leadership that will rally the remnant of every kingdom to stand as one in the final days."

My jaw drops as he speaks. Again with the 'leader of armies' gig! In my frustration I blurt, "Excuse me, but are you serious? I almost died in my first fight."

"I *am* serious. Has the Great King not sent you?"

Just then, I remember the words of the powerful voice that spoke to me in the tavern: "*Who will I send? Who will bring justice to this land and proclaim the end of all evil? Who will fight for the final days?*" And then, "*You are the one I have sent.*"

However, the memory of the voice doesn't bring back the same boldness that overtook me when I first heard it. Instead, I feel small. Incapable. Insufficient.

This is unbelievable. I don't want to lead. I can't even save my father from a sorcerer and a few monsters! How will I ever be able to lead a remnant army against all of Tyrizah *and* the Great Serpent? No can do.

"Don't worry about it now," the man says. His firm gentleness calms my anxious thoughts. "Start with the first step in front of you. Make the most of what you have right now. As you learn and grow, more will be revealed to you."

"I...I suppose. But, why me? I'm nothing special. There has to be *someone* more fit for the task. Right?"

The figure walks toward me and puts a hand on my shoulder. He looks into my eyes with a gaze that radiates with intense longing. "You will protect her for me, won't you?"

I feel my heart lurch. The entire story of *The Princess of the Sea* plays through my mind in the span of a few seconds. I see Melody's innocence, the Great King's love, Eli's faithful companionship, the Serpent's evil, and the big gap at the end just begging for some kind of resolution.

This story isn't over yet.

Now, here's this man clothed in white asking me to play a part in the grand finale.

What will my answer be?

I meet his benevolent gaze with a confident smile and put my hand on his shoulder. "Yes, I will."

The figure's face shines all the brighter. "Wonderful! I promise, there is no one more qualified for this task than you. It will not be easy, but my father and I will be with you every step of the way. It will be the adventure of a lifetime!"

He embraces me, and despite my initial surprise, I gladly return it. I don't know why, but this man seems to be one of those pleasant huggable types.

When we separate, he says, "You know how crafty the Serpent can be. Keep my words as treasures in your heart. They will keep your hope alive when the days of darkness come."

"I will."

He smiles. "Please, tell Melody I love her. Tell her I will come back for her when she calls for me."

"Yes, of course. But, I didn't catch your name."

"Ah, forgive me." The figure tips his cavalier. "I am Eli, the Great Prince of the Sea. Son of the Great King of Marindel."

My jaw drops in the same amount of time it takes Eli to do a superhuman back flip over the side of the cliff and vanish from sight. As I run to the edge to see what happened to him, I hear a triumphant horse whinny and see Eli flying out over the sea on a white winged unicorn. Soon after, he and his steed disappear in a brilliant flash of white light that fizzles out with a cloud of sparkling blue magic.

I'm so awed by my encounter with Eli that I hardly notice as my surroundings blur and fade into darkness.

"CONNOR!" A VOICE calls. "Can you hear me?"

Other voices follow, "He must have! You're so loud!"

"But, what if he's dead?"

"He's not dead! Look, he's moving!"

I open my eyes. I'm in the middle of a circle of blurry faces, and they're all yelling at me. I groan and stretch, ignoring the surprised gasps of those around me.

My body is still strong.

I feel neither the bite of the monster, nor the poison that once ran through me.

Even if my encounter with Eli was a dream, it was definitely real.

I blink and allow my vision to clear enough to where I can recognize the faces surrounding me. I see Jed, the bartender, Devin, Carmi, Peter, and a few others who'd been present in the tavern. I look beyond their faces to see the wooden ceiling of the tavern. I'm inside, safe and sound. Jaedis must be gone, and his Nox Abyssae with him. Good riddance.

But, where's my father?

The thought causes me to bolt upright. "Where's my father!?"

"Careful, lad!" Jed cautions, steadying me with his hands. "Ye don't want to hurt yourself again."

"Where's my father?" I repeat, calmer this time. I see I'm sitting on my coat, which is spread over a tabletop. Moreover, the tavern is emptier now than I've ever seen it. Morning sunlight streams in through the eastern windows, making the place appear much brighter than it had been the night before.

"Yer father is dead," Jed says, gesturing toward the far side of the tavern, where a body wrapped in a brown cloth lies on a table. "We were unable to save him. I'm sorry, lad."

I'm overcome with emotion. All the morning sunlight in the realm can't shine through the fog of grief that sets upon my heart. I fail to suppress a sob.

Carmi gently takes my arm and hugs it, looking up at me with more empathy than I ever thought kids were capable of. A single tear rolls down her cheek.

Many more run down mine.

All of us gathered are silent for a moment. I remember my father's ways. He was strong, very direct, always speaking his mind. A diligent worker, he never slacked in his farming duties. When mother was alive, he was the most caring and compassionate husband in the realm. When she died of pneumonia several winters ago, he grieved long into the spring. But even then, our homestead didn't miss a harvest. His love for beer was ridiculous in my opinion, but he never drank so much at once that he became unreasonable. He was strategic in his thinking, stalwart in his ways, and an all-around great man. He will forever be an inspiration to me.

Jed breaks the silence with a brief eulogy, "He died a brave man, fightin' like no farmer Armavir has ever known to protect the son he loved. His story will thrive as a legend in this countryside; an example of honor that will never be forgotten."

I nod, wiping tears off my cheek. "Very well said."

Just then the door bursts open. A cart loaded with beer bottles clatters into the tavern, pushed by a jolly rotund man. He rings a hand bell and shouts, "Your shipment of ginger Tethysian brew has finally arrived! Fresh from the exotic islands of southern Tethys, and untouched by that horrible storm, I might add!"

We all stare at the beer vendor as if he is the most annoying individual on the face of the mainland.

"Really?" a man with us shouts. "Can't you see we're grieving?"

As the delivery man observes the scene before him, his expression melts into one of profound embarrassment. He pushes the cart a little further into the tavern and quickly shuffles out the door.

Before the ensuing silence becomes too awkward, I say, "Ginger Tethysian brew was my father's favorite. Why don't we all take a drink in his honor?" To the bartender I add, "If you don't mind, that is."

"Not at all brother. Ginger Tethysian brew is on the house today."

With that, all of us, except for the kids, uncork a bottle and drink in silence. The beer is dark, earthy, and bitter, one of the most masculine brews ever imported into Armavir. In fact, there's a popular folk legend that says drinking this beer at least once a day will cause any man without a beard to grow one, and any man who already has a beard will receive a better one. The legend is propagated among Armaviran country folk because Tethysians tend to have the most wondrously sleek and well-trimmed beards in the entire realm. It's no mystery why Tethysian men always get the ladies.

All of that to say, my father was the brawniest of men when it came to Armaviran farmers, and his love of the ginger Tethysian brew only added to his reputation.

After I've had my fill, I set the half-finished bottle aside and glance at the cart. Once unloaded, it could be used to transport my father's body back to the homestead with ease. I take the cart and roll it toward the bar, where I begin placing the remaining bottles of beer. Meanwhile, I call the bartender over and let him in on the plan.

"Go for it, brother," he agrees. "Take a few others with you. It's hard and lonely, burying a body by yourself. I'd offer to help, but I have to clean up shop before heading home. I've been awake for a whole day already, and I have another night shift this evening."

I smile at him. "That's all right. Thank you for everything."

"Anytime brother," He says with a nod.

I turn away from the bartender and wheel the cart over to where my father's body lies on the table, grabbing my coat along the way.

After I've placed my father's body on the cart, Devin pulls on my pant leg. I look at him and ask, "What is it, Dev?"

"I wanna come with you. Can I? Please?"

"No, you should run along home." I kneel to his eye-level. "The storm's kept you here all night; your parents must be worried sick."

"I don't have parents. Can I *please* go with you? You're so *wizard!*"

I hardly notice the compliment. "What do you mean, you don't have parents?"

"They died," he replies quickly. "Pleeeeease?"

I'm wondering whether or not to believe him when I hear Peter's voice behind me. "Devin's right. We're orphans."

"Oh." I feel a wave of compassion for the kids as Peter and Carmi come around me to stand with Devin. I'm an orphan now, too. "Do you kids live in an orphanage?"

"Yeah, in Bayside Harbor," Carmi replies. "We sneak out and come to the tavern to hear stories sometimes. Tavern stories are *way* better than orphanage stories."

"Everyone dies in orphanage stories," Peter mumbles.

"I'm sorry to hear that, but you kids really should head back to Bayside Harbor. I haven't decided where I'm going from here, but wherever it is, it'll be too dangerous."

"But, Bayside Harbor is *boring*," Devin whines.

"No it's not. Have you ever been to the wharf? Traders and fishermen pass through there, many more than here at the tavern. You'll get some great stories out of them."

"They're too busy to talk to us," Carmi explains. "People here are relaxed and will talk to anybody."

As she's speaking, Jed comes to stand beside me. I rise to greet him, and he pats my back and says, "Let's get yer father home before it gets too hot out."

"Yes, let's." I turn to the kids and say, "It was great to meet you three. Now, please go back to the orphanage before your caretakers begin to worry."

"Awww!" They all pout in unison.

The old man chuckles and winks. "You'll see Connor again soon, don't worry!"

"We'd *better* see him again!" Devin points at his eyes with two fingers and points them at me, and then runs off toward the exit. Carmi and Peter wave and follow close behind.

Once they've gone, I breathe a sigh of relief. "Thank you. I was beginning to think they'd follow me around forever."

"Oh, they might," Jed replies.

Fear drops into the pit of my stomach. I imagine being in a situation like last night's, fighting monsters and confronting a powerful sorcerer, while having to worry about keeping kids safe. Absolutely not. Nope, I can't do it. I give Jed a desperate look, begging for mercy.

He meets my gaze for a second before cracking up with laughter. "Ah, lad! I'm *kiddin'!*"

"Hey!" I chuckle, nudging him with my elbow. "You really scared me there!"

"If ye found that scary, ye'd better grow a backbone. The lands beyond this countryside are *very* scary."

"I think I'm more aware of that now than I ever have been."

Jed and I begin guiding the cart toward the door of the tavern. Before leaving, I stop to take one last look at the old place. Who knows when I'll visit again? Perhaps next time, I'll come with an arsenal of stories I can tell from my own experience! I already have one. The story of the sorcerer's storm will surely find its place among the greats as time goes by. With that final thought, we exit the tavern.

Outside, the late-morning sun is shining and birds are singing. The ground is muddy and puddles abound. The air is thick and humid as the grounded water evaporates into the atmosphere. I'm glad I have Jed with me to help maneuver the cart through the mud.

Through the haze of my grief, I think about what I should do next. I can't run the homestead on my own. I'll have to sell it and move to Bayside Harbor, or another village. Once there, I could pick up a new trade. Or if I'm feeling extra adventurous, I could move to another kingdom and start a new life.

Then, as if by lightning strike, I remember Eli's steadfast gaze as he asked me, "Will you protect her for me?"

I shudder. In doing so I jolt the cart, and Jed steadies it before it tips over. He glances at me. "What's on yer mind, lad?"

"I was just wondering…I haven't seen Mara since I woke up this morning. What happened to her?"

"Melody? Ah, she left after savin' ye from Jaedis."

Wait, what?

"That can't be right," I reply. "She was fleeing from Jaedis, wasn't she?"

"Aye. But last night, ye did in her heart what no Seer has been able to do for a thousand years."

I look at him. "What do you mean?"

"Ye gave her hope. Ye gave her a will to fight. Ye gave her a chance to reclaim her authority."

My heart rises at the thought, but I'm still doubtful. It sounds too good to be true. "I don't remember giving her any of those things. In fact, before I left to fight the Nox Abyssae she said, 'I'll watch you fail from here.'"

"It wasn't yer words that moved her heart, lad! It was yer action, the fact that ye went through with it! Though ye were a simple farmer with no idea what ye were up against, out ye went into that storm to challenge the Nox Abyssae with nothin' more than an old spear. Connor, as soon as ye went out the door, Melody got up and rushed to the window. She saw *everythin'*. It was when Jaedis attacked yer father that she finally had enough. Forgettin' her own fear, she went out there and used her magic to send Jaedis away and end the accursed storm over the countryside. She took the poison out of ye before it reached your heart, and she healed your wounds. After that, she left."

My eyes are wide as Jed speaks. When he finishes, I gape in disbelief. "Wait, hold on! Why'd you let her leave? Now I have to find her all over again!"

"Why is that, lad?"

Determination wells up in my heart as I speak. "One, I have to thank her for saving me. Two, I have to tell her Eli loves her. Three, I have to keep an eye on her because all the kingdoms of Tyrizah will want to have her killed, and…"

I trail off as Jed places a hand on my shoulder, his sea-blue gaze as gentle as ever. "Aye, there is a great destiny ahead of ye, but take it one step at a time. Jaedis the Sorcerer is an immediate threat. Ye must confront him and bring him to justice before he finds Melody again. But first, ye will need companions to join yer quest. Ye're no fighter, so ye'll need friends who will fight for ye and teach ye self-defense. Many adventurers pass through Bayside Harbor seekin' to embark on quests such as yours; it won't be hard to recruit a few of them."

"But this isn't just any quest, and you know that!"

"Use yer Seer's gift. It will guide ye in your search."

It sounds hard, intimidating, tedious, and unpleasant, but I know it's what I have to do. I'll sell the homestead and use the money to buy supplies for me and whomever I find to join me, and then we'll journey to the Northern Bluffs to find Jaedis and stop him from hunting Melody and killing innocents like my father.

Finally, I say, "I'll do my best. Thanks, Jed."

We arrive at the homestead. Jed and I take the cart with my father's body across the fields, between the rows of growing barley, and to the side of the house. There is a large oak tree nearby, and just beneath it is my mother's grave. My father will be buried next to her.

Jed and I spend most of the afternoon digging. After we're finished, we place my father's body in the grave and have another few moments of silence before burying him. I search the outskirts of the field for a fitting, perfectly-sized boulder to place at the head of the grave as a headstone. With a chisel and hammer I write my father's name—Marcellus Lightwood—and an epitaph: "A strong, brave man who died protecting his beloved son."

After the work is finished, I invite Jed inside the house and cook the two of us a meal of garlic bread, beets, and beef stew. We eat, talk, and plan how to sell the homestead until nightfall, when we both lie down for a much-needed night of rest.

At sunrise, I pack my bag with anything in the house that might be useful on a long and perilous quest: a rope, tinder kit, small hatchet, canteen, some bread, a bag of several blics, and most importantly, my father's hunting knife. I also find the deed for the homestead, which I give to Jed. Lastly, I change into the most comfortable, yet durable, tunic and coat I can find.

Before leaving, I look around the house one last time. I relish the smell of the old wooden beams and run my hands across the familiar grooves on the plaster-coated walls. I've lived here for as long as I can remember. If life hadn't thrown such tragic circumstances my way, I'd never be willing to sell this property. I hope the next owners will take care of it and enjoy it as much as my family did. Who knows? Maybe I'll come back and visit again someday. Standing on the front porch, with a few tears and a final goodbye, I shut and lock the door of my childhood home.

Jed and I part ways on the road. He travels eastward to Cloud Summit, the capital city of Armavir, where he will work out the details of selling the homestead. Meanwhile, I travel westward to Bayside Harbor, where after all my previous talk of storytelling, I will finally begin to live my own adventure.

8
The Pride of Felidae
Spring, 1418 AIE

~Tarento~

"FELIDAE IS AN ancient land with a rich cultural history, stretching all the way back to the beginning of time. However, it is only within the last hundred years that Felidae has reached realm-wide prominence and taken its place among the most powerful kingdoms of Tyrizah.

"For centuries, the people of Felidae lived in constant fear and affliction, arising from cut-throat competition with the many species of monsters on the island. Over time, Felids have learned to outsmart and outmaneuver their enemies with novel strategies and state-of-the-art weaponry.

"The Samurai warriors of Felidae were born on the front lines. Battle techniques were developed in times of adversity and passed down to the Samurai of the next generations, who not only heeded the wisdom of their ancestors but added to the skills they inherited by developing many unique styles of swordsmanship, archery, martial arts, magical arts, and tactical warfare.

"But everything changed in 1323, when the pinnacle of Felid ingenuity came on the scene.

"An aspiring inventor, skilled with intellect but an embarrassment on the battlefield, Zhemushi endured much suffering early in his life. In a great tragedy, he was unable to save his sister from a marauding jungle troll. Bent on revenge and unwilling to accept his natural shortcomings, he isolated himself and spent many moons indoors.

"Planning.

"Experimenting.

"Model after model.

"Failure after failure, facing ridicule over and over again.

"Finally, twelve years after the death of his sister, it was complete.

"Against all odds, and against the belief of every Samurai on the battlefield that day, Zhemushi planted his great masterpiece, the first of many, within the gates of the budding city of Jinshi. There he waited patiently.

"The jungle trolls advanced, forcing their way through Felid defenses and coming upon the walls of Jinshi. It seemed as though the city would fall, and the people of Felidae would suffer a great loss.

"With a mighty crash, a burly jungle troll sent the gates of Jinshi flying off their hinges and marched inside, bellowing in triumph.

"There, just fifteen feet ahead, was Zhemushi and his greatest invention. With a sly grin, he lit the fuse.

"*BOOM!*

"The troll was scattered everywhere.

"Never before had any man recreated the fire-spitting abilities of a dragon: a red-hot projectile that erupted with infernal fury upon its target.

"No one, man or monster, could stand against the Felid cannon.

"Zhemushi's ingenuity became known across the land, as every village sought to acquire the ground-breaking invention. He made copies of his blueprints for metalworkers, who built factories dedicated to the production of cannons. Meanwhile, Zhemushi himself continued to experiment with new and improved models.

"Bigger models.

"Rolling and rotating models.

"Ship-borne models.

"More explosive models.

"In this way, the people of Felidae began to conquer the entirety of the island they called home. Centuries of blood and sacrifice were finally being avenged.

"Within two decades, the monsters of Felidae were all but extinct.

"The people began to enjoy prosperity, unknown and unprecedented by any of their ancestors. Their numbers doubled, tripled, and quadrupled. Villages and cities expanded rapidly, and trade with other kingdoms budded and flourished. In the span of a generation, the success of Felidae became renowned across the realm.

"In 1325, Zhemushi was appointed king of Felidae, uniting the island under one ruler for the first time. He became an icon of human success and pride. During his lifetime, he was revered by all of Felidae as the greatest man to have ever lived. A hero. A savior. The very reason the kingdom of Felidae existed.

"After his death in 1375, Zhemushi was succeeded by his son Doku, who, unlike his father, was no strategic mastermind. Unable to attain Zhemushi's level of prominence and popularity, he soon became discouraged and was rarely seen outside of the palace. The passive rule of Doku only strengthened the pride of the people in their previous ruler, and some extremists believed Zhemushi was still their true king, even though he was dead.

"Doku ruled Felidae for thirty-nine years before his death, and he was succeeded in 1414 by his son Zetsumei.

"Ambitious, amiable, confident, and showing his love for Felidae and human ingenuity with proactive gusto, Zetsumei has been king for only four years, yet he has seen more economic, military, and artistic development in Felidae than Doku did for all of his thirty-nine-year reign."

The proconsul rolls up the scroll he'd been reading from and looks at us with a gleam in his eye. "The sun couldn't possibly shine brighter over the kingdom of Felidae."

I hold my breath, waiting for him to continue. Surely we weren't summoned here for a history lesson. *Everyone* in Felidae knows the story. It's taught in school to mere toddlers! Felids are very proud of their heritage.

I, however, happen to be more reserved when it comes to these things. I love Felidae, to be sure, but sometimes I wonder if we take it too far. I don't know of any other kingdom that, for lack of a better expression, worships itself.

The proconsul gestures toward the massive sixth-story window behind him. "Look now at the Heavenly Palace."

The cityscape of Jinshi greets us; dozens of ornate pagodas and spires, some with ornate gilded roofs. In the distance is the Heavenly Palace, only the top of which is visible among the other buildings.

The proconsul says, "When Lord Zhemushi had the palace built, it was the tallest and most extravagant structure in the city. But, as you can see, Jinshi has grown up in splendor around it. The city's glory has surpassed that of the dwelling place of our king."

Mutters of discontent are heard among the group of Samurai with whom I stand.

"I have good news," the proconsul continues with a small grin. "Lord Zetsumei is pleased to reveal his intention to honor the legacy of his grandfather by authorizing the construction of a new palace. It will be the tallest structure ever built; a tower that will reach the very heavens."

"Outstanding!" A Samurai says.

"Yes," the proconsul agrees. "It will preside high and strong over the great city of Jinshi. What's more, it will even be visible from Port Beihai. There, every kingdom will see from afar the power and greatness of Felidae."

The others make excited comments while I thoughtfully consider what the proconsul is saying. Port Beihai is on the northern shore of the island, thirty miles from the inland city of Jinshi. Beihai is the only port in Felidae where foreigners are allowed to travel and trade freely.

The news that Zetsumei wants to build a tower so massive that it can be seen from thirty miles away by foreigners is staggering. It's as if he wants to shout to the other kingdoms, 'Look what we can do! See, way over there, that monolith on the horizon? We built it. Don't you wish you could be as amazing as we are, with our intricate golden arches, pointed roofs, colorful banners, and triumphant fanfare? You can watch from afar, but don't come too close or you'll find yourself staring down the barrel of a cannon.'

Such goes the logic of the average Felid. I suppose I'm an exception.

"What do you think, Tarento?" the Samurai to my left nudges me with his elbow. "A tower that will reach the heavens! Impressive, eh?"

His name is Heiban; he's a true Felid if there ever was one. He also happens to be my Samurai partner, and my best friend.

"It's great," I reply, forcing a polite smile.

"Just 'great'?" Heiban laughs. "It's beyond 'great'! It'll be the thing everyone's talking about for the next twenty years, at least!"

Despite a strong urge to say "I wish we had better things to talk about than an ostentatious building," I hold my tongue. It's highly frowned upon to voice one's opinion of Felidae, its king, or its affluence if it isn't equated with the glory of the sun.

The proconsul speaks again, "The public announcement and

ground-breaking ceremony will take place on this year's Jubilation Day, and the grand opening will take place in seven years, as the keystone event of the Centennial Jubilee."

Jubilation Day is the annual celebration of the crowning of Zhemushi and the unification of Felidae. It involves exorbitant feasts and festivals, confetti and fireworks, live orchestras, and of course, a grand parade marching through the heart of Jinshi. The holiday takes place on the summer solstice, which is three days from now. The Centennial Jubilee will be Felidae's aptly-named centennial anniversary, and I dare say it's no coincidence the culmination of Felidae's collective ego will be completed on that day.

The proconsul continues, "Lord Zetsumei has selected each of you, two Samurai from every village, to be present with him when he makes the announcement. He has also given you the honor of being among the first to pay homage to the new statue of Lord Zhemushi, which will be revealed at the ground-breaking ceremony. It will stand with prominence in front of the new palace."

Excited murmurs emanate from the group.

"You must all meet at the Heavenly Palace before dawn on Jubilation Day, dressed proudly in your best ceremonial gear. You will not need heavy combat armor or masked helmets; your village headbands will suffice. Lastly, your attendance at this event is mandatory. Is that clear?"

"Hai!" we all affirm.

"Good. You're dismissed."

"Can you believe it?" Heiban asks as we walk together. "What an honor! Out of all the Samurai in our village, Lord Zetsumei chose *us!*"

"Yes, it's a very great honor," I reply with a nod.

We're on our way to check in to our hotel, where we'll be staying until the ceremony on Jubilation Day. It's on the other side of the city, so we've found ourselves traveling through the narrow bustling streets at noontime. It was Heiban's idea to come this way. I'm overwhelmed by the sheer number of people, the clanging of pots and pans in nearby restaurants, and the competing smells of various stir-fry dishes, amplified by the humid midday heat. Now, to make matters worse, Heiban won't stop talking my ear off about the new palace.

"What motivated him to choose us, I wonder?" Heiban muses.

"Did he hear about the Warrior Tournament last year? We didn't win, but we put up the greatest fight! Or, perhaps he made the decision based on the scope of our abilities. I'm the best with elemental ninja arts, and you're good with weapons. Or," Heiban cracks a playful grin, "he must have heard about the time I rescued you from that Abysso years back. Remember?"

"Oh, come on Heiban," I chuckle. "You would've been killed yourself if Jing Sensei hadn't shown up."

"But *you* would have been killed if *I* hadn't shown up," Heiban asserts.

"Very well, then," I say. "In any case, Jing Sensei might have put in a good word for us. No one is more aware of our progress in training and success in our assignments than he is."

"No doubt about that," Heiban agrees. He sniffs the air and looks over at a noodle shop as we walk past. "You hungry, Tarento?"

Despite my desire to leave this crowded area as quickly as possible, my groaning stomach gets the better of me. "Yeah. Let's eat."

We walk into the busy noodle shop and stand in line while perusing the menu. My eyes quickly fall upon my favorite dish; a large beef noodle bowl garnished with chives and baihua pollen. I never grow tired of the simple things in life.

"*Tarento*," a voice calls.

"Yeah?" I ask.

Heiban looks at me. "Huh?"

"Did you call me?"

"Nope."

"That's odd," I mutter.

"Do you know what you want?" Heiban asks, glancing again at the menu. "I'll buy this time."

"I'll take the usual," I reply as I study my surroundings, looking for anyone nearby who might have called me.

"Got it. Why don't you find us a seat? This place is getting bombarded."

I nod. My eyes had fallen on an empty table a few seconds ago, and I go to claim it.

As soon as I sit, it comes again: "*Tarento*."

"What?" I ask, looking this way and that. Not seeing anyone looking at me, I furrow my brow with annoyance. Someone must be playing a prank on me, and I detest being pranked.

"*Tarento*," I hear it again, and this time I realize the voice is in my own mind. Either I'm hearing things, or someone is speaking telepathically to me.

"*Yes?*" I reply.

"*Why do you hide your feelings about the new palace?*"

A prick of fear stabs my heart. "*What feelings?*"

"*Consider them well. Remember why it is you feel the way you do. Soon you will be launched into your destiny, for I have chosen you.*"

"*What are you talking about?*" I ask, but I hear no response.

As I sit alone in the bustling noodle shop, my initial premonitions about the new palace begin to resurface.

Why am I so disturbed by the news?

Why am I upset with the direction in which this kingdom is headed?

It's ridiculous to me, all this frivolous, flamboyant nonsense. But, why am I the only one who seems to notice?

Well, I may not be the *only* one, but I'll never know for sure because no one talks about it openly.

Unfortunately, it turns out many Felids think Felidae is the only civilized kingdom in the realm. Foreigners aren't allowed to travel here with the exception of Port Beihai. What's more, Felid merchants, diplomats, and Samurai can only leave Felidae with special permission. Therefore, the average Felid's exposure to the other kingdoms is minimal at best, and the pseudo-cultic bias championed by the ruling regime ensures everyone believes they live in the greatest kingdom that ever was, is, or will be.

But I've been out there.

Across the sea, to the mainland.

When I was eighteen—I'm twenty-four now—I was given a rare mission that granted me the opportunity to travel abroad.

Back then, there were rumors about a war with Sunophsis. Pirates were always trying to hijack Felid trade vessels to get their hands on a Felid cannon. Of course, every single time, it was those very cannons that put the pirates in their place. Despite our obvious advantage, the Sunophsians thought they could scare us into a trade agreement by threatening to declare war.

Thankfully, this took place in 1412, at the end of Doku's reign. He had no interest in going to war, so he sent a delegation to Sunophsis to work out a trade agreement, with strict orders *not* to incite war and *not* to give them cannons. As it happened, I was one of the five Samurai appointed to escort the delegation.

The mission lasted eight moons due to the length of time it took to travel to the Sunophsian capital city of Kharduman: first across the sea; and then across a barren, sandy desert.

The negotiations went well, but even so, it was there in Kharduman where I realized what the realm is really like.

The citizens of other kingdoms aren't *nearly* as patriotic as we are.

Crime is everywhere.

Fighting is common. Not against monsters, but against each other.

Living conditions are inconceivable.

The consequences of greed are evident.

Theft, murder, deception, lewdness, substance abuse—all of it is everywhere, just out in the open. Yet, no one seems to give it a second thought.

Sunophsis has a king named Sisera, but he is allegedly a self-absorbed drunken maniac who would rather lounge around and feast than maintain order in his kingdom.

"They took forever, as usual," Heiban interrupts my thoughts, setting our tray of food on the table before sitting down across from me. "By Zhemushi's beard, I feel like I could eat a troll!"

I chuckle. "Did you get the troll noodles? I saw it up there on the menu."

"Nah," Heiban says, picking up a pair of chopsticks and beginning to eat. With his mouth full he adds, "Troll's too expensive nowadays. Besides, this rabbit bowl hits the spot!"

"Glad to hear it," I say, picking up chopsticks and digging in to my own meal.

I wish I could tell Heiban how I feel.

It's hopeless. If there's even *one* person in Felidae who feels the way I do, it's not going to be him. Among the Samurai, Heiban is one of the most outspokenly loyal to the legacy of Zhemushi and to the current king Zetsumei. He'll more likely be the one to betray me if I express my thoughts and doubts to him.

But...he's my partner. My comrade. My best friend.

I have to try.

"Heiban," I begin, as I swallow a mouthful of noodles. "Do you remember when I went on that mission to Sunophsis?"

"How could I forget?" Heiban rolls his eyes. "I was supposed to go too, but I already had my hands tied with a C-level mission for the merchant's guild."

"Don't worry, it wasn't very exciting. Too much traveling with boring scenery." How do I preface this without it coming across as odd? I'm very bad at navigating conversations, especially of this sensitive nature.

"Why'd you ask?" Heiban presses, before slurping another helping of noodles.

"Well, I was just wondering...have you ever thought about what it might be like to live in another kingdom?"

"I sure have," Heiban replies.

"Really?" All right, that was easier than I expected.

"I definitely wouldn't want to. They're missing out on so much, and they don't even know it. We have it made here, Tarento. I'm sure you know that even better than I do."

I frown. That's not the answer I was hoping for. "Well, do you ever wonder if we should...I don't know...do more to help the other kingdoms?"

"We trade with them. What more could they possibly want?"

"No, no, not like that—"

Heiban cuts me off with a light chuckle. "Why are we talking about this, anyway? It doesn't matter what goes on outside of our borders. The other kingdoms can figure themselves out on their own, just like we did. Besides, you were in *Kharduman* of all places. That city tops the list for crime, corruption, and anarchy. The rest of the realm can't possibly be as bad as that."

He still doesn't understand. There's a part of the story I haven't told him yet.

After a few days in Kharduman, and after trying in vain to talk to the other Felids about the horrible condition of Sunophsis, I was so distraught that I set out to find citizens of other kingdoms, non-Sunophsians, to ask if the same was true of their kingdoms.

"It is. It *is* as bad as that," I reply with a grave nod. "It's not the same kind of 'bad' as in Sunophsis, but every kingdom is suffering in some way."

"Hmph," Heiban scoffs. "I suppose you have examples of this?"

I nod. "I spoke with a Tethysian sailor one night. He told me the Tethys Region is scattered and disorganized, a mere shadow of its former self. They fight with each other and are attacked by sea monsters and dragons on a regular basis."

Heiban shrugs. "So?"

"There's more," I continue. "I also met an Armaviran adventurer. His land enjoys the aura of peace, but the economy has been falling for years, and it'll continue to do so until a major breakthrough occurs. They don't have the resources to defend their vast swath of land if it were to be invaded by a neighboring kingdom."

"Sounds like they need to get some factories up and running. Start inventing and building something useful."

"It's not that simple," I reply with a frown. "They don't think the way we do. Sure, maybe they'll have an invention of their own someday, but what if something happens before then? How many innocent people will suffer and die?"

"Hmm," Heiban frowns, "thoughts like that probably keep the king of Armavir up all night. It's *his* responsibility, after all."

"That's not the point," I reply with frustration. "One more, and I've saved the worst for last. I met an Izendoran nobleman who told me his kingdom is terrorized by a deranged king who suffers from extreme mood swings, during which he has innocent people arrested and killed at a moment's notice. The nobleman was a refugee, hiding in Sunophsis to escape the king's wrath."

"The people of Izendor should depose him," Heiban says. "Put a level-headed king in his place. There, problem solved."

"The nobleman *also* told me," I continue, "the king of Izendor has electrokinetic powers that make him as invincible as he is unpredictable. Imagine living under that kind of tyranny! It'd be horrible!"

"Oh, I'm sure it would be." Heiban leans back and places his hands behind his head. "Aren't you *thankful*, Tarento, that we live in a kingdom where we don't have to worry about any of that?"

"Yes. Believe me, I'm very grateful. But, don't you see? Here we are, marching around within our own borders, toting glamorous banners and chanting about how great we are, but we won't lift a finger to alleviate the suffering of other kingdoms. Why is that? What meaning does our success have if it's not shared with others?"

"Shhh," Heiban silences me, holding his hand up, and flicks his chin behind me.

I look to the side, and in my peripheral vision I see that three other Samurai have entered the shop. When I look back at Heiban he whispers, "This conversation is over. If I were you, I wouldn't speak of these things ever again, lest you attract unwanted attention."

I sigh deeply, looking down at my half-empty bowl of noodles.

"Hey, cheer up," Heiban says, cracking a smirk. "We have much to be grateful for. Never forget that, all right?" Without giving me a chance to reply, he stands up and shouts across the shop, "Well, well, well! Looks like three of Felidae's finest warriors have come to join us!"

The other three Samurai exchange brotherly greetings with Heiban and me, and after ordering their food, they sit down at a table near us and we talk about normal things, like our favorite noodle bowls and the latest news in our villages.

But it does nothing to cure the burden of sorrow and indignation in my heart.

9

The Stand

Spring, 1418 AIE

~Tarento~

I OPEN MY EYES to see that I'm floating above the realm of Tyrizah, with the ten kingdoms spread out beneath me like a giant map. I quickly identify Felidae, far south of the mainland. It looks very small and lonely compared with the other kingdoms.

As I survey the realm below, a voice begins to speak, "Long ago, during the Era of Peace, there was a city called Marindel. The Great King of the Sea, the sovereign ruler of this city, sought to ensure peace, justice, and harmony for all of Tyrizah. Royal and powerful though he was, he never considered himself too lofty to walk among the common people. He truly cared for them and was concerned for their welfare."

I feel a burning sensation within my heart. This is the same voice that called me earlier today! It's filled with wisdom and strength, carrying tremendous authority. Who is this, I wonder?

The realm beneath me darkens. A hideous snake-like silhouette spawns in the middle of the sea. Growing larger by the second, it coils around the kingdoms of Tyrizah and covers them in shadow, one by one.

Meanwhile, the voice continues. "The Era of Peace has come and gone, and the Era of the Great Serpent is at hand. For millennia he has deceived both commoners and kings, groups of people and entire kingdoms, to do his bidding."

"What is his bidding?" I ask the voice.

Chapter 9: The Stand

"To oppose the works of the Great King. To incite war, pervert justice, oppress the innocent, and ultimately, to bring death to every living thing. He does this in many ways, but one stands out from the rest, and you know it full well. He fills hearts with pride and vanity, until they forget the fallen state of the realm around them. And once they've brought themselves high upon a cliff, he pushes them down and laughs as they fall into the pit they dug for themselves."

I see now that the snake has darkened all of the kingdoms except for Felidae. It circles the island, spiraling inward, closing in with an evil grin. Suddenly, it opens its mouth and swallows the island whole. The realm below disappears, and I'm floating alone in empty space.

I'm terrified beyond words.

A light appears. It's a warm, blue light, growing as it draws near. I don't know if I should be comforted or frightened by it.

As I keep wondering about the light, I become aware of a hard surface beneath my feet. Then, I notice I'm in a room. It's spacious and peculiar, illuminated with dancing hues of blue, like reflections upon water.

The light settles upon a grand throne atop a flight of wide steps. It takes shape and materializes into the most dazzling figure I've ever seen—an elven king, if his pointed ears are any indication. 'Wisdom, kindness, and majesty incarnate' are the only words I can think of to describe him. No king of Felidae has ever carried such authority by his presence alone.

The figure looks beyond me and speaks with the same voice I heard narrating the story a moment ago. "The final days are drawing near. Who shall I send to alleviate the suffering of the needy, stand up for justice, and speak against pride and vanity?"

My heart lurches within my chest.

Is...is *this* the Great King?

In a flash, hundreds of elves appear on the fringes of the room. They're similar in appearance to the figure on the throne, but younger and less radiant. They sing in unison,

> *"We must find the Discerning One,*
> *Whose heart vanity has not won.*
> *He is ready, it has begun.*
> *The Serpent's fall is said and done!"*

The enthroned king speaks, "At last, I have found him."

The beings around the throne celebrate with shouts of joy and wild dances, putting Felidae's best stage performers to shame.

Who is the Discerning One?

As the beings around the throne end their celebration, the enthroned king looks at me and asks, "Tarento, have you something to say?"

All eyes are on me. I've been taken by surprise, and I feel as though my insides are about to jump out and run circles around me.

Nevertheless, I open my mouth and squeak, "I think...I think what Felidae needs is a noble and selfless king. One like you, Great King—if that's who you are. If Felidae can get a noble king, the realm may yet stand a chance."

The Great King looks at me, his eyes shining like the depths of the sea. "Be encouraged, my son. Your concerns have been heard. I have chosen you out of your people to warn them of the coming disaster. You will help me bring a new Era of Peace to all the kingdoms of Tyrizah."

What?

The Great King chose *me*!?

No! It's impossible!

My jaw hangs limp for a few seconds before I find the strength to speak. "But...how...? I can't do that! I'm just an ordinary man, and I'm terrified of public speaking!"

One of the beings, a beautiful woman, approaches me. She holds a glass chalice filled with a silvery liquid, and says, "Take courage! You are the Discerning One, whose heart vanity has not won. Drink this cup, and your tongue will be anointed with wisdom and power to transform hearts and kingdoms."

Usually, I refrain from drinking strange liquids given by strangers, but something in my heart stirs within me.

Am I really the Discerning One?

There's only one way to find out.

I take the chalice and drink the silver liquid. It slips delicately down my throat, sweet to the taste. I feel it going down into my stomach, where it hits like a fresh heap of coal on a dimly-lit furnace. Within seconds, it feels like fire is blasting through my limbs and out of my mouth! I shout and fall to my knees.

The Great King speaks while I'm on the ground. "My son, I have equipped you with boldness to speak my words to those who suffer. Listen to my voice and follow me, always. As you obey, step by step, you will begin to see the change in the realm you hope to see."

As the initial effects of the silver liquid wear off, I feel a tremendous confidence taking its place. There's a courageous flame burning in my gut, like a reservoir of dragonfire. Somehow, I know it will enable me to speak words more powerful than any Felid cannon ever made.

"I-I will do as you say," I reply, voice trembling. "You are my King now, more worthy of my allegiance than Lord Zetsumei of Felidae. I am now more a citizen of Marindel than I am of Felidae."

The Great King smiles at me; a grand, radiant smile of favor and approval. The elves around the throne erupt with joyous shouts and dancing once more.

Under the benevolent gaze of the King, I stand.

Summer, 1418 AIE

LOUD CHEERS ERUPT from the crowds.

Confetti falls endlessly from the rooftops.

Red banners and flags bearing the gold insignia of Felidae flutter in the wind.

Patriotic fanfare decorates the atmosphere.

Three days have come and gone. Jubilation Day has arrived.

I stand on a roof adjacent to the Heavenly Palace, having just been dismissed from our debrief meeting and rehearsal earlier that morning.

The ceremony will take place at the end of the Jubilation Day Parade around sunset, while the citizens of Felidae are already gathered in front of the Heavenly Palace. Zetsumei will address the crowd from a podium in front of the palace, giving a brief history of Felidae like the proconsul had given us, while we Samurai stand at attention on either side of him. Then he will announce his plan to build the new palace.

Next, he will unveil the gold statue of Zhemushi. One by one, we Samurai will pay homage to it.

Afterward, the ground-breaking ceremony will take place: Zetsumei will light a fuse, we will lead the crowd in a countdown, and the old Heavenly Palace will be demolished. The buildings adjacent to and behind it are tagged for destruction as well; the foundation of the new palace will be *that* massive.

Once the dust has settled and cheers have subsided, Zetsumei will give his son the honor of placing the first cornerstone, a sturdy brick coated in steel and trimmed with gold. For the grand finale, there will be an enormous fireworks show. And the festivities of Jubilation Day will continue long into the night, like they always do.

Those were the plans given to us that morning, but they will not happen that way.

I have spoken with the Great King several times since the first dream. I know what I must do, but I don't know what the outcome will be. For that part the Great King has only said, *"Trust in me."*

"Tarento!" Heiban alights on the roof beside me. "We're all going to get hotpot for lunch before the big event. Come join us!"

I shake my head. "No, thank you. I need some time to think."

Heiban sighs, coming closer and putting a friendly hand on my shoulder. "Hey, I know you're an introvert and all that, but you've been keeping to yourself more than usual. You haven't gone out with us in the past few days, and that worries me. Is something the matter?"

"It's nothing. It's all just...overwhelming, you know?" I gesture with one hand at the Jubilation Day festivities unfolding all around us. "Don't let me slow you down. Go have fun with the others; I'll see you back here for the event."

"You sure?" Heiban tilts his head, eyeing me with concern.

"Yes," I say, putting my hand on his shoulder. "Go have fun, you crazy velospark monkey!"

Heiban grins. "Well, all right. We'll miss you! See you soon!"

I watch as Heiban turns and runs along the rooftop to the other side, where he jumps nimbly over the narrow street and onto the next roof. In that way he travels across the crowded city toward his destination.

As he goes, a single tear rolls down my cheek.

This is not going to be easy.

LATER THAT AFTERNOON, the Jubilation Day Parade is in full swing. The sides of the broad central street are packed with cheering crowds as they behold the colorful procession of parade floats, flag bearers, dancers, military formations, and ox-drawn carts bearing the latest Felid cannon models. The Heavenly Palace is along the parade route in the very center of town. A full-scale orchestra and choir currently occupy the front plaza, playing patriotic music for the parade.

The other Samurai and I, wearing our finest ceremonial

robes, are standing on the outskirts of the plaza. Once the final marchers pass by, the orchestra is scheduled vacate the plaza. At the same time, four taiko drummers will begin to play onstage. The thundering drumbeats will alert the entire city that something important is about to happen, and people will come crowding into the plaza. That's when we Samurai will take our places onstage, and we'll hold our positions until Zetsumei unveils the statue during the ceremony.

I'm sick to my stomach with nervous anticipation.

So many things might go wrong.

I could be pelted with crossbow bolts on the spot.

One of the Samurai might be ordered to execute me.

Maybe Zetsumei himself will execute me.

Or, if everything works out perfectly, all of Felidae will repent of their pride, topple the statue, and forget about ever building a new palace.

But what are the chances of that?

The Great King's voice quells my anxious thoughts. *"Don't worry about what will happen to you or to them. Listen to me and speak the words I give you, and all things will come together."*

"Very well," I reply, swallowing my fear. *"I trust you."*

The orchestra finishes its final fanfare. Right on schedule, they disassemble and scatter. The taiko drummers begin, beating their instruments with passionate force. As crowds are drawn by the booming rhythm, the proconsul shouts, "People of Felidae, come and witness history in the making! The great Lord Zetsumei has an important announcement to make!"

"Let's go! That's our cue!" Heiban nudges me as the other Samurai make their way onto the stage. I follow alongside him without a word. We take our places in a staggered formation on either side of the center podium, where Zetsumei will stand with his adolescent son, Prince Kurai. My position is third from the center on stage-right. Heiban is second from the center on stage-right, next to me.

The plaza quickly fills with excited Felids, murmuring to one another about what the announcement might be.

Soon, two trumpeteers take positions in front of the stage. The drummers pause, and a hush falls over the plaza. As two palace guards open the front doors of the Heavenly Palace, the trumpeteers begin to play the anthem of Felidae. Lord Zetsumei and Prince Kurai emerge from within, and they stride confidently to center stage. At their appearance, we Samurai swivel on our heels to face them, salute with our right hand against our chest, palm facing down, and we shout, "Hail, Lord Zetsumei!"

The crowd erupts with cheers and shouts of "Hail, Lord Zetsumei!" and "Hail, Felidae!"

Zetsumei takes his place at the podium, waves a hand to silence the crowd, and begins with the history of Felidae.

My heart is beating fast. My eyes dart back and forth as I try to discern where in the neighboring buildings the crossbow snipers are hiding. Certainly not in the buildings that will be demolished at the end of the ceremony.

I expel the nervous thoughts and think again about the words of the Great King. My anxiety subsides, but the moment draws near.

Zetsumei finishes the history of Felidae.

The crowd hangs on his every word.

He makes the announcement. "To honor my grandfather's legacy, I have decided to build a new Heavenly Palace. It will be a monument unmatched in splendor and majesty, towering high above every man-made structure in the realm. In seven years, on the Centennial Jubilee, it will be complete. And I promise you, Felidae, there will be a celebration on that day far more extravagant than anything we have ever seen! We will make a name for ourselves among the kingdoms, and all of Tyrizah will acknowledge our greatness. The glory of Felidae will outshine the sun!"

The crowd begins to cheer even as Zetsumei is speaking, but at his final statement the response becomes deafening. Chants of "Hail, Felidae!" and "Hail, Lord Zetsumei!" continue unabated.

As I observe their response, I'm struck with a horrifying revelation. All of this is meaningless, and I'm the only one who seems to notice.

I actively prevent myself from having a panic attack by focusing on the words of the Great King.

Zetsumei begins to preface the unveiling of the statue, which is currently covered in a large cloth on a pedestal immediately behind him. As he speaks, two high-ranking military officers emerge from the Heavenly Palace and position themselves on either side of the statue. When Zetsumei finishes his speech, the officers will remove the cloth.

Then, one by one, we will pay homage to it.

"It will be the most prominent feature in the plaza," Zetsumei says. "Even during the tower's construction, all of you may behold the statue and pay homage to it as often as you wish. Let it serve as a reminder of our great Lord Zhemushi: his story, his struggle, and his legacy. For surely, without him, we would not be the mighty kingdom we are today. And now, without further ado, I present to you the great golden statue of Lord Zhemushi!"

The guards posted by the statue pull the cloth with a fluid sweeping motion, and the entire crowd gasps.

The statue is fifteen feet tall. It features Zhemushi standing proudly beside a prototype model of the Felid cannon. It sparkles and glows in the light of the setting sun.

I swallow hard at the sight of it.

Zetsumei says a few more things I'm too distracted to pay attention to, and then the crowd begins to chant and cheer all the more. The trumpeteers and drummers play, and in the midst of it all, Zetsumei is the first to pay homage to the statue. He bows down and kisses the bottom of the pedestal before saying two quick phrases: "Long live Felidae the Mighty!" and "Long live Zhemushi the Sovereign!"

Prince Kurai goes next. The Samurai closest to the statue on stage-left follows him. Then the one closest on stage-right. Then the second from the statue on stage-left.

Heiban's turn. He struts up to the statue with a confident, jovial smile and pays homage to it as if it were a huge slice of lotus cake. I wouldn't be surprised if he licked it.

The Samurai third from the statue on stage-left pays homage after him.

I'm next.

My heart beats in sync with the thundering drums.

The crowd won't stop shouting "Hail, Felidae" and it's driving me insane.

I hope I don't faint.

Here goes nothing.

I walk to the front of the statue and glance up at it for a second. Then, instead of bowing down, I turn my back toward it and look out at the audience.

Within seconds, the cheering, drumming, and trumpeting subside, as if suppressed by a mighty whisper.

Zetsumei and Kurai, alarmed by the sudden change, turn and look at me with puzzled expressions.

After a deep breath, I speak. "Lord Zetsumei, people of Felidae, listen to what I have to say. I love our kingdom very much, and I'm proud of how far we've come. However, I cannot pay homage to this statue, nor can I condone the project that you, Lord Zetsumei, have planned to undertake."

Silence.

I could be killed by a hailstorm of crossbow bolts at any time now.

Zetsumei turns to face me. He opens his mouth to speak, but hesitates. After pondering, he leans in to Kurai and whispers, "What's his name?"

"Tarento."

Zetsumei recomposes himself, clearing his throat and speaking loud enough for the audience to hear. "Samurai Tarento, I do believe you're making a mistake. Please explain to us why you have the audacity to interrupt such an important moment in the history of our beloved kingdom."

"Lord Zetsumei, I mean you no disrespect. However, I have a message from the Great King of the Sea, sovereign ruler of the Kingdom of Marindel." Even as I speak, murmurs of discontent begin arising from the crowd. "Felidae has come a long way over the last hundred years. We achieved victory over the monsters that terrorized our ancestors, and now our society has grown prosperous. I'm very proud to be a Felid, as we all should be. However, people of Felidae, we mustn't hold our heads above the other kingdoms as if we're better than they. The realm outside our borders is suffering. They long for the help we're able give! Why are we building ourselves up, fattening ourselves to be slaughtered like cattle? If we continue on our current path of vanity and self-veneration, Felidae *will* fall in the blink of an eye, and all of Tyrizah will fall with it. People of Felidae, listen to me! Building a tower to make a name for ourselves will serve no purpose but to keep us blind to our own coming destruction. We *must* be prepared! Something is coming that threatens to end the realm as we know it, and the only way we'll survive is if we reach out to the other kingdoms and help them. Divided the realm will fall, but united we will stand!"

By now, the crowd is boo-ing me. Yet my heart is shielded from the shame of rejection as if by a cloak of cool water.

Zetsumei and Kurai exchange glances. Their fidgeting reveals their discomfort.

The Samurai behind me are still standing at attention, but with disquieted expressions. Heiban, notably, sports a disappointed frown.

Meanwhile, I stand as confidently as I know how, waiting for Zetsumei to speak.

Soon, the king of Felidae raises a hand to silence the crowd. Then he says, "Samurai Tarento, what proof do you have that what you say is true? Please, provide us with the evidence that leads you to believe such a disaster will take place."

I wait for a second, mentally relaying the question to the Great King and hoping he'll give me something profound to say. I speak as the words are given to me. "Lord Zetsumei, all I can tell you is this: if you ignore the words of the Great King and continue with your plans to build a new palace..." I pause, my breath taken by the realization of what I'm saying. "...Felidae's Centennial Jubilee will be its very last."

Silence.

Thick, unrelenting silence.

"Blasphemy!" Someone in the crowd shouts.

"Hail, Felidae!" Another person follows.

As a chorus of "Hail, Felidae" begins to erupt from the crowd, Zetsumei raises his hand again to silence them. He says, "Samurai Tarento, you are guilty of blasphemy and treason against the kingdom of Felidae, against me your king, and against Zhemushi the Sovereign. I hereby sentence you to exile. You are no longer welcome in the great and glorious kingdom of Felidae. Begone with you and your superstitions, so that we may continue the ceremony in peace."

Well, that was anticlimactic.

With nothing more to say, I bow in farewell to Zetsumei and depart from the stage. I avoid eye contact with all of the Samurai as I go.

The silence is present even after I leave the plaza and take a back-alley route away from the assembly. A full minute passes before I hear Zetsumei's voice, barely audible behind me, resuming the ceremony. The protective covering over my heart lifts, and the gravity of what just took place hits me like an arrow in the chest.

I've just been exiled from Felidae.

10
Comrades
Summer, 1418 AIE

~Tarento~

As I APPROACH the gate to exit the city, I hear Heiban call my name. I stop and turn to see him running after me, his expression fraught with anguish. He stops a dozen feet away, panting for breath. No one else is around. The taiko drums thunder in the distance.

"Tarento," he breathes, "What have you done?"

The confidence I felt onstage has long since dwindled. Now, standing face to face with my friend, I struggle for words. I swallow hard and speak what comes to me. "I've done what I must to prevent Felidae from making a fatal mistake. Even though I've failed today, I hope everyone will remember this moment and abandon the path of self-veneration before it's too late."

"You've gone mad!" Heiban shouts. "Is *this* what's been bothering you? How long have you been thinking this way!? Don't tell me it was that blasted trip to Kharduman! That is *no* excuse for plotting treason against your own kingdom!"

"Heiban, please, you must understand! I mean Felidae no harm! The Great King showed me what's coming, and he told me to warn the people—"

"You've doomed yourself, Tarento! I don't know where you got this idea of a Great King from, but you'd better drop it while you still can."

"I can't do that," I shake my head solemnly. "The Great King is my only king now. I've chosen to serve him, so now I must accept the consequences of my actions. Into exile I will go." I turn to continue toward the gate.

"No," Heiban's voice drips with gravity. "The exile is a cover-up to keep the crowd quiet and the ceremony running smoothly."

I stop.

"Tarento, Lord Zetsumei has sent me to kill you."

My heart skips a beat.

Zetsumei sent a Samurai from my own village—my closest friend, no less—to eliminate me behind the scenes. Although it's clear Heiban is regretting every second of this, he hasn't any other choice. To disobey a direct order from the king is a fatal offense.

Even so, I mustn't back down.

Turning again to face Heiban, I meet his gaze with a sorrowful acceptance of fate. "I will not condemn you for following orders, but I cannot revoke my decision to follow the Great King. I will do whatever it takes to avert the coming disaster, even if..." I choke with grief. "Even if I must fight those whom I'm trying to protect."

Heiban sighs deeply, appearing for a moment to be holding back tears of his own. He speaks softly without looking at me, "*You* are the only disaster in Felidae right now. None of this would be happening if you had just stayed quiet, kept your idle daydreams to yourself, and paid homage to the statue like a loyal Felid."

His response irks me. Without quite meaning to, I raise my voice. "Subservience to the image of a self-centered king is *not* the answer! I've made up my mind. I'm going to serve the Great King of Marindel, the only one who can truly bring peace and justice to the realm. In fact," my countenance brightens as the idea comes to me, "W-why don't you come with me? You've *always* wanted to see the lands across the sea. I *promise* you, once you experience life in the other kingdoms, you will understand how important this is. Please, Heiban! Come with me! Both of us can escape now, while the ceremony is still going!"

Heiban is aggravated beyond words, held captive by the conflicting loyalties in his heart. He turns away, tightly pulling on his hair and groaning with frustration.

"Come on, Heiban," I say more gently. "Don't let Zetsumei tear our friendship apart. Don't listen to him. Come with me!"

When Heiban looks at me again, his expression is dark. "Lord Zetsumei isn't the one tearing us apart. *You* are."

I frown, swallowing the urge to weep. "So, you've made your decision, then."

Heiban nods grimly. "I regret it has come to this, my friend."

A distant explosion causes the ground to tremble beneath our feet. We both look to see a column of dust and smoke rise from the center of the city as the Heavenly Palace collapses upon itself.

Compelled by the sound of the blast, Heiban draws his black-bladed katana and rushes toward me.

I step forward and draw my own katana just in time to meet his first attack with a resounding *clang*.

Heiban jumps back, and then comes again with a barrage of strikes.

I skillfully block each swing, stepping backward as he presses his attack.

As heartrending as this moment is—realizing firsthand that my best friend is determined to defy my decision to follow the Great King—I must defend myself and find a way to escape. Heiban may still be reluctant to kill me, but I must treat him as a legitimate threat. I can't afford to underestimate or go easy on him simply because he's my friend.

Defending myself against Heiban is not difficult yet, lending me the mental capacity to think about these things while parrying his blows. Once he starts using elemental ninja arts, it'll be much harder to stay alive. That's his specialty. However, I have one trick up my sleeve that not even he knows about. I just need to get to higher ground.

Ducking away from Heiban's assault, I sprint between the nearest two buildings. I wall-jump nimbly between them and haul myself onto the roof in time to avoid Heiban's pursuing blade.

When I've run halfway across the roof, I turn to see Heiban has jumped after me and is in pursuit.

I jump from this roof to the one adjacent to it, and continue jumping from roof to roof en route for the city wall. One of the guard turrets there will be a high enough vantage point to make my getaway.

At the sound of an ominous whirring behind me, I turn and see a kunai knife flying toward me, radiating with supernatural power. I dodge it ever so narrowly before the weapon careens into the roof several feet ahead. The kunai explodes, sending a cloud of wooden shrapnel my way. I shield my face with my arms and leap over the gaping hole, landing precariously on the other side.

Heiban imbues another kunai with magic and hurls it toward me.

I brace myself, waiting until the last second to jump away from it. The shockwave of the detonation launches me onto the next roof. I land on my feet and keep running.

Heiban continues in pursuit, preparing and throwing explosive kunai at me or the roofs beneath me. His frustration is hampering his technique and precision; his aim isn't usually this lousy. All the same, I know him very well. Judging by his current tactics, I know he hasn't yet decided to kill me.

He's still trying to scare me into changing my mind.

I jump and grab onto the pointed corner of a higher roof, hauling myself up and continuing onward. The wall is nearby, and I have to gain some altitude to get on top.

As I go, Heiban performs several hand signs, the signature feature of elemental ninja arts. He jumps high into the air using a wind technique, flipping and soaring over my head, and he lands in front of me. During his maneuver he had drawn a kunai, and now he throws it at me.

I duck and roll under his attack and run past him, jumping up to the next highest building as I had done previously.

"Where are you going?" Heiban taunts, wind-jumping after me. "Stand and fight like a real Samurai! You opposed Lord Zetsumei to his face in front of all the people of Felidae. Why won't you now stand and face your own comrade?"

"That's just it," I call over my shoulder. "We're comrades!"

"Perhaps we *were*," Heiban replies, stopping to perform a different series of hand signs. "But you have betrayed me, along with every other Felid in the land. Now, I'm afraid the fate of a traitor awaits you." He claps his hands together, and a sparkling blue aura envelops his arms from his elbows down to his fingers.

I don't stop to watch, I know what he's doing. It's one of Heiban's signature elemental techniques. While keeping him in my peripheral vision, I stay focused on my destination. The wall is almost within reach; only a few more roof jumps to go.

Giving chase once again, Heiban points one of his glowing hands at me and fires a blue energy dart from his palm. The dart strikes the wall of a building nearby, and the entire area is encased in jagged ice.

The chase continues, with Heiban sending his icy darts after me. I have to make detours and take cover behind spires and decorative roof adornments as I go, which slows my progress. Even so, I'm closing in on my escape.

One more jump, and I land with a shoulder roll on the wall of

Jinshi. No time to celebrate; now it's on to the nearest guard turret, several dozen feet away.

Heiban wind-jumps onto the wall, landing in front of the turret. He calls into the window, "Guards, this man is a traitor! Get him!"

Four crossbowmen, weapons raised, emerge from the turret and open fire. Two more guards point their crossbows out of second-story windows on the turret and add to the barrage.

Dodging some bolts and blocking others with my katana, I continue sprinting toward the turret.

Heiban releases an ice dart at the ground beneath me as I'm about to step down. The sprouting ice grows up around my foot and traps it there, forcing me to make an abrupt halt.

Having lost my mobility, a crossbow bolt strikes my right arm and elicits a gasp of pain.

"Hmph," Heiban sneers. "Where is your Great King now?"

I can't slow down to wonder. I must press on to my escape.

Using the hilt of my katana, I strike the ice trapping my foot until it breaks enough for me to yank myself out.

Grimacing with effort, I hurl myself at the crossbowmen, who had stepped in front of Heiban and were advancing toward me while I was down. I cleave the first guard's crossbow in half before punching him in the face with my free hand, hardly pausing for breath before I roundhouse kick the next guard in the head and knock him out. I raise my katana to block a crossbow bolt from the third guard before I shoulder-tackle him, sending him staggering back into the fourth guard. Both of them trip over each other and fall backward, and I step on them en route to Heiban.

He has one shining palm pointed at me, and his other hand is on the hilt of his katana. It's the sort of thing he'll do when he doesn't want his opponent to know his next move. However, as his long-time training partner, it won't trick me.

I flick my katana to block an incoming bolt from the guards firing from the turret window, and then I raise it over my head with both hands as if I'm about to cut Heiban down.

He smirks and releases an ice dart point-blank at my exposed chest. It would be a fatal hit, freezing my heart and killing me instantly.

Fortunately, I expected him to go for that move.

I torque my body so the ice dart strikes a plate of armor hidden beneath my ceremonial robe. In the same motion I strike Heiban hard on the forehead with the hilt of my katana to knock him out.

The dart causes ice to sprout like a jagged-petaled flower on my body. Though it didn't hit anywhere that would freeze my heart, my mobility is greatly restricted. It also happens to be insanely cold.

I move quickly out of range of the turret guards before pausing to catch my breath. I look over at Heiban, slumped on the floor nearby. He has a bloody wound on his forehead where I struck him.

"I'm so sorry, Heiban," I whisper with a sigh of regret.

As I look upon my fallen comrade, struggling to overcome the instinctual urge to rush to his side, the Great King says, "*He will be all right. Hurry to the top of the tower. There is little time left!*"

At that moment, I hear shouts of alarm coming from the neighboring turrets along the wall. The other guards must have seen the fighting; now they're coming in from both sides. In a short while they'll be close enough to open fire.

I glance one last time at Heiban before heading inside the turret.

I enter just in time to encounter the two guards who were upstairs a moment ago. Despite my injuries, I manage to give them a sound beating before throwing them outside, shutting the door, and locking them out.

Heading upstairs, I discover a ladder leading to a trap-door on the roof. I climb the ladder, wincing from the pain with every move, and emerge on the roof of the turret.

Now I'm up high enough to make a quick escape.

I pull out a scroll decorated with ancient writing, unravel it, and place it on the ground in front of me. I perform a few hand signs and plant one hand on the scroll, muttering an incantation in the ancient Felid language. In a cloud of smoke, the scroll transforms into a giant golden eagle.

Not pausing to marvel at the bird, I quickly sling myself onto its back and command it to fly. The eagle screeches as it flaps its wings, jumping into the air and grazing the treetops as it secures our getaway.

The incoming crossbowmen shout and try to shoot us down, but the bolts are unable to reach us.

We've made it!

As the eagle gains altitude and turns northward, the fireworks show marking the final celebration of this year's Jubilation Day begins. The cityscape of Jinshi is bright and dazzling, and the flashing and booming of fireworks only adds to the scene.

Nevertheless, as I behold the sprawling city below, I feel great sorrow. The chances of Felidae ever turning from its path of pride and vanity are slim. However, I serve a King who is wise and kind, who seeks to bring peace, justice, and harmony to every kingdom in the realm. I'm willing to do whatever it takes—whatever he needs me to do—to see it happen. Hopefully, as a result of my journey, the kingdom of Felidae will one day be saved.

For now, I hear the Great King beckoning me to the mainland, where I presume I will learn more about him as I follow his lead.

Goodbye, Felidae. When I see you again, may your hearts be soft.

ZETSUMEI SITS UPON a decorated chair in a temporary throne room, his posture tense and his fingers tapping.

Heiban kneels before the king, describing the account of Tarento's escape. "Once he was on top of the turret, he summoned a giant eagle and got away. No one has seen him since. That's all the turret guards were able to tell me."

"Three days later, and still no sign of him," Zetsumei sighs, massaging his chin with one hand. "Do you understand what could happen if we allow his toxic message to spread unchecked across the kingdom?"

Heiban lowers his head in shame. Tarento's escape was *his* fault. He should have killed him without remorse, like he would've dealt with any other target, but he didn't have it in him to kill his best friend.

And what did Heiban get in return for his reluctance?

A bloody forehead and a concussion, from which he woke up merely hours ago, and a very bad reputation with the king of Felidae.

"I should have you executed immediately for this," Zetsumei says.

Heiban releases a defeated sigh, expecting a blade to cleave through his neck at any moment.

"However, I have a better plan for you."

Heiban looks up in surprise.

"In making his defiant stand, Tarento claimed to speak in the name of another king. That leads me to believe he has gone to visit his new king, where I imagine he will conspire against us and bring about the very disaster he so brazenly pronounced upon us."

As Zetsumei speaks, Heiban's face betrays a growing seed of hatred.

"Therefore, Heiban, I am sending you to the kingdoms of the realm to find that traitor and bring him back to me, dead or alive.

If you should also find his king, I order you to kill him and plunder his palace. You may take with you all the men and equipment you need. Until you complete this task, consider yourself exiled from Felidae with the sole exception of Port Beihai. Am I clear?"

"Hai," Heiban whispers, voice quivering. Not with sorrow, but with hate.

"Stand up!" Zetsumei shouts.

Heiban shoots up to his feet and stands at attention.

"I said, am I clear!?"

"Hai!" Heiban shouts.

"Good, good. Now, be gone with you, and let that mark on your forehead be a reminder of who you're dealing with."

Heiban bows to the king of Felidae before turning and taking his leave.

He will never be reluctant to kill again.

11

From the Ground Up

Summary, 1419 AIE

~Connor~

BAYSIDE HARBOR.
PORT of mystery.
Seat of adventure.
Goldmine of stories.

I crest the hill overlooking the sprawling port town, with the morning sun shining behind me. Finally, I have arrived at my destination. Some may say an arduous journey was required to get here, but for me, it has only been one uneventful hour since I parted ways with Jed at the homestead. Though grief for my father still tugs at my heart, a sense of purpose drives me forward—and with it, excitement for the journey ahead.

I stand and behold the city, relishing the cool ocean breeze with every breath. This is where I will find people to join me on my quest. I wonder whom I will encounter? With nervous anticipation, I hurry down the hill and walk through the old stone gateway.

The harbor town quickly kindles within me a thirst for adventure. Unlike the countryside, the roads here are lined on either side with buildings two to three stories tall. Many colorful stands and awnings border the fringes of the road. The smell of cooked fish and freshly-baked bread rides on the breeze, coupled with the sounds of stirring shops and bustling crowds.

More interesting to me, of course, are the people. My curious people-watching side kicks in as I walk along. There are fishermen, craftsmen, metalworkers, lumberjacks, merchants, bakers, farmers, cattle herders, shoemakers, and every profession in between. Most of them look to be from Armavir, but among them I spot a handful of Tethysians and Bothnians, and— whoa!

My heart leaps.

A Pythorian huntsman!

There he is, walking just a dozen feet ahead of me with a bow and quiver slung across his back. He sticks out like a sore thumb with his animal-skin outfit, a deerskin shirt and trousers, both lined with bear fur. His shaggy black dreadlocks make him look even more outlandish. He's middle-aged yet strong, and he carries himself confidently.

I wonder if he'd be interested in going on a quest?

With hardly a conscious decision, I quicken my pace in pursuit of the huntsman. I've never met a Pythorian before; their kingdom is land-locked near the center of the mainland, where they have no need for boats, fishing, or any seafaring activity. To see a Pythorian here in Bayside Harbor is almost as peculiar as seeing a sorcerer in a peaceful countryside.

As I'm about to catch up, he turns left and walks into a general store. I follow behind him and begin browsing through the wares as if I'm interested. Meanwhile, I watch the Pythorian with my peripheral vision.

He goes to a corner of the store where there are maps available for purchase and begins sifting through them.

"There you are!" A girl's voice catches the huntsman's attention. "I've been waiting almost an hour for you!"

The huntsman turns to greet her, a young adolescent who gives him an affectionate hug. He says, "The inn had no vacancy last night due to the storm. Many mouths to feed."

"What'd you catch this morning?"

"Turkeys, pheasants, and rabbits. Cooked 'em all into a big stew with some potatoes, and everyone was happy."

"Sounds delicious! You've got to be their best cook, hands down. No wonder they didn't want to let you leave."

"Yes, they tried their best to dissuade me. But the time has come for us to move on. No one can deny it."

The girl looks down sadly. "Yeah. I'm not looking forward to saying goodbye to the medicine guild tonight."

"It will be hard, Yoko. I know that, and I'll be there to support you. Now, let's focus on the task at hand, shall we?" The huntsman puts a strong hand on the girl's shoulder and holds her close. "You haven't gotten a map yet, have you?"

"Nope," Yoko shakes her head. "Before you came, I got most of the things on our list, but not a map yet."

While they continue discussing what kind of map to get, I think about what I've heard so far. It seems like these two are about to go on a journey somewhere. Their interaction leads me to believe Yoko is the huntsman's daughter, but oddly she doesn't look Pythorian at all. She's fair-skinned with thin dark hair and bright hazel eyes. The huntsman can obviously hunt and cook, and Yoko is presumably a medic. Definitely quest material.

Moreover, as they continue speaking, I realize that though they're dead-set on leaving Bayside Harbor, they haven't decided where they're going. It's all too perfect.

I walk over to them and say, "Excuse me, I couldn't help but overhear your conversation. Why are you leaving Bayside Harbor?"

"None of your business," the huntsman says without turning.

"Khai doesn't like it here," Yoko whispers.

"Ah," I nod. "Yes, I wholeheartedly agree. Bayside Harbor can be boring. I believe what you need is a little bit of adventure."

"More like peace and quiet," Khai mutters.

I continue. "You look like the kind of people who would not only enjoy a journey to foreign lands, but you'd also be very good at it. Khai, you look like—"

He glares at me. "What do you want?"

I gulp. He's certainly terrifying when he's angry. "I, uh, would like to invite you to join me on a quest."

"No."

"But...you don't even know what it is yet."

"I don't care."

"But Khai," Yoko says, "What if it's something fun?"

"Don't encourage him, Yoko. We're not going on any quest. It's time to leave this noisy town and find someplace peaceful to live." With that, Khai snatches a map of Armavir and walks toward the counter.

I look at Yoko and ask, "What's *his* deal?"

"He's been through things," she whispers. "Grew up in Pythoria, enslaved in Sunophsis, killed a bunch of bad guys, that kind of stuff."

My interest is piqued. I look at Khai again while asking, "Do you think he'd share his story if I asked him?"

Yoko shakes her head. "Nope. But I can tell you my favorite part."

"Please do."

Her eyes light up and she whispers, "Get this. He took out a whole tribe of goblins and a shaman. *By himself!* I was there. It was a right before he adopted me. I killed one goblin, but—"

"Yoko!" Khai shouts. "Leave him alone, and bring your things over here."

"Coming!" Yoko shouts, and then to me, she says, "I think Khai's had enough of quests for his whole life. Otherwise, I'd persuade him to join you, and I'd come too. But I guess it just isn't meant to be. Good luck!"

As she scurries off with a basket of things to pay for, I stand there with my mouth agape.

Khai killed a whole tribe of goblins *and* a shaman?

By himself!?

Why in the land of Armavir can I *not* bring him with me to face Jaedis? It'd be perfect! I frown and sigh. Khai and Yoko won't be coming with me, but I shouldn't beat myself up about it. They're only the first two people I've asked, and I'll probably be rejected many more times before I find someone who's interested. I need to get back out there and find people who are both fit for the task *and* willing to go.

With that thought, I turn and leave the general store.

I continue down the main road in the same direction I had been going before my detour. On the west side of town, the road spills out into a spacious public square. Bordered by the wharf on one side, just ahead, and shops on the other three, the cobblestone clearing is bustling with activity. There's a large fountain in the center around which seagulls, pigeons, and children frolic. On the fringes of the square, minstrels play their instruments and beggars seek alms from passersby.

I walk several feet into the square before stopping to strategize.

How should I go about this?

Let's see, who would want to go on a life-threatening quest to save the realm?

My gaze falls on a chubby young man carrying a loaf of bread.

Not him.

Next, I see an elderly woman with a cane walking slower than a turtle.

Not her.

I turn to the right and notice two strong young men carrying an anvil toward one of the roads branching off the square.

Possibly them? ...Nah, they look busy.

I look to the left and see a beggar looking straight at me. When we make eye contact, he grins, exposing a gold tooth that sparkles in the sunlight.

Ugh, certainly not him.

Just then, a light dawns in the darkness.

Lo and behold, strutting across the square is a knight. He is equipped with a sword on his belt and a shield on his back, and white armor that shimmers like ivory.

"Blimey! A Paladin!" I breathe with excitement, and I begin walking briskly toward him.

Paladins are Armavir's greatest warriors. They serve as the guardians of the land, keeping it free from monsters and administering justice as needed. These warriors make up the Paladin Order, with its headquarters in Cloud Summit and the king of Armavir as the commanding officer.

No one messes with a Paladin.

Surely, this *has* to be the person for the job!

"Excuse me!" I call as I approach.

The shining warrior keeps walking. He's on his way out of the square; I have to catch him before he disappears into the crowded streets. I break into a jog. "Sir Paladin, sir! Can I talk to you for a second?"

He keeps on walking.

"Excuse me! Please, sir, it's important!" I catch up and stand in his path.

The Paladin stops and lifts his visor. "What is it?"

I flinch at his frustrated tone and beady eyes. "I-I need help with a quest."

"Step aside. I have no time for quests."

The Paladin moves to go around me, but I stand in his way again. "It's not just any quest! It's probably the most dangerous, daring, adventurous quest the realm has ever known!"

"Not interested," the Paladin turns and walks away.

"Hold on, just hear me out for a second!" I follow. "There's a sorcerer, a very dangerous one, and he must be stopped before—"

The Paladin turns and glowers down at me, speaking sternly, "Listen, commoner! Enough of your childish games! I'm in the middle of an important mission for the king. Now, leave me be!"

The Paladin shuts his visor and barges past me. I stand and

watch, feeling rejected and defeated. I loved hearing stories of Paladins when I was little, but I never thought they would be so rude.

Disheartened, I turn away from the Paladin and walk back to the center of the square. That was rejection number two. Who would be better suited for the job than a Paladin? I can't imagine finding anyone else with more potential.

As soon as I finish that thought, my eyes prove me wrong. There, passing between me and the fountain, is the most fearsome-looking Bothnian man I have ever seen. He is a head taller than everyone else, middle-aged, very muscular, and sports the most amazing golden beard I have ever seen in my life. He totes a massive pickaxe over his shoulder and walks along, whistling contentedly.

Without a second thought, I run after him "Excuse me, sir!"

Surprisingly, this man stops and turns, greeting me with a grand smile. His Bothnian accent is like music to my ears. "What can I do for you, young man?"

I stop in front of him and look up. I can't take my eyes off of his beard, which glistens in the morning sunlight. I wonder how many ginger Tethysian brews he had to drink to get it to do that?

"I, uh..." I struggle for words. "I'm on a quest, and I need some help."

"A quest, huh?" the man strokes his beard. "Tell me about it."

"You see, there's this sorcerer. He sent a storm and—"

"You mean the one from the other night? I had a feeling there was something off about the weather. Such a long storm, that was!"

"Yes, that storm!" Words begin babbling off my tongue in a quick and disorganized manner. "You see, the sorcerer sent a few monsters after a certain woman, who ended up at the tavern where I was riding out the storm. After talking with her, long story short, I went out to fight the monsters, but I almost died. Then my father came to my rescue and we killed one, but then the sorcerer showed up and killed my father, and he almost killed me too but the woman saved me and dispelled the storm before running away. Now I'm looking for courageous adventurers to help me find the sorcerer and bring him to justice."

As I speak, the man maintains eye contact and nods to indicate his understanding. Could he be willing to join me on my quest? I hold my breath while awaiting his reply.

"Young man, that sounds like quite a task—one for which you will require many brave men and women to stand by your side. As for me, I must tell you that I have larger fish to fry." The man looks off into the distance. His beard and pickaxe blade sparkle simultaneously.

I frown. "But, what could be a larger fish than a sorcerer?"

The man lowers his head to my ear and whispers with utmost urgency, "The secret sort of fish that lurk in the deepest waters, unbeknownst to the common man. Even now they plot, they scheme, and they connive. You understand, don't you?"

"Hm...no," I reply, scratching my head.

"That is all well and good. I see you have just begun your journey with the Great King. I too am on an assignment from him, though it is too complicated to explain now. However, I believe we will one day meet again and fight side by side for the glory of Marindel in this present era."

I stare up at the divine bearded man with my mouth agape. I have no words.

"Good luck to you, young man!" he smiles, pats my shoulder, and turns to walk away.

"Wait! One more question!" I side-step in front of him. "Could you at least point me in the right direction? Who do you think would be able to help me?"

"Ah, yes, hm..." the man pauses to think. He strokes his beard like he would a favorite cat. "If I were you, I'd go to the beggars."

"Beggars? Why?"

"Let me ask you something. What's the best way to build a castle?"

I furrow my brow. "With...bricks?"

"No, no," the man shakes his head. "Think about it from a strategic perspective."

Let's see. If I were to build a castle, I would need bricks, yes. I would also need laborers, tools, and a stable foundation. I don't know much about stonemasonry, but I'm fairly certain the foundation is the most important factor, no matter how many laborers, tools, and bricks I have.

That's why my father and I started the wall for our homestead by digging a trench. One must begin with the foundation, then build on top of it.

The best way to build a castle is from the ground up.

I look at the divine bearded man and say, "From the ground up."

"Precisely! Think of your quest like a castle. You can figure it out easily from there."

With one last wink, the man's beard glistens and shimmers before he disappears from sight.

Chapter 11: From the Ground Up

I look around wildly. Did he just...? Where did...? What...?

Suddenly I'm aware of how naked my face is.

I don't know what to believe about my life anymore.

Words cannot describe my feelings of bewilderment as I stand in the square, trying to make sense of my encounter with the amazing bearded man.

I finally manage to snap out of it when I notice the creepy beggar with the gold tooth I had seen earlier. He's crouched at the edge of the square, shaking a cup with a few coins in it, and staring hungrily at an unsuspecting group of pigeons.

While I look at him, the phrase "from the ground up" continues to cycle through my mind. What's the best way to build a castle? From the ground up. My quest is like a castle. What's the best way to build a quest? From the ground up. What does that mean?

There's only one way to find out.

I walk toward the beggar. Before long, he notices my approach and perks up.

"Hello, good sir!" I call out to him, trying my best to sound friendly. The temptation to talk down to him is unbearable, but I remember my previous encounter with Melody, and how I came so close to wrongly insulting her. I know the hardened Melody I encountered two nights ago was the result of many long years of torment and abuse. Perhaps this beggar has a similar story.

He smiles at me, his gold tooth glinting as he extends his cup expectantly.

For the moment I ignore the cup and say, "I'd like to ask a favor of you."

The beggar raises an eyebrow and asks with a raspy voice, "A favor?"

"Yes," I kneel in front of him so we're eye-to-eye. Then I explain the quest to him like I had to the amazing bearded man, and I wrap it up by asking if he'd be interested in joining me.

"Why you askin' an ol' fart like me for tha' kin'a help?" He asks.

"Well, you don't have much to lose. Why not give it a try? It'll be more exciting than sitting around begging for coins. Besides, we might find treasure! Then you'll be set for life!"

The beggar chuckles. "I 'preciate the offer, but tha's all young-people-stuff yer blabbin' about. I'm too ol' n' smelly for that kin'a thing."

"I'm, uh...sorry to hear that," I frown. "I guess I'll be on my way then."

"Wait, hol' on a min'!" The beggar grabs my arm before I can stand up and leave. He pulls me in close and whispers, "If it's a do-nothin' beggar yer after, y'oughta go to the ol' shipyard on the south side'a town. Lots of us hangin' out there, yeh, but it's purty darn dangerous. I hope y'don' have money, cuz if y'do, they'd up an' kill you for it."

I nod. "Old shipyard, south part of town, dangerous, don't bring money. Got it. Thank you very much." I fumble in my pocket and give the beggar my sack of blics. If I can't bring money to the shipyard, he might as well have it. "Treat yourself to something nice for dinner."

The beggar's eyes bulge. "Why, thank ye, fren! Yer so kin' an' hospabitable!"

"Don't mention it," I reply with a smile before rising to my feet.

As I cross the square en route for the wharf, I hear the beggar call out behind me, "Oi! Watch out for them Blue Fox boys! They dun' like trespassers!"

I raise a hand and call in reply, "Yeah, Blue Fox, got it! See ya!" I dismiss the thought immediately.

Something in my soul tries to bring up the 'Blue Fox boys' again, but I quickly shelf it. I don't want to scare myself out of going to the shipyard, so I'll worry about it when I get there.

Sure, I might be a Seer who can probably gain an advantage if I let an epiphany or revelation come to me about the 'Blue Fox boys' before I get there, but once again I reject the thought. It's probably just me, anyway.

Upon reaching the wharf, I turn and walk southward along the boardwalk. At the far end is the old shipyard, where my adventure continues.

12

The First Encounter

Summer, 1419 AIE

~Connor~

HALF AN HOUR passes before I reach the end of the wharf. There I'm greeted by a sign post that says, "End of boardwalk. No trespassing."

Up to this point, the wharf was bustling with people of every sort, passing to and fro among the ships at the docks, bartering and trading their wares. Now that I've reached the end, there's hardly anyone around. The buildings here are weather-worn and dilapidated.

Beyond the sign marking the end of the boardwalk is the old shipyard. It used to be a continuation of the wharf during Bayside Harbor's golden glory days in the 1100s, but since then it has become a place where ships too old or damaged for use are stored away and forgotten about.

I've heard several stories about this old shipyard, all involving mysterious disappearances and ghosts and whatnot. Of all the places I always dreamed of visiting as a child—the adventure-filled islands of the Tethys Region, the vast plains of Pythoria, the enchanted lands of Ibadan—this rickety old shipyard was definitely not one of them.

Nevertheless, here I am, standing at the end of the boardwalk and working up the confidence to enter the creepy place. Thankfully, it's not even noon yet. I think it's safe to assume nothing bad will happen until after dark. I just need to get in there, fetch a few useful beggars, and leave by sunset. That's do-able, right?

I take a deep breath, and then I step beyond the sign and into the shipyard.

After a few steps, the sturdy oak boardwalk officially ends, and I find myself walking on an ancient creaking boardwalk half-covered in sand and with holes broken into it.

The skeletal shapes of old ships tower above on every side, with ropes and torn sails dangling from the masts. Most are to my right in the bay, tied to docks as old and broken as they, while others are to my left on the sand, having been thrown there by ocean storms or king tides. Some ships still look mostly intact, while others are wasted away beyond recognition, half-submerged in the water or the sand with shellfish and barnacles coating what's left of them.

Now, what I find more eerie than my surroundings is the fact that I haven't seen a single person since I entered this place.

I start calling out. "Hello? Anyone here?"

Only a distant seagull answers.

I keep walking along, calling out every now and then, while looking for any signs of life among the ghostly ships.

Soon I come to a dead-end on the old boardwalk. A large ship had been washed ashore, and its massive hull is beached in my path. I also notice an indented path through the sand around the bow of the ship. That must mean it's a commonly-traveled route.

As I follow the path around the ship, I find myself in a large sandy clearing. There are beached ships on all sides, along with what appear to be makeshift shelters. There are many sets of footprints going this way and that. All of them must have been made after the sorcerer's storm, which means there are definitely people around here somewhere.

"Hello?" I call as I step into the clearing. "If you can hear me, please come out. My name is Connor, I'm looking for people to join me on a quest."

Something snaps beneath my foot. I look down, and still my breath.

It's an arrow, the head of which is covered in blood.

Just as I look up from the arrow, something grabs me from behind by the collar of my tunic. I yelp and gag as I'm dragged backward by massive hands into a hole in the hull of a ship. Before I can make another sound, a hand covers my mouth, and a cold iron blade is pressed against my throat.

A stern voice whispers, "What do you think you're doing? Do you have a death wish?"

I try to reply, but it comes out as a muffle.

Just then, I notice an adolescent boy across the clearing, creeping in the shadows. Even from this distance, I can tell he's Izendoran; the people of Izendor have unmistakable silvery-white hair, earthen skin, and burning amber eyes. The boy looks this way and that, and then he stoops down to pick up a small pouch.

An arrow flies across the clearing and clips his arm. With barely a grunt, he sprints back to where he came from, pouch in hand. In that instant, the clearing becomes a battlefield. Shouts and flying arrows fill the air as people emerge from their hiding places and begin to fight.

What in the land of Armavir have I gotten myself into?

My captor holds me steady as the battle intensifies. On the other side of the hull, two bowmen take up positions behind an overturned table and begin firing into the clearing.

"Hide the necklace!" My captor shouts. "Quickly!"

Another person farther back in the hull takes a small box and disappears behind a pile of crates.

"They're coming!" One of the bowmen shouts an instant before a rock strikes him between the eyes, sending him sprawling backward.

Just then, several attackers charge into the hull, waving their swords. I don't see what happens next because my captor tosses me into a pile of hay before going to challenge the invaders. Thinking it better not to move, lest I be killed, I stare up at the ceiling and listen to the terrible sounds of battle. In a moment, as quickly as it began, the fighting subsides and silence ensues.

I sit up with a groan, rubbing an area of my arm that was likely bruised by my landing. That's when I realize three of the attackers, ragged and dirty, are still in the hull with me. All of them have their bows strung and aimed at me.

I slowly put up my hands, smiling nervously. "Look, I don't know what this is all about, nor do I care to be a part of it, so...if you don't mind, I'll just scoot on out of here and—"

"Stand up, peasant," the center bowman rudely replies.

I immediately obey.

"What're you after?"

"I, uh...I'm looking for beggars."

The bowmen exchange glances, and then the apparent leader glares at me. "What for?"

"For a quest. You see, there's a sorcerer, and—"

"The chief sent you, didn't he? You were sent to spy on us!"

"What? No! I come in peace, I promise!"

"Peace indeed. There is no peace here," the leader scoffs. "To the jail with you!"

"Jail?" I ask in disbelief.

"Keep your hands up!" the leader lowers his weapon and walks out of the hull. I hesitate, but the other two bowmen grunt and tighten the draw on their strung arrows, and I'm persuaded to follow him.

I exit the hull after the leader, with the other two bowmen close behind. I'm led along the edge of the clearing, in the shadows of the looming ships, up to a narrow passage between piles of large crates. We go through the passage and come out to a smaller clearing.

On the other side of this clearing is a large galleon, almost fully intact, with a makeshift ramp going up to a hole in the center of the hull. The entrance of the ramp is flanked on either side by tall wooden stakes, each sporting a decorated human skull, and the hole is covered with a blue curtain adorned with beads.

As I look upon the intimidating structure, I begin to wish I was an elite deadly warrior who could subdue these three losers with a flashy set of moves and make a daring escape.

Another day, perhaps. If I get out of this mess alive.

I am led up the ramp and through the curtain. The halls of the old ship are dark, with very little light coming through the small cracks in the wood, but the lead bowman carries on. I suspect he knows these musty halls well, even in pitch darkness.

Soon we come to a door guarded by a large man armed with a mace. The leader speaks to him, "We caught another spy. Throw him in."

"Huhuhuh," the guard chuckles before turning to open the door with a key. After he steps inside, the bowmen behind me prod my back to make me follow. Once I enter, I see the guard opening the door of a small prison cell and gesturing for me to enter. I walk inside without a quarrel, and he locks the gate behind me.

"Enjoy yourself, you filthy rat," the guard says with a snicker as he exits the jail room, locking the door behind him. I listen to the steps of the departing bowmen until they are out of earshot and everything is silent.

"Hey," a voice behind me greets.

Startled, I whirl around to face the owner of the voice. "Who's there!?"

In the darkness, I can just barely see him sitting with his back against the wall of the cell, though not well enough to pick out any of his features.

He chuckles at my reaction. "You're a jumpy one."

"You surprised me," I mutter as I sit cross-legged on the ground across from him.

"Sorry about that. Did they frame you for spying?"

"Yeah. You too?"

"Yep."

"Who are they?"

"A gang of scoundrels."

"A gang? In Bayside Harbor?" The idea sounds strange to me.

"Unfortunately. From what I've heard, they've been here for several moons. They fled from Cloud Summit after the Purge."

I tilt my head. "What's the Purge?"

"You haven't heard about the Purge? It happened around six moons ago. The Cloud Summit police cracked down on all the troublemakers in the city, killing hundreds and displacing many others, including these guys. They believe I was sent by the chief of police to spy on them."

"Blimey," I frown. No wonder these ruffians are paranoid. "What were you doing in the shipyard?"

"I was begging—"

"You're a beggar!?" I gape. "I've been looking all over for you!"

My cellmate is taken aback. "Hold on a moment, I'm no beggar! Or, at least I wasn't—"

"But you are," I insist.

"Stop it," he mutters. "My story is more complicated than that."

Oh my goodness.

This man just said the magic word.

I lean in close with dramatic expectation. "You have a story to tell me, don't you?"

My cellmate is silent for a few seconds, and then after a deep sigh he says, "Well, I suppose we have nothing but time to kill."

"Yes! Don't worry, I'll tell you my story next. That way, we'll be even."

"Fair enough," he replies. After clearing his throat, he begins talking about his life.

Spring, 1397 - Summer, 1419 AIE

MY NAME IS Jake. I was born in an affluent village called Nora, just east of the central Armaviran mountains.

I'm the youngest of three brothers, and by far the most dim-witted of them all. I was my mother's favorite, which caused my brothers to hate me.

It isn't quite the same in western Armavir, but in the east where I'm from, every healthy young boy moves to Cloud Summit at the age of ten to begin training as a Paladin. It's not a rule; just the popular thing to do.

Even though my brothers made fun of me all the time and never let me join them in anything, I always looked up to them. I always dreamt of us standing together as Paladin warriors, fighting side by side for the peace of Armavir.

There's nothing I wanted more than to be accepted by my brothers and counted as one of them.

One by one, as my brothers turned ten, they moved out of the house. Soon it was my turn, and I was very excited.

As he did for my brothers before me, my father took me on his horse to Cloud Summit. It's a difficult four-day journey from Nora. There he signed me up for the Paladin Training Academy, said his goodbyes, and left.

The first level of the Academy is a six-year program involving academic studies, like history, geography, politics, and how to kill various monsters, in addition to being assigned to a Paladin as a page.

Unfortunately, I'm not very bright. I always thought academics were horribly boring, except the lectures on monsters. I could never remember the name of the fissure separating Armavir from Sunophsis, nor could I remember the farthest extent of the Tethysian Empire during the Imperial Era. I could never remember any of that.

My brothers always laughed and told me to quit. But I wanted to be a Paladin so badly, I studied much more than the others. In the end, after many late nights and forfeited social outings, I barely graduated with the minimum requirements.

The next level of the Academy is an intense five-year program involving skills like horseback riding, agility training, swordsmanship, and lance training, along with a promotion to squire.

I did better at this program because I'm a hefty guy, but I always made the most embarrassing mistakes. It turns out I'm very clumsy.

My brothers added insult to injury by mocking me at every opportunity, spreading rumors, and encouraging their friends to do the same.

In spite of all this, I fulfilled the requirements to become knighted as a Paladin, even if only by a hair.

On the eve of the ceremony, I was to don the white armor at Königheim Castle and present myself to King Alphonse V in his court, before all the captains and generals of the Paladin Order. I carried two ceramic jars adorned with silver: one gift of perfume, and another of aged elderberry wine. The former represents the peace of Armavir, and the latter represents the blood of those slain to achieve it.

As I approached the king with these precious items, I slipped and fell flat on my face, accidentally throwing the containers at the king. The jars shattered to pieces and their contents stained his royal garments and his throne.

The king himself didn't seem to mind at first; he was laughing with everyone else. However, my brothers and several other Paladins raised a commotion, shouting things like, "Look at him, what a disaster! He should never be a Paladin! He will ruin us all! How can *he* be trusted with the peace of Armavir? He will shatter it just like the ceremonial jars!" Bennett, the chief of police, joined them and agreed I should never be trusted with the responsibilities of a Paladin warrior.

Swayed by the opinions of the naysayers, King Alphonse declared I was not fit to be a Paladin and ordered me to leave Cloud Summit to avoid further disgrace.

Later that night, my brothers hastened my departure by beating me and chasing me out. They told me if I ever returned, they would kill me.

It took me eight lonely winter days to return to Nora—or, what was left of it.

I arrived to find nothing but a snow-covered field and charred remains. There was a signpost that said, "In memory of Nora and all of its inhabitants, destroyed by dragonfire. May they be avenged," dated in 1415 AIE.

I fell to my knees before the sign.

My hometown was destroyed *years* ago!

How did I not hear of it?

Did anyone escape?

My sorrow was unbearable. I had no idea where to go or what to do.

When night fell, I ran away from that spot into the nearby woods. There I was haunted by a voice that repeatedly told me to kill myself. To be honest, I was so ashamed of my failure, I felt it was in everyone's best interest for me to do so. But every time I touched the hilt of my dagger, I heard another stronger voice tell me to wait.

Soon, exhausted and shivering, I found a small cave to shelter in and cried myself to sleep.

That night I had a dream about Nora and my family. It was springtime. My father went into the woods to hunt, and he discovered an injured woman passed out in a thicket. He brought her home, and he and my mother nursed her back to health. She never told them what her name was or where she was from. In fact, she hardly spoke at all.

The other villagers didn't like the woman. They believed she was cursed and would bring bad luck to the village. However, my parents insisted otherwise and allowed the woman to live with them.

Sure enough, in the middle of autumn, a dragon attacked Nora. It flew back and forth, roaring and spouting smoke, before landing in the center of the village. It asked with a voice similar to the one that haunted me that night, "Where is the girl, condemned to die, that I may devour her? Give her to me, or all of you will perish."

A figure appeared before the dragon, an elven warrior who shone bright like a star. He said, "The Princess of the Sea has fled, and she has taken her hosts with her. She does not belong to you, nor will she ever. The Galyyrim watch over her day and night, and they will not allow her or those who show her favor to fall into your clutches or the jaws of your master."

The dragon roared and breathed fire on the elven warrior, but he turned the fire into steam. Then he disappeared.

In its rage, the dragon burned Nora to the ground and killed all of its inhabitants. Then it left, presumably in search of the strange woman, the one called the Princess of the Sea.

I woke up early that morning with many questions. I wasn't sure the dream was significant, but I hoped it was. I longed for a reason to believe my parents were still alive.

I came out of the cave just as the rising sun cast its fiery glow upon the snow-bound landscape, and there in front of me was the elven warrior from my dream. He was tall and strong, with ginger hair and a large sword. Seeing him there scared me half to death, and I can't say I didn't spring a leak, if you catch my drift.

He chuckled and said, "Hello, Jake. It's good to meet you at last."

"You know me?" I looked up at him from where I was crouched on the ground in my embarrassment.

"Of course," the elf replied. "And I know your parents very well. They are still alive, safe and sound in the town of Herring, southwest from here. Go there, and they will explain everything to you."

I stood up, overcome with excitement. "Oh, thank you! Thank you so much, mister, uh...?"

"You may call me Nuriel," the elf said with a bow. With a note of urgency, he added, "Do not listen to the voice of darkness. He would like to destroy you and thwart your tremendous destiny, but you must stay strong."

Before I could ask what he meant, the elf disappeared in flurry of snow, swept away by the wind. There was no sign he had ever been there, not even a set of footprints.

After locating Herring on a map, I traveled there as quickly as I could. A few days into the journey I happened upon a mining town, where I bought a horse to speed things up.

On my way, I was often terrorized by the voice of darkness. It reminded me of my failure in Cloud Summit and my failure at all sorts of other things, and it told me I shouldn't continue to live. It was difficult to ignore at first, but I came to realize it all sounded like the insults my brothers would use to discourage me. Once I recognized that, I learned not to let it get to me. I had plenty of experience in *that* arena.

I arrived in Herring after twelve days. I found my parents, and after our long-overdue reunion, I told them what had happened in Cloud Summit, and then at the remains of Nora, up to my dream and conversation with Nuriel.

Intrigued, my father told me more about the woman they took in prior to the dragon's appearance. Though she expressed little gratitude for my parents' hospitality at first, everything changed when the dragon came to Nora.

She insisted that my parents grab hold of her hands.

When they did so, they were blinded by a flash of light, and suddenly found themselves in Herring. The woman was no longer with them, and they haven't seen her since.

Some time later, my parents learned of the destruction of Nora, and they sent a letter to my oldest brother explaining everything.

My parents assumed he would share the news with the rest of us, but apparently, my brothers withheld the information from me.

Snooty jerks, the lot of them.

Anyway, I stayed with my parents in Herring until mid-spring.

One warm day, while I was out in the meadows enjoying the afternoon, I encountered Nuriel again. He told me to go to Bayside Harbor and wait for a Seer to come and tell me more about the Kingdom of Marindel. He said it would be the first encounter with my destiny.

So I came.

I arrived in Bayside Harbor two moons ago, sold my horse, quickly ran out of money because I don't know any trade, and resorted to begging.

I heard the shipyard was a safe haven for beggars, but that had ended when the gang moved in and took control. Now there are always fights breaking out and people getting hurt or killed, all for a little bit of extra cash.

I was taken captive a few days ago because they found out I've trained as a Paladin, and in their minds that places me in the same category as Chief Bennett and the whole justice system that's out to get them. So here I am, rotting in this cell, talking to you, and still waiting for a Seer.

Now that you probably think I'm crazy, the floor's open for you to share your story.

13
Trial

Summer, 1419 AIE

~Connor~

I DON'T KNOW WHAT to say.

I stare at Jake in total disbelief.

"Yeah, it's crazy, I know," Jake says. "But I promise, I'm telling the truth. Honest."

"No no, that's not a problem," I reply, struggling to contain my excitement. "I believe you wholeheartedly. But, do you have any idea who you're speaking with right now?"

"Not a clue. Please, enlighten me."

"All right. My name is Connor," I pause a few seconds for dramatic effect, "and I just so happen to be a Seer."

Jake is silent for a few seconds, and then sighs. "I wouldn't have told you my story if I knew you were going to mock me."

"Huh? I'm not mocking you!" Is Jake so accustomed to being made fun of that he doesn't believe a real Seer when one appears right in front of him?

"Then I suppose you have an explanation."

"Yes, of course." I compose myself and clear my throat. "I'll tell you how it all started."

Excited anticipation causes my whole body to tingle. This is the first time I've ever had a story of my own to tell!

My story!

I take a deep breath and I'm about to start, when suddenly I have a strange feeling that I should wait. I shouldn't tell Jake my story at all right now.

At first I want to ignore the subtle warning, especially to defend my status as a Seer, but then I realize it would be very un-Seer-like of me to ignore an impulse that might've come from my Seer gifting.

With that thought, I tell Jake, "I'm sorry, but I'll have to explain another time."

"Why's that?"

At first, I have nothing to say, but as I think more about it, an idea comes to me. It's a strange imaginative scenario not unlike the story of the sorcerer's storm I came up with while running to the tavern the other day.

It's so strange, it might just be true.

I put the idea into words. "In a few minutes, we'll be escorted out of this prison cell and brought before the leader of the gang, where he will accuse us of spying on the gang's activity on behalf of Chief Bennett. He and other gang members will give evidence that there are indeed spies in the shipyard, but it's important for us to tell them the real spies are Felid warriors, who are searching for a fugitive who has passed through here several times recently."

Jake tilts his head. "You really *are* a spy, aren't you?"

"Nope. Just your friendly average Seer."

"You're not still mocking me, are you? Or is this an excuse to get out of telling me your *real* story?"

"How about this. If I'm wrong, nothing will happen in a few minutes. We'll be stuck in this cell indefinitely, and at that point, I might as well tell you my story to pass the time. If I'm right, you'll see for yourself that I'm a real Seer, and then when the timing's more appropriate, I'll tell you my story. What do you think?"

"Hm...that doesn't sound bad to me."

We wait in silence.

Meanwhile, I begin to think about this situation as it pertains to my quest. I've successfully found not just an average beggar, but a beggar who once trained as a Paladin. Now, if I can figure out a way of escape for us, we can be on our way to bigger and better things. I wonder if one beggar will be enough to challenge Jaedis the Sorcerer? I'll err on the side of needing more, but I've had enough of this place. I can't imagine finding any more helpful people around here.

I wonder what time it is now? I definitely don't want to stay the night in this creepy shipyard if it can be avoided. I ask Jake, "Is there any way to tell time around here?"

Jake peers out of a small crack in the wooden wall of the ship. "It's about sunset."

"Blimey." It looks like we're stuck here. Unless, of course, my Seer senses were correct, in which case we should be departing from our cell at any moment now. Regardless, I'll do my best to search for any means of escape. Jake might know a few things about the daily routine of the guards that could help me form a plan of action.

As I open my mouth to ask, the door of the room flies open. The guard enters, holding a torch which illuminates the room with a reddish-orange glow. He unlocks our cell and opens the door. "Come on! Out you go!"

I obey, relieved that the events foretold by my Seer's gift are coming to pass.

Jake is more hesitant, but the guard doesn't give him time to dawdle. He reaches past me into the cell and pulls him out.

"Let's go, let's go! Keep it moving!" The guard nudges us both out the jail door, where we are met in the hall by several other gang members armed with torches in one hand and various weapons in the other. They surround us and force us down the hall with rude shouts and shoves.

The scene is very chaotic. The gang members are obviously worked up about something. While they channel us through the halls of the ship, they continue shouting at us.

"Keep moving, scum!"

"Faster, faster!"

"You'll get what you deserve, filthy spies!"

Despite all of this, in my heart of hearts, I feel a solid sense of peace as if something or someone is near to comfort me. Whatever it is, I feel like it's shielding me from the chaotic energy swirling all around me.

I steal a look up at Jake. This is the first time I have a good look at his features in the light. He has a thickset jaw, strong dirty-blond eyebrows, short ruffled hair of the same color, and earthen brown eyes. I also notice he's much more muscular than I am. His expression is filled with worry and anticipation.

He immediately catches my gaze, and his expression changes to one of puzzlement as he studies my features, no doubt also for the first time. He whispers, "You're not afraid?"

I shake my head. "It's hard to explain, but I have feeling everything will turn out well."

Jake's expression softens as if the calm presence is transferred to him as well. He nods just before a gang member shoves him from behind. "Faster, you oaf! Move it!"

After turning a corner and climbing a flight of old wooden steps, we come into a large room decorated with a flare similar to that of the ship's entrance. Blue banners with painted fox symbols hang from the walls, adorned with strings of beads, feathers, bones, and other trinkets. The walls on either side are lined with torches so that the room is well-lit. The wall in the far back of the room has three large paneled windows, outside of which the nearby skyline of Bayside Harbor is visible.

In the center of the room is a makeshift wooden throne, upon which a lean adolescent boy sits. He wears a leather outfit decorated with animal teeth and claws, in addition to a full wolf skin dyed blue that looks something like a hooded cape.

This must be the gang leader.

It'll be interesting to find out how this youngster came to lead a group of thugs presumably so dangerous that they got chased out of Cloud Summit by the police. However, I don't suppose now would be an appropriate time to ask for his story.

"Kneel before Alpha Blue, you criminals!" a gang member shouts as he kicks the back of my knees, forcing me to the ground.

Another gang member shouts, "The Blue Foxes will never be subdued by the tyrants of Cloud Summit!"

Several of the gang members begin to kick me ruthlessly while shouting taunts and accusations. I cover my face with my arms and stay kneeled on the ground, wincing and gasping with each blow. I sneak a peek at Jake to see that he too is being beaten.

As I endure the attack, I remember my father.

The toughest man I've ever known.

I'm not like him, and I highly doubt I ever will be. But I am his son, so I will be as strong as I must, even when left to the mercy of my enemies.

Suddenly, an image of Prince Eli flashes across my mind, and along with it a series of strange thoughts:

Was he ever beaten like this?

Did the memory of his father give him strength, too?

I'm puzzled. The idea of someone as noble and friendly as Eli receiving a beating seems foreign to me, yet I can't help but feel like I'm identifying with him in some way through this trial.

"Stop," Alpha Blue speaks.

The gang members back off, heads lowered in submission.

"On your feet," Alpha Blue commands us.

I obey, grimacing through the pain. My whole body is battered, and I'm sure I have scrapes and bruises underneath my tunic I'll have to bandage later.

"Tell me," Alpha Blue begins, his eyes piercing like those of a fox, "what does Chief Bennett want with us now? Was it not enough for him to kill half of us and expel the rest? He did to us triple the damage we've ever done to him. We only did what we needed to survive. We were fending for ourselves; hanging on to this miserable life by the skin of our teeth. He thought, in all of his self-righteous bigotry, that the solution to Cloud Summit's rampant crime was to eliminate us with brute force! And now he seeks to expel us from the outer reaches of Armavir? Who does he think he is!?"

"I'm sorry," Jake says.

Alpha Blue glares at Jake. "Don't apologize to me, scum! Answer my question!"

Jake swallows hard and speaks. "I'm sorry, Alpha Blue, for the tragedy you and your people have endured. But there's been a huge mistake. We're not spies sent from Cloud Summit."

"Yes, you are," Alpha Blue says. "We have evidence. You were not brought before me to defend yourselves. You are to tell us the reasons behind Bennett's obsessive pursuit of the Blue Foxes, so we may retaliate accordingly."

"Alpha Blue, sir," I speak up, "With all due respect, the chief of police should be the least of your worries tonight."

"Shut up!" Alpha Blue barks.

I continue anyway. "Is there any other person you know of who might have come through the shipyard recently? A fugitive of sorts, perhaps?"

"That's none of your concern. Listen, scum, *I'm* the one asking the questions, not you. What does Chief Bennett want with us? Answer me!"

"I don't know," I reply.

"Yes, you do! I'm going to have you both killed tonight no matter what. If you want a quick and painless death, you must cooperate. Otherwise, I will make you both suffer."

Jake and I exchange glances. I sense he wants to speak, and I nod to give him the go-ahead.

Jake looks at Alpha Blue and says, "Sir, I lived in Cloud Summit for eleven years, and as your intelligence has informed you, I trained as a Paladin. I had several interactions with Bennett, and I agree with you: he's arrogant and callous. Even so, I don't know why he decided on a course of action so severe. I left Cloud Summit before the Purge took place. I don't know anything about it other than what I've heard from the Blue Foxes."

"If that's the case, then why are you here?"

"I never became a Paladin. I fled the city in shame. I went to my home town first, but it had been destroyed years earlier. I found my parents in another town and stayed with them for a few moons, and then came here to look for someone who can tell me why my home town was destroyed. I was among the beggars in the shipyard when your followers found and arrested me."

"The evidence doesn't line up," Alpha Blue growls. "We *know* there are spies in the shipyard."

"May I request the evidence?" Jake asks. "I'm sure we can help you sort this out."

Alpha Blue studies Jake for a moment before replying, "Over the past few nights, there've been sightings of shadows lurking in the shipyard. Some of my men have reported they're being followed."

Here in this creepy shipyard, it's easier to believe the stalking shadows are ghosts, not police spies.

Jake says, "With all due respect, Alpha Blue, that sounds like mere paranoia. Do you have *material* evidence proving these shadows are in your midst?"

Alpha Blue waves to summon a Blue Fox standing off to the side: the bowman who led me to the jail earlier. He steps forward and pulls out a few items, saying, "These have been found near places where sightings of the shadows took place. They're foreign to us, so they must have been introduced by outsiders, such as yourselves."

Jake studies the items and identifies them verbally. "Two crossbow bolts, and, uh…" he is stumped by the last one.

"Can I have a look?" I ask, leaning over to see the items. The crossbow bolts are steel, with a sleek aerodynamic design. Definitely Felid. As for the third item…

I gasp.

I've heard stories about this.

It looks like a simple glass adornment on a plain string necklace, but that's the ruse. It happens to be the ultimate spying tool.

I don't know the chief of police, but I highly doubt he'd employ one of these to spy on a ragtag group of thugs.

"It's a crystal ornament," I reply with certainty, "and I would suggest breaking it as soon as possible."

The bowman looks incredulously at the ornament, and then at Alpha Blue, who says, "We won't break it until we have all the information we need."

"No, no, that's just it. The crystal ornament is itself a spy. It sees and hears everything going on in this room right now, and whoever brought it to the shipyard must have left it on purpose."

Alpha Blue reclines back with a smug grin. "You see? There *are* spies in the shipyard. The evidence speaks for itself. What do you have to say for yourselves now?"

"We never said there were no spies to begin with," Jake counters, "but you have the wrong guys. We're not the spies you're looking for."

"Here, may I?" I take the crossbow bolts from the bowman and hold them up for all to see. "Everyone, take a look. These are steel crossbow bolts of the finest quality; expertly crafted. The only kingdom that uses technology like this is Felidae. With this evidence, Alpha Blue, might I suggest the spies in the shipyard are Felid warriors?"

"That's ridiculous. Why would Felid warriors spy on us? Unless..." his eyes widen, "Chief Bennett hired mercenaries! That conniving bastard!"

"All of that to say," I continue, disregarding Alpha Blue's comment, "this situation is far more serious than you or I can imagine. Please, I beg you—break the crystal ornament. It isn't safe to discuss anything at all while someone dangerous might be watching and listening to every word." My Seer senses didn't tell me what kind of fugitive the Felid warriors are looking for, but if they're desperate enough to use a crystal ornament, it must be important. If the Blue Foxes really *are* helping the fugitive and the Felids find out about it, I fear they may do the gang more harm than Chief Bennett ever did.

Alpha Blue continues to glare at me.

I take a deep breath, and I repeat the request. "Please break the ornament."

Alpha Blue glances at the ornament, then back at me. What a stubborn idiot!

Jake begins to help. "With all due respect sir, Connor's right. No matter who the spy is, through that ornament they can see and hear everything we're doing. We *must* break it before discussing anything else."

Alpha Blue sighs before saying to the bowman, "Break the damn thing."

The bowman takes one look at the ornament, and then throws it down and stomps on it. The shattered crystal releases a spray of sparks and flashes briefly before becoming dim like shale rock.

Silence follows.

After a moment, Alpha Blue clears his throat and says, "All right, it's broken. Now, what do you have to say?"

I smile at him and nod. "Thank you. Now, this is a question I've already asked once before, but I'll ask it again: is there any other person you know of who might have come through the shipyard recently?"

Alpha Blue strokes the hair hanging down in front of his face before replying, "A tall hooded man has come through a few times to give us food and supplies. He calls himself the Discerning One and says he's our friend. I think he's a loon, but I allow him to come and go freely because he takes care of us. He makes the people of the shipyard happy."

That doesn't make any sense. This "fugitive" seems like a nice guy.

Why would Felid warriors be looking for a charity worker?

There must be more to the story.

"Do you know anything about him?" I ask. "His real name, where he comes from...?"

Alpha Blue shakes his head. "He never talks about himself. I've asked him why he comes, but he always says a bunch of nonsense like he cares about us and wants to help. I don't understand him at all."

"When was the last time he was here?"

"Yesterday."

"How often does he come?"

"Every few days."

"Hmmm," I stroke my stubbly beard. This is getting really tough.

If I weren't a Seer and I hadn't seen any of this coming, I would probably abandon the conversation at this point. In fact, Alpha Blue's claim that Bennett hired Felid mercenaries to spy on him isn't too far-fetched at all. Additionally, there's always the ghost theory.

Now that I think of it, the bit about the fugitive came at the end of my Seer-revelation earlier, just like the bit about the bartender being an ogre in my first Seer-inspired story. Though the premise of that first story was true, it turns out I made up the part about the ogre. Perhaps, in this most recent case, I made up the part about the fugitive. I was right up until the Felid warriors were involved, but then my imagination got ahead of itself and added to the truth.

I must be a really awful Seer.

Chapter 13: Trial

I'm about to speak affirmatively about Alpha Blue's idea, when another gang member rushes into the room, wide-eyed and panting for breath. He speaks without waiting for permission: "Sir, a group of Felids has arrived! They demand an audience immediately!"

14

The Fugitive and the Refugee

Summer, 1418 - Summer, 1419 AIE

~Tarento~

AFTER FLYING FOR a day and a half on the back of the eagle, I arrived at the mainland on the southern coast of Armavir. As desperate for solid ground as I was, I couldn't land at the first town I saw: a seaport village crawling with Felid merchants. Even from the sky, the red fan-shaped sails of Felid vessels were visible all over the bay. Though it was too soon for these Felids to know of my "treachery" back home, I didn't want to take any chances. For my own safety, I decided to stay hidden from Felidae.

I continued inland for several miles until I reached another town at the base of a range of hills. There, I disembarked my summon and spoke a command in the ancient Felid language to dismiss it. Just as suddenly as it had appeared, the eagle vanished in a cloud of smoke. I will not be able to use another such eagle until I obtain another summoning scroll of that type.

My first order of business in that town was to change my outfit and blend in with the local crowd. I sold my ceremonial Samurai clothes, including all of my armor and weapons, and I bought a plain chestnut-colored tunic and a black hooded coat, trousers, and shoes.

Through that process, I learned about the mainland currency

system which Felidae has so far been too stubborn to implement. Felidae's currency is built solely on one gold coin called a jin-kuan, whereas the mainland currency uses bronze "kappes," silver "blics," and gold "krons." As the economy stands now, one kron is worth a hundred blics, and one blic is worth twenty-five kappes. By weight, one kron is worth just under three jin-kuan. Gold is worth far more on the mainland than in Felidae, where the alluring substance abounds.

I spent a few days in that town to familiarize myself with Armaviran social customs and gestures. Armavirans are far more outgoing, boisterous, and dare I say it, *slovenly* than the average Felid. Nevertheless, I found their company quite enjoyable. They have a knack for appreciating the simple things in life, which most Felids all too often overlook. Soon, the Great King told me to travel northward, further into the interior of Armavir.

I journeyed on foot from town to town, spending one to several nights at each place. Everywhere I went, especially as my knowledge of Armaviran culture increased, I was able to help those I met who were in need—and there were *many* of them. On most nights I was invited to stay in the homes of people I met. If not, I slept outside under the stars. I did this because I found it more rewarding to use my money to help other people than to spend it on my own lodging and comfort. On this journey, I learned to rely on the Great King to let me know how and when to use my money to help the greatest number of people in meaningful ways.

For my own safety, I never shared my name with anyone. To those who asked what to call me, I replied, "I am the Discerning One."

Three moons later, as autumn descended upon the land, I journeyed toward the mountains of central Armavir, in the midst of which Cloud Summit resides. At the foothills, in a town called Finch, I met a refugee from Izendor: an adolescent boy who called himself Scourge. I figured he was using a cover-up name to hide his identity just like I was, so I never pressed him for his real name.

He told me he had just left Cloud Summit, where he lived for six moons, due to a growing tension between the commoners and the city law enforcement. When I expressed my passion for justice and peace for all kingdoms, Scourge promptly warned me not to go to Cloud Summit. The mere *mention* of the word "justice" to the wrong person could put me in a very dangerous situation.

I was ready to heed Scourge's warning, but that night the Great King spoke to me in a dream, confirming that Cloud Summit was indeed my next destination. He urged me to depart from Finch soon in order to arrive and settle in before winter, which I had never experienced in tropical Felidae.

The next morning, as I walked with Scourge through a grove of fiery-colored oak trees, I told him of my decision. He was initially alarmed and tried to dissuade me. But when I told him about the Great King, something in his countenance changed. He declared he would only allow me to go to Cloud Summit if I let him come with me.

I wanted to refuse him. I'd come to enjoy the freedom of traveling alone, but I knew it'd be wise to bring someone who knew the layout of the city and the details of the emerging conflict better than I did.

I checked with the Great King, partially hoping he would allow me to leave Scourge behind. But the King said Scourge and I had crossed paths for a reason, and I should make the most of his company. So, I agreed to let Scourge come with me, but I made sure to let him know I liked my quiet time.

We rounded up supplies in order to keep warm and well-fed for the several nights we'd be spending in the mountain wilderness, and then we set out for Cloud Summit.

On the journey, because I realized I would be traveling with Scourge for an indefinite amount of time, I decided to tell him why I was in Armavir. I began with my arrival in Jinshi for the proconsul's announcement of the new Heavenly Palace, and explained everything from then until my arrival in Armavir.

Scourge was very supportive of my situation, even swearing on his honor not to betray me or any information I entrusted to him. However, when I asked to hear his story, he became very uncomfortable and said he didn't want to talk about it. Every time the subject has come up since then, his usually-lively disposition has been replaced with fearful silence. I haven't yet felt the need to pressure him. I will let him tell me when he is ready.

When we arrived in Cloud Summit, Scourge led me to the poorest sector of the city, where he knew a few people. And that's where we stayed.

The winter that followed was harsh. Long nights, frozen streets, and gusting winds—with a blizzard or two every moon. Of course, I had never experienced anything like it, but even the locals said it was worse than the average winter. Conditions were so dreary, even honest people were driven to steal necessities such as bread and clothing.

The police were of no help. They showed no mercy to anyone

caught or suspected of stealing, and many arrests were made. An attitude of bitterness toward law enforcement was already present when I arrived, but I believe it grew exponentially over the course of that terrible winter.

I tried to help as many people as I could, but by then I had run out of money and my resources were limited. I eventually picked up a blacksmithing apprenticeship to support myself and a few others. The need was far too great for me to handle alone, but I received encouragement on a daily basis by speaking with the Great King.

One day, someone asked me why I seemed so peaceful and confident despite the harsh circumstances. It was then when I began to tell people about the Great King and the hope of peace he promised to bring to the realm. Of course, many people had questions: "Where is Marindel?" "Why have we never heard of this king before?" "If he's so great, why does he tarry while we suffer?" I was unable to answer them. My own knowledge of the King is limited, and all the Great King says when I ask him is *"Trust in me."*

Despite the hardship, Scourge and I shared many wonderful moments with our friends in the poor sector. United by our common circumstances, we shared our belongings and resources so that no one person was left lacking. Over time, life in the poor sector began to improve. Winter was almost past, and people became more hopeful every day.

But then, it happened.

I had a dream in which a group of suspicious characters broke into Königheim Castle to steal an important relic. When it was discovered missing, King Alphonse ordered a search to be made for the thieves responsible. Chief Bennett, head of the Cloud Summit police force, was quickly up to the task. But as he walked out of the king's court, I saw a hideous imp resting on his shoulders. It was only there for a blink, and then it was gone.

Things escalated out of control. The police went from door to door, interrogating every person who seemed suspect and arresting many of them for further questioning. People began to resist, and violent skirmishes broke out.

The chief of police, observing a scuffle from atop his horse, said to the police captain beside him, "We have been *so* patient with these depraved vermin, and look how they repay us. Cloud Summit will never be cured of crime and vice at this rate. Let's make an example of this night, shall we? Give your men the order to engage all hostiles."

"But sir, what about the king?"

"Do you not see how the people are fighting against us? Surely the king will approve of our actions if we do what is necessary to curb this violence. Go now! Find those thieves and bring the relic to me!"

"Yessir!" The captain drew his sword, his face cold and dutiful, and galloped into the fight. Over a dozen mounted policemen followed him, brandishing their weapons.

The dream ended there in darkness.

I awoke with a start. The Great King said, *"Time is short. Take Scourge and leave the city. I will protect this sector, but you must go back to Finch. Remain there until I tell you."*

I obeyed the Great King as quickly as I could.

As sleepy-eyed Scourge and I exited through the southern gate and fled across the stone bridge connecting Cloud Summit to the south-bound trade route, clouds of smoke and fire rose up from the city and melted into the darkness of the night. Blood-curdling screams and clanging weapons echoed among the snow-bound mountain peaks. It looked as though an enemy army had infiltrated the city, but I knew in my heart that it was none other than the Great Serpent and those he had deceived into doing his bidding.

We arrived at our destination several days afterward. Cloud Summit residents began trickling into town soon after us. From them, we learned how terrible the Purge really was. Hundreds of people were killed: mostly the poor, homeless, beggars, gang members, and foreign refugees. No part of the city was untouched by the Purge except for the sector where Scourge and I had lived. The Paladin Order intervened just in time to stop the onslaught from progressing any further.

Over the next few days, I often went alone into the woods and wept for Cloud Summit. At first, the surge of empathetic emotions surprised me—I hadn't wept so extensively since I was a child—but I soon realized this was how the Great King felt. He was grieved by what had taken place that night, even more so than I was. Such a flagrant abuse of authority should *never* be permitted to happen in any kingdom of Tyrizah.

One day, after grieving to the point of exhaustion, I asked the King,*"Why does the Great Serpent have the power to cause so much devastation?"*

"Because authority has been given to him to do it," the King replied. *"Take courage, my son. I am sending you to meet another servant of mine who will tell you things about Marindel you haven't*

Chapter 14: The Fugitive and the Refugee

yet heard. Stay in Finch tonight and depart first thing in the morning. Travel west and go where I tell you."

That morning, Scourge and I departed from Finch. We had stayed there for over a moon, and spring was in full bloom. It was finally warm and pleasant enough to travel.

At a certain town we stopped in for the night, we overheard in the local tavern that a group of thugs passed through several weeks ago, having fled from the Purge. They were allegedly on their way to a western port city called Bayside Harbor to get as far away from Bennett's wrath as possible.

I couldn't stop thinking about these survivors, so I asked the Great King if I should go after them. He told me to find them in Bayside Harbor and do whatever I could to help them.

Scourge and I arrived there two weeks later.

Unfortunately, it didn't occur to me there would be Felid merchants in Bayside Harbor.

After some careful planning, I sent Scourge in ahead of me to find out where the survivors were. He returned with news that they had occupied a shipyard in the southernmost part of the harbor. Next, I told Scourge to stay behind while I went to meet them. On my way there, I got several baskets of free bread from a bakery that was about to discard it to make room for a fresh batch.

Upon my arrival, I discovered the thugs were survivors from the Blue Foxes, a gang I'd heard of in Cloud Summit with an infamous reputation. One could even say these were the types of people Chief Bennett was hoping to eliminate. But I didn't let that stop me from helping them.

They were suspicious of me at first and I made little headway, but I showed them as much kindness as I could before leaving at nightfall.

After the first visit, Scourge and I came up with a plan. I sent him in to live with them and learn more about their situation and their needs. I built a shelter just outside the city and have been staying there to avoid attracting unnecessary attention from the Felids at the wharf. We don't want the gang to know of a connection between me and Scourge, so I told him not to talk about me or Cloud Summit. However, every time I visit, he is to be excited and help inspire the others to trust me. Every other night, he meets me outside the city to tell me what he's been learning, so on my next visit, I'll have an idea of how best to engage with the gang members.

The plan worked perfectly for several moons.

A few days ago, as I was walking in the nearby countryside

early in the morning, the Great King spoke to me: *"Be on your guard. Your whereabouts are no longer a secret to Felidae."*

"How did they find me?" I asked.

"You have done well enough to avoid merchants, but those on your trail now are Samurai. Don't be afraid, my servants are on their way. Do not go to the shipyard today. If you do, the Samurai will find you."

Sure enough, later that evening, Scourge came and told me several of the Blue Foxes reported they were being followed, and they thought Chief Bennett had sent spies to find them. Earlier that morning, a local beggar who allegedly trained as a Paladin was imprisoned as a suspect.

Scourge seemed to believe the Blue Foxes about all of this, so I told him what the Great King said about the Samurai. However, I instructed him to play along with their paranoia for the time being, so the Samurai wouldn't be able to use him to discover my exact whereabouts.

For the next two days, I wanted so badly to go to the shipyard, but the Great King had not yet released me to do so. I eagerly looked forward to Scourge's next visit so I could hear how the Blue Foxes were doing and learn more about the Samurai who were searching for me.

Unfortunately, on the evening Scourge was supposed to visit, a fierce thunderstorm hit. I was up all night, hoping Scourge would come after the storm blew over, but when it finally did, it was almost daybreak.

As I watched the sun rise over the drenched Armaviran countryside, the Great King released me to return to the shipyard that day.

On the way, I stopped at the bakery again to grab a few baskets of bread.

For once, the Blue Foxes were overjoyed to see me. I spent the entire day at the shipyard, helping them dry their clothes and blankets in the hot afternoon sun. Their leader, Alpha Blue, approached me and said he appreciated my visits because no one would fight as long as I was around.

Scourge came up to me privately and confirmed this, saying the Blue Foxes often fought with the other beggars and vagrants in the shipyard, but no such fighting ever occurred while I was present.

I stayed with the gang until nightfall, and then went back to my shelter outside the city.

That was yesterday.

I've taken a liking to wandering the countryside, and I've spent today recounting all of the events that have happened since my arrival in Armavir.

Now it's late afternoon. I'm expecting a visit from Scourge, so I head back to my shelter outside the city.

Just as I crest the hill overlooking Bayside Harbor, I notice him running up the road toward me. He's never been this early before, and he's certainly never come out to look for me in the countryside.

Something must be wrong.

I quicken my pace to close the gap between us. He stops short in front of me, panting for breath. He holds his right hand over his left arm, the sleeve of which is wet with blood.

My heart jumps. "Scourge! What happened? Were you caught in a gang fight?"

"Y-yeah," he pants. "But it's all right, the arrow just clipped me. It doesn't hurt too bad."

I take a roll of white bandage cloth out of my coat pocket and begin to wrap the wound on his shoulder. "What were they fighting about today?"

"They've been finding strange trinkets lying around, probably left by the spies. A fight broke out as the Blue Foxes claimed most of them for Alpha Blue."

"*Most* of them?"

Scourge pulls a small pouch out of his pocket and shows it to me. "I was wounded while snagging this for you."

When I finish the bandage on Scourge's arm, I take the pouch and open it up.

My eyes widen.

I pull a tiny summoning scroll out of the pouch. I've never seen one this small before. "Why are they leaving things like this for the gang to find?"

"The Samurai know you were at the shipyard yesterday," Scourge says urgently. "This morning, a crystal ornament was found on one of the masts overlooking the central clearing. The Samurai must have put it there during the storm, which means they were watching and listening during your visit. The Blue Foxes don't know what it is, but once I heard the news, I snuck away to tell you."

"Hm..." I place the summoning scroll in my pocket and look thoughtfully out at the ocean. The Great King *told* me to go to the shipyard yesterday, most likely knowing there was a crystal ornament overlooking the clearing.

"What are you thinking?" Scourge asks.

"I'm thinking..." I trail off into a sigh. This is a very delicate situation. Samurai can be ruthless killers. I can't allow harm to come to the Blue Foxes or the citizens of Bayside Harbor because of me.

"*What do I do?*" I ask the Great King.

"*The shipyard is in danger. Go to them after sundown, and I will tell you what to do from there.*"

I say to Scourge, "We have to warn them. It's my fault they're in danger, so I must do everything I can to keep them safe."

Scourge's eyes widen. "Are you going to fight the Samurai?"

"I hope not, but I will if I must. Go on ahead of me; I'll be there after sundown. Don't tell anyone about this, all right?"

"You got it!" Scourge runs back down the hill toward Bayside Harbor.

I stand watching him until he passes out of sight at the city gate. Once the sun dips down below the sea, I make my way to the shipyard.

15

Shipyard Showdown

Summer, 1419 AIE

~Connor~

JAKE AND I are escorted down the ramp of Alpha Blue's ship with our wrists bound. The air is thick with tension, ringing with shouts of alarm as the Blue Foxes mobilize and gear up to meet the mysterious visitors from Felidae. Orange lights dance to and fro on the wooden ruins as torch-bearing gang members come out of every place of shelter and scurry toward the large clearing where I was captured earlier that day.

Soon we arrive at the edge of the clearing. Dozens of armed gang members already stand on the fringes as they gaze upon the Felids standing confidently in the center.

The first Felid, a slender woman, is clothed with a scarlet robe and a white crystal tiara, from which her wavy hair cascades down to the small of her back. She appears to be in her late twenties.

The second is a harsh-looking man with an exotic horned helmet and a heavily-armored black and green Samurai outfit. Though I've heard in stories that Samurai often wear masks to intimidate their opponents, this man's scowl is so intimidating he clearly doesn't need one.

The third, an adolescent boy, is dressed in a black martial-arts getup and a blue headband. His hair is pulled in a neat ponytail on top of his head.

I also notice none of the Felids appear to have any weapons. That could either be a good thing or a very, very bad thing.

Alpha Blue emerges from the ranks of his followers and steps toward the center. As he goes, a hush falls upon the shipyard. I feel as though I can hear my own heartbeat before the Felid woman finally speaks.

"So, this is the Blue Fox gang. Quite more of a motley crew than I imagined. And you must be the leader, Alpha Blue."

"What do you want from us?" Alpha Blue asks.

"We've come to do business with you," the woman replies, her voice smooth. "I see you're all bit uneasy since we've come unannounced, so allow me to introduce myself and my company. I am Meiling; a fire witch. This here," she gestures to the armored warrior, "is Ibara, a formidable Samurai. And this is Kaze, his Samurai student."

"We know who you are," Alpha Blue growls. "You're mercenaries sent by Chief Bennett! How dare you foreigners degrade yourselves to serve such a monster of a man!"

Ibara rolls his eyes.

Kaze snorts a chuckle.

Meiling smirks.

"Let us give you a message to send back to Cloud Summit," Alpha Blue continues. "Tell the one who sent you that we will not be ousted from our turf again. Not without a fight!"

Most of the Blue Foxes shout in agreement, while a smaller minority are noticeably disconcerted.

Meiling scoffs, "What brazen foolishness! Where did you get such a ridiculous notion? We have no alliance with Chief Bennett or any Armaviran official, and we haven't come to chase you out of your precious turf. However, if you refuse to meet our demands, we may feel inclined to do so anyway."

The Blue Foxes murmur amongst themselves, exchanging uneasy glances.

Alpha Blue narrows his eyes. "If you weren't sent by the chief of police, then why are you here?"

"As you already know well, we've been keeping a close eye on this shipyard. We have determined with absolute certainty that a fugitive of ours is a frequent visitor in these parts, and we have come to retrieve him. If you help us capture him, you will be compensated generously."

Silence.

Alpha Blue looks at me with unhindered bewilderment, likely realizing I was right about the Felids after all. He reins in his surprise and tells them, "Your fugitive isn't here. We don't know where he is."

"No matter," Meiling replies. "When he comes again, as I expect he will, you may capture him and hold him prisoner for us until we return. As I said before, you will be rewarded for your cooperation. What have you to lose?"

At the mention of the reward, Ibara pulls out a bulging sack of coins and tosses it forward onto the sandy ground with a hefty *cling*.

Alpha Blue's eyes widen and his tough demeanor eases as he considers the Felids' offer. The Blue Foxes' murmuring grows louder as they discuss amongst themselves what they think their leader should choose.

"It's not a bad play," Jake whispers to me. "The Felids must know how desperate the Blue Foxes are for a bit of cash."

"Yeah," I agree. Even still, something in my heart burns with indignation at the deal presented by the Felids. They're up to no good, and I hope with all my might that Alpha Blue will realize it and refuse to take the bribe.

After a moment, the gang leader responds, "The man you're looking for has shown nothing but kindness to us. Do you really think we would betray him for a sack of money? We may be scoundrels, but loyalty is a virtue we take *very* seriously."

Many of the Blue Foxes cheer and shout in agreement.

"That is commendable," Meiling replies with a nod. "We too understand the virtue of loyalty. Just as you're loyal to your Blue Fox brethren, we are loyal with unyielding resilience to the great kingdom of Felidae." Her gaze begins to darken. "What you don't understand is that the fugitive has committed high treason against Felidae. We consider such a crime to be unforgivable, so I must warn you that we will do whatever it takes to seize him. It will be in your best interest to help us."

Alpha Blue is silent again, and the Blue Foxes' murmuring evolves into arguing.

I exchange worried glances with Jake. "What are we going to do?"

"You're a Seer, aren't you?"

I roll my eyes. "I don't know *everything*, all right?"

Before Jake has an opportunity to reply, Ibara's voice fills the clearing. "Everyone, listen up! Since you're taking so long to make a simple decision, allow me to explain what's at stake here. If you refuse to help us capture the fugitive, we will reduce this miserable shantytown to a pile of ashes. Now, I'll ask you one last time. Will you help us or not?"

Alpha Blue chuckles. "That's big talk coming from three intruders in the presence of fifty armed gangsters. It might serve you well to think about whose turf you're standing on and choose your words wisely."

Ibara raises his hand in a signal.

Shadows move on the far side of the clearing behind the Samurai as Felid soldiers emerge from hiding, taking positions on the edge of the clearing across from the Blue Foxes. They all carry crossbows, and they're additionally equipped with a three-foot blade in a scabbard on their belts. I count fifteen in all.

I look up at Jake with a nervous frown. "Are you seeing this, Jake? The Felids are going to destroy the entire gang to get their hands on one fugitive!"

"Shh," Jake hushes without looking at me. "Get ready to move."

"One more chance," Ibara repeats.

Alpha Blue scowls. Then he turns to address the Blue Foxes. "Well fellas, what do you think? Will we give the Discerning One to these snobbish brutes, or will we repay him for his kindness by fighting on his behalf?"

Immediately, every gang bowman strings an arrow and takes aim at the Felid warriors. The others all raise their weapons and stand ready to charge on command.

The Felid soldiers respond in kind by raising their crossbows; Kaze takes a fighting stance; and both Ibara and Meiling smirk where they stand.

"You made the mistake of trespassing on our turf," Alpha Blue declares. "My word rules here, not yours. Now get out of our shipyard, or we'll chase you out!"

"Hmph." Meiling reaches into the sleeve of her robe and pulls out a magic wand. "Clearly you don't understand the gravity of our mission."

"Bowmen!" Alpha Blue calls. "Take 'em out!"

The bowmen release a volley of arrows at the Felids.

Meiling raises her wand, causing all of the arrows to pause in mid-air seven feet from their intended targets.

The Blue Foxes gasp in wonderment and fear.

My eyes are wide. "Jake, did you see that?"

"Shh," Jake nudges me.

Meiling lowers her wand, causing the arrows to fall on the

ground like useless twigs. "Very well, Blue Foxes. I see you have chosen your fate."

Ibara raises his hand. "Soldiers—"

"Stop!" A loud voice resounds across the clearing. A hooded figure emerges from the ranks of the Felids and jogs toward the center. He uncovers his head to reveal Felid facial features and shoulder-length black hair. "Ibara, leave the Blue Foxes alone. I'm the one you're looking for."

"Hmph," Ibara smirks. "Just in time, old friend."

Several thick roots emerge from the ground beneath the fugitive to completely immobilize him.

"No!" An Izendoran, the same one who took the pouch in the last gang fight, breaks away from the Blue Foxes and sprints across the clearing toward the fugitive.

"Scourge, stay back!" the fugitive commands.

Ibara looks at Kaze and says, "Get him."

"Hai!" Kaze sprints out to intercept Scourge.

"Let Tarento go!" Scourge throws a flying punch at Kaze, who blocks the hit and returns with four quick jabs to the torso and neck. Scourge promptly crumples on the ground like a rag-doll.

As Scourge is defeated, Alpha Blue shouts to his followers, "Don't just *stand* there! Attack!"

"No! Stop!" Tarento shouts, but his pleas are drowned out as the Blue Foxes shout and surge toward the Felids.

Jake and I are nearly trampled by the charge. Once we're left unguarded, Jake says, "All right, now's our chance. Let's get out of here!"

My first instinct is to agree with his sound logic, but a strong intuition stops me. I feel like there's more to this conflict than we currently understand. My inner Seer is extremely drawn to Tarento the fugitive, and I have to find out why.

Seeing my hesitation, he asks, "What's wrong?"

"We have to rescue Tarento," I declare. "But first, we need to get our wrists untied."

"Are you sure this is a battle worth fighting?" Jake flinches as an arrow careens between us, striking the hull of a nearby ship. "This may be our only chance to escape."

"Very sure," I reply. "It's a Seer thing. I wish I could say more, but all I know is that Tarento is really important and these Felids are up to no good."

"All right," Jake nods. He walks over to the arrow and, turning his back toward it, grabs it with his tied-up hands and pries it out of the hull. He turns his back to me and says, "Cut your rope on the arrowhead."

I don't know who told Jake he was dim-witted. This man's a genius.

"Did you learn this at the Paladin Academy?" I ask while turning my back to him.

"Nope, just common sense. You free yet?"

"Hold on," I turn my head as much as I can to look behind me, and I catch the rope on the blade of the arrowhead. I tug several times, grunting with effort. "This is much harder than it—" The rope snaps, and I face-dive into the sandy ground. I pull my wrists free and stand up quickly. "You didn't see that."

"You're right, I didn't," Jake says, back still turned. "Hurry, cut me loose!"

"I'm on it!" I take the arrow and use it to cut through Jake's binding.

Once the rope snaps, he breathes with relief, pulling his muscular arms apart and swinging them back and forth. "It feels good to stretch after all that time in the jail cell."

"Oh, I'm sure," I agree with a chuckle. "Now, where do you think we can find you a weapon to fight those Felids?"

"Hey, wait a moment. I'm not your personal gladiator; we have to do this thing together."

"I'm not a fighter," I say with a frown. "Did you see what they did to the Izendoran kid? That'd be me."

"You're a Seer, aren't you?"

"You keep asking me that, but it won't help in combat!"

"Can't you see their weaknesses, or predict their next move? Anything like that?"

"I…well…I don't know!" I have no idea if my Seer's gift can help me in those ways, and I'd rather not find out the hard way. All the same, I know I have to be brave. I must do whatever it takes to rescue Tarento whether my Seer's gift kicks in to help me or not.

"The Blue Foxes are getting hammered out there," Jake says. "If we're going to help at all, we have to act fast."

I look out at the clearing. Tarento is still immobilized by roots. His eyes are closed and his head bowed.

Ibara stands guard in front of him, directing multiple plant vines emerging from compartments in his armor. As Blue Foxes rush toward Tarento, Ibara's vines quickly knock them down or pick them up and throw them. The vines also defend Ibara from any archer attacks. I watch with a gulp as one of the vines plunges underground and, several seconds later, resurfaces behind a sheltered bowman and begins to strangle him.

Also fighting in the clearing is Kaze, who spins, jabs, and kicks at everyone who comes near while also managing to dodge or deflect arrows with his palms. He's so quick and agile, he might as well be dancing.

There are smaller scuffles across the clearing between Felid soldiers and the Blue Foxes as they either spar with swords or exchange volleys from sheltered positions. There's already a dozen gang members lying on the ground dead or wounded, but only one Felid thus far.

More sounds of battle echo from beyond the clearing, indicating the fight has grown to envelop the entire shipyard. I suspect that's where Meiling and the remainder of the Felid soldiers have gone. The orange glow of a distant ship's mast going up in flames confirms my intuition.

"Connor! Take cover!" Jake shouts.

With hardly a second thought, I fling myself behind the nearest crate in time to avoid two flying crossbow bolts. Jake had maneuvered behind a broken piece of ship's hull several feet to my right.

I peer out of my hiding spot to see a Felid soldier coming toward us, and then I duck down again to avoid a crossbow bolt to the face.

"Connor, keep him distracted," Jake whispers. "I'll take him when he's not looking."

"O-okay," I nod, peering out again to see the soldier has come closer. Thinking quickly, I stand up and sprint toward another hiding place farther from Jake. Bolts whir behind me as I go.

I dive behind the new spot and peer out again just in time to see Jake barrel into the Felid and bring him to the ground. After a flurry of limbs, grunts, and sand, the soldier falls quiet with his neck locked in Jake's sleeper chokehold.

"Oi!" A voice calls after Jake stands up again. I look to see the Blue Fox prison guard with the mace. He says, "You put up a good show, Paladin. Glad to have you on our side."

Jake calls back, "I never was against you. I hope you realize that."

"You'll be needing one of these," the guard says, tossing Jake a sword handle-first. "Take out a few more of those guys for us, will ya?"

Jake catches the sword and nods. "I'll do what I can."

Even as Jake is still speaking, my heart jumps when I see the sand shifting beneath his feet. I hardly have time to stand and shout, "Jake, beneath you!" before a vine emerges from the ground and coils around his neck. He drops the sword and holds on to the vine with both hands, groaning with effort as he fights to get free.

Ibara calls across the clearing, "Let's see how *you* like being choked to death, big man!"

"Jake!" I rush toward my friend. It doesn't occur to me until far too late that Ibara would see me coming from a long way off, and now there are three vines coming toward me. I skid in the sand in an attempt to alter my course, but I lose traction and fall. A vine coils around my leg and picks me up off the ground. I hang upside-down for two seconds before the vine flicks to release me, sending me tumbling and screaming through the air.

I'm not sure how I survive the landing; I think I owe it to the sandy ground. I land flat on my back, and the whole realm spins above me. My wounds from the beating I received earlier are pounding in step with my beating heart. Maybe it would be best for me to stay here until it's all over, just like the last gang fight. After all, what can I do to help? I'd just get thrown back over and over again.

"Hey, peasant!" Someone shouts nearby.

A face enters my field of vision: the bowman who captured me. After helping me up, he guides me into the shadows of the ship hull where he found me earlier and says, "You were right about everything. How did you know?"

"I can explain later," I reply. "Can you help me free Jake? Ibara's going to kill him if we don't do something!"

"Who, the Paladin? Don't worry about him. Take a look." He points outside, where I see Jake has been freed from his restraints. Now, sword in hand, he cuts through vines sent for him with the help of a few Blue Fox swordsmen and the guard with the mace.

"They'll keep the plant guy busy," the bowman says. "Why don't you make yourself useful and free the Discerning One?"

I nod, swallowing every bit of fear that rises up in my heart. I know it's what I need to do. "I'll do what I can. Do you have a sword I can use to cut through the roots?"

"A sword?" The bowman scoffs. "You don't need a sword! Use this."

He hands me my father's hunting knife.

I gape. I had completely forgotten about the knife, not to mention the rest of my stuff. My father would be *livid* if he knew I abandoned his special knife! I swipe it out of his hands. "How did you get this!?"

Chapter 15: Shipyard Showdown

"You left your pack here when we captured you. Everything's still inside except for the knife."

I look at the bed of hay I'd been thrown in, and there beside it sits my travel bag. I'll come back for it later. Turning to the bowman I say, "All right. Will you cover me?"

"On my honor as a citizen of Armavir," the bowman says, placing one fist over his chest.

I smile and nod before stepping out into the clearing once again.

Tarento is immediately to the left, a little way out in the clearing. Ibara is in front of me, focused on Jake and the other Blue Foxes to my right. Kaze is sparring with Alpha Blue and another gang member. Meiling is still out of sight, but the shipyard is bright with flame as the fires she started jump from mast to mast, steadily devouring the old wooden ruins.

I turn left and creep through the shadows toward Tarento's position. I need to get as close as possible in the cover of darkness to avoid being seen, and then I need to run out there and cut through the roots as fast as possible to free him before—

A Felid soldier springs up in front of me and lunges with a swing of his exotic blade.

An arrow strikes the soldier in the thigh, and although it just glances off his armor, the distraction allows me time to duck and maneuver away from his attack. I turn around to face the soldier again, but I see he's now focused on the bowman, who is stringing another arrow. The bowman shouts, "Keep going! Don't look back!"

After brief hesitation, I turn and continue on my way. Soon I see another soldier in the clearing coming toward me with his crossbow raised. I keep running until I hear the *fwick-fwick-fwick* of his weapon firing, and I dive behind an overturned rowboat.

The bowman, still where I left him, has defeated the first soldier who attacked me and now fires an arrow at the crossbowman. The arrow misses, but it gets the soldier's attention and they begin to fire at one another.

While the soldier is focused on the bowman, I crawl low to the ground along the length of the rowboat. Once I reach the end, I peer out to see I'm as close to Tarento as I can be without going out into the clearing. Now is the time for stealth, precision, and speed. The eight roots binding Tarento will be no match for the serrated blade of my hunting knife, which was crafted to cut through bone. I coil my legs underneath me in preparation to spring into action. With a count to three, motivating myself with thoughts of my father's bravery, I launch out from behind the rowboat and sprint to the roots. Then I immediately get to work.

One... Two...

I see the crossbowman from earlier charge the bowman and shoot him point-blank. The bowman goes down. The soldier rushes up to him, drawing his blade and finishing the job with a swift stab in the back.

I hold my breath and swallow the urge to shout. I can't be discovered. If I don't cut these roots, this fight will be in vain.

Three... Four...

The soldier notices me. Eyes wide, he opens his mouth to sound the alarm, but no sound comes out. He himself seems surprised by it.

I keep cutting. Five... Six...

The soldier fumbles with his crossbow, struggling to reload it.

Seven...

The soldier casts the weapon aside and sprints toward me. His blade glints in the firelight, and his face seethes with angry determination as he closes in to cut me down.

Come on, come on, come on...!

Eight!

Tarento spins around, knocking both me and the soldier backward with the remains of the roots still clinging to him. I only get a glimpse of the lightning-fast kick Tarento delivers to the side of the soldier's head.

Next, not even giving me a passing glance, Tarento sheds off the last of the vines and sprints toward Ibara. The Samurai is taken by surprise when Tarento tackles him from behind, forcing him to the ground, where they begin to wrestle.

"Yes!" Jake shouts, and the Blue Foxes cheer.

Ibara's bulky armor restricts his mobility, but his vines are constricting Tarento like the tentacles of an octopus.

"Get him a sword!" Alpha Blue shouts. Every able-bodied Blue Fox in the clearing begins running toward the scuffle, shouting "Kill the Samurai!"

Kaze intercepts and disarms one of the Blue Foxes before shouting, "Meiling! We need help!"

Tarento and Ibara disappear in a throng of a dozen gang members. While I'm wondering whether or not I should go and join them, suddenly all of the Blue Foxes and Tarento are launched into the air with a shockwave of air and sand.

Ibara springs up into a fighting stance, his fingers locked in a hand sign. His helmet had been thrown off while he was wrestling Tarento.

Meiling re-enters the clearing, her face cruel like that of a huntress. She points her blazing wand at one of the fallen Blue Foxes, releasing a fireball that detonates on its target.

Two Felid soldiers accompany Meiling, raising their crossbows and opening fire on the nearest gang members.

Tarento, enraged, stands up to face Meiling and Ibara. "Why are you being so cruel to these people? This is *exactly* the behavior that will lead to Felidae's destruction. Please, stop this now! I beg you!"

"Silence!" Ibara shouts, stomping one foot.

The ground beneath Tarento lurches, and he falls. Ibara's vines grab him, along with Jake, Alpha Blue, the remaining unharmed Blue Foxes, and...

I scramble to my feet and run from the vines coming after me, but it's no use. They catch my ankles, picking me up and hanging me upside down. From my vantage point, I see everyone is now held captive by Ibara's vines. The remaining Felid soldiers spread out across the clearing, aiming their crossbows at each of us.

Jake, dangling nearby, says, "I'd say we've failed quite spectacularly."

"No," I reply. Despite our current situation, I have a feeling we'll escape from this alive. "We've stalled them just long enough."

Jake furrows his brow at me, but before he can question my response, Ibara shouts, "Blue Foxes, you have been defeated! Your brethren lie dead in the sand, your shipyard is ablaze, and you pathetic few are at our mercy. Do you now realize how foolish it was to stand against us?"

Alpha Blue throws his sword at Ibara, who avoids it with a sidestep. He groans and raises a hand. "Soldiers—"

"Wait," Kaze says. "Ibara Sensei, let's not kill them. We can use them to force Tarento into telling us everything he knows about his new king."

"Not a bad idea, kohai," Ibara agrees with a smirk.

Meiling flinches, but she says nothing.

"You're making a terrible mistake," Tarento warns. "Threatening and killing people will not save Felidae from its coming demise. If you must capture me, then do so, but leave the others out of this."

Ibara growls at Tarento, "Don't you dare take us for fools. We're not just out to get *you*, we're going to kill your king, too. We'll destroy his kingdom just like you threatened to destroy ours."

Tarento shakes his head. "You don't understand. The Great King does not have a kingdom among the ten kingdoms of Tyrizah. In this present era you will not find him or his kingdom, but soon he will unite every kingdom under the reign of his son, and a new Era of Peace will begin."

What?

How does Tarento know about the Great King?

Now I realize why I felt such a strong connection with him earlier.

Ibara spits on the ground and looks away. "This is madness. I can't believe you used to be one of us."

Tarento looks sadly at Ibara.

Ibara continues, "I can no longer blame Heiban for his unwillingness to face you himself. The Tarento we knew is gone, and—"

"Heiban is here too?" Tarento asks, his eyes widening.

"That's enough!" Meiling shouts. "I can't endure another moment of this. Ibara, I'm going to kill him!"

"No Meiling, we—"

"You don't understand!" Meiling shouts, turning furiously on her partner. "Forget about the king! Tarento will never tell, and we'll never find him! We were sent to catch the fugitive. Let's kill him now and be done with it!"

I sense Meiling has a very strong aversion to the Great King and all things Marindel. I wonder why?

Tarento replies to Meiling, "Whether I'm alive or dead, the Great King will recruit others like me to speak out against the pride of Felidae before it's too late."

My heart leaps after Tarento's words. I have nothing to say in response, but I know it to be true.

Meiling scowls. She grips her blazing wand so tightly that her knuckles turn white. She glares vehemently at each one of us as she draws her arm back. The wand leaves a trail of fire in its wake. "Let me show you what I think about your imaginary king!"

She swings her weapon forward, unleashing a deadly inferno upon Tarento.

16
Gathering of Heroes
Summer, 1419 AIE

~Connor~

I WATCH WITH ASTONISHMENT.
The instant Meiling's fiery projectile is released from the wand, it curves aside and detonates on Ibara.

The Samurai warrior hurtles backward. His vines are incinerated at once, and we fall to the ground. After spitting out a mouthful of sand, I look up to see Ibara rolling about. Every compartment of his armor spouts smoke and fire.

Meiling is stupefied. She looks at her wand, and then at Ibara. "H-how in the...?"

Ibara springs to his feet and turns on Meiling with a furious scowl. "What the hell was that all about!? You've burned my vines to the core!"

"It wasn't *me*!" Meiling retorts, pointing her wand at Tarento. "I was aiming for him!"

An arrow strikes the wand, sending it flying out of her hand.

I look in the direction the arrow came from to see a group of people marching out of the smoky fray. The glint of Paladin armor catches my eye; there are three of them. Next, I recognize the fearsome silhouette of Khai, followed by a group of market guards, firefighters, and medics.

"No! This can't be happening!" Meiling searches the sand for her fallen wand. "Ibara, Kaze, do something! Soldiers, open fire!"

One of the Felid soldiers raises his crossbow to aim at the

newcomers, but Khai strings an arrow and sends it into the soldier's heart faster than he can press the trigger.

The other soldiers gulp and step back, lowering their weapons.

One of the Paladins points forward and says, "Seize them!"

Ibara begins performing hand signs. "All Felids, fall back!"

The soldiers turn and run. Jake reaches out from where he lies on the ground to trip one of them, who is shortly apprehended by market guards. Khai shoots and kills one more fleeing soldier.

Kaze stops by Meiling and pulls on her arm. "Come on! Let's go!"

She bats him away. "I'm not leaving without my wand!"

"Crazy lady!" Kaze calls over his shoulder as he continues on his way.

Alpha Blue gets up and runs toward Meiling. He dives with a shoulder-roll nearby and jumps up, brandishing her beloved weapon. "Looking for this?"

Meiling's dark eyes lock onto the gang leader. She draws several throwing blades from her cloak sleeve and flings them point-blank at Alpha Blue, whose mocking grin is immediately replaced with a shocked grimace. She pries the wand out of his hand, spits in his face, and throws him aside. With a short glance at the guards closing in on her, Meiling raises her wand and is enveloped in a whirlwind of fire. She leaves no trace when the fire soars into the air, flying over the burning shipyard and vanishing from sight.

At the same time, once all of the Felids have run past Ibara, he spreads his arms apart and claps. A cloud of smoke erupts before him, obscuring them from view.

"Into the smoke!" The lead Paladin shouts. "Find them!"

Most of the market guards and two of the Paladins disappear into the smoke. The remaining Paladin promptly begins giving orders to the medics and firefighters.

While most forms of magic are banned or largely frowned upon in Armavir, the techniques used by firefighters and medics are an exception. Firefighters use water spells to create small rain clouds above the fires that serve to put them out, and some medics use magic to quicken the healing of patients or dull their pain. I've heard these things in stories before, but this is my first time seeing medics and firefighters in action. I could sit here and watch them for hours.

But I can't.

Reigning in my thoughts, I scramble to my feet and run to the place where Alpha Blue lies contorted on his back. I kneel down beside him. "Alpha Blue, can you hear me?"

Slowly, he turns his head and rasps, "You knew."

I realize he's referring to the Felids. I remember the stunned look he gave me when they made their first demand for Tarento. "I was trying to warn you, but never mind that. Let me find you a medic."

Alpha Blue grabs my wrist. "No. I'll be f-fine."

He has one blade in his chest and two in his gut. Blood runs over his leather outfit and drips onto his blue wolf-skin cape. "I'm not sure I agree with you," I say.

Alpha Blue groans, staring up at the smoke-polluted night sky. "Our home is ruined... again..." he coughs. "I-I should have expelled the Discerning One the first time he... came. He deceived us all."

"Tarento didn't mean for this to happen. He gave himself up hoping the Felids would leave you alone. He was ready to die for your sake."

Alpha Blue is silent with the exception of his raspy breath.

"I *am* sorry about all this," I say, sitting down cross-legged next to him. "I lost my home recently, too. I can't imagine it happening twice."

At that moment, a familiar medic passes nearby. I wave and call, "Yoko! Over here!"

"Huh?" Yoko stops and looks. It takes her a second to recognize me, but when she does, her face lights up. "Oh! Hi!"

"My friend needs help right away," I say as she scampers over.

"All right, move aside," she says, kneeling down next to me and beginning to fumble for supplies in her bag.

"No...I'm fine," Alpha Blue rasps.

"Not yet, you're not." Without warning, Yoko pulls the blades out of the gang leader's body, eliciting gasps of pain, and immediately puts a white fabric over the wounds. She picks up his arms and places them over the fabric, saying, "Hold the webbing down firmly."

Alpha Blue complies with a groan.

Yoko searches for other things in her bag. She takes out three small sacks, and from each one she takes out a different herb. "All right, I need you to swallow these. They won't taste good, but they'll keep you alive."

"What are they?" I ask.

"Western jute sage will prevent infection," she holds it up before slipping it between Alpha Blue's lips. "Cabbit weed will counteract the loss of blood, and horfrost will speed up the healing. Horfrost will also taste the worst, so be careful not to spit it out."

Next, she uncorks a canteen and pours water into Alpha Blue's mouth. "Swallow everything, nice and easy."

He does so, followed by a coughing fit which causes him to move his arms.

"Keep holding the webbing!" Yoko takes his arms and forces them back into position.

"Webbing?" I ask. "You don't mean a spider's webbing, do you?"

"I do! It's a...well, I forgot the spider's name, but their silk is useful for stopping bleeds. It's absorbent, clean, and easy to weave."

"Interesting. You're very knowledgeable about all this."

"Oh, no, I'm just an apprentice. I've been a part of the Bayside Harbor medicine guild since we moved here two years ago, but even before then, Khai taught me a few things. He knows a good deal about herbal remedies. Most Pythorians do."

"I see. Where are you from?"

"Ibadan. Born and raised," she smiles.

"I've never had the pleasure of meeting an Ibadanian before. My name's Connor, by the way."

"Oh, we're nothing special," Yoko chuckles. "Nice to meet you."

"Connor," Alpha Blue whispers.

I look at him. "Yes?"

He speaks much clearer than before; the herbs must already be working their magic. "One of my men told me you came here looking for people to join a quest. Is that so?"

I'm caught off guard. I haven't even thought about the quest since the Blue Foxes captured me earlier that day. Is Alpha Blue thinking of joining me? That would be the finest definition of 'unexpected' I've ever heard. "Yes, I am. Why do you ask?"

"I didn't believe it before," Alpha Blue replies, "but now I know there is more to you than meets the eye. I will give you a tip in exchange for a promise. What do you say?"

I nod. "Yes, of course."

He speaks quietly, but with a gravity that makes my heart burn. "Promise me you will avenge us. Promise me you will put an end to the oppression of the poor and restore Armavir to the paradise it once was. Find the Felids, Chief Bennett, and everyone in Armavir like them and bring them... to..." he struggles to say last word, "justice."

All right. Now *this* is the finest definition of 'unexpected' I've ever heard. Alpha Blue, who once was a notorious criminal in Cloud Summit, is asking me to bring people to justice.

I remember the voice that said to me, *"Who will go? Who will I send? Who will bring justice to this land and proclaim the end of all evil? Who will fight for the final days? ... You are the one I have sent."*

This is the Great King's call to me.

I reply, "On my honor as a citizen of Armavir, the Land of Peace, I promise I will avenge your people, bring justice to those who take advantage of the innocent, and do everything I can to alleviate the suffering of the oppressed."

Alpha Blue smiles ever so slightly, more than I've ever seen him smile before. He says, "I know many people in Cloud Summit who would be useful to you on your quest, but none are more skilled or cunning than the Offspring of Sisera."

"Offspring of Sisera?" I've only heard passing references to this term in a story or two, but I'm not sure what it means. Sisera is the king of Sunophsis and has been for a very long time, but I know nothing of his offspring.

Alpha Blue explains, "Some of them have superhuman abilities; enhanced speed or strength. Some can perform mind tricks and illusions. Others are skilled with levitation, or the manipulation of sound. If you have even one Offspring on your side, not even the Felids will be a match for you."

"Are they criminals?"

"Definitely. They're part of a rival gang called White Sand, but I have something that will grant you respect in their eyes. Medic, will you help me?"

"Sure," Yoko places her hands on the webbing so Alpha Blue is free to fumble in his pocket. He takes out a folded piece of cloth and hands it to me.

I unfold it to see a painted Blue Fox insignia, identical to the one on the banners of Alpha Blue's ship. I ask, "How will this help?"

"It's a token of my favor; everyone in the Cloud Summit underground will recognize it. Show it to the Offspring when you find them, and they shouldn't give you any trouble."

"Do you think they'll still be in Cloud Summit after the Purge?"

Alpha Blue chuckles. "The Offspring of Sisera survive like cockroaches. There's no getting rid of them."

"Connor!"

At Jake's call, I turn to see him coming toward us with Tarento and the Izendoran. I stand to greet him with a handshake and a pat on the back, and then he introduces me to Tarento and Scourge.

"The Great King told me," Tarento says, "I would meet someone who can tell me more about the Kingdom of Marindel. Jake said he was told the same thing," he looks at Jake, who nods in agreement. "Why don't we leave here and spend the night at my shelter outside the city, and then tomorrow you can tell us everything?"

My heart leaps. "That sounds wonderful!"

"I wanna go too!" Yoko says.

"We would love to have you," I say with a smile.

"What's going on here?" Khai asks. He stands behind Yoko with his arms crossed and a less-than-amused expression on his weathered face. "Yoko, when you're finished tending to him, we're leaving. We've wasted enough time already."

"But Khai," Yoko stands to face him. "It's late, and we need to rest. Plus, I *really* want to hear about Marindel! Please? We can leave after that, no problem!"

Khai sighs. Yoko's pleading eyes appear to be melting through his heart like a branding tool through an ice block. "Well, all right. Let's get on with it, then."

"Woohoo! You're the best!" Then she kneels next to Alpha Blue and says, "You keep pressing on that webbing, all right? I have to go, but the other medics will take care of you. Call for help if the pain gets worse, or if you have any other discomfort. Got it?"

Alpha Blue nods. "Thank you."

Seeing this, Khai says to Tarento, "Lead us to your shelter."

Tarento nods. "This way, everyone." We follow his lead through the smoldering shipyard.

The Paladin is standing guard ahead. I say in passing, "Thank you, sir."

He nods in reply.

A surge of excitement rises in my heart. A Paladin just positively acknowledged my presence! The first of many, I hope.

We exit the shipyard using the same route I'd entered through earlier that day. It's now late enough that Bayside Harbor is mostly quiet. There're a few people loitering around the wharf and the plaza, talking about the fire or other important matters, but the streets are otherwise empty, and most buildings are devoid of any light source. Now that we're away from the smoke, the stars and moon shine to illuminate our path.

Tarento leads us to a spot in the city wall where there's a person-sized hole tucked away behind some crates in an alley. One by one we squeeze through the hole, and then we continue skirting the wall on the outside, heading away from the city gate. After covering a hundred feet or so, we come across two sturdy oak trees standing a few feet away from the wall. Tarento's shelter is built out of pieces of wood and cloth, supported and held together by the wall and the tree trunks.

Tarento moves a few things around to create enough space for all of us to lie on the ground in the shelter and sleep for the rest of the night. He spreads out a pile of hay to cover the floor, with a thick blanket over it for extra comfort. Once the shelter is ready, we settle down and fall fast asleep.

We awake to the rays of the rising sun as they pierce through the shelter. Tarento's gone, but as we're beginning to stir, he returns with two baskets of bread.

We sit in a circle in a patch of soft grass in the shade of the oak trees and divide the bread amongst ourselves. During the meal, I share my story, including *The Princess of the Sea* and everything I know about my destiny as the Final Seer. I'm so into the details of the story, I'm unprepared for the response that comes when I'm finished.

"I'll go with you on your quest," Jake says.

I look at him in surprise. This man who trained as a Paladin and fought bravely in the shipyard battle last night wants to accompany me on the journey to the Northern Bluffs to face off against a sorcerer?

As I fumble for words, Jake continues, "The woman my parents took in, whom the dragon wanted to devour—that was Melody. I've been wanting to thank her for saving them."

"I see," I reply with a nod. "Welcome to the team!"

"What's this I hear about a dragon?" Tarento asks.

I chuckle. "You'd better tell your story next, Jake."

"Perhaps I will. But first, let's hear what the others have to say."

"I'm in," Tarento says. "Until now, I've only been familiar with the Great King and, to a lesser extent, the Great Serpent. It seems like the Kingdom of Marindel is more complicated than I first thought. In any case, I know the Great King would like me to join you, so I'll commit my service to the King for this noble quest."

"Wow, what an honor!" I reply. Tarento the Samurai will be coming too!

"Scourge?" Tarento looks at the Izendoran. "What about you?"

Scourge, twiddling his fingers, refrains from making eye contact. "I'm not sure yet."

"What's wrong?" Yoko asks, leaning in close to him.

Scourge shrinks back. "Nothing, I'm fine."

"Leave him be," Tarento says. "I've known Scourge for a while, and I see something about this conversation has brought up traumatic memories."

"Traumatic memories?" I ask.

"It's all right Scourge, you can trust us!" Yoko says.

"He doesn't know us," Khai says. "If the kid's gone through hard times, he's not going to share it with people he met last night."

"Indeed," Tarento agrees. "Let him open up in his own time. Trauma isn't something we ought to take lightly. Not even I know the nature of his past, but it's best for us and for him to avoid it for the time being. There will be a proper time for him to tell us everything."

I study Scourge for a moment. What about my story made him so uncomfortable? He seemed fine up until the part where Jed and I discerned the storm was sent by a sorcerer. He became more unnerved as I described the Nox Abyssae and my encounter with Jaedis outside the tavern.

Do Jaedis and his pets play a role in Scourge's story? Perhaps, but I'll have to be patient. Whatever happened to him must have been very painful if it's still affecting him so severely. He reminds me of Melody in that respect.

"I'm coming," Scourge says, looking up at us. In his eyes, I see he's still disquieted. But behind it, there's a well of fire and lightning. A silent strength in his soul is longing to be acknowledged and believed in. This kid's got something special, and his decision to join our quest will be the first step in his journey of self-discovery. I recognize this to be a Seer revelation, and *that* revelation causes a grand smile to spread across my face.

"There you go!" Jake says, patting Scourge on the back. "We'll be glad to have you."

"I second that," I reply. "Welcome to the team!"

"I wanna go!" Yoko says.

Khai looks incredulously at Yoko. "What?"

"I do," Yoko meets Khai's gaze. "It's a noble quest for a higher cause, and they need our help! Please, we *have* to go!"

"No, we don't. They can manage without us. We'll be going somewhere else, where there are no monsters or sorcerers to bother us."

"But...but I don't want to live a boring life!"

"I don't want you to put yourself in danger."

"I would rather have fun being in danger than die of boredom in a stupid little town where nothing ever happens!"

"There's nothing fun about danger," Khai growls. "This is not a game. You heard Connor; that sorcerer killed his father. If we go looking for him and pick a fight, you can be sure he won't hesitate to kill us too. Their quest is noble, yes, but it's not for us. As your father, Yoko, I will not allow you to go with them."

Yoko's mouth quivers as she searches for words. She glances at each one of us to beg for help, but none of us speak. I, for one, can't imagine challenging Khai on a decision he seems so stubborn about. He does have a point: this quest is not for the faint of heart.

Nevertheless, I have a feeling both Yoko and Khai are supposed to join us. Is it a nudge from my Seer's gift, or do I just really want them to come? I can't tell. It's not as strong as what I was feeling for Scourge a moment ago.

As I'm still thinking, Yoko concedes. "All right. You win."

"Very well, then," Khai wraps one arm around Yoko. "You'll be fine, you'll see."

"I hope so."

I guess it was just me. Oh well.

Tarento asks Khai, "Where will you be going?"

"North along the coast, then east along the Bothnian border. I've heard good things about the Solvys Lake wilderness. Good.

hunting, quiet towns, and no unwelcome disturbances of any kind."

"Yippee," Yoko mutters.

"Well, I wish you a pleasant journey," Tarento says. "Thank you for your help in the shipyard last night, both of you."

"Don't mention it," Khai says, standing up.

Yoko's gaze follows him. "We're leaving *now*?"

"Yep," Khai says while slinging his bow and quiver over his shoulder. "Grab your things."

Yoko fails to repress a reluctant sigh as she stands and obeys.

We say goodbye to the huntsman and his adopted daughter, and all too soon, they take their leave. I presume they'll travel east until they reach the tavern crossroads, and then they'll turn north on the road to Bothnia.

After they've gone, I say, "All right Jake, your turn to share. I bet Tarento and Scourge would love to hear your story."

"Yes, of course." Jake clears his throat, and then pauses thoughtfully. "Actually, I have a better idea."

"What's that?"

"We have to get to Cloud Summit, don't we?"

"Oh, yes! Yes we do!" How could I have forgotten?

"How about we start heading in that direction, and I'll tell my story on the way to help pass the time? If we set out now, we'll reach Willow Creek by sundown. It's a good place to spend the night."

"Sounds perfect," I reply, and the others agree.

"Let's leave immediately," Tarento says. "Willow Creek is in a densely wooded area. It'd be wise to arrive before nightfall to minimize our chances of being attacked by wolves or bandits."

Without further ado, Jake, Tarento, Scourge, and I set out from Bayside Harbor and journey east toward the wilderness beyond the countryside.

While we walk, Jake tells his story. Tarento is particularly interested in Jake's mention of Cloud Summit and Chief Bennett, and he asks many questions about them. After Jake is finished, Tarento tells us about his and Scourge's adventures in Cloud Summit, and the conclusion we draw is that Tarento ought to tell his story next. After all, he owes us an explanation for the Felid invasion of the shipyard.

We arrive at Willow Creek just in time, as the guards at the gate are closing up for the night. We use what little money we have to get a room at the inn, and after laying down on the small bed, I quickly fall asleep.

17
The Felids Regroup
Summer, 1419 AIE

HEIBAN STANDS ON the deck of his ship, running his hand across the barrel of a Felid cannon mounted near the bow of the vessel. He can see his reflection in the cold steel. His expression betrays frustration and a lack of sleep, and the scar on his forehead reminds him why.

At the sound of footsteps, another reflection appears beside Heiban's. He's a high-ranking Felid officer, as indicated by his black, gold-trimmed uniform and wide-brimmed conical helmet. The officer bows. "Sir, Kaze has returned from his mission."

"Bring him to me."

"Hai." The officer leaves.

Heiban turns and walks toward the center of the deck. The ship is docked at the northernmost part of Bayside Harbor, where its unique crimson sails stand proudly among the white masts of the predominantly Armaviran, Tethysian, and Bothnian vessels.

Not far from Heiban's position, four Felid soldiers are sitting around a small table playing mahjong.

Meiling and Ibara sit on crates in the shade of the nearest mast, absently watching the game. As Heiban walks near, they avoid looking at him.

When they returned late that night and recounted the events in the shipyard, Heiban couldn't contain his temper. He remembers the conversation.

"Why didn't you call for backup?" Heiban asked.

"There was no time for that!" Ibara argued. "You should've given us more men at the outset to overwhelm the gang and escape with Tarento before the Paladins arrived. What's more, you should've been there with us!"

"And you," Heiban countered, "should have retreated after securing Tarento, instead of indulging yourselves on the slaughter of worthless vagrants!"

Heiban's bitter recollection is interrupted as the officer approaches again, accompanied by a nervous Kaze.

The Samurai student bows down with his face to the ground. "I have news, Heiban Sensei!"

"Stand up, kohai. Where is Tarento?"

"He's on his way to Cloud Summit with three other people. They're preparing to fight a sorcerer named Jaedis of the Northern Bluffs."

Meiling looks up at them as they converse.

"The Northern Bluffs?" Heiban spits. "Why the blazes is he going all the way over there?"

"I, uh..." Kaze tries to say something else, but Heiban turns and asks the officer, "Commodore Kantai, how long will it take for this ship to reach the Northern Bluffs?"

"The northern waters are unnavigable," Kantai says. "No ship can sail there."

"So be it," Heiban replies. "We will leave the ship here in the care of a few trustworthy soldiers. The rest of us will make the journey on foot to Cloud Summit in pursuit of Tarento."

"You're running low on sleep, Heiban," Meiling says, standing up and walking over to them. "Do you realize how quickly we'd be stopped by the Paladin Order if we marched on Cloud Summit with fifty soldiers in tow? Everyone who sees us will believe we're invading the kingdom. It'll never work. Besides," Meiling smiles and walks up close to Heiban. "What the good commodore said about the northern waters is only true for those who don't know the secrets of sorcery."

"Hmm," Heiban strokes his chin. "What do you suggest, then?"

"I say," Meiling says, drawing close enough to Heiban that he backs away, "You take only Ibara and Kaze with you to Cloud Summit. The three of you can travel much faster than any of us could while easily avoiding unwanted attention. In the meantime, leave the ship in my care. I will ensure we safely reach the Northern Bluffs. If Tarento eludes you long enough to arrive there, we will have him cornered. He'll have nowhere to run."

By the time Meiling finishes, she has Heiban backed up against the rail of the ship with one finger on his chest as if about to push him overboard.

Heiban bats her hand away. "Stop that. Why should I trust you?"

"It's your only chance to catch Tarento. I promise I'll take good care of the ship and your men. Kantai will keep me in check. Won't you, big guy?"

"Er..." Kantai looks at Heiban.

Heiban turns aside to gaze at the open ocean. "I hate to admit it, but you have a good argument, fire witch."

Meiling is silent, twirling a lock of her hair with one finger.

Heiban sighs. "We haven't any other options. We will proceed as you've suggested."

"Hm," Meiling smirks.

Kantai frowns. "But, sir—"

"Kantai, you are in charge of the ship. You are *especially* in charge of the cannons. Meiling, you are not permitted to touch anything, especially not the cannons. You are to tell Kantai whatever he needs to know to navigate the northern waters. You are not to command the ship yourself. Do you understand?"

"Hai," Meiling chimes with an innocent smile.

Kantai's reluctance is masked by his professional demeanor. "Hai."

"Heiban Sensei?" Kaze peeps.

Heiban doesn't hear him. He walks over to Kantai and whispers, "I don't trust her any more than you do. Keep a close eye on her. If she does anything remotely suspicious, you know what to do."

Kantai nods.

"Heiban Sensei," Kaze says again, but he is drowned by Heiban's announcement. "Ibara, Kaze, and I will leave in pursuit of Tarento after nightfall. Once we're gone, Kantai, you are clear to depart. Gather supplies as needed from the city, but be vigilant in doing so. I suspect the Paladins and militia will be looking for those responsible for the mess you caused last night."

"Heiban Sensei," Kaze says again, and this time he is intentionally ignored as Heiban continues.

"Keep the cannons loaded and the men ready for deployment on a moment's notice. We will not tolerate the interference of any third party, be they vagrants, sorcerers, Paladins, or anyone else. We will not lose Tarento again! Am I clear!?"

"Hai," Kantai and Meiling reply.

"Notice me, senpai!" Kaze yells.

Heiban turns on Kaze. "What!?"

"I heard them talking about the Great King."

"Oh? Did they disclose the location of his palace?"

"Kind of. It's on a...a sea turtle."

Heiban raises an eyebrow. "A *sea turtle?*"

"That's ridiculous," Meiling scoffs.

"Yeah," Kaze nods. "One of Tarento's new friends told a story about it. Some kind of Armaviran folk tale, I think."

"Hmph," Heiban folds his arms. He always knew Tarento to be the down-to-earth and reasonable one; definitely the last person he'd expect to believe a simple folk tale and travel across the realm as if it were true.

Unless, of course, there's more to the story.

Heiban places his hand on Kaze's shoulder and directs him toward the pile of crates where Ibara sits. He also beckons for Kantai, Meiling, and the mahjong-playing soldiers to join them.

Once they all gather around, Heiban asks Kaze, "Now, why don't you tell us everything you heard about the Great King today?"

"I'm out." Meiling stands and walks away, muttering to herself.

Heiban watches her go, and after a dismissive wave he continues, "Please, don't leave anything out. Every detail may be of utmost importance to our mission."

18
Trust the Unseen
Summer, 1419 AIE

~**Tarento**~

WHAT AN INTERESTING turn of events.
Everything Connor shared about the Kingdom of Marindel, glorious though it was, gave me more questions than answers.

I can't believe the Great King allowed a human girl to be adopted into his family. I understand his willingness to rescue her from the side of the road, but...to give her royal authority she clearly wasn't ready to handle?

I don't see any logic there.

It was because of her naivety that the Serpent acquired enough power to plunge the whole realm into darkness and instigate tragic events like the Purge.

Did the Great King not foresee it?

Did his sympathy for Melody trump his commitment to justice? It makes no sense.

What's more, up to the present day, Melody is still alive, and the Great King is still trying to get her attention.

All for what?

Connor said only Melody can reclaim her authority from the Serpent, and until she does so, not even the Great King can stop him. While the realm waits for Melody to stop being stubborn, that heinous creature is free to bring death and destruction to anyone and everyone whenever he pleases.

And there's not one thing we can do about it.

"Tarento," Jake's voice breaks my train of thought.

It's late at night, but I've been too troubled to fall asleep. I didn't think anyone else was awake.

I turn my head to look at Jake.

He meets my gaze and asks, "Care to go for a walk?"

My initial reaction is to decline so I can continue processing alone, but something about Jake's persona—even the way he went about asking the question—is so relieving, I can't help but oblige. Nothing sounds better for this moment than a late-night walk.

"Yes," I reply, standing without a sound.

Jake also stands, and we sidle our way between the others' beds and exit the room. We make our way outside the inn and turn right, walking down the dirt road between the wooden buildings of Willow Creek.

The moon and stars are the only sources of light, and the air is alive with the music of crickets, distant frogs, and the occasional hooting owl.

I love being out and about at night.

I take a deep breath, filling my lungs with the cool, moist summer air.

"Feeling better already?" Jake asks as I exhale.

"Yes, very much," I nod.

"Your breathing was troubled back at the inn."

"Is that so?"

"Yeah."

I hadn't noticed my breathing while I was lost in thought, but in retrospect, I was about to weep out of sheer helplessness. I was so disturbed, I didn't realize how disturbed I really was.

"What's on your mind?" Jake asks.

"I'm still processing the story of Marindel. There is much I don't understand."

"I see," Jake gives an understanding nod. "If you'd like to talk about it, I'm here to listen. I can tell you're the silent type, but be careful not to let your worries eat you up from the inside."

Again, my initial reaction is to stay silent and process alone. I hardly know Jake at all, but there's a gentle spirit about him that helps me feel willing to open up, despite my contemplative introversion.

I look at him with a polite smile. "Thank you. Just give me a moment."

We continue walking in silence as I gather my thoughts. I'm

not sure how much Jake knows about Marindel, so I eliminate any expectation that he'll answer my questions. I will simply share what I'm wondering about, and perhaps we can both seek the answers together, whether it be tonight or later, on the journey.

If anything at all, it'd be helpful to know I'm not the only one who has questions.

Soon, I begin to speak. Frustration creeps into my voice with every sentence. "I don't understand why the Great King gave Melody so much authority, just to have it fall into the jaws of the Serpent. I know the Great King seeks to bring peace and justice to the realm, but it seems like he made a mistake with Melody. He trusted a human girl with too much, probably knowing full well she'd be deceived in the end. Only Melody can stop the Serpent, but she won't or can't, and that means no matter how many people I help, the Serpent will continue to destroy lives! I feel so helpless!" I take a deep, trembling breath.

Jake puts a hand on my shoulder. "Easy there. It's all right."

"No, it's not," I mumble.

"Do you remember what happened on the night of the Purge?"

"Yes. It was awful, and there was nothing I could do to stop it."

"No, Tarento. Do you remember what the Great King said to you about the people you helped that winter? You told us what happened."

I sigh. "The Great King protected them. None of them were killed or chased out by the police that night."

"That's right. The Serpent's evil plan was cut short. Had it not been for your presence in Cloud Summit, the Purge might have been much worse."

"How do you know? I reckon the Great King could have protected them whether or not I was there."

Jake is silent for a moment, looking up at the star-filled sky as we walk. When he speaks, his voice is steady and firm. "I don't know everything. I have many questions, like you do. But in my experience dealing with the voice of darkness, there is one truth I've discovered. The Great King has worked it out so that *anyone* who willingly serves and obeys him has authority to challenge the Serpent and bring goodness back into the realm. Tarento, you are an obedient follower of the Great King. He told you to go to Cloud Summit and help those people, and you did. And when he told you to get up and leave, you did. Every person whose life you touched was saved, just like he said they would be. That is a victory. Without you, many of them would be dead today."

I spend a few moments internalizing Jake's response. On the night of the Purge, it was the Paladins who stopped the police. The Paladin Order has authority over city-level law enforcement, so no one would think it odd that they stepped in. However, Jake is suggesting it was my obedience to the Great King that caused the Paladins to show up. No one would see the Great King's direction behind something like that unless they knew him.

From this, I infer the Great King's strategy is to fight the Serpent through regular people who are willing to do what he tells them to do.

Why?

If it's true Melody alone can take back her inheritance from the Serpent, how can it be that any person who serves the Great King can also do something to that effect?

There must be a *very* important piece of the puzzle still missing.

"Do you think we're missing something?" I ask Jake.

"Most likely."

"Doesn't it bother you?"

"Not much."

What?

How can Jake be so unconcerned? Doesn't he feel the weight of the implications of all this? I personally would love to know how I'm supposed to go about saving the realm when there's an evil Serpent in my way that I have no power against, yet somehow have some kind of power against. My mind is bogged down by the weight of the paradox.

I ask Jake, "Why doesn't it bother you?"

"I trust the Great King."

His answer is so simple, it's offensive. I press, "Yes, of course, but there's more right?"

"Nope," Jake shrugs. "That's all there is to it."

"What do you mean? I trust the Great King too, but I still want to know everything. I *have* to know as soon as possible."

"I don't doubt your loyalty to the Great King," Jake replies, "but do you *really* trust him?"

I'm about to say 'Yes, that's what I just said,' but a lump in my throat causes me to pause.

"Do you trust that he knew what he was doing when he adopted Melody and gave her royal authority?"

I'm cornered. He caught me. "I suppose not."

"Do you trust that he is in the right for continuing to pursue

Chapter 18: Trust the Unseen

Melody even today, with every intention of restoring her status as the Princess of the Sea?"

I don't reply.

Jake waits a moment before asking, "How many times has the Great King asked you to trust him?"

Too many to count. Almost all he said during the shipyard conflict was 'Trust me, trust me, trust me.' I did trust him then, and I did my best to do everything he said. Even up to the last time I heard him speak, when he assured me the wounded gang members would be safe in the care of the Paladins and market guards, I trusted him as best as I knew how. Otherwise, I wouldn't be in Willow Creek with Jake and everyone else on a quest to confront a sorcerer.

It wasn't until after Connor told his story that my mind was opened to the idea that maybe the Great King doesn't know what he's doing after all.

Since then, I haven't heard him speak once.

My heart sinks and my mind races as another realization comes.

Melody completely trusted the Great King until her mind was opened to the idea that maybe he wasn't a good and loving father like she thought he was. And that's when the Serpent was able to manipulate her into doing his bidding.

I can't believe it.

My breath quickens, and my hands tremble.

The Serpent has been deceiving me too!

I haven't done anything horrible yet, have I?

Am I still doing the right thing?

Should I stay here or go back to Bayside Harbor?

I am flooded with guilt and fear.

"Easy, easy there!" Jake steps in front of me, grasping my shoulders. I avoid his gaze, but he shakes me. "Look at me, Tarento. Look at me."

I look into his strong dark eyes. When I do, I feel something recoiling within me, afraid of the bold authority this man carries.

"It's all right, Tarento. You're doing the right thing. The Serpent is using your questions to distract and discourage you. Don't give in. You know the King is good. Rest in that truth. Your questions will be answered at the right time. For now, simply do what he tells you. Nothing more, and nothing less. In the midst of it all, trust the unseen."

Jake's words serve to banish my guilt and fear. I've been thrown out of my introspective rut in the best way possible, and now with Jake's help, I'm being built up with truth and hope.

"*Do you trust me?*" The Great King asks.

Excitement flashes in my heart when I hear his voice, but still, he's asking me a difficult question. I reply, "*I want to, you know I do. I have many questions, and I hope you'll answer them for me soon. But until then, I choose to trust you. I will trust the unseen.*"

I feel an inner release as the last of my misgivings disappear like vapor, and a confident sense of peace settles in their place. I take a deep breath.

As I relax, Jake's eyes shine, and he smiles. "All better?"

"Yes. Thank you."

"You're doing well. I'm glad we have the opportunity to go on this journey together."

I smile and nod.

Jake takes a breath and says, "Shall we keep walking?"

"Yes, let's."

We continue through the moonlit village in a much more pleasant silence than before. My mind is much clearer now, and I'm better able to enjoy the sights and sounds of the night. Though neither of us speak for a long time, we're both comfortable enjoying the other's company.

"Pssst!"

I whirl around, tense and ready for a fight. There's a person coming quickly toward us. Though I'm initially alarmed, it only takes a second to recognize her in the abundant moonlight.

"Yoko?" Jake asks. "What are you doing here?"

Yoko stops, panting for breath, and says, "I *had* to come, I *had* to! Khai stopped for a nap a little way north of Bayside Harbor, so I left him a note and snuck away to follow you."

Jake and I exchange glances. I ask, "Won't Khai be worried that you've gone?"

"Is he going to come after us?" Jake asks with some concern.

"Yes, and possibly," Yoko replies. "I told him in the note not to come looking for me unless he wanted to come on the quest. So, if he does find us, hopefully it'll be to join us and not to put arrows in your heads."

"Let's hope so," Jake replies.

"Come on then," I say, gesturing for the three of us to continue walking. "Let's get back to the inn and rest. Connor will be excited to see you in the morning."

We finally approach the inn. I give up my bed for Yoko and lay on my coat on the floor. Despite the hard floor beneath me, as soon as I put my head down, I sink into a peaceful sleep.

OUR STAY IN Willow Creek has drawn out longer than expected. We're sitting around a table in the dining area, awaiting breakfast and planning our route to Cloud Summit. The chefs are taking a long time, and we can't seem to decide on the best route to our destination.

"I'll explain it again," I say, tracing a route with my finger on the map sprawled out on the table. "I came this way from Cloud Summit on my way to Bayside Harbor. It took about three weeks on foot. There are enough towns along this road to stay the night in until we get to Finch," I point at the town in the foothills where I met Scourge. "From there, it's a trek through the mountain wilderness to Cloud Summit."

"Three weeks?" Connor asks. "I didn't think Cloud Summit was so far away."

"Armavir is a large kingdom," I reply.

"I know, but that's *such* a long time!"

I'm annoyed with Connor's negative attitude. I've spent a whole year traveling all over Armavir. Three weeks is hardly anything! I hope he isn't like this all the time.

"Be patient with him," the Great King whispers. *"Not everyone has traveled like this before."*

I remember Connor mentioning yesterday that he had never been further from home than Bayside Harbor. So here, in Willow Creek, Connor is farther from home than he has ever been, and he's only going to go farther.

"Don't worry," I say to him, putting a hand on his shoulder. "I know travel like this is new to you, but soon you'll see it's quite the adventure. Besides, you'll have us to keep you company."

Connor's face brightens. "There can't be anything more epic about a long journey than good company."

"Indeed," I agree.

"Actually," Jake enters the conversation, "we may not have to spend three weeks traveling after all. If we manage to get horses, we can shorten the journey to ten days. Eight, if we're really going for it."

"Great idea!" Yoko chimes.

"How expensive is a horse?" I ask.

"Something like ten krons. Depends on where they're from."

Does Jake have any idea how poor we are? I give him a disapproving look. "Ten krons each, huh? That's *how* many krons to get each of us a horse?"

Jake flinches at the thought. "Well...we don't *all* need one. Some of us can double up."

"That's fair," I reply, "But *how* much money do we have at the moment?"

"Two kappes!" Connor says, holding up the small bronze coins for us to see.

"So," I flick one of the coins out of Connor's hand. "I suppose we won't be getting horses anytime soon. It may work out later if we get a good sum of money for Connor's homestead, but in the meantime, we'll just be walking."

"Hey guys," Scourge pipes up. He is hunched over the map and studying it closely. "It looks like there are a few side roads we can take to get to Cloud Summit faster."

"What do you mean?" Jake leans in and looks at the map.

"If we take this road from Bunting instead of the main road," Scourge traces the route with his finger, "we can shave a few days off the journey. See, it goes straight across and rejoins the main road at Granite Hollow."

"Hm, that may be true," Jake says, "but it would be challenging. Smaller roads go deeper into the wilderness, where there's a greater chance of encountering wild animals. Plus, there won't be any towns to stop in for the night."

"We don't have money to stay in a town every night anyway," Connor says.

"True," I agree. "We may not be able to stay in towns at all, unless someone is kind enough to invite us in for the night."

"I wouldn't count on it," Connor says. "I think we're much too shady to be invited into someone's home for the night."

"What do you mean?" Scourge asks. "Tarento and I stayed the night in people's homes all the time while we traveled together."

"We're a bigger group," Jake explains. "It's one thing to give lodging to two travelers, but quite another to give lodging to five."

"We'll let Tarento do all the talking," Connor says with a grin, "and have Yoko stand next to him and smile. Her innocent demeanor might account for the rest of our shadiness."

"Hey," Yoko pokes Connor. "I can be shady too, you know!"

While the others banter back and forth, I find myself deep in thought. Figuring out where and how to travel was so much simpler when I was alone. Having Scourge as a companion was sometimes difficult, but still manageable. Now, I have four companions who can't seem to agree on anything. How long I will have to deal with this?

I could use some alone time, but I know if I turn around and leave now, they'll follow me and ask what's wrong and all that. Why is this all so complicated, anyway? We can take the main road for the three weeks necessary, and we'll be in Cloud Summit without any further issue. No need to talk about horses or shortcuts or overnight stays or whatever else. Those things are best worked out along the way.

If I were alone, I would've left Willow Creek an hour ago. We're wasting time.

"*Tarento, my son,*" the Great King says, "*listen to me.*"

My interest is piqued. I clear my mind of all distractions and tune my heart to hear him well. "*Yes?*"

"*I have invited you to go on this journey with my loved ones for a very special reason. I intend not only to bless others through this quest, but you also. Please be patient with them. Learn to help them in their weakness and inexperience, as you know you have weakness and inexperience of your own. Remember how Jake was able to help you sort your thoughts and find your trust in me. Be a similar example to the others. They do not see things the way you do, and that is why they need you. You are the Discerning One. They will not always listen, but as you journey on, their respect for you will grow. Do not lose heart. Finally, though you can see much, do not be disheartened by what you cannot see. The broad road may seem right, but you will find that many of the greatest treasures are found on the narrow road. When you are uncertain, trust the unseen. Trust in who I am.*"

I listen to the Great King like a kohai listens to a sensei. As he speaks, I feel the weight of every word, dripping with gravity, yet soft with genuine care. He is rebuking me, yet I must say I've never experienced one of such encouragement. In Felidae, a Samurai sensei will yell, scold, sometimes even beat their kohai pupils as a form of rebuke. But not so the Great King.

Scourge's voice brings me back to the present. "Tarento, what do you think we should do?"

I look at Scourge, Jake, Connor, and Yoko in turn, and then down at the map. I don't know what they were just discussing, so I don't know what exactly Scourge is asking me about. I simply speak the first words that come to mind. "I think we should take the narrow road and trust the unseen."

The four of them exchange glances.

Yoko shrugs. "Sounds great to me."

"Fair enough," Jake agrees.

At that moment, the chefs enter the dining area, each carrying a tray of food. There are two cooked turkeys and two platters of toasted bread with cheese. The delicious aroma immediately makes my mouth water.

"Breakfast is served!" The lead chef says, placing a turkey on the table beside the map.

"Wow, it smells great!" Yoko brushes the map aside to make room for the chefs to set down the other trays.

Connor snatches the map before it falls off the table and rolls it up neatly.

"Thank you," I say to the chefs as I behold the hearty meal. They took a long time, to be sure, but it looks like the wait might have been well worth it. Without a second thought, I say, "There's more than enough for everyone. Why don't you join us?"

The chefs gladly oblige, combining our table with another to make a table large enough for all of us. Not long into the meal, the chefs ask us where we're going, which inevitably leads to conversations about Marindel. They're enthralled by the stories, hanging on every word. At the end, as we tell them of our journey to Cloud Summit, I'm shocked by their response.

"Let me go talk to the innkeeper," the lead chef says, already standing up. "I'm sure there's something he can do to help."

"Oh no, you don't have to do that," I say, but he ignores me and says, "Meet us outside the inn thirty minutes from now, all ready to go."

We spend a short while finishing the meal and talking with the other chefs before we round up our things and gather in front of the inn. The chef, the innkeeper, the assistant innkeeper, and the front desk clerk meet us there, accompanied by three horses.

Three horses!

The assistant innkeeper is donating two of her finest travel horses to our cause, and the front desk clerk is donating his personal travel horse to make it three. He says, "I rarely leave town anyway; she'll be better off in your hands."

The innkeeper himself, holding a small sack, says, "I'm glad to hear there are still people in Armavir who are about the King's business. I give you all my best wishes for a safe journey, and as a token of my support, please accept this gift."

Jake takes the sack; I can hear the clinking of coins as he moves it about. His eyes widen. "How much is in here?"

"You'll never make it to Cloud Summit with only two kappes," the innkeeper says with a wink, "but I think you'll manage just fine with ten krons and two hundred and fifty blics."

"What!?" Connor and I say simultaneously.

I have never been the recipient of such extravagant generosity.

"Is this okay?" I ask the Great King. *"I feel as if we're robbing them. Shouldn't we be the ones giving to them?"*

"I love my children very much, and I will always provide for them. The more you give, the more I will return to you. Receive it gratefully. It is a well-earned gift."

Smiling and looking at the inn staff, I say, "Thank you all *very* much! We're honored by your generosity, and surely the Great King will reward you."

"I'm glad to be of help," the innkeeper says. "Go on, no need to tarry! There's no telling what that sorcerer is up to now."

I reply with urgency, "The sorcerer isn't our only foe in this quest. Please, if *anyone* comes by and asks if you've seen us, don't tell them anything. Clean our room thoroughly, remove our booking from your records, and act as though we never came. It could mean the difference between life and death."

The innkeeper nods. "On my honor as a good citizen of Armavir, I swear your secret is safe with me."

"Thank you," I nod.

Jake, Scourge, and Yoko have ridden horses before, so they each take a horse's reigns. Yoko and Connor share one horse, Scourge and I share another, and Jake is on the third.

Connor raises a hand and says to the inn staff, "Thank you so much, my friends! We won't forget it!"

"Our pleasure," the innkeeper says. "Stay safe, all of you. Armavir isn't the Land of Peace it used to be."

19

The Dungeon Seal

Summary, 1419 AIE

~Tarento~

WE DEPART FROM Willow Creek and travel east. For the rest of that day, to pass the time, I tell my story. They ask many questions about Felidae, finding it particularly interesting that the people of Felidae have scant knowledge of anything that happens outside of their own kingdom. For Armavirans and most others, politics is a topic of profound interest.

In addition, urged by the Great King, I explain to everyone my past friendship with Heiban and Ibara.

Heiban had been my closest friend since I was a child. We grew up in the same village, trained together, and upon graduation from kohai to Samurai, we were partnered together. Since then we've gone on many missions, but he was unable to commit to the Sunophsian diplomacy mission that changed my life. Looking back, the divide in our friendship began there. It became increasingly difficult to connect with him as I became disillusioned with Felidae's grandeur. Finally, on last year's Jubilation Day, my stand against Lord Zetsumei turned Heiban from an estranged best friend into a mortal enemy.

I don't know Ibara as well, but he, Heiban, and I were all kohai under the same Samurai mentor, who we called Jing Sensei. The rigors of training forged a tight bond between the three of us. We were prepared to lay down our lives for one another.

I can imagine two reasons why Heiban recruited Ibara to travel with him in pursuit of me. First, Heiban lost one close friend and perhaps would be devastated to lose another. Second, Heiban may think he and Ibara together can more easily persuade me to surrender, so they won't have to kill me after all.

It's difficult for me to accept the reality that my closest friends have become my greatest enemies. But no matter what my opinion of the matter is, they have set themselves up against the Great King and the values I've come to cherish as I've embraced his calling on my life. I hope one day they will understand there is no way they can persuade me to return to Felidae with them. More than that, I hope one day they will realize the error of their ways and turn to follow the Great King just as I have.

That would be the greatest gift imaginable to me.

In contrast, I've never met Kaze nor Meiling. Kaze is apparently Ibara's kohai, so it makes sense he's along for the ride. Meiling is another matter. Fire witches, though ethnically Felid, are culturally Tethysian. They're at odds with Samurai and the Felid government for many deeply-rooted reasons. Knowing that, I'm unable to discern why Meiling would be interested in teaming up with Samurai to capture me, a Felid traitor. We spend several moments discussing ideas, but soon abandon the topic due to a lack of information. If it's important for us to know, the Great King will tell us in time. Until then, there's no reason to worry about it.

As the days go on, we travel through woodland areas interspersed with meadows, ponds, and hills. Every evening we stop at the nearest village, where we sleep in a stable with the horses. With the innkeeper's generous gift, we're able to buy food at every stop. We've decided it's more worthwhile to buy food than to book a room at the inn because none of us are skilled hunters; it would take up too much of our valuable traveling time.

During our daytime rest stops, Jake begins teaching Connor how to use a sword. Neither has a sword, but they use branches of similar size and weight. "You should know the basics of swordplay before we get to Cloud Summit and buy you one," he says.

Yoko goes foraging for herbs, berries, roots, and other medical supplies. She frequently mentions how she wishes Khai was here to train her with the bow and arrow. We comfort her as best as we can, despite our inability to help. For her sake as well as our own, I hope Khai has a change of heart and comes to join us soon. However, I believe it's more probable he'll come seeking vengeance for our "kidnapping" of Yoko. I ask the Great King to protect us from such a scenario, should it occur.

As for me, I use our rest stops to step away from the others. I don't go so far that they wonder where I've gone, but far enough that I can gather my thoughts and talk to the Great King without distractions.

Sometimes while doing this, I can't help but keep an eye on Scourge. Simply by watching him, I've realized how much he wants to be open with us but is too afraid to do so.

I know it was Scourge who turned Meiling's fireball to hit Ibara.

When he thinks no one is watching, he spawns fire or lightning in his palms and weaves it between his fingers, forming it into different shapes.

No doubt he wishes he had someone to train with, too.

Nevertheless, because he is very protective of his abilities, I choose not to approach him just yet. After all, there's no telling how the others would react if they knew Scourge had electrokinetic powers.

On the fourth day, we depart from the main road to follow the route Scourge pointed out. It's a narrow road indeed, overgrown with bracken and ivy, winding back and forth at the bottom of a steep valley. Our horses must travel at a slower pace, single-file.

Several hours into this new leg of the journey, we come across a staircase carved into the cliff on the side of the road, well-hidden by overgrowth. It goes up to a small ledge high above us, which curves around a bend and out of sight. Both the staircase and the ledge are too small for the horses to travel on.

We pause by the staircase and look up at it for some time.

"There's a castle at the other end," Connor says.

"Hm, that'd be something," Jake replies. "I learned in the Academy about castles that were built during Armavir's Golden Age to protect hordes of treasure."

"Can we go check it out?" Scourge asks.

"We can't leave the horses," I reply, "and it may not be a good idea to split up."

"It's not too far," Connor says. "Just around the bend. We could probably hear each other scream."

"Is there treasure in it?" Scourge asks.

"I can't tell."

"It doesn't matter if there is," I say. "We don't have space in our bags for treasure. Besides, we don't need the extra burden of protecting treasure while sleeping at night. We'd be attracting bandits like a flower attracts bees."

"That is true," Jake says.

Chapter 19: The Dungeon Seal

"Well," Connor raises his voice, "I believe I sensed the presence of a castle for a reason. Are we going to sit here talking about it all day, or does anyone want to come with me to check it out?"

"Count me in!" Scourge says, already dismounting.

"If Scourge is going, I'm going!" Yoko likewise dismounts.

"I'll stay with the horses," Jake offers.

I sigh with annoyance. Are we *really* doing this right now? I don't care to see the castle; it's just a big building. Felidae is full of big buildings, and they've never interested me. I don't care for treasure, either.

As I watch Connor, Yoko, and Scourge climb the staircase, Jake says, "You should go with them, Tarento. They may need you to look after them."

I'm about to say no, but the Great King says, "*I have prepared a treasure for you on this narrow road. Take Jake as well. I will protect the horses.*"

No sense in arguing with that.

I tell Jake, "We're both going. The Great King will protect the horses."

Jake blinks. "Huh. All right, then. Let's do this."

We both dismount, tether the horses to a nearby tree, and make our way up the stairs.

The climb proves to be challenging because the steps are tall, but it's a welcome change of pace from sitting on a horse. Arriving on the ledge, we stop to catch our breath. I can see far down the valley in the direction we came from, where dark green forested hills stretch as far as the eye can see. In the opposite direction the view is the same, except for a cluster of gray mountains just on the horizon. In the midst of those mountains, our destination awaits.

We begin walking along the ledge. It's just over two feet in width, so I focus on balance. To fall from this height would be very unpleasant.

Jake, in front of me, is moving with slow and trembling steps as he sidles along the face of the cliff. I ask, "Are you doing all right?"

"I'm no fan of heights," Jake replies.

"Don't rush; take your time. I'll catch you if something happens."

Soon, the ledge snakes up and around a rocky spire projecting out of the valley wall. Sure enough, perched on a small plateau near the top of the valley, is an old, ruined castle.

When Connor first mentioned it, I imagined it would be like Königheim Castle in Cloud Summit. I'm surprised to see this castle is much smaller and surprisingly quaint. It's so old that most of the wooden parts have rotted away, the stone walls and towers are broken through in several places, and an assortment of mosses and ivy are growing all over it.

A field dappled with summer wildflowers separates us from the castle. The others have finished crossing and, while chattering with excitement, are heading up the steps to the castle's wide-open door. Jake and I jog across the field to catch up to them.

When we arrive at the entrance, Yoko sees us and shouts, "Guys! Isn't this neat? I wonder who used to live here? I would *love* to live in a place like this! Do you think we can fix it up someday? Come on, let's explore!" She runs off.

"We're right behind you, Yoko," Jake says with a chuckle as we follow her inside.

The first room of the castle looks to have been, long ago, some kind of great hall. Holes in the ceiling allow rays of sunlight to come down in several places, where weeds have grown up between the cracks of the brick floor. The decayed remains of furniture, banners, and tapestries lay scattered all over the room or dangling from the walls. Metal objects, like pieces of armor, are also thrown about.

Yoko and Scourge scurry back and forth, picking up curious-looking objects and wondering aloud how they got there and where they must have come from. Connor follows close behind, letting his imagination fly and inventing stories to fuel their excitement.

But, something about this room doesn't feel right.

I steal a glance at Jake, who meets my gaze and nods grimly. "There was a battle here."

"I thought so. What are you thinking?"

"It's very subtle since it happened so long ago, but see the way the armor's lying there, and there, and over there? You could imagine a person inside of it, fallen in battle. The bodies have long since decayed, but the armor hasn't moved. And look there. That table, before the rot, looks to have been smashed by a war hammer."

"You're really good at this," I say, thoroughly impressed.

"I learned it in the Academy, but I'm by no means the best of them. The scene here is only easy because the evidence hasn't been disturbed since the time of the battle."

"Well, you'd better hurry then. The evidence is being disturbed as we speak." I gesture toward our friends. They're touching and picking up every object in sight!

"Indeed," Jake chuckles, and then calls to the others, "Hey, everyone! Don't touch anything more. We're going to solve a mystery."

174

"A mystery?" Yoko asks, her expression curious like that of a kitten.

"Yes," Jake nods. "You see, there was a battle here long ago. If this really *is* a Golden Age castle built to hide a horde of treasure, I bet it was attacked for that very reason. Let's see if they succeeded. Shall we?"

"Yes!" Yoko, Scourge, and Connor shout together.

"All right, then. Stay close and don't make a sound." Jake holds a finger up to his lips and begins walking stealthily across the room.

I admire Jake's ability to make this seem fun. I'm mildly interested in the idea that there was a battle here, but not interested enough to look for whatever lured the attackers here in the first place.

But then I'm reminded of what the Great King said about preparing a treasure for me here.

"I don't want any treasure," I say to the Great King. *"I think you, of all beings, know I've never been interested in gold or silver. What kind of treasure could you possibly have in store for me?"*

"Trust me," comes the King's reply.

"Of course," I force my reply. If the Great King wants to give me treasure, who am I to refuse? I swallow my misgivings and follow Jake as he examines the items around the room.

"There was a scuffle here. See these three sets of armor? One of the helmets is over there; he must have been decapitated. Look, there's still some hair in it."

"Awesome!" Yoko whispers, while Scourge grimaces.

Jake continues, "I believe this armor belonged to the defenders of the castle; it's all similar in design. So, I'm thinking there must have only been one or several attackers, and they were all strong enough to make it past this room without any casualties."

"But what if," Connor says, "the attackers' armor or outfits have long since decayed?"

"Hmm...I hadn't thought of that," Jake admits.

"Suppose for a moment," Connor begins to pace, "that the attackers were ogres. Naked ogres. They'd come in here killing armored troops and smashing furniture with ease. But then, if one of them *did* fall in battle, its body must have decomposed a long time ago. How would we know? We can only wonder."

"Yes," Jake agrees. "What you say is true. The long span of time we're working with is a challenge."

"Might I suggest," I finally decide to speak, "that the attackers could not have been ogres if they made it past this room, because the only door to advance through is too small for them?"

We all look at the door on the far side of the room, which is just a regular human-sized gap in the wall, and therefore could not have been breached by an ogre unless the wall itself had been busted through.

"Aw, I kinda hoped it'd be ogres," Yoko says.

"I don't think you'd ever want to meet an ogre," Jake says, placing a hand on Yoko's shoulder.

"Have *you* met one?"

"No, but I learned about their habits and how to kill them. So, if you ever do meet an ogre, just call for me and I'll take it down."

"Yes! And I'll watch and cheer you on," Yoko clasps her hands together and smiles.

"Of course!" Jake laughs.

While they're talking, I decide to move on to the next room. I walk through the gap in the wall, where a wooden door had long since rotted. This is a smaller cylindrical room, the walls of which stretch upward into a tall tower. The roof is missing, and sunlight pours down into the center of the room to illuminate what looks like a stone shrine. All around it, there are pieces of armor and weapons.

I approach the shrine and begin trying to discern what it is. After my careful examination, the only conclusion I draw is that I have no idea what in the land of Armavir this stone shrine thing is supposed to be.

"Blimey!" Connor says from behind. "That's a dungeon seal! I've heard stories about them. They're used to guard the entrance to something really important, like a treasure vault. Good find, Tarento! I don't think anyone uses dungeon seals anymore. This is amazing!"

"A dungeon seal, huh? How does it work?"

"You have to solve a puzzle, or light it up with magic, or something like that. It's different every time. Usually, the more important whatever it's guarding is, the harder it is to open."

As Connor spoke, Jake had walked up to the dungeon seal and is now studying it. I ask him, "Jake, did you learn about dungeon seals in the Academy?"

"Nothing more than what Connor said. They're archaic, so the Academy instructors didn't think them worth learning about."

"Hm," I begin to study the dungeon seal more closely. There are various rune designs all along the base. Above that is a stone block with a bowl-like indent on the top side. On the sides of the block, there are swirling designs that resemble smoke and fire. I still don't know what to make of it. Ancient Armaviran things are so strange.

"I know!" Yoko says. "I think you're supposed to burn something on top, like an incense altar."

"What's an incense altar?" Jake and Connor ask simultaneously.

"An Ibadanian thing," Yoko says, waving her hand. "But never mind that. I know someone who might be able to help us open it."

"What do you mean?" I ask. "The treasure isn't so important that we need to leave and find someone else to open the seal. We're on our way to Cloud Summit, remember? "

"No, no," Yoko scrunches her face while pulling an acorn out of her bag. "We don't have to go anywhere at all. She's right here."

"An acorn?" Scourge tilts his head.

"It's not the man-eating kind of acorn, is it?" Connor asks.

Yoko rolls her eyes at Connor before saying, "Don't all freak out, all right? You'll scare her." She takes off the crown of the acorn and traces her finger in a circle around the top. The circle glows green and releases a wisp of silvery sparkles. The wisp moves a few feet away and expands into the form of a woman. Her skin is verdant green, and her long hair consists of vines and ferns. Her dress looks to be made of silvery white flowers. She hovers in place six inches above the ground, and she's translucent like a ghost. Despite the oddness of this creature, her face is young and child-like.

I look from the apparition to the acorn and back again. Is this some kind of Ibadanian summoning trick? Maybe they use acorns instead of scrolls. Very interesting.

"What is it?" Jake asks.

"A silver tree nymph," Yoko says with a huge smile. "Her name is Sylva. She's a bit shy, so—"

"I can speak for myself, dearest Yoko," Sylva says. Her voice has an echo to it.

"Oh! Yes, yes you can. Anyway, we're trying to open that dungeon seal. Can you tell us what the runes say?"

"Of course." Sylva floats over to the dungeon seal. Her movements carry the sound of a gentle breeze blowing through a lush mountain forest. She mumbles an ancient language to herself as she studies the runes.

Yoko whispers to us, "Most nymphs can read ancient runes. They're experts on all things archaic."

Connor smirks. "Well done, bringing a nymph along on our quest."

Sylva looks back at us and says, "This dungeon seal requires an offering of maple leaves and foxglove, ignited by the fire of an electrokinetic."

"I saw a few foxgloves in the field outside!" Yoko exclaims, turning and leaving the room.

"I saw a few maple trees near the ledge!" Connor says, following close behind.

I exchange glances with Jake. He asks, "You don't happen to know any electros, do you?"

I remember my conversation in Kharduman with a nobleman from Izendor, when he told me about his deranged electrokinetic king. I shudder at the thought and reply, "Just the king of Izendor, but we certainly don't want *his* help."

"Oh," Jake frowns. "Yes, I remember a bit about him from the Academy. We spent a week or so talking about Izendoran political history. Electros have been on the throne for over a thousand years. Izendor and Armavir have a long history of rivalry and war, but historians say that Izendor's current king is the worst of them all. If *he* were to invade Armavir, there's no telling if we'd come out alive."

"That's...encouraging." I remember the conversation with the Armaviran adventurer who said the economy was declining so much that Armavir wouldn't be able to defend itself in the event of an invasion. Having seen the corruption of leaders such as Chief Bennett, and the poverty and general lack of fighting skills among the common Armavirans, I can't say I disagree.

Anyway, I shrug and say, "Well, I suppose we won't be opening this dungeon seal then."

"I suppose not," Jake replies.

"How come?" Sylva asks.

I look over at her. I had almost forgotten she was here. "We need an electro, but we don't have one."

"Yes you do."

I open my mouth to argue, but suddenly it hits me. I look around the room. "Where's Scourge?"

Jake looks around. "Good question. He was here a moment ago."

"He snuck away," Sylva replies.

"Did you see him?" I ask.

"Yes. He left after dearest Yoko and her friend went to find foxglove and maple. At the time, you were talking about the king of Izendor."

"Do you know where he went?" Jake asks.

"He wishes not to be found at the moment."

Jake raises an eyebrow. "Are you a mind-reader?"

Sylva giggles. "No, but I know facial expressions and body language. Don't you?"

Jake, embarrassed, fumbles for words. "Er...yes...well, maybe just a little."

"Excuse me," I interject. "Sylva, you said we have an electro with us. Is it Scourge?"

"Yes, but he wishes not to be."

"And that's why he left, I assume."

"I assume so as well."

I take some time to think it through. I saw Scourge's ability to manipulate fire during the battle in the shipyard. Kaze's jabs had paralyzed him at the outset, but he was just coming out of it when Meiling and Ibara had us all captive. I saw him wave his hand when Meiling released her deadly fireball. Once he saw it hit Ibara and set us free, he went limp again to avoid being noticed. He hasn't spoken about it since.

More recently, I've seen Scourge playing with bits of fire and lightning while he thought no one was watching. His use of fire *and* lightning removes any possibility he's a fire mage or pyrokinetic. Only an electrokinetic can master multiple forms of elemental energy.

Jake's voice brings me out of my thoughts. "Tarento, will you go find him? He trusts you more than any of us."

"Sure. Don't tell the others yet. Sylva, that includes you."

Both Jake and Sylva nod.

Just as I turn to leave the room, Connor and Yoko come back inside with bundles of foxglove and maple leaves. Yoko says, "We found them!"

"Very good!" Jake replies, and asks them a question. I slip out while they're distracted.

I stand in the center of the first room of the castle. Closing my eyes, I clear my mind of all distractions and focus on my sense of hearing. If Scourge is in this room, making any sort of movement, I will pick up on it. Samurai are trained to use their sense of hearing to locate people who may be hiding nearby.

"Use the small summoning scroll to find him," the Great King says.

That's the one Scourge took from the Blue Foxes and gave to me outside Bayside Harbor.

I take out the scroll, unravel it, and place it on the floor. I perform a few hand signs and place one hand on the scroll, muttering the ancient Felid incantation. The scroll goes up in smoke, and when it clears, there's a rat on the ground in front of me.

A rat.

An ordinary rat.

What am I supposed to do with a rat?

Just then, I look over at a knight's helmet lying on the ground. I remember Scourge had picked it up when we first entered the castle. Now I realize how the rat can be helpful.

I walk over to the helmet and stoop down next to it, beckoning for the rat to come and sniff it. I'm thankful for a summon's ability to understand and obey its summoner's directions, even if it can't speak for itself. Once it's spent a few seconds taking in the smell of the helmet, I say, "Find the person who touched this last."

The rat twitches its nose and scurries to the exit of the castle. I stand and follow it.

Once outside, the rat takes a left and skirts the castle wall. When we've almost gone around to the back, it turns and disappears beneath a large bush.

Unable to see beyond the bush, I walk around it and sure enough, there's Scourge facing away, sitting cross-legged on the ground. His finger's on fire like the tip of a match as he ignites a dead leaf on a rock. The rat is behind him, sniffing his back.

I drag my feet for a couple of steps, so he hears me coming before I speak. "Hello there."

He looks up at me and douses the flame on his finger. "Hey."

I sit down so I'm eye-level with him, and then I speak in the ancient Felid language to dismiss the rat.

Scourge tilts his head. "What?"

"There was a rat summon behind you. From the scroll you gave me, remember? I used it to find you."

Scourge turns to look, seeing nothing but fading smoke where the rat once was.

I take a moment to ask the Great King for wisdom. Then, when Scourge looks back at me, I say, "You know we need you in there."

"No you don't. That treasure probably isn't important anyway."

"Normally I would agree with you about the treasure. But the Great King says it's important, and I believe him."

He looks down at the charred leaf and starts poking at it.

"Scourge, why are you so upset about your powers?"

"I...I don't know."

I wait for him to continue.

180

Soon he begins to shift uncomfortably, and he asks, "Who are the electros you know about?"

"You," I reply. I know that's not the answer he's looking for. "And the king of Izendor."

Scourge sulks and mumbles.

"What was that?"

Scourge says louder, "His name is King Ruslan. And he's my father."

I stay silent for a while. I refrain from making any connections because I want Scourge to tell me his story on his own before I make assumptions. I can't imagine what it must have been like to be raised by a deranged king.

After a moment, Scourge begins to sob. "I can't tell you everything yet."

"That's all right. Just know that whenever you're ready, I'm here to listen."

He looks up at me through watery eyes. "I know. But the others should hear too."

I nod. "You don't have to tell us anything now, but we would appreciate it very much if you would help us open the dungeon seal."

Scourge swallows the last of his sobs and wipes his eyes. "Okay. Let's go open that dumb old rock."

We stand up and head back toward the front of the castle. As we come upon the entrance Scourge says, "Thank you for coming to find me. When I arrived at the bush, the Great King asked me why I was hiding. I was making every excuse not to go back. But that's when you came."

I smile at him. "The Great King cares about you very much, and so do I."

He returns the smile, his face acquiring its adventurous, inquisitive glow once again.

We return to the room where the others are waiting. The foxglove and maple leaves are already piled in the bowl-shaped indent, ready for an electro's fire to turn them into smoke and ash.

"There you are!" Yoko says. "Things were just starting to get boring around here. Tarento, what do you think? Should we try using ordinary fire? I don't think we can find an electro to do it."

I cast a glance at Jake and Sylva, surprised they managed to keep quiet about Scourge while we were gone. Jake winks, and Sylva smiles.

"Well," I say to Yoko while patting Scourge on the shoulder, "I wouldn't jump to conclusions just yet."

At my signal, Scourge walks up to the dungeon seal. He points and releases a bright spark that ignites the offering on impact.

As the foliage burns, the runes on the base of the seal begin to glow bright red. Then the altar stone slides back, revealing a staircase going down into pitch blackness.

Connor and Yoko are looking wide-eyed at Scourge with mouths agape. Jake crosses his arms and smiles with approval, and Sylva flits behind Jake and peers out with a nervous eye on the fire.

Scourge says, "I'll explain my powers and tell my story once we get back to the horses. But for now, please stop gawking at me."

Connor sets his jaw back into place before replying. "I don't suppose you can help us see in the dark corridor down the stairs, can you?"

"Yup. Let's go." Scourge leads the way down into the darkness. As he goes, a steady fireball forms in his palm. It casts an aura of light all around him.

Jake and Connor follow close behind. Before Yoko can go, Sylva maneuvers in front of her. "Dearest Yoko, I don't want to be anywhere near that fire. Can I rest in my acorn again?"

"Oh, yes of course! Thanks for your help!" Yoko pulls out the acorn, uncaps it, and holds it out. Sylva waves goodbye before dissipating into a cloud of sparkles, which the acorn absorbs. Yoko puts the top back on and puts it away.

I watch with great intrigue. Is Sylva a re-usable summon? As we follow Scourge down the staircase, I decide to ask. "Yoko, I noticed you didn't dismiss Sylva like an ordinary— er, Felid summon. Can you summon Sylva whenever you choose? Are all Ibadanian summons like that?"

Yoko chuckles. "Sylva isn't a summon! She's a real silver tree nymph. I rescued her from trappers, and she's been traveling with me ever since. This acorn is the only thing left of her silver oak tree, where she lived for hundreds of years before it was burned down."

"Trappers, huh?" In one sense, I can see Yoko as a person who would go around rescuing magical creatures from trappers, but in another sense, she seems too innocent to win against trappers if it came down to a fight. But then, what do I know about trappers, or Yoko, for that matter?

Yoko summarizes my thoughts, "You'll just have to wait for my turn to tell my story."

"Indeed."

The staircase is long, taking us deep underground. It levels out into a hallway, and after that, we come out into a dead-end room.

By the light of Scourge's fire, we can see a few of its features. It's the same size as the dungeon seal room. The floor, walls, and ceiling are blackened in some areas, as if by fire. It's empty, except for a few sets of armor lying about and some scattered bronze kappes. Because this tunnel has not been exposed to the elements, there are still skeletons inside the armor. I count five in all.

"This armor is different from the armor we've seen thus far," Jake says while examining one of the armored skeletons. "Perhaps these are the attackers?"

"Izendoran soldiers," Scourge says. "It's unmistakable."

"That makes sense," I reply. "They would have had to be Izendoran to get in here in the first place. That is, assuming all electros are Izendoran."

"Look at the walls," Scourge says, holding his light up closer to one of the scorch marks. "An electro was definitely here."

"Do you think this is where the treasure was kept?" Yoko asks, picking up a kappe. "If so, there isn't much left."

"Yeah," Connor agrees. "It looks like the Izendorans got what they were after."

I examine the room again. The treasure is gone, yes, but why did these Izendorans stick around long enough afterward to get killed? Were they looking for something else?

I turn to Jake, who is deep in thought, and ask, "What do you think happened here?"

"I'm working on it," Jake says. "Everything is better preserved in here, which makes it easier." He stoops down and studies the skeleton nearest him without touching it. Then he moves on to the next one, and then a third one. "They were killed by archers; you can see an arrow inside each one. Armaviran arrows, by the looks of it. A group of reinforcements must have followed the Izendoran soldiers in here."

"What about the black areas?" Yoko asks.

"I'm not sure yet. Like Scourge said, it was probably the work of an electro."

"Come look over here," Connor says, pointing at a scorch mark near the back of the room. An armored skeleton is lying in the middle of it.

Jake walks over to inspect it. "...Ooh, good find, Connor. This one is Armaviran, like the ones in the previous rooms. The armor's covered with soot and the skeleton is charred. No arrow, either."

I walk up to the Armaviran skeleton to examine it for myself. It looks like this soldier had been crouching by the wall before he was blasted to death by the electro's fire.

Jake voices my observation, "Now, I wonder why he's crouching like that...?"

The Great King tells me to ask Connor. I turn and ask, "What do you think, Connor?"

"Hmm," Connor narrows his eyes as he examines the scorched soldier. "I bet he was hiding something, like a secret passage to another part of the treasure. He refused to move out of the way even when the electro confronted him. What a brave soul he must have been, dying for something more valuable than himself. If only we could hear his story."

Aha. Just as I thought.

"Thank you for your input, Connor the Seer," I say as I move the charred skeleton out of the way. Sure enough, right where the skeleton's pelvis had been, one of the floor bricks has a strange indent.

"Oh. Wow," Connor says. "I didn't see that one coming."

"You should tell us stories more often," I say with a chuckle.

Jake steps on the indented brick. After nothing happens, he stomps several times. "How does it work?"

"Maybe you have to pull it out," Yoko says, stooping down to give it a try. She can just barely fit her slender fingers in the cracks to grab the brick. She wiggles it back and forth. "It's loose, but it'll be hard to pull out."

"Jake, you've stomped on it too much," Connor elbows Jake.

"Quiet, you," Jake elbows him back, sending him staggering to the side.

"Not fair!" Connor laughs. "Your elbow is much bigger than mine!"

While they banter, I say to Yoko, "It's getting looser. Keep trying to pry it out."

"Here, let me help," Scourge kneels down on the opposite side of the brick from Yoko and slips his free hand into the crack. They work together to wiggle the brick further out of its place. When the top of the brick has come two inches out of the ground, it jams in place. The sound of stone grating on stone fills the room. A nearby section of the wall opens up to reveal a corridor just large enough for a person to crawl through.

"Did it!" Yoko springs to her feet and dashes inside the opening.

"Hey, wait up!" Scourge runs after her.

Jake, Connor, and I follow closely after.

20

The Music of Marindel

Summer, 1419 AIE

~Tarento~

THE CORRIDOR IS alarmingly claustrophobic. Jake and I, the tallest of the group, have to crawl on our hands and knees. The others are short enough to walk in a crouch. Thankfully it's only about twenty feet long, and we soon find ourselves in another room.

Scourge shines the light around to show us our surroundings. The room is circular and much smaller than any room we've been through previously. It's empty with the exception of an elevated pedestal in the center, upon which an ornate white treasure chest, four inches in length, width, and height, proudly sits. On the lid is a silver coat of arms featuring a turtle and crown.

"The treasure!" Yoko shouts, going up to the pedestal and reaching for the box.

"Yoko, wait!" I shout, and she stops several inches short of touching it. "Be careful, there might be traps."

Yoko sighs. "We haven't seen any traps *so* far."

I'm about to reply, but Jake speaks first. "Traps were never used in Golden Age architecture. It wasn't until a century ago when Armavir took the idea from...Sunophsis? Or Tethys? Well, that's not important. What I mean to say is there're no traps here."

Yoko blinks. "Sounds great to me." She takes the treasure chest from the pedestal.

The instant she touches it, images of flashing light begin taking shape before me. Creatures dashing to and fro, cutting trails through a vast blue expanse. I hear sounds of fighting, screaming, yowling and shouting, the whirring of energy and the collapsing stone.

But then, I hear music. It's so beautiful and powerful that it puts all of Felidae's greatest orchestras to shame. It starts out faint, but grows to consume every other sound. Every color I've ever known, and even some I've never seen before, flash before me with increasing intensity until I'm blinded by white light.

I shout and fall to the ground, and all is quiet.

"*Tarento,*" a voice calls. I've never heard this voice before, but perhaps my ears have been blown out by the music.

In my mind's eye I see a man clothed in white with the friendliest face I have ever seen. His eyes shimmer as he sings,

"The Music of Marindel,
A song devoted to the Great King,
Will turn the tide of battle,
Banish the curse from land afflicting,
Pacify the ruthless beast,
And strengthen hearts of those found trembling."

After a pause, he speaks normally, "*In an Era long gone, the Music of Marindel was entrusted only to the Galyyrim. A shorter time ago, it was given to the children of the Great King, and then it was hidden again out of fear. But now, for such a time as this, I entrust this powerful weapon to you.*"

"Tarento!" Someone shouts. I'm being shaken on both sides. My vision clears, and I see Connor, Jake, Yoko, and Scourge crouched around me, looking worried.

"What happened?" I ask.

"You tell us," Jake says.

"Yeah," Connor says. "You just screamed and fell over. Did a bug get you? Was it a centipede?"

I groan. "The music...? Where...?"

"What music?" Yoko asks.

I sit up and rub my head. What in the land of Armavir just happened? As I stand to my feet, leaning on Jake for support, I remember the figure in white. Then I remember Connor's description of Prince Eli: tall and stately, a white nobleman's outfit with a cape and cavalier, dark hair, and earthen skin.

Jake says, "If you need to take a breather outside, just let us know."

186

"No, no." This claustrophobic room is hardly the issue. "I saw Prince Eli."

"What?" They say in unison.

"There was a battle," I explain. "I couldn't make much out, but it looked like creatures were flying around in the sky. Or, perhaps, the sea. And then this beautiful music started. I'm telling you, I've never heard anything like it. And it got louder and louder until all I heard was music, and the battle was consumed by the music and bright, flashing colors, and then I fell down and everything stopped. And that's when he came." I tell them word for word what the Prince told me.

The others are awestruck for a moment before Yoko finally speaks. "That sounds great...but very random at the same time."

"It has to mean *something* important," Connor says.

"Hm," my eyes wander to the pedestal in the center of the room, and then to the small chest held under Yoko's arm. The crazy vision happened the instant she touched that thing. I remember what the Great King said about preparing a treasure for me here.

"Yoko, have you opened the chest yet?" I ask.

"No, it's locked. I said so before you screamed and fell like a weirdo. Weren't you listening?"

I ignore her question. "Let me see it."

She hands the treasure chest to me. It's very light, even for its small size. Nothing rattles inside as I shake it. There's no keyhole, but it has an almond-shaped silver panel where a keyhole should be.

I show the lock to the others. "Have any of you seen anything like this?"

They all shake their heads.

"Hmm..." I take another good look at the chest. "Yoko, do you think Sylva would know how to open it?"

Yoko opens her mouth to reply, but a distant screech makes us all flinch. It echoes in the darkness of the stone corridor. We hold our breath and listen.

A moment later there's another screech, louder than the first.

"That doesn't sound good," Jake whispers.

I nod. "Let's get out of here before it corners us in this tiny room. Yoko, hide the chest in your bag. Don't pull it out, and don't let it go." I give it back to her. "Jake, let's take weapons from the fallen Izendorans."

"Great idea," Jake replies.

We crawl single-file through the small corridor, with Scourge and his light in the lead. As we emerge into the main treasure room, we hear another screech. It's coming closer.

"It sounds like it's in the dungeon seal room," Jake says while prying a sword out of the nearest Izendoran skeleton's grasp.

"You and I'd better lead," I say, taking a sword for myself. "Scourge, come behind us with the light. Connor, stay with Yoko; use your hunting knife to defend her if you must. Yoko, don't lose the chest."

"It's safe with me!" she replies.

"Good. Let's go."

I enter the hallway, holding my sword up and ready. My Samurai-trained senses are on the alert, and my steps quieter than those of any cat that has ever lived. Once we reach the staircase, I stop to watch and listen. Far up at the top of the staircase is the dungeon seal room, which is dimly lit by sunlight. I can hear scuttling, squeaks, and clicks in the room above. No matter what's up there, I realize there must be more than one. I look over my shoulder to say, "They're up ahead. Stay close."

I begin padding up the stairs. The others are close behind.

Five steps up, there's a *thump* behind me and a shout from Jake. Something knocks me from behind, and I fall forward. My sword flies out of my hand as I catch my fall, and it clangs on the stone steps some distance up. At the same time, everyone else shouts, Scourge's light goes out, and the wind is knocked out of me as I'm crushed from above.

Jake says, "Sorry! Sorry, everyone! I tripped."

"You can't be serious," I say with a groan.

A cry so horrid that it hurts my ears comes from the top of the staircase. The light from the room is eclipsed by the silhouette of a creature, which is now barreling down the staircase toward us!

My eyes widen, and every muscle in my body tenses for action. I pull myself out from underneath Jake and everyone else, leap up a few steps to retrieve my sword, and raise it just in time to meet the oncoming assailant.

I'm buffeted by a flurry of limbs and feathers, and the creature's battle cry pierces my eardrums. I strike the creature, but it doesn't go down. It maneuvers past me, and I turn around in pursuit.

Jake has gotten up and now stands ready. He swings deftly at the creature, cleaving a part of it off, and plants his foot on its wriggling body. He shoves his sword into its head to make it still.

"What is it?" Connor asks.

"No time to wonder," I say. "There are more of them up there.

Let's get out of this dark hall and meet them in the daylight." I turn and run the rest of the way up the stairs. I can hear the others following close behind.

When I exit the dungeon seal, I see three creatures in the room. Two are fluttering in the air, and one is on the ground just ahead. They are mostly bird-like, covered in black feathers, but their heads and faces are like that of a woman. A terrifying woman, that is: pale gray skin, solid black eyes, protruding fangs, and shaggy black hair mixed with feathers. Each one is about the size of a large dog.

The grounded creature and I make eye contact. It furrows its brow and screeches so terribly that I wince and hold my hands to my ears, though I'm careful not to drop my sword again.

"Harpies!" Jake says, coming up beside me. "Scavengers from the north. They're never up to any good!"

"Harpies in Armavir?" Connor asks. When he sees them, he recoils. "Yeesh! They're hideous!"

Jake runs at the harpy on the ground, raising his sword with both hands. A flying harpy tackles him from the side, bowling him over with an angry screech.

I shake the fuzziness caused by the harpy's scream out of my brain, lift up my sword and charge into battle.

The grounded harpy had taken flight after Jake went down; I chase after it. When it realizes I'm in pursuit, it squeaks fearfully and dives through the doorway into the main hall of the castle.

"That's right, get out of here!" I shout, following it through the opening. It looks like we won't have to face them after all. They realize we're not afraid to fight, so perhaps they've had a change of heart about attacking us. We'll escort them right out the door and be on our way.

The other two harpies fly squealing over my head. One of their wings is on fire, so it doesn't go far before tumbling down and crashing into a wall.

But when I look up, my breath is robbed by what I see.

The roof of this castle, as I've previously observed, is broken through in several places, where rays of sunlight come down into the main hall. Those gaps are now filled with harpies, perching or hanging in all kinds of contorted positions from anywhere they can grasp with their talons. There are dozens more of them lined up along the horizontal support beams just below the roof.

There must be a hundred of them. At least.

Jake and Scourge arrive on either side of me and follow my gaze upward.

"Oh..." Scourge breathes.

Before another word escapes our down-hanging mouths, the harpies begin screeching madly and swarming like an angry beehive. They dive upon us, attacking with outstretched talons and powerful wingbeats.

"Stand together!" Jake says, putting his back to mine and Scourge's. The three of us take stances in a triangular unit, facing away from each other, and we battle the harpies as they come. Jake and I swing expertly with our swords, and Scourge throws sparks of fire to burn their feathers. The fire is very effective, as it renders them unable to fly and therefore unable to attack or escape.

"Ah! Help!" Yoko shouts.

I turn and see two harpies, their talons fastened around Yoko's arms, lift her up into the air. A third one clings onto her back and rips into her bag.

Connor is being swarmed by harpies just like we are. He's backed up against a wall and swinging his knife in the most undisciplined manner. He shouts, "There're too many of them! They're taking Yoko away!"

"I'll get her," I say just before a harpy shoves me back into Scourge, and we fall together. On the ground, we're mobbed by so many harpies that we can't get up again. All I can do is shield my face from their scathing talons and kick them as they try to pile on me.

"Evil beasts, all of you!" Jake yells, kicking harpies off of us while also attacking those swooping down on him from the air.

Through the blur of feathers all around, I can see Yoko being carried out of the castle. The harpy on her back has just torn her bag open, and the treasure chest falls. Another harpy seizes the chest in midair and flies out of sight.

"No!" I shout, trying in vain to get up. There are too many of these hideous creatures pinning me to the ground, and they're much stronger than they look. "Jake, they have the chest!"

"They won't have it for long!" Jake slashes one harpy out of the air and punches another before sprinting toward the castle entrance.

A group of harpies flies after him, screeching and squealing in triumph.

Connor, who has managed to escape being pinned to the wall, runs after Jake with his own flock of harpies in pursuit.

I don't see what happens after they leave the castle. I'm being sat upon by several harpies, which have stopped attacking and are most likely keeping me prisoner. They smell like carrion, with a side of rotten cabbage. Scourge is nearby, undergoing the same fate.

"Scourge," I say, trying to look over at him.

"Yeah?"

"Can you use your powers to get us out of this mess?"

"Probably not. I can't move."

"Do you need to *move* to create fire?"

"Well, yeah. I have to move my hands and arms in a certain form, like how Samurai use hand signs. I'm not good enough to *think* fire into existence."

"Can you try?"

"Sure, I guess." Scourge is silent for a moment.

All is quiet except for the rodent-like squeaking of the harpies.

"It's not working," Scourge says.

"Well, it was worth a shot." I take a deep breath to calm myself down, and then I ask the Great King what to do.

I don't hear an answer, but what I do hear are the whooping shouts of the others, accompanied by harpies' angry cries.

The harpies guarding me and Scourge begin to stir, their squeaks becoming more anxious. They're no longer focused on keeping me down.

Now's my chance.

I brace myself. Every muscle in my body tenses up for action.

One. Two. Three.

I spring to my feet with a kick-up, bucking all the harpies off of me. Once I have proper balance, I throw a roundhouse-kick at the harpies on Scourge. I only hit a few of them—those that jumped to attack me once I freed myself—but it's enough for Scourge to wriggle himself free and jump to his feet.

Without skipping a beat, I pick up my fallen sword and launch toward the nearest group, attacking them faster than they can avoid me.

In my peripheral vision, I see Scourge electrify another group with a crackling barrage of lightning.

The remaining harpies flee for the exit. I throw my sword at one to take it down, and Scourge throws sparks to bring down a few more. One harpy remains, and it's about to escape.

"Come on!" I say, giving chase.

We cover half the distance across the room before it lurches in mid-flight and plummets to the ground. Once it lands on the castle doorstep, I notice an arrow has pierced the center of its forehead.

We stop immediately.

Khai stands at the doorway, arrow strung and ready to fire. The late-afternoon sun shines brightly behind him.

Scourge and I exchange glances before slowly raising our hands in surrender.

Khai looks back and forth across the room, maneuvering his weapon accordingly. Then he relaxes, lowering his bow and looking at us. "That's all of them."

Scourge and I breathe sighs of relief.

"Come on," Khai beckons with a wave. "Everyone's safe, and the chest has been recovered."

Scourge and I exchange glances once again before walking toward him. Khai pulls the arrow out of the dead harpy as we come, and then the three of us exit the castle together.

Jake, Yoko, and Connor are waiting near the center of the field, which is now littered with dead harpies. The sun, almost ready to set, casts an orange glow on the landscape.

I ask the huntsman, "Did you do all this?"

"Most of it."

"I can't thank you enough," I say. "They were after the chest, something the Great King promised to give me. If they had stolen it...well, I doubt it would've been a good thing."

"Don't mention it."

I ask my next question in a hushed manner as we approach the others. "Have you come for Yoko?"

"I have."

"You *do* realize she's supposed to come with us, don't you?" My voice is laced with confidence as I continue. "She's been a great help thus far. I believe the Great King had us cross paths for a reason, and she knows it well. I know you love her and want to protect her, but *please* don't force her to give up her destiny."

"You almost lost her!" Khai snaps. I believe he's about to say more, but Connor interrupts him, waving his arms dramatically. "Khai! You're *amazing*! You were like, 'fwip!' 'fwip!' And the harpies were like, 'Eeeeeek!'"

"Yeah!" Yoko flies headlong into Khai's fluffy torso for an embrace. "Thank you for saving me! For saving *all* of us. We never could have beaten them without you."

Khai squeezes Yoko, sighing deeply. "You have no idea how much I've missed you."

"If I may," Scourge asks, "how were you able to find us?"

"He's an excellent tracker," Yoko brags. "I knew he'd find us eventually. I wanted him to. Now," she looks at him, "will you come on the quest with us? Please, please, please?"

Khai ruffles Yoko's hair before looking at each one of us. "I *am* an excellent tracker, as Yoko said, but that's not how I found you. The Great King helped a bit. I've known him for a long time, but... you could say we haven't been on the greatest terms."

We watch and listen intently. Yoko grasps his hand.

"After finding Yoko's note, I was livid. There's no way to describe the feeling of losing a daughter. If you haven't lived through it, you'd never understand." He takes a long, trembling breath. "I thought you had deceived her; I was going to find you and kill you. Then, two days ago, a Bothnian man with a pickaxe met me on the road. He said, 'Khai, you've been running and hiding for most of your thirty-nine years of life. On your current path, you will lose the treasure you seek to keep. It's time for you to choose the way of the Kingdom of Marindel. You must accept it, forgive your perceived adversaries, and surrender your fear. Rise up to the challenge! You've performed many great exploits thus far, but your greatest adventure is yet to come. The Great King will guide you every step of the way.'"

"Wow," Connor breathes. "That was the amazing bearded man I met in Bayside Harbor!"

Khai nods. "I knew he was, and I didn't want to believe him. I wrestled with it through the night, and when dawn came, I went off the trail to hunt. In the wilderness, I encountered one of the Felids from the shipyard, but he didn't see me. I followed him back to his companions, the small Samurai and another man I haven't seen before. They were talking about finding you, Tarento, when an ash bear attacked their camp and set them fleeing. You'd think they'd never seen an ash bear before!" He chuckles. "But that's when the Great King spoke to me. He said, 'I am the protector of Yoko, Connor, Tarento, Jake, and Scourge, for they have chosen to serve me. Those who plot against them will be scattered, but those who help them will be given honor.'"

He takes a deep breath again. "That's when I knew I needed to find you. Not to harm you as I had intended, but...to join you. After all, *someone* needs to make sure you kids stay out of trouble."

"Yes!" Yoko shouts, embracing Khai. "Thank you!"

Jake pats Khai on the shoulder. "I'm honored to have you with us."

"I am as well," I say.

"And I," Scourge says, followed by Connor.

"In time I hope to feel the same. Now," Khai hefts his bow. "Sunset is upon us, so we'll set up camp here. I'll go hunt. Yoko, see to everyone's wounds. The rest of you, if you're not being treated, gather wood and brush to build a fire. Oh, and throw the dead harpies over the cliff, before they stink up the place."

We're all together again by nightfall. We've roasted two pheasants over the fire, and now we're sitting in a circle eating slowly and telling Khai what he missed since we left Bayside Harbor. After recounting our adventure in the abandoned castle, I share my thoughts about the chest and the harpy attack:

"I believe the Music of Marindel Eli told me about is somehow contained within the chest. It'll be a great asset to us once we know how to open it, but the real question is this: if the chest was locked away under a dungeon seal for hundreds of years before today, how did the harpies know about it? Clearly, they waited to ambush us until we had the chest in our possession. I don't believe harpies are smart enough to coordinate a move like that on their own."

"And we must wonder," Connor adds, "what harpies are doing in Armavir in the first place."

"Indeed," Jake agrees. "Harpies have *never* lived in Armavir, not even before the establishment of the Paladin Order."

I say to Jake, "You made a comment earlier about them being scavengers from the north. Are you saying they might be from Izendor?"

"Not Izendor," Connor says. "Meiro. I heard a story about harpies from an adventurer who'd been there."

"I believe it," Jake nods. "There is no land more accursed in our time than the kingdom of Meiro."

Huh. I've never heard of Meiro before. "Are you sure about that? Is Meiro worse than Izendor? Worse than Sunophsis?"

Yoko chuckles. "Your Felid lack-of-knowledge-about-the-out-side-realm is showing."

I glare at her. Khai chides her before I find anything to say in rebuke.

"Much worse," Jake says. "There's a curse over the land. It's naught but a wasteland crawling with monsters."

"Where is it?" I ask.

"North of Pythoria," Khai says. "West of Izendor. It's the north-ernmost kingdom on the mainland."

No wonder I've never heard of it. It's geographically as far from Felidae as a kingdom can be, let alone the fact it probably has no trading ports. Felids would never be interested in a place so far away with nothing to offer.

"What that means," Jake says, "is the harpies had to come a long way south to get here. Something's not right about that."

Scourge speaks up. "I know who sent the harpies."

We all look at him.

"Who?" Jake asks.

He fidgets, eyes darting to the ground. "Have any of you heard the story of Meiro before?"

We all shake our heads.

"Do tell," Connor says.

"All right." Scourge breathes deeply. "I promised I'd be the next one to tell my story, but you need to hear this first or you won't understand the context of what I've been through. These won't be light-hearted stories, either. Are you ready?"

We nod.

"Go on," Khai says. "Surprise us."

Scourge takes a drink of water from his canteen before jumping into the story of Meiro.

Spring, 1328 - Summer, 1419 AIE

WHEN YOU HEAR mention of the kingdom of Meiro, perhaps images of a desolate landscape come to mind; a wasteland crawling with monsters, as Jake put it. That's all anyone knows about Meiro, because no one has a reason to go there. Those who venture in have a death wish, and all they find are monsters, famine, disease, and death. That's how Meiro appears to the common outsider, and that's exactly how the ruler of Meiro wants it to be.

As an Izendoran, I know it quite differently. My kingdom of origin has had a complicated alliance with Meiro ever since it became what we know it as today.

In the year 1328, during the reign of King Dmitri of Izendor, a dangerous fugitive came into the land from the southeastern kingdom of Ibadan. He sought the favor of King Dmitri in return for his loyalty and service, and it was granted. At that time Izendor had frequent borderland skirmishes with Ibadan in the south and Dantoneia in the west—Dantoneia is what Meiro used to be called— so the fugitive was able to serve as Dmitri's advisor and a magical wildcard to help Izendor gain the upper hand.

In 1333, it became known that the fugitive was gathering support for a coup d'etat against Dmitri. His greatest following was among the rock trolls that live in the remote parts of Izendor, and even more trolls were crossing over from Ibadan to join his army. When Dmitri learned about this, he ordered that the fugitive be killed.

The fugitive defeated every assassin sent after him. He retaliated by challenging Dmitri to a duel, claiming it would be a horribly bloody affair to pit the armies of Izendor against his rock trolls and other supporters.

Now, keep in mind that Dmitri was an electrokinetic, and any duel against a powerful electro is certain to end swiftly, with a bolt of lightning through the opponent's heart. He thought the fugitive's move was strange, but he accepted nonetheless.

The two were evenly matched, and they battled for nearly twenty-four hours. In the end, Dmitri's fire and lightning overpowered the fugitive's Bygone magic, and the latter was forced to surrender. Dmitri had every right to kill the fugitive, but he had come to respect his magical prowess and decided exile would be a more fitting punishment. The fugitive disappeared, and for a long time no one knew what became of him.

Years later, I believe in 1347, King Dmitri passed away, and his son Alexei became king. In that same year, the border skirmishes with Dantoneia suddenly stopped. Everyone in Izendor hailed it as a sign of blessing over Alexei's kingship. But, in the next year, Izendoran border intelligence brought back news that Dantoneia's entire ruling regime had been usurped and destroyed by the fugitive. Rock trolls had crossed into Dantoneia, reinforcing the fugitive's position as ruler of the kingdom. The sky over Dantoneia grew dark, and every plant withered and died. The sentient residents disappeared completely, while monsters native to the land but kept in check by the previous inhabitants were allowed to roam free as long as they remained loyal to the fugitive.

King Alexei was the first to call it 'Meiro,' meaning 'accursed land.' To avoid making known any involvement Izendor had with the fugitive, in every diplomatic discussion with other kingdoms about what became of Dantoneia, Alexei and his ambassadors said the land was cursed by misfortune, resulting in the death of all intelligent life and the proliferation of dangerous monsters. To this day, Alexei's story of Meiro lives on in the minds of the inhabitants of every kingdom excluding Izendor. The kingdom of Dantoneia has nearly been forgotten.

Even while keeping other kingdoms in the dark with his omissive diplomacy, Alexei was afraid the fugitive would extend his rule into Izendor and cause it to suffer the fate of Dantoneia. He sent ambassadors to Meiro to forge an alliance—three times, in fact—and they never returned. Finally, Alexei himself went and found the fugitive. They created an alliance, and it seemed like Alexei and the fugitive were on good terms for the rest of Alexei's kingship.

The next king maintained the alliance with Meiro, even as monster sightings and civilian deaths became commonplace in western Izendor. When that king died after two decades, the next king addressed the issue by force. He had fortresses built to oversee the western borderlands, and gave orders for any trespassing monster to be killed on sight or chased back into Meiro.

This king ruled for only two years and died of unexplained causes. His son, Ruslan, came to the throne at age fourteen. This Ruslan is the one you've all heard about; the deranged king of Izendor whose frequent mood swings and electrokinetic prowess are a deadly combination even to his own people. Ruslan and the ruler of Meiro are fierce enemies, often sending dispatches of men or monsters to fight each other. Tomorrow, you'll hear more about that in my own personal story.

The reason I've explained all of this is because the ruler of Meiro is none other than Jaedis of the Northern Bluffs, the very sorcerer we are on a quest to destroy. He knew about the Music of Marindel, he knew we were in the castle, and he is the one who sent the harpies at just the right time to take it from us.

WHEN SCOURGE FINISHES, I have nothing to say. My mind is reeling with all the new information, and my heart is stirred with fear at how it all applies to our quest.

Until this moment, I believed Lord Zetsumei was the greatest obstacle in my service to the Great King. But now that I've heard more about Jaedis, he sounds far worse. While Zetsumei is a self-absorbed tyrant blind to his own coming destruction, I can infer from Jaedis' actions that he is a direct follower of the Great Serpent, just as my friends and I are followers of the Great King. That alone makes him our greatest threat.

For the first time, I feel a wave of compassion for the adopted daughter of the Great King. Connor's stalwart enthusiasm to embark on a quest to protect Melody from Jaedis is now fully warranted.

Our previous assumptions of Jaedis as a rogue sorcerer with only a few Nox Abyssae under his command have been shattered, and now we have the accursed kingdom of Meiro to reckon with.

To make matters worse, it seems as though Jaedis has been watching our every move from the start. His ability to time the arrival of the harpies with our finding of the chest causes a prick of fear to penetrate my heart. If he sees us now, there's no way we'll have the element of surprise as we plan our tactics against him.

The others are just as disquieted as I am. Connor and Jake vocalize a few of my thoughts, but it turns out we're too exhausted to discuss anything further. As the fire dies out and the damp, late-night wind causes us to shiver, we decide to turn in for the night.

As I lie down on my coat spread over the soft grass, I look up and admire the stars. The moon has not yet risen, and the darkness magnifies the stunning array of glittering light above us. As I take in the sight, I focus on my breathing. I find it very soothing after hearing such a dreadful story.

Only as I'm drifting off to sleep, in that intriguing realm between reality and oblivion, do I realize the story we'll hear tomorrow will likely be much worse.

21
The Dark Heart of Izendor
Summer, 1419 AIE

~Connor~

TARENTO CALLS MY name, yanking me out of a dream I no longer remember. I stretch with a groan; my whole body is stiff. All the horse-riding, sword training, and yesterday's battle with the harpies have left my muscles burning in pain. I know this is supposed to make me stronger, but I'm not feeling it yet.

"Connor, wake up," Tarento repeats.

I sit up slowly, opening my eyes to see that the sun has just risen. Tarento and Khai are the only ones standing and fully awake. The others are stirring and sitting up as I am.

"It's time to move," Khai says while packing some of our things. "We have several days of travel ahead of us, and there's no time to lose."

"Can we have breakfast?" Yoko asks, rubbing her eyes.

"Perhaps we'll find some fruit along the way," Jake says with a stifled yawn. "Khai's right. We need to get going."

I muster all the strength I have to force myself to my feet. I stagger as I shake off the last of my sleepiness, and then I pick up my coat and bag and begin walking back to the ledge which leads down to the valley where the horses are.

The others follow suit.

We arrive at the bottom of the valley staircase to find our horses exactly where we left them. They look well-rested and well-fed, and they've even made a friend. There are *four* horses instead of three!

"Khai," Scourge asks, "Is that your horse?"

"How else would I have caught up to you so fast?"

Khai's horse is different. While our horses are muscular and mottled with black, white, and dark-brown colors, Khai's is small and sleek, the color of wheat at harvest with a slightly darker mane and tail.

"A Pythorian horse," Jake says, patting it on the shoulder. "Very nice."

"Everyone," Yoko says, "Khai is *so* good at riding horses, you wouldn't believe it! He learned how to ride when he was seven years old! *Seven years old!*"

"Six," Khai says, cuffing Yoko playfully. "It looks like the horses enjoyed their rest and the greenery of the valley. Now they'll be strong and ready to take us through the next few days."

We fill our canteens with water from a nearby stream, and then we all mount and set off at a trot along the valley floor.

There's no conversation at first because we're all still tired. However, to use a metaphor I've heard in a story once or twice, there's a berserker beast in the room.

Scourge's story of Meiro last night was a real downer, almost as bad as the ending of '*The Princess of the Sea,*' and Scourge promised he would elaborate more on the subject today in the context of his own personal story. We know how sensitive Scourge is about his past traumas, so I think we're all reluctant to bring it up. Still, I'd bet ten thousand krons that we want to hear his story so badly that we'd each pay him ten thousand krons to persuade him to tell us.

Or, at least *I'd* do that.

We trot along for an hour in silence. The valley begins to widen and the steep cliffs on either side become shorter. The sun rises high enough that it peers through the trees at the top of the valley and casts dappled light on our path.

We soon come to a spacious area with wild apple trees and raspberry bushes scattered about, and Khai suggests we stop to pick fruit for the journey. We dismount and fill our bags with as much as we can carry.

It's during this brief foraging break that I make up my mind. Once we've started on our way again, I'm going to remind Scourge he promised to tell us his story. He owes it to us and to our quest to be honest and open with any information that might be crucial for our success. It would also help us understand where Scourge came from and how best to help him through his traumatic memories.

Soon, we're back on our horses and on our way again.

As I lick raspberry juice off my fingers, I begin the assault. "Hey, Scourge."

"Yeah?" He says between apple bites.

"I was thinking about the story of Meiro you told us yesterday. Do you think you can tell us more?"

"Oh...yeah..." Scourge takes a huge mouthful of apple.

Jake flanks Scourge from the side. "You did say you would tell us more as we traveled today."

After swallowing, Scourge replies, "Yeah, but I don't mind waiting if you guys don't want to hear it yet. I could tell you were spooked by what I shared yesterday."

Tarento moves in for the kill. "Scourge, there were several times yesterday when you said you would tell us your story. I understand you're not comfortable talking about it, but you can't back out of something so important when you know how much it will help us. You gave us your word."

Scourge's face flashes with surprise. He didn't expect his traveling partner for the past year to put him in a corner like that.

"You promised us," Tarento continues. "You promised *me*, remember? There's nothing you can say that will cause us to look down on you. We're all here to listen and support you. Please, Scourge. We need to hear your story."

Scourge is silent, eyes fixed on the back of his horse's head.

Khai delivers the final blow. "You're not the only one here with a dark past, kid. We've got your back."

"All right, all right," Scourge throws the half-eaten apple over his shoulder.

"Wizard," I say. "Take as much time as you need. We have the whole day."

Scourge closes his eyes and breathes deeply.

Tarento, behind Scourge on the same horse, gives him a firm pat on the shoulder.

I wait with bated breath. I feel like my soul is about to jump out of my body and run in circles around our little cavalry.

Finally, Scourge begins.

Autumn, 1404 - Autumn, 1414 AIE

~Scourge~

I WAS BORN during a thunderstorm.

Legend has it, when an electro is born during a thunderstorm, their abilities have the potential to become twice as powerful.

My father, King Ruslan, was also born during a thunderstorm. You'd think he'd be thrilled his son was born on such a night.

But it was not so.

You see, King Ruslan loved my mother Elena more than he's loved anyone before or since. She was the daughter of a mountaineer; a commoner. But Ruslan loved her so much, he broke the royal tradition and took her to be his wife. He was twenty-three at the time, and she was nineteen.

Ruslan has always been ambitious and infatuated with power, but before my birth, he was much more stable—or personable, you could say. His anger flared when things didn't go his way, but to the untrained eye it was nothing serious. Even so, some of the wise men of Izendor saw the signs of his developing insanity and tried to warn Elena and others. No one listened to them.

Then, it happened: I was born and Elena died on the same night, the night of a thunderstorm. It was believed that Elena was perfectly healthy until she went into labor. As she gave birth, she became very sick. Mere moments after I was born, she breathed her last.

When Ruslan received the news, he didn't believe it at first. He had the messenger killed immediately. When another messenger came and told him the same thing, he went to see for himself. There he saw the midwife holding me, the two of us crying, and Elena on her bed as dead as can be, looking like she had succumbed to a horrible plague.

Ruslan's fragile sanity shattered in that moment. He mourned over her body, screaming and sobbing, until his grief transformed into unbridled rage. The midwife had left moments before and passed me off to a nurse, who took me into hiding.

Ruslan went after the midwife first. When he found her, he accused her of murdering his wife and incinerated her on the spot. After that he called for all the servants who prepared the room or who were otherwise involved in the birthing process, and killed every one of them.

Next, his rage not satisfied, Ruslan utilized the thunderstorm already underway to strike the buildings outside the palace walls, setting them ablaze and destroying a third of Izengrad, the capital city. When that was finished, he went into the mountains and continued to vent his fury.

My father didn't remember me after he returned. When the

nurses finally worked up the confidence to remind him, he was greatly disturbed and told them to 'throw me away.' However, the nurses convinced him to keep me alive for the sake of Elena and for the sake of the kingdom. The name he gave me was Scourge, to remind every citizen of Izendor that it was because of me that his beloved Elena died.

I was raised by the nurses for much of my early life. I rarely saw my father—he never wanted to see me anyway—but I always heard the nurses talking fearfully about his latest mood swing, the people he incinerated the other day, or the apathy with which he sent soldiers on "suicide missions" to the Meiro borderlands. The nurses would look at me and say, "Your father is a horrible man. Please, may you never become like him." So I developed an intense fear of my father at an early age.

When I was old enough to explore the palace on my own, I did so frequently. I also started experimenting with my powers, but every time the nurses found me doing it, they reprimanded me. "Put that away right now! Fire is not a plaything for children. You don't want to end up like your father, do you?" Because the use of my abilities always elicited fear and disgust, I've never been comfortable using them in public.

Sometimes, while exploring the palace, I would cross paths with my father. I always hid from him, because if he saw me, he would mock and insult me. He'd pull me out of my hiding place and throw me across the room, telling me to stay out of his way. I received a few scrapes and bruises from his beatings, but nothing worse. It felt like someone was always there to catch me, though I never saw who it was.

When I was nine years old, my father sent for me for the first time. I was terrified, but I had no choice. I went and knelt before him.

"My son," he said, "you are destined to sit upon this throne and rule as the king of Izendor. You're a disappointment now, and I loathe to even look at you. Nevertheless, I will train you to become worthy of the throne of Izendor, so one day you may be a strong and powerful king, feared by all the kingdoms of Tyrizah."

I didn't want to be trained by him for any reason, and I was afraid, but there was nothing I could do to resist.

Usually, fathers teach their sons how to throw a ball, build a table, or wield a sword. But my father was no ordinary man.

He would take me to the dungeon beneath the palace, where people would be incarcerated for even the smallest crimes. He'd bring me to a prison cell and order me to burn or electrocute the person inside. If I didn't obey him immediately, he'd scold and beat me. I tried to resist and run away, but he always caught and overpowered me. I tried to harden my heart and do what he told me to do, but the guilt was too much to bear. Even more unbearable were the prisoners' screams of agony and pleas for mercy. No matter what I did, felt, or thought, I was trapped.

This went on several times a week for several moons. I hate to admit it, but I became fascinated with my powers. I relished the feeling of unleashing destructive energy on command. But the more I enjoyed my powers, the more I hated myself.

I realized I was becoming my greatest fear.

One night, shortly after my tenth birthday, I was in my room. I knew my father would be coming soon to take me to the dungeon, and I wept and trembled with fear. Through my teary-eyed vision, I noticed a rope coiled in the corner, next to the fourth-story balcony window, and it gave me an idea. I could tie one end of it to the banister, lower myself down, and run away. If I hurried, I'd escape far enough into the mountains that no one would be able to find me.

I made my move, quickly tying the rope to the banister. But when I finished the knot, a wave of despair overtook me. A voice in my mind said, *"You are becoming a monster, just like your father, and there is no escape. The only way to save yourself and every innocent person you will someday kill is to hang yourself from the balcony. Tie the free end of the rope around your neck and jump. You deserve to die."*

I listened to the voice as if in a trance. I tied the rope into a noose, slipped it over my head, and stood on the banister. With trembling breath, I prepared to throw myself down and end the nightmare.

I jumped. I fell. I closed my eyes and braced for my imminent death.

Just as I wondered why it was taking so long, I landed softly in someone's arms. The fragrant smell of jasmine flowers flooded my senses.

I opened my eyes and was awestruck to see that a beautiful elven woman was holding me. I looked beyond her at the balcony and saw that the rope had slipped from the banister, therefore preventing my hanging.

She spoke with the loveliest voice I've ever heard, "Dear friend, why are you so surprised? Don't you recognize me?"

"N-no," I stuttered.

She smiled gently. "I am the one who catches your fall."

I remembered every time my father threw me it had felt like someone was there to catch me. But, surely I would've noticed if a radiant elf-lady was in the room!

"Can you turn invisible?" I asked.

"You can call it that if you'd like," she said merrily, setting me down. "Now, why don't you take that rope off your neck?"

As I obeyed, she introduced herself. "My name is Guinevere. I'm a Galyyr assigned to protect you."

I blinked. "Why?"

"The Great King has seen your suffering, the lies spoken to you, and the injustice committed against you. The Serpent intends to destroy you while you're young, and the Great King intends to resist him. Nevertheless, your greatest trial is yet to come. You must be strong, friend. You have a very good heart. Guard it with your life."

I didn't understand. "What King? What Serpent? What do you mean I have a good heart? I—"

"Hush, don't fret. All you need to remember now is that your life is valuable. You mean something to this realm."

The beauty and authority in her voice gave strength to my weary heart, but I was still confused and skeptical. "I *mean* something to this realm?"

"Yes, dear friend. I am here whenever you need me." The elf smiled and moved to walk away.

"Wait! One more question. Why do you keep calling me 'friend'? My name is Scourge."

Guinevere stopped and turned, blinking curiously. "No, it's not."

"Yes, it is. My father named me after the plague that killed my mother. It's my fault she died, you know."

She laughed. "That is *not* who you are! You are neither a scourge nor a plague. Your true name remains hidden even from me. However, as a citizen of Marindel, I cannot call you what you are not. So, I will call you what you are: a friend."

Just then, my father appeared on the balcony and spotted me. "Scourge! What are you doing down there!?"

My heart stopped. I looked where Guinevere was before, but she had disappeared. Her jasmine-flower scent was quickly fading. I looked up again as my father leapt off the balcony and fell freely for a second before softening his landing with jets of fire from beneath his feet. Then he strode toward me as I cringed for a scolding and a beating.

But when he arrived, he did neither.

Instead, he ruffled my hair and said, "Son, I'm proud of the progress you've made so far. I have a wonderful surprise for you."

"R-really?"

"The next phase of your training." His eyes gleamed with murderous mischief. "We leave at dawn tomorrow. Bring nothing with you."

"Y-yessir."

I hardly slept a wink before my father's soldiers came and took me down to the dungeon. Much to my surprise, they led me past the dungeon and deeper beneath the palace, through halls and passages I never knew about, until we came into a very spacious cavern.

It was filled with soldiers, all equipped and ready for battle.

My father stood on a precipice over the assembly, shouting orders and threats for disobedience. From his yelling, I discovered these soldiers were about to set off on a borderland raid.

Apparently, I was to join them.

My father led the charge down a corridor on the other side of the cavern. The army poured in after him, and the soldiers my father sent to retrieve me made sure I accompanied them.

We traveled underground for a long time; I later discovered it was a total of four days. I never knew Izendor had underground tunnels, but I decided it was reasonable given most of the kingdom's topography consists of steep mountain crags that are nearly impassable, even on a good summer day.

Now, here are a few important things you should know about the Izendoran army.

According to legend, long ago, giants lived in the mountains of Izendor, and they intermingled with the humans there to create hybrid offspring. Though giants have long since become extinct, it's said that the Izendoran people still carry giantish blood, and it gives us extra strength and stamina. Our silvery-white hair and amber eyes are believed to have come from the giants.

Whether the legend is true or not, all Izendoran soldiers are trained and perfected in the areas of endurance and perseverance. No one in the army ever walks or marches to get anywhere. They always run, even with all their gear. They stop for two-hour naps and meal intervals, and then they get up and keep running. This behavior is driven by a pervasive belief in Izendoran culture that it's shameful to show weakness or weariness of any kind.

The small amount of rest and nourishment was not enough for me. Fearing rebuke, I kept silent and tried my best, but I couldn't ignore the fact that I hadn't been trained for this. I could hardly keep up, but every time I was about to faint from exhaustion, I felt strength fill me from the inside. Every time it happened, I smelled the faint aroma of jasmine. Guinevere, though invisible, was traveling with me.

One of my father's soldiers, named Vladimir, was impressed by how I was managing the journey, and he asked how I was doing so well. Not wanting to tell him about Guinevere, I said maybe it was a perk of being an electro. He said that couldn't be it; electros don't have any physical advantage over ordinary Izendorans. He continued to press me on the subject, and because he was the only semblance of a friend I had on that journey, I eventually caved. I thought maybe he could help me understand more about Guinevere.

When I finally opened up, Vladimir was intrigued. He told me about an encounter he had several years ago with an old man in an Izengrad tavern. The man told him a certain Great King was looking for people to stand up for justice in Izendor, and illustrated it with the story we now know as 'The Princess of the Sea.' Vladimir disregarded the encounter at the time, thinking the old man was using a folk legend to demonstrate the need for political reform, but the memory of it had haunted him ever since. He said he always had a lurking thought in the back of his mind that the Great King wanted him to do something, but he was too afraid of Ruslan to seriously consider it.

Vladimir and I talked about the Great King and the Kingdom of Marindel every chance we had. I enjoyed it so much, it became easier for me to endure our hectic pace through the tunnels. I even forgot we were heading toward a place so dreadful, we were not guaranteed to return alive.

Once we emerged from the tunnels—four days after we departed from Izengrad, as I said before—we were only a day's journey from Meiro. Ruslan ordered the army to split into three groups, each taking a separate mountain road toward the borderlands. We didn't slow our pace, even though the roads were treacherous and often so narrow that we had to run single-file. We stopped to make camp when evening fell, and for the first time since our departure, we slept for the length of an entire night.

When dawn came, we got up and ran the final stretch. Meiro was near, just over the mountains in front of us.

In the early afternoon, a mass of thunderclouds barreled over the mountains and covered the sky within minutes. Rain, thunder, lightning and wind came relentlessly upon us.

The third of the army I was with arrived at the foot of the

mountains first, just after the storm hit—and that's when the battle began. Squinting my eyes against the deluge, I saw a throng of nightmarish monsters charging toward us.

The Izendoran soldiers didn't break stride. They shouted against the fury of the storm, drew their weapons, and engaged the hordes of Meiro head-on.

So, there I was, ten years old, having never been in a battle, having never seen a monster in my life, and exhausted from running for nearly five days straight, in the middle of a brutish war between the burliest of men and the fiercest of beasts.

Everything happened so quickly. Writhing bodies were everywhere. Metal clanging, men shouting, monsters roaring, thunder pounding, wind howling. I was overwhelmed with sheer panic, and stood in a daze while everything whirled around me.

The second group of Izendorans arrived from the right, these headed by my father. They charged into battle, attacking the hordes of Meiro from the side. The third group appeared a moment later, attacking the hordes from the left.

Ruslan stood upon an elevated precipice near the edge of the battlefield, where he laughed and yelled and laughed some more. I realized with horror that my father had no intention of participating in the battle himself. He was only there to enjoy the carnal display. I couldn't make out his words, but I could tell by his demeanor that he wasn't giving orders or cheering for his men. He seemed to care nothing for them at all.

Vladimir shouted behind me, "Scourge! Look out!"

I turned to see a massive black shape with three snake-like heads, piercing yellow eyes, and sharp, glistening fangs.

A hydra.

Vladimir jumped in front of me as one of the hydra's jaws came down to snap me in two, and he sliced the creature's head clean off. I was so terrified, I stood still with my eyes wide and my mouth agape.

Vladimir took a stance facing the monster and called back, "Scourge, run! Get out of here!"

As he spoke, the hydra's severed neck grew two new heads, both as fearsome as the last, and the beast attacked Vladimir with all its might.

In my panic, I channeled electrokinetic energy into my fingers and unleashed a barrage of forked lightning upon the hydra. Drenched by the torrential rainfall, it was violently electrocuted and toppled over.

An instant kill.

Meanwhile, a tendril of my lightning had flickered aside and struck Vladimir. The jolt sent him tumbling backward into the mud.

"Ah! Vladimir!" I shouted, rushing to his side.

Vladimir lay face-up, his body covered in burns. None of his wounds looked fatal, but I'd electrocuted enough prisoners in the dungeon to know he'd take a long time to recover. How could I have been so stupid? Vladimir was standing in front of the hydra, but I didn't think about that at all. My mistake might've just cost Vladimir his life.

I should have run, like he told me to.

"I'm sorry, I'm sorry, I'm so sorry," I bumbled, crouching over him and using his shield to protect his face from the rain.

Vladimir smiled and said, "Don't worry, kid. I'll be all right."

"What have you done?" My father's scathing voice asked.

I turned with a start, looking up at his livid face. "I-I'm sorry, it was an accident, I didn't mean to—"

"Silence! *Look* at him!" He pointed at Vladimir. "Vladimir was one of my favorite soldiers, filled with potential, and you took away every chance he had to prove himself! You are a pathetic excuse for a son, let alone a prince of Izendor!" He continued to berate me with many more insults that are not worth repeating.

I cowered in shame and began to cry. I hardly ever looked at my father while being scolded, but in that moment, I glanced at his face in time to see his mood change. If you know him well enough, you can see it in his eyes when it happens. His hateful expression evolved into one of cruel mischief.

"Nevertheless," he said, voice calm, "I am very pleased with how powerful your lightning has become. You killed a hydra with one shot, and even wounded this man here." He paused, pointing at Vladimir once again. "Go on, son. Finish the job."

My jaw dropped. I've never witnessed a quicker and more complete mood swing from my father: scolding me for hurting Vladimir one moment, and encouraging me to kill him the next. I squeaked my reply, "But...you said he was your favorite soldier!"

"Never mind that. Izendoran soldiers are born to die. It's nothing to be concerned about."

"What?" A surge of anger and fear welled up in my heart.

"You heard me!" my father barked. "Finish him!"

"No!" I stood and cast Vladimir's shield aside. Electrical power gathered in my fingertips.

"How *dare* you defy me!? You will do as I say!" My father drew back his leg to punt me.

Everything seemed to happen very slowly. My habitual desire was to hide my face and suffer the hit. But this time, something inside me howled with rage and yearned to fight back. I extended my hands forward to electrocute my father. As I was about to unleash the energy pent up in my fingers, I realized I was responding just like my father would if he were in my position, and I was filled with self-hatred. More than every other feeling vying for control of my heart in that second, I was overcome with fear of becoming my father.

So, I could not attack him that day.

With no time to stop the lightning, I torqued my body and released the bolts into the sky. At the same time, my father's boot met my jaw and sent me sprawling into the mud.

My father laughed. "You pathetic creature! How the *hell* did you miss me at such close range? Oh yes, I remember. You're weak! You're a coward! You hate me from the depths of your heart, but you're too soft and stupid to do anything about it! You will never amount to anything! Never!"

I hauled myself out of the mud and, still crouching, turned to face my father as he came toward me. I was frightened for my life. If a noble soldier like Vladimir was worth nothing to him, then I thought I must be worth ten times less than nothing.

My father pointed at me with his index and middle fingers extended, and said, "I have lost all faith in you. There is no amount of training that can make you any sort of man, any sort of king, or any son of mine. I'm going to deal with you now the way I should've dealt with you long ago, when you killed Elena." His amber eyes burned with vengeful loathing. "From this moment on, King Ruslan of Izendor no longer has a son."

I saw a bright flash and felt searing pain, but only for an instant. The sounds of the storm and battle ceased. I was aware of nothing but darkness.

22
Guinevere's Prophecy
Autumn, 1414 AIE

~Scourge~

WHEN I OPENED my eyes, I was lying on a bed in a stone room. I was too dazed and confused to wonder how I got there. I didn't know if I was dead or alive, asleep or awake. My soul was paralyzed and my heart in great pain because of what I did to Vladimir. I had no motivation to get up, so I stayed with my gaze fixed on the ceiling.

A voice said, "Ah, you're awake. I was beginning to think you were gone for good."

I snapped my head around to see a person standing at the foot of the bed. He was a tall, bald man with a white and blue robe, looking at me with utmost concern. It was Jaedis, but I didn't know it at the time.

"What happened?" I asked.

"Your father tried to kill you. He sent a lightning bolt through your chest."

I looked at my chest to see that not only was I not wounded, but I was wearing a clean set of clothes. "D-did I die?"

"Of course not. I couldn't allow someone with your potential to be discarded so carelessly. When your father left you for dead, I brought you to a safe place. I cleaned you up and healed your wounds. You've been unconscious for two days since."

"Wow," I said, sitting up to stretch my arms. I studied the

room for the first time and saw that it was decorated like a small bedroom. There was a single window, but the view was blocked by thick purple drapes. I wondered what I'd see if I pulled them back to look outside.

"Are you hungry?" Jaedis asked. "Thirsty, perhaps?"

"Oh, very thirsty," I replied. I didn't realize until then how dry my throat was.

Jaedis held out his hand, and a chalice on a nightstand flew on its own into his grasp. Then he waved his other hand in a circle, pulling water out of thin air, and filled it. Then he handed it to me.

At first, I was too thirsty to ask questions about his use of magic. I took the chalice and drank with ravenous gulps until it was gone. I asked for more, and he repeated the same trick to fill it again. After emptying it a second time, I asked, "Where'd you learn to do that?"

"My mother taught me long ago. Simple trick, really."

"Can you make food, too?" I asked. The mere thought of the possibility caused my stomach to growl.

"I thought you'd never ask." He pointed one finger at an empty platter on the nightstand where the chalice had been. A small, comet-like wisp of magic soared from his finger to the platter. It hit with a burst of sparkles, and an assortment of fruit, crackers, and cheese came into being. The food-laden platter flew through the air into Jaedis' hand, and he passed it along to me.

I began stuffing my face immediately. It was delicious!

When I had almost finished eating, Jaedis asked, "Tell me, what do you think about your father?"

I replied with my mouth half-full. "I try not to think about him at all."

"He is a bit rash, isn't he? I don't quite care for him either."

I continued to eat without a word, but soon he followed up with another question. "What if I told you there was a man who knew how to remove your father and bring peace and stability to Izendor? Would you believe me?"

"Nope," I replied, licking fruit juice from my fingers. "My father's invincible. I don't think anyone can stand up to him and live to tell about it. Not even a sorcerer."

"Is that so?"

"Yeah," I set the empty platter down beside me. Then I remembered my conversations with Vladimir about Marindel and the Great King, and without a second thought I added, "Someone from Marindel might be able to beat him. One of the Galyyrim, or the Great—"

Chapter 22: Guinevere's Prophecy

"Silence!" Jaedis yelled, suddenly glowering down at me.

I flinched, caught off guard by his abrupt change in temper.

He quickly realized his blunder and pulled away, composing himself and clearing his throat. "Excuse me, sorry about that. Anyway, whether you believe it or not, I speak the truth."

I raised my eyebrow. "You know someone who can defeat my father?"

"Yes. He is none other than the ruler of Meiro himself: Jaedis, the Sorcerer of the Northern Bluffs."

"Jaedis and my father have been fighting since before I was born," I said with a shudder, remembering the horrific battle I had just been a part of. "If he knew how to defeat my father, he would have done it already."

"Unless, of course," he said with a twinkle in his eye, "Jaedis is much more patient than your father, and is waiting for the right moment to strike."

I tilted my head. "What do you mean?"

"Allow me to explain," Jaedis said, beginning to walk slowly around the room. "To you and to everyone in Izendor, it appears as though Jaedis and your father are at war with each other. That ruse is Ruslan's pride and joy. He uses the borderland raids as a training ground for his soldiers; an arena to weed out the weak and harden the strong. Why, you ask? Because Ruslan, in all his twisted ambition, seeks to take the mainland for himself. He longs to pour his men into every neighboring kingdom and plunder them of their riches until there is nothing left."

"Izendor doesn't have enough men for that. My father kills far too many people to be preparing for an invasion."

"Do you remember the tunnels you used to get to the borderlands? You didn't know about them until few days ago, did you? There are hundreds of tunnels deep beneath the mountains of Izendor, and within them are underground barracks where Ruslan keeps soldiers hidden and waiting for his command. Many of the 'disappearances' you've heard of over the years were not the fault of an invading monster, but of Ruslan himself, who even now is assembling his best soldiers in these locations."

"Are you sure?" I asked. At that time, I didn't believe him at all. "It's an interesting idea, but my father isn't smart enough to *really* plan something like that."

"You're right. He isn't," Jaedis stopped pacing and turned to face me. "I gave him the idea myself."

"What do you mean? Who are you, anyway?"

He smirked. "I am Jaedis, the Sorcerer of the Northern Bluffs."

I quickly made all of the connections: his use of magic to give me food and drink, his abundant knowledge about my father, and the strange fact that he seemed to know who I was. I gasped with horror.

"Oh, come now," Jaedis said with an eye-roll. "If I wanted you dead, I wouldn't have rescued you in the first place. You're safe here with me."

"B-but why?" I asked. "It doesn't make sense. You claim to be the one who can defeat my father, but you're secretly helping him prepare for war against the mainland kingdoms!"

"Absolutely not. You and I have one thing in common, young Scourge: we hate King Ruslan very much. Because of the alliance I forged with your great-grandfather Alexei, I have considerable influence over everything that happens in Izendor. Your father listens to me because I know how to speak to his insanity. I have given him an idea that will bring him to his own destruction. He believes I'm on his side, a supporter of his best interests, but he's fatally mistaken."

"I still don't understand. Do you expect him to die in battle? That won't happen. He'll sooner stand on the sidelines and cheer while every other Izendoran dies first."

"No. I will kill him before any invasion takes place."

"How?"

"Now we're getting somewhere," he smiled. "In my interactions with the kings of Izendor, I've learned much about the electrokinetic powers you all carry. With that knowledge, I have created a beast that can overpower any electrokinetic, no matter how skilled they are. I'm sure you've heard about the magic-resistant pelt of a Felid Abysso, the deadly venom of a Sunophsian wasp, the self-igniting capability of a Tethysian fireworm, the endless endurance of a Pythorian stallion, and the bloodthirsty instincts of an Ibadanian werewolf. These superior qualities have been combined into one creature, perfectly engineered with a sprinkle of sorcery, to be the end of King Ruslan and the beginning of a new Izendor!"

"So, you made a magic-proof, venomous monster that can set itself on fire, run forever, and loves to kill?"

Jaedis' eyes twinkled. "Yes. As Ruslan stands on the edge of the battlefield, gloating and reveling as he loves to do, the Nox Abyssae will emerge from the fray and tackle him head-on. Just one bite, and he'll be a dead man. His trust in me will be the end of him."

"All right...then what?"

"Izendor will be yours, of course," Jaedis finished with a grin.

I met his grin with a frown. "But, I don't want to rule Izendor. I'm not good enough to do something like that. Besides, I'm only ten years old."

"Not a problem. I will teach you everything you need to know."

"That's what my father said before he started taking me to the dungeon every other night to torture and kill people for fun."

"Rubbish! I would *never* force you to do something like that."

"You turned Dantoneia into a wasteland," I said. "An entire kingdom of innocent people and creatures died because of you."

"You speak of matters you can never hope to understand."

I keep going. "Look, I believe you when you say you hate my father and want him dead, but I've heard enough about you to know that you're just as cruel as he is. After you kill my father, what's to stop you from taking Izendor for yourself? You tried to overthrow King Dmitri all those years ago!"

Jaedis chuckled and stepped toward me. "You're a smart boy, very unlike your father, so listen closely. I rescued you because you have potential. Why should you take your father's side? He has never found any reason to value you, but I find *great* value in you. Stand with me, and I will share the riches of Izendor with you. I will give you the recognition you deserve. Say the word, and anything you want in the whole realm will be yours. I will take you in as my own son, and I will care for you and protect you for as long as you live. You will never be abused by your father, or anyone else, ever again."

At first, I hung onto every one of Jaedis' words. He appealed perfectly to all the needs and desires I had deep in my soul. When he said, "I find great value in you," my heart leapt. That was exactly what Guinevere told me to remember. Though it was hard for me to think of myself as having value, I relished the fact that another living person confirmed it for me. His promise to be the protector and provider that my father never was sounded too good to be true.

After giving me a moment to think, Jaedis leaned in to stroke my hair with his ring-laden right hand. "What do you say?"

I opened my mouth to say 'yes,' when suddenly, I saw Guinevere at the far side of the room, behind Jaedis. Her expression was sorrowful, and she disappeared as soon as I realized it. Somehow, in that moment, I knew I had to reject Jaedis' offer. Guinevere had said she was assigned by the Great King to protect me. The sorcerer's promise to be my protector and provider contradicted that statement. *"If I accept his offer, I might lose the Great King's protection. Then, I'll always hit the ground after falling, and always faint from exhaustion after hours of running, and I'll never smell Guinevere's jasmine-flower scent ever again."*

"Well," I began, "I'm grateful that you saved me, and that you see value in me, and that you've offered to give me so much. But I already have a protector and provider, and...well, his name is the Great King of Marindel." As I continued to speak, ideas formed in my mind one after another, and my confidence increased. "I don't know much about him, but he's protected me many times so far and I look forward to learning more about him. Now, if you don't mind, I'd like to go to Armavir where I can be a safe distance away from Izendor and learn about everything my guardian Guinevere has told me. I promise I won't tell anyone what you've said, not even your plans to kill my father. I don't want any part in a conflict between you and him. So please, could you show me the way out?"

Jaedis listened patiently until I mentioned the Great King. From then on, his gaze darkened, even as my confidence increased. By the time I finished, he wouldn't look me in the eyes anymore. He was fidgeting and glancing around, as if seeking to escape. At my request, he pointed with a trembling hand at the door and said, "Go down the stairs two levels, take the left passage, go down three more levels, turn right, and you'll be in the courtyard. A horse will be there waiting, and my guards will open the portcullis for you to make your exit. No monsters roaming my kingdom will attack you as you go."

"Thanks." I hopped off the bed and followed Jaedis' directions. I felt strangely bold, as if I had a protective covering over my heart. Tarento described something similar when he told us about his stand during the statue ceremony.

It didn't occur to me that I had been in a castle until I emerged into the spacious cobblestone courtyard. I think it was Jaedis' castle on the Northern Bluffs, but I didn't stick around long enough to be sure.

In my earlier childhood, the nurses had taken me horseback riding a few times, so I had no trouble hoisting myself into the saddle of the dusty-brown mare and galloping off toward the giant iron portcullis that guarded the exit. It was my first time riding a horse on my own, but I didn't have time to stop and think about that.

Two enormous rock trolls stood on either side of the portcullis. When they saw me, they turned and began pulling on thick chains, causing the portcullis to rise.

I exited the castle and crossed a perilous stone bridge over a deep chasm, at the bottom of which dark blue ocean waves swirled and foamed.

After clearing the bridge, I rode straight ahead. I passed through most of the Meiro wasteland without any trouble. It was like a strange dream. I never saw a single monster, nor did I come across any terrain my horse couldn't pass through.

But it was all too good to last forever.

Eventually, as I was just getting comfortable, the boldness in my heart subsided. I took in my surroundings: flat, dusty, and barren, dotted with a few dead trees and piles of rocks and bones. I could tell it was daylight, but the sky was ashy-gray with clouds and the air was stale. For the first time, I realized I was in the middle of Meiro with no idea where I was going. After all the stories I'd heard about people venturing into Meiro and never returning, I began to fear for my life.

"*Take heart*," The Great King said. I had never heard his voice before then, but somehow, I knew it was him. "*Because you've chosen me in your moment of decision, I have enabled you to escape from the kingdom of Jaedis. However, soon after your departure, his heart was hardened, and he has decided to kill you. Do not be afraid. I will confirm for you with great power that I am your protector and your provider.*"

I didn't know what to think of the Great King's message then, but a few minutes later, I heard ominous howling far behind me. I looked and saw four black creatures pursuing me from a distance. They were closing in fast.

"H'ya!" I spurred my horse to run faster, but it was no use. The creatures continued to gain, and it would only be a matter of time before they overtook me.

I turned aside into a wooded area, hoping to loose them. I sped past hundreds of tall dead trees, with their ghastly black branches stretching across the ashen sky. I never would've ventured into a forest like that on a whim, but I couldn't afford to stay in the open.

Still, the creatures' howls echoed from every direction, as loud as if they were right beside me. I looked around, but I couldn't see them. Despite the Great King's earlier encouragement, I was terrified and urged my horse to run even faster.

A green light appeared in my peripheral vision. I looked and saw a creature running parallel with my horse. The frill of tendrils around its neck, streaming backward as it ran, glowed in the dark. For a second, it was mesmerizing.

My horse buckled and squealed. Clinging to the reins for dear life, I realized another creature had attacked my horse from behind, leaving a gash on its right flank.

The horse skidded to a stop, nearly bucking me off, as another creature jumped in front of us with a vicious hiss.

"Ah! Get away!" I shouted, pointing one hand at the creature to strike it with a branched lightning bolt.

The creature, unfazed by the hit, grinned and chuckled. Its entire body lit up with green flames as it flared its tendrils and yowled.

And that's when I realized I was face-to-face with the Nox Abyssae, the monsters Jaedis specially designed to kill electros.

At first, I nearly fainted with fear. But like all those times before as I ran through the tunnels, I felt strength enter my heart from within, accompanied by the faint aroma of jasmine. I breathed a sigh of relief and thanked Guinevere, but I had little time to revel in my newfound energy boost.

Another creature came from the side, sprinting toward us with jaws wide open. Thinking quickly, I dove off the horse's back seconds before the creature tackled my horse and brought it down. Its squeals of pain were abruptly silenced as all four Nox Abyssae piled on and began ravenously devouring it.

I'd landed with a shoulder roll and took off running. The woods became thicker and darker as I sought to lose myself among the blackened trees. Soon, I heard the creatures howling again as they resumed the pursuit.

I ran as fast as I could. I knew I could neither outrun nor fight them, so I looked desperately for anything I could use to give myself an advantage.

The eerie, green glow on the trees in front of me was the first indication that the Nox Abyssae were upon me. I turned to see one of them, fully ablaze, pounce at me from a low-hanging branch. I gasped and rolled to the side, barely avoiding its attack, and kept running for a few seconds before another creature charged from the side to cut me off. In that instant, I had a brief flashback of my father when he jumped from the balcony and emitted jets of fire from his feet to soften his landing.

Figuring it was do or die, I jumped to avoid the creature's powerful swipe and reached for a branch that was much too high. I focused all my energy into my feet and willed for something to happen.

Just when I thought I was going to fall into the clutches of

Chapter 22: Guinevere's Prophecy

the Nox Abyssae, a chaotic burst of fire came out of my feet and launched me upward, and I nearly hit my head on the branch. I grabbed it and held on tight, rendered breathless by the fact that I just flew.

The Nox Abyssae were neither amused nor discouraged. Two of them lit themselves on fire and started climbing after me, while the other two prowled around the base of the tree. The flames encircling the first two caused the tree to catch fire. The dead branches were so dry that the green inferno scrambled up the tree just as quickly as the Nox Abyssae.

I frantically climbed higher. My amateur fire-boost had launched me fifteen feet up for a head start, but the Nox Abyssae were much faster climbers, and the fire was catching up too. I coughed in the smoke and felt the searing heat as the flames spread and grew. I tried to use my abilities to put out the fire or divert it, but the flames were unaffected. The Nox Abyssae's green fire is just as electro-resistant as they are.

When I was three-fourths of the way up the tree, I knew I had to do something about my pursuers, or they'd catch up within seconds. Thinking fast, I produced a fireball and condensed it into a small blade, which I used to chisel through a branch above me about as thick as my arm. I tore it free just as the first creature dug its claws into the branch I was standing on. With a shout, I plunged the blunt end of the branch into its face. The creature yelped and lost its grip, falling a dozen feet before catching itself on a lower bough.

The second creature was right behind it. I tried the same thing, but this one reached up to catch my makeshift weapon, and pulled on it to make me fall. I let go of the branch before I lost my balance. After letting it go, the monster clambered up and snapped its jaws at my ankles. I jumped to grab a limb above me and swung my feet to kick the monster in the side of the head. It kept its balance and responded with an irritated hiss.

I hauled myself up and created a fire-blade again, chiseling into the branch I was standing on until I could feel it bending beneath my weight. I jumped onto the next branch just in time to avoid the Nox Abyssae.

As my pursuer pulled itself up and hunkered down in preparation to leap after me, the branch gave way and sent the creature hurtling down.

I breathed a sigh of relief, but my victory was short-lived. The green inferno had caught up to me, and I knew I couldn't just bash it down. I climbed higher, with flames licking at my feet. My eyes and throat burned in the thick smoke.

I was near the top of the tree, and running out of options. The branches could hardly support my weight anymore. The two Nox Abyssae were gaining on me again, and I knew they wouldn't be deterred by the same old tricks.

There was only one thing I could think to do.

I climbed as far up as I dared, just high enough to see the darkening Meiro sky above the lifeless canopy of branches, and I yelled for help.

"Great King! Guinevere! Help me!"

I shouted again and again, frequently interrupted by coughing fits.

The branch I was standing on caught fire.

As if things couldn't get any worse, I noticed a flying creature coming toward me from far away. It was enormous; radiant and beautiful, yet terrifying. I knew immediately it was a dragon, and I knew immediately I was as good as dead. Fire below and fire above, dangerous creature below and dangerous creature above. There was no escape.

I felt searing heat around my legs as my tunic caught fire. I screamed, beginning to cry, and clambered higher. As I hauled myself onto the next branch, it snapped, and I fell. Everything around me spun into a blur, and I thought for sure I was about to die.

My miserable life flashed before my eyes. All the running away, the hiding, the beating and scolding, the "Never become like your father" and "Never play with your powers," the torturing and killing in the dungeon, the weeping and despair, the horrors of the borderland raid, my brief friendship with Vladimir that ended when I struck him down, my father's disowning and attempting to kill me, and Jaedis' devious attempt to woo me to his side. Then I thought, *"I'm going to die here in Meiro with no one to see or care, and I'll be forgotten forever. It'll be as if I never existed at all."* Utterly defeated, I closed my eyes and waited for it all to end.

I landed softly in someone's arms.

I was irritated at first and blurted, "Guinevere, why won't you let me die already!?" But when I opened my eyes to see her, my jaw dropped almost completely to the ground.

The dragon caught me.

It was long and serpentine, glowing white like snow when it reflects the sun. Its limbs were small relative to the length of its body, it had a white-feathered tail fluke that expertly guided its flight, and majestic feathered wings on its back that made no sound as they stirred the air.

I was held in the dragon's forepaw, as soft as a rabbit skin. The fire on my clothes had been smothered. And wouldn't you know it, the whole beast smelled like jasmine.

"Dear friend, I won't let you die because you are valuable to the Great King and to me." As Guinevere spoke, the dragon tucked its head under to look at me upside down. Its dove-like eyes carried the same merry charm that Guinevere's had when we first met.

"Guinevere! Are you really a dragon!?"

"No, I am elven. But I can turn into a dragon whenever it pleases the Great King."

"That's...*incredibly* wizard!"

"You haven't seen anything yet!" Guinevere reared her head, purring like thunder, and turned sharply. She held me close to her velvety chest as she descended toward a clearing near the bristly black woods, where a column of smoke marked the place from which I'd been rescued.

"Why'd we turn around? Let's get out of here," I said as Guinevere alighted on the dusty ground.

"The Great King is not finished yet," she replied, setting me down. *"He wants both you and Jaedis to see how much he is, indeed, your protector."*

The dark shapes of the Nox Abyssae emerged from the woods on the far side of the clearing. They spread out, prowling low, with their gleaming eyes fixed on Guinevere. I wondered how much Nox Abyssae venom it would take to kill a Marindelian elf-dragon.

"Guinevere, can you die?"

She snorted as if to laugh. *"That is a topic for another time. Today, let us declare life!"*

Guinevere craned her neck up until it was fully straight, fanned out her feathery wings, and flared her tail fluke. It looked like she was about to roar, so I covered my ears because I thought it'd be loud and terrifying, as dragon roars ought to be. But the sound that came out was anything but that. It was the song of many women singing in chorus, and it was more beautiful than any music I've ever heard.

My heart quickened and my spirit soared.

The Nox Abyssae screeched, their tendrils flailing about like worms, and they bolted off in separate directions.

A beam of sunlight pierced through the clouds and illuminated the center of the clearing. In the center of the sunbeam, a seedling poked out of the dusty ground. It sprouted two leaves as it grew taller, and then a few more, and then some branches. It twirled and swayed to the melody of Guinevere's song. Its trunk solidified into hard wood and continued to thicken. The canopy became laden with vibrant green leaves as it stretched toward the sky. Soon it was larger than any of the dead trees nearby. When its growth slowed, the tree heaved as though taking a breath, and a flurry of pink cherry blossoms opened among the leaves, showering petals all along the ground at the base of its trunk.

When Guinevere finished, the tree was still.

I looked from Guinevere to the tree and back again. "What in the land of Izendor did you just do? That was wonderful!"

"This tree is a sign for all who behold it," Guinevere began, purring softly. *"It is a symbol of the deliverance that will come to all of Meiro in years to come. Just like my song broke through the curse to allow this tree to grow and flourish, so shall the song of many sons and daughters of the King liberate this land and make it even more beautiful than it was in the days of Dantoneia. You, dear friend, will live to see this day, for it is coming soon. The Princess of the Sea will lead the way."*

Guinevere looked to the side of the clearing, where for the first time I noticed Jaedis was standing. I could tell by the mixed fear and loathing in his expression that he heard everything Guinevere said. She now addressed him, though I could hear it as well. *"For you, Jaedis, this tree is also a sign. Though you will seek to destroy it with all your might, not a single leaf or petal will fall from its branches. The Great King will protect it just as he protects his own children. You will not see the day of Meiro's deliverance, for your doom will precede it. The Princess of the Sea will lead the way."*

Jaedis glared back at Guinevere, seething with hatred. As he replied, I heard a second, much more hateful, voice join with his. "The Great King has no power here. This is *my* land. *MY* kingdom! You and your kind have no authority here, the power of the orphan girl is mine alone, and I will continue to control her as I always have. She is mine. Get out of here, and watch from a distance as your words fall like stones to the bottom of the sea!"

Guinevere didn't flinch. *"Your lies are as obsolete as your claim to this realm. You know the Great Prince Eli rescued the Princess of—"*

Jaedis screamed more terribly than a banshee. "She does not

acknowledge it! As long as she believes she is mine, she is still mine!"

"You cannot hide the truth forever, just as darkness cannot hide the light. Deep down, even you know that."

"Wait and see! I will—"

Guinevere roared. And this time, it was a real, terrifying dragon roar.

Jaedis became himself again at the sound of the roar. He screamed and disappeared in a haphazard spurt of water and steam.

I hurriedly covered my ears to prevent myself from exploding like Jaedis did.

Guinevere purred and nudged me with her snout. *"Now we can leave."*

I uncovered my ears and asked, "What was that all about?"

"You will learn soon enough," she replied, lowering one wing for me to climb. As I got onto her back, she continued, *"For now, simply keep my words in your heart, and never let the darkness hide the light."*

"But you said darkness can't hide light," I said, settling between two of Guinevere's neck spines.

"That is true, but it will try. It may even appear for a time that the darkness has won. But take heart; just as you see that tree there, flourishing in the cursed land of Meiro, know that the Great King has every intention of turning all *darkness into light."*

With that finishing remark, Guinevere took to the sky. She soared higher and higher, circling the beam of light cast upon the tree, until she escaped the stifling atmosphere of Meiro through the hole in the clouds. I relished the fresh air, my lungs rejoicing to be out of that nightmarish place. I decided I never wanted to go there again, for any reason, at all, ever...*except* to see the fulfillment of Guinevere's prophecy. That would be wizard.

As Guinevere took me farther and farther from the terrors of Meiro, I snuggled between her neck spines in the comfort of her velvety fur and was lulled to sleep by the pleasing aroma of jasmine on the wind.

23
Pressing On
Autumn, 1414 - Autumn, 1418 AIE

~Scourge~

ALL OF THAT happened about five years ago. The rest of my life wasn't nearly as eventful until I crossed paths with Tarento. Guinevere brought me to northern Armavir, where she said I ought to travel on my own from then on. She said it was time for me to get to know the Great King directly, without reliance on her. I was upset because I had grown so fond of her, but sometimes I'll catch a faint whiff of jasmine as a reminder that she's still watching over me.

Since my escape from Meiro, I've been plagued with nightmares of Jaedis and his monsters, the borderland raid, and the horrors I've experienced at the hands of my father. It's been very stressful for me to be reminded of the past, so I've avoided anything that can trigger those memories—including even the Great King. Just like Vladimir described, I knew in my heart that the Great King wanted me to do something, but I was too afraid to wonder about it. All I wanted to do was forget and move on.

After parting ways with Guinevere, I went to live at an orphanage in Château Pierre, the second-largest city in Armavir, after Cloud Summit. I was there for three years, until one of the older kids caught me playing with my abilities and threatened to tell the adults. He had a reputation for tattling, so I decided not to risk my own safety and ran away that night.

After leaving Château Pierre, I wandered from village to village until it was nearly winter. To avoid traveling in the cold, I joined a smaller orphanage in a town called Stonehaven. I came to enjoy the simplicity and slower pace of small-town life, so I stayed for almost a year and a half. But when I turned fourteen, the adults took me aside and suggested I leave the orphanage to make room for younger kids. They said I could join an adolescent orphanage in Cloud Summit and begin learning a trade. I took their advice and went to Cloud Summit.

It didn't take long to discover the pros and cons of being an Izendoran refugee in the enormous Armaviran capital city. On the bright side, I didn't have to join an orphanage. I was invited to live with a poor elderly couple who were also Izendoran refugees, and they treated me well. On the other hand, I was often picked on by well-off Armavirans and refugees from other kingdoms. Instead of taking up a trade, I got involved with gangs made up of people my age. I saw, and even took part in, skirmishes with law enforcement, though I was very careful not to use my abilities in those situations.

Within a few moons, when autumn was in full swing, I accepted that Cloud Summit wasn't a safe place for me to live. I decided to leave before winter made traveling difficult, so I moved to Finch in the southern foothills. It was only a few days later when Tarento showed up.

I found him interesting because he was mysterious, and I had never met a Felid before. Once he started talking about the Great King, I knew I had to stay with him even if it meant going back to Cloud Summit. Despite the harsh winter and the challenges we faced, I enjoyed living with Tarento and helping the poor district become a better place. I finally began to realize what the Great King is really like.

I believe that's all I have to share. You heard the rest of the story from Tarento, and there's nothing notable from my perspective to add.

Well, there is one thing.

Ever since Connor told us about his encounter with Jaedis and the Nox Abyssae, I haven't been myself. For five years I've tried to forget about my past and live a normal, independent life, but now that I'm on this quest, I can't ignore my past or my weaknesses any longer. I've often thought about leaving the group and running away, but my desire to be a part of what the Great King is doing always gets the best of me. You've all been so kind. You remind me that I *am* valuable, as Guinevere has so often told me, and you prove it by your actions. You remind me that darkness indeed cannot hide the light. I'm a mess and I'm a coward, but I hope one day I'll be as valiant as every one of you. I hope I'll bring a meaningful contribution to our quest to find Melody and defeat Jaedis.

Summer, 1419 AIE

~Connor~

THE SILENCE AFTER Scourge finishes is deafening. His story had us, hook, line, and sinker, from the very beginning.

"I had no idea," Tarento speaks first. "It's hard to believe you've gone through so much at such a young age. No wonder it's had such a damaging effect on you."

"Yeah," Scourge sighs. "Like I said, I'm a mess and a coward, but—"

"But," Jake interjects, eyes twinkling. "I'm so glad you're here with us on this journey, and I apologize for every way we might have taken you for granted."

"Seriously," Yoko agrees, her eyes wide with intrigue. "Now we know why you got so quiet whenever we begged you to talk about your past or your abilities."

"It's still not easy to talk about, that's for sure."

"But we will understand you so much better now," Tarento says, placing a hand on his shoulder. "I'm proud of you, my friend."

Scourge looks back at Tarento and smiles. "Thanks."

"Scourge," Khai speaks up, "One thing about your story is most disquieting to me. If Jaedis created the Nox Abyssae five years ago with the intent to kill your father, why hasn't it happened yet?"

Yoko suggests, "Maybe it *did* happen, but Izendor's trying to hide it, like they hid the true story of Meiro."

"No," Khai shakes his head. "News of Ruslan's death would spread like a wildfire among the kingdoms. There's no way something like that could be hidden for long."

"Hold on, it makes perfect sense," I say, allowing my Seer's gift to piece everything together. "Think about it: Guinevere prophesied the end of Jaedis' rule and the deliverance of Meiro, ending with the phrase, 'The Princess of the Sea will lead the way.' She even caused a curse-defying, indestructible tree to grow in the middle of his territory to prove her words! Jaedis must have realized Melody is more of a threat to him than Ruslan, so he set his sights on her instead. It probably took him a while to find her, but once he did, he sent the Nox Abyssae to kill her. Without Melody, Guinevere's prophecy won't come to pass."

"And the Music of Marindel," Jake adds. "Guinevere said the song of many sons and daughters of the King will liberate the land. Tarento, didn't Prince Eli say that the Music of Marindel has been entrusted to the sons and daughters of the King? I don't know how Jaedis learned about the Music of Marindel, but I bet he knows it ought to be eliminated if he's to keep Meiro for himself."

"That is very possible," Tarento agrees.

"He knew he needed an electro to get in the dungeon seal," Khai says.

"So, he waited for Scourge and the rest of us to do the hard work for him," Jake adds.

"And was ready to snatch it from us once we had," Scourge finishes.

"Well," I grin and clap my hands together, "that didn't quite work out for him, did it? He'll have to try *much* harder to steal from us next time!"

"You bet he will!" Yoko chuckles.

"It's no laughing matter," Tarento says, voice raised in announcement. "As long as we have the chest with us, we're all targets for Jaedis' monsters. No doubt he's quickly learning what we're capable of, so next time he'll try something to exploit our weaknesses. We must stay the course, remain vigilant, and be ready to deal with any obstacle he sends our way. Most importantly, we must listen to the Great King and heed his every word."

I listen to Tarento with awe. He's such a great leader. I remember what Jed told me about one day being a leader of armies, but it seems like Tarento would be a better option for that. He's so introverted that he probably hates leading, but he's *so* good at it!

I'm so busy comparing myself to Tarento, I almost miss what he says next.

"And don't forget, we have a Seer in our midst. When Connor gives us a bit of obscure information about the future or our surroundings, we ought to take it seriously and act accordingly. Let us honor each other as we use our individual talents for the benefit of all. Together, we will be a force to be reckoned with."

"Woo!" Yoko cheers.

"Let's do this!" I shout, throwing in my two-kappes-worth of leadership potential.

"We must press on to Cloud Summit with no more interruptions," Tarento continues. "Jaedis likely won't send monsters to attack the city, so we'll be safe from him once we reach it. Still, we must proceed with caution. Connor, you said something in Bayside Harbor about finding an Offspring of Sisera to join the quest. I now advise against that. It would be too risky and take too much time. We need to find Jed, get money for the homestead, buy our equipment, and leave as soon as possible. Then we'll be headed straight for Meiro."

I'm discouraged by Tarento's advice to forego the Offspring of Sisera, but he does have a point. Alpha Blue said they're all a bunch of dangerous criminals. Even with the Blue Fox gang insignia he gave me, wooing an Offspring of Sisera to leave their life of crime and join a quest centered on bringing justice to a sorcerer will require extensive negotiation. I agree we shouldn't waste our time in Cloud Summit arguing and fighting, so I'd say Tarento wins.

"Sounds good to me," I say, and the others voice their agreement as well.

After our discussion, we spend time pondering everything we've learned. By now, it's late afternoon, and the sun will be setting in about an hour. We rejoined the main road while discussing Scourge's story, so now we're no longer traveling single-file on the narrow road through the valley.

I pull the map out of my bag and open it to see where we are. It looks like we'll easily reach a city called Pomegranate by sundown. I hope we find a place to stay with a bed; my aching muscles could use a bit of pampering after all they've been through these past few days.

"Hey guys," Yoko interrupts my thoughts. "Remember when Guinevere told Jaedis that Prince Eli rescued Melody? What do you think that means?"

What a great question.

I remember when Eli told the Great King he wanted to help Melody reclaim her authority from the Serpent, and the Great King agreed to send him to find her at the proper time. But I haven't heard, or even thought about, whether that's happened yet.

Wait a cotton-pickin' second. When Eli appeared to me while I was unconscious, one of the things he asked me to do was tell Melody, "I'm coming back soon. I will come for her when she calls for me." He's coming *BACK* soon! That implies he already came, which Guinevere must have been referring to. But how? When? What happened? Why is Melody still hard-headed and bitter?

"No idea," Scourge replies to Yoko. "Honestly, I still don't understand most of anything Guinevere's ever said."

Chapter 23: Pressing On

"I've been troubled by this for a while," Tarento says. "There's a gaping hole in the middle of everything we know about Marindel. Jake and I have discussed it a few times. Your concern, Yoko, puts the spotlight of ambiguity on Prince Eli, who we know very little about, aside from his role in *The Princess of the Sea.*"

I speak next, "I think Guinevere meant exactly what she said. Prince Eli already rescued Melody from the Serpent. I don't know how, or when, or what it has to do with anything, but Eli did tell me he's coming *back*, not for the first time."

"Very interesting," Tarento replies.

Suddenly, a thought occurs to me. Yoko and Khai haven't shared their stories yet. Are they withholding any relevant information from us? I have to ask. "Yoko, Khai, I know you haven't shared your stories with us yet and I don't want you to spoil them, but can you say whether or not you've had a significant encounter with Eli?"

"I haven't," Yoko shakes her head.

"Nor have I," Khai says.

"Great," I say with a shrug. "We're stuck with a plot-hole."

"Not to worry," Tarento says. "I have a feeling we'll find the answer to this riddle very soon. In the meantime, let's trust the Great King and press on. He knows what he's doing, whether we understand it or not."

Good ol' Tarento, always seeing the positive side of things. "All right, I'll take your word for it."

"Guys, look!" Yoko points forward, where the gates of a town are visible just over a mile down the road.

"Pomegranate ho!" I declare, pointing like Yoko.

"Dinner!" Scourge declares, also pointing.

"Dinner!" All of us cheer, spurring our horses to quicken our arrival at the next town.

Our stay in Pomegranate is all we could have imagined and more. As soon as we enter the gates, we're met by a well-dressed man who asks if we need a place to stay for the night. He says he's got a few rooms available at his luxurious inn and stable space for the horses, provided we do him a favor: he needs someone to cook dinner for the folks at the inn, because most of the chefs are sick with fever and can't fulfill their duties. We all look knowingly at Khai.

"You've asked the right man," he says with a modest grin.

After we put our horses in the stable, we're led to the kitchen, where Khai teaches us how to cook honey-roasted duck and vegetable borscht, the ingredients for which are provided by the kitchen staff. We crank out pots and pans of the stuff to feed every hungry traveler staying at the inn that night, including ourselves.

After dinner, we're told we've earned a free overnight stay at the inn! We split up two to a room: Jake and I, Scourge and Tarento, and Khai and Yoko. And the best part of it is, we each get our own glorious bed with goose-feather-stuffed pillows and linen sheets!

I fall asleep as soon as my head hits the pillow, and I have the best sleep I've had in years. I'm a little disappointed when Tarento comes knocking on my door at sunrise, telling us we have to get going. Even Jake moans and throws a pillow at the door in protest.

Nevertheless, we all head down to the stables to retrieve our horses, and then we mount and continue on our way. We make a stop at the bakery to pick up fresh baguettes for breakfast, and then we leave Pomegranate to continue our eastward journey.

Over the next few days, the terrain and climate begin to change as we approach the central Armaviran mountains. We see many kinds of pine trees interspersed among the previously-prevalent oak, birch, and maple. The ground is rockier and the undergrowth scraggly. The air becomes drier and the nights a bit cooler.

Most wonderfully of all, we encounter no trouble from Jaedis' monsters, or anything else for that matter. Surely, the Great King is providing us safe passage to Cloud Summit!

We travel quickly and simply, though we still make time for rest stops and practices with our weapons. While Jake and I spar with branches, Khai trains Yoko in archery and Tarento helps Scourge practice his abilities. Though Scourge is still reluctant, Tarento uses Samurai training techniques to challenge him within safe boundaries. It's different from what he's used to getting from Ruslan, but still, Scourge makes progress and grows in confidence.

Three days after our departure from Pomegranate, we arrive in Finch. We stay the night there and continue onward with little trouble or fanfare. That next night, our first overnight stay in the mountain wilderness takes place.

Tarento is the first to suggest we take turns keeping watch throughout the night in case we get attacked by wild animals, bandits, monsters, vengeful Samurai, or whatever else may lurk in the darkness.

I've never stayed the night in the mountains before, so I'm intimidated by the idea of sitting awake by myself in a pitch-dark forest in the middle of the night. All I can think about are the wilderness horror stories I've heard throughout my childhood: ash bears coming out of the woods to rip us apart, or rock trolls causing landslides to wipe us out, or centipedes crawling all over our faces as we sleep.

Centipedes. Yeesh.

Tarento, Scourge, and Jake, who have traveled on this road many times before, say this is the easiest night of all because it's summertime. They say it's nice not having to sleep in a tight crevice in the cliffside a foot away from a campfire to avoid freezing to death in the icy wind and snow.

I see their logic, but their encouragement hardly puts my fears to rest. Bears and centipedes are especially active during the summer. Needless to say, I hardly sleep at all that night.

The next day, we depart at dawn and ride the final stretch to Cloud Summit. As we go, anticipation builds up within me.

I remember Jake's story, with the Paladin Training Academy and his ruthless brothers who chased him out of the city, promising to kill him if he ever returned.

I remember Tarento's and Scourge's stories, with their vivid descriptions of the poor districts, the corruption in the law enforcement, the tension between various gangs and refugee groups, and the Purge headed by Chief Bennett under the influence of the Serpent.

I remember Alpha Blue and his gang's paranoia; they fled all the way to the west coast of Armavir to escape Bennett's wrath.

I remember the less-personal stories I heard when I was a child: about the establishment of the Paladin Order; the numerous fights against invading trolls, dragons, and goblins before Armavir became the first monster-free kingdom in the realm; stories from Armavir's Golden Age, when many adventurers used Cloud Summit as their home base; and last but not least, my father's story of his visit to Cloud Summit in his younger days...about the largest tavern in Armavir and the greatest beer found anywhere on the mainland.

I've heard so many stories about this grand city, and now I finally get to experience it for myself!

Soon, as the sun hangs high in the sky above us, we round the last bend and come upon a massive stone bridge spanning a wide, fog-blanketed valley. On the other end of the bridge, in the very center of the valley, is the humble hill upon which Cloud Summit, the crown jewel of Armaviran civilization, sits enthroned.

24

The Illusionist

Summer, 1419 AIE

~Celine~

LIGHTNING SPLITS THE sky, followed by a resounding thunderclap. Torrential rains stream down from the heavens.

It's the middle of the day, but the sky is so dark, it's no different to us than the middle of the night.

And that's why we're here.

No one would expect us at noonday, let alone in these conditions.

I'm hiding in an overturned barrel in a narrow alley.

Two of my brothers have gone inside the building across the street, which I can see through a small hole in the barrel. The sign on the building says, "Cloud Summit Regional Bank of Armavir." We've never robbed a bank like this before, but we *have* done far worse.

I wait.

They've been inside for a few minutes now. I hope that means they're raking in a plethora of beautiful jewels.

A person in a hooded trench coat walks by. If he turns to go in the bank, I'll make sure he doesn't make it to the door.

He keeps going, past the bank and out of sight. Just a passerby.

It's when the police show up that things get interesting.

Suddenly, the door of the bank bursts open.

A figure clothed in a dark-colored tunic, his head wrapped in a black cloth turban with a slit for his eyes, emerges from the building with a bulging potato sack slung over his shoulder. The sack is so large there could be a person or two inside, but my brother Nebioth carries it as if it were filled with hay.

My, my, that is a big load of goodies.

Abdeel, my second brother, follows closely. He backs out of the building while holding off several bank guards with skillful swordplay. No ordinary swordsman is a match for Abdeel and his scimitar.

Nebioth moves the sack off his shoulder. Looking up to the roof of the building to my left, he swings the bag underhand round and round, picking up momentum, before hurling it up on roof. The sack flies out of my line of sight, but I know it was just caught by another one of my brothers waiting there.

The sack will be passed to several more of my brothers in a similar manner before it finally arrives at the hideout. Works every time.

Now free of his burden, Nebioth retreats down the street and disappears into an alley.

Next, Abdeel flees from the guards and sprints in the opposite direction of Nebioth.

Four guards exit the bank and look around wildly. One points and shouts to pursue Nebioth, another points and shouts to pursue Abdeel, and yet another notices the sack on the roof and points, "The gold! Up there!"

Point though they might, they don't have long to think about who to pursue.

It's my time to shine.

I extend the reaches of my manas'ruh—what we Sunophsians call the psychic mind—and I establish a mental connection with each of them. Then I fill their minds with images of...hmm, what shall I do today?

Spiders?

Ogres?

Swamp terrors?

Hairless cycloptic puppies?

Ooh, I have a good one!

I hijack their imaginations and cause them to see themselves on board a small ship in the middle of a violent storm. Suddenly, an enormous sea monster comes up out of the depths, towering over their pathetic little ship, and screeches like a banshee! Then it opens its mouth wide and plunges down upon the ship, destroying it and everyone on it!

All four guards scream together and collapse on ground.

"Hmph!" I smirk. Once they're unconscious, I sever the connection and leave them be.

Now that I've bought my brothers some time to scatter, I can head back to the hideout. Since those guards were the only witnesses of the robbery, I doubt the police will find out in time to be a threat.

I stand up straight, lifting the barrel over my head and setting it down. Only now that I'm out of the barrel do I realize how stiff my legs have become from crouching for so long. Good thing it's over.

I turn around to head down the alley, but I stop dead in my tracks.

Two policemen have just rounded the corner at the other end of the alley. They're unmistakable in their black-leather, iron-plated uniforms with the blue Armaviran coat of arms displayed on their right shoulders. They, also, stop dead in their tracks when they see me.

I'm wearing a dark tunic and turban just like my brothers, so I'm sure I look mighty suspicious standing here by myself with a group of unconscious guards behind me.

"Hey, you! Stay right there!" one of the policemen says as they start running toward me.

Oh, yes, I'll stay here all right...and so will you.

I extend my manas'ruh toward them. As I'm establishing connections, something sweeps my legs out from under me. I yelp, falling onto the wet cobblestone with a thud, and I hurriedly pull my manas'ruh back together.

As I reorient myself, several hands roll me over so that I'm lying with my face to the ground. I feel a muddy boot firmly placed on my back as my arms are pulled and forced together behind me.

If I didn't know any better, I'd say I'm being arrested.

Not today, pals.

I extend my manas'ruh toward whoever is stepping on me, establish a connection with him, and cause him to see a rattlesnake coiled around his leg.

"Ah! Blimey!" the guy leaps off me.

Not allowing the others any time to detain me, I roll onto my back, twisting my arms away from my captors, and jump to my feet with a kick-up. I sprint out of the alley, barging past a policeman in my way.

My left leg buckles underneath me. A painful cramp has taken residence in my thigh, courtesy of crouching for so long under a barrel.

Wonderful.

Chapter 24: The Illusionist

I fall on the ground, and within seconds the police are surrounding me again. I try to make connections with one or several of them, but the pain in my leg and the distraction of being detained are disrupting my focus.

I've been involved in many robberies, and I've had a few brushes with the police. But now, for the first time, I have a dreadful feeling I might actually, really, be arrested.

It's well-known around here that anyone who gets arrested by Chief Bennett's police force never sees the clear blue sky ever again.

Panic wells up in my heart.

I can't let that happen to me!

I have to escape! *Now*!

Just then, out of the corner of my eye, a lightning bolt strikes a spire on a nearby building. The sheer power of its thunderclap almost drowns the startled shouts of the police.

Before the thunder dies out, acting on instinct fueled by panic, I launch to my feet in spite of the pain, pushing two of the policemen back as I go. Two others come at me from behind, one choking me and the other trying to grab my arms to handcuff me.

I notice the handcuffer's sword hilt within my reach. I snatch and draw the weapon.

The handcuffer shouts and jumps back, while the man choking me squeezes even harder.

My vision is becoming spotted.

Panic swells.

I thrust the blade into the stomach of the man choking me.

Letting go of the hilt, I grab the arms around my neck and pry them off with a shout.

As the man collapses behind me, the other policemen draw their swords.

Now that they realize I'm dangerous, I have enough time to inflict massive amounts of mental pain on them. Still driven by panic, I replicate the illusion of the sea monster I used on the bank guards, only this time I add a bonus ending: they get to spend six years slowly and painfully digesting in its dark and miserable belly.

The policemen scream, falling to the ground and writhing in pain, until they're rendered unconscious. Soon, all I can hear is the heavy rain and the distant thunder as the worst part of the afternoon storm takes its leave.

That encounter was much too close for comfort.

Standing still and breathing deeply, I look upon the policemen sprawled on the ground.

I did this.

I just inflicted six years' worth of pain in three seconds.

They're not dead, but they'll probably be traumatized for life.

Slowly, with bated breath, I turn around to see the man I stabbed.

He's lying on his back with a sword fixed upright in his belly. His eyes stare in endless shock at the dark sky above. The rain causes blood to stream out of the wound and form a cloudy red puddle around him.

He's dead.

I killed him.

I *killed* him!

I back away from the body as guilt washes over me.

I've never *killed* anyone before.

How could I do such a thing?

I'm turning out to be a heinous criminal after all, just like my brothers.

But...is that what I really want?

I trip over something. With a yelp, I fall backward and land on a body. The dead body!? I scream and roll off it before frantically jumping to my feet.

It's just one of the unconscious men, but it scares me enough that I turn my back on the scene and run as fast as I can down the alley.

I've been a notorious thief in Cloud Summit for years now, but today I've picked up a new title:

Celine the murderer.

The first rays of sunlight pierce through the dreary sky as I descend the gutter toward the hidden entrance of our hideout.

When I come to the central hub of the hideout, I'm greeted by the sounds of my brothers and other gang operatives laughing and celebrating the successful heist. They're all sitting on or around a large pile of crates filled with explosives.

"It has to be at least a million krons!" Abdeel says, waving his arms.

"No, no, more than that," Nebioth says. "I saw a few cut gemstones in there. They'll be worth a few thousand krons each."

"It's sure as hell no use counting it," another brother says, running his fingers through the loot.

Another brother cuffs him on the shoulder and says, "The treasury's getting so full, it'd take us the rest of our lives to count it all!"

Chapter 24: The Illusionist

Just then, Nebioth notices me and stands to his feet. "Ah, sister! Job well done, as usual. Another clean getaway!"

Normally I relish the praise of my brothers, but today, the guilt in my heart leaves me feeling heavy. I force a confident smile and say, "They clearly had no idea who they were dealing with."

"Haha," Nebioth chuckles in agreement. "We'll be running this city soon enough. White Sand will be unstoppable."

White Sand is the name of our gang, almost exclusively made up of Sunophsian refugees. We're the most notorious criminal group in Cloud Summit for many reasons, but the main one is because a dozen of us, myself included, have special abilities that give us an edge over all the competition. They're inherited gifts from our common father, King Sisera of Sunophsis. We're referred to as Offspring of Sisera, just a few of Sisera's many, many, many children.

"Hey Celine," Abdeel says as he picks mud off the hilt of his scimitar, "you took your time getting back. Did you grab us lunch on the way?"

"You wish," I reply, taking the sopping-wet turban off my head and letting my long, black hair down. "I stopped to dance with the police, that's all."

"The police?" Nebioth asks, raising an eyebrow and looking at the others. "I didn't see any police out there today. You guys?"

"Nope, nuh-uh, not at all," they all say.

I take a seat on a nearby crate and begin brushing my hair as I talk. "They showed up after I put the bank guards to sleep. I dealt with it, so there's no need to worry."

"Good." Nebioth folds his arms. "The police have been extra nosy lately."

"Nothing we can't handle, I'm sure," I say as I continue grooming myself.

"This isn't something to take for granted, Celine."

His stern tone causes me to pause. "Why? You're not *afraid*, are you?"

"Bah! Of course not!" He jumps down from his crate and walks closer to me. "The glory of White Sand is contained in our ability to always remain one step ahead. But if we lose that advantage for *any* reason, we'll find ourselves in a steaming pile of bear shit."

"Deadly bear shit," Abdeel says.

I roll my eyes. "We're *criminals*. It's an occupational hazard!" Despite my jest, it takes great effort to swallow the resurgent feelings of panic.

I must remain strong before my brothers.

"Nebioth, is your head screwed on right?" One of my brothers asks. "The police are no threat to us at all. They never have been, and they never will be!"

The others laugh and make similar comments.

Nebioth groans and fumbles around in his bag. He pulls out a rolled-up parchment, unfurls it, and shows it to me. "Read it."

I lean in close and read aloud, "Wanted: The Illusionist. Experienced thief believed to be affiliated with White Sand. Very dangerous. Kill on sight. Five thousand kron reward when the body is brought to the Hall of Justice and confirmed to be the culprit." At the bottom of the poster is Chief Bennett's signature. I look at Nebioth and mock a smile. "Aw, you care about me, how cute."

"It's not about *you*," Nebioth says, crumpling the wanted poster and throwing it. "It's about *us*. The police are on to you, Celine. Your strategies are becoming obsolete. If you don't change your act fast, you'll get caught. And they'll be one step closer to catching the rest of us."

I was previously hesitant to tell my brothers I was almost caught, but now I must avoid it at all costs. I shrug and reply, "Come on, brother, it can't be *that* bad. There's no picture on the poster. They have no idea what I look like."

"All it takes is one small mistake. Just one," Nebioth brings his fingers close together as if holding a pea.

"Hey Nebioth," another White Sand operative calls as he enters the room. "Who died and made you gang leader? Leave her alone!"

The newcomer is my boyfriend, Misham. He's also an Offspring of Sisera, but technically he's just a half-brother, so it all works out.

Misham comes and wraps his arms around me. "Great job today, you killed it out there!"

I move to hug him in return, but the phrase "you killed it" almost causes me to fall off the crate. I sputter, "Killed what? I didn't kill anything, nothing got killed, nope, no killing, not at all, never."

Misham lifts an eyebrow. "It's just an expression. Did Nebioth frighten you that badly?"

"Of course not," I say, removing his arms and composing myself proudly.

I hear Nebioth mutter, "Who's afraid now?"

"Shut up!" I shout at him.

The others start chuckling and making comments.

Misham looks at Nebioth and rolls his shoulders. "Hey brother, I told you to leave her alone."

Nebioth narrows his eyes. "You wanna fight, pipsqueak?"

"Any time, any day," Misham says, puffing out his chest.

"Seriously?" I groan.

"Fight! Fight! Fight!" the others chant.

This is the main drawback to being only one of two females in a gang oozing with testosterone. I'm tempted to knock them both out with an illusion, but I refrain. Instead, I'll just walk away and get changed into some dry, comfortable clothing. A bite to eat wouldn't be so bad, either.

I begin to leave, but Abdeel says something to the others that catches my attention. "You can't be so hard on her. She helped us get into Königheim, remember? It was the greatest heist in the history of White Sand!"

Several others laugh in agreement and jump in:

"Greatest heist ever!"

"They *still* don't know we did it!"

"The police went ballistic, killing everyone in sight!"

"As if people didn't hate Bennett enough already!"

"The other gangs were chased out or killed, and now White Sand reigns supreme!"

"Armavirans have been joining our ranks in droves! Bennett's the *real* villain now!"

It was my greatest moment.

We learned through some library research about a powerful ancient weapon kept within Königheim Castle. After some careful plotting, the best burglars among our ranks were sent to steal it.

I was the one who gave the guards an illusion of a Paladin ordering them to reposition themselves in a different part of the castle, allowing three of my brothers to go in and take the relic.

We were long gone by the time anyone found out about it.

Many people died that night.

Many more fled the city, never to return.

Meanwhile, we ate and drank in our underground sanctuary, celebrating the triumph of White Sand.

Never before have I felt an ounce of guilt for my role in catalyzing Cloud Summit's infamous Purge. But now, overwhelming guilt swells in my heart more than I ever imagined was possible.

What's happening to me?

What does it mean?

I hope I'm not going soft...

I shake the thoughts out of my head and leave the hub, navigating through the hideout with ease. Once in my room, I close and lock the door, quickly change into a clean outfit, and there I stay. I ponder the day's events and my strange thoughts while snacking on a stash of raisins, until eventually I fall asleep.

"YOU DESERVE TO *die.*"

I open my eyes. My vision is blurred. I'm not sure where I am.

"You deserve to die."

I feel my body rocking back and forth. No, the floor is rocking back and forth.

"You deserve to die."

I realize I'm still wet. It's raining again. How did I get outside?

"You deserve to die."

I hear the voice.

"Who's there?" I ask, blinking and sitting up.

I'm struck numb with terror when I realize where I am: a small ship in the middle of a violent storm, being tossed about by towering ocean waves. It's the illusion I used on the guards and the police earlier!

I cling to the mast of the ship for dear life as a wave barrels over the deck and nearly carries me off.

"You deserve to die!"

Oh, that stupid voice! Once I know who keeps saying that, I'm going to inflict massive amounts of mental pain on them!

"Who's there!?" I shout. "Show yourself!"

The voice merely chuckles.

The swirling water in front of the ship parts to reveal an enormous sea monster rising from the depths. The instant I see it, all the fight I had in my spirit is vaporized. It's not the same monster I used in my illusion.

Never have I ever imagined such a horrible, hideous Serpent.

It towers over my little ship, flexing its powerful body and flashing its fearsome teeth. It leers down at me with a murderous grin, and as I'm captivated by its emerald-green eyes, I hear its voice again: *"You will die!"*

I scream as the Serpent opens its jaws and dives upon me.

Chapter 24: The Illusionist

"I'M GOING TO die! I'm going to die!" I wake up writhing on the floor, tangled in my bedsheets. Once I realize I'm in my room, I lie still on the ground and breathe until I've calmed down. Then I untangle myself and sit on the bed with an exhausted sigh.

I feel like I haven't slept a single second.

What time is it, anyway?

Someone knocks at the door. If I had to guess, I'd say it's Misham.

My heart leaps. All the horrible feelings from the dream suddenly disappear.

"Coming!" I jump off my bed and scurry to the mirror.

Damn it, my hair is a mess!

I grab a brush and begin working out the knots. After a moment, I give up with an exasperated sigh and tie my hair up in a bun. There! No one will notice its imperfection now.

I grab some beautiful silver earrings studded with emeralds, and a jade-green necklace to match. Oh, and that bracelet is gorgeous! I'll wear that too.

There's another knock on the door.

"Coming, coming!" I finish by wiping a smudge off my face, and then hurry to answer the door.

The person at the door is not Misham at all. She's an older woman, almost unnaturally slender, wearing royal purple garb and excessive amounts of jewelry, even for my taste. Her thinning gray hair is hidden by an elaborate headdress. I take a step back.

It's Shaama, the leader of White Sand.

"Good morning, dear," Shaama greets, her voice shrill and her Sunophsian accent thick.

"Good morning, Auntie," I say with a polite bow. Shaama is an Offspring of Sisera like me and my other siblings, but she's much older than we are. Though the ordinary White Sand operatives call her "ma'am," or "boss," she prefers it when we Offspring call her "auntie."

Shaama looks past me into the room. "I heard you screaming a moment ago. Is everything all right?"

"Oh, uh, yes. Everything is all right," I smile.

"Are you sure?" Shaama stares directly through my eyes and into my soul. In that moment, I'm very glad she can't read minds.

"Well, my hair was a mess, and it made me upset, so I put it up in a bun. You know how frustrating hair can be, right?" I end with a nervous chuckle.

Shaama raises an eyebrow. Then she shrugs and says, "Well,

now that you're up, please come with me. I'd like to have a word with you."

"Y-yes, of course Auntie," I force a polite smile even as my heart revolts. Why in the land of Armavir does she, of all people, want to have a word with me?

I hope it's not about that stupid wanted poster!

Shaama puts a hand on my back as we walk down the hall. "Celine, you must know that I'm very pleased with you."

"Thank you," I reply.

"You're a very skillful thief, one of the best we've ever had, and your illusion skills are a match for none. You fend for yourself well, even as a lady in the presence of your powerful brothers. You are everything I aspired to be when I was your age. And frankly, you're the only person in Cloud Summit I believe I can trust."

"More than Nebioth?" I ask. He's our second-oldest sibling in White Sand and takes the lead on most missions.

"Yes, more than Nebioth."

Soon, we find ourselves in the treasury. It's only a tad smaller than the central hub of the hideout, but it's filled with heaps of coins, gemstones, treasure chests, and valuable items. It's the sum of our robberies and black market dealings over the years, and it's by far my favorite room in the hideout.

"Why are we meeting here?" I ask, picking up a beautiful sapphire and admiring my own reflection in it.

"I have a special assignment for you," Shaama says, taking my sapphire and tossing it aside.

"Oh?" I do my best not to pout.

"Do you remember the relic you stole from Königheim?"

"Yes. Well, I didn't steal it. I helped steal it."

"No matter," Shaama says while examining a nearby treasure chest. "Do you remember what it was supposed to do?"

"A little bit."

"Tell me what you know."

I try to remember. I'm not a huge fan of old relics or weapons or whatever unless they're shiny and can be worn as jewelry. Why is Shaama asking me these questions and not one of my brothers?

"Well?" She presses, continuing to examine treasure chests one by one.

"I don't remember," I concede with a sigh.

"Don't worry, I'll remind you. It's an ancient weapon said to turn the tide of war, cure any disease, and tame any beast."

"Yes, I remember now," I reply half-truthfully.

"And why did I ask you to retrieve it for me?"

"Because...you want to win wars, live forever, and have pet monsters?"

"Leverage, child!" She snaps. "It's all about leverage. With a weapon like that in our arsenal, we can blackmail King Alphonse, Chief Bennett, and all the nobles of Armavir into giving us whatever we want. If they don't comply, we'll destroy the city. We'll be unstoppable. All-powerful; in complete control of Armavir itself!"

"Oh! Yes, yes that makes sense," I say, forcing myself to sound enthusiastic.

"Ah, here it is!" Shaama finds the chest she was looking for. She pulls out a key to unlock the chest and opens it, revealing another treasure chest. The second chest is very small and has no keyhole, but instead has an almond-shaped silver panel where a keyhole should be. She hands it to me. "Here, take a look."

I take it from her and examine it. I guess it's kind of pretty. Ornate, white as snow, light as a feather. The turtle-and-crown design is a little off-putting.

"I bet you're wondering why we haven't used the weapon yet, even though we've had it all this time."

I hadn't thought of that, but she has a good point. "Yes, do tell."

"Well, simply put...I have no idea how to open it."

I finger the keyhole-less panel. "You don't say?"

"I've spent the last six moons trying to figure it out. It can't be pried open, it can't be crushed, smashed, dissolved in water, burned in fire, rubbed like a genie lamp, nothing. I've searched the library, even in the books that tell of the weapon, but there's no clue as to how it opens. However," Shaama acquires a mischievous grin. "I know someone who knows how to open it."

"Really?" I ask, still trying hard to feign interest.

"I have seen, with my gift of Farsight, a certain old man who is very knowledgeable about the myths from which this weapon was created. I read about his kind in a book. They're called Seers. They're much like fortune tellers, only a bit more loony. What I need you to do, my dear, is go to this man and convince him to open the chest. You may threaten him in any way you'd like, as long as you don't kill him or give yourself away. Report to me as soon as you're finished."

"Yes, Auntie. Where is he?"

"Come into my mind and see."

It's a command she can only give to an illusionist.

I establish a mental connection with her, and I allow my

manas'ruh to rest and observe her thought process. I watch from Shaama's point of view as she extends her manas'ruh aboveground, across the city as the crow flies, and settles down in a market square. There's an old man in a sailor's outfit leaning on a cane of polished bone, speaking with a couple of merchants.

"The old man in the sailor's outfit?"

"Correct. Go quickly, before he gets away. Don't tell any of your brothers about this. I want you to go alone."

"Yes, Auntie," I reply, reeling my manas'ruh back in.

"Take the weapon with you. Remember Celine, I believe in you. Don't take my trust for granted. Keep the weapon hidden at all times, and *do not ever* bring it out in public!"

"Yes, Auntie. But, how do I get the man to open it if I can't take it out?"

"Use your head, child! Corner him in an alley. Do whatever you need to do, just make sure there are no witnesses."

"Yes, Auntie. I'll do it right away." I nod and take my leave.

I stop by my room to get a shoulder bag and proper walking shoes. Cute ones, of course. Since I'm not going on this assignment with my brothers, I feel like I have the freedom not to wear the suffocating dark-colored outfit we wear while doing organized robberies and all that. No one will suspect me if I look like a classy Armaviran citizen. Besides, it'll make pickpocketing easier, which I always enjoy doing in crowded areas, regardless of my assignment.

"*You will die,*" the voice from the dream whispers in my mind.

Fear pricks my heart.

I immediately ignore it.

Actually, I think I'll wear a cute hat too. I'm fair-skinned for a Sunophsian, but my dark hair will give me away as foreign in a heartbeat. It'd be wise to avoid unnecessary trouble from the police or other anti-Sunophsian folks by blending in as much as possible. I choose a stylish summer straw hat with a white flower on the front. Once I tuck my bun underneath the hat, I depart from the hideout.

25
Finding Jed
Summer, 1419 AIE

~Celine~

WHAT A LOVELY day for a late-morning stroll down the busy streets of Cloud Summit.

Unlike yesterday, when the summer storm drove most people indoors, the city today is bustling with activity. Because there's only one moon left of summer weather, the merchants and traders are busier than ever, seeking to maximize their profits before cold weather comes to inhibit their travel.

Though most White Sand operatives carry out their assignments at night or other times when the streets are all but empty, I prefer the social scene.

I turn the corner and begin walking down the main street of downtown Cloud Summit, which leads to the market square where the old man was seen.

I'll never grow tired of the downtown area's architecture and artsy flare. The stone buildings, rising at least ten stories on either side, are elaborately carved and decorated with spires, flying buttresses, and lancet windows. The street itself is lined with stalls and shops, like many splashes of color against the sunlit stone, as well as few spherical evergreen bushes. Banners of blue, violet, and gold are hung high on some of the buildings, featuring either the Armaviran coat of arms or that of the Paladin Order. Even the cast-iron lampposts lining the street are elegantly designed.

Königheim Castle dominates the skyline ahead, shimmering in the sunlight as a flock of doves swirls around the magnificent structure.

This is where all the important people in Cloud Summit hang out, and rightfully so. It's my favorite place in the city.

I take a deep breath and smile confidently. It's time to play 'social elite.'

"Don't look down, don't frown, and don't lose step," I coach myself as I go. *"Smile when people make eye contact, always be polite, and for goodness' sake, don't do anything awkward."*

In a minute, I come to an intersection. On the street corner, there's a man playing an accordion for donations, and a nobleman sitting on a nearby bench, listening to the music.

This looks fun, I think I'll join in.

I slow down near the accordion man, as if captivated by the music.

He notices me and smiles, gesturing with his eyes toward the bucket at his feet and giving me a wink.

I smile in reply and pretend to fumble around in my shoulder bag. Meanwhile, I establish a mental connection with him and the nobleman and cause them to see me pulling out a blic. I flick my wrist as if tossing the coin, and they see it fly into the bucket. I don't forget to add the special *clink* sound of the blic hitting its mark.

There are enough coins in there that they won't notice it disappear when I break the illusion.

But I'm not finished yet.

The accordion man smiles gratefully and nods, and I smile in return. Then I casually meander around him and toward the nobleman's bench.

"Beautiful music, isn't it?" I ask, sitting down beside him.

"Yes, indeed," the nobleman says, clearly surprised I came to sit with him. He fumbles for words. I pretend not to notice, but internally I'm very entertained. Finally, he says, "You're very kind, you know—giving him a blic. Not many rich folk in Cloud Summit care for the poor anymore."

"Oh, it was nothing," I answer more truthfully than he'll ever find out. "So, what do you do for a living?"

"Oh, me? I'm one of Prince Oliver's officials. I run errands for him."

"Really?" I tilt my head, showing utmost interest. "How wonderful. It must be so dreamy, working for a prince."

The nobleman chuckles. "I don't know about that, miss. Prince

Oliver is a good man, but his responsibilities grow more and more every day. It's difficult for errand boys like me to keep up with."

"Oh, I see. That's very interesting. What does the prince have you doing today?"

The nobleman tenses. "I-I'm sorry miss, I can't say. It's confidential, you know."

"Don't worry, I won't tell anyone," I say, scooting two inches closer and gazing deep into his eyes. "I would love to help if I can."

He looks away momentarily, failing to hide a blush, and inevitably he succumbs.

It's the hat. I'm so glad I decided to wear a cute hat today.

"W-well," he stutters before clearing his throat and trying to speak like a proper nobleman, "I'm on my way to the Hall of Justice to deliver a subsidy. A rather large one, if you know what I mean."

I notice when he mentions the subsidy, his eyes flicker down at a coin purse which hangs from his belt only a few inches from where I'm sitting.

"Oooh," I widen my eyes. "Yes, that's very important. I promise I won't tell anyone."

"Thank you," the nobleman nods and smiles. "So, what do you do? What's your name?"

Aw, Mister Nobleman wants to get to know me, how cute.

"My name is..." I trail off and look at something behind him.

As he turns to see what I'm looking at, using the mental connection I've maintained since feigning the coin toss, I cause him and the accordion man to see a Paladin approaching. The knight says to the nobleman, "Good sir, I've come with a message from Prince Oliver."

"Oh?" The nobleman composes himself and turns his attention toward the illusory Paladin, and away from me. The accordion man, still playing, is also focused on the Paladin.

"There's been a change in plans," the Paladin begins. "According to the laws set by King Alphonse V upon his ascension to the throne, which are indeed based on the very laws that were established upon the creation of the Paladin Order and the coronation of the first king of Cloud Summit in the year 992 after the Imperial Era, the subsidy cannot be delivered today."

The nobleman's brow wrinkles. "Sir, I don't know what you mean. Prince Oliver himself told me to deliver the subsidy today."

While the nobleman is distracted, I go about my pickpocketing work.

The Paladin replies, "Yes, well, I'm sure you're aware of how the prince's new responsibilities are weighing him down, what with the king's ailing health and all. He is still quite young and makes many mistakes. No insult intended, of course. After sending you off on this important errand, he was reminded by his father's officials that the laws of Cloud Summit, set by King Alphonse V upon his ascension to the throne, based on the very laws that were established upon the creation of the Paladin Order and the coronation of the first king of Cloud Summit in the year 992 after the Imperial Era, clearly state that subsidies due to the chief of police and the Hall of Justice staff are only to be delivered after sundown. Being a man of honor and striving to set a great example to the people of Cloud Summit and to those who serve him, the good prince immediately sent me to find you and cancel the errand."

Oh, yes, yes, *yes*! Sapphires! My favorite!

"Blimey," the nobleman replies. "What an interesting law that is, delivering subsidies after sundown. I almost feel the prince ought not to have gone through the trouble of sending you to find me for such a trivial misunderstanding."

"He is a very good prince, I'd say. His respect for even the smallest laws is something Cloud Summit desperately needs."

"Understood. I will return to the castle at once. Thank you, Sir...?"

I've just finished transferring the last of the shiny blue subsidy into my shoulder bag when I realize the trap the nobleman is unwittingly putting me in. Creating an illusory Paladin is easy enough, as long as it's a fully-armored Paladin without a name or a face. Once someone asks for a name, things get tricky. The fact that this nobleman probably knows many Paladins by name makes it no easier.

I have to think of a name he won't recognize on the spot.

"Sir Reginald," The Paladin nods.

"Reginald?" the nobleman tilts his head. "I've never heard your name before. Where are you from?"

"Château Pierre. I was transferred here a few weeks ago."

"Oh, yes, of course," the nobleman nods and smiles. "I look forward to seeing you again, Sir Reginald. Thank you very much."

"You are most welcome," Reginald nods, and then says the most important phrase for my successful getaway. "Oh, and I must warn you. There's been a rise in criminal activity from the Izendoran refugees lately. You'd do well to keep an eye out for them on your way back to the castle."

"I will, thank you."

"That goes for you too, miss," Reginald says to me. "It would be a great tragedy if a beautiful young lady like yourself had a run-in with those no-good bandits."

I like to throw in a compliment for myself every now and then.

"Oh, thank you, Sir Reginald! Take care," I smile and wave at him.

Sir Reginald nods again before turning and walking behind a building and out of sight. That's when I sever the connection, and Sir Reginald disappears once and for all.

When the nobleman turns back to me, I'm looking at him just as I was before Reginald appeared. I speak with a faint tone of regret, "Well, I suppose you should be heading back to the castle now."

The nobleman picks up on the regret and blushes again. "Yes, well...I could, but I wouldn't mind taking an early lunch. It'd be a pity to start another errand so close to noon. How about you, would you like to join me?"

"Aw, how sweet of you to ask," I say, acting genuinely...like I care or something. "Actually, I was just on my way to the market. I have a few errands of my own to run, and they must all be completed before noon. I've enjoyed talking with you, but I'm afraid I must get going."

I stand up to leave, but the nobleman grabs my hand. "W-wait! I don't even know your name. How will I find you again?"

"Oh, yes of course," I turn to face him, silently reprimanding myself for forgetting such a basic social custom. "My name is Marie. And you?"

"John," he says, shaking my hand. The hand he never let go of in the first place.

"It's so great to meet you, John," I say, smiling. I allow a mischievous glimmer to appear in my eyes. "I would love to see you for dinner at La Belle Rose tomorrow evening. How about six o'clock?"

"Yes, that would be wonderful," John says, gripping my hand harder.

I internally roll my eyes.

"It's a date," I say, gently tugging my hand out of his and turning to leave. "See you then."

"See you then...Marie," John breathes as I walk away.

I imagine he's probably watching me leave with a stupidly lovestruck expression, as the nearby romantic accordion music adds to the mood.

I wonder if I overdid that one a little bit...?

Nah.

Even if I have to meet him at La Belle Rose tomorrow to maintain my cover, I'll get a free meal out of it. And more opportunities to steal his stuff.

Now, I'm back on my mission to find the old man. I hope he hasn't left already. That little side-stop did take longer than I meant it to.

But sapphires are *always* worth it.

I make my way down the main street past two more intersections before I turn left on the smaller road leading to the market square.

As soon as I turn the corner, I bump into a policeman.

"Oh!" I shout in surprise. As I behold the man in front of me, I realize he's a *police captain,* a direct subordinate of Chief Bennett, as indicated by the crest upon his helmet. The panic and guilt I felt yesterday after the murder begin to resurface. Despite those feelings, I quickly collect myself. "I'm so sorry, sir. I didn't see you there."

"Not to worry, miss. I'm in a bit of a rush myself," the captain says, sidestepping me and continuing onto the main road.

As he passes, I slip a few blics out of his pocket and keep going.

Was that rash of me, stealing from a police captain?

Perhaps. But it'll earn me extra rapport with my brothers.

As I continue onward, the small road empties out into the market square, filled with haggling merchants and bartering traders. It's crowded enough to where I can't simply walk straight to my destination on the far side of the market. But that's fine by me.

I walk innocently into the market crowd.

Bump into a lady here. Nice watch.

Bump into a farmer there. A polished stone, not bad.

Bump into a fruit stand. Apple for later.

Bump into the merchant who just ripped off a customer. I'll take those blics.

Bump into the potion guy. Damn it, he's broke.

I stand on my tip-toes to look for the old man. I see him on the far side of the square, sticking out like a sore thumb with his outdated sailor's outfit. He receives a bulging sack of money from one of the merchants, shakes hands with the other, and turns to walk away.

The merchants head a few steps back to their shop. The sign above it reads, "Royal Land Grant Distributors of Armavir." Some kind of real estate firm. Armavir's economy may be failing, but the price of land is still high in most parts of the kingdom. I bet the old man has a halfway-decent amount of gold in that sack of his.

I'll probably take it as a souvenir after I'm finished interrogating him.

I weasel my way through the rest of the crowd, pickpocketing a few more goodies as I go, and hurry after the old man before he walks out of sight.

Thankfully, he's frightfully slow, hobbling around on that hideous cane.

I slow down a dozen feet behind him and follow at his pace, pretending to browse the shops as I come up with a plan.

Let's see. Shaama said to get him to open the box by any means necessary without killing him or giving myself away. Also, I can't reveal the box in public. How can I convince the old man to open the box in a place where no one will see? Where can I lure him, and with what illusion, to make sure everything runs smoothly?

Here's an idea: I'll send him a little boy to ask him everything he knows about...hm. I sure wish I knew more about the context of this stupid box.

Yes, I'll have the boy ask him about the context of the stupid box. Where it came from, who brought it to Königheim, how does one go about opening it, stuff like that. Then, if it's something I can't just do on my own or tell Shaama how to do, I'll corner him in an alley and threaten him until he does it for me.

Perfect.

By now the old man has hobbled away from the crowded market scene, and now we're on a less-crowded side road. I suppose now is as good a time as any to get started.

I extend my manas'ruh toward the old man to establish a connection with him. I cause him to see a little boy come out from a cross-street some distance ahead and run toward him.

"Excuse me, sir," the boy says, stopping in front of the old man. "I have a dilemma."

"Oh, do ye?" the old man says, stopping as well.

As I continue to work the illusion, I wander over to a news bulletin board within earshot and pretend to read it.

"Yes," the boy replies. I make him sound adorable. "I'm studying for the Paladin Training Academy entrance exam, and I need some help. Can I ask you some questions? You look like a wise man who knows *everything!*"

"Oh, well, I don't know about that, lad," the old man says,

reaching forward to pat the boy on the head. I manipulate the man's imagination to make him believe he's feeling the boy's hair.

"Please, sir?" The boy asks with puppy eyes. "If you don't help me, who will?"

The old man chuckles. "All right, I'll give it me best shot."

"Yes!" The boy jumps up and down.

"Come now, lad, let's sit down." The old man reaches to put his hand on the boy's back, and I make him feel as though he has his hand on a boy's back.

How silly he must look to passers-by, talking to nobody and walking with his hand out like that.

The old man leads the boy to a bench on the side of the road, and the two of them sit down. The bench is about nine feet from where I'm standing in front of the bulletin board.

"Ok, first question," the boy says, his eyes gleaming with hunger for knowledge. "What is the most special relic in Königheim Castle?"

"Hmm, I don't know that one," the old man replies. "Can't say I've ever been in the castle, but I hear there are many precious artifacts of great value."

"Well, do you know of any in particular?" the boy presses. "Maybe something really powerful? Like...a weapon? Something the Paladins can use to kill all the bad guys?"

"Hmm...ah, yes, there is one thing. I bet ye're wondering about the Music of Marindel."

"No," the boy shakes his head. "I mean a weapon."

"There is no weapon more powerful than the Music of Marindel," the old man says with a twinkle in his sea-blue eyes. "It can turn the tide of war, cure any disease, nullify any curse, tame any—"

"*Yes!*" the boy shouts. "I want to know about *that* weapon."

The weapon is a musical instrument? In a box that small? How in the...?

"Ah, of course, lad. The Music of Marindel has been available to us for centuries, yet we have all but forgotten its power. It's been kept hidden in places like Königheim Castle, collectin' dust. But ye know, when the Great King gives us a gift, he intends for us to use it. Don't you agree?"

"I don't know," the boy replies, scrunching his face. "If King Alphonse wanted us to use the gift, I don't think he would've kept it in the castle for himself."

The old man chuckles. "Oh, laddie! The Great King is not King Alphonse, or any other king ye've likely heard of. The Great King is nothin' like those kings. He's existed for a very long time; some say even before humans arrived in this realm! And he is very kind."

"Whoa," the boy opens his eyes wide.

Shaama was right, this guy *is* loony. It looks like I'll have to be more specific with my questions.

"So, what *is* the Music of Marindel? How does it work?"

"It is the most beautiful sound in the realm," the old man says wistfully. "At its beck and call, light shines out of the darkness, hope blooms in the midst of despair, and life comes forth out of death."

Both the boy and I are clueless, mouths agape and eyes narrowed in disbelief. After a few seconds I make the boy compose himself and ask, "Well, how does it *work*? Like, if I were to hold a...Music of Marindel...in my hands right now, how would I use it?"

"The Music of Marindel cannot be used in that way. It isn't a physical substance. It's a present reality."

What the hell!? If he keeps up with these vague answers, I'm going to throw something at his face!

No. I have to stay calm.

Deep breath in, deep breath out.

The boy asks a more logical question. "Well, music doesn't come from nowhere, it comes from an instrument. Does the Music of Marindel come from an instrument?"

"Why yes, of course lad," the old man replies.

"Okay, how does the instrument work?"

"Just like any other instrument."

Unbelievable! I've never had a more difficult time interrogating a person in my entire life. I'm almost beginning to wish Shaama hadn't told me not to kill him. I'll be mighty tempted to do so if my frustration causes this illusion to fail.

The boy is silent for a moment as I regain my mental composure.

The old man seems to be waiting patiently.

Soon, the boy looks at the old man again and asks, "What kind of instrument is it?"

The old man looks into the distance, reminiscing on some long-forgotten memories or something. He heaves a nostalgic sigh and says, "I've no idea. I've never seen it meself. It was in Königheim for centuries before I was even yer age. Oh, what I wouldn't give to be one of those chosen to play for the King in this day and age! But, alas, it is not my callin'."

This isn't working. I need a new plan, and fast. Something more direct.

The boy promptly stands up and says, "Thanks for your help, sir! For my next question, would you please come with me? I want to show you something."

"Of course, lad." The old man stands with the help of his cane. "Ye'll have to forgive me, I'm much slower than I used to be."

The boy runs across the street diagonally, dodging a few passers-by, and stops in front of a narrow alley between two tall stone buildings. "This way, sir!"

"I'm comin', I'm comin'," the old man says as he hobbles across the street. "Ye know, many years ago, I was one of the fastest runners in the Tethysian navy. One of the fastest swimmers, too!"

"That's very nice," the boy replies, hopping up and down with anticipation.

I linger near the bulletin board for a moment longer, allowing the old man time to lengthen the distance between us. As long as he doesn't get too far away, I'll be able to keep the illusion running. I just need him to get to the alley first...

Hm? What's this?

My eyes fall on a wanted poster for "The Illusionist." How did I not notice it earlier?

"*You will die*," the voice from my dream says.

The poster is similar to the one Nebioth showed me, but with some added content.

I'm *known* to be a part of White Sand.

I'm accused of murder.

The bounty has been tripled to fifteen thousand krons.

"*Yes, you deserve to die*," the voice says as I peruse the poster.

Panic floods my soul.

Guilt over the man I killed.

Am I really going to die?

No! I don't have time for this right now!

"Now, young lad," I hear the old man's voice across the street, "what is it ye'd like to show me?"

I pull the wanted poster off the board, roll it up tight, and stuff it in my shoulder bag. Then I make the boy say, "This way, sir!" and run into the alley. From the old man's point of view, I cause the boy to run a dozen feet down and disappear behind a tall heap of garbage. Then I sever the mental connection.

I won't be needing that illusion anymore.

As the old man hobbles after the boy, I cross the street after him.

"Laddie? Where'd ye go?" He calls from within the alley.

All right. It's time to get some answers.

I walk down the alley, skirting the garbage heap. The old man is a little further down, perplexed out of his mind. When he notices my approach, he asks, "Excuse me, lass, ye haven't seen a wee lad around here, have ye?"

"I'm afraid not," I reply, still walking toward him.

"Hmmm," he furrows his brow. "There are mysterious things happenin' around here. *Very* mysterious."

When I reach the old man, I snatch that hideous cane of his and toss it across the alley. Then I take him by his shoulders and push him against the cold stone wall, where I hold him steady.

"What're ye doin'?" the old man asks with surprising calm. "Would ye really mug a defenseless old man?"

"Tell me how to open it," I demand, staring into his eyes.

The old man's expression is as strong and peaceful as ever. "Open what?"

"The Music of— ugh," I stop myself. It's no use trying to describe the box with words. I place one hand firmly on the man's chest while using my other hand to open my bag and pull out the box.

"This!" I say, holding it in front of his face. "Tell me how to open it!"

"It wouldn't help ye even if I did, lass."

I establish a mental connection with him, and...hm, where to start?

He's being a nuisance, so I'll shake him up a little.

I cause him to feel as though there are thousands of reaper ants crawling on his legs, biting relentlessly. The old man winces, but he doesn't break eye contact. Not a glint of fear or submission appears in his eyes.

"Tell me how to open it," I repeat. "Don't play dumb with me! I know you know how!"

"Ye have no idea what ye're askin' for."

"Yes I do. See this box? See it!?" I push the smooth panel of the box up against his nose. "I'm asking you to tell me how to open it!"

"What for? So ye can use the Music of Marindel to achieve yer own selfish gain?"

"That's none of your business," I snap.

"Well, then, what is my business?"

"Your business is to tell me how to open it, you ignorant bastard!"

"Ignorant, eh?" the old man smiles. "Fancy that. An ignorant Seer. I've never heard of such a thing."

The fearlessness of the old man makes me very uncomfortable.

I edit the ant illusion by adding the sensation of standing barefoot on burning coals.

"Do not underestimate me," I whisper. "I can reduce your psyche to splinters if I choose! Tell me how to open the box now, or you will regret your very life!"

"All right, all right, if ye're goin' to be stubborn about it," the old man is still hardly wincing. "Don't say I didn't warn ye."

"Out with it!" I shout.

"Press yer right index finger firmly against the panel."

I'm holding the box with my right hand, so I shift my grip until I can place my index finger on the panel. "Okay, now what?"

"That's all there is to it."

"It's not opening."

"It doesn't belong to ye."

"What do you mean, it doesn't belong to me!?"

"It's up to the Great King to choose who will be gifted with the ability to wield the Music of Marindel."

I roll my eyes. "Oh, I see! What you're telling me is that some King of yours made this box for only certain people to open?"

"Aye."

"I don't believe you."

"I know ye don't, lass."

"Fine then," I say, pressing him harder. "*You* open it."

"I can't open it either."

"Still don't believe you," I say, grabbing his right hand and pressing his index finger against the panel.

Nothing happens.

"It's no use," the old man says. "The Great King would never bestow such a wonderful gift to his beloved servants without first safeguardin' it against wicked people like yerself."

I let go of the man's hand and lean in closer, glaring maliciously. "You are the most pathetically insane human being I've ever met. You ought to consider yourself lucky I have orders *not* to kill you."

"Ye should consider yerself lucky the Great King still has his lovin' eye on ye."

What in the land of Armavir?

Is he serious right now?

Someone tell me he isn't serious right now.

I can't take it! It's hysterical!

I burst out laughing so hard, I can't help but shed tears. I say between gasps, "You're hopeless, you really are. No king in their right mind would cast so much as a *glance* of approval on someone like me: a thief, a criminal, a *murderer*, for crying out loud! You know where you belong, old man? A garbage heap! Because everything that comes out of your mouth is garbage. I'm finished with you. I'll find another way to open this box, and I promise, I *will* find a way!"

The old man speaks sternly, "I want ye to stop and think about this conversation, Celine. Look at me, right now. Who of the two of us is *really* hopeless?"

Once he says my name, I don't hear another word. I trash the illusion of the reaper ants and hot coals, and in its place I cause him to see and feel a king cobra bind him tightly from his legs up to his shoulders, and then position itself ready to strike his throat. I ask, "How do you know my name?"

He doesn't even glance at the cobra; his eyes are on me. "The Great King knows yer name."

I roll my eyes. "Oh, and I suppose he told you I'd show up today, didn't he?"

"Aye. Young lad and all."

"Ugh!" I fail to contain my frustration. Anger overcomes my judgment, and I cause the cobra to strike the old man's throat. Obviously, he isn't *really* being smitten by a snake, but his sensory nerves don't know that.

Now, finally, the old man screams and doubles over.

I sever the mental connection and pick him up again, forcing him to his feet. I hold my face close to his and say, "I hate you so much, I'm not even going to use an illusion to dispose of you. You're a total lunatic and I hope you rot in this alley, never to come out again!"

Without waiting for a reply, I reach into his bag and pull out the sack of money he received from the merchants a short time ago. "I'll take this as payment for having to deal with your stupidity."

"N-no," the old man wheezes, "That money is...for someone else...!"

"Too bad. It's mine now," I say, stuffing the sack into my bag.

"Lass, have mercy," the old man pleads.

"No thanks." I grab one of his arms and hurl him into the garbage heap. He lands head-first, disappearing halfway into it with a *splut*. I can hear him mumbling in the garbage as he wriggles his legs about, trying to get free.

"Hmph!" I dust my hands off and adjust my cute hat.

Turning toward the exit of the alley, I kick something on the ground. I look down and nearly lose my breath when I realize it's the Music of Marindel box.

How did that get down there?

I suppose I must've dropped it when I got angry.

"Oh you," I say to the box, stooping down to pick it up. "If Shaama didn't care so much about opening you, I'd throw you in the garbage too." I put it back in my shoulder bag.

Or, at least I try to.

My bag is so full of goodies now that it's hard to fit everything inside. But I *have* to get this box back in there, so I shift things around and shove with all my might. Finally, it fits just well enough that I can close the bag over it.

Phew, that was close.

My bag is bulging and awkward to carry because it's so big and heavy, but it's a small price to pay for the prizes inside.

In any case, I should head back to the hideout and let Shaama know she was wrong about the old man.

"You are going to die."

"Go jump in the garbage," I retort, not even giving the accompanying guilt a chance to distract me.

I regain my composure, taking deep breaths and speaking confidently to myself. Then I emerge from the alley and head down the street, taking a roundabout way back to the White Sand hideout.

26

Broken

Summer, 1419 AIE

~Celine~

I T'S NOW AN hour past noon.

Judging by the rising humidity, I'd guess there's a storm coming, perhaps later this evening.

My goodness, I sure am hungry.

I hope my brothers have lunch. And I hope they're willing to share with me.

As I'm thinking idle thoughts like these, I pass by a small restaurant with outdoor patio seating. A whiff of roasted chicken catches my attention, and I stop to look. Something besides chicken quickly piques my interest.

There's a Felid in the restaurant.

Hmm, I don't see many Felids in Cloud Summit. I wonder what he's up to? Maybe he's rich. Felids who travel to Cloud Summit are usually rich. I'll go check it out.

I walk through the patio area and into the restaurant. I stand there perusing the menu while I eavesdrop on the Felid and his non-Felid companions, who are all sitting together at a nearby table.

"…some of the best chicken ever! It's so good!" A peppy adolescent girl says.

"Cloud Summit is known for good meat," a burly guy across the table replies. "It's a staple in the winter time."

"It's a really good thing we saved the rest of our money for this meal," a scrawny peasant says. "It'll keep us satisfied long enough to find Jed and get the money for the homestead. You guys think we can find him by tonight?"

"Only if your Seer's gift gives us a few leads," the burly guy replies.

My heart skips a beat. Not another Seer! Just after I throw one in the garbage, another one happens along my path! Just great!

I'm going to mess with him. Because, why not.

"The Great King will lead us," the Felid says.

My eyelid twitches.

The Felid is a lunatic too!

I'll get both of them. Hell, I'll get all of them.

The Felid, the burly guy, the scrawny Seer, the peppy girl, the Izendoran kid, and the guy with tacky animal skins and a quiver.

All of them.

I hold back a silly grin as an idea comes to mind. They like roasted chicken, do they? Well, let's see how long *that* lasts.

I establish a mental connection with each of them and hijack their imaginations. Then I turn the Seer's head into a roasted chicken.

They all turn and stare at him.

The peppy girl points. "Connor! Your head! It's...It's...!"

"What? Why are you all looking at me like that?" Connor sinks into his seat.

The Felid speaks next. "Connor, your head is, um...how do I say this... Your head is a chicken."

Connor stares back in disbelief. "What in the land of Armavir are you talking about?"

"Feel your face!" the peppy girl says, still pointing.

Connor strokes his face. I make him feel the hot, steamy, slimy skin of a delectable roasted chicken breast. His eyes widen in horror. "AH! What happened to me!?"

"It's Jaedis! It must be!" the Izendoran kid shouts.

The others shout indistinctly for a few seconds before the Felid says, "Everyone calm down! There has to be an explanation for this."

Everyone else in the restaurant is looking at them like they're crazy. The beautiful thing is, they don't see Connor's chicken-head at all.

The animal-skin guy pokes Connor's face. "What kind of evil sorcery is this?"

"What are we going to do?" The Izendoran kid asks, looking up at the Felid.

Chapter 26: Broken

Before the Felid has a chance to say anything profound, I'm going to smite him with humiliation as well.

Hm, let's see... Aha. Yes.

I turn the Felid's head into a sparkly-eyed pink kitten head.

Those at the table gawk at him.

The peppy girl points her other finger at the Felid. "Tarento! You're...you're so...*cute!*"

Tarento replies, but I cause those at the table to hear nothing but an adorable meow.

The Izendoran kid strokes Tarento's cheek-fur. "So...so soft!"

Tarento says something else, but again I replace it with an adorable meow. Then he feels his own face and flinches, shouting in alarm with a very emphatic meow.

Connor says, "Yeah, Tarento, you have a cat head."

Tarento mews with frustration, but it's the cutest thing anyone has ever seen or heard.

The losers around the table keep trying to figure out why Connor and Tarento have strange heads, but to no avail.

By now, the people in the restaurant are laughing up a storm. It's a very good show, if I do say so myself. I feel like I'm doing the public a favor by giving them an entertaining lunch-hour comedy skit. In fact, I find myself wishing the police would arrive to arrest this group of fools and escort them straight to the insane asylum.

Hey, I can make that happen.

I stretch out my manas'ruh to establish connections with everyone presently watching the show. I can feel my mental energy straining as I struggle to reach everyone, but I won't have to hold it for long. I cause an ordinary-looking Armaviran man to appear on the other side of the restaurant and say, "Hey! The police oughta see this!"

"Yeah!" Another man chips in. A real man, not an illusion.

"I'll go find them!"

"Me too!"

Two people leave the restaurant to find the nearest police officers.

I break the connections then, shuddering as my manas'ruh recollects and taking a moment to gasp for breath. It was difficult, but I believe it will be well worth it.

"My jaws close down upon you. The time of your death draws near."

My silly grin melts away as the voice invades my recovering mind. Panic swells within me once again as I remember the image of the Serpent from the dream, towering over my helpless boat, crashing down upon me with its jaws wide.

Well, this was all fun while it lasted. I'd rather not be here when the police arrive, so I'll be heading on my way. Now that I think of it, I want nothing more than to get back to the hideout and take a nap.

I exit the restaurant, breaking my connections with the freaks. As I walk away, I hear the peppy girl shout, "Your heads are normal again!"

I chuckle. They'll be thrown in the asylum before the sun sets.

I walk a block further down the street before I hear someone speaking behind me. "Hey there, gorgeous, long time no see."

My heart leaps and I whirl around. "Misham!"

He's disguised in a classy Armaviran outfit like I am, complete with a silk maroon cape. He's *so* cute when he wears a cape, and he knows it. Misham embraces me, and I gladly return it. Before I know it, we're kissing passionately.

Abdeel peers out from behind Misham and says, "Celine, you're stooping to a new low."

I look at him over Misham's shoulder. "What's the matter, jealous?"

Abdeel spits. "Hell, no! I'm talking about the restaurant back there. Misham and I saw what you did."

"Humiliating civilians for fun," Misham says with mock disappointment as we let go of each other. "I can't believe you'd do such a thing. You're growing up to be just like your cruel brothers. Who in the realm is your father, I wonder?"

I laugh. "Let's not speak of that old douchebag."

"Quite right," Misham agrees.

"Where you going, sis?" Abdeel asks.

"Back home," I reply, continuing to walk again.

"Us too," Abdeel says, falling in on my left.

Misham falls in on my right.

Their presence comforts me. I'm very thankful that my brothers, though they are often callous jerks, still care enough to travel with me and keep me safe. No matter what the stupid death-voice says, I know my brothers will protect me. My entire gang will protect me. White Sand always sticks together. They would do anything for me, and I would do anything for them.

Anything.

"You're very quiet," Misham says after a moment.

"Hm? Oh, I'm just tired is all."

Chapter 26: Broken

"Someone giving you a hard time, sis?" Abdeel asks. "Give me their address and I'll have their head on a platter by tomorrow morning."

I force a laugh and say, "No, no, that won't be necessary."

I wonder if they would believe me if I told them about the death-voice?

Well, there's only one way to find out.

"Hey guys," I say, taking a deep breath. "Do you ever feel like you're going to die?"

"Nope," Abdeel replies.

Misham looks at me with a raised eyebrow. "Why do you ask?"

"It's just..." Where do I begin? How do I say this? My brothers have never been good at listening to me share my feelings. They just make fun of me for being a girl or whatever. But I've already started this conversation, so now I have to follow through. "Well, say you've just robbed a bank, and one of the bank guards is extra pesky, so you kill him. As you're standing there, looking at his dead body, do you ever feel like...like you should die too? Because you killed him?"

Abdeel laughs. "Girl, I've killed more people than I can count on my fingers, and I never stop and stare long enough to feel sorry for them *or* myself."

"W-well," I stutter, disheartened by his confident reply, "have you ever had a nightmare about it? About someone or something trying to kill you for all the wrong things you've done?"

"Who said I've done anything wrong? The way I see it, I'm doing what I need to survive. If the king or the police want to set laws to try and stop me, that's their loss."

"But have you had a nightmare about it?" I press.

"No, sis. Stop whining, you're just being a girl."

"Shut up!" I retort. "Misham, tell him to shut up!"

"Abdeel, let me handle this," Misham says, and then to me, "Celine, what's troubling you?"

I take a deep breath to steady myself, and then I explain, "Yesterday, after you fled from the bank, the police came and almost arrested me. I only got away because they were distracted by a lightning strike and I killed one of them. I can't stop thinking about it, Misham. I had a nightmare last night that a giant sea monster told me I deserved to die, and all day I've heard it echoing in my mind over and over, driving me crazy! I can't take it, Misham! Tell me how to make it go away!" I grab his arm and hold it tight.

Misham chuckles.

"What's so funny?"

"Voices in your head, Celine? I'm afraid Abdeel's right about this one. You really *are* being a girl."

"What!?" I let go of him. "Take that back!"

"What for?" Misham asks, still chuckling. "It's the truth."

"Misham! I'm serious!"

"Oh, don't worry about it," Misham waves his hand. "You've only killed one person so far. The voice'll probably go away when you kill a few more. No big deal."

"Are you sure?"

Misham opens his mouth to reply, but Abdeel cuts in, "Police! Scatter!"

"Whoa!" Misham wraps himself in his cape and disappears.

"H-hey, wait!" I call after Abdeel, who sprints off and disappears in a nearby alley. I can't keep up with him; he's three times faster than I am.

I'm left all alone.

For the first time, I notice how empty the street is. It's still the middle of the day, but there are no people to be seen—except for a group of policemen a few dozen feet ahead, coming this way. My stomach falls like a rock.

"You will die."

Not wanting to meet and greet them, I calmly turn and walk in the opposite direction.

Only a second later, several more police come out from streets on either side. They're heading straight toward me.

"You will die."

I turn and walk briskly toward the alley Abdeel disappeared into. When I reach the mouth of it, I see a group of policemen coming down the other side.

"You will die."

I back out of the alley and search for another escape route, but I realize with increasing fear that there are none left.

I'm surrounded.

What in the land of Armavir is going on? The police have never done anything like this before!

"You will die."

They've blocked every alley, every side-street, and now they're closing in. I'm caught right in the middle.

Everything turns dark as a billowing thunderhead blots out the sun overhead.

As they form a tight circle around me, those with pikes take stances with their weapons pointed at me. The rest of the police stand at attention as if waiting for something.

I try hard to remain calm. I look around at the police while adjusting my hat and say, "Good afternoon, gentlemen. Can I help you?"

No one says a word. However, a few of them in front of me part to reveal the approach of two other men. The first is John the nobleman, and the second is the fearsome chief of police himself.

"You will die."

John and I make eye contact for a brief second, during which I receive powerful currents of fear, anger, and humiliation. Then he points at me and says, "That's her."

"Thank you kindly," Bennett says with a nod. Then he looks at me and steps forward. He wears a black police outfit, including a cape and a cavalier decorated with a luscious crimson plume. The coat of arms displayed on his shoulder is crimson as well. Bennett's composure is arrogant, and his deep voice carries undertones of self-superiority that make me shudder.

I swallow hard, but stand my ground.

"Miss, I do believe you have something of mine, and I'd like you to return it immediately."

The subsidy.

There's no way I'm giving that bastard my beautiful sapphires without a fight.

I can see there are about as many police here as there were people in the restaurant, so I know for certain I can knock them all out with one illusion. At least, long enough for me to run away.

Bennett speaks again. "You know, I was perturbed when I didn't receive my subsidy on time. As fate would have it, I ran into our friend John shortly after noon. He explained everything that happened between the two of you, with the sincere belief that everything you said was the honest truth." Bennett glares at John, who cowers behind the ranks of police. "There is no such Paladin as Sir Reginald. There is no law dictating the time at which a subsidy can be delivered. There has been no recent criminal activity from any Izendoran in the city. And if I'm not mistaken," Bennett scowls at me, "there is no such person as Marie."

I stare petrified at Bennett. I can't muster the willpower to do anything else. Why did John have to blab about my illusion to *him*, of all the wretched people in Cloud Summit!?

The chief continues, "John was heartbroken when I helped him realize you were to blame. Still, I wonder how you convinced him to believe such *illusory* things in the first place?"

I swallow hard again. Bennett is only a few feet away from me now, and I don't like the look on his face.

"What do you have in that bag of yours?" Bennett asks.

I say nothing. I start spreading my manas'ruh and establishing connections with the nearest policemen.

After a few seconds, Bennett flicks his chin at me.

Three policemen break ranks and come at me from different directions. Two of them grab me, and the third goes for the bag.

"No!" I shout, reeling in my manas'ruh and struggling against the police. I kick the man going for the bag just before he grabs the buckle to open it. Meanwhile, I establish connections with all three of them and make them imagine themselves bound from the neck down in chains.

They immediately stiffen and fall.

I look up at Bennett in time to see his black-gloved fist coming straight at me, and suddenly I'm flat on the ground.

I touch my face, which throbs with pain, and I realize my nose is bleeding.

I also realize my hat has fallen off, so my dark Sunophsian hair is now exposed for the whole realm to see.

Next, and far worse, I realize Bennett is opening my shoulder bag.

"Ugh!" I grunt, performing a kick-up. "Give it back!"

Three pikemen step forward to block my way with their weapons.

Stupid pikemen! I don't need to *physically* walk over to Bennett to screw his head off and reclaim my bag.

I stand there in mock helplessness as I stretch out my manas'ruh to connect with everyone around me, including John. By the time I achieve it, I'm wincing and trembling with effort.

No time to be creative; I'll just put them to sleep. I deliver the command, and everyone keels over as though dead.

I break the connections and fall to my knees, gasping for breath. That was much more difficult than the restaurant. I guess I didn't allow myself enough time to recover before trying a stunt like that again.

Well, now would be a great time for a well-earned nap at the hideout, yes?

"You will die. There is no escape."

Bennett's voice immediately follows the death-voice. "Ah, what's this you have?"

266

My heart lurches.

I look up to see Bennett still standing, and holding the Music of Marindel box. "This looks like the missing relic from Königheim. How kind of you to return it to me, I've been looking all over for it."

I don't understand! Why is Bennett still awake!?

Did I forget to put him out?

Out of all the people here, how could I forget the most important guy?

"You will die. You will surely die."

Bennett pulls out a handful of sapphires, allowing them to run through his fingers and back into the bag. "I'm glad to see you've kept my subsidy safe. Otherwise, how could I afford to keep Cloud Summit free of crime and vice?"

All right, Chief. Time for bed.

I prepare to establish a connection with him, and…my manas'ruh hits a wall.

Wait, what?

I try once more, but once again my manas'ruh comes up against an impenetrable force.

What's going on?

I focus all my mental energy into it. I imagine my manas'ruh condensing into the shape of a drill and forcefully ramming Bennett's mind for entry.

Still, I'm locked out, and this time the recoil gives me a headache.

"Agh," I mutter, rubbing my temples. What do I do now? What's with this guy?

"You will die. Surely you will die."

"Oh, what have we here?" Bennett pulls the wanted poster out of my bag and unfurls it. He reads the poster out loud. "The Illusionist. Experienced thief known to be affiliated with White Sand. Accused of murder. Very dangerous. Kill on sight. Fifteen thousand kron reward. Oh, and there's my signature." Bennett lets the poster fall to the ground and looks at me with a smirk. "At long last I've found you, Illusionist. And I bet you're wondering why I'm not slobbering on the ground with the rest of my men."

Panic overtakes my entire being as he speaks. I take a step back.

Bennett removes his cavalier to reveal a headband crowned with a bright orange topaz. "This headband is enchanted with the power to protect the wearer's mind from any and all outside attacks. I bought it recently in anticipation of our meeting." He puts his cavalier back on and places one hand on the hilt of his sword. "Now, Sunophsian scum, I order you to surrender immediately."

As I stare wide-eyed at Bennett's cruel face, I'm mortified beyond belief.

I'm going to be arrested!

No...I'm going to die!

I can't let that happen to me! I have to escape!

Leaving logic and reason behind, I sprint toward Bennett.

"Hmph." With a smirk, he steps toward me, tightening his grip on the hilt.

I know what he's planning to do.

When I'm five feet away, Bennett draws his sword with a powerful uppercut.

I dodge the swing and reclaim my shoulder bag, containing everything except the poster, in one fluid motion. Now behind him, I quickly close the shoulder bag, hold it firmly under one arm, leap over the group of sleeping police, and sprint as fast as I can down the street.

"Gah!" Bennett shouts. A second later, he whistles, possibly calling for backup.

It's no use, Chief. I'm on the run. And if any of your goons manage to catch up, I'll knock 'em out with an illusion.

I think I may just get out of this one alive.

A loud thunderclap shakes the air.

I turn down a side street toward downtown. That'll be a good place to lose any potential pursuers, what with the crowds and all. Even on this street there are a few people, hurriedly closing up shop before the rain comes.

My running shouldn't look too suspicious here. Others will probably think I'm running home to dodge the rain like everybody else.

"Make no mistake, you will not escape. My jaws close down upon you. Illusionist, you deserve to die, and surely you will die!"

Suddenly, I hear a horse whinny behind me. When I turn to look, I'm overcome with more fear than I've ever felt in my life.

Here comes Chief Bennett, mounted on his burly black steed like a harbinger of death, galloping at full speed after me.

I scream and pump my legs faster. There's no way I can outrun Bennett's horse! What do I do!?

There's an indoor shop up ahead on the right that's connected with another shop on the other side of the building, through which

Chapter 26: Broken

I can get to the main street of downtown. Bennett won't be able to chase me through there.

I reach the door just as the pounding hooves sound like they're about to crush me. I sprint through the shop, barely managing to dodge the surprised people inside, and I use my momentum to crash through the door into the next shop.

"Oi! What do you think you're doing!?" An angry man shouts as I stumble about, trying to regain my balance and continue running.

"Sorry not sorry!" I yell over my shoulder as I run out the front door.

Once on the main street, I turn right and keep running. The street is still full of activity, and it's much more chaotic now that most of the merchants are scrambling to tear down shop and move their wares indoors. It's hard to run at full speed with everyone in the way, but I'm agile enough to duck and dodge when necessary.

Bennett arrives on the street two blocks ahead. He looks around wildly and somehow finds me within the span of a second.

It's my hair.

It's my stupid black hair!

"H'ya!" Bennett urges his horse to charge down the busy street toward me. Everyone in the horse's path shouts and dives out of the way, while Bennett himself is hardly focused on who or what is in front of him.

His menacing eyes are locked on me.

No sooner did he locate me did I turn my back and flee in the other direction. I thought Bennett wouldn't be able to find or follow me in this crowded of an area, but as I've already concluded, my hair causes me to stand out in this sea of brownish-blond-haired Armavirans, and apparently Bennett would sooner trample civilians with his horse than lose a runaway criminal.

Two people are carrying a large wooden table right in front of me. I maneuver underneath the table, but unfortunately, I don't see the man with a wheelbarrow of desk clocks on the other side. I run into the wheelbarrow, causing it to flip over and spill its cargo. I tumble along with it and land among the clocks.

The clock man glowers down at me, his curly mustache bobbing up and down as he talks. "What is the meaning of this? Why don't you watch where you're— ah!" He jumps back as Bennett arrives on the scene, his horse trampling the ground all around me.

I narrowly avoid having a horseshoe print on my face.

Many clocks are not so lucky.

"No! Not my clocks!" The clock man shouts.

As soon as I'm able, I roll backward over my shoulder, springing up and away from the horse's aggressive hooves. Then I flee for the nearest side street.

"You can't run forever, witch!" Bennett growls as he maneuvers to give chase.

I'm painfully aware of the fact that he's right.

I avoid several more people before reaching the side street, and I begin searching for a narrow alley. Anything to get Bennett off that stupid horse.

A strange whirring noise comes from behind, accompanied by the ever-present sound of incoming hooves.

I sneak a glance behind me to see that Bennett has drawn a whip and is swinging it above his head in preparation to lash me with it.

I gasp and run faster. Where's an alley when I need one!?

"There is no escape!"

Intense pain sears my leg as the whip makes contact, ripping through my outfit and drawing blood.

I scream, stumbling and trying to keep from tripping. In spite of the pain, I run as fast as I can.

Bennett's horse gallops ahead and maneuvers in front to block my path. Meanwhile, Bennett hoists his whip and brings it down with a fierce crack. This time, it strikes and rips through my bag, causing the sapphires, coins, and other goodies I've collected to be scattered all along the street.

"No! No!" I cry, torn for a brief second by my fear of dying and distress over losing my stuff.

For the first time in my life, I decide *not* to go after the jewels.

What use are they to me if I die?

With that, I drop the shoulder bag and sprint back toward the main street.

The sound of Bennett's whip flying through the air quickly follows.

Intense pain across my back causes me to double over and tumble along the ground like a rag-doll. I land face-up, sprawled on the cold, hard stone. My vision is spotted and blurry. I groan and move to get up, but the stinging pain holds me down.

Lightning flashes across the sky as Bennett and his steed loom over me. The chief's darkly satisfied smirk conveys to my soul the truth I've been trying so hard to ignore until now:

I *really am* about to die.

"Rise to your feet," Bennett commands.

I obey, staggering and wincing.

Once my head is within his reach, Bennett grabs my hair and pulls me up toward him, almost managing to lift me off my feet.

I squeal helplessly.

Bennett sets his whip aside and draws his sword. He glares at me with condemning hatred and says, "You have polluted this city with your vile tricks and licentious conduct for long enough. Now your body shall rot in the gutter and serve as an example to your filthy Sunophsian cohorts that I will stop at nothing to smite the lot of you, one by one!"

I swear I can hear the death-voice speaking along with his.

"By the authority of King Alphonse V vested in me as the chief of police in Cloud Summit, I herby sentence you to immediate death!"

Bennett hauls me up by my hair and raises his sword in preparation to cleave my head right off.

Whimpering in pain, with panicked tears streaming down my face, I close my eyes. I accept my fate.

I deserve to die.

"Stop!" A powerful voice commands.

Silence.

I'm not dead yet.

"Chief Bennett, with all due respect, there are better ways to handle matters of justice in this fair city."

I know that voice.

I open my eyes, but because Bennett still holds my hair, I can't turn to see whose it is.

"Mind your own business old man," Bennett scowls. "It's my duty to uphold the law, and I will do so in every way I see fit."

No way.

The old man? The same one I just harassed and robbed? It can't be!

"Need I remind ye the law requires a fair trial to be given to every suspect arrested by the police force? Ye seem to have forgotten that since the Purge six moons ago."

Bennett growls incoherently.

"Put the lass down," the old man says.

Silence.

After what seems like a long time, Bennett sighs and releases his grip.

I collapse to the ground.

I feel the old man's presence as he kneels down beside me and places a hand on my shoulder. "It's all right, lass. I'm here."

I tremble at his words.

Why?

Why is he treating me this way?

Does he not remember who I am?

I turn my head to catch his gaze. His face is as calm and confident as ever, a deep ocean full of some mysterious hope I can't begin to fathom.

His words from earlier in the day return to memory: "Think about this conversation, Celine. Look at me, right now. Who of the two of us is *really* hopeless?"

I begin to sob. I can't help it.

"There there," he says, gently stroking my shoulder. He's careful to avoid the gash from Bennett's whip running across my back.

Why!?

I don't understand! I deserve to die; I know I do! Yet this man, whom I threw into the garbage not even two hours ago, has come to my rescue!

"Celine," he whispers, "do ye remember the lullaby yer mother used to sing?"

I shake my head.

The old man sings,

> *"Come, my child, let's sail the sea.*
> *Farther and farther we'll fly,*
> *To where skies are gray no more."*

The melody awakens something in my heart, some kind of distant memory. An intense longing for a life better than the one I know.

He continues to sing:

> *"Come, my child, how glad ye'll be.*
> *We will live, we will not die,*
> *In a land ne'er seen before.*

> *Come, my child, let's sail the sea.*
> *Don't ye cry, I'll tell ye why:*
> *There is life forevermore."*

Thud. Bennett has dismounted and stands over us.

"Step aside old man, or I will arrest you too."

He looks up at Bennett and says, "Only when I have yer word

that her life will be spared until every accusation brought against her has been confirmed in a fair trial."

Bennett hesitates for a second, his eyes darting about uncomfortably, before he bows his head and concedes. "Very well, old man. You have my word."

"Call me Jed." He stands to his feet and backs away from me.

"Chief Bennett!" The police captain I bumped into earlier approaches us with three other men. "Are you in need of assistance?"

"Captain Antoine, perfect timing. Apprehend this prisoner, clean up her mess," he gestures at the scattered goods from my bag, "and escort her to the Hall of Justice—"

"Don't forget her mind powers," Jed interrupts.

Bennett shoots an annoyed glance at Jed, but then clears his throat and says, "I will accompany you in case she tries to escape."

"Right away, sir."

The men surround and lift me to my feet, promptly cuffing my wrists behind my back. I have no willpower left to resist. Antoine secures an iron fetter around my neck with a chain attached, by which he'll be able to drag me around like a dog on a leash. He stays with me while the other officers go to pick up the coins and jewels.

I look earnestly at Jed in an attempt to beckon him closer. Thankfully, he understands the plea in my eyes and comes.

I ask with a trembling whisper, "W-why did you s-save me?"

Jed smiles. "Ye'll understand soon, lass. For now, remember everythin' I've already told ye."

Rain begins to fall as Jed speaks.

The police gather the stolen goods in one bag and hand it to Bennett, along with the Music of Marindel. After stashing them in a saddle bag, Bennett hauls himself up on his horse and says, "Come, let's make haste. I hate the rain."

At his command, the entourage of police escort me toward the Hall of Justice. I turn my head to look at Jed one last time as we depart. He's standing still, watching me with the most truly loving gaze I've ever seen.

This experience has left me broken in more ways than I ever imagined was possible. Everything I thought I was and everything I aspired to be has been thrown out and destroyed in the span of an hour. Even though Jed saved my life today, I know for sure I will be found guilty at the trial.

I still deserve to die.

27
The Seventh
Summer, 1419 AIE

~Connor~

WE ARRIVED IN Cloud Summit at noon. Excited and relieved to have finally made it to the big city, it didn't take us long to decide what to do first. Once we left our horses at a public stable, Jake insisted we follow his lead to the best street-side restaurant in town: The Big Fat Hen. There, we spent the remainder of the money given to us by the Willow Creek innkeeper on some of the best roasted chicken any of us have ever had.

I loved it overall, but I had major complaints about the side effects.

While some restaurant food can cause gas, bloating, diarrhea, nausea, and in some cases death, the food at The Big Fat Hen is another story. To put it plainly, it turned my head into a slimy roasted chicken, and it made Tarento's head into an adorable kitten head.

We were bewildered and helpless, but thank the King, it was all temporary. By the time law enforcement showed up, everything had gone back to normal. Tarento and Scourge were spooked by their appearance, but they seemed civil enough to me. After asking a few questions they told us we were probably victims of a certain "Illusionist" character they were trying to capture.

Remembering what Alpha Blue said about some Offspring of Sisera having psychic powers, I turned the interrogation on the police and asked if the Illusionist was an Offspring of Sisera. They affirmed my suspicion, but ignored the other questions and left the restaurant in a hurry.

Afterward, Tarento reminded me, "We're not going on a wild goose chase for an Offspring of Sisera, especially not one who's a wanted criminal. We need to find Jed, and we don't know how long that'll take."

Just as Tarento finished speaking, one of the restaurant chefs came and placed a folded note on the table, saying, "An old man came by this morning and told me to give this to you."

We all exchanged glances.

Khai tested the chef, "How do you know we're the right group?"

"He told me to find a Felid, an Izendoran, an Ibadanian, a Pythorian, and two Armavirans sitting together at the same table. It's a rare sight; doesn't happen much around here. Enjoy your stay." He gave us a friendly nod before returning to his duties.

Jake took the note and read it aloud: "Connor and friends, meet me this evening at the Bullfrog Tavern on the west side of the city. Yours truly, Jed."

"Yes!" I shouted. It was a secret hope of mine that we'd be able to visit a tavern in Cloud Summit, where we can meet all sorts of people and hear all sorts of stories. The tavern in the countryside had its fair share of exciting visitors, but a tavern in a major city like this is bound to have many more.

Jake asked, "I wonder if Jed'll treat us all to some ginger Tethysian brew?"

"If drinks are on him," Khai said, "I'll go for a Pythorian summer whisky."

Jake chuckled and nudged Khai with his elbow. "You don't mess around, huh?"

"Go big or go home," Khai said with a smirk.

By then a storm had hit, so we stayed inside The Big Fat Hen for half an hour longer to wait it out. Once the rain stopped, we left the restaurant.

Tarento, Jake, and Scourge gave the rest of us a beginner's tour of the most important areas of Cloud Summit. We saw the downtown sector, including the main street and Königheim Castle; we hurried quickly by the Hall of Justice, where Tarento didn't want to linger for long; and then passed through the poor sector where Tarento and Scourge lived last winter. According to them, it looked like things had improved significantly since their last visit. Though the area and its people were still living in poverty relative to the rest of the city, the atmosphere was more cheery than it had been, and some of the worn-down buildings were being remodeled. Amazed, Tarento said, "The Great King continues to protect this place, even after the Purge!"

Many people there recognized Tarento and Scourge and came to say hello, and we found ourselves giving a short summary of our quest several times on our way through. One family even invited us into their quaint dwelling place and served us a modest dinner of vegetable stew and crackers. The hospitality of these people, despite their living conditions, was incredibly humbling. We were all pleasantly surprised by how much they supported our quest and believed the Great King would guide us through to victory. It was hard to leave so soon, but we said our goodbyes and left the sector with our spirits high.

We arrived at the tavern just as the street lamps were being lit by the people who light street lamps for a living. I'm not sure what to call them. Street-lighters? Lamp-oilers? Lamp-lighter-uppers? Lantern folk? Brethren of the Lamping Guild? It's an important job; they must be called *something*! Without them, Cloud Summit would be impossible to navigate at night, and everyone would stumble and fall on the pitted cobblestone roads.

Oh, I know!

Light-bringers.

That's what I'll call them. I'm sure the name'll catch on if I sneak it into a good story.

Now, here we are at the Bullfrog Tavern, gathered at a large table in the center of the lively seating area. I presume Jed will be here any moment now.

As I've been reflecting on the day's events, Khai, Yoko, and Scourge have been playing a game of cards, and Tarento and Jake have been comparing their training experiences as the elite warriors of Felidae and Armavir respectively. I'd been listening to their conversation, but I must have zoned out for a few minutes. Now that I'm tuning in again, I notice they've moved on to a different topic: the consequences suffered by the Cloud Summit police after the Purge.

Bennett's right-hand man, Captain Giles, directly received the order to attack civilians and rallied other policemen to join him. He's the captain Tarento saw in his dream. Giles took the brunt of the blame for instigating the Purge, and he was shortly executed. Many of his men, depending on their involvement, were either imprisoned or executed. Bennett, unfortunately, received nothing more than a stern talking-to from Prince Oliver. Jake thinks Bennett was let off easy because King Alphonse favors him and believes he has no one capable to replace him.

Giles' position was filled by a police lieutenant named Antoine, who was on leave in Verdyth when the Purge took place. Since receiving the promotion four moons ago, Antoine's zeal to redeem the public opinion of the Cloud Summit police force has been evident. However, under Bennett's shadow, there's little he can do.

"You know," Tarento says, "I would promote any Paladin to be chief of police instead of Bennett. Paladins have the ideals of peace, honor, and chivalry drilled into their heads from the time they step foot in the Academy, don't they?"

"Yes," Jake replies, "but that doesn't mean they're always honorable. Many Paladins make fools of themselves when they think no one's watching. Take my brothers, for instance. I wouldn't trust any one of them to be the chief of police."

"Oh yes, I remember. Didn't your brothers say they were going to kill you if they found you in Cloud Summit again?"

"Yep."

"You don't seem too worried about it."

"If I had come alone, I'd be nervous, but now I have all of you with me! I'd like to see them pick a fight with me in the presence of my Samurai, electro, and huntsman friends. Let them try!" Jake laughs, placing one hand on Tarento's shoulder and another on Khai's, who is startled by the gesture and drops his cards face-up on the table.

"I *knew* you were bluffing!" Yoko says.

Khai groans. "Jake! I *had* this game!"

"Oops, sorry about that," Jake says with a nervous chuckle.

Meanwhile, a thought occurs to me: Jake's brothers aren't in Cloud Summit. I get his attention and speak as the words come to mind, "Your brothers are stationed in Eisenstadt at the border with Izendor, so we won't run into them during our stay here."

Jake blinks. "Well, that's certainly good news. Thanks for the tip!"

"I see ye've grown in confidence, young Seer," a familiar voice says. I snap my head around to see Jed standing next to the table, his deep blue eyes shining bright.

"Jed!" I exclaim, overcome with so much excitement that I wrap my arms around him and squeeze tight. I realize how much I've come to love and respect the old man since we parted ways in the countryside nearly two weeks ago. It's almost hilarious to recall how annoying I thought he was before.

"I appreciate yer enthusiasm lad, but I can't breathe."

"Oh, sorry," I let go of him and look at my friends, who by now have stopped everything and are watching expectantly. "Everyone, this is Jed. Jed, this is Tarento, Khai, Yoko, Scourge, and Jake."

"Hi Jed!" Yoko waves.

"Nice to meet you at last," Jake says, reaching across the table to shake Jed's hand.

Jed returns the handshake and says, "Forgive me for bein' late. I had a very eventful afternoon."

"Not a problem," I reply. "Here, take a seat. We saved you a chair."

"Thank ye lad," Jed says as he takes the seat next to me. "So, this is the band of heroes that'll journey to Meiro and challenge Jaedis the Sorcerer. I couldn't have picked a better team myself. What do ye think, Connor?"

"What do I think?" Great question. I look at each person gathered around the table.

Jake, the almost-Paladin.

Tarento, the fugitive Samurai.

Scourge, the electrokinetic prince of Izendor.

Yoko, the medic-in-training and the life of the party.

Khai, the huntsman, archer, chef, goblin-slayer, and probably many other things.

And me of course, Connor, the Seer and Master Storyteller.

I remember the adventures we've had since meeting in the Bayside Harbor shipyard: fighting the Felids, rescuing Tarento, training and sparring on the journey across Armavir, exploring the abandoned castle, fighting a flock of harpies, and a whole lot of storytelling.

Even though we've only been together for a short while, and despite our different backgrounds, personalities, and talents, it seems like we've already grown tremendously as a team. Our allegiance to the Great King of Marindel is the only thing we have in common, and it may very well be our most powerful uniting force.

I reply to Jed, "It was hard at first. A divine bearded man told me to start looking for beggars, because the best way to build a castle is from the ground up, so through a chain of events in the shipyard I met all of these guys. Well, Khai showed up late, but that's beside the point."

Yoko laughs and hugs Khai's arm. Khai kisses the top of her head.

"This isn't what I imagined our team would be like," I finish, "but given everything we've been through so far, I think we'll turn out all right."

"Well said," Jed replies. "The Great King certainly knows what he's doin', and ye're all diligently followin' his lead."

We look at one another warmly and proudly. Blimey, if I don't change the subject soon, I'm going to start weeping! "How about the homestead? Have you sold it yet?"

"Aye. Made it sound like beachfront property, what with Bayside Harbor a few miles away. I got twenty-five thousand krons for it."

"Twenty-five *thousand* krons!?" Jake, Scourge, Yoko, and I exclaim.

"That's unbelievable," Tarento says. He's the least fascinated of us all with material riches, but even he seems like he's struggling to hide his excitement.

"Jed, you're the best!" Jake says. "With that much money, we can buy top-quality equipment for our quest. Swords, armor, arrows, a tool bag, everything we need!"

"Yes, well—" Jed tries to speak, but he's interrupted by Yoko. "I can have a bow custom-made, just for me! I don't have to use Khai's enormous one anymore!"

Khai speaks next. "We ought to stop by a good potion shop. We'll need herbs and elexirs to keep us strong and healthy on the journey. Anti-poison is a must."

Jed is once again about to speak, but this time Tarento interrupts, "Do any of you know a place in Cloud Summit that sells Samurai equipment? I wonder if the Great King would be all right with me having Samurai gear again?"

"I think you *deserve* Samurai gear," Scourge says.

Yoko leans in close to Scourge. "What're you gonna buy?"

"Hm, I don't know. Something simple in case I find myself in close-combat. Maybe a dagger, nothing heavy."

Jake says, "You should find a weapon you can use with your electro powers, like a metal-hilted sword that can channel electricity. Then anything you strike will be electrocuted as well as cut through!"

"That'd be something," Scourge says. "Though, I'd probably still settle for a dagger."

"Lad," Jed nudges me and whispers, "I hate to be the bearer of bad news while yer friends are excited, but I don't have the money at this moment."

"Oh, that's all right," I say. "We won't do any shopping until tomorrow morning. Besides, a tavern is no place to bring a sack full of krons."

"It won't be that easy, lad."

"Why's that?"

"The money's been stolen."

My heart nearly stops. Everything in me comes to a skidding halt, and all I can hear is the echo of Jed's voice. I shake it out of my head and laugh it off before asking, "Sorry, could you repeat that?"

"The money's been stolen."

Tarento overhears him and asks, "Excuse me, what'd you just say?"

"The money's been stolen," Jed replies for the third time.

Tarento and I exchange horrified glances. I ask Jed, "How in the land of Armavir did the money get stolen!?"

"What got stolen?" Yoko asks.

Jed looks at everyone and says once again, "The money's been stolen. Earlier this afternoon I was mugged by the Illusionist, and she took it."

We're all silent for a moment, knowing full well that it was this same Illusionist character who made a laughingstock out of us at The Big Fat Hen.

"What are we going to do?" Yoko asks. "We *need* that money! We can't just show up at Jaedis' front door unarmed and unprepared!"

"Yoko's right," Tarento says. "We'll have to track her down and get it back. Jed, do you know where she might have gone?"

"She ran into the clutches of Chief Bennett, and now both she and yer money are bein' held prisoner at the Hall of Justice."

I've never seen Tarento look so frightened.

I try to be positive. "Well, that doesn't sound too bad. Jed can walk on in there and tell the police his money was stolen by the Illusionist, and they'll give it back. Right?"

"No," Tarento replies, hiding his face in his hands. "It doesn't work that way."

I'm about to argue, but Jake says, "Tarento's right; the police will be of no help in this matter. We'd need solid proof that the money belonged to Jed before it was taken, and even then, we'd be at the mercy of Bennett's...well, lack of mercy."

"All right," I reply, "Why don't we talk to the land grant distributors tomorrow morning? Maybe they can help."

"It's a start," Jake agrees.

"Jed," Tarento says, "You must have seen this coming. There

must be something you can tell us to lead us in the right direction. Something, *anything!*"

Jed leans forward, his eyes betraying no hint of triviality. "Trust me, lads. Ye must do everythin' I tell ye, no matter what. Know without a doubt that I hear the voice of the Great King. What we're about to do is for the glory of the Kingdom of Marindel. Ye must trust the King. Really, truly *trust* him." Jed's gaze lingers on Tarento, who shifts uncomfortably. "Do ye understand?"

We all nod.

"Good. I have somethin' to show ye." Jed reaches into his bag and pulls out a rolled parchment. He unfurls it and lays it out on the table in front of us.

It's a wanted poster for the Illusionist.

"Wanted: The Illusionist," Tarento reads out loud, "Experienced thief known to be affiliated with White Sand. Accused of murder. Very dangerous. Kill on sight. Fifteen thousand kron reward."

Jed pulls out a pen and draws a line diagonally across the poster. "Captured! No longer a threat! Now in the custody of Chief Bennett." He then flips the parchment over and lays it out flat, revealing a detailed sketch of a woman's face. "This, my friends, is the one they call the Illusionist."

We lean in close to look. Unlike the sloppy caricature of a scowling criminal a wanted poster usually features, this sketch looks like it was done by a professional artist. The Illusionist's face is beautiful and her eyes are captivating. She doesn't look angry, or even dangerous for that matter. Dare I say it, she almost looks friendly.

"Wow," I say. "She's prettier than I imagined."

"It's a very good sketch," Tarento agrees. "How did you find it?"

"Yesterday evenin', when I was out for a stroll, I saw a clear image of her face in my mind's eye. Then I walked past the poster, and the Great King told me to sketch her on the back. I took the poster and spent most of the night drawin' her. After I sold the homestead this afternoon, the lass mugged me. And then she was arrested."

"What exactly are you getting at?" Jake asks.

"The Great King is very interested in her. He wants to rescue his daughter, but time is short. The Serpent has nearly succeeded in destroyin' her for good."

"Wait, hold on," Tarento furrows his eyebrows. "The Great King is calling this criminal his *daughter?*"

"Aye."

"But...that doesn't make any sense. Melody is the Great King's daughter, I understand that. I also understand those who follow the Great King can call themselves his sons and daughters. But the Illusionist? She's a criminal! How can *she* be a daughter of the Great King?"

"Let me explain. Do ye remember Scourge's story?"

Scourge tenses and looks at me. I shrug and whisper, "Jed knows everything. Don't worry, he's harmless."

"Yes," Tarento replies, "but what does that have to do with it?"

"Have ye ever thought about how many innocent people Scourge killed before he came to rely on the Great King?"

Scourge begins sinking in his seat.

Tarento glances at Scourge for a moment and then says, "No, but that's beside the point. Ruslan forced Scourge to do those things. It wasn't his fault."

"He could have resisted. He could have let Ruslan kill him instead, but but he didn't. Did Scourge do the wrong thing?"

We're all silent.

Jed continues, "Accordin' to the most literal definition of the Great King's ideal of justice, harmin' innocent people is *always* the wrong thing, even if the perpetrator is coerced into doin' so unwillingly."

"Can you please stop?" Scourge squeaks, now almost invisible under the table.

"I'm not sayin' this to shame ye," Jed replies, disarming his fear with a merciful gaze. "The Great King doesn't hold yer actions against ye any longer. He has forgiven ye, and now ye have been set free from that burden of guilt. Now, bear with me a wee bit longer." Jed now addresses all of us, "Even while Scourge was doin' these things, the Great King didn't abandon him. He saw the potential for good in his heart, and he longed for his son to turn and choose him as his protector and provider. As we know, that moment came when Scourge stood up to Jaedis and fled from Meiro. The Great King certainly did not disappoint in his promise to deliver Scourge from that accursed land."

Jed pauses, eyeing each one of us as we ponder his words. Then he asks, "Have ye caught on yet?"

"I'll give it a go," I say before clearing my throat. "It sounds like the Great King saw Scourge as his son even while he was harming people in the dungeon. So, it shouldn't offend us that the Great King sees the Illusionist as his daughter even though she's a criminal. He wants her to turn to him, but she hasn't yet."

"There ye go!" Jed smiles. "The same is true for each of ye: the Great King saw and loved ye before ye came to know him."

"All right," Tarento says with a sigh. "I think I'm starting to get it. Even in his commitment to justice, the Great King's kindness is greater than we can fathom. But how is that supposed to help us now? The Illusionist has been incarcerated for a very good reason. How will rescuing a dangerous criminal who the Great King apparently loves help us on our quest?"

"I have much to tell ye," Jed replies, "but I cannot tell ye now."

"Why? Why not?" Tarento asks, impatiently gripping his hair.

"It's somethin' every member of yer team must hear."

Tarento looks at us and says, "Everyone pay attention! Jed's going to say something important."

Jed chuckles. "Calm down lad, there's no need to fret. The seventh member of yer team is not yet present. I cannot tell the Great Story until *all* of ye are ready."

"The Great Story?" I ask, eyes widening.

"Aye," Jed nods with a smile.

A fiery swell of excitement rises in my heart. What is the Great Story? I have to hear it! If there's a Great Story out there, I *must* add it to the collection of amazing stories I'll have when I'm as old as Jed, traveling around the realm visiting taverns, telling stories, and sending people on adventures.

My thoughts almost cause me to miss Tarento's question: "Jed, how are we going to find a seventh person? Do we even *need* a seventh person? You just said our team is great; that you couldn't have picked a better one yourself!"

"Hmm," Jed smiles. "Why don't ye sleep on it?"

"But—" Tarento is about to argue, but Jed cuts him off. "I would like each of ye to spend time tomorrow askin' the Great King for clarity. I believe he'll say somethin' to each of ye to help us move forward. Take the poster with ye. This is a delicate situation, so I must warn ye: be *very* sure that what ye hear is from the Great King."

"I feel like I've learned *nothing* so far," Tarento says, once again placing his head in his hands.

"Ye think too much. Don't just listen with yer mind. Listen with yer heart."

"Jed is right," Jake agrees, taking the wanted poster and rolling it up. "We'll heed his advice and think through it together."

"But where will we stay the night?" Scourge asks.

"I have that covered," Jed says. "I got a hotel room for all of ye:

a traveler's suite with six small beds and a kitchen. I booked it for a full week."

"Wait, hold on," I say. Despite my excitement about the hotel room and the beds, his latter comment throws me off. "Are you suggesting it's going to take a *whole week* to sort this out and get back on the road?"

"Perhaps. Take it one day at a time, and don't worry too much."

After a bit more small talk and a round of drinks courtesy of Jed, we depart from the tavern and head for the hotel. It's located downtown just a block away from the main road. In the lobby we part ways with Jed, who goes to his own room. Exhausted from the events of the day, we hardly tarry before turning in for the night.

28
Personal Retreat
Summer, 1419 AIE

~Connor~

THE NEXT MORNING, after enjoying a complimentary breakfast at the hotel, we decide to spend the day doing what Khai described as a "personal retreat."

"Go somewhere on your own, do something you like to do, and collect your thoughts away from other distractions," he said. "If we want to focus and hear what the Great King has to say, that's the best way to do it. We'll meet here at sundown to share what we learn."

None of us have any objections to the idea, so we set off on our separate paths.

It's my first time in Cloud Summit, the largest city I've ever visited. I could go anywhere, see anything! The opportunities are endless! Blimey, why do I only have until sundown to do all the exploring I wanna do!?

Unable to choose between the myriad of options, I decide to go to the first place that comes to mind: The Bullfrog Tavern.

With an excited grin, I stroll inside the tavern and sit down at a two-person table. There I begin to people-watch.

It's not as busy during this time of day as it was last night, but there are still enough people here to keep me entertained. I can already identify people of many different trades, but in order to stay focused, I filter out the normal-looking people and keep my eyes peeled for the shady characters in the room:

The two bald guys gambling in a corner.

The scruffy old man trying to catch flies between his hands.

The aristocratic women standing at the bar, whispering and giggling.

The bartender himself, a massive Bothnian man with a braided red beard, chugging a mug of beer.

The three Sunophsian young men sitting at a table, smoking cigars like they own the place.

Sunophsians.

The Illusionist is Sunophsian, which I've inferred from her involvement in White Sand, so these men might know a thing or two about her. The question is, how do I approach them? It needs to be as natural as possible.

I get up and head over to the bar. As I'm perusing the menu, the bartender sets his mug down firmly and slurs, "'Yello there, small fry. Whattya like to drank?"

I give him a strange look. 'Small fry,' huh? I brush it off. I have to act natural. "How much for your, uh...Pythorian summer whisky?"

"Three blics for a single shot, an' four for a double."

"Ooh," I wince. "Expensive stuff. All right, how about...you know what? I'll take a glass of water."

The bartender snorts a chuckle. "Y' came o'er here for a *glass of water*? Tha's rich! What ya need is a big one a'these!" He picks up his mug and takes a huge gulp.

"Er... no. I came to the tavern to meet and talk to people. But, I just so happen to be broke, so I'll settle for a glass of water."

The bartender roars with laughter. "Ah! Tha's rich! Yer a strange one, small fry!"

"Small fry?" I ask with a furrowed brow. Once is fine, but twice? Hmph! This means war! I hadn't planned on making a show of myself, but this bartender is in no condition to take me seriously, so theatrical tactics may have to win the day. I glare at the bartender and shout with an over-dramatized Western Armaviran farmer's accent, "Who are you callin' small fry, you drunk, drink-mixin', big-nosed, beefy-armed imbecile!?"

Everyone nearby turns to look at me.

The bartender fumbles for words. "I-I'm sorry, I din't mean it, I—"

"Then mind your words, 'big fry.' I may be small, but I've got one *hell* of a fighting spirit!"

"Oooh," one of the aristocrat ladies says.

She's totally into me. But I'm not doing this for the ladies.

Chapter 28: Personal Retreat

The bartender says, "I din't mean t'offend ya, small—er, sir."

I narrow my eyes. "*Smaller* sir? Do you think that just because you're bigger than everyone else, you have the freedom to call people *small* and get away with it? I don't find that very funny."

"Oh, no sir! I was a'merely correctin' myself. You're not *so* small, y'know. Kinda like, more'f an average sorta' man. How's 'at?" He finishes with a big gulp of beer.

"An average sorta' man," I repeat, shaking my head. "I don't appreciate the way you talk down to me, but I suppose I'll let you off easy...*if* you gimme a glass of whiskey on the house."

"Oh yes, a'course! Pythorian summer, ah? Comin' right up!" He sloppily pours a shot of whiskey and slides the glass across the bar toward me.

I catch it in one hand without breaking my narrow-eyed stare. "Now, make sure you remember this day. Never call a person shorter than you '*small fry*' ever again, you hear me?"

"Yes, yes a'course," He says, nodding vigorously.

"Good. And quit drinking on the job." I nod once, turn around, spit on the ground, and stride away from the bar.

I can hear the ladies whispering and giggling amongst themselves, which makes me feel all tingly inside as if I really *am* a dangerously attractive, shady drifter from another land.

But, again, I'm not here for the ladies.

I meander over to the table where the Sunophsians are sitting. I could see in my peripheral vision that they watched the whole thing. As I walk past, I make eye contact with them and shake my head, saying, "Can you believe that oaf?"

The Sunophsians stare back at me as if I'm the one they can't believe.

I slow to a stop as I internalize their cruel stares. With my pride and confidence recoiling into the inner depths of my soul, I point to an empty chair at their table and peep, "Is anyone sitting here?"

They continue to stare, completely unfazed.

After a few painfully awkward seconds, I set the glass on the table, sit in the chair, scoot myself in, and twiddle my thumbs.

The Sunophsians might as well be statues.

"So," I grab the whiskey, "What are you guys up to?" I lean back and take a swig before setting the glass firmly on the table.

Fire scalds my mouth and throat.

Blimey! That's some really strong stuff! I have a hard time preventing my face from contorting as I swallow the amber substance.

One of the Sunophsians puffs his cigar and says, "You're not from around here, are you?"

"No sir, no I am not," I say, still gagging on the whisky.

"Drop the act," a second Sunophsian says. "What do you want?"

Dang it. They're on to me.

Where are my Seer juices when I need them?

I endure another drink of the whiskey to stall for time. As I look at them, the man who told me to drop the act stands out more than the others. He has a neatly-trimmed black beard and a forest-green tunic. As I ponder this, it occurs to me that this man is an Offspring of Sisera named Abdeel.

I open my mouth to tell him I know his name, but the Great King says, "*Don't tout this information yet; ask him about the Illusionist. Keep your Seer's gift hidden for now.*"

Heeding the King's words, I say, "Well, honestly, I'm curious about how the Sunophsian community in Cloud Summit is feeling about the capture of the Illusionist. I know many of you probably looked up to her."

Abdeel glares at me. "You don't know a damn thing about us. What makes you think you can just walk in here and stick your nose in our business?"

"*The gang insignia,*" the Great King says.

Oh! How could I have forgotten?

"I may not know you guys personally, but I have a few friends who do," I say, taking out the piece of cloth and showing it to them.

Their composure changes at the sight of the Blue Fox insignia, but Abdeel narrows his eyes and says, "Where did you get that? You're not a street kid. I'd be able to tell if you were."

"I met the Blue Foxes in Bayside Harbor; they fled there after the Purge. I helped them defend their new turf from a group of Samurai."

"You?" Abdeel asks. "*You* helped defend them against *Samurai?*"

"Yes," I nod. "Yes, I did."

"How? Entertain us."

"That's not important right now. Would you please answer my original question?" I can tell by the look on their faces that they don't remember what the question was, so I ask them again. "How do you feel about the capture of the Illusionist?"

"How do we *feel?*" Abdeel scoffs. "What, are you a shrink or something?"

"Maybe. Come on guys, this is important."

"You wanna know how I feel? All right. I'm angry as hell!"

Chapter 28: Personal Retreat

"Angry at Bennett?" I ask.

"No!" He pauses. "Well, yes, but not just him. I'm angry at her too." He keeps his voice low, but rage emanates from every word. "She blew her own cover. Now we're next on Bennett's hit list, and it's *her* fault! If she cracks and tells him where to find us, I'm gonna go to the Hall of Justice and take off her head before the guillotine does!"

I notice Abdeel revealed himself to be a member of White Sand through his use of 'we' and 'us.' I already figured as much, but a confirmation is always welcome. Treading carefully, I ask, "Do you really think she'd sell you out?"

"I don't think she would, no. But the chief will do anything to squeeze it out of her. He's been looking for us for years with no luck, and this is the closest he's come. He's not going to give up."

"I understand." I take a sip of whiskey.

It's growing on me a little bit.

The pause gives me the time I need to come up with another question, this one more direct. "Do you think, if it comes down to a fight, that White Sand will prevail against Chief Bennett and his police force?"

"Oh, absolutely!"

"How so? Is White Sand quite numerous?"

"No. What we lack in numbers, we make up for with our wits and maneuverability. Plus, a group of us have abilities that will give us an edge over Bennett and his men."

"I'm assuming those abilities didn't help the Illusionist very much."

Abdeel sighs. "As much as we hate to admit it, Bennett becoming smarter with every passing season. The more he learns about us, the more he's able to strike when we least expect him. My brother always says the glory of White Sand is contained in our ability to remain one step ahead. Many of us fear we're beginning to lose that step. And it makes us *very* angry."

I glance at the other two Sunophsians sitting on either side of Abdeel, and true to his word, they look like they hate everything in sight.

"I understand," I reply. "If you don't mind me asking, what are you going to do about it?"

Abdeel takes a long puff his cigar. "None of your damn business."

I try to discern with my Seer's gift if there's anything I should know about their plans, but nothing comes to mind.

"But, trust me," Abdeel smirks and stands. "You'll know it when you see it." He places a hand on each of his companions. "Let's go."

"Leaving so soon?" I ask.

"Good talk, shrink." Abdeel leaves the tavern with the others closely on his heels.

I stay at the table and slowly drink the whisky while pondering everything I learned from the White Sand members.

~Tarento~

I LOVE THIS idea.

Finally, a chance to spend hours on my own without social obligations or distractions.

As we parted ways at the hotel, Scourge had asked, "Tarento, where are you going?"

I had something in mind, but I didn't want him to follow me, so I said, "I'm not sure yet. You?"

"Well, I really wanna go to the poor sector. I know we're supposed to go to separate locations, so I want to make sure you don't have the same idea. If you want to go there, I don't mind. I can go somewhere else."

I smiled. "The poor sector's all yours."

Scourge beamed. "All right! See you at dinner, then!"

After he rounded a corner, I began walking toward my location of choice.

Now here I am, standing at the very top of the second-highest tower in Cloud Summit, surpassed only by Königheim Castle.

Perhaps it's a Felid thing, but there's something very calming and thought-provoking about climbing to the top of a building. While I don't care for tall buildings in and of themselves, I appreciate the views they have to offer.

From my current vantage point, I can see the entire city. I can also see the fog-blanketed valley which surrounds Cloud Summit on every side, and both the northern and southern bridges which connect the city to primary trade routes. Beyond the valley, also on every side, majestic gray mountains tower much higher than I currently stand. They're striped with crystal-white glaciers that glitter as they reflect the light of the ascending sun.

I breathe in the crisp mountain air, relishing my distance from the noisy city below. I could stay here all day.

At least, that is, until I have to relieve myself.

I made sure to relieve myself before climbing up here, so I think I'll manage.

But what if there's a thunderstorm? Then I will certainly have to climb down. Thankfully, in that case I'll see the storm coming from a long way off and have plenty of time to move.

I take several deep breaths and clear my mind of all trivial thoughts. Part of me doesn't want to think about the conversation with Jed last night. It was overwhelming, but I know I must use this time to ask the Great King for clarity.

I begin to feel peaceful as the breeze blows across my face.

Finally, I ask, *"Can you explain what Jed was saying last night in the tavern?"*

"What are you most concerned about?"

What kind of question is that? Can't we start from the very beginning?

I bite back the instinctive reply. With another deep breath, I articulate my thoughts. *"I'm still not sure why you care so much about the Illusionist. I think I understand why you consider her your daughter; Jed described that vividly enough. But what does that have to do with us? What are we supposed to do about it? She stole the money we need to buy supplies, and then she got herself arrested. It'll be difficult to get the money back from Bennett, and what's more, you want us to rescue her somehow. You don't mean for us to rescue her from prison, do you? She deserves to be there. Breaking her out would make us all criminals as horrible as she is, in Bennett's eyes at the very least!"*

"Do not worry, my son," The Great King's mighty whisper stills my quickly-beating heart. *"I do not mean for you to break her out of prison. You're also correct that the Illusionist has appropriately reaped the consequences of her actions. However, I'm not finished with her yet. I see her, I know her, and I love her. Rather than rescue her from prison, I wish for you to rescue her from the voice of the Serpent. You must tell her about Marindel and about my love for her."*

"Is it really that simple? Will she believe me if I visit her in prison and tell her? Or will it be all be vain, like when I stood before Lord Zetsumei?"

"She is not yet ready to receive what I have to tell her. You must wait for the proper time."

"All right." With a sigh, I ponder these things as I gaze upon the beautiful landscape.

Perhaps an hour later, Great King speaks again. *"Heiban will arrive in the city today."*

I frown. *"As if this situation needed to become any more complicated."*

"The coming days will be hard for all of you. I need you to trust me no matter what happens. It's no coincidence that Jed said it over and over again last night. I will tell you again: trust in me. If you lose sight of me and what I'm doing through the events of the next few days, the Serpent will succeed in scattering you and your companions, and your quest will end in failure. You, above all, must be vigilant. Do not be discouraged. Soon you will understand everything about the Kingdom of Marindel that you know is missing. Be strong and brave, my son. I will always be here to strengthen your heart when you're afraid."

I ponder the Great King's warning for another hour before I can bring myself to reply. *"What must I do, my King?"*

"Listen to Jed and do everything he tells you. The knowledge of what will soon take place is too much for you or any of your companions to bear, but to him I have revealed everything. Return to the hotel in the evening and join him in encouraging the others to trust me."

"Hai," I reply. *"I choose to trust the unseen. I will trust you, my King."*

I AM THE first to arrive at the hotel entrance as the sun sets. In spite of my fear that someone might've gotten lost or into trouble, the others arrive within the next few moments. We go together into the hotel and purchase dinner with money Scourge received from the poor sector, ironically enough. Over our meal, we begin to share the information we gleaned from the day.

"I asked a few friends in the poor sector about the Illusionist," Scourge says. "They're all terrified of her. One person told me about his brother's wife's uncle's best friend's sister's fiancé, who works as a stonemason. One day he hallucinated that a pack of goblins came and beat him up, and the next thing he knew, he was on the ground and all of his belongings were gone."

"Sounds terrifying," Jake says.

"And it's not just the Illusionist," Scourge continues. "Since the Purge, White Sand has become the dominant gang in Cloud Summit. With no rival gangs to oppose them, they've evolved into an organized crime syndicate. Many people fear Sunophsian refugees because they might be members of White Sand."

"But not every Sunophsian refugee is a White Sand member," I say.

"Exactly," Scourge agrees. "There are a handful of Sunophsians in the poor sector who are just as fearful of White Sand as everyone else, but they're also burdened with a fear of being arrested or otherwise discriminated against because of their ethnicity."

"Question," Connor speaks up. "Did you ask your friends how they feel about the Illusionist being captured?"

"Yeah. Some were glad, but others were nervous. They think Bennett will be inspired by this victory to make more arrests. While it'd be good to have more White Sand members behind bars, they're not easy to catch. And they won't hesitate to frame innocent Sunophsians if it'll throw the police off their trail."

"Savage," Khai says.

"Indeed," I agree.

"All right, my turn!" Connor jumps in. "I learned a bit about White Sand today as well. You'll never believe this, but I ran into a few White Sand guys at the tavern this afternoon."

"What?" Yoko says, eyes wide.

"Yes, I sure did. There I was, sitting in the tavern minding my own business, when all of a sudden, there they were! Three of them sitting at a table, smoking cigars. It was so suspicious that I just *had* to check it out."

I can't help but chuckle. Everyone is captivated by Connor's story, despite how uneventful it sounds so far. I can't blame them; Connor has a knack for making any story sound interesting.

He continues, "So I said to the bartender, 'I don't appreciate how you talk down to me like that, but I'll let you off easy if you give me a glass on the house.' I took my whiskey and strode all the way up to the White Sand guys. I looked them in the eyes, and I said, 'Can you believe that oaf?' And then they said, 'Yeah man, what a moron, way to put him in his place. Sit down, have a smoke with us!' And I gladly obliged."

Jake chuckles. "Did they really say that?"

"Uh..." Connor's eyes dart about. "All right, maybe not. They didn't say anything when I walked up, and it was really awkward, so I just sat at the table anyway. They were a tough crowd until I showed them the Blue Fox insignia."

"Huh, that worked?" Jake says. "Did they think you were a gang member?"

"No, no. I told them I knew the Blue Foxes and helped rescue them from Samurai. It didn't convince them to trust me and answer my questions, but the main guy said some interesting things."

"Like what?" I ask.

"He's angry," Connor replies. "They're all angry. Abdeel, the main guy, said he believes Bennett will interrogate the Illusionist to figure out where the rest of them are hiding. He was confident they could defeat the police in a direct confrontation, but he's afraid White Sand is losing their preemptive advantage."

Jake asks, "Do you think they might do something drastic in response to the arrest?"

"I asked him something to that effect, but he just said, 'None of your damn business' and 'you'll know it when you see it,' and he got up and left. I think they're planning something big."

"What about your Seer's gift?" I ask. "Have you discerned anything Abdeel didn't tell you?"

"Not much. All I got was his name; he definitely didn't introduce himself to me. The Great King told me not to blow my cover as a Seer, so I played along with whatever Abdeel told me. He doesn't know I know his name."

"That's probably for the best," I reply with a nod. "Great job listening to the Great King."

Connor perks up at my encouragement. "Thanks!"

"Can I go next?" Yoko asks, raising her hand. "I found something really cool!"

"What'd you find?" Khai asks.

"A really neat shop! No, really guys, you're not going to believe this. It's called the Exotic Goods Hub, and it has stuff from every kingdom in the realm! I think we'll find useful items there for our quest, like this!" Yoko pulls out an object and holds it up for us to see. It looks like a key made out of polished jade.

"A key?" Connor asks.

"Not just any key," Yoko says, eyes shining. "It's an enchanted jade key! There isn't a key-lock in the realm it can't open!"

"Really?" Jake and I ask together.

"Yup," Yoko says while pocketing the key. "Or at least that's what the shopkeeper said."

"Wait a second," Scourge speaks up. "Did you buy that?"

Great question. How did Yoko get an item from the Exotic Goods Hub if she didn't have any money? I hope she didn't steal it.

"Nope. The shopkeeper gave it to me in return for a promise to come again soon and buy stuff."

"Could be a counterfeit," Jake says. "Have you tried it yet?"

"Nope."

Jake shrugs. "I suppose we'll find out soon enough. Good find Yoko, we'll keep that shop in mind once we get the homestead money back."

"Woohoo!" Yoko cheers.

Something seems off to me about Yoko's shop. It makes no sense that a shopkeeper would give Yoko something that valuable for nothing more than a promise to return. Any real key that can open any lock in the realm is probably worth thousands of krons at the very least.

What if the shopkeeper who gave Yoko the key wasn't actually the shopkeeper? What if the supposed shopkeeper who gave Yoko the key stole it himself to give it to Yoko?

But why would anyone want to do that?

I turn to Yoko, about to ask for more information, but I realize Khai has already begun sharing about his personal retreat. I was so deep in thought that I missed the beginning, so I shelve my concerns and tune into what he's saying.

"...after walking around and enjoying the park, I found a bench near the fountain and sat down. That's where it happened. There were many birds around the fountain, but I found myself entertained by six sparrows eating birdseed on the ground. A seventh sparrow flew in from elsewhere in the park and landed nearby. Seeing the birdseed, it hopped over to join. However, the six sparrows reacted defensively and chased it away. So, the seventh sparrow flew to the top of the fountain and sat by itself. A moment later, a hawk swooped down and carried it off to a tree. The six scattered at the sight, but soon after, they regrouped and began attacking the hawk. As they kept diving and pecking, the hawk lost interest and fled. The seventh sparrow was injured, but not dead, and the six sparrows stayed near to protect it. As I thought about this, the Great King said, 'You must stand together as a team of seven, or when the enemy comes, you will be scattered to the winds.'"

"Wow," Connor breathes. "You got all that from watching a few birds in the park?"

Khai nods. "The Great King speaks to me through nature. I'm most at peace while observing the simple ways of the realm. It's during those times when I feel closest to him."

"That's wizard," Connor replies, gawking at Khai.

Khai nods, and then looks at all of us and says, "I believe we need to be open-minded about our seventh team member. The Great King knows who it is, and we shouldn't do anything to hinder him or her from joining us. If he or she happens to be in trouble at the talons of a hawk, then we must band together and charge to the rescue."

A horrible thought occurs to me while Khai is speaking.

No, please, no...

"*Great King,*" I ask silently, "*Is the Illusionist our seventh team member?*"

"Hey, guys," Connor says while I'm still relaying the question, "I just realized who our seventh team member is. I don't know how we didn't realize it sooner, but I have a strong hunch it's the Illusionist."

The others are silent.

I hope, just this once, that Connor's Seer's gift is wrong. Imagine the implications! She's in *prison* for crying out loud! It can't happen! It's impossible!

Scourge is the first to break the silence. "I think Connor's right. That would explain why the Great King is so interested in her."

No, Scourge! The Great King is interested in her because he wants her to know him, not because he wants her to join us! Despite the strong emotions flaring up in my soul, I can't bring myself to vocalize my objections.

"I believe you're right as well," Khai says.

No, not Khai too!

I thought I told everyone to forego the idea of finding an Offspring of Sisera for our team. None of those criminals would ever want to join us, and to go looking for one would almost certainly put us in danger. To make things worse, our Offspring of choice happens to be behind bars, and for good reasons to boot. I'm so busy internally panicking, I hardly notice Yoko voice her agreement. As Jake is beginning to speak, I try hard to focus on listening to him.

"I definitely think we may be on to something, but before we jump to any more conclusions, I need to share what I discovered on my walk today. I went all over the city, revisiting all my favorite places: the jousting arena, the park Khai mentioned, the downtown market, and a few others. I didn't get any shocking revelations from the Great King, but if it's true that the Illusionist is supposed to join us, then the small bit of news I have will put us in a very tight spot."

I'm seething with anticipation. I can't bear it. "What is it, Jake? What did you hear?"

"I passed by the Hall of Justice and overheard two people talking. They were members of the jury for the Illusionist's trial. Today, she was declared guilty. Tomorrow, she will be executed."

We are all silent.

Jake continues, "She had the king's missing relic with her when she was caught. She was an accomplice on the night it was stolen."

The silence continues.

Everything within me burns with resentment toward the Illusionist. She's responsible for the deaths of hundreds of people, and the displacement of many hundreds more! How could we even *think* about letting such a person join us!?

"Good evenin' lads!" Jed's voice startles me.

"Jed!" Connor says. "I was beginning to wonder if you were coming."

"Aye, sorry I'm late. By the looks on yer faces, I'd say I've missed somethin' important."

"Very," Jake replies. "Putting our intel together, we've discovered White Sand is the dominant gang in Cloud Summit, but their reign of terror is endangered by the Illusionist's capture. They're planning something big in retaliation, but we don't know what. We've also come to believe our seventh team member will be the Illusionist, although she's set to be executed tomorrow."

"We have to do something!" Yoko says, and then lowers her voice to a whisper, "Do you think we should break her out of jail?"

I elbow Yoko and give her a stern look that says, "absolutely not."

She recoils from my gaze and shifts about uncomfortably.

"Hmm, what a peculiar position we're in," Jed hums. Then he looks me straight in the eye and says, "Tarento, ye haven't shared yet. What's on yer heart?"

I stare back at Jed. 'What's on my heart?' I feel like I'm about to explode! I have nothing good to say right now! I recall what the Great King told me, and I reiterate bluntly, "The Great King wants us to tell the Illusionist about his love for her, Heiban will be arriving in Cloud Summit tonight if he hasn't already, and we need to trust the Great King no matter what, or like Khai said, we'll be scattered and our quest will end in failure."

Everyone stares at me.

I'm too overwhelmed to try and read everyone's facial expressions or ask for their opinions, so I look down at my half-eaten food.

Jed says, "What Tarento said is correct. The Great King loves the Illusionist very much, and he has entrusted us with the duty of tellin' her about him before it's too late."

"What must we do?" Khai asks.

"Heed my words carefully," Jed begins. "Jake and Connor, tomorrow mornin' I'd like for ye to come with me to the land grant lads in the marketplace. We'll work on buildin' a case to get our money back from the police. Meanwhile, I would like Khai and Yoko to go to the Hall of Justice and wait there. As—"

"Are we gonna break her out of jail?" Yoko whispers excitedly.

"Shh," Khai quiets her, much to my relief.

"I think we should," Yoko mutters under her breath.

Jed, unfazed by the interruption, continues, "Tarento and Scourge, I would like for ye to rise early in the mornin' to visit the Illusionist and tell her about the Great King."

I blurt, "But the Great King said she's not ready yet. She won't listen. It's hopeless."

"Careful, Tarento," Jed says. "Don't let fear and anger blind ye. It won't be an easy task, but ye must trust me and go."

"I-I, uh..." I can't stand the position Jed is putting me in right now. I know I have to trust him and the Great King, but *why* do we have to worry about the Illusionist at all? *Why* must I tell her about the Great King tomorrow morning if she will most certainly ignore me? It's not going to change anything; she'll still be destined for the guillotine. I try to rein some degree of control over my emotions, and I heave a deep sigh of defeat. "All right. Sure."

"Very well," Jed says, eyes beaming. "Go to yer rooms and get some rest. Ye'll need every moment of it."

After parting ways with Jed, as we're heading to our room, I pull Scourge aside and say, "Please let the others know I've decided to go for a walk. I'll be back later tonight."

"But Jed told us to rest," he says, looking at me with concern.

"I know, Scourge," I say, trying hard to hide my troubled state. "But I can't rest until I've spent some time alone. I promise I'll come back soon. Don't worry." I force a smile.

"All right," Scourge says with a nod. "Hurry back!"

"I will," I smile again before heading toward the exit of the hotel. As much as I wish I could be with my companions right now, I can't expect them to understand how upset I am about all this. I have to work things out with the Great King alone, and then hopefully everything will be all right.

"Psst," Yoko, kneeling beside Scourge's bed, pokes his shoulder.

Scourge groans and rolls over.

"Psssssst," she pokes him again.

Scourge rolls to face Yoko and opens his groggy eyes. "What...?"

"I have an idea," Yoko says, eyes gleaming.

"Can't it wait till morning?"

"Nuh-uh," Yoko draws close and whispers, "I don't think the others will like it. It's a bit, uh...dangerous, I guess."

"What do you mean?"

"Come with me," Yoko stands up. "Let's talk along the way."

"We have to *go* somewhere?" Scourge moans.

"Shhh!" Yoko holds a finger over her mouth. "Just come on!"

"Fine, all right," Scourge mumbles, rolling out of bed and fumbling with his boots.

Yoko tip-toes over to Jake's bag, takes the wanted poster, and stuffs it in her own bag. Once Scourge is ready, she whispers, "All right! Let's go get our seventh team member!" And she flits out of the room.

Scourge is clueless, but he follows nonetheless.

Tarento is still missing, and they leave without rousing any of the others.

29

The Trap

Summary, 1419 AIE

~Celine~

'*COME, MY CHILD, let's sail the sea.*
Farther and farther we'll fly,
To where skies are gray no more.'

I remember.

My mother's face. So calm and peaceful, yet forlorn and weary.

The rocking of a ship at sea.

The memory came as I was thrust into a prison cell by Bennett and his men, mocked and spit upon before they left.

> '*Come, my child, how glad you'll be.*
> *We will live, we will not die,*
> *In a land ne'er seen before.*'

I remember.

My first sight of this land. Green and gold on the horizon.

The surge of hope and joy.

The memory came as I spent that night weeping all alone, wishing I had my mother's warmth to comfort me.

> '*Come, my child, let's sail the sea.*
> *Don't you cry, I'll tell you why:*
> *There is life forevermore.*'

Chapter 29: The Trap

I remember.

Summer days in Armavir. Freedom from the tyrant at last.

The highest high, from which one can only descend into the depths.

The memory came as I was taken to my trial. It was all a whirlwind.

'Life forevermore?'

My mother died that first winter.

The pain. The agony. The loneliness.

The memory came as I stood before the judge. The only word I heard was the last: *Guilty*.

Shaama took me in.

I was raised by White Sand. They provided for me in my earliest days.

As I matured, they taught me how to survive.

I learned to exploit others before they could exploit me.

I discovered my psychic powers and used them to my every advantage.

I ran and hid from my weaknesses, my fears, my disappointments, and my overwhelming sense of despair. My facade was so perfect that for years I had forgotten about the lonely little girl crying on a dark winter night for her mother who would never answer again.

But now, I remember.

Here I am.

Everything I worked so hard to build has been taken away.

'Life forevermore?'

There can be no such thing. All I know is this:

Tomorrow, I am going to die.

Here I sit, curled up in the dark stone corner of my cell. A fetter secures my ankle with a four-foot chain to the back wall.

I don't know what time it is; there are no windows here. For all I know, tomorrow is today, and in a few moments, I will meet my demise. I certainly deserve it.

I hear noise noise on the other side of the black iron door.

Men talking. Laughing.

I lift my tear-stained face as the door is unlocked and opened. I lower my gaze with dread as Chief Bennett enters with a wooden chair.

I know what's coming.

"Why are you so frightened?" He taunts. Nothing that man says can ever be perceived as relieving or kind.

He sets the chair in the middle of the cell, facing me, and sits. The guards on the other side close the door and lock it.

I cannot bring myself to look at him.

"I'm disappointed," Bennett says. "I spent so long looking for you, Illusionist. Yet now that I've caught you, I fail to understand why I worried myself so. Look at you! You're so pathetic, groveling in a corner. It *almost* makes me want to let you go."

I hate him.

"Pitiful," Bennett scowls. "Absolutely pitiful. It's no wonder you were the first of your gremlin friends to fall. Soon, I will catch them too. It is inevitable."

No, it's not. You have no idea who you're messing with.

"Illusionist, I beg you," Bennett leans in close. "Make this easy for both of us. Tell me, where is your hideout?"

I have no motivation to tell you anything, scumbag.

After I'm silent for a few seconds, Bennett repeats more sternly, "Where is it? Tell me now."

Or what? Are you going kill me? Pfft.

I whisper, "You have no leverage."

Bennett stands abruptly and kicks me in the ribs. While I'm disoriented and gasping in pain, he shouts, "Where is the hideout!?"

I say nothing.

He kicks me again. "Tell me!"

During his second kick, I realize his boots are iron-toed. No wonder this hurts so badly. When I have breath enough to reply, I look at him and say, "Y-You'd never find it...even if...I told you."

Bennett picks me up by my hair, eliciting a shriek and forcing me to my feet. He holds his face close to mine and says, "Tell where the hideout is, and perhaps I'll keep you alive long enough to prove I can."

I spit in his face. "Up yours."

Bennett releases my hair, and before I know what's happening, his fist meets my face and sends me sprawling back into the wall. I collapse to the ground and hold my face, whimpering in pain. I can already feel it swelling.

"Believe me, witch! I will find plenty of leverage to make you talk if you insist on being stubborn!"

I peek through my fingers to see Bennett looming over me with the chair over his head, ready to bludgeon me with it.

Just as I squeeze my eyes shut and brace for impact, the door to my cell opens. A voice calls, "Excuse me, Chief! Sorry to—"

"Can't you see I'm busy!?" Bennett slams the chair on the ground.

"Ah! I, uh, I'm so sorry Chief, but believe me, this is very important."

"On with it, then!"

As they converse, I cower in my dark, stone corner and look away.

"Three men from Felidae are here to see you. They're waiting in the main hall."

"Felidae?" Bennett pauses. "What could they possibly want?"

"They insist their business is personal and refuse to speak with anyone except for you."

Bennett heaves a heavy sigh. "This'd better be good, then. For their sake." He picks up the chair and leaves the cell, shutting the iron door behind him.

He's gone.

I sigh with bittersweet relief, sobbing as everything around me goes dark.

"Celine," a female voice calls me.

"Leave me alone," I groan.

"Celine," the voice is gentle and sweet.

A pinprick of realization pierces my heart.

"M-mother?" I open my eyes.

Standing before me, where Bennett had stood an unknown amount of time ago, is the most beautiful woman I have ever seen. Her radiance illuminates the tiny cell.

I rub my eyes, which have long since grown accustomed to the darkness, and stutter, "A-are you...my mother...?"

"No, dear friend," the woman replies. "But I knew your mother very well."

"Oh..." I trail off, looking down at the ground.

"Celine," the woman calls me again.

"What?" I sniffle, not looking at her.

"You have a beautiful name. Do you know where it came from?"

I've never thought about it before. My brothers used to make fun of me for being the only Offspring of Sisera in White Sand with an Armaviran name. I don't care for it very much. I shake my head in response.

"Your mother gave it to you while she was still in Kharduman.

Celine means 'heavenly light.' To her, you were the embodiment of her faith that there was still good in the realm. She longed to give you the opportunity to discover that goodness and live a better life in a free and peaceful kingdom."

Brief memories of my mother and the boat ride to Armavir flash across my mind.

"You were only four years old when your mother fled from the palace of Sisera. She risked everything to cross the barren desert and secure a forbidden voyage from Sunophsis to southern Armavir."

"So what? She died only a few moons after we arrived."

"Yes," the woman's voice drips with compassion. "She did everything she could to make sure *you* made it safely to Armavir. She knew her life was as good as gone, but until her dying breath, she sacrificed everything to give you freedom from the tyranny she knew in Sunophsis."

"But...but *why*? It's all meaningless. I'm about to die now; she only delayed my death by a few years. She died for...*nothing*!"

"Hush," the woman says, crouching down to place a hand on my quaking shoulder. "Through the faithfulness of your mother, the Great King saved you from Sunophsis. Now, through the faithfulness of one man, the Great King will save you from Armavir."

"Wh-what do you mean? Who is the...the..." I can't bring myself to mention the Great King.

The woman smiles. "You will see soon enough, dear Celine. Be strong and wait for him."

Before I realize what's happening, the woman fades into the darkness of the cell. "Wait!" I cry out, but it's too late.

She's gone.

I'm not sure what to make of any of this, but it doesn't matter. Even if I knew who that ghost-lady was and why she felt it necessary to visit me, it won't change anything.

I'm still going to die.

Just as I curl up on the floor to wait for any wink of sleep I can get, I hear noises on the other side of the door.

Scuffling.

Quiet, muffled voices.

They're coming closer.

I mentally prepare myself for the worst. I bet Chief Bonehead is coming back to finish throwing his chair at me. Maybe this time he'll bring a metal chair. Ooh, it makes me quiver. He'll say, 'How's this for leverage, you dirty witch?' And I'll scream and say, 'Oh, damn it, Chief! Metal chairs are my greatest weakness! I promise, I'll tell you everything!'

Bullshit.

Someone is fiddling with the lock on the other side of the door. They're taking a long time, as if they're trying to pick it.

My heart skips a beat.

Someone's trying to pick the lock!

Have my brothers come to rescue me!? I can't believe it! It's too good to be true!

I sit up and look at the door just as it swings open.

I see two figures. Two short and unassuming figures.

They quickly enter the cell and shut the door on themselves.

What...?

"Okay, Scourge," one of them, a female, says. "Hold a fire up to her face."

I'm blinded by orange-yellow light as a fire ignites mere inches away. I recoil and cover my eyes. "Hey! Stop it!"

"Whoa," the female gasps. "She's so beat-up I can't even recognize her!"

"No kidding," the other figure, who by some strange sorcery is holding a fireball in his palm, studies me intently. "Bennett wasn't messing around when he caught her."

I squint at the two figures. "Who are you, and what are you doing here?"

"I'm Yoko," the girl says, "And this is Scourge. We're here to rescue you!"

Scourge shushes her.

"Oh! Right," Yoko whispers. She then repeats, "We're here to rescue you!"

"Are you crazy?" I blurt. "How did you get in here? Why are you here? Who *exactly* are you?"

"We'll explain more later," Yoko says, taking out a small green object and walking toward me.

"Don't touch me!

"Shh!"

"I'll scream."

"Don't scream," Yoko whispers as she kneels down next to me. "Just relax."

I watch in gradual bewilderment as Yoko inserts the object into the keyhole of my fetter. The object flashes with green energy, and Yoko turns it clockwise. The fetter swings open.

My jaw drops.

That's got to be the niftiest lock-picking trick I've ever seen.

"You're free!" Yoko whispers. "Come on! Let's get you out of here!"

I slowly stand up. My legs are wobbly and stiff from crouching for so long, and all of my wounds are aggravated by the movement.

Yoko scurries over to the door and stands on her tip-toes to look out the small barred window. "I don't see any guards. Now's our chance!"

"Are you crazy?" I blurt. "What the hell do you think you're doing?"

"Rescuing you, duh," Yoko says, rolling her eyes. "Weren't you listening?"

I look at Scourge. He shrugs and says, "She's good at rescuing things. She knows what she's doing."

I glance at the fire floating a couple inches above Scourge's palm. This is all so strange; I might as well be dreaming.

Wait!

I recognize him!

He's the Izendoran kid from The Big Fat Hen! The one with the Seer and the tacky-animal-skins guy and all those other crazies! And the peppy girl! That's her!

I gasp in horror. "What's going on here!? Who are you!?"

"Shh! Come on, we're going!" Yoko says, grabbing my hand and pulling me out the door.

I'm so confused, I can't resist.

We emerge into a cramped stone corridor lit with wall lanterns. Down the corridor both ways are many more iron doors, behind which are presumably cells like mine.

How did they know which door to open to find me?

No matter. Nothing makes any sense right now.

I begin pinching myself as I follow Yoko and Scourge down the left corridor. When we reach the end, I notice two prison guards unconscious on the ground. A strange smell lingers, as if something burned.

I point at the guards. "Did you...?"

"Scourge did it," Yoko whispers proudly. "Don't worry, he didn't kill anyone. He just zapped 'em unconscious."

I look again at the guards. "Zapped, huh?"

"Yup," they both nod.

I pinch myself harder.

We go through the next door, down a few corridors, and up a flight of stairs, passing more 'zapped' guards as we go. When we reach the top of the stairs, we freeze as we hear voices on the other side of the door in front of us.

"Now, what?" I whisper. I wonder what insane trick these weirdos will think of next.

"Scourge," Yoko looks at him. "You don't suppose there are any empty barrels in there, do you?"

"Could be," Scourge shrugs. "But the real question is, can we get to them before anyone notices us?"

I grimace. "What are you talking about?"

Yoko speaks matter-of-factly as if it's the most normal thing in the realm. "On our way here, we snuck past guards and watch-towers by hiding in overturned barrels and walking in them when no one was looking."

I can't believe my ears.

Why am I being rescued by children?

"All right, you two," I say. "We won't be needing barrels to escape. Just hang tight."

I extend my manas'ruh beyond the door to connect with the guards in the next room. Three of them. I happen not to be in a creative mood, so I put them to sleep.

At the sound of the guards slumping to the ground, I say, "Let's go."

"What'd you do?" Yoko asks.

"Put them to sleep. That's all." I open the door and the three of us advance through the next room.

We continue through the maze of rooms and corridors that makes up the Hall of Justice's prison wing. As we go, I become more alert and confident. The dazed fear that crippled my mind in the prison cell begins to recede.

I almost bbegin to believe I might actually escape.

We ascend a flight of stairs, and Yoko makes us stop in front of the door at the top. She whispers, "Okay, now we need to be extra careful. This door leads to the courtyard. We have to cross it using the barrels so no one will see us. We want to reach the double-doors on the far side. Then we'll cross through the court room, then the main hall, and then we'll be free."

I nod, swallowing my strong dislike of barrels. After the bank robbery, it was because I spent too much time crouched in a barrel that I almost got arrested. I don't believe I'll ever be comfortable crouching in a barrel ever again.

Yoko opens the door and peers through the other side. After

looking this way and that, she waves for us to follow and slips through.

Scourge and I follow.

I vaguely remember this courtyard from when I was being escorted to and from my trial earlier today. The ground level, paved with granite, is surrounded on every side by colonnades, and above the colonnades are two levels of balconies. Higher still, watchtowers preside over every corner, each manned by several guards. The moon casts an eerie white light into the courtyard, making it unfortunately very bright for those of us who wish to remain hidden. We'll have to lurk in the shadows of the colonnades to cross the courtyard unnoticed.

"Oh, no!" Yoko whispers.

"What?" I turn and look, but I instantly frown. Yoko is staring at two barrels sitting against the wall.

"We only have two barrels, Scourge! We didn't bring a third one for her!"

While Yoko speaks, the death-voice says to me, "*You have all fallen into my trap. You will surely die.*"

I sigh, dismissing the death-voice, and whisper a reprimand, "We don't need barrels! We just need to stay in the shadows and be quiet!"

Just then, the door behind us opens, and two policemen emerge. They see us right away, and their faces turn ghostly pale.

Aw, I'm flattered to see how much they fear me.

With a little smirk, I establish mental connections with them. But one of them shouts, "She's escaped!"

I put them to sleep, but too late.

Guards on the watchtowers shout, "Look, down there! It's her! Sound the alarm! Call for backup!"

"Now what do we do?" Scourge asks.

"Give up?" I suggest. I know *my* situation won't get any worse now that we're caught.

"No!" Yoko shouts. "We're so close, we have to try!"

Bong! Bong! Bong! The alarm bell begins to ring.

Shouts echo across the courtyard, accompanied by intensifying sounds of tramping boots and clinking armor. Glimmers of torchlight dance on the balconies as guards and police come streaming out to meet us.

"Run!" Yoko shouts, sprinting down the colonnade toward the double-doors on the other side.

Scourge and I follow suit.

Chapter 29: The Trap

Arrows rain down upon us from the balconies across the courtyard. The pillars of the colonnade provide some cover, but not enough.

We keep running.

Just as we're about to reach the doors, they swing open to reveal six pikemen. They step forth and brace themselves to block our escape.

Anxiety rising in my heart, without breaking stride I extend my manas'ruh toward the men in our path and deliver a sleep command. In my haste I only succeed in putting out four of them.

A second later, Scourge zaps the two remaining men with tendrils of lightning emanating from his fingers. They writhe and babble incoherently before falling unconscious.

"Hm, not bad," I say with a curt nod.

"You guys! Look!" Yoko shouts, eyes wide with horror. Over a dozen guards are running toward us from all sides of the courtyard, brandishing their weapons.

"No, don't look," I say as I sprint for the double-doors. "Run!"

I don't check to see if Scourge and Yoko are behind me. If I wait for them to follow, we'll be caught for sure. Instead, I choose to believe that whatever smarts they used to find and free me from my cell will help them keep up with me as I flee.

My body is in great pain—all of my gashes, bruises, joints, bones, and even my guts, for all I know. But my heart is racing, and my blood is pumping. I have all the adrenaline I need to push forward for my escape.

We're in the court room now. It's dark and unlit, but not for long. One of the doors on the left side opens, and torch-bearing guards with swords rush in single-file.

"That door!" Yoko says, pointing at an exit on the far side of the room. "Go through that door!"

I run for it, gearing my mind for an all-out assault on anyone who tries to come through it before I get there.

Something snares my ankles, and very suddenly, I fall flat on my face.

I hear the guards cheer.

I try in vain to stand. Whatever tripped me has tangled my legs together. As I turn to find out what it is, Scourge throws a fireball at the ground between me and the incoming guards, causing them to skid to a halt and shout in alarm.

Yeah, I'd probably react like that too if he did that to me.

During the distraction, Yoko scurries to my side with a dagger and cuts the ropes entangling my legs. I see now that I had been tripped by a bolas.

Once free, I spring to my feet and run the rest of the way to the door.

"Scourge, come on!" Yoko says behind me. "There's too many of— Ah!" She yelps.

I whip around to see what happened.

She's been hit with an arrow in her thigh. She won't be able to run anymore.

"Yoko!" Scourge runs back toward her while hurling another fireball at the incoming guards to keep them at bay.

I notice more men are coming in through the door we entered from. Our enemies are multiplying, and we're running out of options.

I could probably still escape if I left Scourge and Yoko here. The guards would be preoccupied detaining them, and I'd be as free as a bird. That's what I would've done several days ago, before any of this ever happened. Now, guilt consumes me at the very thought of abandoning these kids, especially after they just helped free me from the bolas.

I can't escape without them.

I won't.

Several feet away from the exit, I crouch behind a wooden counter to use as cover. Then I establish a mental connection with Yoko and cause her to feel and believe as though she hasn't been struck with an arrow in the thigh. I give her a shot of courage and determination to hopefully keep her moving long enough for us to escape, despite the reality of her serious leg wound.

Yoko jumps to her feet and shouts, "Run! Come on guys, run!"

Yes! It's working! I turn and head for the door.

I hear Scourge doing something with lightning behind me, and our pursuers gasp. I hope he's running after us, as well as distracting the guards.

Just before we reach the door, arrows begin flying past us again. I fling the door open and shove Yoko through. Then Scourge runs through, and I go last. An arrow clips my arm before I leave the room, but I swallow the pain and ignore it. I have enough wounds trying to bother me already.

Without looking back, the three of us sprint down the final hall toward the entrance of the Hall of Justice. This one is very large, having vaulted ceilings with windows casting rays of moonlight down upon us. Blue, violet, and gold banners featuring the Armaviran coat of arms hang from the walls and ceiling across the entire length of the hallway, and our steps echo on the polished marble floor as we close in on our freedom.

I hear the guards and police shouting and pursuing us a couple dozen feet behind. But at this rate, they will not catch us.

There's no way.

When we exit the Hall of Justice, we'll be on my turf. I can find the darkest and most obscure alleys for us to hide in where they'll never find us.

"There is no escape," the death-voice says. *"The entire realm is my turf. All is lost for you and for those who seek to challenge me."*

I have no time to react to the death-voice.

Three dark figures drop down from the ceiling and land between us and the exit.

I send my manas'ruh forward to put them to sleep.

Before I get a hold of them, the central figure performs a couple hand signs and points his palm at me. A gust of wind throws me back, causing me to tumble on the ground and land face-up. All my wounds are searing from the impact.

Scourge runs ahead, spawning a fireball and throwing it at the central figure.

The figure shields himself with his cape, appearing to take no damage. One of the other figures attacks Scourge with a flurry of jabs that causes him to go limp.

"Not again," Scourge slurs as he falls.

"Oh, no!" Yoko says, gaping at the figures. "Not *you* guys!"

They stand proudly while dozens of guards surround us. More police come in through the Hall's entrance, adding to their number.

There's no escaping now.

I sever the connection I had made with Yoko. She immediately looks down at her leg and falls to the ground. "Oww…"

The central figure steps forward, walking into the moonlight and allowing me to make out his features. He's a Felid warrior, judging by the outfit, and he has a noticeable scar on his forehead.

These must be the Felids who came to see Bennett while he was interrogating me. Perhaps they've been hired as mercenaries to do his dirty work.

That's bad news for White Sand.

The Felid looks down at us, his eyes lingering on Scourge and Yoko. A smirk spreads across his face. "Well, this makes things *very* interesting."

30

The Visitor

Summer, 1419 AIE

NEBIOTH AND MISHAM race down a torchlit corridor of the White Sand hideout.

"We should have been there," Nebioth says. "We could have protected her. Now, things are only going to get worse!"

"Auntie told us clearly enough," Misham says between breaths. "She didn't want to risk any more of us getting caught."

"It's not fair," Nebioth growls. "Our archers were no match for those Samurai! If *we* had been there, we'd have given them a fair fight!"

"Calm down, brother. A few hours ago, we had no idea there were Samurai working for Bennett. I'm sure Auntie will send us to take vengeance on them soon enough."

"How will that work with tomorrow's plan? It's all hands on deck. We're spread thin as it is, and now we have *Samurai* working against us!"

"Hey, let's just ask Auntie what the new plan is, all right?" Misham smirks. "Soon, we'll be drenching the streets of Cloud Summit with the blood of our enemies. It's too late for any Samurai to stop us now."

Nebioth and Misham slow to a walk as they round a corner and approach the treasury. The sound of an unknown voice causes them to stop and listen.

The two Offspring look down the remaining twenty feet of the hall. The treasury is at the dead-end, and through the gaping entrance they see Shaama and a tall, hooded figure talking together. Their voices are too quiet to make out.

"Have you ever seen that guy before?" Nebioth whispers.

Misham shakes his head. "Never."

"Teleport over there and eavesdrop on them."

"What? Why *me*?"

"Your teleportation doesn't make any noise. If we walk any further down the hall, they'll hear us coming and change the conversation before we get there."

Misham groans. "Fine. But if Auntie's just talking about how much she misses our old man, you owe me a keg."

"Fine." Nebioth grins. "If it's anything but that, *you* owe *me* a keg."

"Hey, no fair!"

"Go on!" Nebioth shoves Misham forward, and he disappears.

Misham appears behind an ornate vanity which is half-buried in a massive pile of coins. He peers out to see Shaama and the strange visitor standing at the foot of the pile, only a dozen feet away. The first thing Misham notices is that the visitor is not human. He must be eight feet tall, featuring dark gray skin, black eyes with bright yellow irises, and a ridge of scales along his jawline in the style of a mutton-chop beard. His exotic red and purple robe covers every other feature of his body.

Misham cowers behind the vanity, hardly able to summon his own breath. "*What is that thing!? And what's it doing in our hideout!?*"

"...but it's no concern of mine," Shaama says. "I have everything under control. Stick around past noon tomorrow, and you'll see for yourself."

The visitor's voice is smooth but dark, "I don't doubt your abilities, lady Shaama, nor does my master. I believe the note made everything clear enough."

"Why didn't your master deliver the message himself?"

"There is another being in the city who would sense his presence and jeopardize our efforts. My master thought it best to send an enforcer in his place."

Shaama cackles. "After all these years, you gave up your place in King Sisera's court for a position as an enforcer?"

Misham smirks. "*Ha! She mentioned Sisera after all. That keg is mine!*"

"I love my new line of work," the visitor says with a glimmer in his eye. "If Sisera desired a horde of monsters to do his bidding, I might have stayed. But alas, he is content with his progeny."

"The Offspring of Sisera are more powerful than any monster," Shaama says with a boastful grin.

The visitor matches Shaama's expression. "Oh? If you're so powerful, why did you ask *me* for help all those years ago?"

"You know very well why. But I'm not the girl I was back then. Age has taken my vigor, but my mind is sharper than ever. Tomorrow, I will conclude my father's legacy. All of Sunophsis will hear of it and rejoice! Then, I will finally have the recognition I deserve."

"Very admirable, and I wish you the best of luck." The visitor smiles. "But, do not forget it was *I* who gave you the Glimmerbeast. I have every right to take it out of you if you don't agree to our terms."

"Oh, all right. But since you've come at such an inconvenient time, we'll be performing *our* plan first. Then, we'll eliminate those followers of the Great King." She grins and clasps her hands together. "If they survive our triumph, that is."

"I'm pleased to hear it. I'll return soon to check on your progress. Farewell." The visitor disappears in a wisp of shadow.

Misham teleports back to Nebioth in the hallway. He whispers, "Aha, you owe me a keg!"

Nebioth ignores the comment and places his hand on Misham's shoulder, beginning to walk forward. "Act natural. Don't mention the visitor at all."

The two of them walk into the treasury. Nebioth says, "Auntie, we have news."

Shaama turns to face them. "What is it?"

"Three Samurai foiled the rescue attempt. All of the archers are dead, and Celine was recaptured. The decoys were also caught."

"Excellent," Shaama grins.

Nebioth and Misham exchange glances. Nebioth asks, "You're pleased, Auntie?"

"Certainly. I've been observing the situation with my Farsight. I did not expect Samurai to be involved, but they will be of some use to us."

"What would you like us to do?" Nebioth asks.

"The Samurai are here to find one of their own; they don't *really* care to destroy us. If we find their fugitive first and give him over to them, they'll leave us alone. Nebioth, you're in charge. Kill him swiftly; he *is* dangerous."

Nebioth nods. "It will be done."

"What about Celine?" Misham asks. "Who will rescue her?"

"No one, dear. You see, with the increased security Bennett will have at the Hall of Justice, our objectives will now be much easier. We need not waste our time and resources on another vain rescue attempt. Celine is doing exactly what she ought to be doing: drawing Bennett's attention away from our true target."

"But she'll die!" Misham says, clenching his fists.

"A death of honor," Shaama says, her eyes glimmering. "Run along, now. Our triumph is nigh."

"Come on," Nebioth says, placing a hand on Misham's shoulder.

The two of them depart from the treasury, but not before Misham teleports behind Shaama to pickpocket the note given to her by the visitor.

31
Anointed
Summer, 1419 AIE

~**Connor**~

"**C**ONNOR," KHAI'S VOICE pulls me out of my dream.

I groan and roll over. I was about to finish harvesting the final swath of barley in our field, and my father was going to reward me with an amazing dinner after the day's hard work.

Before I have a chance to doze off again, a gruff hand grabs my shoulder and rolls me onto my back. "Connor! Get up!"

At the urgency of his voice, I shoot up into a sitting position. As I rub my eyes, dismissing my dreams of farming grandeur, Khai crouches next to the bed and looks intently at me. Once the sleepiness is gone and my vision is clear, I see the unsettled look on his face. I've never seen Khai this worried before. I ask, "What's happening?"

"It's an hour after sunrise. Tarento, Scourge, and Yoko are all missing. Jake doesn't know where they went, and neither do I."

I yawn, taking a moment to process Khai's words. I vocalize the first guess that comes to mind, "Maybe they've gone to the visit the Illusionist like Jed asked them to?"

"Are you sure? Is that your Seer's gift at work?"

"Uh…" I didn't specifically try to tap into my Seer's gift. "No, I just thought—"

"This is serious!" Khai says. "Tarento and Scourge might have gone to visit the Illusionist, but Yoko wasn't supposed to go with them. What's more, Yoko couldn't possibly have left so early in the morning without waking us up. You know how loud she is!" He takes a trembling deep breath. "Please, see if you can tell where they went using your Seer's gift."

"O-okay, uh…" Despite being frazzled by Khai's urgency, I focus on my inner Seer to discern where our missing friends might have gone.

"Anything?"

"N-no," I shake my head.

Khai heaves a deep sigh. "This can't be good."

Jake enters the room and says, "The front desk clerk hasn't seen them. Neither have the kitchen staff. They couldn't have passed through the lobby."

Khai stands up and begins to pace. "This isn't good. This is *not* good."

Jake looks at me and asks, "Connor, you didn't see anything?"

I shake my head. "Right now I know as much as you guys do."

"We have to find them," Khai says. "We have to."

"How?" Jake asks. "Cloud Summit is enormous. They could be anywhere!"

I optimistically suggest, "Why don't we hang out here for a bit? Maybe they'll come back soon."

"No!" Khai shouts. "Do you not understand? Three of our companions are missing, and none of them let us know where they were going or when they would return. This isn't like them! This isn't like *her!*"

It's disquieting, I'll admit. Even when Yoko left Khai to join our quest, at least she left him a note. I begin pacing the room as well, thinking out loud. "Jed told Tarento and Scourge to go early in the morning to the Hall of Justice to tell the Illusionist about the Great King. If Yoko wasn't a part of the equation, it would be sensible to say that's where they went. But Yoko *is*, in fact, a part of the equation, and that means either she disobeyed Jed's orders and went with them, *or* all three of them went somewhere else and got into trouble."

"You know," Jake says, "Tarento wouldn't have allowed Yoko to go with him and Scourge to the Hall of Justice. He's not one to encourage disobeying orders."

"That sounds right," I agree. The more I think about it, the more shady it all seems, and the more I begin to understand Khai's urgency.

Where in the land of Armavir could they have gone?

Suddenly, Tarento enters the room, followed by Sylva, the tree nymph.

Immaculate timing, if I do say so myself.

The three of us look at them and are stunned by the grief and terror on their faces.

"Tarento?" Khai asks.

Tarento swallows hard before announcing, "Scourge and Yoko tried to rescue the Illusionist. They failed, and now they're set to be executed alongside her. *Today*."

My heart drops like a rock.

"What!?" Khai thunders. "But...how...why...!?"

"Were you there?" Jake asks. "Did you get away? Tell us! What happened?"

Tarento heaves a trembling sigh before telling the story, "I went out last night after talking with Jed, as you know. I was reclining on a rooftop sifting through my troubled thoughts, and then I must have dozed off. The next thing I knew, the alarm bell at the Hall of Justice was ringing. I had a feeling the Illusionist was involved, so I jumped the rooftops to get there and have a closer look. The Great King told me to stop a few buildings short, and for a good reason. Heiban, Ibara, and Kaze were all there. They'd just piled five bodies in the middle of the street, and they went into the Hall of Justice. Shortly after, the bell stopped. I couldn't bring myself to move after that; I never saw them leave the Hall.

"At dawn, I watched from my hidden location as several guards came to remove the bodies in the street. I overheard them talking. The bodies were White Sand archers, thought to have been waiting in ambush to help the Illusionist finalize her escape. Now, here's the truly horrifying part. They mentioned the Illusionist was released by an 'adolescent girl' and an 'electrokinetic boy,' and with the help of the Samurai, both were captured with the Illusionist." Tarento takes a deep breath, having not stopped for a proper one during his entire discourse. "Sylva found me and confirmed everything. One of the policemen accidentally released her from the acorn, and Yoko told her to get help."

All of us are speechless.

Scourge and Yoko are in prison?

For trying to rescue the Illusionist?

What came over them? What were they thinking?

"I can't believe this," Khai says. "I know how much Yoko enjoys setting creatures free, and people too. But this? This *can't* be! Why would she...risk her life...?!"

"There's more," Tarento says grimly. "Chief Bennett and a few of his men came at daybreak to speak with the guards and have a look at the White Sand bodies. Bennett declared the Illusionist and her accomplices will be publicly executed today. He ordered his men to heighten security in the surrounding area, and he sent a courier to Königheim to ask for Paladin assistance. Once they left, we hurried back here as quickly as we could."

Khai shakes his head incredulously. "Is Bennett so blind? What makes him think executing an Ibadanian girl and an Izendoran boy will have any effect on deterring White Sand?"

"It sounds like they were framed," Jake says. "How else would White Sand have known to stage an ambush outside the Hall?"

"Well, no matter how it happened," Tarento announces, "Clearly, neither White Sand nor our companions counted on the involvement of Samurai. My pursuers have allied themselves with Chief Bennett, so now we must take that into account as we form a plan of action."

"What about Jed's orders?" Jake asks.

Khai says, "I hate to say it, but they've become obsolete. The stakes have risen. If we don't get Yoko, Scourge, and the Illusionist out of prison soon, they will all be killed."

I feel a strong wave of uneasiness as Khai speaks.

"Are you suggesting we break them out?" Jake asks, eyes widening.

Khai picks up his quiver and slings it on his back. "Whatever it takes."

"It won't be easy," Tarento warns. "Heiban will be expecting us to make a rescue attempt."

"Hey guys," I speak up. "I agree that this is a dire situation and we need to act as soon as possible, but I strongly believe we should ask Jed for advice. Otherwise, we'll be heading into a trap."

"I agree," Tarento nods.

"That'll take too long," Khai growls. "The time for planning is over. We have to take action! Time is running out!"

"But Heiban—" Tarento's reply is cut off when Khai says, "Tarento, I'll kill him myself if it'll make you happy. Let's go!"

"Hold on, Khai," Jake says. "We have to be smart about this, or we'll be put in danger. Let's go talk to Jed first."

"No Seer is going to help us free our friends!" Khai shouts.

I can't take this anymore! Khai is out of his mind!

"Don't be discouraged," the Great King whispers. *"Here, let me teach you an important Seer tactic. Say exactly what I tell you to."*

In response to the Great King, I step forward and say, "Khai, *stop!*"

Khai looks at me. I can see the fear and anger in his eyes. I see a deadly Pythorian huntsman who can and will overcome any enemy who crosses his path. If it weren't for the Great King's confidence steadying my heart, I'd slink away and hide behind the couch. Nevertheless, I speak. "Khai, I understand. You want to rescue Yoko, the daughter you see as your own. You lost one daughter already, and you can't bear to endure the pain a second time."

A glimmer of surprise appears in his face.

I continue, "You're allowing yourself to be consumed with vengeance. That was your life before you encountered the Great King. He showed you how to forgive and how to let go. We need you, Khai. Don't let vengeance have its place in your heart again. Yoko's still alive, and we need you here with us to make sure she stays that way."

Khai closes his eyes and breathes deeply.

Tarento and Jake stand aside, watching in awe.

Sylva floats behind them with a curious gaze.

"Trust the Great King," I say, approaching Khai and placing my hands on his shoulders. "He knows how you feel, and he knows *exactly* how we can rescue our friends. But he needs you to trust him to make it happen. Can you do that for me? For us?"

Khai nods without a word.

"Great," I say with a smile, firmly patting Khai's arm before turning toward Tarento and Jake. "I'll go ask Jed what to do. You guys prepare our things so we can get moving when I return. A few snacks wouldn't be so bad, either."

They exchange glances and nod. I've never seen them look so impressed with me before.

"*That was wizard,*" I say to the Great King. "*Let's do it again sometime.*"

As I leave the room, I beckon for Sylva to follow. "Sylva, with me."

As we journey down the hall, she says, "That was beautiful! How did you do it?"

"I'm a Seer, so the Great King shows me things every now and then."

"Astounding! I don't believe you understand how wonderful it was to hear you speak to Khai in that way."

"What do you mean?"

"I was with dearest Yoko when Khai found her. He was, as you said, very troubled by the loss of his own daughter years before, and he was on the dark path of vengeance. My heart breaks for dearest Yoko even now, but I cannot imagine how Khai must feel. It's no wonder he reverted back to his old self. But you steadied him more gently than anyone I've ever seen. No one has stood up to Khai like that before."

I ponder Sylva's words. The situation we're in now, with Yoko mere hours away from certain death, is likely the worst situation Khai could imagine. It caused him to succumb to old thought patterns of fear and vengeance, likely magnified by the Serpent to disrupt our team unity and prevent us from thinking clearly and taking appropriate action. The Great King just used me to bring us back together, at least for the time being. I hope now we can figure this out and free our friends before it's too late.

Just then, I reach the door to Jed's hotel room. I knock and wait a few seconds. As I stand there, I realize I can hear Jed inside... shouting?

What is he shouting at?

"Hello?" I knock again. "Jed, it's me!"

More shouting. I don't think he hears me.

"Jed!" I call, testing the door. It isn't locked, so I open it a crack and peek inside.

Jed is crouched on his knees by the bed, facing the window, bawling harder than I've seen anyone bawl before. His face is red with weeping and wet with tears as he pounds the ground with his fist, shouting, "I trust ye, I trust ye Great King! Sovereign are ye! Mighty are ye! Yer plans are wise, and I trust ye! I trust ye! I love ye and I trust ye!"

He continues shouting these phrases and others like them as I stand in bewilderment at the entrance of the room. Under normal circumstances, I'd probably close the door nice and quietly to make sure he never knew I intruded on him in his most vulnerable state, but blimey, these are *not* ordinary circumstances and I bet he knows it better than any of us.

I walk over and sit on the ground beside him, placing a hand on his shoulder. Sylva settles down on his other side and begins rubbing his back.

Once he realizes we're here, he stops shouting and simply breathes and weeps. Slowly he calms down, and within moments he looks at me with a friendly grin. "How are ye, lad?"

"I'm...not doing too bad. What about you?"

He chuckles, wiping a trail of snot from his nose with a

handkerchief. "I've been better, I'll say that. But the Great King is good! He is *very* good!"

The lively vigor in his voice is surprising. I'm impressed by Jed's ability to stay positive, despite his apparent anguish. His trust in the Great King must be realms above mine or Tarento's or anyone else's I know.

"My friends," Jed stands to look out the window at the Cloud Summit cityscape. Sylva and I rise on either side of him. "There is no time to lose. Our original plan won't work the way we intended, but no matter. We never placed our trust in a plan to begin with, did we?"

"So, you know what happened last night?"

"Aye, every detail," Jed replies with a nod. "Ye came to ask for direction, did ye not?"

"Yup. Direct away."

For once, he gets right to the point. "I would like for ye and Jake to go to the item shop where Yoko found the jade key. The shopkeeper from whom she received it is an ally of White Sand and gave it to her knowin' she would try to rescue Celine. Look around—"

"Celine?" I ask.

"The Illusionist. That's her name."

"Ah. Carry on."

"Look around the shop for clues to help ye discover White Sand's next move. Bennett believes they'll try to sabotage the execution, but I'm afraid they're up to somethin' far worse."

"All right. Then what?"

"Go to the Hall of Justice. Ye'll know what to do from there."

"Great. What about the others?"

"Tarento cannot venture anywhere near the Hall of Justice today. He must stay at the hotel until the Great King tells him to move."

"He's not going to like that," I frown.

"He must, for his own sake. The execution is a baited trap. The Felids will be watchin' for disruptive activity, and if Tarento goes there he will be caught. He'll endanger himself and all of ye with him if he disobeys this order."

"Blimey, that's rough," I frown. "I'll make sure he understands."

"The Great King will help him understand. I know Tarento listens very well."

I nod. "What about Khai?"

"He must take his horse to the park fountain and wait. He'll know what to do when the time comes. And Sylva," he looks at the tree nymph, "I'll be needin' that jade key. Ye saw which of Bennett's men took it, did ye not?"

Sylva nods. "The same man who released me from the acorn. I know his face well."

"Bring it to me, and then join Khai in the park."

"Of course."

I'm unnerved by Jed's mention of the jade key, and it reminds me to ask him a very important question. "Jed, what are *you* going to do?"

He looks at me with a twinkle of mischief. "I'm goin' to find a messenger dove and a slingshot."

"What for?"

"I'm goin' to sabotage the execution."

My jaw drops.

Jed takes his polished-bone cane and hobbles past me, patting me on the back as he goes. "Don't ye worry about me, lad. The Great King knows *exactly* what he's doin', and he is *very* good!"

I promptly turn and grab Jed's arm. "B-but, how? You just said the Felids are out there, and White Sand is out there, and the police, and the Paladins too! How will you even get close?"

"He has a way."

"But, what is it?" I press. "Do you even know what it is?"

"Does it matter if I know or not? The Great King knows, and that's enough for me."

"Do you realize how crazy that sounds?"

"Connor," Jed grabs my shoulder firmly. Once I've been silenced by his gaze, he says, "Ye must know I am very proud of ye. In such a short time, ye have grown tremendously in bravery, wit, strength of heart, and trust in the King we serve. Ye're a very gifted Seer, lad. The Final Seer, and the greatest of us all. Don't be discouraged by the events that must take place. Trust in the Great King always. The others will look to ye for strength and direction, just as ye have looked to me. Do not fear that responsibility. Ye must accept it and carry it proudly. Ye're a necessary part of the Great King's plan to save Celine, to save yer friends, to save Melody, and ultimately to save all who call themselves citizens of the Kingdom of Marindel. Never forget who ye are. Never forget yer identity as a son of the Great King. It is yer greatest strength. Never, ever forget."

As Jed speaks, my soul is electrified by the sheer power of his words. It's as if the Great King himself is speaking to me. All my doubts and questions are silenced for the moment, and all I can do is stand in awe.

Jed takes a small vial out of his pocket and pops it open. He takes a drop of the contents—oil, I think—onto his finger and rubs it horizontally across my forehead. He places his hand on my head and says, "I anoint ye, Connor Lightwood, son of the Great King, to carry with valiance the mantle of the Final Seer. May the mysteries revealed to me pale in comparison to the mysteries he will reveal to ye. May he be yer greatest protection against any threat the Serpent pits against ye, and may he ever be yer greatest friend. Connor, I give ye my blessin'. I know and believe ye will fulfill yer destiny and prepare the way for Melody to return home to Marindel, at last."

By the end of Jed's speech, I'm trembling and my eyes are welling up with tears. I feel a power I can't describe coursing through my body. My knees buckle and I fall to the ground. I'm unable to move and unable to speak. I open my mouth to say something—anything—but I just gasp and weep.

Despite how pathetic I probably look, I feel...amazing.

I've never felt so free, so wonderful, so full of confidence and strength!

I'm not sure how much time passes while I'm on the ground, but when I finally look up, Jed is gone.

I stand, bracing my wobbly self on a nearby coat rack. If I wasn't an official Seer before this moment, I'd venture to say I am one now.

Sylva floats up beside me and asks, "Are you ready?"

"I...well, did you see where Jed went?"

"Don't worry about him. He knows what to do." Sylva embraces me with one arm to help me stand. Something about her gesture brings more vitality to my body than any human touch I've felt. It must be a tree nymph thing. She continues, "But what about you, young Seer? What are you going to do?"

I take a deep breath, standing up straight and shaking the last of the wobbliness out of my limbs. "As difficult as it seems, I'm going to do what Jed told me to do. I'm going to tell the others what he said, and we're all going to trust the Great King together."

"Let's go," Sylva says, "and may the King's guidance be ours to the fullest."

"Indeed. Thank you, Sylva."

We hurry back to the others. The Great King's got an amazing plan, and we're all eager and ready to spring into action.

What could possibly go wrong?

32
The Shopkeeper's Riddle
Summary, 1419 AIE

~Connor~

WHEN WE ARRIVE back at the room, I give our orders for the day as we scarf down the potatoes and sausage Jake brought up from the kitchen. I don't mention Jed's parting words to me personally—I'm having a hard time figuring that out myself—and I leave out any mention of Jed's plans to sabotage the execution. The others accept their orders without difficulty, and without further delay, we split up and get to work.

It's been half an hour, and Jake and I are racing up and down the streets of Cloud Summit to find the Exotic Goods Hub. Our anxiety increases by the moment. The day is drawing on, and all we've succeeded in doing is getting lost!

Jake studies a map of the city while muttering, "I could have sworn it'd be on Fourth and Cypress. Hm, maybe it's on Fourth and Pine. Connor, have we tried Fourth and Pine?"

I look at him with utter disbelief as I point to a sign post on the street corner where we stand, which indicates we are in fact standing on the corner of Fourth and Pine.

Jake looks at the sign, and then shoves the map in my face and says, "Your turn!"

I take the map with a sigh. "You've lived here for over ten years and still can't read a map of the place?"

"The Exotic Goods Hub isn't on there! All I can do is guess, based on what Yoko's told us about it."

"Which isn't much," I concede. As I study the map, I'm quickly overwhelmed by the number of names and places I've never heard of. Jake is right, that blasted shop could be anywhere! Its absence from the map is quite shady. Maybe it's not a legitimate shop? Could it be an outlet of the black market?

There's only one way to find out.

I quickly fold the map and shove it in Jake's hands. "Here, hold this."

Jake tries in vain to give it back. "Hey, you didn't even try!"

"We'll never find it on a map like that," I say as I walk toward the nearest passerby, a nice-looking man coming our way down Pine street. When I've gotten close I say, "Excuse me, sir. Could you help us with directions?"

The man tilts his hat in greeting. "Good day, what're you after?"

"We're looking for a place called the Exotic Goods Hub. Do you know where that is?"

"Never heard of it. Sorry, mate." The man continues on his way.

"Hmm," I look around for another person. Across the street I see a minstrel playing the accordion for donations. I figure he, who likely performs all over Cloud Summit to maximize his earnings, knows the city better than most. I wait for a horse-drawn cart to pass, and then I cross the street toward him.

Jake calls from behind, "Connor, if it's not on the map, who else is going to know about it?"

I ignore him. I have a feeling this guy will know. "Excuse me, sir!"

The minstrel looks at me and smiles, playing with more enthusiasm. I guess he thinks I've come to listen to his music. Unfortunately, I haven't.

"Sir, may I ask you a question?" I ask as I come upon the street corner. "Please, this is important."

He stops his music and says, "Of course, young man. Are you wondering about my accordion? I'd love to tell you—"

"Sorry to interrupt, sir. Your music is great, it really is, but I have another question. We're looking for a shop called the Exotic Goods Hub. Do you know where it is?"

"Ah," the minstrel taps his foot. "I've heard that name. Let me think..."

Jake comes up alongside me as I wait.

"I've got it!" the minstrel says. "It's on Seventh Avenue between Elm and Aspen. Easy to miss, but just look for the purple awning."

Chapter 32: The Shopkeeper's Riddle

"Great, thanks!" I reply, pulling out a kappe and tossing it into the bucket.

"You're most welcome! Would you like to stay for a moment and hear a song? I've got a special one for you!"

"Sorry, another time," I say with a wave. "We're in a bit of a hurry. Thanks again though!"

"Thank you, sir!" Jake says as we both turn and run toward the location given by the minstrel.

Within a few moments, panting for breath, we arrive on Seventh Avenue where there's a purple awning over a hole-in-the-wall shop without any windows. There's a worn-out placard, displaying the shop's name, propped up on a crate by the entrance. No one just passing by would notice it.

"How did Yoko find this place, anyway?" Jake wonders aloud.

"Beats me," I say with a shrug before opening the door and gesturing for Jake to enter.

"I guess we're about to find out," Jake says, stepping through the doorway.

I follow close behind him.

We descend a few steps, walk down a short hall, and pass through a beaded curtain before entering the main room of the Exotic Goods Hub. It's quite large, with five more halls branching off in different directions. The entire place is decorated with beads, feathers, strange paintings and sculptures, and shelves loaded with a myriad of exotic items. It's illuminated by torch-holsters farther up the walls that are not holding torches, as one might suppose, but glowing stones. Some of the stones are purple, and others are orange. The light of these stones casts an eerie glow in the shop.

A few seconds after we enter, an old lady enters through one of the other hallways and throws her arms wide with a shrill greeting, "Welcome to my store!"

The woman looks just as exotic as everything else in here. She wears a purple robe, excessive amounts of jewelry and piercings, and a small pair of glasses. Her skin is pale, as if she never ventures out to see the light of day, and her voluminous white hair is frizzy and maniacal.

My left eye twitches. Is this the shopkeeper we're looking for?

"Feel free to look around at all the wonderful items within these halls," the woman says, clasping her hands together. "Here you'll find goods from every kingdom in the realm. If you see something you like, bring it to me and we'll discuss a price."

"Thank you, ma'am," I say with a curt nod. "We—"

She continues, "And if you break something, you'll pay a large fee in addition to its value. So, don't go romping around like berserker beasts in a pottery shop!"

I open my mouth to speak, but again she sharply interrupts, "And don't you even *think* about stealing! You won't get away from me if I catch you doing something crafty. Are we clear?"

"Yes, ma'am," Jake and I reply.

"Good. Now, I'll leave you two be. I'm taking inventory at the moment, but come find me if you'd like to make a purchase." The shopkeeper turns and flits down the hall from whence she came.

I sigh with relief when she's gone.

Jake whispers, "Let's look around first. We'll find some clues, meet up here in a few minutes, and feel it out from there."

"Sounds good," I say with a nod.

Jake immediately goes toward one of the halls and disappears behind a beaded curtain.

I stay for the moment to look around. There're many useless-looking items on these shelves. Perhaps not ironically, they seem like trinkets eccentric old ladies tend to hoard. Small figurines of people, animals, and monsters; necklaces and bracelets; colorful rocks and crystals; artsy ceramic jars, cups, and plates; decorative glass items; wind chimes; wooden carvings…

Aha! Finally, something useful!

I see wooden plaques above each of the five hallways branching from this room. On each sign are the names of two kingdoms. I presume the items within each hallway will be specific to the kingdoms listed on the sign.

I look at the sign above the hallway where Jake disappeared to. The kingdoms listed are Armavir and Izendor.

Inspired to explore, I look at the other hallways and their plaques. There's Pythoria and Ibadan down one hallway, Tethys and Murumbwé down the second, and Sunophsis and Felidae down the third. The final hallway is sealed off with planks of wood. By the process of elimination, I assume this hallway would house items from Bothnia and Meiro.

The shopkeeper had gone down the Tethys-Murumbwé hallway, so I'll avoid that one for now. If it's clues about White Sand I'm after, I'd better check the Sunophsis-Felidae hallway first.

I walk through the beaded curtain and down the dozen-foot-long hall. I emerge into a smaller room loaded from floor to ceiling with items, and I gasp in awe.

The room is illuminated by yellow and red stones much brighter than those in the main room. The effect is multiplied by the sheer number of golden and crystal items, which reflect and intensify the light. The ceiling is very high, allowing for enormous statues of ancient Sunophsian kings to stand in two of the corners on my right. The wall between the statues is filled with shelves, which in turn are filled with Sunophsian artifacts, treasures, weapons, and other things. The wall on my left is completely Felid, with their unique weapons, Samurai gear, exotic carvings and paintings, pagoda sculptures, and much more. The wall in front of me is divided in half, with Felid items on the left and Sunophsian items on the right.

My eyes grow ever wider as I behold the sight.

No wonder Yoko wanted to bring us back here! *Look* at all this amazing stuff!

I run over to the Felid side and pick up a sheathed katana from its holster. I speak aloud, unable to contain my excitement, "I've never had a chance to hold one of these before!"

Then, out of the corner of my eye I see an enormous red jewel on a pedestal. I set the katana down and rush over to it. "This is the biggest ruby I've ever seen! It reminds me of the story of the adventurer who went looking for treasure in a Sunophsian tomb guarded by..."

I gasp, setting the ruby down and rushing over to a two-foot-tall obsidian statue of a beastly warrior with a scimitar and a shield. "The Ifrit of the Darker Sands!" I pick up the statue as I continue, "According to legend, this is the monster who turned King Sisera into a Shade all those years ago!"

"Shall I fetch the shopkeeper for you?" A deep voice startles me, and I almost drop the statue. I whirl around to see a middle-aged Murumbwéan man at the entrance of the room, holding an armful of glittering necklaces and a round shield coated in what appears to be black leather. With his curious gaze he looks at me as if I'm lost.

"Oh, uh," I fumble with the statue, putting it back where I found it. "Nope, no need. I'm just looking."

"Hmph," the man smirks as he goes toward the Sunophsian side to hang the necklaces on a display rack. "It sounded like you were about to tell me a story about the Ifrit of the Darker Sands."

"Hm, well, I got a little excited," I reply, scratching my head. "I mean, if you *want* to hear a story, I'd love to tell. I have a few good ones up my sleeve, now that I'm an adventurer."

"Adventurer, huh?" The man says as he continues to hang necklaces. "When I was young, I wanted to be an adventurer. I left

Murumbwé in search of a prosperous life in Armavir, but I soon discovered it's not the Land of Peace it used to be. Now, I work here at this shop. It puts food on the table, at least."

I tilt my head as he speaks. What a depressing adventure story; leaving his home far across the sea to come here and end up in a dark hole working for a crazy old lady.

The assistant says, "Can I help you find anything, young adventurer? There must be a reason you've come."

I'm about to say, "No thanks, I'm just looking," when I hear the voice of the Great King, *"This man has no knowledge of the shopkeeper's White Sand affiliations. It is safe to seek information from him."*

As I ponder the message of the Great King, the assistant finishes his task of hanging necklaces and turns to see me standing still. He asks, "Is something the matter?"

"No, no, nothing's wrong. I'm just..." I trail off, wondering where to start. My eyes settle on the assistant's shield, so I point at it. "What's that shield you've got there? I've never seen one like it."

"Oh, this?" The assistant hefts it up for me to see. "It's a fire shield. Steel round, with a coating of Abysso hide."

As he goes to hang the shield among the Felid items, something clicks. I'll eventually be going up against a sorcerer, who uses magic. If he were to throw an energy attack at me, such as fire, then an ordinary shield would hardly protect me. That shield, coated with the magic-resistant hide of a Felid Abysso, would be much better protection than any other shield. In fact, according to Scourge, Jaedis gave Abysso-like traits to his Nox Abyssae so they'd be effective in battle against King Ruslan and other electrokinetics.

I *need* that shield.

I'll have to come back later when I have money. Besides, there's no time to waste on shopping. I have a job to do.

The assistant turns to see me standing still once again. He raises an eyebrow. "You are a very *strange* adventurer."

I straighten up, refusing to be perceived as strange, and I ask him another question. "You know, I've noticed you have a few jade sculptures here among the Felid items, but I don't see any *enchanted* jade items. I've heard incredible stories about their magical qualities, and I was hoping to check them out. Do you have any in stock?"

"Ah, enchanted jade," the assistant beckons for me to follow. "This way, please."

As we enter the main room and turn toward the Pythoria-Ibadan hallway, he says, "You were not far off in assuming they would be found in the Felidae category, since jade is found there in abundance. However, we like to keep our enchanted items together in the Ibadan category. Felid jade is regularly exported to Ibadan and used for the enchantment of every sort of trinket."

We arrive in the Pythoria-Ibadan room, which is illuminated by green and white stones. Pythorian items are on the left, and Ibadanian items on the right.

"Here they are," the assistant says, leading me to a display full of jade items. "I'll be around if you need any more help."

"Actually," I say, "Would you mind staying for a bit? I might have a few more questions."

"Not at all, sir."

I browse the jade items. Amulets, bracelets, totems, and even a dagger, but no keys.

Interesting.

I allow my Seer's gift to guide me as I launch into a battery of questions. "You don't happen to have any *jade keys* lying around, do you?"

"We had one, but we sold it to a customer yesterday. I'm sorry."

"Aw," I snap my fingers, feigning surprise. "Something like that would be useful to unlock any treasure chests I find on my adventures. Where do you think I can find another one?"

"Ibadan, most likely."

"Where did you get yours?"

"Amaash, our shopkeeper, brought it in two days ago."

"Did she say where from?"

The assistant shakes his head. "No. Come to think of it, she never explains where things come from. New items arrive every day, but I never see her talking or trading with merchants."

"Sounds shady, don't you think?"

"I believe she knows what she's doing."

"Does she ever leave the shop?"

"Yes, of course. Why wouldn't she?"

"Have you ever *seen* her leave the shop?"

He pauses for a moment. "No, I haven't. That's very strange, now that I think about it."

"Definitely strange," I agree. "How much of your day do you spend here?"

"I come in shortly after sunrise, and leave just before sunset."

"Have you ever thought about staying here past sundown?"

He shakes his head incredulously. "Why would I want to do that?"

"To see what Amaash does while the city sleeps. Solve a mystery, have an adventure...you know, that sort of stuff."

"Hmm..." the assistant appears thoughtful.

At that moment, Amaash comes in and says, "Kamau! I don't pay you to loaf around and socialize! Hurry up and finish putting away our new items!"

Kamau nods and replies with surprising calm, "I was just helping our customer, ma'am. I'll get right back to it."

"Hm," Amaash looks at me as if she hadn't noticed me until then. "Did you find something you like, dear?"

With Amaash here, I feel more nervous about asking probing questions. It takes me a while to tune into my Seer's gift and decide where to start. Meanwhile, Kamau leaves the room to finish putting away the items.

"Well?" Amaash presses. "We're very busy today, so if you're not going to buy something, hurry up and get out!"

"All right, all right," I say, putting my hands up. "You see, I'm an adventurer, and I go on all sorts of quests across the land. I just thought I'd check and see if you have any enchanted jade keys in stock. You know, so I can open all the treasure chests I find."

"We're fresh out of jade keys," Amaash says.

"Yes, Kamau told me. But he also told me you *did* have one yesterday, until a customer bought it. Might I ask where you got yours, so I can go there myself and get one? Do you have adventurer friends who go around collecting things, or do you have merchants who supply you with daily shipments, or—"

"You will find one in Ibadan, I'm sure."

"*Connor,*" the Great King says, "*There's little time left. You must press into this matter without fear. Do not be afraid; I will protect you.*"

"All right," I nod, taking a deep breath. Yoko, Scourge, and Celine's lives are at stake, and possibly others if I don't figure out what White Sand is up to and put a stop to it. With a fresh jolt of determination, I begin my interrogation. "So, why did you give away the jade key for free?"

Amaash is taken aback, surprised as to how I knew that.

I don't wait for her to verbalize her confusion. I nod and continue, "Yeah, the girl you gave it to is one of my good friends. Did you know she got arrested last night for trying to rescue the Illusionist with the key you gave her?"

"Hmph. What are you going to do, sue me? She must have been very stupid to think she could get away with a stunt like that."

"I agree with you wholeheartedly. If Yoko made this decision on a whim, it would indeed be very stupid of her. However, I believe she was played into it. I think White Sand manipulated her into trying to rescue the Illusionist. What do you have to say about that?"

"Nothing. I gave her the key in return for a promise to bring my shop more business. That's the only reason."

"How are you helping your shop by giving away something as valuable as an enchanted jade key? You could have sold it for thousands of krons."

While Amaash fumbles for words, Jake enters the room and stands beside me. We exchange glances and nod in greeting; I'm glad to have his strong presence with me. Now, it's time to up the ante on the shopkeeper. I jump right in. "I ran into a buddy of yours the other day who expressed his fears about the Illusionist's arrest. He thinks the police might get cocky and start rounding up other White Sand members. Oh, and get this: there're Samurai in league with the police now. With their help, Bennett will find the White Sand hideout in a matter of days, if not sooner. What better way to avert such a crisis than by rescuing the Illusionist? She could put down the Samurai no problem, and it would kick Bennett's morale in the nuggets. What do you think?"

The shopkeeper's eyes twinkle, and her wide grin sends chills down my spine. "You're a clever boy, I'll say that. But you're still far from the truth."

"Tell us," Jake demands, taking a step toward her. "Tell us everything you know about White Sand's motives. What are they planning?"

Amaash cackles and clasps her hands together. "How about we play a little game?"

"No games," I say. "People's lives are in danger. Tell us everything. Now."

"Connor," Amaash addresses me by name, which catches me off guard. "You do remember the legend of Sisera, don't you? Now, why don't you think about it for a while and use it to solve my riddle? Then perhaps you'll understand the goal of White Sand. But you'd better hurry up! Time is ticking, and your friends don't have long to live!"

"Just spill it, you black-hearted witch!" Jake lunges forward to grab her, but I step between them. "Jake, it's all right! Amaash, just give us the riddle."

"Yes, yes," Amaash rubs her hands together as she speaks. "There was a group of rock trolls living in a lonely mountain range. They'd been living there since the dawn of time, but suddenly, they were wiped out by a single beetle. How is that possible?"

"What kind of riddle is that?" Jake asks, clenching his fists.

Amaash turns to leave with a cackle and taunts, "Tick-tock, tick-tock!"

I watch her go, taking a deep breath to calm myself and focus. I repeat the riddle, "There was a group of rock trolls in a lonely mountain range. They'd been there since the dawn of time, but suddenly, they were wiped out by a single beetle. How...?"

Jake sighs. "I can't believe this!"

"We can do it, Jake. I'm a Seer, remember?"

"Do you know the answer already?"

"No, not yet. Did you find anything interesting in the Armavir-Izendor room?"

"Armor and weapons, mostly. Things I'd buy if I had money. There was a model of Königheim Castle in the center of the room. I thought it was neat, until I noticed the roof of the main hall was missing and there were scribbles on the columns inside. We could probably get a discount for the damage, but it's so big it'd be a hassle to carry through these narrow halls."

"Huh," I ponder. "Yeah, that is a little strange. But anyway, back to the riddle. Let's talk through the legend of Sisera. Did you learn about him in the Academy?"

"Yes, but I don't remember much."

"All right. I know most of the story, but let me know if I forget anything. Got it?"

Jake nods. "Let's do this. Quickly."

I take a deep breath before launching into the story: "In 1140, during the Golden Age of Armavir, there was a war between Armavir and Sunophsis. At the climax of battle, the king of Sunophsis was killed and most of his army decimated by the Paladin Order. The king's son, Prince Sisera, was devastated by his father's defeat. He was visited by a desert mage who told him of a great power that dwelt in the deepest levels of the Tomb of Kings, where most of Sunophsis' ancient rulers were buried. An ambitious young man, hungry for power and driven by a desire for vengeance, Sisera went on a daring quest into the depths of the Tomb of Kings, where he encountered the Ifrit of the Darker Sands. The Ifrit promised to share with Sisera his powers of immortality and Bygone magic, but only at the price of his very soul. He agreed, and the Ifrit turned him into a Shade, the most powerful to have ever lived. When the Ifrit commanded Sisera to recite an oath to become his eternal slave, Sisera fought back. He used his new powers to seal the Ifrit in one of the ancient tombs. Sisera returned to the surface, and after his coronation as king, he led a vicious campaign against Armavir. He plundered many of the southeastern villages and cities, stopping just short of Cloud Summit in 1142. For unknown reasons, he and his troops fled back to Kharduman, and there he's been up to the present day. Now, as we know, he's a bumbling drunkard who seeks only to please himself with feasts, women, and entertainment. His soul is dead and gone, and he knows not how to get it back."

Jake is pacing back and forth, deep in thought. "I don't understand. What does any of this have to do with trolls and beetles?"

"We must be missing something," I say, beginning to think. Rock trolls live in mountains, that's very normal. Rock trolls being exterminated is only normal if a Paladin or skilled warrior goes into the mountains to slay them all. But a beetle? What kind of beetle can wipe out a group of rock trolls? And what does Sisera have to do with it?

I have an idea.

"Jake, do you remember how to kill a rock troll?"

He grins. "Yes! Let me see. Rock trolls have a tough hide that makes them difficult to cut down. The best spots to go for, where their skin is thinnest, are the armpits and inner thighs. Once immobilized, a stabbing blow between the eyes should finish them off.

I listen, nodding and processing Jake's response. Then I ask, "Do you know of any beetles that nest in armpits? Or inner thighs?"

Jake grimaces. "That sounds horrible! I hope they don't exist."

"Me too," I agree.

Just then, Kamau enters with a basket of small items and begins putting them away, one by one. As I watch him, Jake wonders aloud, "It would be helpful if we could find a connection between the legend of Sisera and the riddle. Let's see, are there rock trolls in Sunophsis? No, I remember. They're native to the mountains of Izendor and Ibadan."

Jake's train of thought, coupled with an item I notice in Kamau's basket, gives me a brilliant idea. I snap my fingers with resolve. "You're right, Jake. There are no rock trolls in Sunophsis, but there are definitely beetles." I walk over to Kamau and take the item that caught my attention: a silver scarab figurine.

Kamau looks at me and says, "You know, if you want to see something I have, you could be polite and ask."

"Sorry about that. Would you mind telling me about this beetle?"

He looks from me to the beetle and back again, clearly offended by my brashness—what can I say? Time is ticking!—but he clears his throat and says, "The figurine is a Sunophsian bomb scarab. They're small for scarabs and they live in caves for most of their lives, but they're best known for their parasitic breeding cycle. They find warm-blooded hosts and burrow into them, and they lay their eggs and die in the host's body. The dead beetle releases a poison in the blood of the host, causing their extremities to swell with boils. While the host is distracted by the boils, the eggs mature. When they hatch, they explode. The host dies, and the newborn scarabs feed on the carcass until there's nothing left."

Jake and I exchange disgusted glances.

Bomb scarabs sound even nastier than centipedes! Yeesh!

"Well," I say, "Do you think a bomb scarab can wipe out a group of rock trolls?"

"It'd work," Jake agrees. "Rock trolls aren't so tough on the inside."

Kamau interjects, "Bomb scarabs aren't found in the mountains. They thrive in hot desert climates."

I begin thinking aloud. "Yes, but suppose a bomb scarab found itself in the mountains. Maybe it burrowed into a migrating bird, and the bird was flying over mountains when the eggs exploded, so all the baby beetles fell onto the mountains. Lacking sustenance from their host, they quickly sought out the biggest and most warm-blooded creatures they could find: rock trolls. Soon, every troll in the mountain range was infected with bomb scarabs, and one by one, they exploded."

"Sudden death," Jake finishes.

Kamau shakes his head in disbelief. "Why are you so interested in bomb scarabs and rock trolls?"

"No reason," Jake says. "Go ahead and finish what you were doing. Don't mind us."

"Jake," I whisper, nudging him with my elbow, "He can help us out. Don't scare him off!"

"You *trust* him? He works for the shopkeeper!"

"Just a hunch."

"I can hear you," Kamau says.

I turn and ask, "Kamau, are there any connections between bomb scarabs and the legend of Sisera?"

Kamau crosses his arms. "I don't want to answer any more of your questions until you tell me what you're up to."

I sigh, trying hard to hide my annoyance. I spend a moment tapping into my Seer's gift before I explain. "All right. Jake and I, both adventurers, are here as detectives to figure out what White Sand is planning in response to the Illusionist's capture. Amaash said she'd help us out, but you know how much she likes to play games! She gave us two clues: the legend of Sisera, and a riddle that goes like this: 'There was a group of rock trolls in the mountains, and they'd been there since the dawn of time, but suddenly, they were wiped out by a single beetle. How is that possible?' With your help I think we've solved the riddle; now we need to connect it with the legend of Sisera."

Kamau chuckles. "You're by far the *strangest* adventurers I've ever met. What reason do you have to stick your noses into White Sand's business?"

"They're going to harm innocent people," I reply. "Jake and I are adventurers who prevent evildoers from harming innocent people."

"Detectives," Jake adds with a nod.

"Hmm," Kamau looks at the ground. "Honorable, I'll admit. But foolish."

"I think we'll all be a little less foolish and a tad bit wiser if you wouldn't mind helping us out here. What do you know about the legend of Sisera?"

Kamau grins. "I thought you were going to tell me that story."

I sigh. "But I already...! Blimey, you weren't here! Fine, all right, I'll tell it again."

I tell the legend of Sisera again, albeit quicker, given my developing impatience.

"Impressive," Kamau says after I've finished. "You're a very good storyteller."

"Yes, yes, I know that. Do you have anything to add? Anything at all?"

"There is one thing," he says, taking the bomb scarab figurine and beginning to polish it with a cloth. "White Sand has become formidable because a handful of its members are Offspring of Sisera. Do you know where they fit into the story?"

"Assume I don't." Telling him what little I know about them would be a waste of time. I'd rather he just get to the point.

I hope time is going by slower than I feel like it is right now.

Kamau explains, "The legacy of Sisera lives on through his Offspring, the biological children he's brought into the realm through the concubines he's taken over the years. Each Offspring contains a fraction of his power: physical strength, superhuman agility, short-range teleportation, levitation, psychic powers, and other dark arts. One might say the Offspring have done more damage to the realm than Sisera himself ever did. However, not one Offspring has yet accomplished their father's ultimate goal."

"What do you mean?" Jake presses. "What goal?"

"The conquest of Cloud Summit."

When I hear those words, everything begins to click. I pace and speak quickly as my Seer's gift fills in the blanks. "That's it. That's what White Sand is trying to do. They want to complete Sisera's legacy by taking down the capital of Armavir. Their strategy is like the bomb scarabs in the riddle. They're not from here, but here they are in our mountains, lurking in the darkness and burrowing beneath the city, mobilizing and preparing. They're using Celine as bait; the scarab who must die so the protectors of the city, the police and the Paladin Order, are well distracted. Meanwhile, White Sand will execute its greatest move yet. They won't show up in the extremities of the city, where the diversion is. They're not going to sabotage the execution. They'll come up somewhere unexpected, somewhere mostly unguarded. They'll show up at the heart..." I pause, my eyes widening as the concluding revelation comes. "Oh, no..."

33
The Great Sensei
Summer, 1419 AIE

~Tarento~

IT'S ALMOST NOON.

I'm reclined on the couch in the hotel room, repeatedly bouncing a ball off the nearby wall and catching it again.

I can't bear the suspense.

I haven't heard from anyone since they left. To avoid being seen, I haven't looked out the window, but I've left it slightly ajar with the hope that I might hear a passing bit of conversation about how the execution has gone or is going. The city is unusually quiet, and I've heard nothing of interest. All I can do is wait, and it's killing me slowly from the inside out.

With a grunt of frustration, I throw the ball across the room and stand up, beginning to stretch. I wish I could at least go for a walk! All the tension and suspense is giving me more nervous energy than I know what to do with.

"Some exercise will help," the Great King says.

"Good idea." I can't believe I didn't think of that sooner.

Without delay, I rearrange the furniture in our traveler's suite, pushing everything against the walls to open up the center of the room. I also pick up the ball and put it in my pocket so I don't lose it. Once the room is set, I drop to the floor and begin doing push-ups.

Four, five, six...

Twenty-eight, twenty-nine, thirty...

Fifty-one, fifty-two, fifty-three...

Ninety-six, ninety-seven, ninety-eight...

One-seventeen, come on... one-eighteen... you can do it... one-nineteen... one more! ...one-twenty!

I collapse on the ground, where I stay to catch my breath. Phew, I'm not as strong as I used to be. Back in Felidae I could do over a hundred and fifty without breaking a sweat. What a wake-up call! I need to be more intentional about training regularly, especially if I'm loafing around in a big city all day.

"*Would you like me to train you?*" The Great King asks.

"*Er, what do you mean?*"

"*Allow me to be your Sensei.*"

Intriguing.

Having the Great King as a sensei sounds too good to be true. I can't wrap my mind around it.

The Great King explains, "*I know all things. I have wisdom and experience to pass on that is infinitely more comprehensive than the subset of experience in Felid martial arts. I know every form of battle that was, is, or will be. If you allow me to guide your steps and your strokes, even down to the smallest of your movements, you will become the greatest Samurai in the realm: a true Samurai of Marindel.*"

I smile. "*I'd be honored to train as your kohai.*"

"*Splendid! Let us begin. First, I would like you to get up and grab the fireplace iron.*"

"Interesting choice of arms." I stand and follow the King's directions.

"*Walk to the window,*" he instructs, and I do so.

I continue to follow his directions fluidly as he gives them.

"*Turn your back to it.*"

"*Walk six paces toward the center of the room.*"

"*Defensive stance.*"

"*Upward swing.*"

"*Right step.*"

"*Block the downward stroke.*"

"*Jump left.*"

"*Strike the knees.*"

"*Fist-jab the solar plexus.*"

"*Jump-kick the jaw.*"

"*Duck.*"

The instant I crouch, there's a loud crashing noise behind me. A javelin soars inches over my head, across the room, and impales the door. In total shock, I stay put as glass from the shattered window falls all around me.

"*Turn.*"

I blink to refocus, and then turn to see two fully black-clad figures swing in through the broken window, expertly landing with shoulder rolls and leaping up to attack me with their scimitars.

By now, my entire being is on high-alert, and my Samurai senses have kicked into full gear. I'm ready to fight.

"*Duck and roll to the left.*"

I obey the King. My attackers miss.

The Great King's commands come at just the right tempo for me to execute every move.

"*Jump and strike right.*"

I spring to my feet and attack, scoring a direct hit on the head of the closest attacker.

"*Kick his ribs.*"

I send him sprawling back into his bewildered partner.

"*Pursue and disarm.*"

I step toward them and strike their wrists with two succinct blows of the fireplace iron, causing them to drop their weapons.

"*Take the nearest scimitar. Keep the iron.*"

I slip the tip of my boot beneath the blade of a scimitar and toss it up, catching it by the hilt with my left hand. For my personal preference, I switch hands so I now wield the scimitar with my right hand and the iron with my left.

"*Jump back and duck.*"

A second javelin breaks through what remains of the window, soaring just over my head and impaling into the wall.

"*Who in the land of Armavir can throw a javelin with such force, and so precisely?*" I ask.

"*Don't think about it now. Face the window and jump back.*"

When I do so, three more attackers swing into the room. One of them is directly in front of me.

"*Iron forward strike.*"

I notice the surprise in the attacker's eyes before I strike his outstretched right arm, eliciting a shout of pain as his shoulder joint is jarred out of place.

"*Duck, turn right, leg-sweep.*"

I do so and trip an attacker I hadn't seen coming.

"*Step over him. Scimitar defensive stance.*"

I follow through in time to block a strike from the third attacker.

"*Iron stab.*"

I pierce the attacker's belly with the fireplace iron. He shouts in pain and staggers backward.

"Jump back, jump left, scimitar strike."

I notice one of the first attackers had gotten up and is crouching to pick up the scimitar I hadn't taken. The second jump lands me in front of him in time to strike the scimitar out of his grasp.

"Jump-kick to the nose."

Direct hit.

He staggers back with a shout of surprise, holding his hands over his bloody nose, and trips and falls backward over a nightstand.

"Throw the scimitar out the window."

I turn and do so just as another attacker is about to swing into the room. The flying scimitar cuts the rope, causing the attacker to fall short and crash into the wall just below the window. I hear him scream as he falls for two seconds, and then a thud.

With a lull in the Great King's commands, I pause to look around. All five of the attackers are sprawled in contorted positions on the floor, moaning and holding their wounds. Now that I have time think about it, I realize these are all White Sand fighters. The questions come flying in.

Why are they after me?

How did they know I was here?

"Run toward the window."

"Hai." I go.

"Skid feet-first."

A javelin flies through the window. As I skid, I look up to see it clip a small portion of my hair.

"Spring up and out the window."

Just before hitting the wall, I use the momentum from my skid to roll forward, jump back to my feet, and dive out the window.

In free-fall, I notice a two-horse-drawn cart loaded with sacks of potatoes passing under me. How convenient. I land on the heap of cargo, allowing my momentum to carry me down the side of the cart amongst a few displaced sacks. Finally, I land on the cobblestone ground with a shoulder roll and spring back to my feet.

The driver of the cart stops the horses and looks back at me with a scowl, shaking his fist in the air. "Oi! What d'ya think you're doin!? You'd better put those potatoes back on the cart!"

I'm about to reply when the Great King says, *"Look up."*

A White Sand fighter leans out of a window with a javelin in his hand, taking aim to throw it at me.

My muscles tense for action.

"Oi!" The cart driver calls. I see him in my peripheral vision as he hops off the cart and saunters toward me. "Are you deaf?"

My attacker's eyes flick several times between me and the driver.

I know what he's going to do.

"Potato sack," the Great King says.

In the same fraction of a second that the fighter throws the javelin, I take one step forward while crouching down, stooping just low enough to grab one of the sacks. Then I spring up while swinging my potato-laden projectile into the air at the incoming javelin.

The sack of potatoes hits the javelin midway down the shaft, causing it to veer off course several feet from its intended target: the cart driver.

When the javelin stakes into the ground, breaking through the mortar between the cobblestones, the cart driver realizes his dangerous position. He turns and runs with a terrified shout, arms over his head.

"To the cart," the Great King instructs.

I turn toward the cart, but when I do, another White Sand fighter appears out of thin air, standing on top of the cargo. He strings an arrow and takes aim.

I tense, ready to dodge or deflect if necessary.

A second later, I hear a thud behind me. Turning my head to look, I see the javelin-thrower has jumped down from the window and is now coming toward me. Somehow, he managed to make the jump without getting hurt.

I notice another White Sand fighter appear from a nearby alley, and yet another from the other side of the cart.

They all look the same, dressed in full-black including turban-like head coverings, but they all have different weapons. There's the javelin-thrower, the archer, the dual-scimitar fighter, and the...uh, circular-saw-blade-weapon fighter.

The javelin-thrower cracks his neck and says, "You're worth the hype. I see now why even your own countrymen want you dead. Very impressive."

I ask, "What do you want from me?"

"The same thing everyone else wants: your head."

"You're making a mistake," I warn. "I've taken out six of you already. I don't reckon you have many more to lose."

"There are more of us than you think," he replies. "Now, we will see if you have what it takes to hold your ground against White Sand's *greatest* warriors."

I glance around briefly. We're on a road in downtown Cloud Summit at noonday. The potato cart, upon which the archer stands, is a few feet away from me. The two horses at the head of the cart are pawing the ground impatiently. By now, a few passersby have stopped and are murmuring amongst themselves. Others are peering down from the windows of nearby buildings. I don't see any police, market guards, or Paladins in the area, but if we start brawling in the street, I don't expect them to be absent for long. We're causing a scene, and under no circumstance do I believe that's a good thing.

"*What's the plan?*" I ask the Great King.

"*You're surrounded by four Offspring of Sisera who intend to kill you. The javelin-thrower, Nebioth, has enhanced physical strength. The archer, Misham, can teleport across short distances. The scimitar fighter, Abdeel, has enhanced agility, stamina, and speed. The saw-blade fighter, Kindar, has levitation abilities. Your goal is not merely to escape or defeat them. You must make your way north on the main road. Use the cart to get there quickly.*"

"What's wrong, Felid?" Nebioth taunts. "You scared?"

I turn to face him, my back now toward Misham. "Well, it's not every day I get to dance toe-to-toe with Offspring of Sisera. I'm actually quite honored. I can't help but take it all in."

"Indeed," Nebioth says with a nod. "It's not every day we get to test our strength against a Felid Samurai. Do us a favor and stay alive longer than a couple seconds, will ya?"

"Give it your best shot," I say, twirling the fireplace iron as if it's the most powerful weapon in the realm.

Nebioth chuckles, casting his javelin aside and walking toward me.

As he comes, the Great King says, "*Feint tackle Nebioth. Potato sack. Spinning throw at Kindar.*"

I sprint toward Nebioth.

Likely thinking I'm giving him an easy target for his brute strength, Nebioth raises his fists in a boxing stance, ready to knock me out on contact.

Half a second before I reach him, I dive onto a sack of potatoes resting a few feet from where he stands. In the same motion, I avoid a jab from Nebioth that would have busted my head clean off my shoulders.

I roll with the potato sack, grabbing the tied mouth of the bag as I go. When I spring to my feet, I use the momentum to spin, swinging the bag to prepare for a throw.

After seeing me dodge Nebioth, Misham looses his arrow. Due to the timing of my spin, the potato sack takes the hit instead of me.

I let go of the sack and send it flying into Kindar, who has no time to react and is knocked backward.

Once I finish the maneuver, Nebioth, Abdeel, and Misham are all staring wide-eyed. I don't blame them; that stunt hardly took more than a second.

"Go now, take the cart! Use the iron to spur the horses!"

I sprint toward the cart.

Misham, still standing on the cargo, curses and fumbles with his bow as I come. He teleports away as I jump onto the cart.

Nebioth shouts, "He's getting away! Abdeel, stop him! Kindar, on your feet!"

I clamber over the potato sacks to get to the front of the cart. I raise the iron and strike each horse on the hindquarters, shouting, "H'ya!"

The horses yelp and break into a fast gallop, forcing me to crouch and hold the edge of the cart to avoid being thrown off.

All too soon, I hear a voice behind me say, "Don't think you're getting away so easily!"

I turn to see Abdeel, scimitars crossed above his head, coming down the mound of cargo.

"Don't move. Hold on to the cart," the Great King says.

Despite a flicker of alarm, I stay still as Abdeel comes. Just then, the cart runs over a sizable pothole. The jarring causes Abdeel to slip and tumble off the cart along with several sacks. He also loses one of his scimitars, which spins up into the air and stakes itself in a potato sack near me.

"For you, my friend," the Great King says.

"Why, thank you," I reply with an amused grin as I take the weapon.

The horses, as if driven by the Great King himself, turn north onto the main road. I stand on top of the cargo, looking back as the cart continues onward. We've left Nebioth and Abdeel in the dust; however, I can see Kindar some distance behind, roof-jumping with his levitation powers and quickly catching up.

"Duck."

I crouch in time to avoid an arrow speeding through the air where my torso used to be. A second later, the cart passes a second-story balcony on which Misham stands, stringing another arrow. I hardly need the Great King's guidance when he fires again; I block it with the scimitar.

"I can't believe this guy!" Misham shouts before disappearing from his position.

Shortly after, I notice Abdeel further down the road, sprinting after the cart. He's running faster than any Samurai I've ever seen. Faster than any horse, even.

"*Lose the potato sacks. The cart will travel faster with less cargo.*"

"*Got it.*"

Setting down the fireplace iron, I pick up potato sacks one by one and throw them off the back of the cart. As an added bonus, I aim with the intention of tripping my pursuer.

Abdeel impressively manages to avoid every obstacle I throw his way. Once he gets close enough for me to throw sacks *at* him, he's still able to duck and dodge with ease. His eyes glimmer with confidence as he continues the pursuit.

There are only a few more sacks left in the cart, and Abdeel will be upon me in seconds. I doubt I'll last long against him in direct hand-to-hand combat. Gripping my scimitar, I ask the King, "*What do I do now?*"

"*Relax. Breathe deeply. Clear your mind. Focus. Focus. Focus.*"

I close my eyes.

I allow the Great King's gentle yet powerful voice to wash over me. My muscles relax, my thoughts slow down like a quiet stream, and all becomes silent except for the Great King as he speaks to the rhythm of my heartbeat, "*Focus. Focus. Focus.*"

In this state of meditative quiet, a fighting sequence plays through my mind's eye. Now I know exactly what to do.

"*Ready...Go.*"

I open my eyes just as an arrow from Misham is loosed toward me. I duck and move to dodge it while snatching up the fireplace iron.

In that same second, Abdeel leaps onto the cart and comes at me with a flurry of slashes and kicks. I parry each one, just barely able to keep up with his speed, and then I give him a few strikes of my own. Even with his one weapon he's able to defend himself against my attacks, but our fast-paced dance soon causes him to place one foot on a certain sack of potatoes. Seizing the moment, I slice the sack open, follow up with a kick to the solar plexus, and jump back away from him.

As potatoes spill out of the opening, Abdeel loses his balance and is unable to defend himself from the attack. He staggers back and tumbles over the edge of the cart.

That takes care of him, but it's not time to celebrate yet.

I turn and face forward to see Kindar land in the cart's path. He performs a twirling high-jump as a prelude to throwing his saw-blade. It comes buzzing toward the cart with frightening speed.

Without pausing for breath, I cut the left horse free from the cart reigns and jump on its back, immediately leaning left. The horse squeals and jerks left in time to avoid the saw-blade, which flies vertically into the cart and slices it in half.

I don't look back as the cart is destroyed behind me. That was the end of the fighting sequence the Great King showed me. Now I keep the horse charging at full speed toward Kindar.

Kindar reaches out his hand, stopping my horse with an invisible grip. The horse whinnies in defiance. The oppressive force restricts my movement and prevents me from dismounting. To make matters worse, I hear the buzz of the saw-blade as it comes for a returning pass.

The Great King hasn't given me new orders yet.

"What do I do?" I ask, panic rising.

No answer.

I turn my head to see the saw-blade coming in fast from above and behind. I won't be able to avoid it in time.

An arrow clips Kindar's outstretched arm, causing him to recoil and look in the direction from whence it came.

I regain some mobility and steer the horse to the side. At the same time, the saw-blade buckles in flight and misses us by mere inches.

Khai, mounted on his Pythorian steed, gallops into view from a side-street up ahead. He fires another arrow at Kindar, who side-steps it before catching his returning saw-blade, spinning with the momentum, and hurling it his way.

"Throw the fire iron."

I throw it, striking the saw-blade and sending it wobbling into a building on the street corner.

Khai gives me a nod before firing at Misham, who just appeared further down the road. Misham teleports aside and fires back at Khai, who also dodges.

"Release the horse. You're better off on your feet."

"Agreed." I slide off the horse and slap its hindquarters to send it galloping on its way. Then I turn to see Abdeel coming toward me at full speed. His appearance surprises me, and I brace for action.

An arrow flies over my head toward Abdeel, who dodges it with a jump and a skid before launching himself toward me.

I parry two blows from him before a gust of wind throws him off to the side. I look to see Sylva with one arm outstretched. Her entire being glistens with green magic.

"Kindar's after his weapon. Take it before he does."

I nod thanks to Sylva before sprinting toward the building where the saw-blade is stuck. Kindar is attempting to pry it out with his levitation powers. My feet make hardly a sound as I race across the cobblestone.

Kindar turns to face me just as I land a flying kick in his face. He flails backward with a grunt and lands on his back.

"Kick the stone where the weapon is trapped."

I steady myself with a stance before kicking repeatedly at the corner of the building, inches away from where the blade is stuck. The stone cracks, and small chunks begin to fall. Soon, the saw-blade shifts and slides out of its rut, falling on the ground with a clang.

I pick it up by the rotating handle in the center. It's much heavier than it looks; I won't be able to throw it very far.

"That's not yours," a voice says behind me.

I turn to see Misham standing five feet away, arrow strung and ready to fire.

I open my mouth to reply, just as one of Khai's arrows strikes Misham in the left thigh. He doubles over with a pathetic shout.

Khai gallops toward me, stringing another arrow and firing over my head.

"Agh!" I hear, prompting me to turn and see who was hit. Abdeel is just a dozen feet away, clenching his teeth and gripping an arrow in his shoulder.

"Impressive," I say, looking at Khai. "Good shots, all around."

"They're easier to hit when they're after *you*," Khai says with a smirk.

The saw-blade is suddenly yanked out of my grip and into that of Kindar, who is standing again. He reaches one hand forward to hold both me and Khai in place as he draws his saw-blade back to throw it at us.

Sylva comes from the side, sending dozens of small vines to envelop Kindar's saw-blade arm.

"What the—" Kindar's curse is cut off as he's slammed into the side of a building, and then on the ground. When Sylva lets him go, it's clear he won't be getting up again.

Wow, I didn't think she had it in her to do *that*.

Picking up on our shock, Sylva grins sheepishly. "Was that too much?"

"Not at all," Khai says.

"If our lives are in danger, that is," I clarify.

"*You did well for your first round of training,*" the Great King says.

"*Thank you,*" I smile. "*I'm honored to be your kohai. That reminds me, what happened to Nebioth?*"

"*Don't worry, I took care of him. But keep your wits about you; this is far from over.*"

"Well," Khai says, "Now that we're finished here, I have dire news."

"What about? The execution?"

"No. Worse," Khai extends his hand toward me. "Come up. We have no time to lose."

34
The Day of Reckoning
Summer, 1419 AIE

~Celine~

"**T**HIS IS IT," the death-voice says as I'm dragged outside by two aggressive prison guards. "*It's time for you to die.*"

It takes my eyes a few moments to adjust to the bright noonday sun. The first thing I'm aware of is the sound of a crowd gathered nearby. Then I realize I'm being led up the steps of a stage set up in front of the Hall. On center stage awaits a large, imposing, terrifyingly familiar instrument.

The guillotine.

"*Are you excited?*" The death-voice asks. "*I'm very excited. I've waited a long time for this day. Ever since you were born.*"

I respond with a sigh as the guards lead me up to the guillotine and have me stand next to it. Other guards bring Scourge and Yoko to stand beside me. All three of us are secured with iron fetters around our necks, and our hands cuffed behind our backs. Yoko's eyes are wide with fear as she beholds the guillotine, while Scourge looks at it with a somber gaze of acceptance.

I wish they hadn't tried to rescue me.

There's nothing anyone can do about it now.

Blinking as my eyes grow accustomed to the light, I look out at the crowd gathered before the stage. Hundreds of people have come to see this; citizens of Armavir from every strata of society. The crowd fills the enormous walled plaza in front of the Hall of Justice, near the center of which is the stage on which we stand.

Chapter 34: The Day of Reckoning

The Paladin Order is here as well. I count fourteen ivory knights standing guard on the fringes of the crowd. Behind the plaza, out on the street, I see four mounted Paladins armed with double-bladed pikes.

Yet another man, impressive at first sight, presides on horseback among the mounted Paladins. He's stately and dazzling, dressed in white with a silver crown upon his head.

Prince Oliver? What's he doing here?

I wasn't aware I'd become so notorious that the crown prince himself has found it fitting to spend his afternoon observing my decapitation.

On a much less exciting note, there are scores of police standing guard in, around, in front of, and behind the crowd. I quickly spot Bennett on horseback on the left side of the courtyard, with his stature and appearance in striking contrast to Prince Oliver. I look away before he has a chance to notice my gaze.

Next, I look up at the roof across the road from the plaza, and I see one of Bennett's pet Felids crouched like a gargoyle next to a chimney. I suspect the other Felids are stationed on rooftops nearby.

All things considered, if my brothers have any inkling of a desire to rescue me, it sure as hell won't be easy.

"No one's coming for you," the death-voice says. *"They have already forgotten you and left you for dead."*

"Shut up, will you?" I groan inwardly.

At that moment, the executioner makes his entrance. He's a short, heavyset man with a scraggly goatee and a voluminous black robe. If I weren't so miserable, I'd give a snarky comment about his lack of fashion sense. As he walks toward front-center stage, he motions to me and points at the guillotine. "Hook her up."

His voice is more intimidating than his appearance, I'll give him that.

The guards push me onto the guillotine, laying me face-down on a wooden platform with my head over the edge, so when the blade drops it'll slice my neck straight through. The guards secure my body to the platform with ropes, and they remove the fetter from my neck, only to replace it with wooden stocks.

Meanwhile, the crowd begins to cheer.

It's hard for me to see from this angle; it hurts my neck to look up for more than a moment, and my unkempt hair shrouds my view. Instead, I stare down at the empty basket, which longs for my severed head, and I listen as everything takes place.

I hear the crowd hush after a few seconds.

The executioner fumbles with something made of paper—a scroll, I think—and begins to speak. His deep voice gives me chills. "Citizens of Cloud Summit, capital citadel of Armavir, the Land of Peace! Welcome to the long-awaited execution of this dangerous and elusive criminal, the Illusionist!"

The crowd cheers again. I hear someone near the front shout, "Death is no illusion!" Many others shout louder in agreement.

Death is no illusion.

When I hear it, all the panic and guilt associated with my first murder erupts within me like a fountain.

Before that day, everything I did was an illusion. All I did on White Sand raids and robberies was cast illusions. Harmless illusions, right? Perhaps, depending on one's point of view.

But the day I killed a policeman, it all became real.

That was no illusion. He's certainly dead.

Now, I deserve the same fate.

But…I don't *want* to die!

I realize I'm trembling with anxiety, sweating profusely, and my breath is shallow and constrained.

I still hear the executioner's droning voice, with a chorus of applause every now and then, but I don't understand a word he says.

I repeat as if entranced, "Death is no illusion. I'm gonna die."

My heart thumps relentlessly.

I feel like I'm going to vomit in the basket.

"Look at you," the death-voice purrs. *"Only moments from your demise do you realize your inescapable fate. Yes, tremble with fear! You are going to die, unloved and unwanted, despised and soon to be forgotten. You pathetic, rotten, selfish thief! You murderous, devious, licentious witch! Finally, the time has come for you to meet your doom!"*

As the death-voice rips into my soul, and tears stream down my face, I silently shout the cries of my soul:

I can't take it anymore!

It's too much! Make it stop!

Help! Somebody, help!

I don't want to die!

Make it *STOP!*

"STOP!" The word echoes across the plaza and silences everything both within and around me.

"Stop!" A voice repeats. It's coming from just outside the plaza.

Another voice jumps in, "Prince Oliver, Your Majesty! Please, hear us out, it's important!"

The crowd begins to murmur.

I hear Yoko whisper, "Scourge, look! It's Connor and Jake!"

Connor and Jake?

The scrawny Seer?

"What is it?" The prince asks.

"It's White Sand," the first voice says urgently. "They—"

"My friends," Oliver interrupts with a chuckle, "White Sand cannot possibly interfere with this event. Relax and be at peace."

"That's just it, Your Majesty," the second voice replies. "White Sand isn't going to attack here. They're going to attack Königheim!"

The voices are muffled by some derisive laughter and an increase in murmuring from the crowd.

"No!" The first voice shouts. "Prince Oliver, with all due respect, you need to believe us! Please, send the Paladins back to the castle right away! If we don't act fast, people are going to die!"

I hear Bennett's angry shout next, "Königheim is safe, you insolent peasants! Prince Oliver, there is no need to fear. Captain Antoine and a detachment of his best men have been assigned to guard the castle in your absence."

The noise of the crowd becomes deafening. Tension in the atmosphere rises like the coming of a powerful storm.

I crane my head up as far as it will go, and I manage to blow my hair partially out of my face so I can watch events unfold.

My gaze is first drawn to a white dove that flies over the crowd and lands on the arm of the Felid sentry on the roof. The Felid takes a piece of paper from the dove's talons and reads it for a few seconds before pocketing it, motioning with his hand, and disappearing over the other side of the roof.

One of the other Felids briefly crosses my field of vision as he follows the footsteps of the first.

"Gah!" Bennett shouts. "How dare those useless mercenaries abandon their post!"

"Perhaps they went to check on Königheim," one of Bennet's subordinates suggests.

Bennett rebukes him sharply with words I can't make out. Then he shouts at the executioner, who's been standing helplessly onstage this whole time, "Executioner, this is merely a distraction! Finish her!"

I gulp.

"Right away, sir!" the executioner fumbles with the scroll. "Now, where was I?"

"Forget the preamble!" Bennett shouts. "Kill her!"

"I can't do that, Chief! It's standard protocol to read through the— ah!" He flinches as a small projectile strikes his hand, causing him to toss the scroll into the front of the crowd.

Several people, already fraught with fear, witness the event. They point and shout, "White Sand is attacking! Run!"

Cries of panic multiply. Within seconds, the crowd is scrambling to flee the plaza.

Bennett shouts, "No one leaves!"

At his order, a group of police maneuver into the plaza entryway, standing as a human barricade with their weapons and shields up so the crowd cannot push through. But that doesn't stop them from trying.

The Paladins stand by, exchanging glances and fidgeting. Prince Oliver is distracted arguing with Connor and Jake, so he hasn't yet given his knights orders to intervene. I presume they're not sure whether to help the police or stop them.

I hang my head limp again to give my neck a rest. I listen for a moment as the panicked shouts of the crowd and the angry yells of the police become more intense. I can't help but marvel at the amazing work of my brothers in somehow orchestrating all of this. Now that the Felids are gone and the police are occupied, all they have to do is drop in and get me out of this thing.

"Excuse me, lads," a familiar voice comes from the far side of the stage.

What?

It can't be!

I look to my left, and sure enough I see the crazy old man hobbling up the steps toward the four prison guards standing with Scourge and Yoko. He says, "It looks like they need ye down there. Why don't ye move along and help, while I keep an eye on the prisoners?"

The guards exchange glances and nod before jumping off the stage and disappearing in the tumultuous crowd.

"Jed!" Yoko exclaims once the guards have gone. "Are you going to rescue us!?"

"Shhh," Jed, whispers, his deep blue eyes twinkling. "Play along, now. Don't move until I'm done releasin' all of ye." He pulls out a glimmering green object and begins picking the lock on Yoko's handcuffs.

That's the same thing Yoko used to rescue me last night! How did Jed get one? Damn it, I want one too!

I'll have to steal it after he releases me.

"That was you with the slingshot, wasn't it?" Scourge whispers. "The one that hit the executioner?"

"Aye," Jed smiles as he moves on to Yoko's neck-fetter. "I trained with slingshots all the time when I was a wee lad. I could hit a sparrow from over twice the distance of this plaza!"

"Wow!" Yoko breathes. "Can you teach me?"

"Perhaps one day," Jed says, moving on to Scourge. "But not for a long time."

"Aw," Yoko frowns.

After undoing Scourge's bonds, Jed approaches me. I avoid his gaze and lower my head.

"Celine," Jed says as he picks the lock on the stocks. "Have ye thought about what I said the other day?"

I can't bring myself to reply. Why does this lunatic care about me so much?

After undoing the stocks and my handcuffs, Jed draws near and whispers, hardly above the din of the raging crowd, "Remember well the events of this day, but do not be discouraged. There is a love stronger than death, and it is with that love that the Great King will set ye free."

I remember the words of the ghost-lady from last night: "Through the faithfulness of your mother, the Great King saved you from Sunophsis. Now, through the faithfulness of one man, the Great King will save you from Armavir."

I open my mouth to ask Jed about the ghost-lady, but I stop when the most terrifying man in Cloud Summit shouts, "Oh, you've got to be kidding me!"

Sure enough, Chief Bennett has dismounted and is coming this way, glaring at me with unbridled loathing.

"Lads," Jed says to Scourge and Yoko, "Now is the time. Run away from here as fast as ye can, and don't look back."

"But—" Yoko tries to argue, but Jed shouts, "Go!"

I don't look to see if they obey him. My terrified gaze is fixed on Chief Bennett as he climbs the steps on the far side of the stage.

The executioner, who had just arrived onstage after retrieving his scroll, stands in Bennett's way. "It's all right Chief, I got it back! We can now resume the— ah!"

Bennett grabs the executioner by the collar of his robe and throws him off the stage. Two strides later, he draws his sword and says, "The fates seem to be very protective of you, Illusionist, but no scum of the depths can avoid the day of reckoning forever! Justice *will* prevail!"

"No!" Jed stands between Bennett and the guillotine, arms stretched wide. I can't see his face, but I can imagine his sea-blue gaze as calm and steadfast as ever. "Chief Bennett, I urge ye to reconsider! There are more important matters at hand than the execution of a common criminal! This is *not* true justice!"

"You've interfered on her behalf for the last time, old man!" Bennett raises his sword and brings it down upon Jed.

The sound of the blow drowns out that of the tumult beyond the stage.

Drops of blood fly through the air.

Jed falls to his knees, arms still outstretched, and he collapses face-down on the stage as Bennett steps over him, unfazed.

I hear Scourge and Yoko scream. They must have seen it.

I saw it, too.

And I'm next.

Bennett, now four feet away, points his bloodied sword at me and says, "Forget the guillotine. I will destroy you with my own blade!"

I scream, struggling with all my might against the restraints. The stocks are loose, but the ropes hold me in place.

Bennett raises his sword with both hands.

I scream louder, squeezing my eyes shut. The end has come.

BOOM!

A thunderclap rends the heavens, and the ground quakes.

A breathless hush falls over the plaza.

Three seconds later, another two: *BOOM! BAM!*

I open my eyes.

Bennett stands over me, sword still raised, but he stares off into the distance with wide-eyed bewilderment.

Only once the not-so-distant rumble of crumbling stone fills the air do I realize that was no thunderclap.

"They've done it!" A man shouts. "Königheim is coming down!"

"White Sand is attacking!"

Panic ensues once more as the crowd begins to scatter. This time, the police are either panicking themselves, or too stunned to react.

My restraints loosen.

I look to see that Scourge has cut the ropes with a small blade of fire. He doesn't wait for me to thank him; he runs offstage and disappears.

Without a second thought, I spring off the guillotine and follow suit.

I maneuver swiftly through the scattered crowd, fleeing as fast as my weary legs will carry me as far from the Hall of Justice as possible. While I cross the road, I steal a glance at the center of the city where Königheim proudly stood only a moment before. Now, it's a half-ruined disaster, a mere shell of its former self, belching up a column of smoke that rises tall and imposing into the mountain atmosphere.

The greatest architectural gem of Cloud Summit has been destroyed, and the king of Armavir presumably along with it.

But I couldn't care less about that.

Another man died today, one much more noble and kind than any ruler I've ever known or even heard about. This man, crazy though he was, never backed down from any confrontation and always stood his ground. He loved me more than anyone I've ever known, even after how wrongly I treated him. He was not ashamed to stand up for me, though I was a criminal condemned to die.

There was no reason for him to do it.

But still, he loved me.

Now, because of that, he's dead.

Jed died because of me.

It's all my fault.

35
Aftermath
Summer, 1419 AIE

~Connor~

THE WHOLE REALM spins out of control as I sprint across the plaza.

How did it come to this?

It all escalated so quickly!

Once Jake and I discovered White Sand's plot, we rushed to the Hall of Justice to tell someone—anyone—in the hope that they would believe us.

At first, I thought it was a stroke of luck that Prince Oliver was at the back of the crowd. Jake and I thought for sure he would be the one to heed our warning.

We were wrong.

The prince and the Paladins recognized Jake from his years in the Paladin Training Academy. They remembered all too well how he failed his own knighting ceremony, and they treated us with scorn.

We had only spent a moment arguing with Oliver before a riot was in full swing all around us. I was so determined to save Königheim and everyone in it, I didn't realize the magnitude of the situation until one of the Paladins said to Oliver, "Sir, things are getting out of hand. What are your orders?"

Oliver looked around, as if he also had just noticed the uproar. His eyes locked onto the stage and he asked, "What does that moron think he's doing?"

Chapter 35: Aftermath

I followed his gaze in time to see Bennett throw the executioner and draw his sword.

My heart stopped when Jed stood between him and the guillotine.

Everything I'd ever heard about Chief Bennett from Jake, Tarento, Scourge, and Alpha Blue became very real and personal to me as I watched him slay Jed in cold blood.

Jed. The crazy old Seer. My friend and mentor. The kindest, most gentle man I've ever known. An *innocent* man.

Everything around me ceased to exist in that split second. As much as my heart screamed for me to look away, I couldn't bring myself to do it. I stood there in shock, not even able to shout. I vaguely remember Jake trying to shake me out of it, but it wasn't until the first blast that I came back to the present.

It got everyone's attention. With a silence that could be felt, we all looked eastward at the highest towers of Königheim, only a mile down the road. Smoke had begun to rise, billowing and black like death itself.

With the next two blasts, the towers buckled and collapsed.

As the crowd erupted in pandemonium, Prince Oliver spurred his horse and ordered the Paladins, "To the castle! Now!"

They departed in a flurry of hooves and clinking armor. A somber urgency drove them away in a matter of seconds. None of them cast us a passing glance as they went.

I looked again at the stage. Bennett was enraged, yelling and cursing as he kicked the vacant guillotine and struck it with his sword.

Celine got away.

But, so help me, Great King, Chief Bennett won't be so lucky.

"Connor," Jake said, placing a hand on my shoulder.

I brushed it aside without a glance, and began my sprint for the stage.

Dodging people here and there, I pass the abandoned sword of a policeman and stoop down to take it.

"Connor!" Jake shouts from behind.

I ignore him. I'm almost upon the stage, ready to jump up there and attack that murderous chief with every bit of malice he deserves!

He doesn't see me coming. He's fuming and snarling, pacing back and forth and trembling as if he's about to explode like Königheim.

If only he would.

As I jump and pull myself onto the stage, Bennett trudges down the steps on the other side and heads for the entrance of the Hall of Justice.

I stand up and give chase without a word.

Still unaware of my pursuit, he enters the Hall and slams the double-doors shut behind him. I arrive two seconds later, hoping to fling the doors open again, but to no avail. They're already locked.

"No!" I pound on the door several times and shout, "Bennett! Come back here, you murdering coward!"

Even as the words escape my mouth, I become aware of my behavior. A wave of grief smothers the flames of my vengeful anger. I collapse to my knees, dropping the sword and dragging my fist down the door, and I begin to sob harder than I ever have before.

Why did this have to happen!?

Why did Jed stand in the way!?

Why did he have to die!?

"Connor," A gentle hand touches my shoulder.

I turn my head to see Yoko, looking at me with teary-eyed concern. She wraps her arms around me, and I immediately turn and embrace her, sobbing all the more. I can tell she, too, has been traumatized by Jed's sudden demise. Such a sight of cruelty should never be witnessed by a girl her age, but nevertheless, here we are.

The sound of footsteps approaches, followed by Jake's voice, "We can't stay here. We have to find a place that will be safe for us."

"I'm not leaving Jed," I mumble between sobs.

"I'm so sorry, Connor, but we don't have a choice." Jake kneels down beside us. "The police are scattered now, but they won't be for long. They'll try to arrest Yoko and Scourge again."

"We can't leave Jed," I repeat, pulling away from Yoko's embrace to look at Jake. "Not after everything he's done for us."

Jake nods, looking down at the ground. "I understand. Let's see what we can do. Come on," he stands and extends a hand toward me.

I take his hand and allow him to help me up, and then I do the same for Yoko.

We walk toward the stage again, ascending the steps and passing the guillotine to where Jed lies face-down in a pool of his own blood. I can hardly bring myself to look at him.

Scourge is already there, looking down at the body with a single tear running down his cheek. He holds the jade key and a slingshot close to his chest. As we approach, he looks up and says, "He saved us. Yoko, me, and Celine. He risked his life to set us free."

"I know," Jake says, placing a hand on Scourge's shoulder. "He was a very brave man, deserving of the greatest burial of honor."

I wholeheartedly agree. However, it won't be as easy as it was when Jed and I buried my father in the open countryside. Here, everything is made of stone. There's no place to dig into the ground. With a deep sigh, I say, "We'll have to take him into the mountains, away from the trade routes where he won't be disturbed. He can rest in peace there."

As the others ponder in silence, I realize that in hardly three weeks' time, I've lost both my father and my mentor at the hands of heartless murderers. My father's death was grievous enough, and I still haven't overcome it. Jed's death, now, is already so much harder to bear because of that. How has this same thing happened to me all over again? *Why* did it happen? Who's next, I wonder? Jake? Tarento? Anxiety rises in my heart like a dangerous tide as I think about it.

Should I have gone on this quest alone after all?

Do I put my friends and everyone I meet in danger?

Scourge interrupts my train of thought as he replies to my previous answer, "We don't have to leave the city. Why don't we cremate him right here? I can provide the fire."

"We don't have a funeral pyre," Jake says, "or wood, for that matter."

"We can improvise," Scourge says, pointing at the guillotine.

Aside from the blade and a few gears, locks, and latches, the death machine is completely wooden. It's not a bad suggestion.

With another deep sigh, I nod. "All right. Let's do it."

Together, we gather around Jed's body to pick him up. There's not a dry eye among us as we maneuver him onto the guillotine platform and set him down on his back.

His face, frozen with an eternal look of steadfast determination, is in stark contrast to the unsightly gash running diagonally from his right shoulder to the left side of his abdomen. None of us can bring ourselves to look. It's much more horrible up close.

"Wait a second," Jake says, running and jumping off the stage. He takes two abandoned coats from the ground, returning to place one coat over Jed's legs and the other over his torso and face. All of us help tuck him in the coats, and then we back away and look upon the body on the guillotine.

After a moment of silence, I clear my throat and begin a eulogy. "Jed was a very strange man. In fact, he was the most vague, the most annoying, and the most unforgivably obscure man I've ever known. But all the same, he was a very good man. He lived a full life marked by obedience to the Great King. He was very wise, very brave, and he loved everyone his eyes fell upon. It's because of him I came to know the Great King, and it's because of him we're on this quest. I only hope one day I'll be as great a Seer as he. His presence among us will be forever missed."

I turn and nod at Scourge, who nods in return before sending a bright spark to ignite the guillotine. The fire starts small, but it quickly grows to consume the wooden frame and the body resting upon it.

Tears run down my face once again.

This did *not* need to happen.

I understand now the degree of Chief Bennett's heartless corruption. The knowledge has touched me deeply and personally, in many ways more so than that of Jaedis. The sorcerer is expected to be heartless and corrupt, and certainly he ought to be challenged and defeated. This chief of police on the other hand, a man in authority over a city of innocent people who desperately need to be governed and protected, is all the more disgusting for his abuse of power and perversion of the meaning of justice.

That man, as much as I hate to admit it, deserves to die.

The sound of approaching hooves is audible above the crackling of the fire.

We all look to see a police captain on horseback coming toward us. My stomach plummets at first, but as he comes closer, I notice his outfit and worried face are covered in soot. In addition, he holds his right arm as if it's been injured.

Jake leans in and whispers, "It's Captain Antoine; he must be coming from Königheim. Let's build rapport with him and find out what happened."

After we nod, Jake turns and greets the incoming officer, "Captain Antoine! Are you all right? What happened over there?"

Antoine pulls his horse up alongside the stage and looks at us. At first, I wonder if he'll question why we're standing next to a flaming guillotine, but he's far too shaken to care about that. He says, "It's madness. My own men turned against me. They helped White Sand load Königheim with explosives. I...I still can't believe it. I was hardly able to escape."

That's a new plot-twist. Police in league with White Sand.

"What about the people in the castle?" Jake asks. "And King Alphonse? Are they all right?"

"The king and many others were rescued by a Samurai, a

nymph, and a huntsman. But...it...wasn't enough. Many people died in the blast. We were woefully unprepared."

"Tarento, Sylva, and Khai?" Yoko asks, her face acquiring some of its former inquisitive glow.

"Sounds like it," Scourge agrees.

Antoine continues, "Prince Oliver and the Paladins are there now, helping people out of the rubble and searching the area for insurgents. He sent me back here to tell Chief Bennett about the traitors within our ranks."

"I don't suspect he'll be happy about that," Jake says with a frown.

"That's what I'm afraid of," Antoine winces. Then he looks at the guillotine and asks, "Is that the Illusionist?"

None of us speak. We look everywhere except Antoine's clueless gaze, and I clench my fists as anger rises within me once again.

No, you law-enforcing muttonhead, that is *not* the Illusionist.

That is Jed, my friend and my mentor, whom your police chief senselessly murdered without a single thought of mercy. Celine has escaped, and if I'm honest with myself, despite everything we've gone through for her sake, I wish she had been killed instead of Jed.

She deserves to die more than he did.

So much more.

"No," I reply, still refusing to look at Antoine. I gesture with one hand at the fiery guillotine and say, "this is my friend, Jed. He was a great man who lived to love other people. I...he..."

As I struggle to find words, I feel my Seer's gift stir within me. The Great King says, *"Antoine can be trusted. Be honest with him."*

I sigh as I reign in my emotions. Then I tell Antoine about Jed's goal to sell the homestead, Celine's interference, our dilemma with the money being in Bennett's hands, Yoko's acquisition of the jade key and subsequent arrest, and the events of the execution as they unfolded, up to our decision to use the guillotine as a substitute funeral pyre.

I can tell my friends are unnerved by how much I'm revealing, but I press on. I'll tell them it was a Seer thing later.

Once I've finished, Antoine is silent for a long time. He stares past us at the guillotine, deep in thought. Finally, he straightens his posture and clears his throat before gesturing toward Yoko and Scourge. "These two, by the standard of the law, should be apprehended immediately and their death sentence upheld."

We are all silent.

Really, Great King? After all that explaining, Antoine *still* wants to be a law-enforcing muttonhead?

"However," Antoine continues, wiping his sooty brow with a handkerchief, "I do personally sympathize with your efforts. In the wake of the disasters that have taken place today, no one would find it odd if the lot of you escaped just like the Illusionist, and the guillotine so happened to go up in flames. Just be sure to avoid any further suspicious activity."

We all relax and sigh with relief.

"As you were," Antoine nods cordially before spurring his horse and setting off at a trot. As he crosses the plaza, he whistles to Bennett's horse, which had been standing where its master left it. The hefty black stallion snorts gratefully and follows Antoine out of the plaza and out of sight.

As the afternoon matures into evening, dark clouds advance across the sky like a funeral procession, bringing with them steady rainfall and distant thunder.

Jake, Scourge, Yoko, and I make our way back to the hotel. Our pace is hindered by Yoko, who can only limp, due to an arrow wound she received during the rescue attempt. Once we arrive, we're disappointed to find it roped off and guarded by seven police guards and two Paladins. As we come closer, I notice that within the roped-off area there's a body face-down on the ground, clothed in a full-black garb. A third Paladin is crouched next to it, doing detective work like Jake had done in the abandoned castle.

"Look," Jake says, pointing above the crime scene at a broken window on the third floor. "That's our traveler's suite. Tarento must have been attacked."

Aw," Yoko sighs. "Where are we going to sleep?"

"We'll find a place," Jake assures her. "But first, we need to find Tarento and Khai. Connor, do you know where they might be?"

I pause for a moment, taking a deep breath as I discern their location through my Seer's gift. Königheim is my first guess. Remembering Tarento's compassion for the Blue Foxes at the shipyard, I assume he'd want to help as many people as possible. However, as I think more about it, another location stands out even more. "The Bullfrog Tavern. That's where we'll find them."

"Then that's where we'll go," Jake says.

We walk in silence down the dreary and mostly-abandoned

streets of Cloud Summit. We're drenched from the rain, but it doesn't seem to bother any of us. Our hearts are much heavier than our sodden clothing.

In contrast, the bleak circumstances don't hinder the light-bringers. They're bustling about as they always do at this hour, lighting every lamppost to illuminate our path. I'm sure no one would blame them if they refrained from lighting the lamps after a day like this, but even so, here they are. I'm thankful for their company and their warmth, even though they never come near or speak a word as we walk by.

We enter the tavern. Despite it being as busy as always after dark, the atmosphere is dismal. Everyone sits and talks quietly amongst themselves, while on the performance stage at the back of the tavern, there are three minstrels playing melancholy music—two violinists and a cellist.

I quickly identify Tarento and Khai sitting alone at a large table with a half-empty bottle of Pythorian summer whiskey between them. They're both covered in rain-smeared soot and look just as despondent as we are.

"Hey guys," Jake greets as he approaches the table.

Khai looks up, his eyes landing on Yoko, and he smiles.

"Khai!" Yoko hobbles over and tackles him with a hug.

"I'm so glad you're safe," Khai says, returning the embrace and burying his face in her hair. "If I had lost you as well, I would have lost *everything*."

"I'm glad you didn't blow up with the castle," Yoko replies with a tearful whimper.

Tarento, his absent gaze glued to the table, doesn't react to our arrival.

We take seats and sit in silence for a moment. Grief holds us with a grip that seems to take our breath away.

"Jed was killed," Jake finally says with a sigh. "Celine escaped."

More silence ensues.

Tarento takes a drink from the whiskey bottle.

I hardly let it touch the table again before snatching it and taking a swig myself. The burning spice of the drink is a pleasant distraction from the horrors of the day.

"Tarento was attacked," Khai says, "by White Sand."

We all look at Tarento, who refuses to make eye contact with any of us.

I don't blame him.

I have another drink of whiskey and slide the bottle across the table toward him. He takes it and drinks.

"What happened at Königheim?" Jake asks Khai.

He sighs before beginning to tell us the story from his perspective. "Sylva and I were in the park as Jed instructed. We saw a group of police escorting a caravan of draped carts up the road toward Königheim. We followed them and discovered they were collaborating with White Sand to bring explosives into the castle. I knew we couldn't stop them alone, so we went back to find Tarento. There he was, coming our way with three Offspring of Sisera on his tail. After fighting them off, we went to Königheim to speak with the police. They found it more fitting to fight, so we battled past them and entered the castle, where we saw the explosives piled around support columns in the main hall. The police were keeping the room closed off to those inside the castle to hide the surprise. Antoine and his loyal men were held captive there, guarded by White Sand fighters. After we rescued them, Tarento went to the throne room to save King Alphonse. Antoine and Sylva stayed to make sure no one detonated the crates, and I went throughout the castle telling everyone to evacuate. Antoine told me how to get to the bell tower, which I could use to sound the alarm. A group of castle guards and Paladins joined me as I went, but when we reached the bell tower, White Sand was ready for us. We weren't able to get close to the bell. They struck down everyone who came near as if it was their greatest treasure. An Offspring of Sisera with superhuman strength was their champion. Though I put an arrow in his chest, it was only seconds later when the first blast signaled our failure."

As Khai was speaking, I waved the bartender for a bottle of ginger Tethysian brew. Once he brought it, I began chugging it down.

"How did you escape?" Yoko asks.

"Only with the favor of the Great King. The bell tower is behind the castle, far from where the explosions took place. One of the walls caved in, but nothing more. White Sand killed far more people in the bell tower than the collapse did."

"How many people didn't make it?" Scourge asks.

Khai shakes his head. "It must have been at least a hundred."

Silence follows. Can today get any worse?

"Where's Sylva?" Yoko asks.

"I don't know," Khai says. "I haven't seen her."

"Oh, no," Yoko buries her face in Khai's shoulder.

I finish the Tethysian brew.

"We knew," Jake says, his tone solemn. "Connor and I. We knew Königheim was in danger, but Prince Oliver didn't believe us."

Khai places his elbows on the table and hides his face in his hands. "It seems like we were meant to fail from the start. Didn't Jed see *any* of this coming?"

"I...I'm not sure," Jake says. "It seemed like he did, at least... until..."

"He knew," I say, reaching across the table for the whiskey bottle. "He knew. When I saw him this morning, he was sobbing." I drink several gulps of the whiskey, set the bottle down, and wipe my sleeve across my chin. "Jed knew everything. But it didn't help a single one of us, not even him."

I notice the others are looking at me with concern. It's unnerving. "What are you all looking at?"

After no one says anything, my anger flares and I shout, "Jed deserved to live more than all of us! He shouldn't have died! Why didn't the Great King save him? He didn't have to die! Bennett should have died, and Celine should have died, and maybe all of us should have died too, but not Jed!"

"Connor," Jake says. I can't interpret his expression because my vision is spotted, but I'm sure it's nothing good.

"No!" I shout. "Don't tell me what to do!"

"Connor, we understand," Scourge says. "We're upset too; we're disheartened and confused. I don't know why things happened the way they did, but—"

"Wait a second," I say, pointing across the table at Scourge. "You were there! *You* let Jed die!"

"What do you—"

I interrupt Scourge's pathetic defense with the unbridled truth. "You could have saved him! You're an electrokinetic, for crying out loud! You should have killed Bennett to save Jed!"

"You *know* I could never do that!"

"Well, you *should* have!" I retort, standing up.

"Stop fighting!" Yoko shouts.

"You!" I point at Yoko. "*You* risked your life to save Celine, but what about Jed? Huh!? Why didn't you risk your life to save Jed!?"

Khai stands to defend Yoko, "Hey! Cut it out!"

"No! *You* cut it out! All of you cut it out!" I turn to grab a chair and throw it, but in the middle of my stunt everything spins out of control and I feel myself falling amidst a chaotic din of shouts before all goes deathly black and silent.

"WHAT THE HELL were you thinking?" Chief Bennett growls, pacing back and forth across the meeting room.

Heiban stands off to the side with his head bowed, rubbing his temples in frustration. He didn't think working with the chief of police would be so difficult. "I already told you, Chief. A messenger dove brought me a note with your signature and orders to capture a White Sand insurgent in downtown Cloud Summit."

"I ordered no such thing! It's because you left when you did that everything escalated so far out of control. Ultimately, it's because of *you* that the Illusionist escaped!"

Heiban sighs, pulling out a piece of paper and unfolding it. "Look."

Bennett takes the paper and reads it aloud, "'An aggressive White Sand insurgent has been spotted in downtown Cloud Summit. Capture him immediately'...followed by my signature." He tears the letter apart. "It's fake! Who did this!?"

"I have no idea," Heiban says. "However, fake or not, there's a silver lining to all of this. Though you've lost the Illusionist, you've gained another prisoner."

"Hmph. What are you talking about?"

"My comrades Ibara and Kaze are currently pulling intel out of the insurgent mentioned in the note. Before you summoned me, I learned his name is Nebioth and he is one of the most influential members of the group."

"The gang leader?" Bennett asks with a raised eyebrow.

"Possibly, if not someone close to him."

"Hmm...can you make him talk?"

"He looks like a tough nut to crack, but," Heiban smirks. "We have *special methods* for dealing with people like him."

"Find out all you can," Bennett instructs, "and then lock him up. Report to me everything he tells you, and with that information we will prepare a counter-offensive."

"Lock him up?" Heiban scoffs. "Chief, let us dispose of him. We'll get away with it much easier than you can. After all, who will question the death of a high-ranking White Sand insurgent after a disaster like the bombing of Königheim?"

Bennett grins. "I like the way you think, Felid. Do with him as you see fit."

"Very well," Heiban bows. "I will report to you first thing in the morning."

"I look forward to it. Don't fail me again, or our deal is off."

"You have my word."

"THIS IS ALL *your* fault!" Shaama says, throwing her arms up in frustration. Dim firelight illuminates the small stone room where Shaama converses with the strange visitor. "Our magnificent display of terror wasn't the ultimatum it was supposed to be. King Alphonse should be dead! Prince Oliver should be dead! Every nobleman, every one of the king's servants—*dead!*" She takes off the white-haired wig she'd been wearing and throws it on the ground, exposing her nearly-bald scalp.

"I tried to tell you," the visitor says with a shrug. "Every person who interfered with your plan was on the list I gave you. My master wants them destroyed for a very good reason. Had you postponed your plan until they were eradicated, things might have turned out in your favor."

"Hmph. Since it appears we have a common enemy, why don't you help me?"

"I have been given orders not to intervene. You have everything you need to get the job done." The visitor's yellow eyes twinkle. "Moreover, due to our change of circumstances, my master has requested that another name be added to the list."

"Oh? And what name is that?"

"The Illusionist, Celine."

Shaama's eyes widen, but she quickly hides her surprise with a scowl. "What makes you think I'd be willing to eliminate one of my greatest assets?"

"My master's wisdom is not to be questioned on this matter. He sees her as a threat, and she must be treated as such. Besides, you were content with her being executed today, were you not?"

"The execution was one thing. She got herself into that mess, and we had our hands tied with the bombing of Königheim. If she had died at the guillotine, it would have been a noble end. Now that she's returned, I will *not* simply dispose of her because some faraway sorcerer thinks she's a threat."

"Oh, but you will. You'll do *anything* to win your father's approval, will you not? If you hope to take another shot at the royalty of Armavir, you'd better do what my master asks of you. Otherwise, these followers of the Great King will foil your plans at every turn. I assure you, dear Shaama, your victory rests in the hands of my master."

Shaama looks at the ground. Her face at first softens into that of a lost and grief-stricken child, but then she blinks, and her expression turns cold. Wiping what would have been a tear, she says, "We will let them come to us. They'll have nowhere to run, and nowhere to hide. The Glimmerbeast will feast on their flesh."

The visitor grins. "That's more like it."

Misham is hiding in the hall outside the room. He hears every word of the conversation.

36

A Realm at War

Spring, 105 IE

~Connor~

I OPEN MY EYES, heavy like stone.

I'm greeted by a murky featureless sky.

Is it already daylight? I must've been unconscious all night.

I didn't plan on drinking so much. But I was so upset it just felt...*necessary*.

Unlike Jed's death, which was *completely* *un*necessary.

I cough, sitting up to rub my forehead. The air is dry and my throat is parched. I could use a drink of water. But when I look around to see where I am, a parched throat becomes the least of my worries.

I'm in the middle of a desolate expanse of scorched grassland, stretching out over rolling hills on every horizon. Ash falls gently like snow, and the wind blows with irregular gusts to kick up clouds of gray dust. The air is oppressive, smelling of smoke. A sense of foreboding anchors my heart as I stand to my feet.

What is this place? Could it be Meiro?

"Hello?" I ask, peering about.

I hear nothing but the wind and the distant cawing of crows.

I'm alone, at least for now.

I begin walking to the top of the nearest hill; my feet kick up clouds of ash as I go. Both curiosity and apprehension grab hold of me as I take in my surroundings.

What happened?

How did I get here?

Am I...dead?

The agonized shout of a woman breaks the forlorn silence. Someone's in trouble, and it's coming from the other side of this hill! The shout grips my heart so readily, I break into a sprint. When I finally crest the hill, the scene before me is staggering.

I behold a sprawling expanse of stone ruins, leveled to the ground, with pockets of smoldering flame and smoke rising into the dreary sky. "Whoa," I mutter. "What in the land of..."

My gaze falls upon a black-robed woman among the ruins. Her weeping makes my blood run cold. Soon after I notice her, she turns toward me. Even from this distance I recognize her, and my stomach lurches.

Melody.

"Hey!" I wave to get her attention. "Melody! It's me, Connor!"

She doesn't notice. She turns away with a shrill cry and continues to weep.

"Melody!" I shout, running down the hill toward her. After a few steps, something snaps beneath my foot, and I stop to look down. It's a blackened banner holster with a charred flag still bound to it. The insignia, a silver dragon on a black background, is preserved well enough that I immediately recognize it.

The Tethysian Empire.

But...the Tethysian Empire existed over a thousand years ago.

Now I'm *really* confused! Where am I, and *when* am I!?

"This is a realm at war," a voice behind me says.

I whirl around to face the owner of the voice, who stands atop the hill; a male elf about my height, studious in appearance. He wears a pair of spectacles and carries a large tome beneath his right arm.

The elf looks mournfully at the burning ruins as he speaks. "Destruction. Chaos. Agony. Suffering. Death. These are the weapons of war used by the Great Serpent in his final days of denial." He sighs. "Loss of life is a great tragedy and a horrible misfortune—the cost of living in a realm at war."

I tilt my head. "Who are you?"

He nods in greeting. "My name is Penn. I've been sent by the Great King to tell you about the ruins you now see, and much more."

"You're from Marindel?" I ask. "One of the Galyyrim?"

"Yes. Come with me," Penn turns and walks down the hill.

"But, what about Melody? Shouldn't we help her?"

"She cannot see us. As you've correctly discerned, this happened over a thousand years ago."

"Oh." I glance back at Melody and the ruins before running to catch up with Penn. "Why does the Great King want me to know about the ruins? What do they have to do with anything?"

"You'll see. Your heart is in great anguish, is it not?"

I bow my head, remembering Jed's death with a long sigh. "Do you know what happened?"

"Yes. Do you?"

I fail to suppress my scathing reply, "Of *course* I do! I was *there!*"

"But you don't know *why*, do you?"

I pause. "No, I don't. It didn't need to happen. It was all a terrible mistake. Why did he get in the way? Why did he—"

"Hush. I understand. I promise, the Great King is just as sorrowful about Jed's death as you are. I've come to bring a message of hope to carry you and your friends through these troubled times."

"A message of hope," I say slowly, "about a burning city and a crying girl?"

"Yes."

"What could *possibly* be hopeful about that?"

"With your limited vision of the situation, your cynicism is to be expected. To have hope, you must see as the Great King sees. You must know the purposes of his heart and the methods by which he works. Only then, even in this realm at war, with the Great Serpent gasping for his every breath, will you understand hope even in the most terrible of circumstances."

I ponder for a few seconds. "You've mentioned the Serpent twice now, as if he's dying. What do you mean by that?"

"All will become clear after you hear the story I have to tell."

"A story?" I ask, my spirits perking up just a bit.

"Yes. Have you ever heard of the kingdom of Rhema?"

I briefly search my memory bank of epic stories, but the name doesn't sound familiar. "Nope."

"Perhaps you've heard it called the Ancient Isle, or the Forgotten Kingdom?"

"Doesn't ring a bell," I say with a shrug.

"That is to be expected. The Serpent has gone to great lengths to erase the memory of this land."

I look again at our barren surroundings, and I remember the sight of the ruins. "So, this is the kingdom of Rhema?"

"Yes. As the Final Seer, the Great King has entrusted you

with the knowledge of this kingdom, its history, and its role in the coming days."

I look at Penn to ask him a question, but when I see the glimmer of excitement in his eyes, my tongue is stilled. What's he so happy about?

"This is not just any story, mind you," Penn says with a grin.

I then remember the words of Jed: "Calm down lad, there's no need to fret. The seventh member of yer team is not yet present. I cannot tell the Great Story until *all* of ye are ready."

My eyes widen. "Are you going to tell me the Great Story?"

"No, I've come to do much better than that. I'm going to *show* you the Great Story."

"Wow! Really? But…Celine hasn't joined us yet. Jed said—"

"Ah," Penn raises a hand to silence me. "*Now* is the time!"

"Well, all right, if you say so!" Penn's contagious excitement is igniting my soul already, and the story hasn't even begun. "So, where do we start? You said you were going to show it to me. How're you going to do that?"

"You're here, aren't you?" Penn gestures with one hand. "This is the kingdom of Rhema in the year 105 IE. You will see and feel the whole story as you see and feel your surroundings now. Of course, the story begins long before the ruins, and indeed, long before the kingdom of Rhema came to be. It begins immediately after the events in your favorite story, *The Princess of the Sea*."

"Really?" My heart leaps.

"You've been waiting a long time to hear that, haven't you?"

"Of course I have! *The Princess of the Sea* ended so horribly, what with Melody disappearing over the horizon."

"That's correct. Do you remember the conversation between the Great King and Prince Eli in the forbidden room?"

I remember. As I recall the words of the conversation, our surroundings blur together and darken until we're walking in the midst of a black void.

The Great King said, "My son, you must understand. Melody has done a very terrible thing by surrendering her inheritance to the Great Serpent. Tyrizah will not be the same. It will be filled with chaos, perversion, destruction, and death. There is no easy solution, for as long as the Serpent has Melody's inheritance, none of us can stop him. Moreover, only she can reclaim what is rightfully hers."

"Will she?" Eli asked.

"No. Not without help."

As Eli thought about the memories he shared with Melody, his love for her burned like a zealous flame in his heart. He stood and declared, "I will help her! Send me, Father! I'll do whatever it takes to save Melody and help her reclaim her inheritance."

"Very well, my son. When the time is right, I will send you to the realm above to find her. In the meantime, prepare yourself and wait patiently."

Penn says, "Everything the Great King said came to pass. With the power granted by Melody's inheritance, the Great Serpent was unstoppable, and he asserted control over every living thing in the realm. Wars broke out, natural disasters and horrible monsters ravaged the land, and diseases spread unabated. The Era of Peace came to a swift end, and in its place came a terrible era of darkness and despair."

As Penn speaks, a huge window opens up before us. Through it I see illustrations of his words: scenes of war, plagues, storms, and monsters.

"Unfortunately," Penn continues, as do the illustrations, "not even the Kingdom of Marindel was safe. Soon after his release, the Serpent mobilized an army of powerful monsters and hideous creatures from the Bygone Era, and he led them in a direct assault against the Great King and the Galyyrim to destroy the Kingdom of Marindel once and for all.

"The Great King, wise and sovereign in his leadership, knew the Serpent could not be stripped of his power through outright confrontation. He also knew that the Kingdom of Marindel could not safely exist in a realm subdued by the Serpent. To save what he could of the city and those loyal to him, he ordered the Royal Orchestra to play the Music of Marindel. The song of thousands of voices and instruments, playing in perfect harmony unto the King, repelled the Serpent's dark forces and caused the Kingdom of Marindel to vanish from the realm of Tyrizah. No living creature has seen it since.

"For many centuries, it seemed as though the Serpent reigned unchallenged. Marindel was gone, the Great King was nowhere to be found, and every creature on land and under the sea was subject to the Serpent's heartless cruelty with no hope for a better future. However, the Great King hadn't forgotten about the realm he loved so fiercely, and he had a plan to rescue it from the Serpent's grasp."

Penn pauses, looking at me. "Do you know what his plan is?"

I feel as though I should. I remember my vision of Prince Eli while I was unconscious from the Nox Abyssae poison. I remember my conversation with Jed on the road from the tavern to the homestead later that morning. My mind connects the dots, and with confidence I say, "The Great King wants his daughter back. He longs for Melody to remember who she is and reclaim her inheritance, and he sent Prince Eli to help her understand that."

"Yes. Our story begins with the King's lost daughter, who'd been hurled by the Serpent into the realm above the sea. There she was chased around and mistreated for no reason at all, except for pure hatred. The lies the Serpent spoke to her on the day of his release were driven deep into her soul. She believed she was despised by the Great King and could never return to Marindel, even if she wanted to. As a result, she lived her life independently and full of misery, knowing she deserved to die for all the darkness she unleashed upon the realm.

"In time, the Great King began whispering to her. His gentle voice in her heart began melting the callousness caused by the Serpent's lies and others' harsh treatment of her. She began to realize there was something she was made for, some sort of purpose, but she couldn't discern what it was. The Serpent kept her blind to it.

"When Melody had the appearance of fourteen years of age, around the year 1200 BIE, she obeyed a prompt from the Great King to travel to a new land. As she journeyed across the mainland, many people joined her on her quest. The Serpent retaliated by sending enemy armies and bloodthirsty monsters to dispel the group, but the Great King protected them from every attack as they followed his lead.

"From the southern shore of what is now Sunophsis, Melody and two hundred adventurers set sail into unknown waters. Following directions from the Great King, they happened upon a pristine island paradise in the middle of the sea. There they settled and built towns, villages, and cities. Melody named the island Rhema, in honor of the gentle whispers of the King who led her there.

"In the early years, Rhema was the most peaceful land in the realm. Though little was known or understood about the Great King at that time, everyone on the island acknowledged him. Many years passed, and the people of Rhema multiplied and prospered.

"Unfortunately, so too did the seed of pride in Melody's heart.

"She wanted so badly to believe she was important and self-reliant, but with the lies of the Serpent so deeply rooted in her soul, she couldn't cure her sense of guilt and worthlessness. The Serpent took advantage of Melody's thoughts and slowly convinced her that she'd built Rhema all on her own, and she deserved to be its rightful queen.

"When she had the appearance of sixteen years of age, without giving any thought to the will of the Great King, Melody asserted herself as the Queen of Rhema and declared it to be an official kingdom. This happened in the year 618 BIE. From then on, though they maintained the appearance of prosperity, Melody and her people forgot about the Great King. They became entangled in the affairs of other kingdoms. Alliances were made, battles were fought, and worst of all, the Serpent's corruption saturated the hearts and minds of the citizens of Rhema. Melody and her appointed officials, poisoned with arrogance, ignored plight of the poor and denied justice to the innocent. They even encouraged other kingdoms to do the same.

"During that time of slow decline, several Rhemans remembered the Great King and everything he did for them. These individuals were empowered to be the first Seers. Over a period of several hundred years, they warned Melody that if she and her people didn't follow the ways of the Great King as they had done before, Rhema would be subject to an onslaught of the Serpent's cruelty.

"Melody never listened to the Seers. She came to despise them for meddling in her affairs and never having anything good to say. In time, she ordered for them to be exiled or killed as enemies of the kingdom.

"The final Seer of those days, before his execution, pleaded with Melody, 'Your father, the King, remembers you, and he loves you! The Prince of the Sea is coming soon, and he will deliver you from the power of the Serpent once and for all! Remember the Great King and follow his ways! He doesn't want you to continue in your suffering, but to return to Marindel as the bride of the Great Prince!'

"'Kill him,' Melody said, and the deed was done.

"Two centuries later, when Melody had the appearance of nineteen years of age, the kingdoms of Tyrizah were terrorized by the rapid expansion of the Tethysian Empire. As you've likely heard, they were notorious for their use of dragons in military combat. Most kingdoms hadn't the means to resist such a novel strategy."

"The ruins," I say, thinking back to the desolated city where Melody was weeping. "The Tethysians destroyed Rhema, didn't they?"

"Not until much later, and perhaps not for the reason you think. As the Empire's expansion brought war closer and closer to

Rhema, Melody and her officials were terrified. To avoid an attack they feared was imminent, in 57 IE they sent ambassadors to the emperor to form a compromise. The terms of the treaty allowed the Empire to occupy Rhema and use it as a launch point into modern-day Sunophsis, while sparing the citizens of Rhema and allowing Melody and her regime to remain in power, albeit under the higher command of the emperor."

Penn looks at me with a twinkle in his eye. "During this dark period of history, the stage was set for the next phase of the Great King's plan:

"The adventure of a thousand lifetimes.

"The most incredible romance ever recounted.

"The greatest battle of all time.

"The beginning of the Return of Marindel."

At this point I feel as though I'm about to die of suspense.

The window before us, through which I've been watching Penn's narrative play out, collapses and disappears. Dancing hues of blue begin moving about all around us as if we're deep beneath the sea. The air grows colder, and I shudder.

I hear the voice of the Great King thundering all around us. "My son, the time has come. Melody is of age, and the kingdoms of the realm are aligned according to plan."

"I'm ready, Father," the voice of Eli replies.

Penn wasn't kidding when he said he would *show* me the story. We exchange glances, and he lifts his eyebrows with knowing excitement.

The King says, "Before you go, you must understand—Melody's heart is harder now than ever before. She's not the same little girl you played with in the palace gardens during the Era of Peace. She will not recognize you, nor will she want to. You must surrender your powers and your Marindelian heritage to become just like her in every way. Lower yourself to love her and bring her heart out of the slimy pit in which the Serpent has buried it. Show her what it means to care deeply for the welfare of her people. Though you will have no power of your own, I will be your guide and your source of strength. In this way you will set an example not only for Melody, but for all sentient creatures in every kingdom of Tyrizah for years to come. Do you understand?"

"Yes, Father. I'll do whatever it takes!"

The Great King's voice quivers with emotion. "Remember, I will never abandon you, and my love is always with you. Go now! Tell my daughter everything that is stored up in your heart."

As the King's voice fades with an echo, so, too, do our surroundings.

I wait eagerly for the Great Story to unfold.

37

The Prince of the Sea

Summer, 104 IE

OVER THE VAST expanse of the sea, from a place no one could fathom, came a small sailboat driven by a southbound wind. Entering the harbor sheltered on either side by tall wooded hills, not a single alarm did sound. Laying anchor at the busy docks of Carnelian Cove, no one so much as lifted their head.

A young man stepped off the boat, clothed in nothing more than a brown commoner's tunic. His raven-black hair, sprinkled with sea salt, shone in the sun. His stature was strong and stately, yet gentle. In his amber eyes was a fiery hope that could not be quenched.

He looked out at the sailors, farmers, merchants, craftsmen, and soldiers who went about their business on this ordinary day in the kingdom of Rhema.

Not a single person acknowledged him.

Indeed, for the first time in this man's life, not a single knee bowed.

He spared no time, for he knew exactly what he had come to do. Approaching a pair of sailors, he greeted them, "Good afternoon, gentlemen. Do you know where Melody is today?"

"Ah, lucky for you she happens to be in town. I think she'll be having an important meeting with the Tethysians."

The other sailor narrowed his eyes. "Why do you ask, stranger? You aren't hoping to meet her, are you? She's not the friendly type. Doesn't take well to commoners, they say."

"That's not the Melody I know," the man replied. "She has

forgotten who she is, and the family to whom she belongs. But I will help her see."

"What are you talking about?" the second sailor scoffed. "She knows full well who she is: the Queen of Rhema, head of the aristocratic snobs, and a pawn of the Tethysian Empire. You're wasting your time! Go back to wherever it is you're from."

"I will not go until I fulfill my mission," the man replied. "I will not leave her a victim of darkness any longer. It's time for Melody to remember where she belongs as true royalty."

The sailors laughed at him.

"Go on, then!" the first sailor said. "Make a fool of yourself before the officials of Rhema and the Empire!"

With a parting nod, the man left the sailors and went into town.

MELODY STEPPED OUT onto the front balcony of the town hall. With an exasperated sigh, she leaned against the stone banister and looked out at the city. She could see all of Carnelian Cove from there because the town hall was built on higher ground at the back of the cove.

Two of Melody's appointed officials, elders in the royal court, came out shortly after her.

"What hope is there?" Melody asked, as they stood on either side of her. "I'm losing my kingdom and everything I've worked so hard to build."

"Milady, don't be worried," said one of the elders, whose beard was angular and silky-white. "For the good of Rhema, we *must* cooperate with the Tethysians. They're stronger than we are, but with their protection, we can rest content beneath their wings."

Melody sighed again. "I know, but I *hate* it. I wish I could change the way things are."

"There may be nothing you can do," the white-bearded elder said. "But no matter what comes, we will always stand with you as your advisers and friends. We live and breathe to serve you and the people of Rhema according to the royal traditions of this great kingdom."

The other elder, having a big nose, spoke next. "Milady, you know better than anyone how far we've come as a kingdom. How many trials have we overcome through your vast resources and intelligent strategies? Don't be worried! Even this will soon come to—"

"Look," Melody interrupted, pointing over the side of the banister. "Who's that?"

The three looked down at the cobblestone road to see a man approaching them.

"Hmph. Just a commoner," the big-nosed elder said.

"What business does a commoner have at the town hall?" Melody asked.

"None whatsoever," the white-bearded elder said, leering down at the man.

The newcomer waved and called, "Melody! How great it is to see you!"

"What do you want?" Melody called back.

"You may not remember me," the man said, standing below the balcony, "but I'm an old friend. Come and see for yourself!"

"I'm not going *down there*," Melody said, curling her lip.

"Leave the queen alone," the big-nosed elder called.

"Wait a moment, just hear me out," the man said, his face beaming. "My name is Eli, and I've come from the Kingdom of Marindel."

Several emotions flashed across Melody's face, but she suppressed them at once. Lifting her chin, she said, "I don't know who you are. Go away."

"I can help you remember."

The white-bearded elder said, "How dare you oppose a direct order from your queen! We know everything there is to know about Marindel, and you are most certainly *not* from there. Begone with you!"

Eli ignored the elder. "Melody, please. If you only knew how much my heart has yearned for this day—the day the Great King has sent me to find you! I'm Prince Eli, your friend! Come walk with me, and I'll show you."

"No! Go away!"

A small part of Melody's soul did remember Eli, but she didn't want to believe he was the one addressing her now. To her, Eli was only a distant memory that died when the Serpent claimed her mind and her heart.

Eli, though visibly saddened, nodded in concession. "All right. But Melody, I want you to know that I love you, and I'm not giving up on you. My father and I will never give up on you."

"Ugh!" Melody turned and stormed back into the town hall.

The white-bearded elder glared down at Eli. "Look, now you've done it! Begone with you, and never show your face around here again!"

Eli replied, "You think you're Melody's greatest protectors and her sole source of guidance, but in reality, you are the Serpent's blind puppets. You're leading her and the whole kingdom of Rhema to its destruction."

At that, Eli turned and walked away, back down the hill.

The elders were shocked. They exchanged glances, and the white-bearded elder asked, "Did you just hear that?"

"Poppycock," the big-nosed elder scoffed.

"Blind puppets, indeed! Have you ever seen a man more drunk than he?"

"Not one."

"Hmph. Well, at least we know we won't be seeing *him* again. No self-appointed suitor from any kingdom, honest or drunk, would dare pursue Melody after a rejection like that."

The two elders chuckled as they turned and vanished into the town hall.

AFTER THAT ENCOUNTER, Eli left Carnelian Cove and began traveling on foot to Diamond City, the capital of Rhema. Around midnight, as he was walking through the woods, the Serpent spoke to him.

"Well, if it isn't the Great Prince himself, come to grace my realm with his glamorous presence."

Eli ignored the Serpent and continued onward.

"What are you trying to prove?" the Serpent pressed. *"You left your cozy palace, your whole family, and all your powers behind, just to be rejected again and again by a worthless human girl."*

"The Great King's plans are far greater than you can imagine," Eli said.

"Oh no, if I were you, I would watch my tongue. You're on my turf now. Melody is mine, Rhema is mine, the whole realm answers to me. You ought to give up now while you have a chance. Acknowledge your defeat and bow to me."

"I answer only to my father, the Great King. Your ownership of this realm is only a shadow. Even *you* know that shadows must flee when the light comes."

"Ha! You couldn't defeat me even if you came with all of your power, and all of the Galyyrim by your side. How do you, a mere man, expect to challenge me?"

Eli ignored the Serpent and continued onward.

"*Tell me, Prince,*" the Serpent hissed as a supernatural darkness fell upon the woods. "*Why did your daddy really send you here? Don't bother defending him; you know it's true. He disowned you and sent you away. There's no other explanation. You see, the girl* willingly *surrendered her authority to me. I am in power now, forever, and for all time. She traded her inheritance for a death sentence. A slow, painful, all-consuming death. That is her inheritance now, forever, and for all time. And it can never be undone.*"

Eli stood still.

As the Serpent continued, dark forms moved about in the shadows, and the sound of rustling insect wings could be heard. "*Face it, my noble adversary. There is no path forward for you here. The Great King knows better than anyone that the human girl cannot be saved. Can't you see? He sent you here to die. Come now, give up and go home. Why must you give yourself to such a miserable fate?*"

"Be quiet!" Eli's rebuke sent a tremor through the darkness. "I've come willingly to this land, following the guidance of my father the King, to take Melody's inheritance upon myself. *I* will take the punishment for the wrongdoing she has unleashed upon herself and the realm."

"*Hmph. Hmhmhm... Hahahaha! You really are a fool! I must say, I expected better from you. But how can I refuse? The Great King has chosen to save his human pet by slaying his blood-born son, the heir to the throne of Marindel. Ha! Hahahaha!*"

The shadows, creeping closer, laughed in chorus with the Serpent.

Eli clenched his fists. "Are you finished yet?"

"*I'm afraid not, oh mighty Prince. I'm only getting started.*" A thin tendril of darkness caressed Eli's cheek. "*I will take you up on your offer. But, lest you convince yourself you're doing something noble, allow me to let you in on a little secret: I will make it hurt. I will inflict upon you excruciating pain unlike anything you've ever imagined. And what's more, I will rip your father's heart out of his chest and shred it to ribbons with the way I will dispose of you. I'll destroy everything the Great King loves most, beginning with you.*"

"That's enough! Begone!"

The darkness recoiled and disappeared.

Alone in the woods once again, with the stars casting faint dappled light through the canopy, Eli said, "Father, I trust you."

And he continued on to Diamond City.

Along the way, Eli made frequent stops in the towns and villages along the road. He spent time with the common people, told them stories of the Kingdom of Marindel, helped those who were in need, and spoke out against injustices committed by Melody's officials, who often sought to challenge him. Eli did these things, cherishing the people in every village he passed, just like his father, the Great King, did long ago.

TWO WEEKS LATER, Melody was walking through the Diamond City marketplace with a few of her officials in tow. As she browsed the various fruit stands where farmers displayed their seasonal goods, she grumbled to herself, "No one knows how to grow high-quality fruit anymore. It's all mushy, spotted, and rotten, and it costs *twice* as much as it's worth! What has become of this kingdom?"

One of her officials was close enough to hear the complaint. He said, "Milady, you could pass a law about that; a decree for the price of fruit to be dropped to what it's worth, or a command to simply grow better fruit. You know, most farmers probably keep the good fruit to themselves, and they only sell what they don't want. How selfish of them, wouldn't you say?"

"Very much so," Melody agreed, glaring at the farmers who sat behind the fruit stands. Her eyes locked onto a man selling pineapples, and she went toward him.

When she came near, the farmer looked up and gasped. "Oh, Milady! What a pleasant surprise! Please, have a look at my—"

"Rubbish, peasant! I *did* have a look at your foul-smelling crop, and I hated every second of it! What's the matter with you!?"

Melody's words hit the farmer like a mallet on a tent peg, until only the top of his terrified face was visible behind the stand. "I-I don't understand why you're not pleased, Milady..."

Melody picked up a pineapple and pointed at a blemish. "What is this!?"

"It's, uh...it's a unicorn hoof-print."

"A unicorn hoof-print!" Melody spat. "What in the kingdom of Rhema was a unicorn doing stepping on your pineapples!?"

"They live in the fields around here, surely you know! They aren't careful as they—"

"You idiot! Build a fence! Get a dog! Do *something*! How do you expect anyone to buy this garbage!?"

"I-I, uh..." The farmer, his face beet-red with embarrassment, sought words in vain.

The officials stood behind Melody, pointing and laughing at the farmer's humiliation.

Melody continued, "Why don't you do the whole kingdom a favor and cut the price? How about you sell them for one kappe each? Then, maybe a starving child would buy it—to throw at his brother and knock him out to claim the last grain of rice!"

"Milady, I'm so sorry! I'll do whatever you'd like, just *please* have mercy!"

Melody scoffed. "Mercy? I'll show you mercy!"

She raised the pineapple, ready to smash it over the farmer's head.

"Melody!" a voice called.

Her arm stopped as if someone had grabbed it.

Everyone standing within a twenty-foot radius of the spectacle went quiet.

The officials exchanged bewildered glances. Melody looked at them, wondering which of them had called her, but they shrugged and shook their heads.

The crowd adjacent to the officials parted and Eli stepped forward. His voice was fraught with sadness as he spoke. "Melody, what are you doing?"

She recognized him from Carnelian Cove. She hadn't been able to shake the thought of him since that encounter, and seeing him now caused her heart to drop. She tensed and glared at him. "Why do *you* care?"

Eli stood alongside the officials. "I care deeply when my father's people are abused by the one he chose to protect them."

"Hmph. What are you talking about?"

"Why were you about to hit that innocent man in the face with a pineapple?"

Melody was caught off guard by his frankness. She held up the fruit and pointed at the blemish. "Look. He let a unicorn step all over his field and this is what happened. Now he expects everyone to pay an outrageous price for his mistake. He's far from innocent and deserves a beating for his conniving, selfish attitude!"

"I don't see a blemish," Eli said.

"Well, you're blind then," Melody sneered. "It's big and obvious, right—" she gasped.

The blemish was gone.

People in the crowd gasped and muttered amongst themselves.

The pineapple farmer rose out of hiding to see what was happening.

Eli kept his gaze on Melody. "You were saying?"

"Huh?" Melody turned the pineapple around and around, searching for the missing blemish to no avail. "It was just here! I saw it! You all saw it, right?" She looked to her officials.

They stood by without a word. They were as stunned as she was.

"Wow!" a woman in the crowd said. "Those pineapples look delicious!"

Everyone looked at the pineapple stand, which was now filled with the most delectable pineapples that ever graced the kingdom of Rhema.

The farmer's jaw dropped wide open as he beheld his crop.

Melody couldn't believe her eyes. She turned on Eli and asked, "What did you just do!?"

"My father is pleased to bless a simple man, as well as to set an example of mercy for those to whom he has given authority."

The crowd began surging toward the pineapple stand to buy the delicious fruit. The officials stood in the way, shouting, "Don't buy from this man! His crop is cursed! You saw what happened with your own eyes! Where's your common sense?" But the people barged past them, waving handfuls of coins in the air and shouting over one another to barter for the fruit. The officials were so caught up in trying to dissuade the crowd, they didn't notice Melody and Eli conversing nearby.

Melody stepped up close to Eli and glared at him. "Who do you think you are? And who is this father of yours?"

Eli met her gaze firmly. "I've already told you, but you didn't listen. I'm Prince Eli of Marindel, and my father is the Great King."

"You're crazy! Get out of here!"

"Melody, you know it's true. I see it in your eyes. Please, let go of your unbelief and trust me."

Melody trembled at his words. This peasant's persistence was frightening. When she could finally mouth a reply, she said, "You don't know me, and you don't know Eli. You're a monster sent to destroy me!"

"No." Eli put his hand on Melody's quaking shoulder. Their faces were inches apart now, and the chaotic marketplace faded into the background. "I know you, Melody. I've known you since the day you were brought into Marindel, the city on the back of a sea turtle. Don't you remember? It was I who gave you a tour of the palace halls and the gardens. It was I who taught you to sing and play piano. It was I who used to play with you every day; all sorts of games. Your favorite has always been hide-and-seek," Eli chuckled and smiled.

Melody stood still, looking down at Eli's tunic to avoid his overwhelming gaze. His words quelled her rebellious spirit like a lullaby quiets an anxious child. In her heart she knew everything he said was true. She didn't resist as Eli placed a hand under her chin and lifted her face. She was surprised to see tears in his eyes.

"You've been hiding for a very long time, Mel. Won't you come out?"

At his words, Melody was flooded with flashbacks. She saw herself in the palace of Marindel, saying, "How about you count to a thousand while I hide, and then you have to come find me. Sound like fun?"

Eli replied, "Great idea, Mel! I'll go to that corner and get started. One, two, three..." his voice became distant, and she heard him calling, "Melody! Melody, where are you?"

The Serpent said, "*You haven't much time. Use your magic to unlock the door. Then come inside, and I will give you power.*"

"*All right. Here I come.*"

"Melody? Melody!?" Eli's voice called.

"*Hurry, inside!*" the Serpent said.

The massive doors slammed shut, silencing Eli's call. The flashback faded with the Serpent's echoing laugh.

Just when she thought it was over, she heard her own voice squeak in the dark, "What in the realm of Tyrizah am I doing?"

"What in the realm of Tyrizah am I doing?" Melody whispered. And then she broke.

Melody threw her arms around Eli and began to sob.

Eli returned the embrace and rested his face against hers. "It's all right. I'm here. I've found you."

Melody cried into his shoulder until she found the breath and courage to look at him again. She asked in a choked voice, "Why did you come for me?"

Eli took her by the shoulders and said. "Because I love you, Melody. And the Great King loves you, too."

Melody suppressed a sob. "That's impossible. He hates me. I'm a horrible daughter."

"I love you, Melody," he repeated, eyes glimmering. "And the Great King loves you, too."

"But..." Melody's lip quivered.

"Hey!" The big-nosed official yelled. "Get away from her!"

His shout alerted the other officials, who then saw Melody

teary-eyed in the arms of Eli. They all shuffled toward her, shouting and waving their arms.

Eli whispered in Melody's ear, "Come find me in the apple orchard tomorrow at sunrise."

Two officials grabbed Eli and tore him away from Melody. They shouted, "What do you think you're doing!? You've offended the queen! Filthy peasant, how dare you!? Where are Tethysian soldiers when we need them? Quick, find the nearest guards! This is grounds for arrest!"

Eli slipped out of their grasp and disappeared into the marketplace.

"After him! Don't let him get away!" Several officials ran in pursuit.

Those who stayed behind swarmed around Melody. They wiped her tears, fixed her hair, asked if Eli had done anything malicious, and vowed to ensure he was properly disposed of. She ignored them, watching Eli until he disappeared from sight.

38

The Prince of Mystery

Summer, 104 IE

E ARLY THE NEXT morning, Melody awoke with a start. She remembered the events of the previous day, and a tingling apprehension laced her thoughts. Had Eli really come to find her? Could it even be possible?

There was only one way to find out.

She put on a simple blue tunic and a translucent shawl to cover her head, and she departed quietly. Exiting Diamond City through the eastern gate, she skirted the city wall until she came upon the apple orchard, which sprawled over the nearby hills.

As Melody wandered through the orchard, anxiety welled up in her heart. "*What am I doing? This man knows much about Eli and about me, but what if he's a fraud? My officials don't trust him, so maybe I shouldn't either.*"

Just then, she realized she was alone.

For the first time in many years, Melody had ventured outside of the palace without anyone to escort her. She began to feel very small and lonely. "*What if something bad happens? Something bad always happens when I'm alone!*"

Melody peered around as she went. A myriad of birdsongs filled the air, and the dew on the grass reflected the dawning sky. The air was cold and crisp, with a breeze so gentle it was hardly noticeable. The branches stretching overhead were laden with green leaves and ripe pink apples.

Melody took a deep, calming breath as she took in her

surroundings. She never realized mornings could be so beautiful. In fact, she tended to sleep in on a regular basis. The anxiety she felt a moment before, dwindled away as she discovered the charm of the early morning.

She quickened her stride as she ascended a hill. She could tell from the light touching the treetops that the sun was just beginning to rise, and she wanted to get a perfect view.

Once at the summit, Melody was astounded. She had a clear view not only of the sunrise, but of the entire countryside: rolling green hills speckled with trees and patches of wildflowers. As the sun cleared the horizon, it cast golden rays of light on everything in sight. The drops of dew on the grass twinkled like stars as they reflected the rising sun.

It was the most beautiful thing Melody had seen in a very long time.

"Wonderful, isn't it?" Eli's voice came from somewhere nearby.

Melody gasped and whirled around. There he was, leaning against a tree and looking out at the countryside. The light glistened in his eyes.

"Yes, it's lovely," Melody replied. She fixed her eyes on the landscape, still finding it uncomfortable to look at him.

They watched the sunrise for a moment before Eli asked, "Melody, what do you love about the sun?"

"I, uh..." Melody looked at the ground. Truthfully, she didn't like the sun at all. She never liked being hot, and she hated sweating and getting sunburns. She spoke her mind, "I don't really love anything about it."

"Really?" Eli asked. Melody expected him to mock or judge her in some way, but he didn't. Instead he asked with genuine interest, "How can you behold a sight as beautiful as this, and not have a single thing come to mind that's lovely about the sun? You did say yourself it was lovely."

Melody looked again at the countryside. The sun hovered above the horizon, bathing the landscape in golden light. She said, "Well, I do like the way it makes other things look more beautiful."

"Yes, that is a grand quality of the sun, isn't it? More than just aesthetics, the sun gives life to all living things. The plants grow and the flowers bloom because the sun shines on them. It gives warmth and comfort, light and life. It sends water to the sky to become clouds, and when the clouds become dense, the water returns as rain to quench the thirst of the land. Everything we do in this realm is dependent on the sun. We owe it our very lives."

"You sound like a philosopher," Melody said. She realized her tone might have been offensive, so she added, "I mean, not in a bad way. You just know things about the realm, and you talk about them in a way that makes others want to listen."

Eli picked an apple from a branch above him and tossed it to Melody. "Let's sit down for a bit."

She furrowed her brow. "In the wet grass?"

Eli picked an apple for himself and said, "Of course not. Come, this way." He walked a short distance down the hillside to a pile of smooth boulders in the shade of a larger tree. He gestured toward one of the smoothest rocks for Melody to sit on, and he sat cross-legged on one across from her. Once they were both settled, he asked, "Have you ever tried one of these apples before?"

Melody shook her head.

Eli smiled. "Oh, you must! They're the best in the land!"

Melody inspected the large pink apple. It *looked* good, but she was bothered by thoughts of how dirty it must be, and the possibility of worms or parasites inside.

"There's nothing wrong with it," Eli said. "Go on, try it."

She took a bite, and her eyes widened as the flavor exploded in her mouth. Its juicy crunchiness surpassed that of any fruit she could remember!

"Mmmmh!" Melody took another bite and chewed voraciously.

Eli chuckled. "Good, huh?"

"Mhmm," Melody replied, taking a third bite.

They enjoyed their apples together in silence for a few moments.

"Ahh," Melody breathed as she threw the core into the grass and leaned back against a neighboring boulder. "That was amazing. I've never had an apple like *that* before."

"Really? Never in your life?"

"Nope. To be honest, I hated apples before you gave me this one."

"How come?"

"I don't know, I just did," Melody shrugged.

"So, you hated apples, and now you don't. And you hated the sun, and now you don't. Is there anything else I can help you un-hate?"

Melody chuckled. "Oh, I don't know. I hate many things. Almost everything. When you've been through as many hard times as I have, it's hard to find a reason to love anything. Much less any*one*."

"Is that a challenge?" Eli asked with a smirk.

"Why do you care?" Melody tried to come off as indifferent, but she couldn't tame the small bit of her heart that rejoiced in how much this man took interest in her.

"I care about everything, and everyone," Eli said, looking out at the countryside. "I care because the Great King cares."

Melody rolled her eyes. "Runs in the family?"

"Not necessarily. To care—that is, to love—is a choice we all have. It's a decision in the face of circumstance. It doesn't matter who you are or what you've been through. Every sentient creature has a choice to love or to hate, to care or to ignore. Ultimately, the state of the realm we live in depends on that choice."

"Given the state of the realm right now, you might be the only person alive who cares."

Eli looked at Melody and said, "You may be right. But that's why I'm here."

"Hm," Melody looked thoughtfully at the ground. Then she stood up and said, "I'm going to get another apple."

Eli shot to his feet and took her hand. "No, no, allow me."

"Hey!" Melody pulled her hand away from his. Then she composed herself and said, "Okay, fine. Just don't touch me."

Eli didn't take offense. He jumped up on a few boulders to reach a branch, picked an apple, and came back to hand it to her. "For you, Milady."

"Don't call me that!" Melody snapped, taking the apple and sitting again. "Everyone and their mother calls me that."

Eli sat as well. "All right. What should I call you, then?"

"Melody's fine." She took a bite of the apple. "Mmmmh. Oh, so good! Mmmh..."

Eli watched with delight as Melody enjoyed the apple. When she was almost finished, he said, "Melody's a good name."

She acknowledged his reply with a hum as she took one last bite of the apple. Then she said, "You can call me Mel, too, I guess."

Eli smiled and nodded. Then he stood up and said, "Care to take a walk?"

"Maybe. Where to?"

"Jasper Village is just down the hill. I was there a few days ago, and I'd love to show you around."

"*You're* going to show *me* around my own kingdom?"

"Yep. You can't deny you don't get out much, and when you do, how much do you *really* see?"

Melody was offended, so she fumbled for a reason to back out of it. "I don't think I can. My officials are probably wondering where I am, and they'll stress themselves out searching the whole city until they find me."

"Why do they worry so much about you?"

"Because I'm the queen, of course. They keep me safe, they help me make wise decisions, and they help enforce the rules around here."

"Do they care about you?"

"Of *course* they do! Why wouldn't they?"

"Be mindful when you're with them," Eli said. "They're more influential than you think. Though they may seem concerned for your welfare, they're far more concerned with their own prestige."

No, they're not, Melody wanted to say, but something within her kept the words from coming out.

"Come with me," Eli urged, reaching his hand out for Melody to take.

Melody looked from Eli's hand to his beaming face and back again. As much as she didn't want to, the small, untamed part of her heart longed to take his hand and go wherever he took her. It wasn't even so much about the village, she just wanted to be with him.

What? Am I falling in love with him? Melody blushed, struggling to hide her conflicting thoughts and emotions. She had *never* fallen in love before. She hated people far too much for that nonsense. Besides, even if this man standing before her *was* Prince Eli from the Kingdom of Marindel, she'd never been attracted to him in that way. Eli was just a friend and a brother back then.

Of course, he's much older now...and more handsome...

Melody scolded her own heart, *"For goodness' sake, control yourself! It's just a casual morning walk. You can do that, can't you?"*

She took his hand.

Eli helped her up and said, "All right! Let's go!"

The two of them walked down the hill and skirted the edge of the orchard until they came across a road, and they began traveling north.

Along the way, Melody remained thoughtful. She couldn't decide if she believed this man was Prince Eli. And if he was, what was he doing talking to her? Wouldn't the real Eli be disappointed in her? There's no disputing the fact that she caused the permanent ruin of both Marindel and the realm of Tyrizah by her one mistake. The real Eli would have plenty of reason to hate her.

But still.

This man knew things about her not even Seers had been able to discern. It was like he was there in the beginning, during the Era of Peace, while she grew up in the courts of Marindel. Such knowledge of her past was impossible for anyone except the real Eli.

After all, before this man, only Eli had ever called her Mel.

Melody shook those thoughts out of her head and belittled herself, "*What are you thinking, you idiot? There's no way this could be Eli. He's a man, for crying out loud! Eli is supposed to be an elf. How could you even let the possibility cross your mind? He's nothing more than a Seer. A good one, I'll give him that, but a Seer, nonetheless. I know what I'll do: I'll play along with his little ruse and keep him entertained, but I'll be watching and waiting for him to make a mistake. When he does, I'll exploit it to uncover his fraudulent act and have him arrested and killed like every Seer before him. Yes, that's what I'll do.*"

"What's on your mind, Mel?" Eli asked.

"Oh, nothing."

Eli stayed silent. When the tension became uncomfortable, Melody sighed and said, "Okay, I'm a bit nervous. Nothing major. It just comes with walking alone with a stranger to a random village when you're the queen and many people don't like you."

"You're afraid to trust me," Eli said.

Melody tensed. In five words Eli effectively summarized her entire dilemma. "*He's one hell of a good Seer,*" she thought.

Eli said, "I understand what troubles you, and that's why I'm taking you to Jasper Village. If you're willing, come and see for yourself that I am who I say I am, and more importantly, believe what I've come to tell you."

"What if I'm not willing?" Melody challenged.

"I won't force you to come. You can go back to the palace whenever you'd like."

Melody was surprised Eli didn't sound angry. She was used to others reacting in fear or anger when she tried to be difficult, but thus far, Eli had only treated her graciously. As she thought about it, the part of her heart that was fascinated with him grew a teeny bit larger.

No! Melody rebuked herself and repressed her emotions. "*Perhaps I should turn back now, lest I be seduced by him and betrayed in the end! That's what men do, after all!*" But even as she considered it, she realized how ridiculous her thoughts were in light of what she knew about Eli's—or whoever he was's—character.

Finally, she made her decision. "I'll come with you for now, but at noon I'm going back to Diamond City."

"Very well," Eli said, smiling. "I'll enjoy your company for as long as you choose to stay."

The two of them reached Jasper Village soon after their discussion. In total, they had only been walking for half an hour.

The road ran through the center of the village, and most of the buildings were aligned on either side. There were many people bustling about, and Melody groaned at the thought of being surrounded by commoners. On the far side of the village was an imposing stone tower, adorned with black banners featuring the insignia of the Empire: a silver dragon with a gold spear.

"What's so special about this village?" Melody asked.

"You'll see."

"I don't see anything," Melody said under her breath.

A few seconds later, an excited little boy scampered toward them. "Mister Eli! You're back!"

"Hey there, buddy!" Eli said, stooping down to meet his flying hug head-on. He stood and lifted the boy into the air, who laughed with glee.

Melody stood by with a stupefied look on her face.

Eli put the child down, who turned and ran toward a pregnant woman who was approaching them. "Mommy! Eli's back!"

"I see that, dear!" the mother replied. Then, smiling at Eli, she said "It's so good to see you again!"

"And you as well, Trisha," Eli replied.

A man followed Trisha, holding a little girl who looked a couple years older than the boy. He said, "Welcome back, Eli! Are you hungry? We're just cooking breakfast, and we'd love to have you."

"Auben, that's very kind of you!" Eli looked at Melody and asked, "Are you hungry, Mel? What do you think?"

Melody couldn't speak. Who were these people? How did they know each other? And why were they offering to feed Eli?

Just then, the little boy approached her and looked up with a blank expression. "Who are you?"

"Who am *I*?" Melody asked, taken aback. She looked up at the boy's parents and sister, who also stared blankly at her. She looked down at the boy, then at Eli, then back at the parents. Exasperated, she said, "Don't tell me none of you know who I am!"

"We've never met, have we?" Trisha asked. "Are you a friend of Eli's?"

"Of course we haven't met, but how could you not know who I am? I'm Melody, the Queen of Rhema!"

The parents' eyes widened.

Auben fumbled for words, "Well, um, greetings, Your Majesty. Please forgive our ignorance."

"I didn't know we had a queen," the boy said. "I thought we had an emperor. Are you the emperor's wife?"

"Trevor, come here," Trisha beckoned. To Melody she said, "I'm sorry we didn't recognize you, miss. We've never seen you before, that's all."

Melody's pride was wounded. She couldn't believe these commoners had no idea who she was. She was also indignant that their son believed the Tethysian emperor was the sole ruler of Rhema.

Eli broke the silence by properly introducing her. "My friends, this is Melody, the Queen of Rhema. I've brought her here to meet you and to show her around the village."

"Oh, that's wonderful," Trisha replied, forcing a smile. "Will both of you join us for breakfast? We'd be honored."

"No, thank you," Melody said. "I'm not hungry. Besides, I have to get going at noon. Eli, we'd better keep moving if you want to show me around the village."

Eli looked at Melody with a glimmer of sadness, but he nodded and said, "All right. Thank you, Trisha. Another time."

"Aw!" Trevor shouted. "Mister Eli, don't let her ruin your fun!"

"Hey!" Melody snapped.

Eli put a hand on Melody's shoulder and said to Trevor, "It's all right, bud, I'll be back soon. I promise we'll spend a whole afternoon playing together. How's that?"

"Okay!" Trevor ran and hugged his father's leg.

"Eli, before you go," Auben said, "I want to thank you again for saving our daughter's life. If it weren't for you, Lia wouldn't be alive today." He looked endearingly at the girl he held in his arms.

Eli smiled and nodded. "She's very precious, and the Great King loves her very much."

"Please come back soon!" Trisha said. "We would love to hear more about you and the Great King. Our home is always open to you!"

"Of course, I look forward to it! Good day, all of you!"

The family waved goodbye as Eli and Melody continued further into the village.

Once the family was out of earshot, Melody took Eli's arm to stop him from walking. She spoke sternly, "What in the kingdom of Rhema was that all about!?"

"They're good friends of mine, that's all. They saw me and came to say hello."

"How do you know them? You're an outsider! You came here from...somewhere, be it Marindel or another place. Yet somehow, they had no idea who *I* was! That is unacceptable! Embarrassing! Humiliating!"

"Melody." The authority in Eli's voice quieted her. "I stayed a couple days in Jasper Village before I arrived in Diamond City to find you. That family invited me into their home, and I stayed the night. We got to know each other very well. Melody, when was the last time you went to a village to spend time with the people there? To get to know them and understand their way of life?"

Melody was too stubborn to answer. She would never lower herself to the level of a commoner. It was unthinkable.

"What I want you to see," Eli said, putting his hands on her shoulders and looking into her eyes, "is that these people are loved and valued by the Great King. They are worthy of being loved and valued by you, by me, and by everyone. You must not think yourself higher simply because you're a queen. Even the Great King, the greatest ruler of all, spent time with the common people. The Serpent has brought much hatred into this realm, but I have come to set an example for you and for others who will believe in me."

Melody avoided eye contact with Eli. She squirmed out of his grasp and pouted.

"Mel, I'm not disappointed in you. I know how hard it is for you to understand these things. All you need is a bit of time, and there's nothing wrong with that. Besides, I'm not finished showing you around yet."

Melody remained silent.

"Come on, cheer up," Eli said, gently brushing her cheek.

She finally made eye contact with him. The intensity of his gaze made her heart skip a beat.

"There's more to see," Eli said with an adventurous glimmer in his eye. "Let's go!"

She nodded. Most of the stubbornness in her heart melted away, and she felt peace. Deep down, she greatly appreciated Eli's patience and tact. No one had ever shown her this much kindness before.

As they continued to walk, Eli reached out and took her hand.

This time, Melody didn't refuse him.

As they went along the main village road, people greeted Eli from left and right. Melody was surprised he was so well-known for only having stayed in the village for two days. He must have said or done something extraordinary to get the whole village's attention. As she thought more about it, a possibility came to mind that piqued her interest. Remembering the transformation of the pineapples Eli caused in Diamond City, she asked, "Eli, what did you do to save that family's daughter?"

"Ah," Eli smiled as he recalled the memory. "On the day I arrived, Lia had been sick for a week with a high fever, vomiting, and tremors. She wasn't responding to treatment, and the medic said she would die very soon. When I heard about it, I went to see her for myself, and my heart was broken. I knew Lia was a victim of the Serpent's cruelty, so I placed my hand on her forehead and sang of my father's love for her and his desire that she be healed. When I finished, she was well."

"That's incredible," Melody replied. "So, you *do* have some sort of powers after all!"

Eli shook his head. "I have no power of my own. I knew my father the King wanted to heal Lia, so I responded in obedience to his will. His power healed her, not mine."

Melody scoffed, "Would you say his power healed the pineapples, too?"

"Yes," Eli agreed. "Whether it involves pineapples or people, the Great King lets those who love and obey him tap into his power to create opportunities for others to get to know him."

Melody was puzzled. "What do you mean?"

"For example, when Lia was healed, quite naturally, everyone was shocked. Just like you assumed, they thought I had magical powers. I took the opportunity to tell them about the Great King and his love for them. Most were touched by what I had to say. Some weren't; they thought I was a lunatic. Regardless, everyone can now call to mind the time when a little girl, destined to die, was healed by a humble nobody who came along at the right time and sent the sickness fleeing in the name of the Great King."

Just as Eli finished speaking, someone up ahead shouted, "Well, well, if it isn't the sorcerer of Marindel!"

Melody looked and saw five Tethysian soldiers coming down the opposite side of the road. She tensed at the sight of them.

"Captain Matthias," Eli greeted the leading officer.

"Hmph," Matthias flicked his chin as he came closer. "You've got some nerve, coming back here after what you did."

"Leave him alone," Melody said, standing between Eli and the incoming soldiers.

"Shut up, Princess," Matthias said as he barged past her. The other soldiers surrounded Eli, their expressions proud and scoffing. The captain asked Eli, "What did we tell you about showing your face around here again?"

"I answer only to my father, the Great King."

"Don't give us that phony gimmick again! You're no prince, you don't come from no King, and you don't belong here in Rhema. This is your last chance, so listen up. Take your magic tricks out of here pronto, or you'll face the tooth and claw of the Tethysian Law."

The other soldiers chuckled.

"I love that rhyme," one of them said.

Matthias elbowed that soldier.

Eli stood confidently and said, "You so-called protectors of the land are selfish and proud. You have no regard for the plight of the people of Rhema, and when someone comes to meet their needs, you chase them out. Is there *any* bit of kindness in you?"

"See here, you ignorant little—" Matthias was cut off as Eli spoke over him, "The Serpent will treat you just as you treat those under you unless you turn to the Great King, follow his ways, and trust in him."

"I've killed serpents uglier than you with this very sword, so mind your words!" Matthias placed a hand on the hilt of his weapon. "In the name of Emperor Flavian the Bright, ruler of the Tethysian Empire, you are under arrest!"

Before Matthias finished speaking, Eli slipped between the soldiers and ran. "Come on, Mel!"

Melody had been standing off to the side, unsure of what to do. When Eli called, she ran after him.

"Get him!" Matthias yelled. He and his soldiers gave chase.

Eli slowed enough for Melody to catch up, and he took her hand and led the way through the busy village streets.

"Why are you provoking Tethysian soldiers!?" Melody asked, panting for breath as she kept Eli's pace.

"Sometimes standing up for what's right will provoke those who seek to exploit others for their own gain," Eli replied.

"But they're *Tethysian soldiers*! You know they can kill you, right!?"

"They can kill me, but they can't challenge truth and expect to win!"

"You're crazy!"

"Maybe just a little!"

Eli turned and took Melody through a small alley between two buildings, scattering a flock of chickens as they passed. Emerging from the other side in a flurry of feathers, Eli ran toward the Tethysian fortress on the far side of the village.

Melody dug her heels into the ground. "We can't go that way! That's their fortress!"

Eli stopped and looked at her. "Do you trust me, Mel?"

"Not really!"

"There he is!" Matthias' voice called from the mouth of the alley they just passed through.

Melody panicked and yelled, "Okay, yes! Yes, I trust you!"

"All right, let's go!" Eli ran toward the fortress with a panting Melody in tow.

The soldiers emerged from the alley single-file and chased after them. There were fewer people walking about the closer they came to the fortress, so it became harder for Eli and Melody to stay hidden.

When they were around fifty feet away from the entrance, Eli turned left and went down another alley. This one was much longer and led to a smaller street, from which there were many more alleys branching off. Eli led Melody through the maze, zig-zagging this way and that.

"Where'd he go?" a soldier shouted.

"Let's split up!"

"Flush him out!"

The soldiers went down separate alleys with the hope of trapping Eli, but to no avail.

Eli and Melody soon emerged from the alleys and found themselves at the edge of the village, running through a field of tall grass. The Tethysian fortress was to their right, and in front of them were only a few buildings and fences separating them from the sprawling Rhema countryside.

"Where do we go now?" Melody asked.

"We'll lose them in the group of mansions ahead," Eli replied.

Melody wasn't sure what Eli was getting at, but she didn't see the point in arguing.

They passed between the first two buildings, and Eli immediately turned right. They were heading toward a manor, and Melody looked up to see a Tethysian banner hanging above the door.

"We're not going in there, are we?" Melody asked.

"Yes, we are!"

"You're crazy! That's a *Tethysian* manor!" Melody pulled her hand out of Eli's grasp. "Let's go around it! We can hide in the tall grass just beyond." Without waiting for his response, she changed course and began circumventing the building.

"Melody! Wait!" Eli called, running after her.

"I know what I'm doing! Just follow me!"

She approached a wooden fence attached to the back corner of the building. With some effort, she jumped and hauled herself over it.

"Wait! Melody, stop!"

When Melody landed on the other side of the fence, she broke into a sprint. There was only a short stretch of grass in front of her, then one more fence, and then freedom.

"I'm gonna make it! We're gonna make it! This is exhilarating!" Melody grinned. She'd never had this much fun running from trouble before.

An angry growl banished her cavalier thoughts.

"No! Not a guard dog!" Melody looked aside, expecting to see a dog running after her. But what she saw instead caused her heart to skip a beat.

A vibrant orange dragon crouched thirty feet away, looking straight at her. It was snarling and pawing the ground, ready to pounce.

39
The Prince of Wonder
Summer, 104 IE

WHEN SHE SAW the dragon, Melody screamed and ran. The dragon yowled and bounded after her faster than any guard dog could ever hope to run.

There was no way she'd escape in time.

When the dragon was a second away from snatching Melody, Eli tackled her to the ground. The dragon soared overhead, buffeting the two of them with its wings and sending them tumbling together through the grass. Even after they stopped moving, Melody clung to Eli with her eyes squeezed shut.

"Mel, are you all right?" Eli whispered.

"No!" Melody trembled. "Eli, there's a dragon! A *dragon*!"

"I know. Hang on, watch this." Eli stood to his feet.

The dragon had turned and was facing them again, its head low and wings spread wide, tail lashing like a cat's. It was small for a dragon, but still twice the size of a horse; limber and muscular. It was orange, as Melody observed earlier, with a golden underside and maroon tiger-like stripes across the length of its body and wings. Its tail had fan-like appendages for enhanced flight. Its face was smooth and aerodynamic.

Eli wasn't the least bit intimidated by the dragon. He walked toward it and began to sing.

Melody stayed low, afraid to do anything but watch.

The dragon hissed at Eli, arching its back and pawing the ground.

Eli sang louder.

His voice tugged at Melody's heart. Eli was singing in Elvish, a language she had long since forgotten, but the sound of it filled her heart with peace.

The dragon inched closer to Eli, still growling and poised to attack.

Eli was undeterred. He sang beautifully, looked the dragon in the eyes and extended his hand toward it.

As the gap between them closed, the dragon's eyes softened, and its wings folded.

"*No way,*" Melody thought as she looked on.

The dragon's head swayed back and forth to the lilt of Eli's song. The closer he got, the more relaxed the dragon became. When Eli reached the dragon with his hand stretched out, it chirped and pushed its muzzle against his palm.

Eli smiled. "There you go, boy." Then he called over his shoulder, "Come here, Mel, it's all right!"

Melody stood and approached them. "Are you sure?"

When the dragon noticed her, it hissed.

"Ah!" Melody flinched. "Eli, it still hates me!"

"Whoa, hey," Eli said, rubbing the dragon's neck. "You'll have to sing for it. Remember how I taught you?"

"No," Melody retorted. "I don't sing, and you never taught me to sing."

"Yes, I did. You don't remember?"

"No."

"I *know* you can do it. You have the most beautiful voice!"

"Oh, you're talking about teaching me to sing in Marindel, aren't you?" Melody scoffed. "Well, of course I don't remember now. It was *so* long ago!"

"I know you can." Eli removed his hands from the dragon and backed away.

The dragon faced Melody and crouched low with a growl.

"Eli, what are you doing!?"

"Come on, I won't let it attack you. Trust me."

Melody gulped. She murmured in a sing-songy voice, "I'm looking at a dragon, a really scary dragon, that wants to bite my face off—"

The dragon yowled and pawed the ground, flaring its wings out.

"Different song, Mel!" Eli called. "Remember how I taught you!"

"I don't remember, okay!?"

"Yes, you do! I believe in you!"

The dragon yowled again, preparing to pounce.

"Remember, remember, remember!" Melody didn't know how to remember something like that, but she had to!

She thought about how Eli sang. It had a quality unlike any song she had ever heard. She closed her eyes and imagined she could hear it. She focused on an image of Eli singing in a garden with fountains, looking at her with a sweet and tender gaze. This was the son of the Great King. Her brother. Her best friend.

"Let it flow," Eli had said. "Don't think about the words. Just focus on the Great King. Think about how much he loves you. Let your heart rejoice in the freedom of knowing who you are and whose you are."

She remembered.

With hardly another thought, she opened her mouth and began to sing. She could hardly believe what was coming out of her mouth! Elvish words she didn't know she remembered, knitted together in the most wonderful tune! Remembering what Eli did before, she walked toward the dragon with her hand outstretched.

The dragon calmed down quickly. Before Melody could even place her hand on its head, it rolled over and exposed its belly for her to pet.

Eli chuckled. "I think it likes you more than me!"

"What's going on out here?" a voice called. It belonged to a middle-aged Tethysian man who stood bewildered at the back doorway of the manor. "What did you folks just do to my dragon? And, my lawn...!"

"The lawn?" Melody looked at the grass around her and saw it was speckled with purple flowers. "Whoa, did *I* do that?"

"You sure did," Eli said, walking over to stand beside her. He looked at the Tethysian man and said, "Good to see you again, Caruso."

"And you as well, Eli," Caruso said with a nod. "Though, I'm perplexed as to why you've intruded upon my dragon keep. If you wanted to say hello to Hunter, all you had to do was knock and ask."

"It's my fault," Melody said. "We were running from soldiers who wanted to arrest Eli. Friends of yours, maybe. I thought this would be the fastest way to the tall grass on the other side, but I didn't know there was a dragon here. I'm sorry."

Eli looked proudly at Melody and put his arm around her.

"No friend of mine wants to arrest Eli, I'll say that," Caruso replied. "This man helped me a great deal a few days ago. I would never accuse him of any treachery."

"Even though he healed a girl?" Melody tested. "Even though he says he's a Prince from Marindel? And his father is the Great King?"

"Noted, and irrelevant. Now, can you please explain what you did to Hunter? He's acting like a kitten!"

Melody looked at Eli. "What happened to the dragon, Eli?"

"We tamed him with the Music of Marindel. A song of wonder and reverence unto the Great King."

Caruso blinked. "I have no idea what that means, but it seems effective. No Tethysian has ever tamed a dragon like that, especially not a dracoviper. They're very loyal and territorial."

Eli nodded. "Dracovipers are also perceptive. They realize quickly whether a person is a friend or foe. Anyone with an honest heart can tame a dracoviper with ease. I can tell he respects you."

"Hm," Caruso smiled at the compliment. "Hunter here could fly away any time and never come back, but he knows his place is here with me. I never have to worry about leashing or caging him." He paused for a moment, stroking his stubbly chin. "Can you teach me? The music, I mean?"

"The Music of Marindel is not yet for the creatures of the surface to know. However, a time is soon coming when it will be available to every one of the Great King's followers."

"Hmm..." Caruso was completely clueless. He shrugged and said, "Well, since you two are here, you can give me a hand. I have a talongrunt dragon on the other side of the fence there, and she's got a nasty temper. Could you tame her, too? I'd appreciate it."

"I think we've seen enough dragons for one day," Melody said, turning to walk away.

Eli held her close and said, "No, let's have a look."

Caruso led Eli and Melody to the other side of the yard, where there was a gate in the fence. He pulled out a key to open the lock, and then opened the door to peek inside. He said, "She's leashed up, but that won't stop her from breathing fire. Don't aggravate her."

Eli looked at Melody and asked, "Do you think you can handle her?"

Melody quickly shook her head.

"Come on, Mel, I know you can!"

Melody threw her hands up. "Why do we have to do this, anyway? What's the point?"

"You'll see. Trust me."

Melody looked desperately at Eli. "You're making it very difficult for me to trust you."

Eli smiled in return. "I *know* you can do it. Don't be afraid, I'll be right here."

Melody steadied her beating heart with a deep breath. "*Fine. If he wants to see me tame a dragon, then I'm gonna tame a dragon. I'll show him.*" Then she said, "Okay, I'm going. But be ready to save me if something happens."

"Of course," Eli nodded.

"All right. Here I go," Melody stepped through the door and into the talongrunt's pen.

It didn't take long to locate the dragon, which was leashed with a chain to a thick post in the back corner of the pen. A bit larger than Hunter, she was bird-like in appearance, with two sturdy hind legs, wings instead of forearms, a whip-like tail, and a swan-like neck with a small head. She was green and scaly, rougher-looking than the dracoviper, and as the dragon's name insinuated, she had fearsome black talons.

"Her name is Kaya," Caruso said.

"Kaya. Suits her well," Melody muttered as she beheld the dragon.

When Kaya saw Melody, she straightened her posture and flared her wings out, squawking a warning.

"*All right. Time to sing.*" Melody closed her eyes and tried to focus on her memory of Eli from earlier. A second later she heard Eli yell, "Look out!"

Melody opened her eyes in time to see Kaya spit a ball of flame in her direction.

"Ah!" Melody jumped back, narrowly escaping the fire, and stumbled backward onto the ground.

"Stay alert!" Caruso called. "I wasn't kidding about her temper!"

"Thanks for the warning," Melody grumbled, standing up. She looked at the black scar on the ground where the fire had burned the grass, and then she looked at the wooden fence and the wooden manor. "Caruso, why do you keep an angry, fire-breathing dragon in a pen made of wood?"

"It's Tamaha wood. Fireproof."

"Oh, you've thought of everything, haven't you?"

"Come on, Mel, give it another try!" Eli said.

"All right, all right," Melody looked again at Kaya. When the two made eye contact, Kaya squawked and bared her needle-like teeth.

"Stop it, Kaya!" Melody shouted. "Bad girl!"

Kaya shot another fireball at Melody, who was better prepared for it this time and ran out of the way. She went closer and said, "Kaya, stop!"

Kaya tried to charge Melody, but the chain leash held her back. Her claws scored deep gouges in the dirt as she pulled on the chain.

"Isn't she supposed to sing?" Caruso asked Eli.

He didn't answer. He was intently watching Melody.

"Kaya, calm down," Melody said.

Kaya shot another fireball, and Melody dodged it just in time. She wasn't fazed by the danger anymore; she boldly approached the dragon. "Kaya, calm down!"

Kaya took a step back with an angry squawk.

Melody stopped a dozen feet away and said, "I'm not afraid of you."

The dragon growled in defiance, tugging to escape from the chain.

Melody took a deep breath and began to sing, just like she did earlier.

She didn't appear responsive to the song.

Melody stopped and said, "Eli, it's not working!"

"Keep going! You can do it!"

Melody continued. While she did so, the burnt scars on the grass began to heal.

Kaya's behavior changed slowly. She stopped tugging at the chain. She threatened to shoot fire, with smoke steaming from her nostrils, but the calming magic of the song quenched her aggression. She squawked and stomped with frustration.

"Just a little more," Eli said.

Caruso was watching with eyes wide.

As Melody continued singing, she walked closer.

Kaya folded her wings and lowered her head. Her expression was still hostile, but the battle in her mind was evident. Soon, the dragon crouched, wrapped her tail around herself, and looked down at the ground.

Melody moved to place her hand on Kaya's snout, but she recoiled with a stubborn grunt. Melody said, "It's all right, you can trust me. I'm not going to hurt you."

Kaya looked at Melody from the corner of her eyes.

"You're so silly, you know that?" Melody cracked a grin. "Come on, let me pet you."

Kaya groaned and lowered her head, but still kept it just out of Melody's reach.

Meanwhile, Eli had walked over and stood behind her. He said, "Tell Kaya you love her."

Melody glanced at Eli, and after a pause, she said to the dragon, "Kaya, I love you."

Though Melody's demeanor was nowhere near as gentle and kind as Eli's, Kaya was perceptive enough to realize Melody's words were truthful. With a hesitant warble, she craned her neck forward and touched her snout to Melody's hand.

Melody smiled and giggled, reaching up to stroke Kaya's jawline. "See? That wasn't so bad! What took you so long?"

Eli chuckled. "Well done!"

"Thanks!" Melody turned and shoved Eli playfully. "But I still think you're crazy for making me do that."

"Hey," Eli grinned. "I sought only to call out the strong, brave woman I know you are."

"I could've died, you know."

"I knew you wouldn't. I'll never put you through something you can't handle."

Melody failed to restrain a blush.

"You two wanna take them out for a ride?" Caruso asked. "They haven't had a chance to stretch their wings in a few days."

Eli looked up at the sun. "I'm not sure we have the time. It's almost noon, and Melody would like to be in Diamond City by then. We should start heading back."

Melody was overcome with regret at Eli's response. He was right; it was indeed almost noon, and she'd wanted to go back to the palace to alleviate any potential concerns of her officials, who didn't know she'd gone out to meet Eli. She was just beginning to enjoy his company, and her appreciation of him was growing by the hour. Plus, she was still very curious to find out if he was right in claiming to be the Eli of Marindel, the Great Prince of the Sea. Part of her still doubted his claims, and she was still paying close attention to his words and actions to find fault in him. But the more she spent time with him, the more she believed.

"*Surely my officials can't be too worried about me yet,*" Melody thought. "*If Eli really is the Great Prince, they would be amiss to be upset with me for spending time with him. It would be in our best interest for me to continue investigating this matter, so when I return to the palace, I can give them a clear answer about his identity. Who knows? If all of this works out, and I eventually come to...marry him...* She blushed at the thought. *Perhaps we'll become strong enough to resist the Tethysian Empire. We can do away with them forever."*

"What do you think, Mel? Would you like to start heading back?"

Melody smiled and said, "Nah, I don't need to go back yet. Wouldn't you rather show me around the rest of Rhema? What's one village compared to the whole kingdom?"

Eli's eyes glowed with delight. "I would be honored."

"I'll ready the saddles then," Caruso said with a nod. "Would you like anything to drink in the meantime?"

"Water, please," Melody replied.

"Got it," Caruso turned and went back into his manor.

Melody leaned up against Kaya and stroked her head. The talongrunt responded by closing her eyes and purring gently. After a moment Melody asked, "Eli, do you remember when you asked what else you can help me un-hate?"

"Yep. What about it?"

"Well, I think dragons are growing on me. They've attacked me many times before; I've had too many near-death experiences to count. I've considered them monsters, and I think most people in the realm would agree with me." She looked at Eli while stroking Kaya's neck. "But I never knew they could be friendly if you treated them right. They even have personalities, like house pets."

"Like people, even," Eli added.

Caruso returned, bringing two glasses of water. After handing them off, he said, "I'll saddle up Hunter first. I'll be back for Kaya."

Melody took a big sip of water and said, "I think dragons may be easier to tame than people."

"Is that so?"

"Mhmm," Melody nodded. "People don't change. They're mostly horrible, with a tiny speck of goodness here and there. The speck is so small, it doesn't count in the end. People *say* nice things, but they *do* horrible things. It's been that way for as long as I can remember."

"What makes you say that?"

"Well, it's true, isn't it?"

"Perhaps," Eli poked Melody on the forehead. "What do you see in yourself?"

She paused, frowning slightly. "I'm horrible. And don't you dare say I'm not."

"I won't argue with you," Eli said, much to her surprise. He went on without any hint of condescension. "You're prideful and stubborn. You look to serve yourself, with no regard for the needs of others. However, I see your pain and the lies the Serpent has woven into your soul from the very beginning. Remember how you approached Kaya in a way that diffused her temper, so you could make peace with her? She reminds you of yourself, does she not? That's why you share a connection with her."

Melody listened thoughtfully.

"I see the speck of goodness in your heart, Mel. And I believe in its potential to grow and triumph."

Melody sighed. "You are an extremely complicated individual."

"Eli!" Caruso called, holding a saddle and running up to them. "There are soldiers at the door looking for you. Here's Kaya's saddle, and here's the key to unleash her. I'll keep 'em busy, and you two fly out of here as soon as you can. Got it?"

Eli received the items. "Will do. Thank you for all your help."

"I'm only returning the favor," Caruso said with a nod before going back into the manor.

As Melody watched him go, she asked, "How did you help Caruso?"

Eli told the story while saddling Kaya. "When I was in town a couple days ago, he was in the general store looking to buy supplies, and the shop owner and some of the customers were giving him a hard time. One of your officials was there, too, instigating the whole thing. They didn't want to sell anything to him because he's a wealthy, dragon-owning Tethysian. I came in as they were arguing, and I diffused the situation. One cannot rightly classify all Tethysians as imperial overlords. Caruso has a good heart, as you've seen, and I helped the people in the shop understand that. The only person who wasn't happy in the end was your official, who left when the shop owner agreed to do business with Caruso."

"It's a good thing you showed up before any Tethysian soldiers did. That would've ended badly."

"Agreed," Eli said, just then releasing Kaya from her leash. "Speaking of soldiers, Kaya's ready to ride. Would you like to take her or Hunter?"

Melody's eye twinkled. "Who's faster?"

"Definitely Hunter." Eli raised an eyebrow. "Are you *sure* you want to take the faster dragon?"

"Yes!"

Having heard his name, Hunter leapt over the fence and landed proudly in front of Melody.

"Whoa!" Melody jumped in surprise.

Just then, they heard Matthias shout, "I hear someone in the back! Don't tell me no one's here, I *know* there is! You're acting in defiance of the Imperial Law!"

"Hurry," Eli whispered. "We have to move."

"Okay." Melody clambered onto Hunter's back. "Wait, Eli, how do I ride a dragon?"

"It's a bit like riding a horse."

"But there are no reins."

"See the handles in front of the saddle, strapped to his neck? Hold on to those and tilt to turn. He'll take care of the rest."

"All right," Melody grabbed the handles.

"Now tell him to fly," Eli said. "You go ahead."

The sound of a door flinging open preceded a soldier's voice, "The dragon's missing!"

"Ahhh! Fly!" Melody shouted in panic.

Hunter took a short running start and bounded into the sky with a powerful thrust of his wings. Melody screamed, unprepared for how fast Hunter could really fly.

"Come on, Kaya! Let's go!" Eli and Kaya took off after Hunter.

Matthias and his men charged into Kaya's pen seconds later. Matthias stomped his foot. "Damn! They got away!"

Caruso stumbled in after them, feigning surprise as he saw the dragons flying off in the distance. "Oh my, they've taken the dragons. I'm sorry, sir, they must've jumped the fence. You were right all along."

"Of *course* I was right," Matthias grumbled, heading back toward the manor.

"What, might I ask, are you going to do with them when you catch them?"

"We'll make him pay. With his life, if necessary."

"He hasn't done something deserving of death, has he?"

Matthias whirled around and snapped, "Use your brain, you aristocratic twit! He practices sorcery and claims to be some sort of Great Prince! The commoners are fascinated with him, and do you know what that means?"

"I'm sure if you talk with him, you'll see—"

"It means he's up to no good! In the name of Emperor Flavian the Bright, I will see to it that he is silenced before he turns the hearts of this kingdom against the Tethysian Empire."

Caruso remained calm. "All right. What will you do with the queen, then?"

"Hmph. Once her valiant vigilante is out of the way, she will once again be a pawn in the hands of the governor."

412

Caruso frowned, hardly able to contain his dismay. He cleared his throat and said, "Well then, you'd better get moving if you hope to catch them. Can I get you and your men anything to drink on your way out?"

40
The Prince of Legend
Summer, 104 IE

HUNTER SOARED INTO the sky, pumping his wings and relishing every moment of his airborne freedom.

Melody held on to the handles for dear life, crouched low and cringing with fear. The shawl that had been covering her head now trailed behind like a scarf, and her curly hair was a frazzled mess. "Hunter! Slow down!" She cried.

Hunter grunted in apology and relaxed his energetic pace, leveling out and allowing the wind to carry him forward.

"Much better," Melody said, though she remained tense.

A moment later, Kaya and Eli caught up to them. "I told you he was fast. Did he surprise you?"

"Just a bit," Melody said, sitting up straight to look unafraid. "I've never gone so fast before, that's all."

"It's all right. You've never flown a dragon, and I'd say you're already doing well for your first try."

"Thanks."

Eli took a deep breath and spread his arms wide. "Look at this view! Have you ever seen the kingdom of Rhema from this high up?"

Melody looked down. At first, she felt a nervous cringe in the pit of her stomach, but she quickly realized what Eli was talking about. Rolling green hills stretched below and around them in every direction, dotted with small trees and laced with dirt roads. A few villages were visible from this high up, as well as some distant wooded areas. Diamond City was beneath them as a sprawling stone maze, glistening in the noonday sun. Jasper Village was small in comparison. The sky was dotted with plump, white clouds, which cast moving shadows upon the landscape. Melody held her breath as she beheld her kingdom. "Eli, it's beautiful!"

"You've lived here for hundreds of years, and never thought to ride across the kingdom on a dragon?" Eli chuckled. "Well, I'm honored to be your guide for the day. Hang on to those handles and follow me!" With that, Eli urged Kaya to fly higher and faster.

Melody was buffeted by a gust of wind from Kaya's wings as they passed over her. She told Hunter, "Don't let us fall behind!"

Hunter grunted and turned upward, once again pounding the air with his wings.

The two of them flew higher and higher until they were level with the clouds. They flew all around and between them, the dragons' wings gracing the edges and sending spurts of mist into the air. Eli whooped and hollered, directing Kaya to swoop up and down with corkscrews and loops. Melody didn't participate, but she enjoyed watching Eli have so much fun. She even recalled vague memories of Eli performing all sorts of tricks and maneuvers throughout the flooded palace of Marindel.

"Eli has always been a thrill-seeker," Melody thought with a smile. *"Never timid. Always bold and ready to try something new."*

Hunter looked back at Melody and tilted his head.

"What? ...Oh, no, I'd rather not join in."

"Hey, Mel," Eli said as Kaya pulled up underneath them. He was reclining on her back with his hands behind his head and his legs crossed. "You feeling all right? Come on, let's have some fun!"

"I'm fine, thanks," Melody replied.

"Are you sure? You can't keep Hunter forever, you know. This might be our only chance to fly dragons together."

"I, uh..." Melody trailed off. She understood what Eli was saying, and part of her wanted to throw fear into the wind and have fun with him, just like they did when they were kids. But another part of her, a significantly larger part, remembered what happened the last time she played a game with Eli. She cringed and shook her head. "I'm sorry, I can't."

"I'll be here with you," Eli said. "You can trust me. I wouldn't ask you to do anything too dangerous."

Melody took more time to think about it.

"It's your choice," Eli said, sitting up and shrugging. "But it won't be as much fun without you."

"Well, I..." Melody looked down at the ground again. They were higher up now than the last time she looked, and she shuddered.

Hunter grumbled impatiently.

"All right, all right. I trust you." Melody looked down at Eli, made eye contact, and said again, "I trust you."

"Very well then!" Eli grinned, braced himself in the saddle, and patted Kaya on the neck. "All right, girl, let's go!"

Kaya screeched and dove into a downward spiral.

"Hunter," Melody gulped. "Please be careful."

Hunter yowled and plummeted after Kaya. Melody screamed the entire way down.

The two dragons ended their dive with an upward swoop, careening into a large cloud. When they shot out the other side, Eli was whooping joyfully, and Melody's scream had evolved into a nervous laugh.

Kaya did a corkscrew and then plummeted down, folding her wings and legs close to her body to enable the fastest possible descent.

"Oh no," Melody said as she watched Kaya. "Hunter, please, no."

Hunter looked back at Melody with one mischievous eye, and then turned in a corkscrew to dive after Kaya.

Once again, Melody screamed.

Hunter, more aerodynamic than Kaya, was able to catch up. As they sped past, Eli said, "Having fun yet!?"

"I'm trying!" Melody shouted mid-scream.

"Stop trying and just enjoy it!"

They were descending fast. A jagged coastline was beneath them, with crashing waves and sharp rocks awaiting their arrival.

Melody yelled, "Hunter, pull up!"

Hunter swooped into level flight just before hitting the ocean. With extreme speed, he turned sideways to avoid a jutting rock spire, and then curved in closer to the water and flew parallel to a breaching wave. His wing gently graced the inside of it. Seawater sprinkled Melody's face as they went.

"I will not be afraid of this," Melody declared to herself. "If Eli's not afraid, there's no reason I should be!"

Hunter cleared the wave and flew up over a cliff topped with a thick woodland. He skimmed above the canopy, only several feet above tallest trees, and looked back at Melody.

"What? Are you wondering if I'm having fun, too?"

Hunter shook his neck, wiggling the handles of the saddle. Melody caught on and asked, "You want me to steer you?"

Hunter affirmed with a grunt.

"Okay," Melody gripped the handles tighter. She tilted to the right, and Hunter turned right. She tilted harder to the left, and Hunter turned a sharper left. Melody smiled and said, "All right, let's go back to the water."

Hunter, guided by Melody, flew back to the coastline. He dove down the cliff and between two towering rock spires before beginning to skim the water.

Now, finally, Melody was laughing. She felt free at last.

There was a fishing ship some distance off the coast, and Melody decided to fly in for a closer look. She steered Hunter toward it, keeping low and close to the water. Then, as they were mere seconds from crashing into the hull, she let loose a "Woohoo!" and pulled up on the handles, causing Hunter to curve upward. The surprised crew was buffeted with a gust of wind and a spray of seawater as they went.

"Keep going up!" Melody shouted, keeping Hunter on his current course. When they had flown up high, she steered Hunter back around to behold her kingdom. She could see the beautiful, wooded coastline, jagged in every area except for one place far to the right. It was Carnelian Cove, surrounded on every side by tall, smooth, green mountains.

"Wow," Melody breathed.

"Finally enjoying yourself, I see!" Eli called from below.

"Yeah," Melody replied with a blush.

"What do you say we take a closer look at the cove?"

Melody smiled. "I would love to!"

"All right! Let's go!"

Eli, Kaya, Melody, and Hunter flew to Carnelian Cove. They skirted the mountains and dove down the forested cliffs sheltering the bay, all the while staying far enough from the city to avoid attracting unwanted attention. They rested for a while at the top of the highest mountain, and then they were off again.

Over the next few hours, Eli did not disappoint in his assignment to show Melody around the kingdom of Rhema. There wasn't a single part of the island kingdom they didn't fly through. Melody grew confident in her ability to ride a dragon, and more importantly, she became more comfortable with Eli's guidance and leadership. The adventure led Melody to become very fond of Eli, even to the point where her fondness outweighed her skepticism.

Despite her progress, Eli knew she still had her doubts. For the last leg of their tour of Rhema, he knew exactly where to take her.

"Mel," Eli said, eyes glimmering, "there's one last place I want you to see."

They were now reclining in a grassy field near a west-facing cliff. The ocean foamed far below, sparkling blue and silver against the molten sky, which was fiery with the coming of sunset. Hunter and Kaya drank heartily from a stream nearby.

Melody looked at Eli and asked, "What do you mean? I thought we've seen everything already. Besides, wouldn't you say it's getting late?"

"I saved this one for last because it's very special to me. It's an ocean cave not far from here. It can only be accessed during low tides, and this is the perfect hour to go."

"All right," Melody replied, standing up. "Let's go, then."

The two of them mounted their dragons and took off. Eli led the way down to the ocean and skimmed the edge of the cliff for a short distance before he had Kaya hover in place.

Hunter hovered beside Kaya as their riders beheld the cave. It was a yawning, black void with dark blue water pulling in and out, which echoed in the most ominous manner.

"*That* cave?" Melody asked.

"Yup, that's the one. Now, we'll have to trust our dragons to guide us through. They have good night vision, so they'll know where to go."

"I thought you wanted me to see something in there. How will I see anything if it's dark?"

"You'll see." Eli winked. Then he nudged Kaya and said, "To the back of the cave."

Kaya disappeared into the yawning cavern.

"You too, Hunter," Melody told her dragon, and Hunter flew inside.

To Melody, it seemed like they were flying for several minutes through the pitch-dark blackness. She could tell the cave was narrowing by the sound of the dragons' wingbeats echoing off the walls, and by the sound of the stirring water below. Melody stayed low against Hunter's back, fearful she would hit her head on the ceiling of the cave.

Suddenly, there was a splash as Hunter landed in the water. Melody yelped in surprise, thinking Hunter was going to sink and take her along with him.

Eli's voice called from just ahead, "It's all right, Mel! The water's shallow enough here for the dragons to walk. Kaya, how about some light?"

A second later, thanks to a steady flame in Kaya's mouth, Melody was able to see her surroundings. The cave in front of them was too narrow for the dragons to fly through, but since the water was shallow, they could walk perfectly well through the tunnel. The water looked to be about four feet deep.

"This is why we need a low tide," Eli explained as Kaya and Hunter ventured deeper into the cave. "Otherwise, this part of the cave would be submerged."

"Have you been here before?" Melody asked.

"No. Only one person has come here."

"Do you know him? Or her?"

"I did."

"Oh. Is he or she dead?"

"Yes, he's dead."

"High tide?" Melody guessed.

"No."

"Oh." Melody looked at Eli, whose countenance had fallen. "Were you close friends?"

"Yes."

Soon, they emerged into a massive, cavernous space. The floor sloped upward, so the dragons surfaced onto packed, sandy ground. High on the vaulted ceiling, in addition to the many stalactites, there were small crevices through which weak shafts of light came down in rays. The cave was so large, Kaya's fire couldn't allow them to see to the other side.

"This is it," Eli said, sliding off Kaya and landing with a thud on the sandy ground.

"A dark, empty cave?"

"Not quite." Eli pointed into the darkness ahead. "Ignite the basin."

Kaya squawked and launched a fireball into the darkness. It careened through empty space for a second before hitting a stone basin carved into the wall of the cave. The projectile burst with a unique display of orange and blue sparks. The basin filled with liquid blue fire, which spread rapidly down small troughs extending along the base of the wall. The cavern brightened to acquire a mystical, shimmering blue glow.

Several troughs on the right side of the room extended up the wall and ran along the ceiling. The blue fire in these troughs illuminated a peculiar pattern at the back of the cave.

Melody squinted her eyes at the pattern as it came to light. She gasped in surprise. "It's...it's a mural! A *huge* mural!"

"Go on, take a closer look!"

She slid off Hunter and ran toward it. Eli, Hunter, and Kaya followed close behind.

Melody stood in front of the mural, awestruck by the enormous piece of art before her. "Eli, I've never seen anything like it! Your friend was a true artist, and in a cave, no less!"

"Indeed," Eli agreed. "What do you see?"

"Hmm," Melody studied the mural. There were many things going on, so she began with the focal point in the very center. "There's a man in the center...no, an elf. A grand, wise-looking elf, and he's sitting on a throne. The Great King," Melody said, looking at Eli for confirmation. Then she continued, "On either side of him are two more thrones. On the right is..." she trailed off.

"Who?" Eli pressed. "Who is it?"

Melody stepped closer to the mural. She was three feet away from it now, staring up at the dazzling figure sitting on the right throne. "It's me."

"That's right."

"I-it's the most beautiful painting of me I've ever seen."

Even as she was still processing, her eyes drifted to the throne on the left. When she realized who was sitting there, she held her breath. "It...it can't be, can it?" She looked at Eli, her eyes demanding an explanation.

"What do you see?" Eli asked.

"I know what I see, but I...I can't believe..." Melody looked again at the figure on the throne. "Eli, it's you. But, it's *you* you. *Human* you, just like you are right now. A bit shinier perhaps, but still *you*."

"Yes," Eli said, standing next to Melody. "What else do you see?"

Melody was overwhelmed, but she continued to examine other parts of the mural. "Well, surrounding the thrones, there are four creatures. Titans, right? One is like a wheel of fire, the second is like a whirling thunderstorm, the third is like an erupting volcano, and the fourth is like a breaching wave. All around them are groups of shiny elves playing instruments. Galyyrim, I think. And below it all, there's the realm. The sea, the land, the trees, the clouds, even cities," Melody walked up to place her finger on a painted city. After a moment, she turned to face Eli. "Who did this?"

"His name was Uriah. Do you remember him?"

Melody shook her head.

"You killed him."

Melody's jaw dropped. "W-what do you mean I killed him?"

"Do you remember what he told you before he was executed?"

Melody became flustered. "Wait just a minute! You're talking about those Seers, aren't you?"

"Yes," Eli said, his eyes filled with sorrow. "He was a zealous, passionate follower of the Great King. A wonderful fellow. He fled from your officials when his actions caused them to seek his life. The Great King showed him to this place, where he spent twenty years in hiding. During that time, he painted this mural, so the mysteries revealed to him would be saved for future generations. Then, the Great King led him to confront you one last time, and he was killed."

Melody wanted to unleash a violent rant upon Eli about how much she loathed Seers, but her heart stopped her. The part of her that loved Eli and everything he stood for came alongside her frustrated ego and sang it a lullaby, like taming a dragon. Then she remembered Uriah and what he said: "Your father, the King, remembers you, and he loves you! The Prince of the Sea is coming soon, and he will deliver you from the power of the Serpent once and for all! Remember the Great King and follow his ways! He doesn't want you to continue in your suffering, but to return to Marindel as the bride of the Great Prince!"

As Uriah's words cycled through her head, Melody looked again at the thrones in the center. The painting of her was the most stunning portrayal of herself that she had ever seen. The painting of Eli was likewise staggering to behold. He was handsome and regal, yes, but he looked *exactly* like the Eli who was in the cave with her now: in appearance, simply an ordinary man.

Everything began to make sense.

The Great King gave Uriah such extraordinary wisdom, he was able to paint this intricate mural down to the detail on Eli's face.

Uriah lived two centuries ago, but somehow, he knew.

He knew Eli was coming.

More than that, Uriah knew Eli was coming as an ordinary man.

Bringing it to a crescendo, Uriah knew Eli was coming as an ordinary man to court Melody and take her back to Marindel and marry her, making her a Princess of the Sea once again and a legitimate daughter of the Great King.

This is what he was trying to tell her all along, he and all the Seers before him. And she had them all killed for it. Her eyes welled up with tears. "What have I done?"

Eli came alongside Melody and took her hand. She immediately hugged him tight and began to sob. "I'm sorry, I'm *so* sorry!"

"Don't worry, Mel," Eli said softly, "I forgive you."

"I deserve to die," Melody mumbled.

"No. You are forgiven."

Melody continued to weep as her thoughts and emotions shifted. Inner walls came down, doubts were washed away, and lies were cut down. The iron hold the Serpent kept on her soul for so long finally began to lose its grip. Finally, at long last, she spoke.

"I believe."

"What's that?" Eli asked, pulling out of the embrace to see her face.

"I believe," she repeated, meeting his gaze. "You are Eli, the Great Prince of the Sea. The Son of the Great King."

Eli smiled and hugged her again, he himself now beginning to weep. "At last, you're beginning to understand!" He chuckled, resting his head against hers. "The Great King has revealed this to you, and you must treasure it with all your heart. Do not let this seed of belief be taken from you. By it, you will be saved, and I will take you to Marindel with me to live with our father, the Great King, forever."

It was late at night when Eli and Melody returned to Diamond City. They flew Kaya and Hunter up to the balcony of Melody's room and had them perch along the banister. There, Melody dismounted and said goodbye to Eli.

"When will I see you again?" Melody asked, looking up at him.

"Meet me tomorrow at noon in the marketplace, by the textile shop." His eyes glimmered. "We'll have a great time!"

"I can't wait," Melody replied, returning his loving gaze.

"Goodnight, Mel. I love you."

"Goodnight."

Eli looked at her a moment longer before nudging Kaya to push off the balcony and glide into the starry night, back to Caruso's manor where the dragons belonged.

Hunter crawled onto the balcony to give Melody an affectionate nudge before he jumped after Kaya.

Melody watched them go until she could see them no longer. She sighed deeply, smiling as she recounted the exciting events of the day.

"That man is something else," she thought. *"He doesn't just know about me. He knows me. He sees me, as I am, right now. Every thought, every feeling. I'm an irredeemable mess, desperate for affection, yet unable to really earn it. But still, he wants me. He enjoys me. Today, Eli's piercing words and penetrating gaze tore down my facade, leaving me vulnerable before him. I should have been terrified. But, never before have I felt so...safe. He is so gentle, and so kind! His presence is like a shield, protecting me from every outside threat. When I'm with him, I feel like I can do anything. I rode a dragon today, for crying out loud! Who can this man be, if not the Prince of Marindel? Oh, I can't wait to see Eli again! I'd better get some rest before our next adventure!"*

Giddy and beaming, Melody walked into her room. It was dark inside, so she went to light the oil lamp on her nightstand. When she did, she yelped at the sight of a person sitting on a chair in the corner. She didn't grow any less tense when she realized it was one of her officials, the elder with the white beard.

"Where were you today?" he asked.

"Visiting other villages in the kingdom. Why, did you miss me?"

"What were you doing in those villages?"

"Having fun. You know, queen stuff."

"What came over you that caused you to traipse around Rhema without your wise council to escort you?"

"I needed a break. You guys don't give me much space, you know."

"But you *weren't* alone, were you?"

By his tone, Melody supposed he already knew the answer, so there was no reason to deny the obvious. "Nope, I was with my new friend, Eli. You know, the Prince of Marindel? He's actually really great."

"Have you gone mad?" The elder stood. "That man is no prince! He's a troublemaker! A peasant who's had too much wine to drink!"

Melody laughed. "Yeah, he gets that a lot. Someone called him a sorcerer today. That's a new one, huh?"

"Milady, this is serious! We've been receiving complaints about him from all over the kingdom. He's meddling in everyone's affairs, performing magic tricks, and fostering division between us and the Tethysians. And let's not even mention the whole Prince of Marindel nonsense."

"Oh, loosen up. You just have to get to know him, that's all."

"Rubbish," the elder spat. "Listen carefully. I don't want to see or hear of you spending time with that man ever again. Do you understand?"

"No."

"Then you'd better take tonight to think about it," the elder said, wagging his finger. "If this continues, there *will* be consequences. As your appointed officials, we cannot allow any threat to the peace and security of Rhema. You ought to tell him to leave, and leave quickly."

"All right. Shall I go with him?"

"And abandon your people and the entire kingdom? That's absurd! You're not going anywhere!"

"Well, what if I marry him and become a queen of Marindel? Rhema will become a state of Marindel, and then we won't have to negotiate with Tethysians anymore. We could fight them and win."

"Milady, listen to me!" The elder stepped closer and enunciated his words very clearly. "He is *not* the Prince of Marindel!"

"Yes, he is!" Melody enunciated with equal clarity.

The elder pointed his finger at Melody's face and glared at her. "One more chance. Just one. If we see or hear of you participating in his ridiculous antics again, you will be placed under house arrest. *He,* on the other hand, will be dealt with as we see fit."

"Challenge accepted."

"Hmph." The elder turned to leave, saying more politely as he went, "Good night, Milady."

After the elder shut the door, Melody thought about the tense conversation. Despite her initial resolve, she knew his threats were legitimate. He would stop at nothing to make sure Eli ended up with the same fate as all the Seers before him.

But this time, it would be different.

"They can't arrest him if I don't let them," Melody reasoned. *"I'm the Queen of Rhema, and they ultimately have to do what I say. If they disobey me, they'll be guilty of treason, and I can convince the Tethysians to back me up on that. Not that I'll be needing them, though. Eli is clever enough to avoid my officials already, but I'll have to warn him tomorrow when I see him."*

With those thoughts, Melody prepared herself for bed and went to sleep with eager anticipation for the day ahead.

OVER THE NEXT few days, Melody continued to spend time with Eli. She warned him of her officials' hatred toward him, but that didn't stop Eli from being himself. That is, from spending time with the people of Rhema, serving them in practical everyday matters, healing diseases and injuries, telling stories about Marindel, and teaching values of justice, humility, and love for one another.

As Melody accompanied Eli on these adventures, she discovered the sole motivating force behind everything he did was a genuine love and respect for all people. The more Melody spent time with Eli, the more his loving spirit began to take hold of her as well. Melody found herself seeing people more favorably, and much to her surprise, she became more willing to talk and spend time with them.

One afternoon, Eli and Melody visited Jasper Village to have lunch with the family they encountered before: Trisha, her husband Auben, the little boy Trevor, and his older sister Lia. The family was amazed at how open and friendly Melody had become, and of course, they reckoned Eli was the reason behind the change. Melody thought the afternoon was very pleasant, and upon departing, she wondered aloud, "Why did I refuse to spend time with them on our first visit here?"

Eli said, "Don't worry, Mel, I knew your heart wasn't in the right place yet. Today was the perfect time for it. Besides, if we had stayed with them, we wouldn't have gotten to ride dragons." He gave her a playful wink.

During this time, Eli and Melody had many close calls with the Rheman officials and the Tethysian soldiers. Both groups were becoming more suspicious of Eli's strange activity, and they were afraid he and Melody were spending far too much time together.

Melody's officials, under ordinary circumstances, were well respected by the common people of Rhema. However, it was an unspoken truth that they cared little for the people, and Eli was bringing that truth to light. As a result, the people favored Eli with growing resolve. This effect was multiplied when Melody herself sided with Eli instead of her officials, thereby stripping them of their legitimacy before the people.

In addition, though the officials tried to place Melody under house arrest, she wielded her authority as the Queen of Rhema to go wherever she pleased. They knew very well how stubborn she could be, though they'd never experienced her attitude working against them before. This was something they sorely resented.

As for the Tethysians, many of them weren't concerned with

Eli's good deeds and bouts with the officials as much as they were with his statements about the Great King, and his "sorcerous" actions. The Tethysian Empire as a whole, having conquered half of the realm by 104 IE, had many experiences dealing with sorcerers and political instigators. The two qualities combined in one person, who also had favor with the common people, was a triple threat in the Empire's eyes. Nevertheless, despite the incredible zeal of some officers like Matthias, they were unable to muster enough support for a successful attempt at capturing Eli. The Tethysian governor, specifically, had no interest in giving a mandate to catch a charity worker.

However, in spite of these things, the Great Serpent was closing in on his illustrious target, knowing exactly what to do to tilt events in his favor.

And he would not relent, not even for a second.

41

The Prince of Love

Summer, 104 IE

MELODY WAS STANDING with Eli on a cloud high in the sky. He took her by the shoulders with a grand smile and said, "Melody, I want you to jump. Can you do that for me?"

Melody shook her head. "That'd be insane!"

"Come on, Mel! Trust me!"

She thought for a moment, and then shrugged. "Well, all right. But you'd better protect me!"

"I will, don't worry," Eli said, grasping her hands tightly.

"Here I go!" Melody jumped off the cloud. She fell for what seemed like an eternity. The sprawling Rhema countryside was below, glistening in the noonday sun. It was so beautiful, Melody forgot she was falling.

Her eyes locked onto a small gray speck on the landscape below. When she did so, suddenly, the speck grew into an enormous metal dragon's head, mouth gaping wide and filled with sword-like teeth.

With a surge of panic, Melody screamed and flailed about as the dragon's jaws closed over her like a steel trap.

MELODY AWOKE WITH a horrified shout. Breathing hard, she took in the safe and familiar surroundings of her room.

It was just a dream. An utterly terrifying dream.

Even knowing that, Melody's heart was hurt. She put her trust in Eli, and in the end, it resulted in her death. Didn't Eli know there was a giant metal dragon head down there waiting for her? How could he tell her to jump like that? Eli would never do such a thing!

"*Or would he?*" the thought entered Melody's mind. It was the Serpent speaking, but he used a voice resembling Melody's own. "*It will only take one mistake, one moment of misplaced trust, to end up in the jaws of death.*"

Melody sat on her bed with her arms wrapped around her knees, pondering this terrifying revelation. Eli had proven to be trustworthy thus far. But, what if, just one time...?

"*You cannot place your trust in others,*" the Serpent said. "*If, when you place your trust in Eli, he turns and stabs you in the back, you have only yourself to blame. Only you can protect yourself.*"

Melody shook her head and banished the thought. "*How crazy. Eli would never do such a thing. He never would! It's not like him. He loves me. I know he does.*"

"*Then you'd better not fail him and change his mind.*"

"Rubbish," Melody said aloud. "I can't believe I'm thinking like this. Eli has loved me since we were kids. He's been waiting all this time to see me again, and now he's finally here. After all the wrong I've already done, I can't do anything to make him change his mind. He knows me completely, and he loves me unconditionally."

"*We shall see,*" the Serpent hissed, leaving Melody to her own thoughts.

After calming down, Melody went to sleep again. The next day, she met Eli in the apple orchard and spent time with him as usual. She didn't act any different, but deep down, she couldn't forget the imagery of her dream and the terror it struck in her inmost being.

Throughout the next two weeks, Melody had many similar dreams.

One night, she dreamt that Eli had stopped to help a young woman with a hunched back. He healed her back so she could stand up perfectly straight, and the girl became inexplicably beautiful. Thereafter, Eli returned every day to visit her, and when Melody questioned him about it, he said, "Melody, I've decided I love her more than I love you."

Using that dream, the Serpent planted envy in Melody's heart. From that night on, as Eli continued visiting villages and helping people, Melody became jealous whenever Eli gave others more attention than her, even if just for a moment. But she never said anything about it because she didn't want to appear selfish.

The more these dreams came, the more Melody began to doubt

Eli's character and her worthiness in his eyes. Outwardly, she still followed him, but she didn't tell him or anyone else about her doubts because she didn't want to be thought of as incompetent or weak for doubting him even after everything they'd been through.

This, of course, was all the work of the Serpent as he manipulated her thoughts and exploited her past wounds to cast doubt on what she thought she believed was true.

ONE EVENING, ELI took Melody to the apple orchard. Though they had spent many hours in the orchard before, this was their first visit after sundown.

"How are you feeling?" Eli asked as they walked through the trees.

"I'm well," Melody replied, looking up at the dark branches against the twilit sky.

"Is that so?"

"Mhmm."

"You've been quieter the past few days. What's on your mind?" Though Eli already knew of Melody's doubts, he wanted her to admit she had them. Otherwise, her heart wouldn't be open to his encouragement and affirmation.

Melody couldn't discern Eli's intentions, so she kept her thoughts to herself. "Nothing really. I mean, all of this is still new to me. I'm still...taking it all in, you know?"

"I see. Well, tonight, I have a surprise for you."

"Really?" Melody asked, her interest piquing.

"Yes," Eli replied, his face glowing. "You've never ventured around the countryside at night before, have you?"

"Nope. It's too dark, too scary."

"Perhaps. But I'll be your guide tonight, so you have nothing to fear."

Melody smiled. "All right, if you say so." She had a tiny prick of doubt even as she spoke, but she repressed it.

"Great," Eli grinned and began to run. "Come on, follow me!"

"Wait, where are we going?" Melody called as she went after him.

"You'll see!"

They ran between two hills laden with apple trees, and then took a right and ran up another hill and down the other side, zigzagging around boulders and tree trunks the whole way. It wasn't long before Melody was panting for breath. It was also very dark, and she was afraid she'd trip.

"Come along! Just a little further!" Eli called. "Don't lose sight of me!"

Melody was becoming frustrated with Eli for leading her on through a gloomy forest. Though she was getting exhausted and longed for a place to rest, she kept her gaze on him. It was strange; Eli seemed to be brighter than anything else she could see, almost as if he were glowing. When she looked at him, she could run effortlessly without any worry. But when she looked away, at the rough terrain below her feet or the dark forms of trees and boulders all around, she became frightened and exhausted. Even then, all she had to do was look again at Prince Eli, and she found her strength quickly renewed. It didn't take Melody long to realize this, so she remained focused on Eli for the remainder of the journey.

Eli stopped.

Melody skidded to a halt behind him, gasping for breath. They were now standing on the rim of a large pond, the waters of which were still and reflected the starry night above.

"Shhh," Eli whispered, "Look, over there."

Melody followed Eli's gaze. There, on the other side of the pond, was a majestic unicorn, shimmering in the starlight, feeding on the apples hanging from a tree.

"Beautiful, isn't it?" Eli whispered. "We have a perfect view! I don't think she's noticed us yet."

Melody stayed silent. Deep down, she greatly resented unicorns. Every time she had an encounter with one, it tried to attack her. She and her officials considered unicorns to be pests because they roamed about freely, trespassing into farmers' fields, eating their fill, and trampling whatever remained.

"Have you ever petted a unicorn, Mel?"

Melody shook her head.

"Oh, they're *so* soft! Let's get a closer look. How about it?"

Melody hesitated. She didn't want to refuse him, but she also didn't want to get any closer to the unicorn. She searched for an excuse. "I-I'm not sure it's possible to get over there. See, the pond is in the way, and there's thick underbrush growing all along the edge. The unicorn will hear us coming and run away long before we can touch it."

"We can make it across that pond easily. Do you trust me?"

"Uh..." Melody wasn't sure what he was asking her to trust him to do. Crossing the pond would be unpleasant, muddy, and cold.

"Do you trust me?" he repeated.

She wanted to. Despite her doubts, she was still incredibly fond of him. He had never let her down before, at least not in the waking realm. Remembering his love for her and drawing strength from her seedling of love for him, she mustered all the courage she had to say, "Yes. I trust you."

Eli smiled and reached forward. "Here, take my hand."

Melody took his hand, blushing as she looked into his eyes.

"Now, just look at the unicorn," Eli said, pointing at it. "How marvelous! Do you know much about unicorns?"

"No, not really. I've never liked them much, and they don't like me, either."

"I understand. Let me tell you something about unicorns, Mel. They're far more perceptive than horses, or even dragons! A unicorn can see the intentions of a person's heart; whether they're good or evil. They will react accordingly to what they see in your heart."

Melody whispered sharply, "What are you trying to say?"

"I'm saying you've changed for the better. I've seen the ways you've grown as we've spent time together. Your spirit has become gentle and loving. Every passing day, I see more of the innocent little girl I once knew, perfected in all the beauty my father saw in you from the very beginning. You've endured a very painful life on the surface, and you've made many unwise and selfish choices. But, Mel, *all* of it can be redeemed. From the ashes of your soul can come a beautiful vine more fruitful than it was at first, before the release of the Serpent. That is what I've come to show you."

Melody listened, her gaze fixed on the unicorn. On an intellectual level she had no idea what Eli meant, but her spirit leapt and grabbed at every word. She felt understood by him. More than that, she felt loved and appreciated, despite her dark past and her present rebellious nature.

She looked at Eli to say something, but when she did, she realized they were standing atop the surface of the pond, a dozen feet from the shore.

"Eli! Wh-what!?" Melody clung to Eli.

"Melody, it's all right! Don't be surprised to find yourself doing impossible things when you put your trust in me and the Great King. Remember when we ran through the orchard earlier? As you fixed your eyes on me, you didn't need to worry about what path to take, or whether or not your feet would slip. It works the same in every matter of life. It has pleased the Great King tonight to allow us to walk upon this pond so you may know even more what it's like to trust me."

"Whoa." Melody slowly let go of Eli and stood freely upon the surface. Their footsteps hardly rippled the pond at all, but the water around their feet glowed with beautiful hues of dancing blue.

"Look," Eli pointed at the unicorn, which had noticed them when their voices raised. It stood still, watching curiously with its ears perked and its tail swishing back and forth.

Melody cowered at the sight of it. "You're not still wanting to touch it, are you?"

"I have a better idea," Eli said, cracking an adventurous grin. "How about we ride it?"

Melody's eyes widened. "What's with you and riding things!? Why in the kingdom of Rhema would I want to ride a wild unicorn!?"

Even as she spoke, Eli began walking across the pond toward the unicorn.

The unicorn leaned forward and wiggled its nose to take in Eli's scent. Then it trotted several steps into the pond to meet him, ears flicking happily.

Once they met, Eli brushed the unicorn's snout with his hand and said, "Hey there, wanna go for a run tonight? Stretch your big, strong legs?"

The unicorn whinnied and nudged Eli's face with its nose.

Eli chuckled, and he called, "Come on, Mel! There's nothing to fear."

"But...didn't you say it sees my heart? What if it doesn't like me? I told you unicorns don't like me."

"What else did I tell you?"

Melody knew what Eli wanted her to say, but she was still fighting her dislike of unicorns.

While she delayed, Eli slung himself onto the unicorn's back. He looked at Melody with excitement in his gaze and stretched out his hand. "Come with me!"

"But, Eli..." Melody trailed off as she looked at him. She was captivated by his eyes, the way his hair glistened in the starlight, the way he smiled at her and sat upon the unicorn's back, calling her to join him. Eli *wanted* her to join him. She couldn't help but blush, and she threw her hesitation aside. "All right, all right. Only because you're with me." She took his hand.

Eli pulled Melody up onto the unicorn's back, and she sat behind him.

The unicorn snorted and flicked its ears, adjusting its stance to accommodate the weight on its back, but it didn't seem at all frustrated with Melody.

"Hold on tight," Eli said over his shoulder. "Are you ready?"

Melody wrapped her arms around Eli's waist. "Yeah."

Eli spurred the unicorn on. It whinnied and set off at a gallop, sending up a spray of water as it moved out of the pond and into the darkness of the orchard.

At first Melody was dismayed that they were once again traveling through the trees, but her disappointment didn't last long. A moment later, they emerged from the orchard and galloped into the rolling, starlit grasslands of Rhema. They were heading east, in a perfect position to witness the rising full moon. A cool breeze blew over the tall grass, bending it in gentle waves. Flashing pinpricks of light shimmered across the countryside; hundreds of fireflies in every direction. As Eli and Melody rode forth, the insects skittered before them like windblown sparks.

Eli directed the unicorn with skill and expertise. Whether it was dodging a boulder here or jumping a pond there, he did so with a calm trust in the unicorn's ability to overcome every obstacle. He never reprimanded the animal, but nudged and spoke simple words to guide it on its way. As a result of Eli's expert riding, Melody was able to forget her dislike of unicorns and take in the experience. It happened quicker on this night than on the day they flew dragons.

Melody relished the nighttime air, the enchanting chorus of crickets and frogs, and the sparkling lights dancing to the rhythm of the unicorn's hoofbeats. But, however impressed she was by this mesmerizing dreamworld, she was most fascinated by the man sitting in front of her. The only man who had ever *truly* loved her, wanted her, and protected her.

"Eli," she said after a few moments, "This is truly wonderful."

Eli turned back to smile at her. "I knew you would enjoy it, Mel."

"I mean it," Melody insisted, wrapping her arms tighter around him. "I'm really happy to be here with you tonight."

Eli's face brightened even more. "And I'm glad to be with you, my beloved."

For another half an hour, Eli and Melody rode the unicorn through the moonlit countryside. They hardly spoke a word, but for once, it wasn't because Melody was lost in thought. She was enjoying the present moment with Eli, whom she loved, and all she could think about was how much she loved him and couldn't wait to marry him. She had never met another man like Eli, who cared for her and pursued her like she was the most precious treasure in the realm.

Eli brought the unicorn to a stop at the summit of a high hill upon which stood a massive camphor tree. The gnarled trunk and branches of the tree towered above everything else in the grassland, and its luscious green canopy was dense like a cloud. From the foot of the tree, with the help of the moonlight, Eli and Melody could see endlessly in every direction: the firefly-speckled fields, a few trees here and there, dark forested areas further on the horizon, and from whence they came, the faraway dimly-lit stone edifice that was Diamond City.

Eli hopped down from the unicorn's back and helped Melody down as well. Then he said to the unicorn, "Thank you, friend. Go frolic as you please."

The unicorn whinnied, shaking its silky mane, and trotted away into the night.

Melody looked around, her gaze lingering on the tree nearby. "What is this place?"

"It's one of my favorite spots in all of Rhema," Eli said, his voice reverent.

She looked around again, but saw nothing interesting. "Why?"

"This is a place where the presence of my father, the Great King, dwells strongly. I come here almost every night to commune with him. He gives me strength, confidence, focus, and direction."

"It's quite far from the city."

"Yes. I prefer to seek my father in solitude, where I can devote myself to hearing his voice."

"Is that why you never sleep in the city?"

"Yes. But tonight, I would like to share this moment you."

"Oh? What kind of moment?" Melody asked, stepping closer to him.

"This intimacy I have with my father," Eli said, taking Melody by the hand, "is something I would like to pass on to you."

"That's...great," Melody replied, not understanding what he meant. "How?"

"Do you remember the gift he gave you back in Marindel? The royal power and authority sealed within the amulet?"

"A little bit, maybe." She didn't want to remember. It was because of the amulet that the Serpent was released. With its power, the Serpent was able to cause unmitigated death and destruction. Melody didn't want to have that power again. "*I don't deserve it,*" she thought.

"In the near future," Eli said, "the power and authority bestowed by the Great King as an inheritance will not be confined to any particular amulet, nor will it be set apart for one person. It will dwell in the hearts of all who choose to follow the Great King. These he will, like you, adopt to become his sons and daughters. In that way, the Kingdom of Marindel will triumph over the Serpent and his dark forces, once and for all."

"Wait, so…" Melody was confused.

"I know it's hard to understand now," Eli said, poking Melody on the nose. "But keep it in mind for another time."

"Why are you telling me this if you know I'm not going to understand it?"

"Because I'm confident you will *someday*," Eli said with a gentle smile. "I believe you will."

"Okay." Melody blushed.

"Now, you've seen the things I've done here in Rhema. You've heard my words, and you've seen the power of the Great King released through my actions."

"Mhmm." Melody stared into his eyes. "There has never been another man like you, and I don't believe there ever will be."

"I've done these things to set an example for you and for those who will soon believe. I have no power of my own, but because I watch and listen for the nudges of my father the King, and I do what he says, he lends me his strength to do the impossible. You've experienced it as well; have you noticed? When you sing unto the Great King, the power of life flows around you and causes plants to grow and bloom."

Melody thought back to when she tamed Hunter and Kaya, and how the grass around her had bloomed and scorched grass was healed. She nodded. "Yeah, I did notice that."

"This is what I've been trying to show you. The Great King's power is available to you, just as it is to me, when you listen for his voice and step out to do what he says. Do you remember, long ago, when you set out to find this land? The Great King led you here because you listened to him. Since then, you and your people have forgotten the Great King and have governed according to your own wisdom. The consequences of your actions have become evident. However, the Great King doesn't want you to be destroyed by the cunning schemes of the Serpent, who is currently the tyrant of this realm. The King has created a way for you, and soon, for all sentient beings, to escape from the control of the Serpent and enter into the Kingdom of Marindel."

"And that way is you," Melody said, wrapping her arms around his shoulders. "Isn't it?"

"Indeed," Eli said, embracing her. "It is."

"Oh, can we be married already?" Melody asked with a longing sigh, resting her forehead against his. "Take me away from this place, from all the horrors of politics and people-pleasing, and the death and destruction that follows me everywhere I go. Take me to Marindel, where I can be beside you forever."

Eli held her close, looking deeply into her eyes. "Do you know that I love you, Mel?"

"Yes. I know you love me very much."

"Do you know I will never stop loving you, no matter what happens?"

"Yes," Melody said, placing her hand on Eli's head and stroking his hair. "No matter what comes our way, your love will endure forever."

Eli smiled. A single tear rolled down his cheek.

"You're...crying? What's wrong?"

Eli's expression evolved into a mixture of joy and grief. "If only it was *that* simple."

"What do you mean?"

For a moment, Eli appeared to have an inward battle in his mind. He glanced at the ground while several tears streamed down his face. He said almost inaudibly, "Father, I trust you." Then he looked at Melody and said, "No matter what happens, Mel—no matter *what* happens—remember I love you. You *must* remember I love you."

Before she could reply, Eli moved in to kiss her. Melody surrendered, holding him tight and returning the kiss with passion.

After a few seconds, they separated and stared into each other's eyes again. Melody's gaze was giddy and bright with adoration. Eli's gaze was strong and loving, gentle and wise—yet, there were undertones of sorrow.

"You look like you need another kiss, mister," Melody said with a grin.

Eli stepped out of her embrace and took her hands, holding them tight. "Mel, there's something I must tell you."

"Yeah?"

"I will not be here for much longer. Soon, I must return to Marindel."

"Oh..." Melody took a moment to ponder before replying, "Well, this is great news! I'm so excited to go back to Marindel with you to be married! Then Rhema will be your kingdom, and Marindel will be mine. Together, we can resist the Empire and every enemy who comes against us. And we can live happily ever after."

Eli didn't respond the way Melody thought he would. She thought he'd be joyful and confident, but instead, Eli was troubled. He sighed deeply and looked at the ground.

"Eli, what's wrong?"

"Mel," Eli said, looking deep into her eyes. "We *will* be married. I promise, one day I will be fully yours, and you will be fully mine. You will take your rightful place as the Princess of the Sea at the right hand of our father, the Great King. But first..."

"First...?" Melody whispered, willing for him to continue.

"I must return to Marindel alone. Where I am going, you cannot come. Not yet."

Melody's eyes widened. She couldn't believe what she was hearing. "What do you mean? You're going to...*leave* me?"

"No. Though you may not see me for a while, you must remember I will never abandon you. I will never stop loving you, and I will always, *always* remember you. Just as I came for you this time, so I will come again when the time is right. But many things must take place before then."

Melody was distraught. "B-but why? *Why* can't I come with you?"

"It's too much to explain now. One day, you'll understand."

"But I want to understand *now*!"

"Shh," Eli said, brushing her cheek with his hand. "Just remember, Mel. Always remember I love you. Never forget, no matter what. Can you do that for me?"

Melody fumbled for words, her lip quivering. "I, uh...yes. Yes. I think so."

Eli smiled and nodded. He stooped down to pick up a fallen berry from the camphor tree, picked out the seed, and dug a small place for it in the ground. After burying it, he stood and looked at Melody with endearment as another tear rolled down his cheek. "Then let us trust the Great King together. His plan is wonderful, his ways are good, and his leadership is wise."

42

The Prince of Sorrow

Summary, 104 IE

MELODY JERKED AWAKE with a gasp for breath, her heart pounding relentlessly.

Another nightmare.

It had been two nights since she last saw Eli, and on both nights, she was plagued with terrible dreams. In every case, unbeknownst to Melody, the Great Serpent had been working to disrupt the very foundation of her trust in Eli. Though she still loved Eli and longed to see him, the knowledge that he would soon be leaving without her was too much to bear.

Now, on this night, the stage was set for the Serpent's plan to be launched in full.

"Mel!" she heard a distant call.

She quieted her breath and listened. "Eli?"

"Mel, where are you?" the voice called again.

Recognizing his voice, a surge of joy overtook her. She cloaked herself in a night robe and hurried onto the balcony. She looked over the banister and called, "Eli, I'm here!"

No answer.

Melody looked, but she saw no one. "Eli?"

"Over here!" The voice came from inside the palace.

She went back across her room and opened the door to peer down the hallway. It was dark and eerie, with the waning moon casting pale white light through the windows on the vaulted ceiling. With a nervous frown, Melody ventured down the hallway. She was careful to ensure her bare feet made no noise on the marble floor, lest she wake her officials or alert the guards.

"Come, this way," the voice called ahead of her.

She followed the voice, passing through several halls and rooms as she went. Oddly, she noticed the voice never seemed to grow louder or quieter. She wondered what Eli was up to. After all, this wasn't like him. Eli wasn't the evasive type.

Melody rounded a corner and continued down the hall toward the palace library. The door was cracked open, and the orange glow of a fire danced within. Someone must have lit the fireplace. Her heart soared; she had always wanted to show Eli the palace library. Perhaps he beat her to it.

"Melody! I'm here!" Eli's voice called from within the library.

"I'm coming!" Melody called, running down the hall and bursting through the door.

As she supposed, the fireplace in the library was roaring heartily, casting its burning light all over the room. It was a spacious library, with books lining every wall, and several rows of bookshelves in the back of the room where the light of the fire was dim. Melody expected to see Eli somewhere inside, waiting for her with open arms and his brilliant smile.

But he wasn't there.

The white-bearded elder was sitting in an armchair facing the fire, with a large book on his lap, appearing to be reading. At Melody's sudden entrance, he looked up at her and they exchanged startled glances.

The elder said, "Oh, Milady! What a pleasure to see you. Is something the matter?"

"Uh, no, I, uh..." Melody took a few steps back. "I was just..."

"You look troubled," the elder said, gesturing to an armchair nearby. "Come, sit down."

Melody hesitated at first. But after looking around and seeing no one else in the room, and then glancing at the elder's concerned expression, she went and sat in the armchair.

"You cannot sleep, I presume?" the elder asked, marking his place in the book and closing it.

Melody nodded. "I was...I thought...well..." She couldn't bring herself to mention Eli.

"Milady, don't worry, I know what ails you. It's that renegade peasant, isn't it? The so-called Prince of Marindel?"

"He *is* the Prince of Marindel!" Melody snapped.

The elder coolly played along. "Oh, yes, of course. You know him better than I, so I'll take your word for it."

Melody's gaze settled on the warm fireplace. Questions cycled through her mind. *"Why did Eli lead me here? Where is he? Is it all just my imagination? Maybe he's playing games with me. No, he isn't like that. I should just go back to bed."*

Melody was about to get up and leave when the elder cleared his throat and said, "You know, Milady, I'm sorry I've been so narrow-minded concerning him. If he is your preferred suitor, then by the royal laws of the kingdom of Rhema, your appointed officials ought to accept and support your decision."

Melody looked at the elder with wide-eyed shock. "What? Really?"

"Yes. After all, perhaps a married alliance between the kingdoms of Rhema and Marindel would be most strategic on our part during this troubling time in our history."

"Thank you," Melody nodded, grateful, yet puzzled. "I can't believe it. Why did you change your mind?"

"Eli and I have little in common, as you know. I won't go into detail about that, but I've decided it isn't appropriate for your officials to keep you from making this decision for yourself. You are the queen, after all. It's our duty to serve and advise you, not to control you."

"I can still hardly believe it," Melody said, unable to keep from smiling. But then she remembered what Eli told her: that he soon had to leave for Marindel, and she couldn't come with him. The thought caused her smile to fade into a sullen frown.

"Hmm." The elder studied Melody's face. "You don't look as thrilled as I would have thought. You two have spent much time together. Has he not expressed his desire to marry you?"

"Yes, he has," Melody replied. She opened her mouth to speak again, but her lip quivered and nothing came out.

Melody saw it play through her mind over and over: the sorrowful Eli telling her he had to leave. Her heart grew heavier by the second. She remembered other things Eli said, but her heart's slippery hold on those memories was torn by the crafty Serpent, who spoke through her thoughts, *"He doesn't love me. I am unlovable. I don't deserve someone like him, and that's why he's leaving me. He changed his mind about marrying me, so he's looking for a way to escape."*

Melody internalized every word.

Finally, she said to the elder, "Eli is going to leave. He says he wants to marry me, but he's going back to Marindel first—without me. He wouldn't tell me why."

The elder looked disappointed. "That is strange behavior, coming from a prince. He won't take you with him?"

Melody shook her head.

"I'm terribly sorry, Milady," the elder reached out to put a hand on her shoulder. "I can only imagine what it must be like: led on by an amazing man for several weeks, just to have him suddenly run off to his next adventure as if nothing ever happened. Your heart must be in so much pain."

"It hurts, it hurts so much." Melody teared up as she continued. "Every night, I have nightmares of Eli letting me down. He hadn't let me down before, so I always thought they were just dreams. But after that night, when he said he'd leave me...what if...what if he never comes back? I don't think I can handle it! How can he do this to me? I've never loved *anyone* as much as I love him. Why is he taking me for granted?" By the time these words came out, Melody was sobbing.

"What a shame. I hate to see you in so much grief. Please, tell me, is there anything I can do to help?"

"I don't know!" Melody snapped. "Make him stay! Tell him he has to marry me right now, or not at all!"

"Ooh," the elder winced. "That's a very rash decision, Milady. I understand you're upset, but I'd advise you to think longer about a course of action like that. Think of the implications! What—"

"No," Melody interrupted. "I've thought plenty about it already. Eli says he loves me, but he can't just *say* things like that without proving it. If he says he loves me but still has it in him to go back to Marindel without me, how can I trust him?"

"That is a very good point," the elder said, nodding slowly. "I'm sorry to say this, Milady, but it looks like my fears about Eli are materializing all too quickly. From the very beginning, I've seen his reckless and unrefined nature, and it has made me very reluctant to trust him—not for my sake, but for yours. After all, it's our duty as your appointed officials to advise and protect you at all costs."

Melody sniffled.

"You must know that everything we do is for you," he continued. "We've been at odds with Eli because we saw his potential to hurt you, and we couldn't bear the thought of it. We love you, Melody, too much. We would hate to lose you to someone who would take you for granted."

"Do you really mean that?" Melody asked, looking up at him.

She was particularly caught off guard when he called her 'Melody' instead of 'Milady.'

"Every word. You are our queen. Without you, what would we be? Our sole reason for existing is to serve you. It may not always be in ways you like or appreciate, but you must trust our judgment. We are *always* looking to protect your best interests, and the best interests of our kingdom."

Melody sat quietly, staring at the fire and pondering the elder's words as the last of her tears dried on her face.

The elder placed his hand on hers. When Melody looked at him, she was surprised to see his eyes had welled up. She had never seen him this emotional before.

"Melody," the elder said, "tell us where to find Eli. We will bring him in for questioning and determine his true intentions. If he wants to marry you, we will make it happen. And if not..."

Melody looked again at the fire. Her heart was torn. She wanted so badly to believe Eli at his word, but the storm in her soul was so chaotic, she couldn't bring herself to do it. She knew it was very unlike this elder to be so kind, and she remembered Eli telling her not to trust her officials. But now she didn't know whom to believe or whom to trust.

Questioning wasn't such a bad idea, after all. It seemed like a good place to start. If her officials could convince Eli to marry her and take her to Marindel with him, it would be more than she could ever ask for.

Melody took a deep breath before she spoke. "He spends the night in the countryside beyond the apple orchard, on a hill with a giant camphor tree."

"Very well," the elder nodded. "We will make preparations tomorrow, and in the evening, we'll set out to find him. In the meantime, please, go back to your room and get some rest. You've had a very emotional night."

"Thank you," Melody said, standing up. "Your help means so much to me. I'm sorry I've been so stubborn and rude."

"You are forgiven. Good night, Milady."

"Good night." Melody smiled and exited the room.

"Oh," the elder called as she left, "Please close the door behind you. I'm going to finish a chapter of my book before retiring to my quarters."

"Of course," Melody replied before shutting the door.

The elder opened his book to the marked page and began reading as before.

Several seconds passed.

Shadows moved in the back of the room as several figures emerged from behind the bookcases.

The elder spoke without lifting his gaze. "Did you hear that?"

"Every word," Matthias said, coming into the light of the fire. The figures behind him were his soldiers.

"We must handle this delicately. As enthusiastic as we are to dispose of Eli, we must do so with the perception of Melody's approval every step of the way. More importantly, we must avoid the public spotlight, or we risk the possibility of rebellion."

"Noted. What would you like us to do?"

"Send word to your soldiers at Point Nex. Have them prepare quickly and quietly. At dusk tomorrow, take your men and bring Eli here. We will do everything under the cover of night while the city sleeps."

"Excellent," Matthias said with a cunning grin. He turned to his companions and said, "You heard the man. Rest up, eat your fill, and ready your weapons. When darkness falls tomorrow, we ride."

AFTER RETURNING TO her room, Melody could hardly sleep. Nightmares tormented her every time she shut her eyes. She kept trying even after the sun rose, but to no avail. At noon, she gave up and thought, *"Maybe a nice walk around the city will help."*

She put on a simple tunic with a head shawl before leaving the palace. She took a roundabout way through smaller streets to the marketplace, which, to her surprise, was bustling more than usual.

"This is odd," she thought. *"Is there an important event today?"*

As she made her way through the crowd, she heard shouting and jeering. Everyone was watching something just up ahead. She maneuvered through the crowd, eager to see what was going on. When she finally arrived at the front, she gasped in horror.

A giant Tethysian man was attacking Eli, who at this point was on the ground and bloodied almost beyond recognition. The Tethysian sneered and laughed as he stomped on Eli's chest, saying, "You do not belong here! This realm is mine, and now you will pay the ultimate price!"

Melody recognized the voice, and it sent horrified chills down her spine. It was the voice of the Great Serpent.

As she stood there, unable to look away from the terrible sight,

Eli turned his face toward her. Everything around her went quiet, and even ceased to exist, as Eli whispered, "Mel...*why?*"

Melody's vision went black, and she felt herself choking and gagging. She tried to scream, but the darkness was so thick, no sound came out of her mouth.

"No! No!" MELODY flipped off the bed and landed with a thud, flailing about. When she realized where she was, she groaned and held her arm, which she had landed on, and stood up slowly.

She'd had many nightmares about Eli over the past few weeks, but this one was different. The image of Eli being tormented was seared in the forefront of her mind, and the slightest thought that it was her fault made her feel sick to her stomach.

When she remembered her conversation with the elder the night before, it struck her to the very core.

The Serpent said, using Melody's voice, "*If Eli is hurt when your officials find him, it will be your fault.*"

Melody bit her lip as she thought about it. She whispered to herself, "I didn't believe him. I don't believe him. I still don't. I hope...I..." She looked out her window, realized the time of day, and gasped.

Late afternoon. Sunset would take place in one hour.

Something in her heart told her she had little time to spare.

She thought aloud, "I don't care what the elder said. I know he doesn't like Eli, and there's no telling what kind of 'questioning' they're going to bring him into. I have to make sure they don't treat him unfairly."

With that, Melody put on an elegant white dress, which she reserved for important political meetings. She washed her face and fixed her hair, and then went out to find her officials.

She searched the palace high and low. Every room, every hallway. Her officials were nowhere to be found. When she asked the palace guards, they said the officials left early in the morning and hadn't returned since.

After taking a moment to think, Melody decided it would be best for her to go to the camphor tree and tell Eli that her officials sought to question him. She asked the guards for a horse and set out immediately.

By the time Melody left Diamond City, the sun had set half an hour before. She skirted the apple orchard and rode northeast across the grassland, in the direction Eli had taken her on the unicorn. As the sky darkened with the coming of night, the landscape was different than it had been before. The grass was still, the fireflies were absent, and not a sound could be heard, except for the pounding hooves of Melody's horse. The moon had not yet risen, and most of the stars were veiled by wispy clouds above.

Melody thought little of her surroundings as she pressed onward. She hoped with all her might that she would reach Eli before her officials did. Maybe she could change his mind about leaving Rhema, and then they wouldn't have to question him. After all, the elder said they were willing to let her make her own decision.

When Melody reached the hill with the giant camphor tree, the horse whinnied defiantly and refused to go up, so Melody dismounted and ran the rest of the way.

Near the top, she saw Eli and two others on the far side of the tree trunk. At first, panic surged in her heart because she thought the two visitors were her officials. But then she slowed to a stop, eyes wide, because these visitors were radiant. She didn't recognize them, but there atop the mountain were Nuriel and Guinevere, speaking encouragement to Eli and strengthening him with their company. She could faintly hear their voices, but couldn't discern what they were saying.

Melody rubbed her eyes in a daze, but when she looked again, the Galyyrim had vanished. She stood perplexed for a moment, not sure what to make of it. But at the sight of Eli alone on the hilltop, she cleared her thoughts and continued up to greet him. "Eli!"

He turned at the sound of her voice. It was too dark to see him well, but Melody could tell by his countenance that he was despondent. Nevertheless, he smiled and greeted her. "Melody, it's good to see you."

Melody ran straight into his arms and held him tight. She nuzzled her face in his hair and kissed his cheek. "It's good to see you, too."

After they separated, Eli said, "Mel, it's time for me to go."

"No, it's not," Melody blurted. She checked herself and clarified, "Eli, *please* don't go. I can't bear it. My officials have finally agreed to let us marry. Isn't that good news? Take me with you! Please, I beg you! What's stopping you now?"

Eli was silent for a while, and he choked up. Now that Melody was mere inches from his face, she could see the pain in his eyes. He reached up and stroked her face. "Melody, never forget. Please, never forget."

"Never forget what?" Melody pressed.

"How much I love you."

They stared into each other's eyes for a moment.

The night was silent, and the whole realm held its breath.

"I won't forget," Melody whispered. "I promise."

Eli's voice trembled as he spoke. "When you fully understand my love and call for my return, I will come for you."

Melody didn't know what he meant, but she nodded. "I *won't* forget."

Eli smiled once more, several tears streaming down his face, as he pulled away from Melody and took several steps back.

Melody's eyes widened. "Wait! You're not leaving *now*, are you?"

Eli said nothing.

The sound of rushing wind broke the silence of the night. A stream of fire came down from the heavens and carved a wall of flame between Melody and Eli.

Melody jumped back with a yelp and looked around wildly. She heard the wingbeats and snarls of dragons coming from every direction in chorus with the jeering shouts of men.

Another stream of fire drew a circle around Eli, trapping him in a flaming arena. Three talongrunts landed within the ring, each mounted by a Tethysian soldier. Two larger wyverns landed next: russet-brown frightwings, each carrying four soldiers. The Tethysians dismounted and drew their weapons, and together they and their dragons surrounded Eli, taunting and snarling.

Another dragon arrived, and the ground shook with its landing. This one, a thunderbeast, was burly and fearsome, resembling a winged black crocodile with a blunted snout and horns like a bull. Matthias rode proudly on its back. With a wave, he shouted, "Good evening, Prince Eli! Fancy running into you out here!"

Eli looked steadily at Matthias. "There's no need for a show. What do you want?"

Matthias slid down from his dragon's saddle and stepped forward. "We're looking for a wanted man who's guilty of sorcery, inciting rebellion against the Tethysian Empire, and falsely claiming to be the prince of a nonexistent kingdom. You know him?"

"What is this rebellion you speak of?" Eli asked.

Melody was overwhelmed with panic. She could but partially understand what was happening on the other side of the fire, which was too hot to approach, and she had a dreadful feeling about it all. She yelled, "Captain Matthias, stop! I command you as the Queen of Rhema to stop this now!"

Matthias responded to Eli, "The rebellion I speak of is shouting on the other side of the fire, telling me to stop. You've turned her against the will of the Empire, and for that alone, not to mention everything else you've done, you are worthy of the most excruciating death."

Melody didn't hear what Matthias said, but a surge of indignation came over her. She marched toward the ring and extended her hand forward, causing a magical blue divide to part the fire like a curtain as she passed through. She stood among the Tethysians and repeated, "Matthias, I command you as the Queen of Rhema to stop this immediately!"

The Tethysians were agape at Melody's use of magic and muttered amongst themselves, "She's a sorceress! That troublemaker has taught her how to use his powers! This can't be good! We must arrest her too!"

"Melody!" Eli called before anyone could address her. "Stand down. It's all right."

"What do you mean its...?" Melody trailed off as she looked at Eli's face, as loving and kind as ever, but with a stubborn determination that couldn't be moved. He said, "I must go with them; it's the will of the Great King. Go far away from here and be safe. The forces of darkness have come to eclipse the light, but soon the light will return. Be strong, Mel, and always, *always* remember my love for you."

"Eli..." Melody stood wide-eyed and mouth agape. She couldn't bring herself to move, let alone speak.

Matthias grabbed the front of Eli's tunic and pulled his face up close to his own. "You taught that woman sorcery!? How dare you defy the Empire by equipping its enemies with forbidden dark arts such as your own! Now, we will have to dispose of her, too!" He shoved Eli to the ground, eliciting a chorus of laughter from his troops. Then he looked at Melody and said, "I don't know what *you're* upset about, Princess. Your officials sent us to capture him after *you* so kindly told them where to find him. What's more, tonight you led us right to him. We couldn't have caught him without you!"

Fear and extreme guilt flooded Melody's soul as she realized the danger she put Eli in. Her most recent nightmare was beginning to come true, and it really *was* all her fault!

Matthias continued, "Yet, after all you've done to help us catch your phony prince, still you stand before me in defiance of the mighty Tethysian Empire. I believe, when Emperor Flavian hears about this, he will allow us to make a smoldering ash heap out of the kingdom of Rhema. That would be fun, wouldn't it, boys?"

The soldiers snickered in agreement.

"Matthias," Eli said, standing up, "If you take me, you must leave Melody alone."

"You're in no position to bargain!"

Eli took one step toward Matthias, and by some invisible force, all of his men, and even the dragons, stumbled and fell. He said, "I'm the one you're looking for! Take me and do what you must, but you will leave Melody alone."

Matthias was taken aback. After composing himself, he said to his men, "What are you doing on the ground? Get up! Move the girl aside and bind the traitor!"

"No!" Melody pleaded. "Eli, don't!"

Eli looked at Melody with a loving smile. "Remember."

A Tethysian punched Eli in the face, forcing him to the ground.

"No! No!" Melody ran toward Eli, but a talongrunt grabbed her with its talons and tossed her backward, sending her tumbling down the grassy hill.

After scrambling to her feet, she looked up to see the flames on the ground extend their reach into the canopy of the camphor tree. Meanwhile, the dragons took to the sky, illuminated by the raging inferno, with their riders shouting and laughing in triumph. She saw Eli dangling from the talons of Matthias' thunderbeast as they disappeared into the murky darkness of the night.

"Eli!" Melody cried, falling to her knees and weeping uncontrollably.

43
Penumbra
Summer, 104 IE

ELODY FELT SOMETHING nuzzle the back of her head. She
groaned and rolled over, rubbing her groggy, tear-stained
eyes. She blinked a few times before she recognized the
snout of her horse, hovering inches above her face.

Upon seeing her stir, the horse snorted and nuzzled her again.

"Ugh, stop, stop it," Melody said, pushing the horse's snout
away and sitting up. She rubbed her eyes once again before looking
around. It was a gloomy, overcast day. The air was thick and humid,
and there was a grim silence that could be felt.

"I must have cried myself to sleep," Melody said. Then, when
she saw the blackened remains of the camphor tree standing atop
the scorched hill, she remembered what had happened. With a
gasp, she jumped to her feet. "It's daylight already! Who knows
what those horrible Tethysians might have done to Eli by now? I
have to go back and help him right away!"

"*What's the use?*" The Serpent's words intruded on her thoughts.
"*You trusted your officials with Eli's location, and they gave him
over to Matthias and his men. This is all your fault. You should
have trusted Eli, but now it's too late.*"

Melody internalized the venomous accusation. "This is my fault.
I never should have told my officials anything about Eli. I should
have known they were up to no good." She took a deep breath and
looked toward Diamond City, just on the horizon. "I have to help
him. I can fix this. I'm the Queen of Rhema. I can fix this."

Something rustled in the grass nearby.

She looked and saw nothing; the grass was still. She heard it again from another direction, but again, there was nothing. A faint snickering noise seemed to jeer at her confusion.

"Stupid jackals," Melody muttered. Swallowing her fear, she swung herself onto the horse and urged it forward at a quick gallop. On the journey, Melody thought through what she could do to rescue Eli. She also kept an eye out for the jackals. For some reason, she couldn't shake the feeling that she was being watched.

Arriving in Diamond City, Melody sensed that something was off. The city was bustling as usual, but everyone seemed more fearful and skittish. When they saw Melody coming, they avoided eye contact and shuffled out of the way. She was disconcerted by their behavior, but tried her best to ignore it and continued on horseback to the palace.

When she arrived at the gate, she asked the guards stationed there, "Where's Eli?"

The guards exchanged fearful glances but said nothing.

"What have they done to him?" Melody pressed. "Where is he?"

"Y-you're serious? You don't know?" one of the guards asked.

"I just got here. Please tell me."

The guard cleared his throat and explained, "Eli was arrested last night. The Tethysians and your officials came together here and put him on trial. He was unanimously sentenced to death."

Melody gaped. "What!? No! This isn't right at all! This isn't what I wanted!"

The guard backed away two steps. "Er, that's the interesting thing, Milady. The officials made it clear that *you* gave the order for his arrest. They made sure everyone in the city knew this was *exactly* what you wanted."

"What?" Melody realized the people were afraid of her when she arrived because they thought she betrayed Eli. She fumbled for words, "N-no, that's not what I wanted at all! I was just...I...I wanted Eli to stay! And the elder, he...! No! Oh, no!" Melody broke down in tears. "What have I done!?"

The guards exchanged glances again before slinking into the palace.

"Melody!" a familiar voice called from inside the gate.

She looked and saw Caruso coming toward her, bustling past the guards as they left. He looked distressed, but nevertheless, glad to see her.

"Caruso!" Melody slid off her horse and ran to embrace him. She wept and said, "It's all my fault, it's all my fault!"

Caruso held her tight and said, "There, there. Don't be hard on yourself, it's all a terrible misunderstanding."

"Did you see him? Were you here when it happened?"

"Yes. I was a part of the council the governor called upon for the trial last night. I tried to have him set free, but..." He shook his head and sighed.

"Where is he?" Melody asked. "Is he still alive?"

"Yes, but not for long. They flew off to Point Nex an hour ago. He'll be dead before the sun sets, I reckon."

Melody knew what Caruso meant by Point Nex. It was an isolated ocean bluff on the eastern coast of Rhema, which the Tethysians used for execution by means of a local sea monster, called Nex. The Tethysians trained it to come to the bluff at the sound of a certain gong, and they would watch as the prisoner, bound near the cliff's edge, was tortured by the monster's secretion of flesh-dissolving acid and subsequently eaten. It was a punishment reserved for Rhema's most dangerous criminals. She asked, "What are we going to do?"

"I'm not sure there's anything we *can* do. Melody, I'm so glad you weren't here to see the way they treated him. Even well-esteemed Tethysian aristocrats I know personally acted like animals, yelling and chanting and spitting at him. And the soldiers! They were a terrible disgrace to the Empire, and even to the human race itself! They beat Eli without mercy until he could hardly stand. Then they forced him to face Matthias' thunderbeast in the courtyard, mocking him and telling him to sing to it. Eli stood his ground even as that bully of a dragon knocked him down, time and time again. If it weren't for the governor, Matthias and his men would have killed Eli then and there. Your officials stood by and cheered from the sidelines as if it were a bull fight. Everyone was stark-raving mad! It's as if a greater power has taken control of their minds to destroy that one man."

Melody wept as she listened to Caruso's words. At the end she whimpered, "It's all my fault. I have to do something. I won't be able to live with myself if Eli dies because of me."

"Don't say that. You know Eli wouldn't want you to think that way."

Melody nodded absently, hardly having heard him. She was thinking as hard as she could of a way to save Eli, and within a moment, an idea came to her as quick as a lightning bolt. "Caruso! Where's Hunter? Can I borrow him?"

"He's…well, actually, he escaped last night. With all the ruckus caused by Matthias' dragons, he and Kaya flew the coop. They could be anywhere by now."

Melody took Caruso by the arms and said, "I *need* him! Right now! Caruso, if I can make it to Point Nex before Eli is killed, I can sing to Nex and stop it from attacking him. You know I can do it—you saw me tame Kaya! Then I can turn Nex on Matthias and his cronies to get rid of them. It'll work if I get there in time, and Hunter might be the only dragon fast enough!"

"Nex has a much worse temper than Kaya, I'll tell you that," Caruso said, shaking his head in disbelief. "And there's no guarantee you'll get there in time, even with Hunter's help. Are you sure about this?"

"Yes. I have to try."

"All right then. I'll call Hunter, but he may be too far off to hear it."

"Please, just do it!"

"All right, all right! Here goes nothing." Caruso put two fingers in his mouth and whistled.

After a few seconds, Melody asked, "How long will it take?"

"It depends on how far he is. Perhaps ten seconds, perhaps ten minutes."

"Oh, I hope he knows to hurry!"

"Well," Caruso glanced around, "I'm afraid I have to go back in to finish a report on the trial. I came out here for a short breather, you see. Go with Hunter and do what you must. I wish you luck, Melody." Caruso nodded goodbye and went inside the palace.

As he left, Melody searched the cloudy sky for any sign of Hunter. She tapped her foot and twirled a lock of her hair with impatient suspense.

"*It's no use,*" the Serpent mocked. "*Try as you might, you will not be able to rescue Eli. All of Rhema will remember the role you played in his tragic and most untimely death. And they will utterly despise you.*"

"No," Melody said to herself, still unaware it was the Serpent speaking in her mind. "I can fix this. I know it's my fault, but there's still time. I have a plan, and it's going to work."

The only reply was the eerie snickering Melody heard earlier in the countryside, accompanied by scuffling and rustling. She froze and looked around, listening intently. It seemed to be coming from several places nearby.

"Jackals wouldn't have followed me into the city," Melody muttered, anxiety welling up in her heart. What could be making that noise if not jackals?

"Hello?" Melody called out. "Is anyone there?"

Two snickers answered her from opposite directions. The scuffling continued.

Melody stood as still as a deer as she observed her surroundings. No one was around, not even her horse; it had left while she spoke with Caruso.

A distorted voice whispered, "You betrayed him."

Out of the corner of her eye she saw movement. She looked, but saw nothing more than the shadow cast by the rampart near the palace gate.

"Who's there?" Melody squeaked.

"You are to blame," another distorted voice answered.

"No!" Melody yelled, running away from the palace gate and into the midst of the crowded buildings. Even then, she couldn't seem to escape the scuffling and snickering. It was coming from everywhere all around her. To make things worse, she thought she saw movement in every shadow she passed.

"Stop following me!" Melody yelled.

"You cannot escape your guilt!" a voice answered.

Up ahead, a shadow detached from a bulletin board and raced across the street into a dark alley. Melody skidded to a halt, and with trembling breath she said, "If this isn't sorcery, I don't know what is. Show yourself!"

"You don't remember us?" several voices asked together. "We remember you. We're altogether like you: servants of the Great Serpent."

Melody gulped. "I-I don't know you, and I'm nothing like you."

Derisive laughter was the only response.

Melody backed away from the alley where the shadow had gone. When she turned to go back to the palace, she saw movement in another shadow behind a crate. She watched with horror as a creature materialized out of the darkness.

It had the overall likeness of a baboon, standing four feet tall, with its body and long arms covered in mangy black fur. It had bulging white eyes, a pudgy snout like that of a pig, a crown of bony spines on its head, a set of locust-like wings on its back, curved yellow claws, and a naked rat-like tail. As it crawled into the light, the creature's wings buzzed to create the rustling sound.

Melody was petrified, her face drained of all color. She'd never been interested in folk legends, but if she had been, she would've recognized it. It was a creature from Murumbwéan ghost lore: the lukúba.

It spoke with a voice like grating stone, "What's the matter—scared?"

Melody screamed and turned away, but quickly realized that three more lukúba had appeared behind her. She was surrounded!

"Leaving so soon?" they taunted, snickering and bearing their hideous, rotting fangs. "Stay with us, and enjoy the dying of the light."

"Leave me alone!" Melody shouted, voice trembling, as she whirled around looking for any means of escape.

The sound of a rushing wind echoed over the rooftops, followed by a fierce dragon yowl. Hunter dropped out of the sky like a preying eagle, and he collided with three of the lukúba. The impact sent them tumbling down the road with shrieks of surprise.

Hunter skidded to a stop, wings flared open wide, and motioned with his head for Melody to get on.

She wasted no time, breaking into a sprint toward Hunter. Hearing the snarls of the first lukúba as it gave chase, Melody leapt onto the dragon's back and clung to the saddle for dear life. "Go, go, go!"

Hunter yowled and turned, thwacking Melody's pursuer with his tail, before taking several bounds and launching upward. He flew straight into the cloud cover and disappeared from sight.

The lukúba got up from where they'd fallen, their bodies regenerating from broken bones and other injuries. They erupted with a chorus of laughter as they disappeared into the shadows from whence they came.

AROUND THE SAME time Melody had woken up in the countryside, the Tethysian soldiers and Melody's officials arrived with Eli at Point Nex.

Just as Matthias had ordered, the seaside arena was prepared ahead of time for Eli's arrival. The granite-paved plaza was three hundred feet in diameter, with a two-hundred-foot drop down jagged ocean cliffs on one side and tall, forested mountain crags flanking it on every other.

At the back of the plaza, several wooden bleachers and dragon landings had been set up, where spectators could watch the execution from a safe distance. The bleachers were adorned with Imperial Tethysian banners. Many Tethysians, and even a few Rhemans, already sat waiting.

At the front of the plaza, close to the cliff, there was a granite platform elevated ten steps high. The only feature on top was a thick, wooden frame. Two poles stood about twenty feet tall and fifteen feet apart, with a third pole bridging across the top. There was a set of chains and shackles hanging down the middle. The frame was adorned with skulls and bones of every sort, from human to goblin to dragon.

Off to the side of the plaza was an enormous gong, about twelve feet in diameter, with a black skull painted in the center.

Seagulls and vultures circled the site and rested in the high crags, waiting for the grisly show, soon to come.

A group of dragons, carrying prominent Tethysian and Rheman officials, crested the mountain crags and glided down toward the arena. They landed on the dragon platforms and let their riders down. Upon their arrival, the crowd began to cheer.

Matthias and his thunderbeast, which held Eli in its talons, descended toward the center of the arena. The dragon dropped Eli from several feet above ground before landing with a skid and a proud grunt.

A Tethysian soldier ran out to greet Matthias. "Sir! The arena is prepared and ready, just as you ordered."

Matthias slid down from his dragon and said, "Good work. It looks better than I've ever seen it."

The soldier looked at Eli and winced at the sight of him: bruised and bloodied, eyes swollen shut, clothes torn, and lying motionless on the ground.

Matthias followed the soldier's gaze and scoffed. "Don't worry about him. He's the Prince of Marindel; he can take a beating."

"Forgive me, sir, but will he bleed to death waiting for Nex to come? He looks like he's been mauled by a dragon."

Matthias chuckled. "Oh, you should've seen it!"

The thunderbeast snorted, eyes gleaming with amusement.

The soldier paused. "I suppose I should have. Shall we commence the execution, then?"

"Yes. Get your men over here and have the prisoner bound to the altar."

"Right away, sir." The soldier turned and ran back to the bleachers.

Matthias stepped onto one of his dragon's forelegs and held onto a spine while pointing at the bleachers. The thunderbeast jumped and flew to a vacant landing platform while Matthias rode on its arm.

Two of Melody's officials, the elder with the white beard and the other with the big nose, staggered toward Matthias, as though drunk.

"I don't know how you Tethysians do it," the white-bearded elder said between breaths. "I never want to fly on a dragon ever again."

"Quit your whining. Take a seat and enjoy yourselves; our hard work is about to pay off."

"I hope so," the big-nosed elder said. "I feel rotten."

"I don't want to hear it," Matthias said, barging past them and heading toward the top of the bleachers, where distinguished guests were allowed to sit.

The elders followed, complaining and bickering amongst themselves.

Meanwhile, three Tethysian soldiers ran out onto the plaza toward Eli. Two of them got on either side of him, picked him up, and dragged him toward the altar. The third soldier ran straight for the altar to ready the chains.

As they were dragging him, one of the soldiers asked in a whisper, "Eli, can you hear me?"

Eli opened his eyes and looked at him.

"I'm sorry about all this," the soldier said, voice trembling. "It's not fair. Prisoners of the Empire, even those condemned to die, are supposed to be treated with honor and dignity. Not like this. I...I do believe you're the Great Prince of Marindel. There's no other reason why they'd be doing this to you. Please, forgive us."

"You can't be serious," the second soldier scoffed, having overheard. "This bastard is getting exactly what he deserves." He addressed Eli. "You hear me, you piece of shit? You're getting *exactly* what you deserve! Every bit of it!" He jabbed Eli in the ribs with his elbow, eliciting a gasp of pain.

"Stop it!" the first soldier scolded. "Don't forsake your honor as an imperial soldier! We're better than that."

"Hmph. It's *because* we're better that we must crush our enemies without mercy!" The second soldier jabbed Eli in the ribs again.

Eli cleared his throat and coughed up blood. Then he said to the first soldier, "I hear you, and I will forgive you. The Great King welcomes you with open arms as his son." He turned to the other soldier and said, "And you will see with your own eyes the master of darkness, and then you will die."

Neither of the soldiers had time to comment because they arrived at the steps of the altar as Eli finished speaking. The third soldier helped them carry Eli up the steps, and up a wooden step-stool to reach the chains. They shackled his wrists, and then they removed the stool to let him hang. Once Eli was secure, they jogged back to the bleachers.

When the Tethysian officials saw Eli in place, they gave a nod to the executioner, who then stood on the highest platform of the bleachers where everyone could see him. He raised his hands in the air as a signal for everyone to be silent. Within seconds, a hush fell over the entire assembly.

The executioner began, "Privileged and highly-valued citizens of the Tethysian Empire, hear my words! You have, no doubt, gathered here today to witness the execution of a very prominent criminal: the traitorous Eli, the Great Prince of Marindel!"

Many in the crowd laughed at the executioner's evident sarcasm.

"This man is guilty of sorcery on many accounts, and for inciting rebellion within the kingdom of Rhema, not the least of which includes turning Queen Melody against the Imperial Tethysian crown."

The crowd booed. Some shouted, "Long Live Emperor Flavian!" and "Long Live the Empire!"

"What you are about to see, valued citizens, is one of the many punishments for disloyalty and treachery within the domain of Emperor Flavian the Bright. May this carnal display serve as a dire warning: let not even your own thoughts cause you to betray the Tethysian Empire, or you will suffer this very same fate." He paused, and then shouted more passionately, "But in addition, may you be endlessly entertained by the misery of this traitor at the jaws of the king of the southern sea, the mighty sea monster, Nex!"

The crowd cheered, some shouting, "Strike the gong!" and others chanting, "Long Live Emperor Flavian!" and, "Long Live the Empire!"

The executioner let the crowd go on for a moment before he gestured toward the gong, where a man stood wielding an enormous mallet. At the signal, the man hefted the mallet and struck the gong.

The sound emanating from it was jarring. It echoed off the nearby crags and continued on for many seconds before it dissipated.

The crowd sat with bated breath, scanning the surface of the sea for any sign of Nex's arrival. Melody's officials, who had never seen an execution like this, were on the edge of their seats. The white-bearded elder, in particular, bit his nails with suspense.

The wind changed first.

It blew in from the sea, a stale and foreboding wind that rustled the trees in the mountains, creating an ominous whisper to accompany the pounding of the waves on the cliff.

The sky grew dark. The cloud cover thickened until it was as dark as twilight.

The vultures and the seagulls took to the sky and fled. Not even the gulls cried as they left.

The dragons grew restless. They crouched low on their platforms and whimpered, fidgeting and flicking their tails.

Matthias noticed even his prized thunderbeast was nervous. He narrowed his eyes. "Something's wrong."

The crowd began to murmur as an ocean swell appeared on the horizon. As it approached, those who had seen executions at Point Nex before stood and squinted their eyes. They muttered to themselves, "That's a very large swell." "Has Nex grown?" "What's happening?"

Eli hung from the chains on the altar, watching the swell as it loomed closer. Despite his condition, his eyes glimmered with determination. "Father, I trust you."

Suddenly, one of the talongrunts screeched in fright and took off. The noise triggered a similar reaction from all the other dragons, which roared and squealed as they fled despite the surprised or reprimanding shouts of their owners.

The executioner glanced around with wide eyes as all these things took place. He looked at the incoming swell and declared with surety in his voice, "That's *not* Nex!"

Matthias watched as his dragon fled with the others, and then he looked at the swell in time to see the creature beneath come to the surface.

An enormous head rose out of the sea: the head of a fearsome, terrifying sea monster, with a crown of spikes all around its neck. It continued to rise, attached to a dark serpentine body, with seawater cascading down from every crevice of its mask-like face. The beast towered over Point Nex, its head alone half the size of the plaza. With bloodthirsty green eyes it peered at the tiny spectators on the bleachers. Then, it bared its teeth in a grin and roared many times louder than the gong which sounded moments before.

At the sight and sound of this monster, everyone was struck with sheer terror. A third of them, including Matthias, fainted on the spot. The rest, including Melody's officials, scrambled and tumbled over each other, shouting and screaming for their lives as they fled behind the bleachers and between the mountain crags, down the only footpath out of Point Nex.

The soldier who mocked Eli, in his haste to escape, tripped down the bleacher steps and split his skull on the granite plaza. What Eli had said about him came to pass, because this monster was none other than the master of darkness, the Great Serpent himself.

44
Umbra
Summer, 104 IE

HUNTER AND MELODY soared through the clouds, having just escaped from the lukúba. After catching her breath, Melody said, "You were just in time. Thanks for saving me."

Hunter chirped pleasantly.

"We need to get to Point Nex right away. Do you know how to get there?"

Hunter grunted, steering left so they were headed in that direction.

"Good. I can't see anything in these clouds, so I won't be able to guide you. But you need to fly fast, all right? As fast as you can!"

They flew on for a few moments with no interruptions. Melody was too focused on her mission to notice when the atmosphere changed, but Hunter wasn't. He slowed to a glide and sniffed the air to check their surroundings. When he picked up strange scents on the wind, he snarled.

Melody blinked. "Huh? What's wrong?"

A lukúba darted out of the clouds with a shriek, locust-wings buzzing, and tackled Hunter from the side. Hunter buckled in flight.

"Ah! Hey!" Melody shouted, holding the handles tight. She looked around for the creature, but after hitting the dragon, it had disappeared into the clouds. To their dismay, Melody and Hunter could hear buzzing and creepy laughter all around them.

"How were those things able to catch up? I don't like this, Hunter. See if you can—ah!"

Another lukúba latched onto Hunter's wing, and he struggled in flight. As the creature scratched and gnawed at his wing membrane, Hunter yowled and tried to throw it off.

Melody yelled, "Get off! Let go of my dragon!"

Hunter managed to free himself from the first lukúba, but only seconds later, two more came from opposite directions. One tried to go for Hunter's other wing, but he saw it coming and dodged. Meanwhile, the second one grabbed onto Hunter's flank and began crawling up toward the saddle.

Melody screamed, jumping and kicking her legs out behind her to hit the lukúba. The stunt was a direct hit, sending it flying back into the clouds from whence it came.

Another lukúba came from up ahead, braced for a head-on collision, but Hunter spun out of the way just in time. Melody crouched low on the saddle and hung on tight. After that she said, "Hunter, we need to get out of these clouds. I think they can see us, but we can't see them. Can you fly up above?"

Despite the pain of his injuries, Hunter veered upward and began pounding the air with his wings. As they went, the jeering and buzzing of the lukúba echoed all around. It got louder and louder until it was almost deafening. Then, Hunter and Melody broke into a large cavern within the clouds.

To their horror, they beheld a massive swarm of lukúba. Hundreds of them, swirling like a vortex! Before Melody and Hunter realized what they'd just flown into, a handful of the creatures broke away from the swarm and careened toward them.

"Ah! Hunter! Fly! Fly!"

The dragon tucked and dove to achieve maximum velocity and escape from the pursuing creatures. Plunging back into the clouds, he continued his rapid descent for a few seconds before pulling up to fly level.

It was no use.

Three lukúba tackled Hunter from the right side, and he rolled in flight. This time, Melody was thrown off the saddle and went hurtling into the abyss, screaming as she fell.

Hunter quickly reoriented himself and dove after her.

As Melody fell, a lukúba intercepted her and attempted to fly away with her. Melody didn't make it easy. She screamed and flailed about, kicking and punching at the creature. It squealed and hissed as it tried to subdue her, but soon it lost its grip. Less than a second later, Hunter snatched the lukúba and ripped it in half with his jaws.

Finally closing the distance, Hunter swooped underneath Melody so she could land on his back. She grabbed the saddle and clung to it, breathing hard and trembling. The terrifying fall left her feeling nauseous, and she yearned for the attack to be over.

But there was much more terror to come.

A lukúba grabbed the end of Hunter's tail, and two more clung to his underside. Creatures came in from everywhere, overwhelming Hunter until he was unable to fly. He tumbled downward, yowling and thrashing to free himself.

In the midst of it all, Melody did her best to throw off lukúba without letting go of the handles. She kicked several off before one perched in front of her and began pounding her with its fists, hissing and spitting in her face. She gagged on its putrid carrion-breath.

The two of them were so preoccupied, they hardly noticed when a fireball sliced through the clouds and struck the creatures on Hunter's tail. The resulting blast sent all but three of the lukúba hurtling off and out of sight.

Kaya swooped down with an indignant screech, picking off one of the remaining lukúba with her powerful talons. She tossed it toward an incoming lukúba, causing them to collide and spiral out of sight.

Regaining his aerial balance, Hunter flicked the second-to-last lukúba off his wing. As Hunter's flight stabilized, Melody gained the courage to punch the face of the creature assaulting her. It lost its balance and fell into the clouds.

Hunter and Kaya exchanged happy chirps and grunts. Melody looked up and said, "Kaya, I've never been so happy to see you in my whole life."

Their celebration was short-lived. The two dragons flew headlong into an oncoming swarm of lukúba, and a battle ensued. The creatures maintained their strategy of clinging to the dragons to disable their flight. However, now that Kaya was present, neither dragon was overwhelmed for long. Kaya shot down lukúba with her dragonfire before they could attack Hunter. Likewise, Hunter veered, dove, and snatched any lukúba going after Kaya.

As much as Melody was impressed by the dragons' teamwork in aerial combat, she hadn't lost sight of her goal. During a lull in the attack she said, "Hunter, Kaya, we need to hurry on to Point Nex. These things are distracting us while Eli is in trouble!"

The dragons chirped back and forth as if discussing a plan. Then Hunter turned and flew level in the direction of Point Nex.

Kaya took a position above and behind Hunter so she could see any lukúba that might try to sneak up on him.

For a moment, all was quiet. Melody began to think they had finally escaped from the hideous creatures.

They came in from above, behind, and both sides. They were organized and precise. They'd been preparing their formation for some time out of sight, and now they performed flawlessly.

Four lukúba attacked Hunter, targeting his wings.

Kaya saw them coming and shot them down with a couple of fireballs.

While she was busy, five lukúba landed on her back and began tearing into the joints of her wings. She screeched and began flailing about to throw them off.

Before Hunter could turn to rescue her, six lukúba came from all directions and attacked him just as ruthlessly.

"No!" Melody screamed. For the first time ever, she was fearful for the lives of these dragons. Memories flashed in the forefront of her mind. She remembered her first impression of Hunter when she trespassed into Caruso's backyard. She remembered when Eli tamed him, and she tamed him as well. She remembered what a big deal it was for her to tame Kaya. It was an accomplishment she was very proud of. Then she remembered flying all over Rhema with Eli. Though she began that day hating all dragons, by the end of it, she'd grown especially fond of Hunter and Kaya. Eli helped her see their personalities, their loyalty, and their persevering nature.

Melody's eyes welled up as she realized the danger she had put Hunter and Kaya in. After all, they were only being attacked by the lukúba because of her. With a shout, she began fighting the lukúba nearest her with all her might.

It was no use.

Melody heard Kaya's blood-curdling shriek in time to see her fall into the clouds, hardly visible in a mob of lukúba.

"No! Kaya!"

Hunter let out a desperate cry as he also began to fall.

"Hold on, Hunter! Hold on! We have to go save Kaya! Come on, you can do it!"

A final shot from Kaya careened through the clouds and struck the creatures on Hunter's underside, causing most of them to tumble off. Hunter yowled with effort and performed a tight dive and corkscrew to fling off the rest of the lukúba, and then he stabilized and began to glide as best as he could.

Melody was shocked to see how badly Hunter was injured. His

wing membranes were shredded and dripping blood, and his tail and neck were pock-marked with bites and gouges. His flight was shaky and unstable. He wheezed for every breath.

"Hunter, oh Hunter!" Melody placed her hand on his neck. She paused, reflecting again on her role in the dragon's suffering, and she began to cry. "I-I'm sorry, I'm really sorry. I did this to you, and to Kaya. It's my fault. I was so stubborn, and so needy, and so…I'm sorry, Hunter! I'm—oh! Look out!"

As Melody spoke, they had descended out of the cloud cover, and now they were quickly approaching forested mountain crags. Hunter yelped and tried to maneuver out of the way, but he ripped through a tree on the mountainside and spun out of control. He was too injured and falling too quickly to reorient himself. A crash-landing was imminent. Melody shut her eyes and held on tight, knowing and accepting she'd probably not survive the impact.

HARDLY A MOMENT after the Serpent's grand entrance, Point Nex had been completely vacated. Only the unconscious remained, strewn about the bleachers and surrounding area as though dead.

The Serpent rumbled with contentment as he looked down on Eli, who was still chained to the altar. For the first time, the Serpent spoke aloud: "I've been waiting a long time for this day, mighty Prince. What a pleasure it is to see you in chains before me at last."

Eli revealed no hint of fear or surprise.

The Serpent continued, "Now, on this dreadful day, I will destroy Marindel once and for all by eliminating the only heir to the throne. Then I will become the Eternal Overlord of all things above and below the sea. How does that make you feel, Prince? I couldn't have done it without your naive cooperation and misplaced faith in that foolish human girl."

Eli winced with effort as he spoke. "You've become very powerful, Serpent, but pride will be your downfall. The Great King is not blind to your schemes, nor am I."

"Well then, you must already know what I have in store for you.

"Do you really believe that by killing me you will have the victory?"

The Serpent chuckled. "Oh, you *are* clueless. My victory is certain, that is a given. Future generations will look back on this hour of history and tell with appropriate fear the story of the darkest of days. However, they will not speak of the Great Serpent killing the Great Prince. No. *I* will not be the one to kill you."

Eli stared at the Serpent, waiting for him to continue.

The beast glanced across the plaza and grinned, eyes twinkling maliciously. "*She* will."

Hunter's distant yowls echoed on the mountain crags, accompanied by the twisting of branches and the breaking of boughs. The dragon made his entry into Point Nex by crashing through the canopy of a large tree and scuffing the top of the bleachers, dismantling the highest levels and sending several Imperial banners to the ground. Upon Hunter's contact with the setup, Melody was thrown off the saddle and sent tumbling down the bleachers like a rag-doll. Hunter skidded and rolled on the granite plaza in a flurry of wings and limbs, and then was still.

Melody groaned, hugging herself pitifully. Her white dress was dirty and torn, and her hair was a windblown mess. She had bruises from the beating she endured from the lukúba, and a few scrapes from her encounter with the bleachers.

Eli glared up at the Serpent. "I told you not to harm her!"

"She puts herself in harm's way," the Serpent purred. "That spoiled, selfish girl will do anything to get what she wants, and you know it."

Melody was roused by the Serpent's thundering voice. She'd gotten a mild concussion from the landing, and her senses were distorted. Groaning with effort, she sat up and observed her surroundings. There were the wrecked bleachers, at the foot of which she landed. She saw the bodies of those who had fainted strewn all around her. Beyond that, she saw Hunter's crippled body and gasped. "Hunter!" She tried to stand, but she was too dizzy and fell to her knees.

Looking beyond Hunter, across the plaza, Melody saw the altar. At the sight of it, she realized where she was and why she wanted so badly to arrive there. "Eli!" She moved to stand again, but stopped immediately when she noticed a massive, dark shape beyond him. She slowly looked above and behind the altar, and through her blurred vision she could just make out the terrifying face of the Serpent, leering down at her.

"Oh...my..." Melody's blood ran cold as the horrible memories of her first encounter with the Serpent flooded her mind.

The Serpent grinned. "Hello there, my beautiful friend. It's been a long time. I was beginning to miss you."

Though immensely frightened, Melody said, "It's...it's you! *You're* behind all this!"

"I'm flattered, but I must disagree. I'm only a spectator here. Eli and his daddy are behind all of this."

"No," Melody said, wobbling as she stood. "*You* started everything. *You* tricked me into releasing you. *You* turned everyone against Eli so he would be arrested. *You* sent those creatures after me and got Hunter and Kaya killed. You've ruined my life, and now you're ruining his!" She noticed a spear next to a fainted soldier, and she went to take it. Then she looked at the Serpent and said, "You have to leave. As the Queen of Rhema, I order you to leave now, and let Eli be."

The Serpent laughed, eyes glittering. He said to Eli, "Did you hear that? Your little girlfriend believes she can challenge me. There's only one problem with that, as I'm sure you're aware. She has no authority from Marindel to do so. She gave it to someone... me, I believe. Oh! And *you* gave up your authority as well, in a sad attempt to rescue her. Neither of you have any authority at all, yet here I am with all the power in the realm!"

"Leave her out of this. Your quarrel is with me."

While the Serpent was speaking, Melody heard the rustling and snickering of the lukúba. She looked around, and to her dismay, she saw them coming out of every shadow on Point Nex. Even high up in the crags, they perched in the treetops and hung on the cliffs. There were hundreds, if not thousands, of them. And they were closing in on her.

Trembling with fear, Melody backed away from the lukúba, toward the altar. She held the spear in front of her as if it would help deter the fearsome horde.

The Serpent watched Melody with a low purr. He said to Eli, "Before you go, you must realize how misplaced your faith in your father is. He found it wise to dismiss *me* from the royal court, and then he turned and gave his inheritance to an abandoned human girl, unwanted even by her own parents. Do you not realize the fallacy of his wisdom? Do you not realize how easy it was for me to take that power away from her? Do you *really* believe that by taking her punishment you will make life better for her, or for any other creature in the realm? What an ignorant fool you are! As long as I have this power, I have the freedom—no, the right—to resist and destroy the Kingdom of Marindel, and your father freely gave it to me through that girl. Now, he is disposing of you, leaving the throne vacant for me to take. And believe me, I will gladly oblige.

What further evidence do you need? Your father the King is not so great after all, is he?"

Eli replied, "You are wicked beyond redemption. You have no place among the Galyyrim in the presence of the Great King. Your powers are nothing more than death, darkness, and despair. Today, you reign in glory. But what have I told you? Even shadows must flee when the light comes. The power you stole will be taken from you once and for all, to be returned not only to Melody but to all who choose to follow the Great King. They will be sons and daughters in the royal court, but you and your kind will be destroyed forever."

"Hmhm, the words of a lunatic. If you will not believe me when I tell you of the power I possess, then I'll just have to *show* you." He maneuvered his face toward Melody, who stood a dozen feet away from the altar.

Melody froze in place. The sliver of boldness she had to challenge the Serpent earlier was vaporized by the enormous monster's scoffing gaze.

The Serpent's focus remained on Melody as he addressed Eli, "Witness now, glorious Prince, as the most devastating forces above and below the sea come together in the soul of this weak and selfish creature you love so wrongfully. Witness now as my superior powers of darkness and chaos destroy every lie you've planted in her pathetic little brain and reduce her to the ruthless animal she truly is. Witness now, with fear and reverence, as the beloved daughter of the King bows before my sovereign might. Death will consume you as it consumes every mortal, and in the wake of your meaningless life, death will consume the entire realm under my command!"

The Serpent lowered his head so that his snout was at the edge of the seaside cliff. He summed up his monologue with one last phrase, "Try as you might, dear Prince, there is no way to save her. The girl belongs to me."

At his words, the lukúba erupted with a raucous cacophony. They screeched and yowled, pounding their chests or the ground with their fists, and picking up nearby items to bang together.

Spines on either side of the Serpent's head vibrated to emit a continuous high-pitched ringing. His brow furrowed and his pupils contracted as he focused on Melody, tilting his head slowly back and forth.

This chaotic racket was a twisted version of the Music of Marindel, conducted to achieve the opposite purpose. It was the Din of the Serpent.

Melody yelped and cringed, holding her hands to her ears and falling to her knees. The spear clanged to the ground beside her. The Serpent established a mental connection with her and drilled into her psyche, subduing all her positive thoughts and emotions to replace them with his own.

Melody screamed and thrashed about in vain resistance. Her will to trust Eli and remember his love hadn't been strong enough before. Now, under the destructive hypnotism of the Serpent, there was no hope. Melody was confronted with all her memories of Eli, including those from her nightmares, and they blended together as one.

Over the memory of Melody and the forbidden door, the Serpent reminded her, "*Eli was not there to warn you. Your naivety is all his fault.*"

Over the memory of Melody being tortured and cast out of Marindel by the Serpent asserted, "*Eli was not there to protect you. Your pain and your exile are all his fault.*"

Over the memories of Melody's first millennium on the surface, before she came to Rhema, the Serpent continued on, "*Eli was not there to comfort you. Your loneliness and your misery are all his fault.*"

Over the memories of the Tethysian occupation of Rhema, the Serpent accused, "*Eli was not there to give wise counsel in your negotiations with the Empire. Your loss of freedom his all his fault.*"

Over the memory of Melody's interaction with the pineapple farmer, the Serpent's words dug deep, "*Eli humiliated you in front of your own people. You were left exposed to public ridicule. It's all his fault.*"

Over the memory of Melody and Eli running from Matthias and his men in the village, the Serpent proclaimed, "*Eli roused the fury of the Tethysian Empire against you. They will destroy you, and it will be his fault.*"

Over the memories of Melody and Eli at the camphor tree, the Serpent tore into every word Eli said about leaving. "*He doesn't care about you. He doesn't love you. He led you on this whole time. You were right to turn him in to your officials.*"

Over many other memories, the Serpent imposed his lies and removed the small seedling of loyalty Melody had for Eli. At the same time, fed by the Din of the Serpent, Melody's fear, pain, and rage were amplified to new heights. Soon, she stopped resisting and lay still on the ground.

In the background, unbeknownst to anyone, Matthias was

roused to consciousness by the noise. He looked up from his place on the ground and watched with terrified bewilderment as everything took place.

Once Melody's soul was subdued, the Serpent introduced the final thought: *"Eli deserves to die. Kill him."*

"Eli deserves to die," Melody whispered, raising her head to look at him with unbridled hatred. Trembling under the weight of her emotions, she took up the spear, rose to her feet, and closed the distance between herself and the altar.

The lukúba screeched, howled, and pounded with passionate frenzy. The Serpent looked on, his hypnotic gaze level with the plaza, eager not to miss a single detail. The climax was imminent.

Melody walked around the altar and into Eli's field of vision. Then she ascended the steps toward him.

When Eli looked into Melody's eyes and saw what the Serpent had done, tears began flowing down his face. Nothing hurt him more than seeing how much pain Melody was in.

When she reached the top of the steps, Melody took a deep breath and hefted the spear. Her words epitomized everything she sincerely believed in that moment.

"Eli, I hate you."

"Mel..." Eli sobbed. His anguished expression showed her words were a direct hit. But, in spite of his pain, he whispered, "I forgive you."

Melody plunged the spear into Eli's chest, through his heart, and out his back.

Eli gasped. His eyes stayed locked with Melody's for one more moment before he lowered his head.

The Din of the Serpent ceased. The forces of darkness held their breath.

Time stood still. The wind and the waves were silent. Not a sound could be heard except for Melody's heavy breathing as she stood with a white-knuckled grip on the spear in Eli's body. Blood ran down the shaft of the weapon and onto her hands, even dripping down onto her soiled dress.

"He's dead." The Serpent maneuvered his massive head closer to Eli's body, with the tip of his snout only inches away, and sniffed to confirm his observation. He straightened his neck, towering over Point Nex once again, and declared with confidence, "The Great Prince is dead!"

The lukúba laughed, cheered, and rustled their wings in chorus.

Upon hearing the Serpent's proclamation, the trance on Melody broke off. She shook her head and blinked, taking a few seconds to realize where she was and what she was holding. She jumped away from the spear and stared agape at Eli, who she saw up close for the first time since his arrest on the hilltop. "Eli…! No…!"

The Serpent looked at Melody with a smug grin. "Yes, my darling, your eyes do not deceive you. The Great Prince is dead, and I have no one to thank more, than you."

Melody's voice quivered, "H-how…how *could* you?"

The Serpent laughed. "'How could *I*?' How pathetic! Do you need me to spell it out for you? *You* killed him! *You* are to blame! He was condemned to die because of *you*!" He tore into Melody's psyche once again, causing her to feel the full weight of guilt and the ultimate responsibility for Eli's death.

Unable to bear the Serpent's tormenting accusations, Melody wept and wailed, clinging to Eli's dangling body and shouting, "No! Why!? I should have died instead! I deserve to die, not him! It's all my fault! It's all *my* fault!"

The Serpent was ecstatic. He said to his minions gathered all over Point Nex, "The Great Prince is dead! The sovereign reign of the Great Serpent, and the sovereign reign of death over every living thing, begins *now*!" The Serpent flexed his body and waved his tail fluke in the air as he roared long and loud in triumph.

The lukúba took to the air, screeching and howling with glee, and swarmed in a vortex around the Serpent as he roared.

Matthias, still on the ground and afraid to move, saw everything. There was only one thing he could say as he observed the terrifying celebration of the dark forces. "What have we done?"

Melody was still clinging to Eli and weeping when two burly lukúba came from behind to pry her away from the body.

"No! No!" Melody struggled to break free, but they were too strong. They dragged her down the steps and tossed her on the ground, laughing and spitting on her. Utterly defeated, Melody hid her face in her arms and sobbed.

The Serpent looked at Eli's body with a prideful sneer. "I mustn't allow my noble adversary to become carrion for the vultures. I will rid the realm of the sight of him." He opened his jaws and vomited a glob of sticky black tar onto the altar. The substance solidified within seconds.

Then, the Serpent turned to Melody and lowered his head toward her, saying "Oh, look at you, groveling on the ground like the useless worm you are! There is nothing great about you at all. Nothing special. There's no room in my dominion for a creature as hated and worthless as you. Give up all hope of ever ruling this kingdom, let alone living peacefully anywhere else. In my mercy, I will not kill you, but you will spend the rest of your long and useless life with me. After all, no one else will understand what you've done. I alone will keep you safe and out of trouble. In my very being, you will find rest."

He extended his forked tongue toward Melody. When it touched her, hundreds of fleshy tendrils shot out and wrapped around her, cocooning and absorbing her into the tongue. As this occurred, Melody was still. She only muttered to herself, "I *am* worthless. I deserve to die."

Once Melody was completely engulfed by the Serpent's tongue, he retracted it and straightened up again. To his minions he said, "My loyal followers, Rhema is ours! Let us enjoy ourselves and feast upon it!"

The lukúba howled and cheered. The swarm dispersed as groups of the creatures scattered everywhere, disappearing in the shadows. Their cackles were fading away as the Serpent said, "First, we will afflict Rhema. And then, all of Tyrizah."

At that, the Serpent looked up and ascended into the sky. His long, coiling body trailed behind him, showering Point Nex with a downpour of seawater as he passed over. His sinister laugh echoed off the crags as his dark form disappeared in the clouds above.

45
Void
Summer, 104 IE

MATTHIAS STAYED ON the ground for several hours after the dark forces departed from Point Nex. Finally, as his surroundings turned ebony with the coming of night, he mustered the strength to stand. He lit a torch and crossed the plaza to inspect the mound of tar concealing Eli's body.

He walked a complete circle around it. He noticed not a single portion of the altar was left uncovered, not even the steps.

He tapped it with his foot. It was definitely solid.

After looking about to make sure no one was around to see his curiosity and make fun of him, he placed the torch on the ground and drew his sword. Taking a deep breath and gripping it with both hands, he swung his weapon at the mound. The sword bounced off the tar with tremendous recoil, and with a shout of surprise, Matthias spun and fell to the ground.

Groaning with annoyance, Matthias stood and prepared to lunge at the mound again, but a spark of ingenuity caused him to pause. He sheathed his sword and picked up the torch. He held it up to the mound with the flame burning against the smooth, black surface to see if it would melt or catch fire.

"You there!" a voice called from across the plaza.

Matthias jumped, dropping the torch and turning around. A Tethysian cavalry had arrived, illuminated only by the lanterns they carried. As they approached, Matthias recognized them to be high-ranking military personnel from nearby Carnelian Cove, and he supposed they'd been sent to scout the area after those who fled from the Serpent arrived there and caused a scene. After all, anyone who'd never seen the Serpent wouldn't know to believe anyone who claimed there was a Serpent in the first place.

But Matthias knew.

He saw the way Eli died.

The lead officer asked, "What in the name of Flavian the Bright happened here?"

Matthias opened his mouth to speak, but no sound came out. He looked around, pointed at the mound, bumbled a few nonsensical words, and then his eyes rolled back, and he fainted.

The lead officer scowled. "Well, we shouldn't have expected an intelligent answer from *him*." To his companions he said, "Round up the unconscious and wounded. Keep your guard up and your eyes open for those monsters."

THAT NIGHT WAS the longest and darkest night in the history of the kingdom of Rhema. By the power of the Great Serpent, a supernatural void sat heavily upon the island kingdom. The moon and stars failed to shine, and dawn never arrived.

The lukúba roamed freely, causing mischief and havoc in every village and city across the kingdom. Tremendous fear was in the hearts of all who saw and heard them. People shut themselves in their homes and barricaded the windows and doors to find refuge from the onslaught of terror. Undeterred, some lukúba flitted as shadows under the doors to torment those inside. They derived enjoyment from eliciting fear, vandalizing belongings, and provoking fights with anyone who sought to challenge them.

The Tethysians resisted the lukúba at first. But once they realized the monsters couldn't be killed, they too shut themselves in their fortresses and manors. Even the dragons hid, because they sensed and feared the presence of the Great Serpent.

The Rheman officials, after finding their way back to Diamond City through the lukúba-infested grasslands, wanted nothing more than to hide in the palace and forget about the events of the past few days. However, only moments after they arrived—thirty-six hours after Eli's death—they were called by the palace guards to see something outside. Weighed down by a lack of sleep and haunted by the guilt of what they had done, the officials crept into the courtyard and onto the balconies, and they stared up at the sky in horror.

The Great Serpent floated above Diamond City, all but blending in with the night, except for his fierce green eyes. Everyone in the city beheld the enormous beast, and they were paralyzed with fear. Once he had their attention, the Serpent said, "Citizens of Rhema, I have come to claim this kingdom that is rightfully mine. Eli is dead, and Melody is gone. There is no one left to protect you now. You *all* belong to me."

The Serpent opened his jaws to unleash a torrent of black sludge on the palace.

46
Antumbra
Summer, 104 IE

A ROUND THAT TIME, Caruso was prompted by the Great King to go to Point Nex and pay respects at the altar. He had barricaded himself in his manor to escape the lukúba, and the last thing he wanted to do was go outside. He didn't know it was the Great King speaking to him then, and he had neither dragon nor horse to make the journey in good time. Nonetheless, he mustered what little courage he had and departed from the manor.

Even with the help of a lantern, he couldn't see more than five feet in front of him. Every fiber of his being willed him to turn back and hide, but ultimately his loyalty to Eli superseded every fear in his heart, even if only by a hair.

Just after he left the village, a unicorn galloped into view. It pawed the ground with a whinny, urging him to get on. Intrigued, Caruso mounted the unicorn and allowed it to take him to Point Nex.

Lukúba tried to distract and intimidate them on the journey. But to Caruso's surprise, the creatures were unable to approach them. Confused and annoyed, the lukúba turned and squabbled with each other. Caruso's fear of the lukúba diminished over time, and he began to wonder what greater power was at work.

Arriving at Point Nex, the unicorn took Caruso to the mound where Eli's body was concealed. Caruso dismounted and looked sadly at the mound. He thought about Eli's life: everything he had said and done, the smile he always carried, his compassion for all people, and his determination in the face of hardship. The thoughts moved him to tears. "Eli, we desperately need you. We're facing a judgment we certainly deserve, but can never hope to survive."

At the sound of approaching hooves, he turned and saw two more horses enter the plaza. He recognized them to be friends of Eli from Jasper Village: Auben, his wife Trisha, and their kids Trevor and Lia. Auben and the kids were on one horse, while pregnant Trisha was on the second.

Caruso greeted them with a nod as they came near. "It's a dark time to be out and about with kids."

"It'd be worse to leave them in a village crawling with monsters," Auben said as he dismounted. He turned to help his kids down, and then went to help his wife.

Trevor ran toward his mother and hugged her leg. "Mom, where's Mister Eli?"

"Hush," Trisha caressed his head. She said to Caruso, "Auben and I had a strange feeling we were supposed to visit Point Nex. It was so unshakable we decided it must be significant. We took the kids and came as fast as we could."

"The same happened to me," Caruso said, stroking his chin. "How peculiar."

Seconds later, another man on horseback arrived; the pineapple farmer from Diamond City. Then a talongrunt landed nearby, carrying the soldier who had apologized to Eli en route to the altar. Both men dismounted and joined the others, admitting the same premonition had come upon them as well.

Over the next few minutes, several others from all over the kingdom came and stood before the mound. The two things they all had in common were a belief in Eli as the Great Prince of Marindel, and a mysterious feeling that they needed to go to Point Nex, despite the rampant forces of darkness that plagued the land. Once they'd all gathered, they began wondering what they were supposed to do there.

"Maybe we can break this rock open and get Eli's body out," the pineapple farmer said. "Give him a proper burial."

"How do you suppose we do that?" Auben asked.

"I brought a hammer," a blacksmith said.

"My sword might do the trick," the soldier suggested.

"Hmm." An elderly lady knocked on the mound with her ear up close to it. "This substance is both solid and elastic. It won't break easily, but perhaps fire will melt it."

A cattle herder said to the soldier, "Tethysian, try your dragon!"

Chapter 46: Antumbra

The soldier beckoned the talongrunt with a sharp whistle. "Everyone, stand back," he said as the dragon hopped toward them. At the soldier's command, it shot several fireballs at the mound. After the smoke cleared, some held their lanterns up to see if any damage occurred. To their dismay, they found it hadn't softened a bit. It was stone cold to the touch.

"It's cursed," a sailor said. "There's no way we'll be getting Eli out of this."

"What are we going to do?" a young seamstress asked.

"Mommy, I'm scared," Trevor whimpered.

"We'll think of something," the blacksmith said.

A voice familiar to most of those gathered answered from across the plaza, "We'll ask the Great King."

Everyone peered into the darkness, where a single pinprick of lantern-light was approaching.

"Is that...?" the soldier asked, eyes widening.

"No, it can't be!" Caruso breathed.

Sure enough, when the newcomer came close, everyone saw that it was Matthias who had come to join them. He looked shaken and embarrassed to be there, but determined, nonetheless. He repeated, "We'll ask the Great King. He brought us here, and he'll tell us what to do next."

The others agreed, though evidently shocked that it was Matthias, of all people, who suggested it.

"All right. Here goes nothing." The elderly woman cleared her throat. "Great King, what have you brought us here to do?"

The group waited in silence. No one knew what to expect:

A thundering voice?

A messenger pigeon?

A courier on horseback, or riding a dragon?

A fairy or nymph?

What if there was no answer at all?

As time went by, the same thought crossed every person's mind, though it was discounted by almost all. It was so simple, so counter-intuitive, given their circumstances. But as the thought persisted, one person dared to suggest it.

"We should sing," Lia said.

No one commented for a few seconds, but Lia persisted, "Mister Eli loved to sing. I think he'll be happy if we sing, too."

"I believe the lass is right," the sailor admitted.

"I had the same thought," the seamstress agreed.

"But what do we sing?" the soldier asked.

Lia replied as if it were obvious. "Eli's *favorite* song!"

"What is it, baby?" Trisha asked.

"It goes...hmm, I think it goes like this:

> *When there is doubt, I know that hope is best.*
> *When others grieve, a song of joy I'll sing.*
> *When storms abound, in peace my heart will rest.*
> *I know and trust my father, the King.*"

"Oh, I remember now!" Trevor said. "Eli sang that all the time. All over the house!"

Caruso chuckled. "Would you kids like to lead us?"

"Sure!" They began singing Eli's favorite song.

Others in the group joined in, quiet at first. It was hard to take the song seriously because no one felt any semblance of hope, joy, or peace. However, as they sung it again and again, their hearts began to warm as they felt those emotions growing within them.

Matthias was the only one who had yet to sing. The thought of singing in general, much less a simple childish tune, grated against his pride. However, Trevor noticed his lack of participation and called him out, "Matthias, the Great King wants to hear your voice, too!"

Matthias nearly choked at the authority in little Trevor's voice, and he started bumbling the words. After repeating the song a couple times, he relaxed, as even he became more hopeful, joyful, and peaceful.

The group continued to sing, but aside from the psychological benefits they reaped, nothing in their surroundings changed. Soon, their voices becoming hoarse, they stopped.

In the ensuing silence, they could hear the rustling of the lukúba all around them. There was a conversation between two distorted voices:

"They stopped."

"Yes. They realize it's no use."

"The Music of Marindel is not for mortal beings. There's nothing to be concerned about."

"Perhaps so, but clearly they are not frightened enough by our triumph. We must convince them otherwise."

"In time, they will learn. Darkness will rule forever."

"Forever, and ever,"

"And for all time."

The voices cackled, and a distant chorus of laughter echoed all around them.

As the noise faded, Caruso said, "We should go now."

"Where to? What's the point?" the cattle herder asked. "There's no escaping those zombie-monkeys no matter *where* we go. We'll never be safe! You heard 'em!"

"To my manor," Caruso replied. "There's room enough for everyone. We'll last much longer if we stay together, even if this darkness *does* drag on forever."

"Aye," the sailor agreed.

"I'll make sure those monsters don't attack us along the way," Matthias said, placing a hand on his sword hilt. To the soldier he said, "You and your dragon stay sharp!"

"Yessir!" the soldier replied, hurrying over to his talongrunt.

"I have a sword as well," Auben said to Matthias.

"Good. Keep it ready."

Everyone talked quietly amongst themselves as they left the mound where Eli's body was hidden. As they went, the hope, joy, and peace they just sang about evaporated from their hearts.

Only Lia remained where she was.

She sang Eli's song again, continuing with a few verses she remembered in that moment.

> *"When there is fear, I'll stand with daring eyes*
> *When others hate, a song of love I'll sing.*
> *When death prevails, in light I will arise.*
> *I know and trust my father, the King."*

"Lia!" Trisha called. "Come on, baby! We're leaving!"

"Coming," Lia answered. With a regretful sigh, she went to join the others. After covering half the distance, she looked back at the mound one last time. When she did, something glittering in the darkness beyond caught her eye.

A small, blue butterfly fluttered toward Point Nex from the sea. To say the butterfly was bioluminescent would be an understatement. It was radiant, sparkling like a star, dancing magnificently in great contrast to its bleak and dreary surroundings.

Lia watched with great intrigue as the butterfly meandered toward the mound and landed at the foot of it, close to where she'd just been standing. She called, "Mommy, look!"

"Lia, come here!" Trisha's back was turned as she endeavored with Auben's help to get up on the horse. "Oh, I can't wait to have this baby already!"

Lia glanced at her mother for a second, but then continued to watch the butterfly. It was too beautiful to ignore.

Soon, Lia began to feel tremors in the ground beneath her. To her amazement, small cracks appeared in the mound, quickly spreading and widening. Beams of light pierced through the cracks, intensifying in brightness, and a quiet whirring sound escalated as they spread.

Caruso noticed first and shouted, "Lia! Get away from there!"

Lia obeyed without question. The butterfly also fled, and then the mound shattered from the inside with a brilliant flash of light and a thunderous boom!

Everyone shielded their eyes from the blinding explosion, and several people were knocked down by the shockwave. Fragments of the mound fell upon the group like a hailstorm, but upon contact with them or the ground, the shards disintegrated into black dust and caused no harm.

It took a moment for everyone to become accustomed to the light emanating from the spot the mound once occupied. Soon, they were able to make out the figure of a man standing in the center of the light atop the steps of the altar, the wooden part of which was dismantled behind him. The man was impressive and dazzling, dressed in a stunning white outfit complete with a cape and cavalier. His face was humble and friendly, eyes glimmering, easily recognized by all.

When Caruso rubbed his eyes and looked closer, he lost his breath. "I...I can't believe it! It's...! It's...!"

"Mister Eli!" Trevor and Lia shouted, sprinting toward the altar with joyful shouts.

"It *is* him!" the elderly woman said. "I see him there with my own eyes! He's alive!"

"Eli!" Caruso ran to the altar, followed by almost everyone else.

"Auben!" Trisha yelled after her husband. "Help me off this horse!"

"Oh, right! I'm coming, love!" Auben returned to help his wife off the horse, and they went to the altar together.

As the kids ascended the steps, Eli smiled as big and bright as ever and stooped down to meet them, arms wide. "Trevor! Lia! It's great to see you!"

"You survived!" Trevor shouted, squeezing him tight.

"Not quite, bud. I was dead, but now, by the power of the Great King, I am alive!"

"Wow!" Trevor pulled away from Eli's embrace and ran down the steps toward the others. "Hey, everybody! Eli was dead! But now he's alive!"

Eli chuckled as Trevor ran off, and then to Lia he said, "You have a wonderful singing voice, my dear. Thank you for listening to the Great King. He and I are very proud of you."

"Thanks," Lia replied, burying her face in his chest.

As everyone gathered around the altar to behold him, the sky began to brighten with the first gleams of dawn. In the midst of this, Eli stood and said, "Hello, my friends! Do not be alarmed, your eyes do not deceive you. The Great King has breathed new life into my body, bestowing upon me the inheritance he has in store for those who follow his will to the very end: the power to triumph over death."

Everyone murmured amongst themselves, hardly able to comprehend Eli's words.

He continued, "I will explain more to you soon. Meet me in the apple orchard outside Diamond City, and there I will speak with you one last time before I return to Marindel. Now, I must finish the work my father started."

Eli looked beyond the group, where hundreds of lukúba were gathered. They'd been creeping out of hiding ever since the mound shattered, but no one noticed until Eli turned his attention to them. They were gawking and pointing, squabbling and shrieking, unable to look at Eli but evidently confused as to why he wasn't dead.

Eli leapt with a front flip, soaring over his friends, and landed in the midst of the lukúba. He looked at them with a smirk, bold and unafraid. "What's the matter? Surprised?"

They screamed and shielded their eyes, scrambling backward to distance themselves from him.

Eli sang a verse, his pure Elvish words dripping with magical strength, and a sword of light formed in his right hand. With blinding speed, he turned on the nearest three lukúba and sliced them in half. They slumped to the ground, turned pasty-gray, and disintegrated like windblown ashes.

They were most certainly dead.

Seeing this, the lukúba in the plaza dispersed at once. Many more jettisoned from the crags and trees surrounding Point Nex, and all of them fled in retreat.

"You won't get far!" Eli called, flipping his sword in his hand and beginning to run toward the exit of Point Nex. He cleared the plaza in a few seconds before jumping onto the crags, where he leapt from rock to rock and from tree to tree. He was faster than the lukúba, even as they flew helter-skelter in panic. Whenever he caught up to one, he killed it.

The unicorn, watching all of this, whinnied with delight and galloped after Eli. Its mystical powers enabled it to run faster than any ordinary horse.

Eli's friends watched with awe, rendered breathless and unable to say a word.

Once he reached level ground beyond the mountains, Eli ran through the woods. His focus was unbreakable, and the zealous fire in his eyes, unquenchable. Nothing could deter him from his mission, the beauty he sought to rescue.

As he broke out of the woods and raced across the grassland, the unicorn caught up and ran alongside him. Seeing it, Eli jumped onto its back and began to sing. Tendrils of light enveloped the sprinting unicorn and caused it to grow larger and more radiant. Magnificent, feathered wings sprouted on the unicorn's body, and at the conclusion of Eli's song, the magical steed launched into sky with incredible speed and a jubilant whinny.

The Serpent's minions across the land were flushed out of the shadows and forced to flee by the brilliant light of Eli's presence. Singing once more, Eli crafted his sword into a bow and sent arrows of light after the fleeing lukúba. The projectiles were able to spear multiple creatures at once. Many of them perished in their haste to escape the risen Prince.

En masse, squealing for their lives, the lukúba fled toward Diamond City.

"PUT ME DOWN!" The Tethysian governor writhed and dangled by the nape of his tunic, which was secured in the jaws of the Serpent. "Help! Somebody, help!"

The Serpent purred with delight, reveling in the terrified screams of the governor as he shook him back and forth. He tossed the governor high in the air and said, "You're not having as much fun as I thought you would. Does this game bore you? Don't worry, I have a better idea for you, just like I did for your white-bearded friend. I can feel my belly rumble as he fights to escape. Come and join him!" The Serpent opened his mouth wide, ready to catch the governor and swallow him whole.

A shriek caught the Serpent's attention, and he looked for the source. The governor landed on the Serpent's head, tumbling down the length of his neck before falling and landing in a sticky pile of sludge.

At that time, Diamond City was in the midst of a slow and dreadful destruction. The palace was a wreck, covered in sludge and crushed beneath the weight of the Serpent, who coiled comfortably upon its ruins. The lukúba had caused widespread devastation across the rest of the city. However, such things were only visible now that the sky glowed pink and blue with the coming of sunrise.

The shriek that distracted the Serpent also caught the attention of his minions. Hearing the distant squeals of their brethren in panic, they, too, began to screech and take flight. Giving no heed to the will of the Great Serpent, the lukúba scattered in frenzied haste to escape the return of the light.

So great was their fear of Eli.

As the lukúba dispersed, the Serpent squinted to see what all the commotion was about. Beyond the incoming swarms of terrified creatures, backed by the rising sun as it peeked over the horizon, the Serpent saw the brightest light he had ever seen—and in the midst of it all, a man on a winged horse.

The Serpent immediately knew who it was. He blinked hard, gaping in unbelief. "What? No! *Impossible!*"

As lukúba zipped past him, the Serpent heard them screaming the name of Eli in sheer panic. He roared at his minions, unable to contain the fear in his voice, "Where do you think you're going!? Come back here! Hold together!"

The lukúba ignored him.

The Serpent looked at Eli once more, eyes wide. The Great Prince was approaching fast, his vengeful gaze locked on the Serpent.

"Agh! This cannot be!" The Serpent yowled, maneuvering his enormous coiling body out of the palace ruins and beginning to fly upward in a tight spiral.

Eli watched as the Serpent flew higher and higher. He pat the neck of his steed and said, "We're not letting him get away. After him!"

The winged unicorn veered upward, its wings and hooves pounding the air in pursuit.

The Serpent flew so high that the entire island of Rhema was visible from his altitude. When he saw Eli hot on his trail, he turned to face him. The Serpent flexed his body, flaring every one of his fins, flukes, spines, and tendrils. The thin yellow markings on his body radiated with magical power. The Serpent opened his mouth wide, allowing an orb of iridescent energy to form within, and he launched the orb at his pursuer with supersonic speed.

Eli sang once again.

The Serpent's attack shattered on an invisible barrier in front of Eli and the unicorn. The impact of sparks and smoke hid them for a moment, but they shot out of the fray undeterred.

"No!" The Serpent curled his lips, bared his teeth, and roared. "Who do you think you are, Great Prince!? How *dare* you defy the laws of death and challenge me!"

Without slowing his approach, Eli said, "I am the son of the Great King, whom you have defied from the very beginning. You've taken something precious from me, and I'm going to take it back!"

"You can't! I claimed this power and authority fair and square! You know it's true! Only the girl can take it back, and you and I know she *never* will!"

"I took her place, remember? Now it's mine to reclaim." Eli smirked, drawing his bow. "Besides, I wasn't talking about *that*."

The Serpent had no time to react before Eli planted a light arrow in his face. The impact of the bolt ripped off one of the Serpent's neck spines, and he yowled in pain.

As the winged horse passed over the Serpent, Eli jumped and dove straight into his mouth.

His yowl ending in a muddled choke, the Serpent tried to clear his throat and unwittingly began hacking like a cat with a hairball. After several seconds of this, the Serpent's face contorted. Tears of pain welled up in the corners of his eyes. His entire body convulsed, and he vomited, spewing a mixture of blood and black dust along with Eli and his own severed tongue.

While in free-fall, Eli used his sword of light to cut into the Serpent's tongue, and he extracted an unconscious Melody from its fleshy bowels. Once he had an arm wrapped securely around her, he transformed his sword into a lasso, which he tossed at his incoming winged horse. When the lasso snagged around the horse's neck, the rope retracted to pull Eli and Melody up onto its back.

In denial, despite his great pain, the Serpent howled and dove after them.

Down they went, falling toward Diamond City, sprawled beneath them. As they plummeted, Eli used the lasso to secure Melody to the horse's back. Then he said, "Take her safely to the ground. I'll be back."

Eli jumped backward off the horse and allowed himself to be swallowed by the Serpent, this time going well past the throat.

Almost at the ground, the winged horse slowed its descent and alighted on the wall of the city. Then it turned to face the Serpent.

Realizing he had eaten Eli, the Serpent sneered and slowed his descent as well. Taking a position facing the winged horse, he tried to speak, but only gurgled and spewed bloodied black dust from his mouth. Growling angrily, he spoke telepathically instead. *"The poor Prince put up a grand fight, but he will not survive. Seven thousand times more potent than the saliva of Nex, surely my stomach acid will devour him and his hideous, glowing glory within moments."* He lowered his head, furrowed his brow, and bared his blood-stained teeth in a snarl. *"Put the girl down NOW! I'm taking her back, and no one will see her ever again. She is mine! She will ALWAYS be mine!"*

The horse stood its ground with a snort, brandishing its horn and flaring its wings.

The Serpent roared, rearing up in preparation to strike. At the moment of climax, just before he crashed down upon them, the Serpent's belly was split clean open by a ray of light. The fissure spread like a jagged lightning bolt all the way up to his throat. The Serpent's eyes widened just before his head exploded. What remained of his hovering body disintegrated into black dust and was dispersed by a strong wind.

From the blast that impacted the Serpent's head came Eli, flipping through the air, sword in hand. After landing beside his steed, he reached up and caught another object flying from the explosion. He opened his palm to admire the item.

Melody's amulet. Her inheritance from the Great King.

He tucked it away in his pocket, dismissed his sword, and looked up with a grand smile and arms stretched upward. "Father, I've done it!"

"Well done, my son," the Great King answered, his voice resounding across the blue sky. "However, this is far from over. It is only the beginning."

47
The Prince of Victory
Summer, 104 IE

THE PEOPLE OF Diamond City soon realized the danger was gone, and they came out of their hiding places. Hardly anyone saw Eli battling the Serpent, and those who did were unable to recognize him. Even so, they celebrated, relieved that the monsters were gone and the daylight had returned. By then, Eli and the winged horse had already left the city.

At noon on the same day, Eli's friends arrived at the apple orchard. Everyone was on horseback except for the soldier, who rode his talongrunt, and Matthias, who was reunited with his thunderbeast shortly after the lukúba fled. They found Eli reclining against a tree trunk, munching on an apple. The winged horse grazed nearby, and Melody lay asleep in a soft bed of green grass. Everyone dismounted and gathered around him, still hardly able to express their awe. Eli rose to greet them, hugging and shaking hands and smiling like he always did. Together, they celebrated the events of the day.

Matthias was the sole exception. He was filled with remorse for the role he played in Eli's arrest and death, so he stood at a distance. He didn't believe Eli would want to see him because of what he did.

Soon, Eli looked at him and asked, "Matthias, what troubles you?"

Breathing hard, trying in vain to hide his fear, Matthias walked

Chapter 47: The Prince of Victory

up to Eli and got down on one knee. He looked him in the eye and said, "Prince Eli, I...I'm *so* sorry...for everything."

Eli smiled and extended his hand.

After a moment's hesitation, Matthias took Eli's hand and allowed himself to be pulled up. He was caught off guard when Eli embraced him. Slowly, he returned the embrace and began to weep. Then Eli took him by the shoulders and said, "I forgive you, friend."

The others cheered, coming to pat Matthias on the back and continue celebrating. They enjoyed apples from the tree in abundance, since they hadn't eaten for the duration of the Serpent's attack on Rhema.

"You did it, didn't you?" the seamstress asked Eli as they ate. "You killed the Great Serpent!"

"Not quite. I destroyed his physical form and robbed him of his power, but his spirit still lives. He will continue in his devious ways to gain back his strength and defy the Kingdom of Marindel until the very last day." He took out Melody's amulet and held it up for all to see. "The Great King would like for you to carry this authority in your hearts as you live your lives, day by day, listening to his voice and caring for others just like you saw me do. Follow in my footsteps and teach others to do the same. As you do, you will prepare the way for the return of the Kingdom of Marindel."

Eli clasped his hands over the amulet and rubbed them together. He opened his hands to breathe deeply upon it, and then he tossed it up as if releasing a dove. The amulet soared like a shooting star, before exploding into millions of magical sparks, which dispersed as far as the eye could see on every horizon. Some of the sparks lingered and were absorbed into every person present.

As they beheld the wondrous spectacle, Eli declared, "Now, *all* who declare allegiance to the Great King will be adopted into his family as sons and daughters of royalty! Those who choose to receive their inheritance will be victorious in this realm, and in the Kingdom of Marindel when it returns. But always remember: just as the Serpent deceived Melody into surrendering her inheritance, so the Serpent will try to deceive every one of you. Be vigilant and resist him at every opportunity, looking out for one another and covering each other's weaknesses. As children of the Great King, you're more powerful than that foul beast, but he will try to blind you to that truth. Never forget who you are. And never forget my love for you, nor the love of our father, the Great King."

"How long will you stay with us?" Trisha asked.

"The time has come for me to return to Marindel. Though I'll be gone for a while, you must begin undoing the works of the Serpent by loving others, standing up for the innocent, and telling all sentient creatures about the Great King so they may come to know him."

Eli turned and walked toward Melody, his beloved. He knelt close to her and whispered, "I love you, Mel. I will always love you, and I promise I will return for you when you call for me." He kissed her forehead.

Melody breathed deeply, though she didn't wake up.

Eli stood and addressed the others, "Take good care of her in my absence. The Serpent will continue to deceive her, and she will continue to be stubborn, but the seeds of renewal have been planted in her heart. Nurture them well by proving the Great King's love for her until the final day. I promise, I will return!"

After he finished speaking, Eli went out to the field and mounted his horse. Caruso followed him and asked, "Will we ever see you again?"

"Yes, but not here."

Caruso looked away sadly. "You're the best thing that's ever happened to Rhema. We will all miss you."

"Cheer up!" Eli said with a twinkle in his eye. "I cannot stay, but I'll tell you who can: two friends of yours who gave their lives resisting the Serpent and his dark forces."

Caruso looked at Eli with a raised eyebrow.

Eli smiled. "I know how much they meant to you. Consider it a parting gift."

The yowl of a dracoviper prompted Caruso to turn around. Sure enough, Hunter and Kaya were flying toward him, chirping and yowling with glee.

"Ah! Hunter! Kaya!" Caruso shouted, running to meet his dragons as they landed in the grass and tackled him. "Oh, I'm so glad you're all right! I thought I would never see you again!"

Eli laughed, and then he said to the others gathered, "I bid you farewell, and I look forward to the day we'll meet again. Always remember, though you will not see me, I will always be with you. And I will always love you, my friends and fellow heirs to the throne of Marindel!"

Without further ado, Eli urged the winged horse to fly, and with a triumphant whinny, it launched into the sky.

As the others watched him go, Matthias ran toward his thunder-beast and said, "Let's go see him off!"

"I'm in!" the pineapple farmer said, running after Matthias.

"And I!" the sailor followed the pineapple farmer.

"Me, too!" Trevor shouted.

"You're too small to ride a dragon," Auben said with a laugh.

"You and the kids can ride Kaya," Caruso said.

Auben turned serious, clearly not fond of the idea, but Trevor and Lia's excited whoops convinced him. He looked at Trisha for approval, and she said with a chuckle, "Just this once."

As Eli soared higher and higher, many of Eli's friends followed him: Matthias, the pineapple farmer, and the sailor aboard the thunderbeast; the Tethysian soldier aboard his talongrunt; Caruso aboard Hunter; and Auben, Trevor, and Lia aboard Kaya. Everyone else watched from below, looking up at Eli's departing figure until he vanished from sight.

Those flying after Eli last saw him disappear between two cumulus clouds. As they went through the clouds after him, all they saw in the blue sky beyond were glimmers of fading magic. They heard Eli's voice echo on the wind, "Remember, I will always love you, my friends and fellow heirs to the throne of Marindel!"

Summer, 1419 AIE

~Connor~

I STAND SPEECHLESS as our surroundings darken with the conclusion of the Great Story. I was so enraptured, I didn't even think to interrupt with questions or comments.

Everything makes so much sense now.

Eli has already defeated the Great Serpent. We, those who follow and serve the Great King, have been adopted as his sons and daughters and have each been given a royal inheritance. Eli won it for us when he took upon himself Melody's inheritance of death, overcame that fate by the power of the Great King, and challenged the Serpent head-on to take back what was lost. He reclaimed Melody's original inheritance and made its power available not only to her, but to all of us.

I look at Penn for the first time since the Great Story began. Teary-eyed and smiling, he says, "The Great King is very good, isn't he?"

I nod, holding back tears of my own. "Yes, he is."

"The events of the Great Story, as I mentioned earlier, marked the beginning of the Return of Marindel. Since then, Marindel has been advancing and taking territory from the Serpent. However, as you know, the war is not without its casualties. There is nothing benevolent about the way the Serpent opposes his own destruction. Let me tell you about the events following Eli's victory."

A window opens in front of us, and just like before, images and scenes illustrate Penn's words.

"When Melody finally awoke from her comatose state, Eli's friends were jubilant. They told her about his resurrection and how he rescued her and the kingdom of Rhema, but she was offended and refused to believe them. To their dismay, she went back to the remains of the royal palace to rejoin her officials.

"Melody tried to forget about Eli, but her heart was torn with lovesick devastation and guilt. She spent those days indoors, shunning all who came to see her and responding with furious outbursts to those who persisted. She became unfit to lead her own kingdom and cared nothing for the people.

Meanwhile, followers of the Great King multiplied across Rhema as Eli's friends shared the Great Story with everyone they knew and everyone they met. The Rheman officials tried to put a stop to it by imprisoning or punishing them, but to no avail. They had little support from the Tethysians at that point because Matthias was able to win their favor. By the time word reached Emperor Flavian in the Tethys Region, one-fifth of the kingdom of Rhema had declared allegiance to the Great King.

The Serpent caused fear and anger to rise in Flavian's heart. The emperor decided the rebellion ought to be quenched before it spread to other territories of the Empire. The messenger who told Flavian about the happenings in Rhema was killed on the spot, and the emperor discreetly signed an order for the kingdom's destruction. Not even the Tethysians stationed in Rhema were to be warned of the impending attack.

"Before the infamous Draco Fleet arrived, the Great King warned many of his followers through dreams, visions, and Seer revelations to flee the kingdom. No one knew the reason why, but they trusted the King's leadership well enough to obey. Those who were more hesitant were persuaded by the urgency of their friends and family.

"The Draco Fleet struck before sunrise, while the island was still asleep. The last of the followers of the King were just escaping as hundreds of dragons with immense firepower passed over the kingdom, mowing it down with billowing torrents of flame. Everyone remaining on the island perished."

490

"Except for Melody," I say, remembering the sight of her weeping among the ruins.

"Yes, except for Melody. Eli's friends tried to convince her to flee with them, but she refused. Though the Great King protected her from harm, she could do nothing but watch as her kingdom was razed to the ground. The island paradise that had been her home for centuries was no more.

"Those who escaped the destruction of Rhema scattered abroad into every kingdom of Tyrizah, where they continued to tell the Great Story and serve the Great King. The Galyyrim appeared to certain individuals and gave them royal instruments, with which they could play the Music of Marindel. The instruments were critical in helping the King's followers overcome impossible odds as the Great Serpent, through the Tethysian Empire and a host of other enemies, relentlessly tried to exterminate them.

"Once Emperor Flavian realized the Great Story survived the destruction of Rhema, he signed an order for all books, scrolls, and tablets with mention of Rhema, Melody, or the Great King to be destroyed. As time went by, the Serpent nearly succeeded in removing knowledge of the kingdom of Rhema from the annals of history.

"In step with this, as time went by and the generation of those who knew Eli passed away, the vigor of the followers of the Great King grew cold. Many of them were deceived by the Serpent into passivity or unbelief. One by one, the royal instruments were set aside in museums or treasure vaults. By the end of the Imperial Era, as the realm recovered from the vise-grip of the Empire, it seemed as though the Great Story never happened at all. The memory of it has been all but forgotten.

"Meanwhile, Melody returned to her former lifestyle of roaming as a vagabond, attacked and chased around by those the Serpent stirred up against her. The Great King has sent Seers to remind her of Eli and his love for her, and though they've been largely unsuccessful, their persistence over the last fifteen hundred years has weakened her resistance. Do you remember what Jed told you about your own encounter with Melody?"

I nod. "Melody saved my life. My determination to help her despite the danger posed by the Nox Abyssae empowered her in a way no Seer before me has been able to do."

"That's right. You didn't do anything different from other Seers per se, but the times are changing. The final days are upon us. The forces of the Great King and the forces of the Great Serpent are mobilizing and squaring off across the realm as we speak. The Great King has chosen you, Connor Lightwood, to bring Melody back to the camp of the Great King and unite his followers against the vengeful tide of the Great Serpent."

I ponder this for a moment. Both Eli and Jed have told me about my destiny before, but for the first time, a new question comes to mind. "I really *am* the Final Seer now, aren't I?"

"Yes."

I frown. What a lonely calling. "Did Jed know he was going to die? Even back at the countryside tavern when he told me I was a Seer?"

"Not quite. Every man dies, Jed knew that. He also trusted you, Connor, to take the Seer's torch and run farther with it than he did. Jed was ready and willing to die if necessary. It wasn't until after your friends failed to rescue Celine when the Great King invited him to demonstrate his love for her by giving his life."

I nod thoughtfully. Knowing this about Jed's death helps me make peace with my tumultuous feelings, and it does bring my heart a small flicker of hope. However, there are so many things left to worry about. We still have to find Celine and convince her to come with us. What's more, after the destruction of Königheim, who knows what sort of city-wide conflict we'll find ourselves in? I ask, "So, what now? What are we supposed to do?"

Penn smiles. "Trust the Great King, and you will know what to do when the time comes."

Great. Of course. I swallow my misgivings and nod.

Our surroundings begin to take shape, and soon we find ourselves once again in the rolling green countryside of Rhema. The sun shines warmly in the blue sky above.

"What are we doing back here? Is there a part of the story we missed?"

"No," Penn says, looking fondly at an enormous camphor tree presiding atop the nearest hill. "This is the Ancient Isle, the kingdom of Rhema in your present time."

I look around, eyes wide. There's no sign of the devastation wrought by the Tethysian Draco Fleet. As my eyes linger on the tree, I remember when Eli planted a camphor seed in the ground. This must be the tree that grew from that seed!

"I have one last thing to share before we part ways," Penn says. "From the time of its destruction until now, the Serpent has kept the Ancient Isle hidden to prevent anyone from rediscovering the site of his embarrassing defeat."

A terrifying roar thunders across the heavens, and I drop to my knees. A red dragon flies overhead, so massive that each of its wings are longer than the tallest towers of Königheim. It continues on toward the eastern horizon, roaring as it goes.

Yup, if I accidentally discovered the Ancient Isle and saw that dragon coming to meet me, I'd turn the other way immediately.

Penn continues, "The Serpent's hold on the island is weakening. The time is soon coming when Rhema will take its place among the kingdoms of Tyrizah once again. Here on this land, you, Melody, and every follower of the Great King will make your final stand against the Great Serpent and his dark forces."

I open my mouth to ask a question, but Penn raises a finger. "Don't worry about it now, young Seer. Store these words in your heart for a future time."

I nod. "Thank you so much for this, Penn. I really mean it."

"The pleasure is mine," Penn nods with a grin. "Take care. We will meet again."

48

Back in the Ring

Summer, 1419 AIE

~**Connor**~

A WOODEN CEILING GREETS my gaze. I'm lying face-up on a straw bed in a small, quaint room. Late-morning sunlight pours in from a window on the opposite wall.

I yawn and stretch. My limbs are incredibly stiff!

My stomach roars like the dragon I saw flying over the Ancient Isle.

Blimey, I sure am hungry! And my mouth is dry, too.

I don't know where I am, but I hope there's food and water available.

I slide off the bed and stand up, taking a moment to find my balance before walking to the closed door of the room. I turn the knob and open it, thankful it's not locked, and proceed into the next room.

Tarento, Khai, Jake, Yoko, and Scourge are sitting in a circle along with three people I don't recognize. We're in what appears to be a living room combined with a kitchen. I don't know when we all got a house, but I'm so hungry and thirsty, I don't care about the details!

"Can I have a bite to eat?" I ask.

Everyone looks at me, wide-eyed with shock.

"Connor!" Yoko jumps to her feet and runs toward me. "You're awake!"

I smile, bracing myself to meet Yoko's embrace. "Yup, I'm awake!"

"Thank goodness!" Jake says, also standing to come. "The medic said you'd be out for days, if not...you know, forever."

"Medic?" I ask, exchanging a handshake and pats on the back with Jake.

"You've been asleep for almost two days," Tarento says. "We sent for a medic after you didn't wake up yesterday. She said you'd fallen into a coma."

"I was asleep for that long?" I ask with an embarrassed chuckle. "No wonder I'm so hungry!"

"There's a pot of stew over the fire," a pleasant old lady says. "And there's a jug of water right next to it. Take a seat, I'll serve you some."

"Thank you!" Stew sounds like the most amazing food in the realm right now. I walk over to a place on the floor and sit to join the circle.

"I'll fill you in on what you missed," Jake says as he goes back to his own spot. "After you passed out in the tavern, we decided to find a place to stay in the poor sector. This family here has been very generous and hospitable." He gestures to the three people I don't know.

Scourge speaks next, "This is where Tarento and I stayed when we wintered in Cloud Summit. Their names are Lim, Ella, and Dan. They're the best!"

"Yes, well," the old lady, Lim, chuckles as she comes with a bowl of stew and a cup of water. "You've been great friends to us as well. It's our pleasure to return the favor."

I eagerly take the bowl and cup. I down the water in a few gulps, and then I have a spoonful of stew. Either I'm starving to death, or this is the best stew I've *ever* had!

While I enjoy the food, Jake continues, "Yesterday, Khai and I went out to see if we could learn anything more about the Königheim attack. Unfortunately, the situation grows worse with every passing day. Bennett had twenty-seven of his men executed for treason and allegiance with White Sand. There was no fair trial; just a cruel beheading with an axe, one by one."

"That's awful," I say between bites.

Jake nods. "I cringe at the thought of how many might've been innocent, and how many of the real traitors remain among Bennett's ranks."

"On another note," Khai says, "Alphonse and Oliver are looking for Tarento, Jake, you, and me to ask us about the bombing and thank us for our roles in trying to prevent it."

"That's great." I'd gladly receive an apology from the prince for how staunchly he argued against our news of the impending attack. "You haven't gone to see them yet?"

"No," Tarento replies. "Heiban is still out there, and White Sand is still out there. Public recognition is the last thing we need."

"Also," Jake says, "Yoko and Scourge have their own wanted posters now. Bennett still wants them dead for attempting to rescue Celine."

"Blimey. So, you've all just been laying low the past couple days?"

"With the exception of our little excursion," Jake nods, "Yes."

"Well then," I look at each person in the room as I set aside my empty bowl.

"Would you like some more stew, dear?" Lim asks, beginning to get up.

I extend a hand toward her. "No, no, it's all right. It's my turn to share what all of *you* have missed."

Yoko tilts her head. "What do you mean? You were in a coma!"

"You're not wrong." I pause for suspense as the others look curiously at me. "Do you remember what Jed said about the Great Story a few days back?"

"He mentioned it, I think," Jake replies.

"Yes, well," I can't help but smile. "During my coma, I saw the whole thing. And now I'm going to share it with you."

For the rest of that day, I tell my friends the Great Story as it was shown to me from beginning to end. We only take one short break in the evening to eat some stew and light a few lanterns, and then I dive back into it. Everyone is captivated, asking questions and commenting the whole way through. By the time I finish, it's late at night, and all of us are awestruck by the goodness of the Great King.

"This is incredible!" Tarento says after I've finished. "We knew we were missing crucial details about Eli's role in the Great King's plan. Now, finally, everything makes sense!"

"Yes, but what does it mean for us?" Khai asks. "What are we supposed to do?"

"Two things," I reply. "One, we must keep it close to heart. Now that we can see our circumstances from the Great King's perspective, we can be bold and courageous no matter what we face. Chief Bennett, White Sand, Jaedis the Sorcerer, dragons, trolls, or whatever else. In the face of uncertainty, we can trust him to guide our path.

"Two, we must be proactive in sharing this Great Story with others. The Serpent has gone through great lengths to hide the evidence of defeat, and it's up to us to oppose him with the truth. Celine is one person who needs to hear the news. Melody is another. And there are countless others, friends and foes alike, who need to know just how much the Great King loves them and is willing to bring them into his family, if only they would acknowledge him and follow his ways."

"Connor," Jake says, pulling out the small treasure chest we found in the abandoned castle. "This is one of the royal instruments, right? Do you know how it works?"

"Let me see," I say, extending my hands forward. Jake tosses it to me, and I examine the chest while listening to my Seer's gift for any leads. Nothing comes, so I shrug. "I'm not sure."

Scourge says, "I wish we had remembered to ask Jed before... you know..."

"It's all right," I reply. "Whenever it's time for us to use it, we'll find a way."

"You still haven't answered my question," Khai says. "What should we do now? How will we find Celine and get out of here before the whole city blows up?"

A grin spreads across my face as the answer comes to me. I know they won't like it, but in honor of Jed, I just *have* to say it! "It's quite late. Why don't we all sleep on it?"

"*No!*" Tarento, Scourge, and Yoko all shout in dismay.

"Yes," I say with a chuckle. "I mean it. I'm good on sleep for a while, but you all need to rest up. Tomorrow we'll be doing much more than laying low, I can guarantee that."

Everyone reluctantly agrees, so we retire to our beds spread out around the small poor-sector home, and we fall asleep.

EARLY THE NEXT morning, as we're all beginning to stir, there's a knock on the door.

I come out of my room to see Dan, a man in his mid-twenties, check through the peep hole in door. He tenses and whispers, "It's the police!"

"What?" Tarento sits up from his bed on the floor.

"How did they find us?" Yoko asks.

Despite still being groggy, I have a sense of peace about the situation. With hardly a thought I say, "I'll get it."

Khai whispers sharply, "What do you mean, 'you'll get it'? If they see Yoko and Scourge here, they'll be arrested!"

"They'll be fine." I look at Scourge and Yoko and say, "Go hide in my room."

"Okay," Yoko crawls out of bed and tip-toes over to the room. Scourge follows close behind, and they close the door.

Once they've gone, I approach the door and open it.

Captain Antoine is there, with two of his men behind him. The captain holds his helmet under his arm, and for the first time I get a good look at his features: ruffled dirty-blond hair, hazel-brown eyes, and a narrow jaw. I also notice one of his men is holding a loaded potato sack.

Antoine nods when I open the door. "Greetings."

"Good morning, sir. What can I do for you?"

"Nothing. I have something to say." Antoine takes a breath. "On behalf of the Cloud Summit police force, I...I want to apologize for the death of your friend. It was a rash mistake, and I wish there was something we could do to make it up to you, but...I know such things cannot be undone, nor friends replaced..."

I get a sense he remembers my attitude in front of the Hall of Justice: grief-stricken, angry, and vengeful. He's afraid he might trigger those feelings again by mentioning Jed's death, but instead, I'm honored. Antoine made the effort not only to find us, but to admit Jed's death was a mistake and apologize for it.

I have none other than the Great King to thank for my change of heart.

I smile and extend a hand. "I accept your apology. Thank you very much."

Antoine is speechless, looking from my face to my hand and back. A smile spreads across his face as he takes my hand and shakes it.

"You have a good heart," I say on a Seer-led impulse. "Cloud Summit needs more men like you."

"Hm," Antoine nods. "I appreciate the compliment."

"I mean it," I insist. "And, while you're here, I'd love to hear about your defensive stand at Königheim. My friends told me you helped guard the explosives to delay the blast. That's some serious bravery, standing guard with *how* many men in a room full of explosives?"

Antoine chuckles. "Five. I had five men left who were loyal to me. After the Pythorian and the Samurai cleared the room of insurgents, I stayed behind with my men and the nymph while they went on to clear the rest of the castle. Soon, more insurgents arrived with a cart full of bombs meant to set off the explosives. We prevented the cart from getting inside and defeated many of them. Three of my men fell in battle; these two behind me are the only ones who survived. When an insurgent got past us with two lit bombs and climbed up on the crates, we knew the castle was lost. We escaped just in time to avoid the collapse."

I smile and say, "The Great King honors your courage and valor."

Antoine tilts his head. "King Alphonse?"

"No," Tarento says, coming up from behind me.

Antoine's eyes widen when he sees Tarento. He mustn't have known he was here.

Tarento continues, "However, speaking of Alphonse, I would like to second Connor's compliments. I was able to rescue him from Königheim, but only with the extra time you bought for us. If it weren't for you, neither the king nor I would be alive today. You, captain, are the true hero of Königheim. Sincerely, I thank you." Tarento bows in that Felid way of his.

Antoine smiles, struggling to contain his embarrassment. Clearly, he's not used to getting so much positive attention. "Thank you very much, Samurai. Though, forgive me, I must ask: are you the one the other Samurai are looking for?"

"I am."

"I see. Well, unlike them, you've proven your honor well enough. Your secret is safe with me."

"Thank you, I appreciate it. However, I would appreciate it even more if you wouldn't mind telling us how you found us here."

"Oh, yes. The medic you called for the other day is my cousin, Valerie. She told me about you. Don't worry, I've come on my own accord. No one else knows about this."

"I hope not," Tarento says. "Would Valerie tell anyone else about us?"

"She won't, I'm sure of it. On my honor as a citizen of Armavir, the Land of Peace, I trust Val with my life." Antoine nods. "Anyway, we've gone on quite a tangent, but there's another reason I've come. I have a few things for you."

He turns to fumble around in his companion's sack. First, he takes out a smaller sack full of coins—I can tell by the clinking sound the contents make in the bag—and hands it to me. "This belonged to your friend, I believe."

"No way!" I exclaim, taking the sack. It's the homestead money! I can't believe it! "Thank you! Thank you *so* much, Captain Antoine! I don't think you understand how great this is!"

"I don't think I do either," Antoine says with a chuckle. "But that's not all. The Illusionist had another item with her when she was captured, and King Alphonse would like his rescuer to keep it as a gift of gratitude. Here you go," he gives a small treasure chest to Tarento.

Both of our eyes widen. *Another* royal instrument!?

"How did the Illusionist get her hands on this?" Tarento asks.

"It's the stolen relic from Königheim. We returned it to the king after the bombing, but he decided it would be better off in your possession."

"This is amazing," Tarento says. "Thank you so much, Antoine. I really mean it."

Jake comes up from behind. "For a conversation with the police, I'm hearing a suspicious amount of excitement. What's going on?"

Tarento and I present our gifts to Jake. As he looks from one to the other, his eyes widen like saucers, and a goofy grin spreads across his face. "Ohhh hohoho! Your excitement has been validated! Carry on, please!" He turns and walks inside with a fist-pump. We chuckle as he goes.

"Two more things," Antoine says, first pulling out Yoko's bag and handing it to Tarento, and then Scourge's bag and handing it to me. "These were taken from your friends upon their arrest. Don't worry, I'm not here to capture them."

"Wow, thanks again," I say.

"Here's a question," Tarento says, pulling out Sylva's acorn. "Did you see what happened to Sylva after Königheim came down?"

"She's in there," Antoine says, pointing at the acorn. "She found me yesterday and asked to be let inside. She didn't look well; probably traumatized by the blast. I reckon all she needs is a good rest. When you get a chance, tell her I appreciate her help. I'm certainly *honored* to have fought alongside a tree nymph."

"We will," Tarento says with a nod.

He smiles. "All right. I have other duties to attend to, but I hope you enjoy the rest of your day."

Antoine begins to walk away, but he stops. Then he looks back at us, his expression serious, like it had been when I first opened the door. He comes near and whispers, "One last thing. Chief Bennett will be leading an attack on the White Sand hideout at midnight. If you're still interested in rescuing the Illusionist, you'd better get her out before then." He looks at Tarento and says, "You'll have to be careful. The other Samurai will be with us."

Tarento and I exchange glances and nod.

"Thanks for the tip," I say.

"You didn't hear it from me." Antoine puts his helmet on, turns, and leaves, with his men close behind.

We go back inside, closing the door behind us.

Khai is sitting in the far corner, armed and ready with his bow. Jake is standing nearby, his eyes shining with excitement because he already knows what we have. Our hosts are spread out around the room, fearful and suspicious. Dan is sitting on a folded blanket that conceals a sword, holding the hilt and ready to wield it, if necessary. Scourge and Yoko peek from behind the door of the private bedroom.

After making eye contact with each of them, I grin joyfully as I lift the sack of money with both hands. "We have *MONEY!*"

"*YAY!*" Yoko screams, bursting out of the room.

Khai stands up, breathing a sigh of relief and setting down his bow.

"What happened?" Scourge asks.

"It's the homestead money! Antoine knew it belonged to Jed before Celine stole it, so he brought it back for us."

Jake claps once and says, "Can somebody *please* make that man the chief of police!?"

"I second that motion," Tarento agrees.

"We have another royal instrument too," I say, pointing to the chest held by Tarento. "That'll be useful once we know how to open it. But," I pause until I have everyone's attention. "Antoine also told us about Bennett's plan to attack the White Sand hideout. We need to get Celine out of there before midnight, or things are going to get messy for everyone."

"How are we going to do that?" Khai asks.

"Give me one second." I begin to pace, and I ask the Great King, *"Please, show me what I need to know."*

After a few seconds I begin verbalizing what comes to mind, "Khai, Tarento, Yoko, Scourge, Jake...everyone but me, I guess. Go to the Exotic Goods Hub with the homestead money and buy the equipment we need. The shopkeeper's out today, but her assistant, Kamau, will be there. He's a solid guy. After that, come back here and wait for my return."

I turn to Lim and say, "You have a friend on the other side of the sector who knows an ex-gang member. He knows how I can contact Celine without walking into the hideout like a duck into a pond full of crocodiles. Please show me to this friend so I can talk to him."

Lim seems surprised by my Seer knowledge, but she smiles and nods. "Of course, dear."

"Great." I turn to Jake and say, "I need you to get me a short sword and a Felid fire shield."

"Got it," Jake nods. "Armor?"

"Tough leather to wear over my tunic, nothing heavy. Oh, and gloves would be great."

"Got it."

"Also, I'll be needing five hundred krons."

"Of course." Jake helps me count five hundred krons into a smaller sack, and then he takes the big one and I take the small one.

Once we're finished, I raise my fist and say, "All right, we're back in the ring! May the Great King be with us all!"

49
Gearing Up
Summer, 1419 AIE

~**Connor**~

WITH LITTLE TROUBLE, I learned from Lim's friend that the ex-gang member is a blacksmith with a shop in the northernmost sector of Cloud Summit. Now I'm walking down the main street in that sector, which is very different from any other place in Cloud Summit I've visited thus far. Judging by the shops I see—carpenters, leatherworkers, stonemasons, tailors, and the like—I'd guess this is a crafting sector. The atmosphere is robust, filled with the sounds of hard-working folks in their shops and customers haggling for prices.

It doesn't take long to find my destination: a large smithy at the end of the road, marked by an anvil-shaped sign with the words "Matvei's Metalworks."

The front of the shop is entirely open, so I walk inside. There are many blacksmiths here, working away at their individual benches, but it hardly proves difficult to find the man I'm looking for. Matvei, after whom the shop is named, is an older Izendoran man with a peg leg. I see him at the back of the shop hammering on an anvil, so I approach him and wait. Once he pauses I call, "Matvei! Have I caught you at a bad time?"

He looks at me, his face and silvery hair smeared with grime, and speaks with a thick accent. "Not particularly. What're you after?"

"My name is Connor," I say, stepping closer so we can hear each other amid the noisy din of the smithy. "I'm a detective-adventurer working to gather information on White Sand. Do you mind if I ask you a few questions?"

"Hmm," Matvei squints. "You're a bit young to be doing that kind of work. Did Chief Bennett send you?"

I shake my head. "I'm here on my own accord. I heard you were once a gang member; what was that like for you?"

"Don't remind me," Matvei grumbles. "I left that life behind years ago."

"Not fond of those memories?"

"No. I was a fool back then, surrounded by like-minded fools with no aspirations in life."

"What do you mean?"

"All we did was steal, vandalize, and fight. And all for what? We lived like rats, scraping by to survive, yet we thought we were the most powerful beings in Cloud Summit. We acted the part, and we expected others to treat us that way. What fools we were!"

"I see. Did something happen?"

"I lost my foot, if you haven't noticed," Matvei says, balancing on his good leg to lift up and wiggle his peg leg, "in a fight with a rival gang. A heavy crate fell on me while I was down. None of my brothers stayed to help me. That night, I realized how fragile and meaningless the brotherhood of my gang really was. That was the night I became wise."

"Wow," I'm becoming genuinely interested in Matvei's story. "What did you do next?"

"Once I had my foot amputated and replaced with a peg, I chose to hone a craft to make a living. I did some smithing as a boy, so I found a local blacksmith to train me as an apprentice. Now, twenty years later, I have a successful smithy with a dozen apprentices of my own."

"Did your gang ever try to bring you back in?"

"Oh yes, very often in the first few years. They tried to kill me several times."

"How did you get them to leave you alone?"

"I learned how to fight. Professionally, I mean. The brother of my mentor was a Paladin. He taught me how to defend myself and outsmart my enemies. After they realized I was dangerous, they left me alone. Of course, that was on the condition I didn't give away any of their secrets."

"Secrets like," I silently thank the Great King for this

conversational segue, "a method of communication? Something only criminal insiders would know about?"

"Yes, secrets like that."

"Can you tell me more?"

Matvei hesitates. "I...would rather not. I don't want any trouble if the wrong people find out. I hope you understand."

"Hmm," I pause to think through my next move. "What was your gang called?"

"The Red Hawks."

"Are they still in Cloud Summit?"

"Not by that name. They disbanded years ago. Many of them went to join other gangs that were stronger at the time. I believe most joined with the Blue Foxes."

"Oh, the Blue Foxes," I say, pretending for the moment I don't know them. "Are they the ones you think would come after you if you shared their secrets?"

"Yes."

"You don't think they got chased out during the Purge?"

"I hadn't thought of that. It's possible, but I'm not going to find out for you, if that's what you want."

"No need," I say, pulling out the Blue Fox insignia to show him. "Their leader, Alpha Blue, gave this to me when I ran into them on their new turf in Bayside Harbor. If most of the Red Hawks joined the Blue Foxes, it's probably safe to say they'll never find out if you spill the beans about their communication techniques."

Matvei's eyes widen at the sight of the insignia. He looks at me and says, "You're a bit young to be traveling so far for a piece of cloth like that."

"Some may think so, but that's a story for another time. During the Purge, in case you're not aware, all the gangs were chased out or destroyed. The only exception was White Sand. They might've been a simple gang like the others before the Purge, but now they've risen to the level of an insurgent criminal organization. The bombing of Königheim was their doing, and they'll stop at nothing to bring Cloud Summit to its knees. That's why I need to figure out how to stop them."

"Hmm," Matvei looks at his work bench.

I wait for his response. I get a sense he's afraid of losing the dream he's worked so hard to build. I hope he realizes that if White Sand continues to terrorize Cloud Summit, the loss of his dream is most likely inevitable.

Matvei fumbles with a few things on his work bench, presumably in order to get back to work.

I walk closer. "Matvei, please, I really need your help. I promise, on my honor as a citizen of Armavir, the Land of—"

Matvei interrupts me with a hand. "No need. Wait one moment."

I stop, looking to see what exactly he's doing. He's clearing out a shelving compartment at the back of his work station. After that, he inserts a crowbar in a crevice in the back wall of the compartment and pulls it open. He reaches deep inside, leaning over his anvil, and pulls out a dusty wooden chest. He looks this way and that, and once he's sure nobody's watching, he opens the chest and presents its contents: a gargoyle figurine, about three inches tall and wide, with a dull ruby embedded in its forehead. He says, "This is the secret messenger of the Cloud Summit underworld."

"How does it work?" I ask.

"It's enchanted—or, it's supposed to be. There were many of them spread throughout the catacombs beneath the city. They were sent with messages to communicate secretly with other gang members. The gargoyles could blend in with their surroundings, so no one would notice them until they sought to be noticed."

"Wizard," I say, taking the gargoyle out of the box. "If I give it a message for a certain member of White Sand, will it know who to take the message to?"

"You will have to enchant it first. The gargoyles are all connected by their enchanting force. If even one gargoyle down there is still functioning, and it knows of the person you seek, then this gargoyle will carry out its mission flawlessly."

"Wouldn't that be dangerous for you?" I ask, holding up the gargoyle to face Matvei. "If this gargoyle sees you, that means all the other gargoyles, and therefore, all the other gang members, can see you too, right?"

"Yes. That's why I had it disenchanted after I left the Red Hawks."

"I see. And you've held on to it for all this time?"

Matvei nods. "I always had a feeling it would be of use again someday."

I smile. "Well, if you don't mind, I'd like to use it. Can I?"

Matvei nods. "It's all yours. But remember, until you have it enchanted, it's just an old statue."

"Do you know any enchanters in the city?"

"Do you have map on you?"

"Yes." I take out the map of Cloud Summit and hand it to him.

He unfurls it, grabs a small piece of coal from his work bench, and makes a circle over a certain building not far away. "You'll find an enchanter here. Tell him I sent you, and he'll take care of the rest. Don't show the gargoyle to anyone else. It's top secret."

"Got it. Thank you so much, Matvei."

"No problem," he nods. "Is there anything else I can help you with?"

"Not now. I'll come again if I need anything else. In fact, I'll recommend you to my friends for all our blacksmithing needs."

"I'd appreciate it. Stay safe, adventurer-detective," Matvei smiles, before turning back to his work.

"Wait, hold on," I say, grabbing his attention again. "One last thing. Do you know where I can find a high-end clothing store?"

~Tarento~

I WALK WITH my companions toward the Exotic Goods Hub with a spring in my step. I can't get over how wonderful it is that Connor was able to share the Great Story with us!

There was certainly no better time for it.

Despite being successful in my objective to rescue King Alphonse from Königheim, I was torn with grief for the people who remained in the castle when the explosives were detonated.

The days that followed were devoid of hope. I didn't hear the Great King speak once from then until just before Connor awoke from his coma. He said, *"Today, all of your questions about the Kingdom of Marindel will be answered."* I didn't believe him at first. But as Connor shared the Great Story, I felt the grief and despair drain from my heart.

Now, knowing finally the authority we have as followers of the Great King to resist the Great Serpent, I no longer feel like I'm striving to save people in vain. Even in the case of the Königheim bombing, from which many people did not escape, I've come to thank the Great King for the lives of those who did. Through our efforts, many people were rescued. The psychological effect of the bombing on the citizens of Cloud Summit, though still large, was mitigated.

Now, we have a chance to make things right again.

"There it is!" Yoko says, pointing at the inconspicuous shop.

"Let's make this quick," Khai says as we head toward it.

We step in through the door, walk down the hall, and emerge through a beaded curtain into the spacious central room of the shop.

This being my first visit, I take in the sight of the eclectic collection of trinkets lining the walls.

"Each room contains items from two kingdoms," Jake explains, pointing at placards mounted above the halls. "Kamau is around here somewhere; he's knowledgeable about most things for sale here."

"I appreciate the compliment," a man says, presumably Kamau, as he emerges from the Tethys-Murumbwé hall followed by a Murumbwéan woman. "Welcome to the Exotic Goods Hub. Our shopkeeper is out today, but if you need any assistance, my sister, Irena, and I will be happy to help you."

"Thank you," we all say together.

"Let's split up and find whatever we need," Jake says. "Then we'll meet here and pay for everything at once."

"Good plan," I agree.

"I need a bow," Yoko says to Kamau, "Just the right size for me!"

Kamau nods. "We have an excellent selection of bows available from several kingdoms."

"Let's get her a Pythorian bow," Khai says.

"Very well. Follow me," Kamau leads Yoko and Khai down the Pythoria-Ibadan hallway.

As they leave, Jake asks Irena for recommendations on a good sword and armor. She takes him down the Armavir-Izendor hallway, and Scourge follows.

Now alone, I look with longing at the Felidae-Sunophsis room. I want to go, but I feel bad about it. *"Great King, when I arrived in Armavir, you directed me to sell my Samurai gear. You've protected me well since, but...is it...can it really be time for me to take up a katana once again?"*

"Go and see for yourself," the Great King says.

With bated breath, I proceed down the hall and into the room, filled wall-to-wall with shining treasure and artifacts. My eyes are drawn to the left, where the familiar items of Felidae are displayed. When I see what presides in the center of it all, my heart skips a beat. I nearly fall to my knees in sheer disbelief. "C-can it be?"

"Go and see."

I walk toward it. The gleaming blade rests upon its stand, brighter than anything else on the wall. I recognize the smooth divots running down its length and the slight wear in the criss-crossing fabric on the hilt.

I stop in front of it, unable to believe my eyes.

This isn't just any katana.

It's *my* katana!

"*But, how...why...?*" I can't find any other words to speak to the King.

"*I kept it hidden for you until this moment. You have followed me well without your gear ever since you left Felidae. Now, my son, I believe you will do just as well with it as you did without. Take back your katana and use it to defend the innocent and fight for justice.*"

"*I don't know what to say.*" I take the katana by the hilt, holding it up as a single tear runs down my cheek. "*Thank you, thank you so much.*"

"*Take other items as well; don't be shy. You must be well prepared for tonight's battle.*"

"*All right,*" I take my sheath from behind the stand and slide the katana inside before standing back to behold the other items. "*What else do I need?*"

"*Combat gloves, forearm and shin armor plates, a sturdy belt, a bag of kunai, and a tiger hound summoning scroll.*"

I gather the items as the Great King lists them. When I come to the last item, I'm surprised to see there's a huge basket full of summoning scrolls. All of them are different sizes and lengths, depending on the creatures they're meant to summon. As I search through them for a tiger hound scroll, I find a giant eagle scroll like the one I used to escape from Felidae. "*Are you sure I won't be needing any more of these?*"

"*For now, all you need is a tiger hound.*"

"*Very well.*"

"*You may also take the fire shield Connor requested. He will need it.*"

Once I've gathered my items, I head down the hall toward the main room. Scourge passes me as I go, asking, "Did you see any Abysso-hide items?"

"In the right corner on the Felid side," I reply. After emerging from the hall, I join Jake and Irena, who are standing in the center of the room.

"Did you find everything you were looking for?" Irena asks.

"Yes, thank you." I ask Jake, "What did you find?"

Jake smirks. "Oh, you're going to love this. Irena showed me this sword they've had for a long time. Take a look."

I set my items down so I can take the sword from Jake. It's a claymore by design, but much more exotic than anything I've seen in Armavir. There's a smooth-cut emerald in the center of the cross-guard, and a line of glyphs etched into the blade itself, running from the hilt to the point. I hand it back to him. "What a peculiar sword."

"It's one-of-a-kind," Jake says. "Its name is Menouthis. It was found in an Izendoran treasure vault, believed to have been looted from an Imperial Tethysian general. What's more, it's an *enchanted* sword that deals extra damage on monsters."

I raise an eyebrow, glancing at Irena. "Are you sure it works?"

Jake scratches his head. "Well, I still have to try it out."

"According to my brother," Irena says, "Menouthis has been here for many years. Not many people go on adventures to slay monsters anymore, so there's been no need for it."

"Hmm," I ponder Irena's words. Because the sword has been here for a long time, it *would* be tempting for a shop owner trying to get rid of it to fabricate stories of where it came from and what it can do. On the other hand, if Menouthis really *is* an enchanted monster-killing blade, it'll come in great handy when we face Jaedis and the hordes of Meiro.

The Great King says, *"Just as I kept your katana hidden for you to find at this time, so I have kept Menouthis hidden for Jake to find. It is a sword with a grand history and an even grander future. Jake must take this blade and use it to serve me, just as you'll use your katana to do the same."*

"*I understand.*" I say to Jake, "The sword does work as Irena said. The Great King would like for you to have it."

"Wizard!" Jake slides the sword into a scabbard he already wears on his back. It's a scabbard that only covers six inches up the point of the blade, and it has a holster for the cross-guard at the top. Jake only needs to pull it up six inches out of the scabbard before swinging it into action.

"Sir," Irena says, "If I'm not mistaken, you just mentioned the Great King. When Kamau and I lived in Murumbwé, our elders told us about him. We haven't heard about him since coming to Armavir, but you know him! Do all of you know him?"

Jake and I exchange glances, and we nod.

"How wonderful! I would love to hear more about the Great King sometime."

Just then, Khai, Yoko, and Kamau emerge the Pythoria-Ibadan hallway.

"I found one!" Yoko says, hefting a bow.

"Great! I can't wait to see it in action," Jake says.

"Did you get anything, Khai?" I ask.

"Stocked up on better arrows. That's all I need for now, though I would still like to visit a potion shop before leaving the city."

"Right," I nod.

Scourge comes with several Abysso-hide items: gloves, a vest, a belt, and boots. He also holds a small, curved Sunophsian blade.

Kamau asks, "Have you all found what you came for?"

"Yes," I reply, along with everyone else.

"Let me see the items, one by one," Kamau says, taking out a book and a pen.

Jake goes first, showing off Menouthis, the scabbard, an iron kite-shield featuring the Armaviran coat of arms, a long-sleeved chain-mail vest, an open burgonet helm, combat boots, and the items Connor requested.

Yoko is next, showing off her new bow, quiver, and arrows, along with Pythorian bison-leather gloves, vest, and boots.

Khai follows with his arrows, Scourge follows with his items, and I go last, showing my items and Connor's shield.

Meanwhile, Irena packs our items in large potato sacks for easier transport once we leave.

As Kamau records our purchases, he says, "Together you're buying more from this shop than all other customers have bought in a moon's time. What's the occasion? Are you going off to war?"

"Something like that," Jake replies.

"The other day," Kamau says to Jake, "you and your other friend were here asking about White Sand. Königheim was attacked, just as you thought it would be. Is it something to do with that?"

Khai steps in front of Kamau. "Why are you so interested in our business?"

"Khai," I say, pulling him back. "It's all right. Kamau and Irena are good people. But," I look at the two shop assistants, "we can't tell you everything. It's too dangerous. We know the shopkeeper is affiliated with White Sand, so it's better for you not to know what we're doing. We don't want to put you in harm's way."

"On that note," Jake adds, "Please don't tell Amaash who bought these items."

Kamau nods. "Of course. We will honor your request and help in every way we can."

Irena adds with a pleasant smile, "Yes! And may the Great King be with you always."

"Indeed," I agree.

"How much for everything?" Jake asks, pulling out our sack of money.

The Epic of Marindel: Chosen

"Hmm," Kamau takes a moment to think, glancing at the notes in his book. "Priced individually, these items are worth twenty thousand krons. But for you, I'll give a group discount. How about fifteen thousand krons?"

We exchange glances, nodding and shrugging, and then Jake says, "Not a bad deal. We'll take it."

As Jake and Kamau count fifteen thousand krons out of the bag, Irena comes to me and whispers, "Kamau's offer is very generous, because he knows you're noble adventurers with good hearts. Menouthis alone is worth thirty thousand krons, but he's letting you have it for *free!*"

I smile and nod at Irena. "Thank you so much for your help."

"All right," Jake says, taking the smaller pile of krons and putting it into a smaller sack, while Kamau fills the larger sack with the fifteen thousand. "We're good to go. Shall we return?"

"Right away," Khai agrees.

"Do you think I can practice with my bow when we get back?" Yoko asks.

"If we have time, we'll think of something," Khai replies.

As the others talk amongst themselves, I have a strong desire to stay at the shop. Irena showed interest in hearing more about the Great King, and I believe Kamau would enjoy hearing it as well. Knowing what we currently know about the Kingdom of Marindel, we'd be doing them a disservice if we didn't take the opportunity to tell them more. Prince Eli loved sharing about the Great King with anyone who'd listen. As followers of the Great King who are to follow his example, I don't see why we shouldn't do the same.

"Everyone," I say, "Why don't three of you take the gear back and wait for Connor to return? One of you can stay with me to tell Kamau and Irena about Marindel. What do you think?"

"I'll stay," Scourge offers.

"Don't tarry for long," Khai says with a nod.

Khai, Jake, and Yoko take our gear and leave the store. Once they do, with some help from Scourge, I share an abbreviated version of the Great Story with Kamau and Irena. Once we've finished, then and there, the shopkeeper's assistants declare their allegiance to the Great King and to Prince Eli. The feeling I get when it happens is like a refreshing spring rain. Scourge, also, seems jovial. I'm glad he's here to practice with me. It won't be this easy when we get around to telling Celine, or other White Sand insurgents, or far more dangerous individuals in the future.

"That future is nigh," the Great King says. *"You and Scourge must return to the poor sector immediately."*

With that, we say goodbye to our Murumbwéan friends and depart from the Exotic Goods Hub.

It's late in the afternoon, and a silent tension hangs over the city.

50
The Notes
Summer, 1419 AIE

~Celine~

WHEN I RETURNED to the hideout after fleeing from the Hall of Justice, it was completely empty. Not a single one of my brothers or fellow operatives were there to greet me, congratulate me on my escape, or share details of how they came up with that wonderfully elaborate plan to rescue me.

I mean, seriously! They blew up Königheim for *me*!

I had been hoping to let loose and celebrate with my brothers that evening, but since I was so exhausted, I didn't allow their absence to disappoint me. I went to my room and collapsed on the bed, falling asleep immediately.

The next day, I discovered that over thirty White Sand operatives had been critically injured or killed throughout the events of the previous day. To make matters worse, two of my brothers were among those killed. The bombing of Königheim was more costly to White Sand than anyone was willing to admit—and our failure to eliminate King Alphonse only added insult to injury.

But it's not over yet.

Shaama called a meeting in the central hub of the hideout. Over a hundred operatives were present, including Armavirans we've recruited since the Purge. She announced that the Felid mercenaries were able to coax Nebioth into revealing the location of our hideout. Now, the police are preparing a counter-offensive. We must be ready to meet them. The enemy has strength in numbers, so we must make every possible use of our home-turf advantage.

We've spent the last two days working hard to fortify and weaponize the hideout. With our stockpile of explosives finally cleared out, there's plenty of room to set up our defenses.

Because of my injuries, I haven't been able to help with heavy lifting or construction. But I *have* been able to set static illusions to hide all of the hideout's entrances. That'll throw the police off our scent and buy us more time to prepare.

I've just finished setting the final illusion, and now I'm on my way back to the central hub.

I round a corner to see Misham coming toward me. I smile and open my mouth to greet him, but before I say a word, he pulls me aside and pushes his lips against mine. For several seconds we kiss. My spirits soar, and my heart bursts with happiness! Afterward, he holds me close, focusing his dark, mysterious eyes on mine. My goodness, I love his eyes!

"Hi there," I say with a blush.

He smiles. "Is anyone coming down the hallway?"

"Hmm," I peer over his shoulder. A group of five operatives passes by, shouldering bundles of javelins and quivers of arrows. I watch them until they disappear around a corner. With a smile, I say, "All clear."

"Good." Misham draws near to kiss me again. I gladly lift my arms to wrap them around his shoulders, but he catches one of my hands and slips a folded paper into it. With his mouth against my ear, he whispers, "Take this note to your room, read it, and burn it."

"Ooh," I peck his cheek. "Did you write me a letter?"

"Something like that," Misham says, pulling out of our embrace and holding my shoulders. "I'm glad you made it back, Celine. Take care of yourself, all right? Things are getting weird around here."

"I will. You too, handsome." I give him a playful shove.

"Ow! Hey, careful," he says, stumbling and wincing. "I got an arrow in my thigh the other day. Still hurts like hell."

I chuckle. "Aww, are you going to cry about it?"

"Of course not!"

"You'd better not," I poke his nose. "Let me tell you about *my* injuries. I was whipped, pulled by my hair, punched in the face, and kicked with an iron-toed boot, just to name a few. I didn't cry once."

It's not a complete lie. I didn't cry because of the physical pain from those injuries, I cried because of the emotional pain. But Misham doesn't need to know that.

"Strong and beautiful, as always," Misham says, punching me in the shoulder.

After another embrace, we part ways. I return to my room with eager anticipation to read the letter Misham gave me. What could it be? Did he write it while I was imprisoned? Is it a list of his deepest romantic desires? I hardly *ever* get a glimpse of Misham's heart through his tough-guy exterior. I can't wait to read it!

I close and lock the door behind me, recline face-up on the bed, and unfold the note. I read it aloud.

"Dearest Shaama—"

I immediately frown. This letter isn't addressed to me! And this handwriting is far too neat to be Misham's. What was he thinking, stealing a letter from Auntie and passing it off to me? Despite the disappointment, my curiosity piques. Who would send Auntie a letter? Who even *knows* she resides deep beneath Cloud Summit? I continue reading.

"Even from the northernmost reaches of the realm, I've heard of your reputation and that of your insidious criminal organization. It pleases me to know you have a strong presence in Cloud Summit and an insatiable thirst to eradicate the outdated order of the kingdom of Armavir. As a fellow magician enamored with the Bygone arts of the Great Serpent, I would like to ask a favor of you. Six adventurers who pledge allegiance to the Great King are currently staying in the city. I would like you to slaughter them by any means necessary. My servant Typhon, with whom this letter was sent, will explain everything in further detail. If you do this one simple thing for me, I will ensure the victory and everlasting prosperity of White Sand. I will bestow upon you, great Shaama, liberal portions of my knowledge, riches, and legacy. I look forward to hearing of your success.

"Warm regards,

"Jaedis, the Sorcerer of the Northern Bluffs."

I blink, reading the name again. Where have I heard that before?

I flip the paper over to see another note. This handwriting is *much* harder to make out. Definitely Misham's.

"I've been eavesdropping on Auntie and this Typhon guy for a few days. They're old friends from Sunophsis. After the Königheim bombing, he convinced her to kill you. I don't know why. You'll hate me for this, but please stay in your room until the police raid is over. Use illusions to stay hidden if you have to. Auntie has a monster called the Glimmerbeast, which I think she'll use against the Great

King followers—whoever they are. I'll find out more and keep you updated. Watch your back."

"Love, Misham."

I read Misham's note one more time.

Auntie wants to kill *me*?

Why? Have I done something wrong?

And now I have to hide in my room?

But...I can't! There's so much left to do! The police are coming, and we have to be ready! I *need* to help in order to prove my worth and loyalty to White Sand.

I pause, and then I laugh. There's *no way* Auntie is going to kill me. I'm one of her best operatives, and I'm the only person in Cloud Summit she can trust. She said it herself. Misham must be playing games with me.

Aha, that's it! He's just trying to keep me safe during the police raid. He almost lost me at the execution, and he can't bear the thought of losing me again. He'll come after the attack and tell me it was all a ruse. Oh, Misham. He thinks he's *so* clever. I chuckle once more and breathe a sigh of relief. Everything is going to be all right.

"*Let me tell you a little something,*" the death-voice says. "*You'll never be good enough. Not for Misham, not for Shaama, not for anyone. Your mistake was fatal. It's only a matter of time before they'll kill you.*"

"*Do you ever shut up?*" I ask. "*You keep saying I'm going to die, but you're always wrong. You're just trying to scare me.*"

"*I don't need to scare you. You're terrified, and you know it.*"

"*You don't know me!*"

"*Yes, I do. You belong to me.*"

"Shut up!" I shout, jumping off my bed and hurling a pillow at the wall. The sudden motion causes my wounds to stab me with pain, and I grimace.

The death-voice laughs. "*You are terrified, and rightfully so. Those you trust will betray you, and then you will die.*"

"I'll prove you wrong," I say, kicking the pillow I just threw.

The death-voice doesn't answer. My mind is quiet once again.

"I'm not afraid," I say to myself. "I'm confident. I'm strong and beautiful, just like Misham said."

There's a knock on my door.

I frown. I hope whoever that is didn't hear me screaming and talking to myself like a weirdo. "Coming," I say, putting my pillow back on the bed and approaching the door to open it.

When I do, I see nothing more than the dimly-lit hall connecting my room with several others in the hideout. There's no one there.

"That's odd," I mutter, looking this way and that before shutting the door again.

I go back and sit on the bed, when suddenly a movement on the ceiling catches my attention. A terrifying creature materializes into being, crawling like a lizard or a bat on the ceiling, making its way to the wall nearest me.

Screaming, I roll backward and behind the bed while grabbing a shoe in preparation to throw it. "What the hell!? Get out of my room!"

The creature crawls along, unfazed by my shouting. I realize it's a gargoyle, and there's a folded paper strapped to its back. Has Misham sent another note? I've heard about enchanted gargoyles being used to send secret messages, but I've never seen one for myself. Nevertheless, my fear diminishes as it scuttles down the wall. I ask, "What do you want?"

The gargoyle stops at my eye-level, pulls the note off its back, and holds it out for me.

I hesitate at first, but when it glares and shakes the note, I sigh and take it. After unfolding it, I read aloud: "Greetings, Celine. I would like to talk with you about Jed. Meet me at La Belle Rose this evening at sunset. Please, tell no one. See you soon."

I read the note again silently, my heart burning with I-don't-even-know-what. This isn't Misham's handwriting. I glare at the gargoyle. "Who sent you?"

The gargoyle makes rings with its index fingers and thumbs and places the rings over its eyes.

I stare incredulously at it. "Someone with glasses?"

The gargoyle shakes its head, still pretending to wear glasses.

"A raccoon."

The gargoyle points two fingers at its own eyes before pointing them both at me.

"You can see me?"

The gargoyle shakes is head, and then does it again.

"The person can see me?" I narrow my eyes. "They sent you to spy on me, didn't they?"

The gargoyle throws its arms up in frustration before jumping on my shoulder and taking the note from me. Before I can scream, it jumps from my shoulder onto the bed, and then it scratches something on the paper with its claw. After a few seconds, it holds up the note for me to read. Torn across the length of the note is the word "SEER."

A Seer?

The I-don't-even-know-what feeling returns, mixed with a heaping dose of anxiety. I've only ever known of two Seers in my life. One is dead, and the other...well...

The gargoyle stuffs the note into my hand, apparently too impatient to watch me think, and performs a triple-jump from my bed onto the wall nearest the door. Then it looks at me as if asking to be let out.

I walk over to the door, opening it just enough for the gargoyle to crawl out the same way it probably entered, and then I close it again.

I sit on my bed and pout.

Why La Belle Rose? What is he trying to pull?

It doesn't matter if it's my favorite restaurant when it comes to both flavor and class. I don't even know this guy, and he's just about forcing me to go out with him. To talk about Jed, I guess. Which is... could be...*mildly* important.

I look at a small desk clock on a nightstand next to the mirror. It's almost three in the afternoon.

I sigh, laying back and staring up at the ceiling.

To go, or not to go? Let's see, what are my options?

I can stay in my room for the rest of the day like Misham told me to, thinking in circles about boring stuff until I fall asleep.

Or, I can go to La Belle Rose to meet this weird guy, endure his weirdness for an hour or so while eating delicious food I'll force him to pay for, and I'll get a nice walk in for the day.

I like that idea better already.

I'll have to be sneaky if I decide to go aboveground, though. I run the risk of being arrested again, and White Sand *definitely* won't be happy about that.

But...Misham doesn't *really* expect me to stay here and do nothing, does he? I appreciate his concern, but I did enough sitting around in the Hall of Justice. Besides, I'll be out of harm's way if I'm *not* in the hideout when the police raid happens.

All right then, it's settled. I'm going! But I'll have to be smart about it.

I open my wardrobe and browse through my many outfits. After some thought, I settle on a royal-blue ankle-length summer dress. It's comfortable, classy, and long enough to hide the bruises and scrapes on my legs. I can pair it with a wide-brimmed hat, under which I'll hide my hair, and a black shawl to cover the bruises and scrapes on my shoulders.

Speaking of bruises and scrapes, I'm going to need several coats of makeup! That's all right; I have yet to try the eyeliner I stole a couple weeks ago.

I spend the next two hours making myself look gorgeous. I can't help but include some lovely silver bracelets, sapphire earrings to match the dress, apple-red lipstick, a generous dose of perfume, and silver heels.

Hmm...on second thought, nope, not gonna do the heels. If I need to run, I'm going to need to *run*. I choose a pair of silver flats instead.

Finally, I'm ready to go! I can't wait to get out of this boring room, see the city, and eat some free food! I'd die for a glass of wine, now that I think about it!

Just then, I notice the Seer's note and Misham's note lying on the bed. Whether I'm in any kind of danger or not, one thing's for certain: I can't let anyone see those! I take both and crumple them together. Then I pull a match out of the matchbox in my nightstand, strike it, and light the paper on fire. I set it on the stone ground to burn, and I go to retrieve a boot from my wardrobe. Once the paper ball has been blackened, I stamp out the fire with the boot. Lastly, I take a broom and sweep the ashes under the bed. There! All gone! The room smells like smoke, but it can always be attributed to the snuffing of a candle.

After a final room check, I depart, taking a circuitous route to exit the hideout. I round a corner, just about to make it, when unfortunately, I come face to face with Abdeel. He's stunned for a moment, looking me up and down. "Hey, sis. What's with the getup?"

"I'm bored," I say with a shrug. "Gonna go get some air."

He rolls his eyes. "If you get caught again, we're not rescuing you. You know that, right?"

I roll my eyes back at him. "I'm not gonna get caught. Just don't tell anyone you saw me, okay?"

"Why shouldn't I?"

"I'll be back in a couple hours; no one'll miss me." I smile and ask in a mildly seductive manner, "Would you like me to bring you dinner?"

Abdeel's face brightens. He tries to hide how happy he is by acting tough, but it's no use. "Hmm...Meat. Lots of meat, and a beer."

"I'll bring you meat if you keep this a secret. Don't tell anyone, or you'll have to share with them. Got it?"

Abdeel sighs. "Whatever. Just don't be gone for long, or Auntie will have a fit."

"I won't," I say, walking past him. "See ya."

"Hey, don't forget my beer!" he shouts as I walk away.

51
Dining with a Seer
Summer, 1419 AIE

~Celine~

I ARRIVE AT LA Belle Rose just as the sun is about to set. It's a beautiful two-story restaurant on a street corner just a block away from the main street. My favorite part of the building's exterior is an oval stained-glass window on the rounded corner of the building, just above the entrance, featuring two red roses with their stems crossed over one another. On the ground level there's a garden-patio seating area underneath a few awnings, and there at the door stands a waiter outfitted with a formal black suit and white cravat.

With a confident stride, I walk through the patio to address waiter. "Good evening, sir."

"Bonsoir," the waiter greets with a smile. "Your name is Celine, if I'm not mistaken?"

I tense. My instinct is to deny it and give a false name instead, but I think better of it. I smile and reply, "Yes, it is. How'd you guess?"

"Your friend told me you'd be wearing a blue dress tonight. He's inside now, saving a table for you."

"Oh, lovely!" I smile to hide how monumentally creeped out I am.

The waiter opens the door and gestures for me to enter. "This way, Mademoiselle, and one of our staff will show you to him."

"Thank you, sir." I walk into the restaurant, where I'm greeted by a waitress and asked to follow her to my seat. Meanwhile I focus on deep breathing and self-talk to quell my rising anxiety. "*It's not a big deal. It's just a casual talk over dinner with a really weird guy. It'll be over before you know it. Smile and nod, make eye contact, be polite, and for goodness' sake, don't do anything awkward...or violent.*"

We ascend the stairs to the second floor, where the upscale seating is located. This room is illuminated by an exquisite chandelier, and on a stage in one corner, a pianist and string quartet play ambient music.

The Seer—I forgot his name, but I recognize him—sits at a two-person table in front of the stained-glass window. When I see him there, my anxiety wells up all the more. How does he know I like that window so much!?

As I approach, he stands to greet me. I'm stunned to see he legitimately dressed up for this. He wears a simple black suit and trousers with a white cravat, his hair neatly brushed, and his face clean-shaven. "Good evening, Celine. I'm glad to see you got my message."

I smile in spite of my fear and shake his hand. "Yes, I did. How kind of you to invite me to dinner."

Once we're both seated, the waitress asks, "Can I get you anything to drink?

I say immediately, "Yes, I'll have an Ibadanian cabernet, please."

I chose it because it's expensive, and I want Seer-Mc-Weirdo to pay for it.

"Of course," the waitress says, writing down my order. "And for you, sir?"

"I'll have that too."

"Great, I'll be back in a moment."

Once the waitress is out of earshot, I look at the Seer and ask, "So, what's the deal?"

He tilts his head. "What do you mean?"

"Why are we here?"

"To talk about Jed."

"Sure, but...why here? Why like...*this*?" I gesture at his formal getup.

"I wanted to meet you on your own turf, where you'd be comfortable. This is your favorite restaurant, isn't it?"

Despite how much I'd like to say no, I can't bring myself to do it. I *really* hate Seers! They know everything! I simply nod.

"Oh, I uh," the Seer straightens his posture and clears his throat, "I forgot to introduce myself. My name's Connor."

"Nice to meet you," I say with a smile. I refrain from adding, *"You know my name already, along with many other strange things."*

The waitress returns with our glasses of wine and a basket of bread rolls. Then she asks, "Are you ready to order?"

"I am," I say. "I'll have the lamb stew."

Lamb dishes are among the most expensive items on the menu; I chose it on purpose. I study Connor's face to see how he'll react.

He glances briefly at the menu, and then says, "Make that two."

Very interesting.

"All right, I'll get that started for you," the waitress says, taking our menus as she goes.

Connor asks, "How are you doing?"

"Quite well. You?" He can't seriously believe I'm going tell him how I *really* feel about this!

"It's been a crazy day," he says with a chuckle before sipping his wine. He looks at the glass and says, "Hm, not bad. Vibrant spice profile and a hint of elderflower. Good choice."

"You like to drink?"

"Every now and then. I enjoy visiting taverns to meet and talk to people, and recently I've come to enjoy trying different kinds of drinks while I'm at it."

"That's neat." This Seer seems to be quite sociable; it may be the first thing we have in common. Interesting, but not any less weird.

"What about you?"

"I don't drink much, except for wine. Like you, I prefer it while talking with people."

He becomes excited when I mention common ground between us. "Have you visited the Bullfrog Tavern? There are all kinds of interesting people to meet there. I enjoy it every time I go."

I shake my head. "The tavern's not my style. I prefer outdoor markets, and upscale places like this. Wherever all the important people are."

"I should have guessed," he says, taking another sip of wine. "I first met Jed in a tavern by my homestead in western Armavir."

"Really?" I ask, only mildly interested.

"Yup. I was a boy then, so I didn't think anything of it. But I saw him there again a few weeks ago, and...well, that's when my life changed forever."

"How so? Did he teach you to be a Seer?"

"A little bit. I was a Seer all along, but he was the first to call it out. He gave me a few guidelines, but I mostly had to figure it out on my own. He was always so vague and mysterious."

"Tell me about it," I chuckle, remembering how difficult it was for me to interrogate him.

"Did you know him very well?" Connor asks before biting into a bread roll.

"No. I..." I pause. I don't want to *tell* him about my experience with Jed, I want to test him. I raise an eyebrow and ask, "Why don't you tell me what you already know?"

"Oh, sure," Connor looks away briefly before continuing. "You mugged him. He saw you get arrested, and he died trying to protect you from Bennett during the execution."

"Anything else?"

"Nope."

"You missed a bunch." I tell him how Jed saved me from Bennett the first time, allowing for me to be arrested instead of killed on the spot. Then I tell him about my mother's lullaby that Jed knew about. On a whim, I tell him about the ghost-lady and what she said about a faithful man rescuing me from Armavir. Lastly, I tell him what Jed said and did on the execution stage up until his death.

Connor listens intently, his face gradually changing from easygoing whatever to awe-stricken disbelief. After I'm finished, he blinks and asks, "Celine, are you serious?"

I nod. "Yeah, why?"

"You don't see it yet!?" He plasters his hands against his forehead.

I furrow my brow. "What don't I see yet?"

"How much the Great King loves you!"

I try very hard not to snort with laughter. I cough it off and fan my face with one hand. "Excuse me, what?"

"Celine," Connor leans in close. "The Great King loves you. That's what Jed was trying to tell you, but you didn't believe him. He gave his life to save you from the death you deserved, so you could come to understand the King's love."

"Hey," I hold up one hand, "I'm just as confused about Jed's death as you are, but it can't have been because some weird king loves me. I mean, come on! *No one* loves me like that, and I'm okay with it."

"Jed loved you."

I pause, thinking again about Jed's caring, fearless gaze. "I know. Well, I *know*, but I don't know *how* or *why*. I certainly wasn't ever nice to him."

"That's what I've come to tell you. I'm sure you're wondering how I know so much about you: your favorite restaurant, the color of your dress, and how much you like this stained-glass window. There's no way I would've known any of those details if it weren't for the Great King. A Seer only knows what the Great King reveals to him."

Connor goes on to explain how Jed saw my wanted poster and drew my face perfectly on the back of it the night before I mugged him.

I think he's bluffing. "Do you have the poster?"

"As a matter of fact, I do." Connor pulls the poster out of his bag, unfurling it and laying it on the table with the sketch facing up.

My eyes widen. That *is* me! "I-I don't believe it, not for one second. You drew this, didn't you?"

Connor flips over the poster and says, "This is an older poster, one that was up before you were accused of murder. See?"

Sure enough, it's the same version of the poster Nebioth showed me after I returned from the bank robbery. Shortly after that, I suppose all of these were taken down and replaced with the updated version. Jed would have had to find this and draw my face on it before I encountered him on that fateful afternoon.

I glare at Connor. "What do you want from me?"

He's about to speak, but something behind me catches his attention.

I follow his gaze to see the waitress coming with our food. "Here're the lamb stews."

"Thank you," I say, taking my bowl and beginning to devour it by the spoonful. It's delicious! I haven't eaten food of this quality since before I was arrested!

Connor doesn't seem fazed by my incredible appetite. Once the waitress leaves, he goes on to say, "I have a quick story for you. It's about a woman not much different from you. She did many bad things, but still, someone loved her and gave his life for her."

"I'm listening," I say between mouthfuls of stew.

At first, I'm only half-listening. I'm far more interested in my food than I am in the elven sea turtle kingdom, which apparently is where the Great King is from.

I start paying more attention when he talks about the Great Serpent. I remember the nightmare I had a few nights ago, with the giant sea serpent towering over my tiny ship in a violent storm, declaring I deserved to die.

I remember the death-voice.

I bite my lip, suddenly losing my appetite, and I stare blankly at Connor's cravat while listening to the rest of the story.

Hearing of the Serpent's manipulation of Melody into betraying and killing Eli makes me sick to my stomach.

And then...Eli wins?

And defeats the Serpent?

And *still* loves Melody?

But...how?

After finishing, Connor tilts his head and asks, "Are you feeling all right?"

I shake my head. His story was nice, but I don't think he understands how real and terrifying my personal darkness is. But the slight chance he *might* know how to deal with it causes me to blurt, "Connor, there's a voice in my head. I hear it almost every day. It tells me how worthless I am, and that I deserve to die."

"That's the Great Serpent. You don't have to—"

"If your story is true," I challenge, "and Eli came back to life to defeat the Serpent, then why is it still talking to me?"

"Because you haven't decided to follow the Great King. The spirit of the Serpent is still at large, and he's as much of a trouble-maker as he's always been. Eli's victory allows for followers of the Great King to resist and overcome him. However, those who don't follow the Great King have no authority to resist. Remember what happened when Melody challenged the Serpent at Point Nex? She didn't stand a chance. If you want to be free from the voice in your head, you have to declare allegiance to the Great King. And why wouldn't you want to? He's the greatest and wisest King of all, who protects all who come to him!"

I shake my head with scorn. "Do you have any idea how crazy you sound right now?"

Connor shrugs. "I think I have an idea, yes."

I roll my eyes. "All right, well, let's say I believe you. What next? What *exactly* do you want from me?"

"Well..." Connor trails off, reaching up to scratch the back of his head. "Jed had this crazy idea that you were supposed to come with me and my friends to defeat a sorcerer, Jaedis of the Northern Bluffs. He's after Melody, who's still alive. It's my duty as a Seer to help her understand the Great King's love for her, much like I'm doing with you now."

Jaedis. He's the sorcerer who wrote the note to Shaama. I narrow my eyes. "You want me to help you fight a *sorcerer?*"

"That's not quite the end goal of this conversation, but...yes, that'd be great."

"Not interested."

"Really?"

"Nope."

"Why not?"

"Well," I laugh at how naive he is for continuing to press this on me, "Even if we grant that I believe you, why should I leave my home city to go who-knows-where and fight a sorcerer I have no business fighting? What's in it for me? I'm doing well enough in Cloud Summit. There's no reason to leave."

"Really?"

"Yes," I nod. "I have a good life here."

"Uh huh," Connor nods slowly.

I shift my posture. "Sure, it's risky and dangerous, but I like it that way. It keeps things interesting."

Connor raises an eyebrow.

"My brothers take good care of me. They're hard on me sometimes, but I like it because it challenges me to improve my skills. Overall, they're very supportive."

"If that's the case, where were your brothers when you got arrested?"

I immediately see where he's going with this. Nevertheless, I reply, "Misham and Abdeel were there, but when the police came, they fled without me."

"Where were your brothers when you were in the Hall of Justice?"

"Plotting to rescue me," I say with a proud smirk. "They would have done it, I'm sure, if those other kids didn't show up first."

"Are you sure?"

A dreadful feeling springs up in my heart. *Am* I sure about it? I always assumed they would rescue me, but now I remember what Abdeel said earlier today: "If you get caught again, we're not rescuing you. You know that, right?" Sure, there's merit in refusing to rescue me if I get in trouble for the second time. The real the question is, did they share that sentiment the first time as well?

"Let me tell you something," Connor says. "On the night Yoko and Scourge tried to rescue you, there were five White Sand archers waiting in ambush outside the Hall of Justice. They were there to help you escape by picking off any policemen who chased you outside the Hall."

Chapter 51: Dining with a Seer

"See? I told you," I fold my arms. "If those Felids hadn't gotten in our way, we would've made it."

Connor nods. "That might be true. Now, I know you won't take my word for it, but I have to warn you. The Königheim bombing wasn't as successful as White Sand hoped it would be. Since then, for reasons I can't discern, they've been convinced that you're a liability. A weak link. Now, they're seeking to kill you."

"What?" His response flusters me. "How could you suggest such a thing? White Sand operatives *never* turn on each other. It's against our code of loyalty!"

"I'm afraid there's a greater ambition in the heart of your leader that supersedes loyalty to any one person. Celine, I'm telling you as a friend. Don't go back to the hideout tonight."

Misham's note about Shaama wanting to kill me crosses my mind, but I shove it aside and cross my arms. "Why shouldn't I?"

"Trust me. If you go back there, you may never come out."

"Pfft!" I laugh. "What are you talking about? The police raid? We're *so* ready for them. In fact, I *want* to be there when it happens." I look both ways to make sure no one's listening, and then I whisper, "I want to see Chief Bennett die a gruesome, agonizing, and very well-deserved death."

Connor sighs. "I understand, Celine. I really do. I can't tell you what to do, but please, don't forget anything I've shared with you tonight."

"How can I? I'll be laughing all night thinking about it." I stand up.

"Leaving so soon?"

"I've been out long enough. My brothers will begin to wonder where I've gone." I turn to leave, but a second thought causes me to pause. I look at Connor and say, "I like you as a person more than I thought I would, so I won't torture you with an illusion for all the crazy things you've said. Consider yourself lucky."

Connor smiles. "I appreciate it."

I smile and wave. "You've got the bill, right?"

52

Into the Underworld

Summer, 1419 AIE

~Tarento~

IT'S TEN O'CLOCK at night when Connor returns. By now, the rest of us are ready and eagerly waiting with our gear. Upon his arrival, Yoko points out his formal attire. "Connor! You're a fancy, rich man!"

Connor sighs, pulling off his cravat and tossing it aside. "Apparently, not fancy enough."

"Did you find Celine?" Jake asks. "Did you talk to her?"

"Yup. I told her the Great Story and everything, but she didn't get it. She's gone back to the hideout."

"Stubborn girl," Khai grumbles.

"What now, then?" I ask. "We only have two hours before the guillotine falls on the White Sand hideout."

"That's not what I'm afraid of," Connor says. "I have a feeling White Sand is planning to kill her before then."

"Blimey," Jake frowns. "What should we do?"

"Hope for the best, get there as fast as we can, and get her out of there."

I nod. "If the Great King wants her to come with us, he'll protect her long enough for us to rescue her."

"Agreed," Connor says. He looks at Jake and asks, "Did you find my gear?"

"Sure did," Jake points at Connor's room. "Everything's in there."

"Great. I'm gonna go suit up." Connor disappears into the room.

Khai stands. "Everyone, grab your weapons. When Connor's ready, we need to move."

"Wait," Yoko says, "Do we even know where we're going?"

That's a great question. I have no idea. A quick glance at everyone else tells me they don't know, either.

Connor's voice comes from within the room, "Sorry, I forgot to ask her about that!"

"We'd better figure it out quick," Khai says.

"Let's ask the Great King," I say. "All of us, together."

"Together!" Yoko says.

Jake looks at me and nods.

Scourge also looks at me, his eyes glimmering with admiration.

"Very well," Khai says. "Connor, can you hear?"

"Yup!"

"All right," I close my eyes and take a deep breath. "Great King, you've asked us to rescue your beloved daughter Celine, but we don't know where to go. Time is short; please help us. Show us where to find the hideout."

We're silent for a few moments. I hardly notice as Connor slips back in, fully equipped with his gear, and sits on a chair nearby.

Soon, the King says, *White Sand expects an attack, and the hideout is heavily fortified. There are several ways to enter, but the safest is through the Exotic Goods Hub.*

"Intriguing."

"I heard something!" Yoko says. "Jake, you need to go tell Prince Oliver about the attack."

Jake almost falls out of his chair. "W-what?"

"I had that sense too," Connor says. "Bennett planned his move without consulting the prince or the king. We'll need Paladin assistance, and Jake, you're the only one who knows how to talk them into helping us."

"Well, um..." Jake shifts uncomfortably. "They don't like me, remember?"

"The Great King will be with you," Connor assures him. "Obey him, and see what he can do. If you don't, we'll all be killed in the hideout. You know, no big deal."

"Right," Jake says with a frown.

"You've got this, Jake," I say. "We believe in you. There's a reason the Great King chose you for this task."

Jake swallows and nods. "All right. I'll do my best."

"Good." I tell the others verbatim what the Great King told me.

"That's what I heard too," Scourge says. "Exotic Goods Hub."

"Great," I look at the others. "Anything else?"

Everyone shakes their head.

"All right," Khai shoulders his bow. "Let's move."

"Let's move," I echo. "Single-file. I'll lead; Khai, take the rear."

With somber urgency, we maneuver through late-night Cloud Summit, dimly lit by the lamps lining the streets. On an average night, hardly anyone is out at this hour. Tonight especially, the streets seem abandoned. The atmosphere is heavy with tension.

A storm is about to break.

We arrive at the Exotic Goods Hub. There we part ways with Jake, who continues on to the Paladin Training Academy. He believes Prince Oliver might be staying there due to the destruction of Königheim.

Connor tests the doorknob of the shop. "It's locked."

"Not for long. Stand back, everyone." I wield my katana, and with a well-aimed upward slash I strike through all three of the door hinges, causing the loose slab of wood to fall on the ground. I step over it, beckoning for the others to follow, and enter the shop.

The inside is dark. The stones that illuminated the shop before are not currently glowing.

"Scourge," I say over my shoulder.

He forms a condensed fireball in his palm to light our path.

I look around. How are we going to find an entrance to the hideout in a place like this?

"There," Connor says, pointing at a hallway blocked off with planks of wood. "That hallway's bound to be hiding something."

"Scourge," I say again.

He splits his fireball in two and hurls one at the wooden barricade. Within seconds, the dry wood is engulfed in flames.

"Get low," Khai says. "That smoke'll choke us out if we're not careful."

We all crouch to avoid breathing in the smoke. After a moment, I see the wood has burned enough to be easily broken through. "All right Scourge, put it out."

Scourge waves his hand over the fire, absorbing it back into his palm.

I hold my breath, stand up, and step forward in a stance. Then I cut twice through the half-burnt barricade: once on the left, and once on the right. The planks fall to the ground.

One by one, we walk, half-crouching, into the hallway. I allow

Scourge to take the lead since he has our light. We emerge into a room identical to the other item rooms, except this one is empty.

"Spread out," I say. "Look for any strange tiles or bricks. Anything suspicious."

We spend a moment searching the room. I wiggle the empty shelves mounted on the wall, hoping they'll give way and reveal a clue, but nothing happens.

"Connor," Khai says, "Any hints?"

"Not yet," he replies, crouched to inspect the bricks making up the floor. "Everything seems normal about this room so far."

"Hmm," I stop to think. We were all so sure it'd be in this room, but we could be wrong. Perhaps we should go back and search the other rooms for clues.

I'm about to make that suggestion when the Great King stops me. *"Do you remember the ball you had in the hotel room a few days ago?"*

"Yes...why?"

"Take it out and throw it against the walls."

I furrow my brow. What an odd suggestion. Nevertheless, I take the ball out of my pocket and begin bouncing it on the walls.

It doesn't take long for the others to notice how weird I've become.

"Ooh, a ball!" Yoko says. "Can I play?"

"If you can catch it," I say, throwing it harder so it bounces across the room.

"I got it!" Yoko shouts, giving chase.

"Tarento," Khai says, "what are you doing?"

"Obeying the Great King."

"Ah." Khai shrugs. "Carry on, then."

"Tarento!" Yoko calls. I look to see her pointing at the wall. "The ball disappeared!"

"Huh?" I walk over. "What do you mean?"

Scourge brings his light closer and asks, "You're not hiding it, are you?"

"Nope. It bounced this way, and then, poof! It disappeared!"

"Hm," I look at the wall. It doesn't take me long to notice something strange about that particular spot. My eyes narrow. "Scourge, back up a little. Yoko, scoot an inch to the left."

When they move, my intuition is proved correct. Yoko's shadow cast by Scourge's fire stretches across the ground, but ends abruptly at the corner where it meets the wall.

"Look," I say, pointing at the shadow. "Yoko's shadow should be cast upon on the wall as well as the floor, but it's not. And that means..."

Connor's eyes widen. "The wall is an illusion!"

"Very clever," Khai says.

"Well, not clever enough for us!" Yoko says, walking toward the wall and disappearing into it. We hear her voice a second later, "Come on, guys! It's a secret tunnel!"

Scourge goes first. The illusion doesn't put his light out, so we can still see as if the wall weren't there. We follow single-file, and sure enough, there's a tunnel stretching out before us, sloping down and ending in pitch blackness.

"I found the ball," Yoko says, bringing it back to me.

"Thank you," I say, taking it and putting it back in my pocket. "I never thought something as simple as a ball would help us on a quest, but I suppose there's a first time for everything."

Onward we go, down the lengthy tunnel. Soon we reach the end, where there's a well-like opening in the ground with a rope ladder suspended from the ceiling above it.

"Scourge," I say, looking at him. "Whatever you do, don't burn the ladder."

"Got it. I'll have to put the fire out when it's my turn to climb down."

"I'll go first," Khai says, taking off his quiver. "Scourge, you can ride on my back. Hold the flame away from the ladder."

"Good idea," Connor says.

"Here, I'll hold your things," I say, taking Khai's bow and quiver and slinging them onto my back.

Khai crouches down so Scourge can easily wrap one arm around his shoulders and secure his legs around his waist. Scourge holds his other hand with the fireball out behind him. Then Khai stands, approaches the well, and grabs the ladder.

"This is really sketchy," Scourge says.

"Get used to it, kid," Khai says as he begins his descent. "This whole operation is sketchy."

Khai's got a point. Forget the rope ladder and the deep pit it leads into; we're breaking into the fortified hideout of a sinister criminal organization. What's more, not long from now, the hideout will be invaded by a police force that happens not to be entirely friendly. I've been on numerous missions as a Samurai in Felidae, but this might be the riskiest mission of them all. Not even my trip to Kharduman compares with this.

534

Chapter 52: Into the Underworld

Our surroundings darken as Scourge's light goes farther and farther down the well.

Yoko stands at the edge and looks down. "Wow, it's really far!"

Connor says, "Their hideout must be deep underground if it's gone undetected for so long."

After a while we hear Khai shout from below, "We're down! Who's next?"

"I'll go," Yoko says, jumping on the ladder and scurrying down at twice the speed Khai had gone.

Connor goes next, his scabbard strapped to his belt and shield slung over his back.

I'm last, with my katana sheath fastened to my belt and Khai's weapons slung over my back. The ladder leads me down the narrow well, and then into a very spacious underground room. By Scourge's light, I see it's paved on the walls, ceiling, and floor with very old bricks, chipped and worn with age. The room is mostly featureless, except for a broad staircase on the far side leading up to an open entryway flanked by six knight statues, all of which are broken in some way or another.

"What is this place?" I ask as I alight on the ground. "White Sand didn't build it, did they?"

"No," Connor says. "These are the catacombs of ancient Armadeaux, built before the Imperial Era."

"Impressive," Scourge says, looking around in awe.

I'm not one to appreciate architecture, but I can't fathom the amount of work it must have taken to build something like this underground, especially so long ago. Nevertheless, I'm aware we have no time to admire our surroundings. I return Khai's weapons and say, "Come on, everyone. Let's keep going."

We walk to the staircase and ascend toward the entryway.

"I've heard stories," Connor says, "of adventurers walking through a room just like this, when all of a sudden, the statues come to life and attack!"

Yoko gasps, glancing at the imposing statues we're currently walking between.

"Connor," Khai says, "Unless that's your Seer's gift at work, please keep those thoughts to yourself. We need to focus."

"Sorry," Connor replies, scratching his head. "I just got excited."

"We have much more disturbing things to worry about than statues," I say as we pass through the entryway.

We walk through a broad hall with no features of interest except for the steadily-growing sound of rushing water up ahead. When we clear the hall, we find ourselves in another room on what appears to be a stone balcony. Twenty feet below, a strong current races along the bottom of a rocky chasm. The other side of the chasm is that same distance away, where an entryway into the next hall is visible. The remains of a stone bridge on both sides indicate that what once was our ticket across is no longer viable.

"Now what?" Scourge asks, peering down at the rapids.

Yoko picks up a stone and throws it into the chasm. After it disappears in the torrent, she says, "Well, there's no invisible bridge."

We spend a moment studying our surroundings and thinking of solutions.

"Khai," Connor says, pointing up at the ceiling, "Do you see that?"

We all look up. On a certain brick, partially covered by old roots and cobwebs, is a small hole with a painted blue rim. It seems out of place, as if it was built more recently than the rest of the catacombs.

"I sure do," Khai says with a smirk. He strings his bow, aiming carefully at the strange hole, and fires. The arrow hits its mark.

The ground trembles, and from both sides of the chasm, thick stone slabs extend outward to meet in the middle, creating a bridge.

"Good eye, Connor," I say with a pat on the back.

"I heard about that kind of switch in a story once. It's a Sunophsian thing. White Sand must have put it there."

As we begin crossing the bridge, Scourge asks, "Connor, didn't you say Sunophsians were the ones who started rigging their dungeons and tombs with traps?"

"Hmm," Connor strokes his chin. "I think it was Jake who mentioned it, but you have a good point. In the last few centuries, Sunophsian dungeons have become notorious for their use of traps."

My stomach plummets. "I bet that's one way White Sand fortified the hideout."

Connor winces. "I wouldn't put it past them. We'd better be careful."

"Stay close," Khai says, bringing Yoko near to walk by his side. "Don't touch anything suspicious."

We exit the room with the chasm, next entering another hallway. We turn left, walk straight for a moment, turn left again, descend a flight of steps, and then turn right.

From there, we emerge into a much larger hall: broad, high, and long. It's lined with dozens of columns and stone coffins on either side. The entryway on the far side is so distant, it's hardly visible by Scourge's firelight.

"*Stop!*" The Great King says.

I skid to a halt and put my arms out to block the others from advancing.

"What is it?" Khai asks. "You see something?"

"I heard something," I whisper. "The Great King told me to stop."

"*This hallway is heavily weaponized. You alone must pass through first to deactivate the traps.*"

My blood runs cold. "*You know I'm not invincible, right?*"

"Tarento?" Connor says. "You look like you've seen a ghost."

"*Trust me,*" the King says. "*You know what to do. Step forth.*"

I swallow my fear and say to the others, "I'm going first. Wait here."

"Hold on," Khai says. "There might be traps. Let's think this through."

"I know. The Great King asked me to go first, so that's what I'm going to do. I'll be fine...hopefully."

"Be careful," Scourge says.

"I will." I look forward, close my eyes, and begin advancing down the hallway.

"*Focus,*" the Great King's soothing voice calms my racing heart. "*Breathe deeply. Clear your mind. Focus. Focus. Focus.*"

I breathe.

Something shifts beneath my foot.

"*Duck and roll.*"

Opening my eyes, I get down and roll with lightning speed. I feel the wind of the arrows as they cut through the air above me.

From there, all is chaos. Listening to the commands of the King, I obey every prompt he gives me.

"*Jump up, dodge left.*"

I avoid an enormous brick falling from the ceiling.

"*Draw your katana and block right.*"

I deflect several arrows fired from the wall.

"*Run forward, duck and roll, then jump high.*"

I dodge a torrent of flame bursting out of a coffin, then a flurry of arrows as they soar over my head. A tile gives way beneath me as I jump, revealing a host of deadly spikes.

"*Katana strike left, sprint forward, jump left, duck and roll.*"

I deflect several arrows before running just fast enough to avoid a coffin that's launched from its place and shatters to bits where

I once was. Then I evade two flying javelins that would have torn through my head and my chest respectively.

"Run, zigzagging left and right three times each, then a spinning katana strike, and jump back."

As I dart back and forth, the ground crumbles beneath me into a deep chasm. I spin with my katana to block a flurry of arrows from both directions, and by jumping back I avoid being crushed by another brick from the ceiling.

"Jump on the brick, dive off and roll, and sprint to the end!"

I dodge a javelin while I'm on the brick, and a final volley of arrows as I roll. While I sprint, columns from either side fall behind me, coffins are ground to dust as javelins rip through them, and towers of flame erupt from beneath.

Finally, panting for breath, I reach the other side.

"Well done, my son. You will make a formidable Samurai yet."

"Thank you," I sheath my katana. *"That wasn't so bad after all. White Sand should try harder to kill us next time."*

"It's not over yet, but this hall is now safe to cross."

I look back at the others. I see them all, illuminated by Scourge's flame, with jaws agape and eyes bulging wide. Between here and there, the hallway is littered with shattered stone, sliced arrows, javelins stuck in the walls, pitfalls with spikes, and a chasm in which there are only several sturdy platforms to jump across. One of the flamethrowers down the hall sputters fire and smoke. It's an incredible sight, to say the least.

"Come on down," I say. "It's not as bad as it looks."

The others come without a word. It's so amusing, I have a hard time repressing a grin.

Connor arrives first. He gives me a sack with a few krons inside; I presume the remains of the five hundred he took earlier. "Here, take my money."

Khai arrives next, patting me on the shoulder as he passes.

Scourge and Yoko follow. Both of them stop to look up at me. "What?"

"You," Yoko says, "are my hero."

"Teach us your ways," Scourge says.

I laugh. "They're the Great King's ways, not mine. Come on, let's go." I place one hand on each of their shoulders and lead them through the next entryway.

Another series of halls later, we emerge into a large room. For the first time, this room is already lit by torches interspersed throughout, giving us enough light to make out the room's features.

It's round and tall, with eight thick columns equally spaced near the walls and a wide-open central area. There are a few crates and barrels stacked near the walls and around some of the columns. Three more halls branch off from this room.

"Stay alert," Khai says. "We're here."

"You're here!" A voice greets from down one of the halls. "We're so glad you made it!"

Khai draws his bow and aims down the hall, and the rest of us draw our weapons and stand ready.

"Oh, *so* welcoming." A White Sand insurgent, clothed in black but lacking the signature turban-mask, strolls into the room. His possession of two scimitars leads me to believe it's Abdeel.

"Hey shrink," he points his chin at Connor. "Did you come to ask about our feelings again?"

"Where's Celine?" Connor asks.

"Celine?" Abdeel spits. "Don't tell me you came all this way just for *her*."

"Answer me!"

"Or what? You're on *our* turf now. Why don't you turn back and go home before somebody gets hurt?"

"We're not leaving without her."

Khai looses his arrow.

Abdeel raises a scimitar to block it, and a smirk spreads across his face. "Itching for a fight, eh? That can be arranged."

At his words, twelve insurgents emerge from the other halls. They all look alike in their dark outfits and turbans.

Yoko gulps. "This is it, guys."

"We've got this," Khai says, stringing another arrow and holding it ready.

"I've never been comfortable attacking people with my powers," Scourge says, condensing his fireball and holding it ready between both palms, "But for the sake of my friends, I'll make an exception."

"Remember why we're here," Connor says. "We're here in the name of the Great King who leads us, and of Prince Eli, whose authority we carry. As citizens of Marindel, we'll stand up for the innocent, and bring every evildoer to justice."

I nod, gripping my katana. "The Great King is our strength and our defense. No matter what happens tonight, we must trust him completely and without exception. Then, and only then, will we be victorious."

"THE TIME IS now," Bennett says, his solemn face illuminated by the torch he carries. "The city is silent, the night is still, and the ground quakes beneath the boots of my soldiers, marching in grand assembly to their rendezvous with fate. Tonight, at long last, the pride of Armavir will be avenged. Tonight, at long last, the vermin within our walls will be obliterated. Tonight, at long last, I will be vindicated and granted the honor long due me as the chief of police in Cloud Summit. It will be said of me, 'Hail Chief Bennett, protector of the law, arbiter of justice, and bane of all deplorable beings in our fair city.' Then, at long last, the crown jewel of Armavir will thrive in safety and peace."

Bennett, on horseback, rides proudly at the head of his procession. To his right is Antoine, also on horseback. Beside them, Heiban, Ibara, and Kaze travel on foot. The former two are fully armored with Felid battle gear and scowling Samurai masks, and Kaze wears a White Sand outfit. Behind them, rank-and-file policemen march in unison: pikemen, swordsmen, and archers in their respective formations. Their shadows, cast by the torches they carry, move like phantoms across the stone buildings.

Roused by the tramping boots, civilians indoors shut their windows, shutters, and curtains to hide from the impending conflict.

White lightning flashes in the distant mountains, and the sky is a dark black abyss.

53
Dance of the Offspring
Summer, 1419 AIE

~Celine~

I WALK DOWN THE hall toward the treasury, my heart filled with anticipation.

When I returned to the hideout earlier tonight, it was clear something had changed. My fellow operatives scurried about, shouting to one another and carrying weapons and other items this way and that. From their shouting, I discovered the police raid will be taking place tonight.

"I came back just in time for the action," I thought.

After giving Abdeel his meat and beer, which he was very excited to receive, I went to change into my White Sand outfit and turban.

When I got to my room, there was a note on the bed. Another note! It said: "Hey Celine, meet me in the treasury when you get back. I want to spend time alone with you before the raid, just in case things don't go our way. Love, Misham."

My heart leapt. The very thought of seeing Misham again, after everything Connor said, made me smile. Misham is someone who loves me, without a doubt.

Just then, I arrive in the treasury. The heaps of gold, silver, and jewelry are piled as high as ever. I skirt one of the heaps of treasure and call, "Misham? It's me, I'm here!"

"Over here," Misham's voice calls from deeper in the room.

I follow his voice, passing a few more piles as I go.

Whoa! What have we here?

I stop and gape at an enormous emerald sitting amidst a host of other beautiful gold things.

I'm sorry, I can't control myself.

I change course, maneuvering through the other items to pick up the emerald. It's almost as big as my head! I love it! I'll have to stash it somewhere safe so I can come back for it later.

Looking this way and that, I see a black obsidian dresser at the foot of a nearby pile of treasure. I step toward it, saying, "Sorry, I'll be right there! I found a beautiful emerald that I have to hide so no one takes it."

"You're obsessed," Misham quips.

"Shut up." I open the top drawer and place the emerald inside. The drawer is just deep enough that I can shut it. I sigh with relief.

Hands wrap around my waist from behind, and I jump. "Hey!"

"Caught you," Misham says. He must have teleported behind me while I was distracted by the emerald. I hate it when he does that! Nevertheless, I relax in his embrace and turn to face him. He's wearing a dark outfit just like I am.

"How are you feeling about tonight?" He asks, eyes as deep and mysterious as ever.

I wrap my arms around his shoulders. "I'm *excited*! I can't wait to prove myself during the battle. My illusions will bring scores of Bennett's men to their knees, defenseless against the finishing blows of our brothers and fellow operatives."

"I like your confidence," Misham says, taking off his turban-mask so I can see his face. "It's one of the most beautiful things about you."

I blush, taking off my mask as well. "I'm so glad you think so."

Misham pauses, closing his eyes and resting his forehead upon mine.

I stroke his back. "We'll be all right. We're Offspring of Sisera. We're going to survive this, and we're going to win."

Misham begins trembling and breathing hard.

I frown. Something's not right.

It's not like Misham to be so afraid.

Under ordinary circumstances I'd poke fun at Misham's weakness, but now I refrain. He has a right to fear tonight's battle. Nothing like it has ever happened in the history of White Sand. We've always been untouchable; invisible; dancing one step ahead of our enemies. Now, it has come to an invasion of our hideout that many of us may not survive, even if we *do* win.

"It's all right," I whisper, pressing my cheek against his. "We'll get through this together."

Misham breathes heavily in response.

I continue stroking his back, hoping to ease some of his discomfort.

"Celine," Misham's voice trembles, "I...I love you."

"I love you too," I whisper, kissing him gently on the lips.

He hardly responds to the gesture. This is very unlike him.

"What's wrong?" I ask. "You can tell me. I won't make fun, I promise."

"I...I..." he stutters, gripping me hard with one arm while his other hand leaves my back.

"You what?" I press, gazing into his eyes.

"I'm..." Misham straightens his posture. "I'm going to miss you."

My eyes widen.

I establish a mental connection with Misham and cause him to feel his wrists bound together behind his back. At the same time, a cold blade slices across my left shoulder blade. I scream in response to the searing pain. Misham steps back. A blood-soaked dagger clanks on the ground beside him, having been dropped as he was ensnared by the illusion. I don't think he was aiming for my shoulder blade. My mind reels with horror and disbelief.

Connor was right.

"Misham," I gasp. Tears begin streaming down my face. "Misham, *why?*"

"I had to, Celine," Misham says, avoiding my gaze. "I'm sorry. I had no choice."

"What do you mean!?" I shout. "I thought you loved me! You've been trying to protect me, remember? You gave me that note and everything!"

"That's just it, child," Shaama says.

I look to see Shaama walking toward us. The expression on her wrinkled face is harsh and cold, and her eyes burn with savage bloodlust. She says, "Misham dipped his nose in business that was never his to understand. I saw it all with my Farsight. He was foolish to think he could get away with it."

"W-what are you talking about?" I ask, looking from Misham to Shaama and back. Misham lowers his gaze in defeat, while Shaama grins. "After he gave you my note, I cornered him with a very simple choice: continue meddling in my affairs and suffer the consequences, or perform a simple task for me and be redeemed. You'd be surprised how quickly he chose the latter. He values his own life and reputation *very* much. And of course, you can guess what I asked him to do."

My eyes widen. I remember Misham's note. He warned me that Shaama's old friend Typhon, now a servant of Jaedis, convinced her to have me killed. Shaama must have known Misham was eavesdropping on her, and she sent him to kill me to test his loyalty to White Sand.

"B-but," I fumble for words, "Auntie, *why*? You need me, don't you? You trusted me! You said so yourself!"

"That was before your arrest, dear. In your carelessness, you have become a liability. Now, I will do what needs to be done—as will your brother, Misham."

I look at Misham. "You don't agree with her...do you?"

He avoids eye contact. "It's...it's for the good of White Sand, sis."

"Wh-what?" I can't believe what I'm hearing! The family that took me in and raised me, for whom I've risked my life countless times, has decided I no longer belong! Does this Typhon character *really* have so much influence over Auntie? Over White Sand?

"You were warned about this," the death-voice says, *"but you didn't listen. Oh, you wreched girl, why won't you accept your fate?"*

My heart races. Panic swells. My left shoulder blade seethes with pain. I feel drops of blood trickling down my back, soaking my outfit. "But, you blew up Königheim for me. What changed? Why so fast? Who cares about Typhon, anyway? Why does he want me dead!?"

Shaama laughs. "We didn't blow up Königheim for *you*, dear! The conquest of Armavir has been White Sand's goal from the very beginning. Typhon was an inspiration to me when I was your age. He is very wise, and I trust his judgment. Really, I *am* disappointed it has come to this—but I will do what needs to be done. When an Offspring of Sisera sits on the throne of Armavir, the legacy of our father will be forever complete. And I will gratify our father at *any* cost."

"I hate you!" I step forward to lunge at her, but I'm blocked by Misham when he appears in front of me. His arms are no longer bound by the illusion; my shock at his betrayal must have caused me to lose the connection.

Shaama cackles. "I'll let you two have at it. There are other matters begging for my attention. Don't you hear? The battle has begun."

Now that she mentions it, I notice the faint echoes of shouting men and clinking weapons coming from down the halls.

Chapter 53: Dance of the Offspring

"Oh, and Celine," Shaama looks at me, "I know you have a soft spot for that Seer. He's come to the hideout to find you. Don't worry, you won't be apart for long. I'll send him to meet you in the realm of the dead."

I remember again the note Misham gave me. Jaedis asked Shaama to slaughter six adventurers who pledge allegiance to the Great King. I remember there had been six people around the table at the Big Fat Hen. One of them was Connor. Two of them were Yoko and Scourge, who risked their lives trying to rescue me.

They're here to rescue me again, and Shaama is going to kill them for it!

I'm overcome with a surge of anger, and I stand to my feet. "Don't lay a hand on them!"

"I won't," she says as she turns to leave. "The Glimmerbeast will."

No way. I won't let her unleash the Glimmerbeast, whatever that is. I'll put her down where she stands!

Just as I'm about to establish a mental connection with Shaama, Misham grabs my left arm.

"Let go of me!" I shout, reeling in my manas'ruh and tugging away from him. My shoulder wound throbs with terrible intensity. I turn to face Misham, but he disappears.

Two seconds later he appears again, holding a scimitar in each hand. "Celine, you must understand. If I don't kill you, Auntie will kill both of us."

"You're a monster! How could you do this to me!?"

"I have to, you know I do," he says, tossing me a scimitar handle-first. "But I'll give you a fair fight...and with it, a chance to kill me first."

I catch the hilt in my right hand. "You said you loved me, Misham. Doesn't that mean anything to you?"

"I did, sis. I do. But some things are more important than love. White Sand *always* comes first."

My lip quivers. "Wh-what has Shaama done to you?"

"Watch your back," Misham says before disappearing.

I whirl around just in time to raise my scimitar to meet his.

Did Misham ever love me at all? I thought he was the only one who cared. The only one who was glad to have me back from the brink of death.

I can't believe how wrong I was.

I extend my manas'ruh toward Misham, but he teleports away.

I whirl around, breathing quick and short, in search of his next appearance.

Here he comes, lunging toward me, scimitar raised for a diagonal strike.

I meet him with an equal but opposite blow, jarring my body and causing me to grimace from the pain. He disappears again.

I don't know how much longer I can do this.

I hear the clinking of treasure behind me and turn to see Misham coming in with an uppercut. I shift aside to avoid the gleaming blade. But his foot hooks around mine, and he yanks me off balance so that I fall to the ground.

"Faster, sis," Misham says, disappearing again.

I stagger back to my feet. "Enough with the teleport, you sick coward!"

"I'll do whatever it takes to survive," Misham's voice comes from no discernible location. "That's how we were raised. You know that."

"Ugh! You're nothing but a selfish, cold-hearted bastard!"

"I agree. We all are, if we're honest."

Misham appears within my peripheral vision. I move to avoid his attack, and then I lunge forward with a counter-strike.

He dodges my blow and brings his leg up in a spinning kick.

I lean back, allowing his foot to pass, and then I slash at him while he's off balance. I scrape his thigh, and he falls, but vanishes upon hitting the ground.

The clinking of metal reveals his location, and I look to see him standing atop a nearby treasure heap. He jumps and slides down, causing an avalanche of coins in his wake. Once his feet touch the ground, he sprints toward me with a double-handed horizontal swing.

He meant to distract me with that stunt, but instead, he's given me a great opening to catch him with an illusion. Eyes wide with mock surprise, I begin establishing a connection.

Misham seems to recognize his mistake and disappears before I have a chance to connect.

Damn it!

He knows me well enough to avoid staying in one place for too long. He also knows my body language when I'm working to achieve a connection. I have to distract him if I'm going to get out of this alive.

"Misham!"

"No more talking, sis." He appears to my left and comes in with another strike.

Chapter 53: Dance of the Offspring

I block his attack. "We don't have to do this!"

"Yes we do," he says before disappearing. Then he comes from behind for another attack. I only notice because I see his reflection in a nearby gold pot.

I leap forward out of range, and then I turn to face him. "Don't listen to Shaama. We can take her down together!"

"No we can't," Misham says, walking toward me.

I notice his limp.

I remember he mentioned being shot with an arrow in the thigh. All this fighting must be wearing him down. That's where I gotta get him.

"Yes, we can," I say, taking a defensive stance. "The only power she has is Farsight. She can't resist us if we attack her together."

"Shaama has much more going for her than Farsight. It's no use."

I begin establishing a mental connection as I speak. "She can't teleport. She can't cast illusions. She has no strength, no speed, no levitation, no other abilities to compete with ours. She's just a creepy old hag!"

"It's no use," Misham says. "She has the Glimmerbeast."

"Maybe if you quit messing around, we can defeat her before she releases it."

Mental connection achieved.

"Impossible," Misham says with a shudder. "It's *inside* her. You can see it in her eyes. Haven't you noticed? It's terrifying!"

"Terrifying, huh? You mean like...*this*?"

At the last word, I cause him to see a giant goblin head floating up above me, with its jagged teeth in a hideous snarl, and with half of its wrinkled skin ripped off.

Misham's face drains of all color as he gapes at the floating head.

I waste no time. Sprinting forward, I tackle him while thrusting my knee in his left thigh, driving as much force into the blow as I can muster.

Misham shouts, flailing about as I take him down. I land on him, knocking the wind out of him with the impact, and I pin him to the ground with my knee on his abdomen. I throw my scimitar aside, freeing up my good arm, and with it I punch him in the face over and over again.

I bust his lip and his nose before he has the sense to disappear from under me. I stagger to my feet.

"You wanna play like that?" Misham asks, his voice coming from no discernible location. "All right. We'll play like that."

I don't hear his appearance this time. An intense sensation of pain blazes across the small of my back. It hurts *so* much worse than the first. I gasp and collapse forward. Everything spins out of control. The metallic taste of blood comes up from my throat, and I cough.

Through my blurred vision, I see my scimitar on the ground a few feet away.

My death may be inevitable, but I'll take Misham with me if I can.

"It's over, sis," he says, now standing over me.

Looking up at him, I begin inching away in the direction of the scimitar.

"Like I said before," he says, following me with a more pronounced limp as he grips his blade with both hands. "I'm really gonna miss you. We had some good times, and I'll always remember them. If only you hadn't been so careless, you could be allowed to live...and we could still be together."

Misham is the *worst* human being in the whole realm of Tyrizah.

I release a sputter of blood as I give my response. "Up yours."

Misham hardens his gaze. He lifts his weapon to deal the final blow.

As he brings it down, I uncoil my legs from beneath me, shouting with effort as I close the distance between me and the scimitar. Grabbing it at the end of my sloppy maneuver, I throw it at Misham's exposed belly.

The flying weapon meets its mark.

We stare wordlessly at each other for a couple of seconds.

In his eyes, very briefly, I see the Misham I knew and loved.

The sword drops from his hands. His injured leg buckles and he topples over.

"Misham..." I collapse on the ground as well. My breathing has been reduced to inconsistent wheezing. Everything hurts. All I see, smell, and taste is blood.

Is this it?

Am I really about to die?

"*Come, my child, let's sail the sea,*" the death-voice whispers the words of my mother's lullaby. "*Don't you cry, I'll tell you why: your life is mine forevermore.*"

54

The Battle of the Catacombs

Summer, 1419 AIE

~Tarento~

"ONE LAST CHANCE," Connor says. "Give us Celine alive, and we'll leave you alone. Otherwise, we *will* engage."

"I'm excited to see you try." Abdeel points one of his blades forward.

The twelve White Sand insurgents charge, shouting battle cries and flashing their scimitars.

Khai plants an arrow between the eyes of the frontmost attacker.

Scourge releases his fireball at a group of three, blasting them across the room and setting their clothes on fire. They retreat, screaming and rolling on the ground.

Yoko fires an arrow, hitting one of the attackers in the shoulder.

I run forward and swing my blade at two of the attackers, but they duck and roll to the side. While they're doing so, I wield a kunai and throw it at an insurgent halfway across the room. The projectile strikes him in the thigh, causing him to tumble and roll with a shout.

One of the attackers who dodged comes in fast with a downward swing.

I deflect it with my katana before giving him a kick to the head. *"Behind you."*

Continuing with the momentum of my kick, I turn and strike the second attacker on the head with the hilt of my weapon.

With both of my attackers neutralized, I notice the rest have all been dealt with by my companions. Even Connor and Yoko succeeded in taking down one insurgent each. Not a bad start, but the battle has barely begun.

"Bunch of damn freaks," Abdeel says, backing away from us.

"Not so fast," Khai says, shooting an arrow at him.

Abdeel dodges it with ease. "Actually, I'm *very* fast. Wanna see?" He turns and flees, disappearing down the hall before Khai can string another arrow.

"After him!" I shout, beginning to give chase. We're not going to let that coward have his way tonight. I can tell by the sound of footsteps behind me that the others are on my heels.

As we navigate the twisting hall, Connor says, "Heads up, everyone. Soon we'll be entering a huge room. There are wooden platforms suspended high up on the columns, where archers are waiting. Scourge, get a fireball ready to throw at them when we arrive. Khai, do what you do best. Everyone else, stay in the cover of the columns until the archers are down."

"Got it," Khai acknowledges.

"They won't know what hit 'em," Scourge says.

We come out of the hall into an enormous rectangular room. The ceiling is supported by columns lining the wall. Just as Connor said, there are platforms built around the columns, upon which White Sand archers stand ready. They're so high up, we wouldn't have noticed them without the advanced warning.

Scourge throws a screaming fireball at the nearest wooden platform. The archers shout and scatter, but much too late. The fireball blasts the platform in half, launching several of the archers in a shower of flaming wooden debris.

The other archers are stunned by our preemptive strike. Khai takes out three of them before they have a chance to take cover and return fire. By that time, we've taken cover behind the columns nearest to our entrance. Scourge and Khai continue attacking from their sheltered positions, and Yoko also takes a few shots.

"Ground forces are coming soon," the Great King says. *"You'll be surrounded and overwhelmed before long. Now is a good time to split up."*

I spend a moment thinking of a plan, and then I tap Connor on the shoulder. "Come with me. We need to draw the archers' fire away from Khai, Scourge, and Yoko so they can take clearer shots."

"Got it," Connor says with a nod.

We begin maneuvering from column to column, farther down the length of the room and farther from our friends' position. At first, we do so subtly, crouching as we move. But at a certain point I say, "Now we need the archers to notice us. Let's—"

A silly grin spreads over Connor's face as he holds up a finger to silence me. "I got this, Tarento. Watch and learn." With that, he steps out into the open between two columns. He puts his arms on his hips and puffs his chest out before shouting, "Have any of you fine gentlemen seen my cowardice? I seem to have lost it somewhere!"

The archers stare in bewilderment, but quickly respond with a murderous volley of arrows.

Connor runs and dives out of the way just in time, holding his shield up over his head.

Well, now that we've seen Connor's uniquely daring style of drawing enemy fire, it's time for a bit of mine. I run further down the length of the room before hurling a kunai up at the nearest archer, striking him in the chest. The smitten archer tumbles over the wooden guard rail and falls the ground.

By the time the other archers turn to see who threw the kunai, I've already taken shelter behind a column.

I repeat the same trick again, bringing down a second archer as I run back toward Connor. This time several archers notice and shoot after me.

As a welcome confirmation that our strategy is working, a fireball careens into a platform nearby. The resulting blast causes the platform to bend, crack, and come crashing down. The accompanying archers fall screaming along with it, and all are lost in a shattered heap of wood and flame.

When I rejoin Connor, he says, "Tarento, listen—do you hear that?"

"Hear what? The sound of Scourge getting after it?"

"Yes, but no. There's something else."

I take a second to still my adrenaline-pumped senses, and then I listen.

I hear the sounds of crackling fire, our groaning enemies on the ground, our shouting enemies above, the *twang* and *fwip* of soaring arrows, and the *clink* of arrowheads glancing off solid stone.

More noises, far more ominous, grab my attention. Crumbling stone, blasts of fire, screams of men, crunching metal, and tramping boots. I look in the direction of the sounds and I see an entryway on the side of the room opposite of our current position.

I exchange glances with Connor.

He nods. "Bennett's here."

"It doesn't sound like they're having much luck with the traps," I frown.

Just then, I hear a different sort of *clink* on the ground nearby. I look down to see a spherical object rolling toward us, complete with a sparkling fuse.

"Look out!" I grab Connor by the collar of his tunic and throw him on the ground before diving on top of him. The shockwave of the explosion sends waves of heat and debris over our sprawled bodies.

A couple of arrows clink on the ground next to us. We're in range of the archers! "Get up, get up!" I shout, pulling disoriented Connor up to his feet and pushing him behind another column as the enemy fire intensifies. I look up to see an insurgent light another bomb and throw it at us.

"We have to keep moving," I say, forcing Connor to run ahead of me. "They won't let us hide behind the columns anymore."

We flinch at the bomb's explosion behind us.

"That's not all we have to worry about," Connor says between breaths. "The police are here!"

I look aside to see Bennett's soldiers staggering in from the opposite hall. Some are on fire, and others have multiple arrows sticking out of them. A few collapse on the ground as they come, gasping and moaning in agony. On their heels, many unharmed policemen march forth. Spurred by the gruesome sight of the traps, their faces hardened with readiness to spill the blood of their enemies, they charge into the room with swords flashing, shields and pikes raised, and bows strung ready for action.

The White Sand archers, now with many targets to choose from, immediately get to work. The police archers respond in kind, toppling several insurgents from their lofty positions. From another adjacent hallway, White Sand battle cries fill the air as fleet-footed insurgents come streaming in to meet the invaders.

As the battle unfolds and grows to consume the entire room, the Great King says, "*Send Connor ahead to find Celine, with your tiger hound to guide him. The rest of you must stay here and fight.*"

I ask Connor, "Do you have anything Celine touched recently? Something with her scent on it?"

"Hmm...yes I do," Connor says, fumbling in his bag and pulling out the Illusionist wanted poster. "Why do you ask?"

"I have something to help you find her," I say, pulling out the tiger hound scroll.

"A summoning scroll?"

"Yup. Cover me." I unfurl the scroll and crouch on the ground. After performing the summoning ritual—the hand signs and incantation—the scroll goes up in smoke to reveal the tiger hound. It has the overall likeness of a wiry hunting hound with the coloring, stripes, eyes, and tail of a tiger. The summon stands a head taller than Connor. Its stature is strong and limber, fierce and deadly, commanding respect from all whose eyes fall upon it.

"Whoa," Connor takes a nervous step backward.

"Hey, buddy," I place a hand on the hound's neck. "I need you to help my friend find someone." To Connor I say, "Let him smell the poster."

Connor presents the poster to the hound. After a few sniffs, the animal recoils and flicks its ears in apparent frustration.

I frown. "There must be too many scents on it. You, Celine, Yoko, Jake, Antoine, and perhaps others have held it. I don't think the hound knows which scent to follow."

Connor thinks for a moment, and then his eyes widen and he snaps. "Celine was wearing perfume. Do you smell perfume, boy?"

The hound sniffs the scroll again, this time flaring its nostrils and grunting with a low bark.

"Lead Connor to her," I say. "Listen to his every command, and protect him from anyone who attacks him. Understand?"

The hound snorts, pawing the ground and whipping its tail.

"Aren't you coming?" Connor asks me.

"No, the others and I will stay here to fight. You go on ahead, and may the Great King's guidance be with you."

"All right. Good luck!" Connor turns to the hound, hefting his sword and shield. "Let's go!"

The hound sprints across the room toward the entryway of a large hall.

"Hey, wait up!" Connor runs after it.

Once I see Connor has made it to the entryway, I turn my attention to where I last saw Khai, Scourge, and Yoko. They're no longer hiding behind columns; now they're engaged in close combat with both White Sand and the police.

I run toward them, dodging arrows and avoiding skirmishes along the way. I've nearly closed the gap between us when the sight of Yoko in trouble causes me to sprint at full speed.

She's been knocked down by an aggressive police pikeman, who steps on her bow and glowers down at her, saying, "You've escaped once, filthy scum, but you won't get away this time!"

"Don't count on it!" I say, flashing my katana.

The pikeman tenses, pointing his weapon at me. "It's *you*! The fugitive they're looking for!"

I catch the hook of his pike with the blade of my katana and yank it away, flinging it behind me. I point my blade at his big red nose and say, "Let the girl go."

The pikeman stutters, slowly backing away and raising his hands.

A scimitar flies out of my peripheral vision and gores the pikeman in the stomach. The color drains out of his face, and he slumps on the ground mere inches away from a terrified Yoko.

"Aha!" Abdeel shouts, sprinting over to reclaim his weapon. "Watch out, Felid! You're next!"

I grab one of Yoko's arms and swing her up and behind me before stepping between Abdeel and his scimitar. Pointing my katana at Abdeel, I say, "By the Great King's power, I beat you once. If you don't back down now, I'll do it again."

"Not a chance!" Abdeel sneers, coming at me with a super-human jump and a scimitar strike aimed for my head. I block it, and with the Great King's help just as before, I engage with him in a fast-paced series of strikes, blocks, kicks, jumps, and evasive maneuvers. I'm greatly relieved to have my katana this time around. My movements are much more fluid and precise than they had been with the scimitar and fireplace iron.

Our tense exchange continues unabated for a moment before finally, at last, I pass Abdeel's guard and land a perfect heel-stomping kick on his chest, sending him sprawling back with a grunt of surprise.

Still maintaining my stance, I ask between breaths, "Have you had enough yet?"

Abdeel regains his balance, breathing hard and scowling. "I won't let an ordinary person beat me so easily."

"He is no ordinary person," a familiar voice says.

Cold chills run down my spine.

Abdeel and I turn to see another Felid coming toward us. He's fully armored, sporting an Abysso-hide cape, and wielding a black katana that already gleams red with blood. His face is covered with a Samurai war mask, but I don't need to see his face to know who he is.

"Heiban," I greet.

"It's been a long time, old friend. I was beginning to think I'd never find you."

Chapter 54: The Battle of the Catacombs

"Aw, *hell* no," Abdeel rolls his eyes. "You two have at it. I'll play winner!"

Two arrows zip past Abdeel, courtesy of Khai and Yoko. They'll keep him busy while I focus on Heiban.

I face my former Samurai partner and say, "I take it you've come all this way to finish what you started on last year's Jubilation Day?"

Heiban nods. "It will be quick, if you cooperate."

"I will not surrender. Not to you, not to Lord Zetsumei, not to anyone. The Great King is my King now and forevermore. I hope you, if no one else, will one day accept that."

"Foolish Tarento!" As Heiban speaks, we begin to square off like jungle cats vying for territory. "I've heard all about this Great King of yours, and I must say I'm terribly disappointed in you. What possessed you to believe a childish folk tale is more important than the legacy of our kingdom, our people, our very way of life!?"

"All those things are more important to me than you'll ever know. However, I cannot ignore what I've seen and heard. The Great King is very real, Heiban, and unfortunately, so is the darkness of the Great Serpent. That darkness is coming for Felidae, and I...I..."

Quite by surprise, I begin choking up. Now that I've heard in the context of the Great Story how heartless and cruel the Serpent can be, I can't bear the thought of my beloved kingdom suffering in the jaws of such wanton destruction. I look at Heiban straight on, allowing the tears to stream down my face. "I *really* don't want it to happen. Heiban, I *really* don't. That's why I have to do everything the Great King tells me to do, all in the hope that one day Felidae will turn from their wicked ways and declare allegiance to the Great King. Only then will the desolation of Felidae be averted."

Heiban is silent for a few seconds. I presume he's choosing his words carefully. Finally, he says, "Let me grant to you this disaster is going to happen. Let me also grant it was some ethereal King who asked you to do his bidding for seven years in order to avert it. If that's the case, how do you expect to save Felidae from all the way over here in Cloud Summit, following a ragtag group of losers on a quest to defeat a sorcerer in a land as far from Felidae as is geographically possible?"

I frown. "I wish I could give you a good answer, Heiban."

He snorts. "When did you find it fitting to abandon logic and reason?"

"The greatest logic is that which is bestowed by the Great King in the context of a personal friendship with him."

"Ugh. You really *have* gone mad! There is *no* Great King, there is *no* disaster Felidae cannot overcome with its own resources, and *you* are a disgrace to the way of the Samurai and to the kingdom to which you swore loyalty. I, on the other hand, will do whatever it takes to defend Felidae from those who seek its ruin." As he points his weapon at me, his finishing words drip with gravity. "I promise, Tarento. This time, I will *not* hold back."

I blink away the last of my tears, setting my face like flint and taking a stance with my katana ready. "So be it, old friend."

Seconds pass.

We stand facing one another, muscles coiled and tense. The Battle of the Catacombs rages all around, but the sights and sounds of it drown in the backdrop of our standoff.

In perfect sync we launch toward one another, sprinting as fast as our legs will carry us, our katanas drawn back as we breach the very last threshold of reluctance.

The first clang of our weapons echoes across the room, dwarfing every other sound in the battle.

Heiban and I engage in a series of strikes and maneuvers. The Great King doesn't instruct me like he has in recent skirmishes, but I have no time or will to question it. I have a sense he trusts me to make the right moves for now.

I quickly discover Heiban has been training since our last encounter. He is stronger and faster than I remember, and it takes all my energy and focus to stay toe-to-toe with him. He isn't as fast as Abdeel, but his strikes are significantly more powerful. In spite of this, it doesn't take me long to notice a flaw in his form.

He's wearing heavier armor than usual: defensive armor a Samurai uses in combat against multiple assailants. Though it's not a bad choice for the invasion of the White Sand hideout, Heiban's attack-oriented fighting style is made clumsy by the bulky suit. The flaw is so subtle, only the trained eye of a Samurai would ever notice.

I continue dancing with Heiban, waiting for the perfect opportunity to exploit his weakness.

There it is. He put his left foot out just a bit too far.

I slide my right foot up next to his, and after deflecting one of his blows I slide left, sweeping his leg out from under him so he falls on his back. Wasting no time, I raise my katana to stab him in the shoulder. As I bring it down, Heiban deflects my blow with his armored forearm, causing my blade to hit the stone floor instead. I jump backward to avoid his kick-up.

Once on his feet, Heiban performs several hand signs and claps his hands, after which his arms glow with a brilliant blue aura. I've seen this before, yes, but the aura is much whiter than it used to be. He picks up his fallen katana, and when he does, the aura overtakes his weapon as well.

This I've never seen.

"What am I getting myself into?" I ask the Great King.

"Heiban has been training his elemental ninja arts. His techniques are more developed now than when you last fought. Be on guard."

He swings his blade, sending a cluster of magic ice darts toward me.

"Whoa!" I dive out of the way just in time. The projectiles soar through the air until they hit a nearby column, bursting and blossoming into terrifying displays of jagged ice.

One of the darts hits a hapless insurgent, encasing his head in ice and allowing a police pikeman to deliver the final blow.

Heiban runs toward me, swinging his weapon yet again.

I dive and roll to avoid the second barrage, and I run to meet him with a mighty swing of my blade.

"Conserve your energy," the Great King says as our weapons clash. *"The greatest test of valor is yet to come."*

55

True Justice

Summer, 1419 AIE

~Connor~

I RUN DOWN THE hall, propelled by a surge of indignation and a heaping dose of adrenaline. Celine is in trouble, and there's no time to lose.

The tiger hound leads the way, guiding me through a maze of broad corridors. White Sand insurgents have tried to stop us, but at the sight of the tiger hound they falter before meeting their demise with a brutal swipe to the throat.

I think about the day it all began: the moment in the countryside when the thunderstorm struck. Back then, I was bored with ordinary life on the homestead. I longed for something important to happen in my life. I wanted to live a story worth telling.

Now, I've got what I've always dreamed of.

It's been exhilarating as well as terrifying, and definitely not without its costs. However, without a doubt, I've never felt more alive than I do now: serving the Great King as a Seer, defending the innocent, and bringing justice to evildoers.

This is what I was made to do.

We enter a larger hall, similar to the one that had been rigged with traps. There're no traps here, but it's filled with the chaos of battle. The tiger hound presses onward, dodging to and fro on its course to the other side.

I follow much less spectacularly, ducking and flinching as arrows fly over my head. I gag when a policeman falls in front of me and is decapitated by an axe-wielding insurgent. I tremble and cower as a bomb explodes nearby, buffeting me with hot wind and dust. An insurgent and a policeman locked in a sword duel pass in front of me, and I barge between them with my shield overhead. "Sorry! Just passing through!"

I notice Ibara up ahead, taking on several insurgents at once with his vine techniques. He wields two Felid short-blades to eliminate any insurgent who makes it past the vines. I pass him quickly, hoping he doesn't notice me and engage.

The tiger hound barks up ahead, and I look to see it has tackled a policeman to the ground. His helmet has fallen off, and I recognize him to be Antoine.

"Hey! Stop!" I sprint toward them. "Tiger hound, stop! Leave him alone!"

The hound, formerly poised to rip Antoine's throat, looks at me with a questioning glance before stepping away from the police captain.

When I arrive, I reach out a hand to help Antoine up.

"Thank you," he says, picking up his helmet. "Is this *your* dog?"

"For the moment. Tarento summoned it to help me find Celine. You haven't seen her yet, have you?"

"I'm afraid not, but you'd better hurry. Bennett's after her too."

"Thanks for the heads up. Stay safe, all right? I hope to see you around after this."

"Same to you," Antoine nods. "I'll cover you as best as I can."

I nod in reply before turning back to the hound. "All right, boy, let's go!"

We weave our way through the rest of the embattled hall. There's an entryway just a couple dozen feet ahead.

The tiger hound skids to a stop.

I stop behind it. "What's wrong?"

The hound sniffs the air, whines, and takes a few steps back.

Just then, we're buffeted by a warm, dry wind. One by one, the torches on the walls are blown out. Behind us, the sounds of battle fall silent.

The tiger hound lowers its head with a growl and lashes its tail. It sees something. I squint my eyes to look, but the entryway is hidden in darkness. The smoke from the extinguished torches lingers like mist.

A familiar cackle echoes down the hall.

My hair stands on end, and my muscles tense. Where have I heard that laugh before?

"Who's there?" Antoine says, coming to stand beside me.

A handful of Antoine's men line up alongside us, weapons ready. Seconds pass without any response.

An orb of magic glows pink down the hall, held in the hand of that horrid shopkeeper from the Exotic Goods Hub. She wears a different outfit and a headdress now, and her creepiness factor has increased at least sevenfold. Her grin makes me sick with fear.

She says, now with a thick Sunophsian accent, "Welcome, one and all, to my humble abode! It's not often we have special guests, so I'd like to express my gratitude with a gift."

Antoine steps forward. "You must be Shaama, the head of White Sand. Your days of villainy have ended. Cease your use of magic and put your hands up!"

I whisper to Antoine, "Don't aggravate her! There's something dark and sinister about her. I can feel it! I'm not sure what to make of it, but—"

"A simple magician, no doubt," Antoine says. "We came prepared to fight Offspring of Sisera. We can take her."

Shaama laughs. "The Seer speaks the truth! You cannot prevail against the high powers of darkness, no matter the strength of your forces! Fight if you will; run if you may; cower in fear! I will see to the destruction of every last invader in my sanctuary. You will be the first to partake in Armavir's inescapable torment!"

With that, Shaama's magic orb condenses into the shape of a dagger, and she plunges it into her own chest.

"Blimey!" I wince. That move was unexpected. The collective gasps from the police echo my sentiment. What is that crazy hag up to?

Blood runs down Shaama's robe, and for a few seconds it looks like she's about to keel over dead. Then her dagger flashes once before darkening to the color of a starlit sky. Coils of smoke slither out of the wound and surround her in what quickly becomes a swirling vortex. The old woman's eyes widen, and she releases a blood-curdling scream as the vortex grows to consume her.

Antoine shouts, "Archers, open fire!"

The police archers fire their rounds at the darkness, but the arrows do nothing to stop the hideous mass as it heaves and swirls, growing larger, hissing and howling with great intensity. A glowing pink face appears, a murderous scowl, as it expands more and more.

"What is that thing!?" Ibara shouts from behind, and the police make similar nervous comments as they begin to back away. The tiger hound whines and barks, sounding more like a puppy than a fearsome beast.

The ground begins to tremble. Cracks appear in the walls, illuminated by spurts of pink and blue energy thrown about by the dark mass. With a thunderous crash, the walls give way to release torrents of gold and silver coins, glittering gemstones, and other treasures. Absorbed by the vortex, the precious metals are molded and formed like liquid into various shapes.

I'm so transfixed by the dazzling display, I hardly notice Antoine shouting behind me, "Fall back! Fall back!"

The shouts of fleeing policemen are drowned out by the scream of the beast taking shape before me. The smoke condenses into a tangible substance, blacker than ebony, almost entirely coated in a golden exoskeleton. A slender body sprouts six insectoid legs, a whip-like tail, forearms with scythe-blades like those of a mantis, and blue and pink energy spines up the length of its back. Most terrifying of all, its head is crowned with energy spines, six ruby-like eyes, a radiant sapphire on its forehead, and a wide mouth filled with rows of silver teeth. The hallway is illuminated by the beasts' kaleidoscopic radiance.

"Great King, help us all," I whisper in a daze. I've always had an aversion to centipedes, but this behemoth is more terrifying than any bug I've seen or heard of in my life.

The beast releases a terrifying shriek, rearing up and slicing the air with its forelegs before stabbing gouges in the stone ground less than a dozen feet in front of me.

"Connor!" Antoine calls from behind.

The tiger hound barks and whines, looking back at me for orders.

As terrified as I am by this creature, it isn't fear alone that keeps me from running. I know what I need to do.

"*I trust you, Great King.*"

The beast comes down on the tiger hound, snapping its jaws over the summon and throwing it against the wall. The hound yelps, and upon contact with the wall it dematerializes in a cloud of smoke.

I lower my gaze and drop to my knees, setting my sword and shield on the ground. Then I bow with my face to the ground and stay perfectly still. I watch the hues of pink and blue on the floor as they shift with the beast's movement. The ground quakes under the weight of its insectoid legs. With its scythe blades it carves up the ground all around me, and I can feel its hot, damp breath as it roars and hisses over me.

In my heart, I feel peace.

I also, for a brief second, notice a whiff of jasmine.

The ground trembles all the more as the beast passes over me.

"Here it comes!" The police shout. "Run!"

I hear the beast shriek again, accompanied by the sounds of metal grating on stone and the terrified shouts of fleeing men. The hall darkens and the sounds fade into distant echoes.

I pick up my weapons and stand again, breathing a sigh of relief. I have no words to express how thankful I am that the Great King protected me from that beast. Now, it's back to finding Celine.

No longer having the tiger hound to lead the way, I tap into my Seer's gift.

The hall is dark again, but because the walls were torn down by Shaama's transformation, the torches in adjacent rooms emit just enough light to see. The left wall breach stands out to me the most, so I clamber over the rubble and into the room.

It's enormous, similar in size to the area where I parted ways with Tarento, but it's filled with mountains of treasure. The amount of gold that tore through the wall to give the beast its armor was only a small fraction of the room's bounty.

Following my intuition, I skirt several piles of treasure as I walk deeper into the room. Everything is silent. The padding of my footsteps and the clinking of coins is deafening.

I gasp when I see them.

Two insurgents lie on the ground in pools of blood. Both of their heads are uncovered. One is male, with a scimitar staked in his body. The other is female.

"No, oh no!" Overcome with anguish, I sheath my sword and sling my shield on my back before running toward the bodies. I crouch near Celine first, taking her arm and feeling for a pulse. "Come on, come on, come on..."

It's very weak.

I check the man's pulse as well. He's dead.

I place a hand on Celine's forehead. "Great King, what do I do?"

"*She has lost a lot of blood. She is moments from death, but you can save her.*"

"What do you mean? I'm not a medic!"

The answer comes in the form of a memory: Yoko treating Alpha Blue with webbing and herbs after the shipyard battle. I don't have medic supplies with me, but I can find *something* to stop the bleeding. I rip off a portion of the other insurgent's garment and press it on the deep wound across the center of her back. Then I roll her flat facing up, hoping the ground will keep the garment firmly in place. I'll have to ask Yoko later if that works; I don't have time to wonder about it now.

I brush Celine's matted hair out of her face. Her faded makeup does little to hide how pale she has become.

"Don't die on me," I whisper. "The Great King loves you, and I love you."

Celine's eyelid twitches.

"As a friend," I say with a nervous chuckle. "I love you as a friend and a brother."

She doesn't respond.

I frown, holding her hand and beginning to hum.

Why am I humming?

It seems familiar. I know this tune.

"Hm hm hm hmmm, hm hm hmmm. Hm hm hm hmm my father, the King..."

Prince Eli's song! Of course!

I sing,

> *"When there is doubt, I know that hope is best.*
> *When others grieve, a song of joy I'll sing.*
> *When storms abound, in peace my heart will rest.*
> *I know and trust my father, the King."*

Celine coughs, releasing a spurt of blood from the corner of her mouth.

I rip another piece of garment and clean the blood off her mouth while continuing with the next verse,

> *"When there is fear, I'll stand with daring eyes.*
> *When others hate, a song of love I'll sing.*
> *When death prevails, in light I will arise.*
> *I know and trust my father, the King."*

At the steady clapping of one person, I tense and look up. I see no one, but a deep voice confirms the presence of another in the room. "What a staggering, beautiful performance. I almost shed a tear."

"Who's there?" I ask, standing and placing a hand on the hilt of my sword.

"Don't be rash, there's nothing to fear. I'm one of the good guys."

I hear footsteps behind a nearby treasure mound, and Chief Bennett saunters into view. He wields a sword and an arrogant grin.

Definitely not a good guy.

"She's hurt and dying," I say. "No threat to you or your men."

"You're defending her?" Bennett sighs with an eye-roll. "Why in the land of Armavir does *everyone* step in to defend this one pathetic criminal?"

"She's harmless. She needs a medic, not a jail cell."

"How dare you suggest such a thing. What will become of her when she recovers? Will she not continue in her criminal ways? Will she not terrorize the citizens of Cloud Summit with her psychic witchcraft?"

I shake my head. "She won't go back to that; I *know* she won't. When she recovers, she'll be a different person."

"Hmph," Bennett scoffs. "Not a chance. I've seen it all before. The criminal lifestyle is all she knows. She'll return to her wicked ways like a dog returns to its vomit. The only way to keep the city safe from the Illusionist is to destroy her, once and for all."

"You're wrong," I say, gripping my sword hilt harder as Bennett nears. "The Great King can change her heart. No matter what her past was like before, from this night on, she will be a daughter of the King."

"Oh, you naive young man. You've been taking the same drugs as that old Seer fellow, haven't you? He had a special affection for the witch just like you do. Remember what became of him? Do you *really* think I'll falter in my duty as the chief of police every time someone stands in my way with the foolish notion that a criminal can be redeemed?"

Bennett's cold mention of Jed causes my blood to boil. Indignation rises in my heart like a furious tide. With one swift motion I draw my sword and shield and take a defensive stance over Celine's body. "Enough of this! You see yourself as an arbiter of the law and the savior of Cloud Summit, but you're driven by selfish ambition and hate! You pursue and destroy so-called criminals without any regard for the innocent who cross your path! Your ways are sickening to the Great King, and to me! I will not stand for it, do you hear me!?"

Bennett's expression darkens. He flips his sword in his hand and says, "I will not tolerate your insubordination. If you don't stand down immediately, you will die along with her."

"Whether I live or die, the justice of the Great King will prevail."

"Agh!" Bennett leaps toward me with his sword raised high.

I raise my shield to block it, but I'm caught off guard when Bennett's iron-toed boot comes instead, sending me sprawling backward.

He's fast!

Chapter 55: True Justice

I scramble to my feet, shaking off the impact, and run toward Bennett just as he stands over Celine with his sword raised.

"Get away from her!" I shout, tackling him with my shield.

He staggers aside, managing to keep his balance, and then he swings his sword at me. This time, frantically remembering the basic moves Jake taught me on the road, I raise my sword in defense.

Success!

Yes! I can fight!

Bennett sweeps my legs out from under me and I fall to the ground. My tailbone takes the brunt of the landing and I gasp in pain. As Bennett's blade comes down to impale my exposed belly, I roll out of the way just in time.

Bennett pulls his sword up and swings again, and I continue rolling away from him. He growls with frustration and kicks my ribs. "Stay put, you little rat!"

"Ah!" I shout. His kick would have been worse if I hadn't been wearing a leather vest. Still, having never been in a fight like this, I'm not used to getting battered around.

I have to swallow it and keep going.

I roll toward Bennett this time instead of away, causing him to step backward. I jump to my feet, holding my shield up in front as I swing at Bennett with my sword. He blocks my blade with his before raising his foot to kick my shield. I see it coming this time, so I maneuver around the kick and tackle him shield-first while he's standing on one leg. With a grunt he stumbles back, and then springs forward with a double-handed downward strike.

I jump back and run away. He pursues me, continuing to swing his weapon. I stay just far enough to evade his attacks.

"You were so brave a moment ago," Bennett says, stopping to fumble in his pocket, "And now all you do is run. Have I beaten you so easily?"

"I'm hoping I won't have to attack you. Will you leave Celine alone, please? Your men need you out there; did you see what happened to Shaama? She—" I flinch at the crack of Bennett's whip.

"Silence! I will *not* stop until that witch is dead! Now, put your sword where your mouth is or accept your fate!"

I frown, raising my sword and shield in a stance once more.

Bennett walks toward me, casting his whip and bringing it down with frightening speed. Even though I dodge it, I can feel the sting of the air as it passes just inches away. My current evasion tactics aren't going to work as long as he has that whip.

I run toward Bennett as he draws the whip back, thinking it will have less of an impact at close range. I'm so focused on the whip, I don't realize until too late that he still holds a sword in his other hand.

Seizing the opportunity, Bennett thrusts the blade forward. I dodge in time to avoid being gored, but it cuts my left arm, eliciting a gasp of pain as I stumble into Bennett and onto the ground.

"Hmph," Bennett smirks, pulling back his foot to kick me.

I raise my shield to take the brunt of the hit. I jump to my feet in time to raise my sword and block a strike from Bennett's, but I fail to avoid his fist, clutching the handle of his whip, as it plows into my face. I sprawl back with a grunt and fall into a pile of treasure.

Bennett pursues and raises his foot to stomp on me. I try to roll out of the way, but I realize in panic that the treasure makes it far too difficult to do so. His boot lands on my wounded arm, and I scream.

Before I know it, Bennett's sword is drawn back for a thrust, and I barely manage to move my shield in the way so his sword glances off of it.

"Give up yet?" Bennett asks, raising his foot to stomp on my shield. I'm crushed beneath it, and I wince. "This is what happens to those who defy me. It feels great, doesn't it!?" He stomps on my shield yet again.

I wince through the pain, trying to think of a way, any way, I can get out of this. The sharp sensation in my arm is so severe I can hardly focus. Terror seizes my heart. I'm about to die by the sword of Chief Bennett, and all for what? A condemned criminal who the Great King loves? Is it all really worth it?

Bennett spits in my face, and I grimace. He says, "It's over, peasant. You were hardly a worthy opponent. Your only success was to delay the death of the Illusionist by a few minutes. What *shame* you must feel, having failed so miserably."

Without a second thought, I say, "What shame *you* must feel, leaving your men while you fret over one girl who the Great King will not allow to die before her time."

Bennett chuckles. "She *will* die, just like you and just like the old man. No one can stop me, not even the Great King."

Bennett's mention of Jed stirs my heart once more.

He notices the change in my temperament. With a grin he continues, "I spared the old man once, you know. He asked me not to kill her when I caught her. I listened to him then, but when he asked a second time, I thought better of it. It felt good to get him out of the way. What a *nuisance* he was..."

Bennett continues, but I no longer hear him. I clench my fists, gritting my teeth through both the physical and emotional pain holding me down. I plead silently, "*Great King, give me strength, even if only this once, to stuff Bennett's words back in his slimy mouth where they belong!*"

An idea comes in response.

While Bennett is still speaking, I shout and throw my shield at him.

The shout distracts him well enough that I score a direct hit on his forehead. His cavalier flies off with the shield, exposing a headband with an orange gem that is now cracked in half. The headband probably saved him from getting knocked out, but even so, the impact sends him staggering back with a grunt.

Wasting no time, I scramble to my feet, taking my sword in my good hand, and I charge toward Bennett. I deliver a series of basic moves I learned from Jake, and I do it with driven passion. I shout with every strike:

"This is for Jed!"

"For Celine!"

"For Alpha Blue!"

"For everyone killed in the Purge!"

"And for the Great King of Marindel!"

Bennett, stepping back as I pursue, blocks the first four blows with tremendous surprise in his eyes. The fifth blow lands with such power that it strikes the sword out of his grip.

I follow with a sixth blow, slicing him across the shoulder, and he falls back into a heap of treasure. He tries to squirm away as I walk toward him. "W-wait! Hold on just a moment!"

"I was in your position just fifteen seconds ago," I say, pointing my sword at his throat. "What reason do I have to wait, you callous monster of a man?"

"I-I..." Bennett stutters, his face lit with shock.

Words drip off my tongue like blood. "If anyone deserves to die for all the evil things they've done, it's you."

"B-b-but...I..."

I raise my sword. I feel my inner Seer trying to stop me, but my indignation has risen to such a level that I refuse to comply. "Chief Bennett, I won't let you hurt anyone else ever again."

He stares back in fear, lip quivering, unable to avert his sudden demise.

56
Glimmerbeast
Summer, 1419 AIE

~Tarento~

THE SHRIEK ECHOES from the depths of the hideout.

My katana meets Heiban's for the hundredth time. With our blades crossed, we stop and listen.

The ground trembles beneath our feet.

I look at the large entryway through which Connor had gone some time ago. The distant sounds of grating stone, clashing metal, and screaming men can be heard coming this way. The White Sand insurgents flee at once, cowering silently into the other halls and out of sight.

I ask Heiban, "Is this a trick of yours?"

"No. Yours?"

"Nope."

Just then, several policemen far down the hall round a corner and come sprinting this way. Even from afar, it's no secret they're terrified for their lives. I'm surprised to see Ibara running with them. They're causing such a commotion that nearly all of us are watching.

Suddenly, an enormous golden beast comes around the corner in pursuit. It picks them off one by one: staking a man to the ground with its scythe-like forearm, then grabbing another in its jaws and casting him aside.

"Retreat! Retreat!" I recognize Antoine's voice as the police pour into the room.

Chapter 56: Glimmerbeast

The beast stops at the entryway, its gaze raking across the room at all of us. It knifes the ground and emits a murderous battle cry.

Everyone flees. They begin to crowd the hallways in a panicked frenzy to escape.

The sapphire on the forehead of the beast radiates with intensifying light, and in a few seconds, it fires a beam of blue energy at the wall above one of the hallways. The resulting blast collapses the entryway, burying anyone unfortunate enough to be running through at that time.

"This way!" Those who remain shout, all crowding toward the other hallways.

The beast fires a beam to collapse a second hallway. Then a third one. Then a fourth. Now there are no escape routes left, save for the broad hallway through which the beast arrived. It charges toward the closest group of people and attacks.

"*Great King,*" I ask, my eyes locked with horror on the beast, "*What is this monstrosity? What do we do!?*"

"*This is the Glimmerbeast, the Great Serpent's emissary of greed and vengeance. It is far too powerful for any one of you to challenge alone. You must band together to stop it.*"

"*Band together?*" I ask, glancing at Heiban. "*Are you serious?*"

"*There is no other way.*"

Heiban meets my gaze.

We stare wordlessly at each other for a second before I say, "Monster first?"

Heiban hesitates, but after cringing at the blood-curdling scream of a dying policeman, he nods. "Monster first."

We both turn to face the Glimmerbeast.

Scourge runs toward it, harnessing electricity between his fingers and unleashing a lightning bolt at the side of the beast's head. The electric attack merely draws its attention, and with a vicious shriek it charges after Scourge.

"Uh-oh." Scourge runs away.

"Scourge!" I run after him, wielding a kunai and flinging it at the beast. The projectile glances off the armor without even serving as a distraction. The beast is closing in quickly.

"Hey!" Khai shouts from elsewhere in the room, firing an arrow at the beast from behind. The arrow pierces between two armor plates on the back of its head, causing it to recoil and hiss.

Heiban runs up next, katana aglow, and releases a group of darts at the beast. Jagged ice sprouts up across the length of its torso, but shatters quickly; the darts do nothing to restrict the beast's movement.

Ibara sends a vine to tether one of the beast's forearms and pulls on it hard. The beast reacts by flicking its arm, snapping the vine and catapulting Ibara across the room toward Khai.

Khai jumps out of the way, and Ibara lands on his feet with a rough skid.

As all this is happening, the Great King says, "*Tell Scourge to melt the beast's armor around the joints.*"

"*Got it.*" I head over to Scourge and say, "That thing's armor is made of gold. Can you get your fire hot enough to melt it?"

Scourge shakes his head. "I've spent too much energy fighting the White Sand archers. It'll take more than the fire I have left to melt that armor."

"We're going to need you to do it anyway. Focus your firepower on the joints. If you can weld the armor together in its legs, it'll lose mobility and become easier to fight."

"A-all right. I'll try my best."

"No," I say, grabbing his shoulders and looking into his eyes. "*Do* your best. We need all the firepower you can muster. This is no innocent dungeon prisoner; this is a soul-less monster created by the Great Serpent to destroy us all. If we don't defeat it, we are *all* going to die. Do you understand?"

Scourge's eyes are wide with fear as he nods vigorously.

"I need more than that!" I shout, patting him on the shoulder. "You have what it takes! You can do this! You *have* to do this! Can you!?"

"Hai!"

"Good! Give it everything you've got!"

"Aaaah!" Scourge runs past me, condensing an orb of fire between his palms.

"*Find Antoine next,*" the Great King says.

I look to the fringes of the room, where most of the police are clustered amongst the columns, and I pick Antoine out of the crowd.

On my way there, Heiban flies in front of me, having been thrown by the beast, and skids to a stop. An idea comes to mind when I see him. "Heiban, try the exploding kunai. Aim for the joints to melt the armor."

Heiban nods, pulls out a kunai, and begins imbuing it with magic.

When I reach Antoine, I'm shocked to see him talking with a White Sand insurgent. They both look at me as I arrive.

Chapter 56: Glimmerbeast

"Tarento," Antoine greets.

"Hi," the insurgent waves at me.

I raise an eyebrow at the insurgent's non-aggressive behavior, and I quickly notice the eyes beneath the turban-mask are Felid, not Sunophsian. "Kaze?"

"Yup."

"Here, use these." Antoine hands me a sack full of items. "They were left here by White Sand."

I take the sack and open it. My eyes widen when I see there are five unlit bombs inside. My first thought is that the bombs will be useful to melt the Glimmerbeast's armor, but the Great King says, *"Give four of them back to Antoine. He must use them to blast through the hallway you entered through so those who wish not to fight can escape. Then, he must rally those of his men who remain, and attack the beast with courage and valiance."*

I take one bomb and hand the sack back to Antoine. "One's all I need. Use the rest to blast through that hallway," I point at the one my companions and I entered through, "so your men who don't want to fight can escape safely."

"Brilliant idea," Antoine says, taking the sack.

I can tell by the look on his face that he means to escape as well, so I continue, "Captain, I remember your bravery during the Battle of Königheim. You were a hero to us all because you fought and led fearlessly in the face of insurmountable odds. If you retreat tonight, I won't think any less of you. But please, keep in mind we need men of your courage to fight against the beast. If you can muster a group of your men to stand with us, it could mean the difference between victory and defeat."

Antoine nods, his face solemn. "I understand. I'll see what I can do."

"Good luck."

As Antoine turns to tell his men the plan, the Great King says, *"Give Kaze the fifth bomb. He must tie it on the head of the beast to destroy the sapphire."*

I grab Kaze's shoulder before he can follow Antoine, and I hand him the bomb. "This is for you, kohai."

"What am I supposed to do with this?"

"None of us here can match your agility. While the beast is distracted fighting the rest of us, we need you to get up on its head and tie the bomb to the sapphire."

Kaze's eyes widen. "The sapphire that shoots rays of death!?"

"Yes, *that* sapphire."

"Well, all right. I should probably ask Ibara Sensei first, though."

"Ibara Sensei will understand. He and Heiban will be *very* impressed with your bravery. You don't even have to tell them it was my idea. The credit's all yours."

"Ohh..." Kaze looks at the bomb, and then back at me. "I'll do it! Look, I even have a rope to tie it with."

"Good! You got this!"

Kaze runs toward the beast, which is now in the center of the room enduring bombardment from Scourge on one side and Heiban on the other. Its movements are less fluid; some of its leg joints have already been welded.

Khai and Yoko are likewise surrounding the beast, shooting arrows into nooks between the armor plating. It doesn't look like they're having much success.

The Great King says, "*It would be wise for Yoko and Khai to save their arrows at this stage in the fight; they will be more useful later on. Ask Yoko to release Sylva to help restrain the beast.*"

I run toward Khai and Yoko.

The Great King continues, "*Tell Ibara and Sylva to bind the beast's two back legs on the left side.*"

"*Got it.*"

I reach Khai and deliver the King's command, which he relays to Yoko. They both fall back to save their arrows, and Yoko releases Sylva from her acorn. The tree nymph has had ample time to recover from the Battle of Königheim, but she's terrified at the sight of the Glimmerbeast and cowers behind me.

"Come along, Sylva," I say, beginning to run toward Ibara. "We need your help to stop it."

I arrive beside Ibara to deliver the King's orders. He, unlike anyone else thus far, offers strong resistance. "Why should I listen to anything you say, traitor!?"

"We need your help, Ibara. The beast is too fast and too strong for us to hit with our weapons. Scourge and Heiban are working to weld the joints in its armor, but your vines will be much more effective. Even if you never listen to anything I say ever again, *please*, just this one time!"

"If you won't listen to him," Sylva says, "Then listen to me. You *fight* like a tree nymph, but if you don't *protect life* like a tree nymph, you're unworthy of your magic power! If you have *any* respect for your plant techniques, listen to my dearest Tarento and engage the beast this very instant!"

Ibara hesitates for a second, but with a hardly-noticeable nod at Sylva, he sends three vines toward the beast's two back legs on its left side.

Sylva sends her own vines, smaller but more numerous, in assistance.

"*Anyone else?*" I ask the Great King.

The beast caterwauls with frustration, sapphire aglow, and it rears up to face Scourge.

"Look out!" I shout.

Scourge rockets backward with jets of fire from his feet just in time to avoid incineration by the beast's death ray.

The Glimmerbeast turns sharply around, flicking its tail at Heiban to send him tumbling across the room.

"Damn it!" Ibara yells. The beast's movement caused him and Sylva to lose the legs they were trying to bind.

It turns toward Kaze next, sapphire glowing for another shot.

"Kaze!" I shout, running toward him.

Sylva's vines shove Kaze out of the way just in time to avoid the death ray. The vines themselves are obliterated.

BOOM!

The explosion comes from the hallway across the room, where Antoine has detonated the bombs to clear the rubble blocking their exit. The police cheer and make haste in their escape.

The beast stops at the sound of the blast. During the three seconds it stands still, Ibara and Sylva secure their hold on its two back legs. Then, with a bloodthirsty hiss, the beast scuttles toward the hallway.

"Oh no you don't!" Ibara says, tugging on the vines that had wrapped around two of its legs. Thanks to the efforts of Ibara and Sylva, assisted by the joints that have been welded, the beast stumbles and falls en route to the hallway.

Kaze seizes the opportunity. He jumps onto the Glimmerbeast's back and scales its torso, taking care to avoid the energy spines in his path. His ascent is made difficult when the beast rises with a shriek and bucks to throw him off.

"Hey!" Scourge throws a fireball in the beast's face and waves his arms. "Come and get me!"

The beast glowers at Scourge, the sapphire beginning to glow again.

An explosive kunai hits the side of the beast's torso.

"No, me!" Heiban shouts.

Nostalgia pierces my heart when I see Heiban's face; his mask had been broken when the beast hit him. A prick of guilt flashes when I see the scar on his forehead, which I dealt with the hilt of my katana as I secured my escape from Felidae.

The beast turns and fires its death ray at Heiban, who jumps aside with a wind technique.

"Whoa!" Kaze shouts, clinging to the top of the beast's head. "I can't do this if it keeps shooting like that!"

"Kaze is right," the Great King says. *"It's your turn now. The beast will continue its current tactics as long as its focus is on Scourge and Heiban. You must go up close with your katana to buy Kaze time to secure the bomb."*

"All right," I say aloud so the others can hear me, "I'm going in." Drawing my katana, I sprint toward the Glimmerbeast.

As I come, the beast faces me with a shriek and gouges the ground with its forearm scythes.

"Dodge left and skid."

I side-step left to avoid a strike from the scythe, and then skid underneath its belly. As I do, I notice there are sections of armor with cracks in them, likely caused by Scourge and Heiban's earlier attacks.

"Strike underneath the right front leg."

I jump to my feet and swing my katana, cutting through the crack and splitting the armor open.

"Avoid the counter-attack, then strike underneath the third leg on the right."

The beast reacts to my first attack by trying to stake me to the ground with its pointed legs. I duck and swerve to avoid several impalements on my way to the third-right leg, where I strike again.

"On fourth-right leg, strike the second joint from the top."

I jump to the side and hit my next target.

"Duck and roll."

I obey as the beast tries to strike me down with both of its forearm scythes.

"Turn, side-step left, and strike the side of its head."

The beast bows to grab me with its jaws, but I dodge and retaliate with a well-aimed blow on the side of the beast's head, where one of Heiban's kunai had left a mark.

"Run back under the beast, strike the crack between its two front legs, and continue on to strike the crack at the base of its tail."

As the beast screams in response to my head-strike, I dart underneath it once more to hit both cracks mentioned by the Great King.

"Duck and roll, and get out of there."

Chapter 56: Glimmerbeast

I get down just in time to avoid a tail-whip, and after jumping to my feet, I sprint away for a few seconds before turning back to look.

The beast has turned to give chase and moves to do so. The sapphire, now with a bomb tied over the center of it, begins to glow.

"Kaze, get down!" Heiban shouts.

The kohai slides down the beast's torso and lands nimbly before running toward his superior.

As Kaze makes his exit, the death ray ignites the bomb. The beast's head goes up in a cloud of smoke, fire, and blue sparks. The Glimmerbeast reels back with a scream. As it staggers along, the armor on its head and torso comes undone and clangs to the ground.

Now, with most of its armor removed, we see that the body of the beast is black like a material abyss, with spines of pink and blue bristling on its back, neck, and head. The cracked sapphire on its forehead is dull and gray, emitting a wisp of smoke. Its legs, forearms, and tail are still armored as before.

I notice a pink hourglass-shaped spot on the monster's abdomen.

"That's your next target," the Great King says. *"Now, all of your weapons— swords, bows, and magic—are fair game."*

I raise my voice in announcement, "Do you all see the hourglass on the underside of the beast? That's its weak spot. Give it everything you've got!"

"Yeah!" Scourge shouts, his fingers crackling with electricity.

Khai and Yoko come to join us, stringing their bows.

Ibara and Sylva stand ready with vines poised to strike.

Heiban grips his katana and smirks.

Kaze pulls out two kunai and holds them ready.

"Tonight, at long last," Antoine says, joining our ranks, "We few will band together to defend the citizens of Armavir from the tyranny of darkness. We will avenge the fallen, and we will fight bravely for the survival of those who live. We will not back down until this evil has been vanquished."

As Antoine speaks, a dozen of his men draw their weapons alongside us.

The Glimmerbeast screams, bristling its spines and breaking free from Ibara and Sylva's bindings as it comes toward us. Despite the welding in its joints, it's much faster without its body armor.

"Attack!" Antoine shouts, leading the charge.

"For the Great King!" Yoko shouts as she looses her arrow, securing the first hit on the beast's abdomen.

A bolt from Scourge comes next, hitting the hourglass with deadly accuracy.

A volley of arrows from Khai and the police follows, but the beast blocks the arrows with its forearm blades.

Those of us with swords, katanas, pikes, and vines rush forward to meet the beast as it comes. From there, the chaos of battle ensues.

I run underneath the beast with Antoine, dodging one of the scythe-blades as it comes down on me. Together we both score a hit on the abdomen and run out of the way, dodging the beast's piercing legs as we go. Ibara and two policemen are knocked down by the beast's tail, and wasting no time, I run in for another pass. I can tell by the sound of footsteps that Antoine is behind me.

As I come, Khai fires two arrows at point-blank range before sprinting away to avoid the beast's snapping jaws.

Ducking and rolling to avoid the beast's sweeping tail, I jump and strike the hourglass before running out of the way again.

Antoine lands a blow right behind me.

Heiban comes in after us, striking the hourglass *twice* on his pass, and also deflecting one of the beast's insectoid legs with his katana on the way out. He looks at me with a competitive smirk.

I roll my eyes and grip my katana, searching for my next opening.

Kaze scores a hit, jumping and spinning to avoid the beast's gouging attacks.

Scourge prepares to strike with a bolt of lightning, but the beast's attention is caught by the sparkling light and it retaliates with a tail-sweep.

A group of vines encircles the beast's body and forearms, constricting and trapping the blades to the beast's upper torso. "Aha!" Ibara shouts as he and Sylva send more vines to reinforce the first ones. Sylva recites an incantation which serves to thicken both of their bindings.

Three police pikemen rush in at that moment, thrusting their weapons into the beast's abdomen as far in as they'll go. They abandon their pikes and fall back immediately.

Glimmerbeast emits a deafening scream, rearing up and writhing in pain. Khai takes advantage of the beast's tantrum by getting three shots in. Yoko and the police archers get a few hits as well. Scourge throws a condensed fireball at the abdomen. The resulting blast sets the arrow shafts and pikes on fire.

The beast thrashes about, fighting to break free from its constraints and snapping its jaws at anyone who comes near.

Antoine looks at me and says, "Let's go in for another hit. I think we've almost beat it."

I nod. "Let's go!"

Antoine and I sprint toward the struggling beast. We approach from the front, away from the menace of its tail and through the open door provided by its immobilized forearms.

The beast sees us coming, of course, and it snaps its jaws madly while Ibara and Sylva pull back to keep it at bay.

Once underneath, each of us give the hourglass several strikes. Antoine was right; the hourglass is going dim, which hopefully signals the approaching defeat of the Glimmerbeast.

I hear gasps and shouts of alarm accompanied by a series of snaps. Suddenly, the beast is upon me and I'm knocked aside. I scramble back to my feet to see that the beast has freed itself and is now bearing down on Antoine, who lies face-up on the ground beneath it. The beast raises its scythe-blade and impales him.

"Antoine! *No!*" I shout, immediately sprinting toward the beast. It flicks Antoine aside before turning to face me.

Heiban falls in on my right, and Scourge on my left.

Arrows soar over our heads en route for the beast's abdomen, but it deflects them with its forearms before rearing up to strike us. I prepare myself to dodge the incoming assault.

The beast turns sharply. By the time I know what's happening, its tail slams into all of us with immense force.

I feel searing pain in my ribs as I tumble through the air, and more pain in my left hip as I skid along on the ground. "Gah," I groan, wincing as I try to get up. The pain is so great, I'd venture to guess my ribs are broken.

Heiban sits up, holding his arm, and glances with a frown at his katana, which rests twenty feet away from his position.

Scourge lies still on the ground.

"No..." I try in vain to stand; the pain holds me down.

The beast scuttles toward us with a wicked hiss.

Khai steps in front of us with three strung arrows aimed at the beast. Yoko takes a position beside him, as do all of the police except for three.

Sylva and one policeman, I see, are kneeling next to Antoine.

The other two are sprawled on the ground, along with Ibara and Kaze. I didn't see them get injured, but I suppose it happened when the vines snapped.

The Glimmerbeast now has the upper hand. There isn't much Khai, Yoko, and our remaining police allies can do to stop it. Why are they still fighting to defend us?

"Everyone, get out of here!" I say, my voice laced with panic. "Save yourselves while you can! We're finished!"

"Not a chance," Khai says without looking at us.

"Not until we avenge our captain," one of the policemen says.

"And everyone else who's fallen in this battle!" another policeman finishes.

Khai and the police archers fire their rounds, but the beast deflects them all.

Now the beast is upon us. I ask the Great King, *"What hope is left for us? Have you abandoned us to die here?"*

Shouting comes from down the hallway.

Tramping boots and clinking armor.

The beast turns, its ruby-red eyes gleaming with anger at the interruption, and it scrapes the ground with one of its scythe-blades.

Have the police brought reinforcements?

Those of us who are conscious look toward the hallway as the sounds grow louder.

"I haven't left you," the Great King says. *"I have given you victory over the Glimmerbeast, though not for you alone. It is time now for Jake and the Paladin Order to shine."*

At the Great King's words, Jake comes rushing out of the hall, brandishing Menouthis and his kite-shield with a mighty shout. Behind him, Paladins pour into the room with surprising speed, wielding an assortment of swords, javelins, and double-bladed pikes.

The beast screams and charges forth to fight its new adversaries.

"The hourglass!" I shout. "Aim for the hourglass!"

The Paladins spread out as they rush forward and surround the beast, forcing it to choose a target. They take turns distracting it while the others attack its weak point as we had done.

I'm amazed as I behold the Paladins in action. Every move is accurate and precise. One would think their armor would slow them down, but they're much faster and more agile than they look. They may not be as quick as Samurai, but I must admit their coordination is better than any Samurai team I've ever known. Samurai work best in pairs or threes, while it seems like Paladins have mastered formations of a dozen or more. I'll have to ask Jake more about this later, when we're not battling for our lives.

Two Paladins are thwacked by the beast's tail. The rest of them up their ante in response. One of the Paladins is taken in the beast's mouth and cast aside, but the ivory knights don't skip a beat.

My eyes fall on Jake, who stands out as the only one without a full suit of armor. He goads the beast to attack him, voluntarily playing the distraction so the others can slip underneath and deliver their blows. Indignation rises within me as I watch. I don't believe Jake should be the one distracting the beast. He needs to give that thing a taste of his blade.

"*Tell him*," the Great King says, confirming my intuition.

"Jake!" I shout. "Get in there!"

"I don't know about that," Jake says, eyes glued on beast. "The Paladins are more experienced than I am. I'd just get in the way."

"No, Jake! Get in there!"

"I'm not a Paladin!" He dodges a blow from the beast's scythe-blade.

"You may not be a Paladin of Armavir, but you *are* a Paladin of Marindel!"

"The Great King hasn't told me anything of the sort!"

"He's telling you now, trust me! Get in there and kill the beast!"

Khai joins in, "Come on, Jake!"

"Go Jake! Go Jake!" Yoko cheers.

After dodging another blow, Jake says to the Paladin nearest him, "Cover me." He maneuvers out of the beast's field of vision and searches for an opening. He's hesitant at first, breathing deeply. But he says, just above the din of battle, "I *am* a Paladin of Marindel. I *can* do this!"

The Glimmerbeast picks up a Paladin in its jaws and throws him at a column with a sickening crunch.

Urgently, Jake casts his shield aside and grips Menouthis with both hands before charging beneath the beast, narrowly dodging its pointed legs. With great force, he pierces the center of the hourglass. The gem on the hilt of Menouthis flashes green, and the beast buckles as if enduring contractions.

Jake pulls out the blade, shimmering green like the gem, and stabs again.

And again.

And again.

I cringe at the beast's agonized scream. It rears on its back legs, flailing its forearms and exposing the obliterated hourglass for all to see, before it topples backward and thrashes about like a dying cockroach. Its body simmers and boils, giving off a sickly red vapor. Within seconds, its final shriek fades into a hissing whisper as the Glimmerbeast melts into a pile of bubbling black sludge.

"Whoa," Yoko says.

The remaining Paladins stand around the puddle, still tense

as if they expect it to regenerate. Perhaps in the Academy they've learned about monsters that can do that. Thankfully, this is not one of those monsters.

Jake stands among the Paladins, still gripping his glowing green weapon.

For the first time since we entered the White Sand hideout, everything is silent except for our heavy breathing and sighs of relief.

57

Allegiance

Summer, 1419 AIE

~Celine~

I FEEL COLD.

I open my eyes. All I see is a dark and swirling mass of blue. Where am I? Am I...wet?

I'm rocking back and forth?

"Do you remember where you are?" The death-voice asks.

I groan, rubbing my eyes and blinking away the heaviness. I'm on a small ship being tossed about in the midst of a violent storm. When I recognize it, I immediately feel sick.

"On your feet."

I comply, getting on my knees and grabbing the mast for balance to pull myself up. In doing so, I realize I'm not injured. My back doesn't hurt anymore. I reach to feel where the wound should be, and I'm surprised to find it's no longer there. *"Am I dead?"* I ask.

"Not yet. Before receiving you into my dominion, I would like to have a word with you."

I frown. *"You've been having 'words' with me ever since the last time I had this dream."*

The sea in front the ship bulges and parts to reveal the sea monster from last time, rearing up high and tall, flexing its powerful body and flashing its fearsome teeth. With sharp green eyes it leers down at me and grins. This time, having heard Connor's story, I recognize the monster for what it is. "You're the Great Serpent, aren't you?"

"I am," the Serpent says. "The Seer told you about me, but he hasn't painted me in the greatest light."

"Well, you *are* a bit of a jerk."

"It's all a matter of perspective, my friend. I've brought you here to offer you a chance to live again."

"But," I speak slowly, "you said I'm not dead."

"Correct. Only my mercy keeps you alive for now. But when you accept my offer, I will empower you to live again with greater strength and beauty than ever before. You will be more powerful than any of your siblings, even more powerful than Sisera himself. Whatever you desire in all the realm will be yours for the taking."

"Really?" I raise an eyebrow. "What's the catch?"

"All you have to do," the Serpent lowers his massive head to my level, "is swear loyalty to me. It's very simple. I will let you do whatever you'd like. You'll have freedom to pursue the dreams of your heart, seize the riches you desire, and live like a queen for all the days of your long and prosperous life."

I tilt my head. "That sounds too good to be true. Connor said—"

"He does not know of what I speak. He and his cohorts are blinded by the Great King to many things. The Great King doesn't grant his followers freedom; he enslaves them. If you declare allegiance to me, I will grant you *unlimited* freedom. No one will be able to resist you for as long as you live."

I think about the Serpent's offer. Every fiber in my being leaps and grabs at his words. Oh, how I would *love* those things! The freedom, the power, the beauty! It's everything I've ever wanted, everything I've ever aspired to achieve. White Sand would be unable to control me any longer. I could leave Cloud Summit, travel to better lands, and live my life in peaceful bliss.

Yet...my heart is wary. Something's not right about this.

I remember what Connor said about the girl, Melody, who was deceived by the Serpent through a promise of power much like this one. What will happen if I accept it?

"Why do you hesitate? Does my offer not please you?"

"Well..." I trail off, taking a deep breath. "You once offered power and freedom to Melody, and her life is *still* messed up as a result. How can I trust you not to do the same thing to me?"

The Serpent chuckles. "There is no such person as Melody. Her story is merely a myth devised to slander me. Rest assured, I will do you no such harm."

"All right. Well, Connor said that Eli said you're a liar and a deceiver."

The Serpent flinches at the name of Eli, and he narrows his eyes. "Let me tell you—"

"Wait, hold on," I raise my hand with a smirk. "Connor also said that...*Eli* said—"

"QUIET!" The Serpent's movement causes the ship to buckle in the waves.

I yelp, clinging to the mast to avoid being thrown off. After steading my composure, I say, "You really don't like him, do you?"

The Serpent growls. "He's dead. Do not speak of him ever again."

I shrug. "All right. However, Connor said *he* already defeated you, and you have no power left to do anything except deceive people."

The Serpent laughs. "What lunacy! Surely you know that isn't true! Look at your own life. See the destruction, the chaos, and the death I've brought about! I have more authority than any follower of the Great King will ever know, and *no one* can take it from me. The realm is mine to command!"

Through this mildly entertaining conversation, I've realized something very important. The Serpent is horrible at denying the truth when he's faced with it directly.

Melody doesn't exist? Oh, please. I've never seen her, but if everything else Marindelian exists, like the Great Serpent and the Music of Marindel box, why wouldn't she?

Eli's dead? If that's the case, why is the Serpent so angry when I say his name?

The realm belongs to the Serpent? If so, why haven't the Seers been eradicated? What's stopping him from doing that?

And what's taking the Serpent so long to kill *me*, even though he's told me a hundred times I'm going to die? Doesn't it mean something that every time I'm about to die, a follower of the Great King rescues me?

Does the Serpent not even have authority to take my life?

"I grow impatient," the Serpent says. "Would you like to live, or would you like to die? Choose now."

I look up at the hideous snake and say, "I decline. Kill me if you can."

The Serpent narrows his eyes, baring his teeth in a furious snarl. "For what reason do you seek to defy me?"

"You're an asshole."

The Serpent hisses. "Do you think petty insults will have any effect on—"

"Eli."

"NO!"

The ship buckles and rises out of the sea. I look over the side to see that the Serpent has picked it up on the fluke of his tail, and now his snout is a dozen feet away.

I face him with confidence. The longer I spend in his presence, the less I fear him.

"Do you know where your powers come from?" The Serpent asks.

"Sisera. Why?"

"No, they come from me. *Mine* is the art of deception and illusion. Everything you are and everything you've become is because of *me*. Do you not realize I can take it all away from you? What will you be without your illusions? Come now, tell me."

I cross my arms. "Look here, Serpent. You just backed down from your initial plan to kill me. If you can't even take my life, how can you take my powers?"

"Foolish girl. I'll kill you *and* take your powers!"

"I dare you."

"Oh, I will do *so* much worse," the Serpent says, fanning out the spikes that crown his neck. "If you will not declare allegiance to me, then I have no choice but to use force."

I laugh. "Yeah, good luck with—"

A deafening, high-pitched ringing fills the air. I scream at the sound, dropping to my knees and holding my hands over my ears.

I feel a powerful force invading my manas'ruh like a thundering cavalry, sweeping through my mental defenses and seizing control of my psyche. The pain is immense. I try to gather my manas'ruh for a counter-offensive, but it's too late.

"You put up a grand fight," the Serpent says, "but you forgot one simple truth that makes all the difference: you still belong to me."

I'm powerless to resist. Before losing autonomy of my thoughts and feelings, I remember one thing that shakes me to the very core.

This is how Melody killed Eli.

Afterward, all is darkness in my soul.

I feel nothing. I think nothing.

All is quiet, save for the infinite ringing.

"*Right now,*" the Serpent speaks in the auditorium of my soul, "*Connor and Bennett fight for the right to take your life. When you awake, to save yourself, you must kill them both.*"

"N-no," I whisper.

"*You must,*" The Serpent encroaches further on my will. "*Bennett seeks to destroy you; that is obvious. Connor is far worse. He befriends you now, only to send you to your death in Meiro.*"

He doesn't care about you; he wants to use you. Kill Connor. Kill Bennett. Kill them all!"

I mutter, "Kill...everyone..."

"Yes. Everyone deserves to die. Every last one of them."

"Everyone..."

"Celine." The voice cuts through the Din of the Serpent.

"Kill them all."

"Celine," the voice calls again.

I open my eyes to see a bright light. Blinking through the wind and the rain, I notice the light has a face: a ruddy, handsome face with the friendliest eyes I've ever seen.

"Celine, look at me."

My eyes widen. I can make out his features perfectly now. He crouches in front of me, looking into my eyes with one comforting hand on my shoulder. Though I've never seen him before, I know exactly who he is.

"E-Eli?"

He smiles. "The one and only."

"No," the Serpent growls.

I look beyond Eli at the Serpent's enormous face. His eyes are narrowed and neck-spines quivering as he seeks to maintain control over my psyche. His words become stronger: *"Kill Bennett. Kill Connor. They deserve to die!"*

"Kill..."

"Don't look at him," Eli says. "Look at me, Celine. Look at me."

I look again at Eli.

"There, that's it," Eli's smile brightens. "Let me tell you something, Celine. The Great King loves you, and I love you."

I stare back at him, mouth agape. Tears trickle down my face in the midst of the driving rain.

Jed has been telling me that since the day I mugged him. After Jed's death, Connor took his place. I must've heard it a dozen times, but I never believed it. Now, seeing and hearing Eli himself saying those words to me, I finally understand.

I finally understand.

"Do you receive it?" Eli asks.

I nod, my lower lip quivering and tears flowing freely.

"Will you follow the Great King? Will you commit your life to him?"

I burst into a fit of sobbing, but I reply as best as I can, "Yes!"

"Celine," Eli says, wrapping his arms around me as I collapse into his embrace. "You are a wonderful treasure, and a precious daughter of the Great King. Don't you ever forget it. Don't you ever, *ever* forget it!"

"*Stop this now!*" the Serpent says. His voice is much quieter now, and I can hardly hear the ringing anymore. "*You are not worthy of his affection! Don't you remember what you've done? You thieving, murdering, conceited wretch of a girl!*"

"Resist him," Eli says.

I begin to garner my mental defenses. I find that now, remarkably, the ground I take within my psyche is immediately given up by the Serpent. It's as if I've been given a lantern, and now I'm chasing the darkness by simply walking into it.

"*No! Stop! You're making a mistake!*"

"*Shut up! You're not welcome here anymore. I don't want to hear your voice or your lies ever again, you hear me!? I declare allegiance to the Great King, and I defy you! Go away!*"

The Serpent recoils with a furious roar, dropping the ship back into the sea.

Eli holds me steady as the ship falls. Then he looks at me with a brilliant smile. "Well done!"

I return his gaze with a stupid, weeping grin. "Thanks."

"Come, let's stand," Eli says, rising to his feet and helping me up as well. He allows me to hold his arm and lean on him for support.

The Serpent turns to face us with his fins and spines fanned out. He snarls, "You cannot prevail, Great Prince. She still deserves to die!"

"Not anymore. She has been forgiven of her crimes and is now a legitimate daughter of the King. Celine no longer belongs to you. Begone!"

The Serpent hisses, recoiling in shame like a disobedient child who's been caught with nowhere to hide.

Eli looks up at the sky and nods.

I follow his gaze to see three bright lights diving toward the Serpent. They pass over with frightening speed, releasing a volley of energy bombs on him. He writhes and thrashes under the attack, and with a defiant shriek, he melts into a pillar of black sludge before disappearing among the waves.

"Wow," I say between sniffles.

"The Galyyrim will keep the Serpent in check. As long as you keep your trust in me and in the Great King, there's nothing he can do to come against you."

"B-but," I sniff, "Am I still going to die?"

Eli shakes his head. "Your wounds have been healed. When you awake, you'll be a new person. Join forces with Connor, Tarento, Scourge, Yoko, Jake, and Khai. They will be your new family. They will take care of you and teach you about Marindel. You, also, have much to teach them."

"Okay," I say, standing on my own. "I'll do it."

"Wonderful," Eli says, smiling once more. "Before you go, I have one final thing to say."

"Yes?"

The sheer power of Eli's gaze is overwhelming in all the best ways, and it fills me with strength and confidence. He says, "Remember my love for you. Always, *always* remember my love for you."

BEFORE OPENING MY eyes, I hear Connor's voice: "If anyone deserves to die for all the evil things they've done, it's you."

Then Bennett's voice. "B-b-but...I..."

A sense of urgency launches me to my feet.

Connor stands over Bennett with his sword raised. "Chief Bennett, I won't allow you to hurt anyone else ever again."

I shout, "Connor! Stop!"

Both of them look at me, eyes wide.

"Bennett's defeated," I say. "You've already won. Don't stoop to his level by taking his life."

Connor looks bewildered for a few seconds before nodding and sheathing his sword. "You're right. I'm sorry."

I see the look in Bennett's eye. He thinks I'm doing him a little favor.

Well, guess what else I see?

A busted headband. Fancy that.

I establish a mental connection with Bennett.

"Are you all right?" Connor asks, coming toward me.

Bennett jumps to his feet and lunges after Connor with an angry shout. I make him believe his wrists and ankles are shackled together, so he curls up mid-lunge and falls.

Connor whirls around, gaze dropping to see Bennett on the ground. "What just happened?"

The chief grits his teeth and says, "This is an outrage! Let me go at once! The Illusionist cannot escape again!"

"Hey, Chief," Connor says, "She let you live. That's more than I was about to do, and definitely more than you would've done. Why don't you give her a break?"

"Never! She's my prisoner!"

I chuckle. It's hard to take him seriously while he's curled up with his butt in the air like that. "You're *our* prisoner, now."

"Our?" Connor asks, looking at me in surprise.

I wink and say, "Let's give Bennett a taste of his own handcuffs, shall we? Then we'll go see if your friends need our help."

"*Our* help?" Connor scratches his head. "Are you feeling all right, Celine?"

"Better than ever," I say, pickpocketing Bennett for a pair of handcuffs and three blics. I hand the cuffs to Connor. "Snap these on him. I'm gonna go find a chair."

Bennett looks at me with wide eyes. He remembers.

"Leverage," I say with an innocent smile before walking off.

58
Never Forget
Summer, 1419 AIE

~Tarento~

T HE SILENCE IS broken by Yoko, who slings her bow over her shoulder and says, "I'm going to help Antoine!"

"Go ahead," Khai says.

She scampers across the room to where Sylva still comforts the wounded captain. I can tell he's talking, which means he's still alive. That's a good sign. The police need a leader like him to look up to.

"You hurt?" Heiban asks. He stands near me, having retrieved his katana.

"I might've broken a few ribs. How's your arm? I noticed you were holding it earlier."

"It's not bad."

I catch the sinister gleam in his eye just as I'm lifted off the ground and constricted until the pain causes me to shout.

Ibara's vines.

"Hey!" Khai says, drawing his bow.

Heiban kicks Khai's bow out of his grip and points his katana at me with a smirk. "The monster's dead. Now, you're mine."

My stomach falls like a rock. While fighting the beast, it felt like Heiban and I were allies again. I'd let my guard down. I should've known he'd turn around and do this.

"Heiban! Ibara!" Jake shouts, running toward us while flashing

Menouthis. "Unless you want to end up like that monster, you'd better put Tarento down!"

Kaze intercepts Jake and takes him down with a series of paralytic jabs.

Ibara chuckles. "You did well, Jake, but don't get cocky."

"What's going on over there?" A Paladins asks. They're coming this way now.

Heiban looks at them and says, "This is Felidae business. You need not interfere."

"Is that so?" another Paladins asks. "Do you really think we'll let you have your way with the hero who saved our king?"

"Stand down, knights of Armavir. No good deed performed by this man will clear him of guilt in *my* kingdom."

"You're a long way from home, bud. Felid rules don't apply in Cloud Summit."

"Mind your words, you disrespectful morons!"

"Heiban Sensei," Kaze backs away from the advancing Paladins. "Maybe we should—"

"Kaze!" Heiban snaps, and then to the Paladins he says, "We made a deal with Chief Bennett. We helped him defeat White Sand, and now we'll be leaving with our prize. We have no quarrel with you or with Armavir, but if you stand in our way, we'll have no choice but to..." he trails off. His eyes widen and he stands still, as if in a trance.

Ibara's vines set me down and retreat back into his armor. Both he and Kaze are also entranced.

"Er," Heiban clears his throat. "Ynes, yes, Lord Zetsumei. It will be done." All three of them begin stomping and waving their arms in sync with one another. I...I think they're trying to dance.

"What are they doing?" Khai asks, gaze narrow.

One of the policemen ventures a guess, "Is it a Felid ritual to reap our souls?"

"No," I reply. "They're out of their minds."

"You just noticed?" Khai chuckles.

After a series of humiliating moves, the Samurai straighten like boards and fall on the ground.

"Can it be?" A policeman says, pointing down the hall from whence the beast came. "Look! Over there!"

We all look to see Connor and Celine walking toward us, escorting between them a handcuffed and grumpy-looking Chief Bennett.

590

"The Illusionist!" The police and some of the Paladins reach for their weapons.

"It's all right, everyone!" Connor says. "She's not going to harm you."

"Perhaps not," Celine says, "but an obligatory flash mob is always an option."

"Don't tease them," Connor whispers to her.

"Sorry," Celine says with an eye-roll.

A policeman steps forward and asks Bennett, "Chief, what happened? You've...arrested yourself?"

"Of course not, you idiot. In fact, I order you to release me, and arrest all of these criminals at once. Paladins, help him."

"I hereby veto your command," a voice replies from down the other hall.

We turn to see Prince Oliver coming in at the head of a troop of Paladins, royal guards, and medics.

"Prince Oliver!" Bennett's eyes widen. "Please, have some sense! Don't you see this madness? They've arrested me, and the Illusionist stands freely right beside me! Everyone here is in league with her!"

Oliver ignores him for a moment as he orders his fighting men to search the hideout and capture any remaining insurgents, and the medics to begin treating the injured. Then he approaches Bennett and says, "You've avoided the consequences of your crimes for long enough. My father thought it well to let you off easy after the Purge, but you've crossed the line once again. Neither the king nor I authorized you to launch a full-scale invasion of the White Sand hideout. If it weren't for this fine young man here," he gestures toward Jake, "I wouldn't have heard about it in time to send reinforcements and clean up your mess."

"Your Majesty, please! I've only done what is necessary to uphold the law in the city. It's my duty! How can you blame *me* when we have scum like *her*," he glares at Celine, "running the streets with their lawless corruption? Someone has to stand against them, and I have done just that!"

"Save your breath. We'll discuss things further in the context of a fair trial. Men," he looks at the policemen standing with us, "take Bennett and his mercenaries to the Hall of Justice for solitary confinement."

The police exchange dumfounded glances at the thought of putting their fearsome chief behind bars. "Yes, Your Majesty, right away!"

The Felids, still entranced, stand and hold their arms forward for the police to handcuff. Then they're escorted out of the room.

"You'll regret this, Prince Oliver," Bennett growls as his own men take him away. "You're still young, and you have much to learn about justice!"

"Not from you." Oliver turns away from Bennett's departing figure and goes to speak with the Paladins who fought the Glimmerbeast.

Just then, Valerie, the medic, kneels beside me. "Where are you hurt?"

My heart sinks. I don't think she'd be offering to help me if she knew what happened to her cousin. She shares many physical attributes with him, now that I think of it: dirty-blond hair, hazel-brown eyes, and a narrow jaw. I reply, "Ribs and hip. I think they're broken."

"All right. I'll have to put you to sleep, then. Do you mind?"

"Not at all. But first, I have something to tell you."

"What is it?"

I pause to think through my wording. Meanwhile, Connor stands beside Valerie and eyes me with concern. I nod in greeting, and then say to Valerie, "Your cousin fought bravely tonight, but he's been critically injured. Please tend to him as quickly as you can. Another medic will take care of me."

Valerie's face turns pale and she looks up to search for him.

"Yoko and Sylva are tending to him now," I say, "But he'll need your help to make it through. I dare say he'll make an excellent chief of police after his recovery."

She looks back at me. "Do you really think they'll promote him?"

"There's no better man for the job. I haven't met a single person in Cloud Summit more valiant than Antoine."

"I second that," Connor says.

Valerie smiles, blinking through her tears. I can tell she's trying to keep her composure for my sake, despite how terrified she is for the life of her cousin. "Are you ready to rest?"

"Yes." I'll make this as simple as possible for her.

"All right. Lay down on the ground, face up...take deep breaths... watch my fingers..."

I comply, allowing my mind to decompress as I watch her hand hover above my face. It's a very calming experience. The last thing I'm aware of is the sound of her snapping fingers.

Chapter 58: Never Forget

~Connor~

W‌HILE V‌ALERIE PUTS Tarento to sleep, I scan the room to find Antoine. There he is, about halfway across. I see Yoko and Sylva, as Tarento indicated, with a few policemen gathered around as well.

Valerie flags down another medic and says, "This man has a broken rib and hip; I've already put him to sleep. Can you take over? I need to find my cousin!"

"Of course ma'am," the medic says, kneeling beside Tarento and unpacking his supplies.

I tap Valerie's arm and say, "Antoine's this way. Let's hurry!"

We run together across the room. En route to Antoine, we pass multiple bodies on the floor, both White Sand and police, both injured and dead. We pass the still-burning rubble of a fallen archer platform, and we have to watch our footing to avoid gouges in the ground presumably left by the beast Shaama transformed into. That battle couldn't have been a pretty one.

Arriving beside Antoine, we both gasp. He's lying on his back, eyes closed, face drained of all color. His helmet and the armor plating on his torso have been removed, and the area from his armpits down to his lower abdomen is covered with a blood-soaked white cloth. A cluster of vines hold the cloth in place. Sylva's hands are on Antoine's forehead while she mutters an incantation. Four of Antoine's men, helmets off, look on in somber silence.

"I don't have any more cabbit weed!" Yoko says, digging frantically in her bag. "It must have been lost when the harpies got me, or when the police arrested me, or—"

"Here," Valerie interrupts, kneeling beside them. She pulls out a small sack and hands Yoko a sprig of cabbit weed.

"Thanks," Yoko takes the herb and slips it between Antoine's lips.

The police captain makes little effort to swallow. At the sound of Valerie's voice, he opens his eyes. "Val..."

"Antoine!" Valerie takes her cousin's hand and holds it tight. Tears begin dripping down her face.

In my peripheral vision, I see Scourge has come to join us, using a broken pike as a crutch. I offer my arm for him to lean on, and he looks at Antoine with a sad frown.

"Antoine," Valerie sobs, "*Please* don't die! You have to pull through, you *have* to!"

Antoine's voice is raspy and quiet. The cabbit weed is visible on his tongue as he speaks. "I'm sorry, Val, I—"

"Swallow the herb!" Valerie says, uncorking a canteen and moving it toward Antoine's mouth.

"Too late," Antoine whispers, refusing to drink. "It's all right."

Yoko speaks up, "You'll be okay, Antoine! Hang in there! Sylva's magic will keep you alive."

"I'd be dead already without her," Antoine's lip curls in a weak smile. "I'm glad I can see you...one last time...Val...Connor..." He looks at me.

Meeting Antoine's gaze, I choke up.

When I talked with Antoine earlier in the battle, I expressed my desire to see him again after the fighting was over. But I didn't expect to see him like this.

"Antoine, no!" Valerie shouts. "Cloud Summit needs you! *I* need you! Please, don't go!"

My heart breaks for Valerie. I don't know her story, but I have a feeling Antoine may be the only close family member she has left. I remember when I lost my father. Everything changed, then. I have no home left to return to. Maybe Valerie has a similar story.

Tears trickle down my face as I think about it.

I know deep in my heart that this is Antoine's final moment.

Antoine's gaze lingers on me. He says, "Good luck, Seer. Stay strong."

I nod, suppressing a sob. "Thank you, Antoine. For everything."

Antoine looks again at his grieving cousin. "Val, I...I love you. Never forget...Verdyth..."

"Antoine!" Valerie cries.

Sylva stops her incantation and frowns, removing her hands from Antoine's forehead.

His eyes have glazed over.

Captain Antoine is dead.

No one speaks for a moment. Valerie weeps quietly, her tears dripping on Antoine's body as she cradles his arm.

Scourge crouches beside Yoko, who immediately embraces him and weeps.

I look at the ground, away from the scene.

Three deaths, now. Three.

"Great King," I plead, *"Will this ever end? Must all good people be destroyed by evil?"*

I remember Penn's words, "Loss of life is a great tragedy and a horrible misfortune—the cost of living in a realm at war."

"Verdyth," Sylva whispers. Her tears have a honey-golden hue to them. "I saw Antoine's memories as he spoke. He and his family saved many magical creatures from trappers. Those who hired the trappers retaliated without mercy. Only he and Valerie escaped."

"Ugh!" Yoko clenches her fist. "That's pure evil. I *hate* those guys!"

"Who would do such a thing?" One of Antoine's men asks.

There's a pause.

Valerie speaks, voice trembling. "There are those in this realm who seek to exploit people and creatures to achieve their own twisted ends. After what happened in Verdyth, Antoine and I vowed to do anything in our power to save as many lives as we could. Me as a medic, and him...as a police officer." She chokes up.

The Great King says to me, *"Those who take a stand against evil understand the risk involved. They commit themselves to the task of challenging darkness, wherever it may appear—no matter the cost. No loss of life will be forgotten. No sacrifice will be in vain. The lives of Marcellus, of Jed, and of Antoine will be remembered in this realm for eras to come. As the Final Seer, you must understand this. Before the final days are over, many more lives will fall victim to dark forces. But they will not be gone forever. Encourage your friends in their grief. Stay strong, no matter how bleak the circumstances. You know the hope which overcomes even death. I will be with you to the very end."*

"You will be with us to the end," I affirm, blinking my tears away and composing myself. I kneel beside Valerie and say, "Even in the short time I knew him, Antoine was a man of honor and integrity, unlike anyone I've ever known. In his duties, he went far above and beyond what was required of him. Never once did he back down from conflict. Not in Königheim, and certainly not here. He gave his life to save the people of Cloud Summit from the tyranny of White Sand. He gave his life for you, for me, for all of us." I look at Antoine's men, who nod in response. "We won't forget his sacrifice. We won't forget what Antoine stood for. We'll keep fighting against the darkness, and we'll do so with the power and authority Prince Eli won for us when he gave his own life to save Melody. To save all of us."

I tell a short version of the Great Story, with emphasis on Eli's willingness to submit his own life to the destructive powers of the Serpent. I go on to explain how, when Eli was raised to life by the Great King, he reclaimed Melody's lost authority and distributed it across the realm. "Now, all who pledge allegiance to the Great King have the power to resist the darkness of the Great Serpent. The war will not be without its casualties. But to the very end, the Great King will never abandon us."

"It may appear for a time that darkness has won," Scourge says, paraphrasing the words of Guinevere, "But take heart, and know that the Great King has every intention of turning all darkness into light."

Valerie, still beside Antoine, rests her face on his. She whispers, "I will never forget. For the sake of our family, and for everything we love and hold dear, I will never stop fighting. I will *never* forget Verdyth. I will *never* forget this night. Goodbye, cousin. I hope I'll see you again someday."

"Well said," Scourge says. "I believe you *will* see him again."

Just then, Antoine's men shoot to their feet and stand at attention.

"At ease," Prince Oliver says, coming to stand among us with two royal guards in tow. He frowns at the sight of Antoine's body. "I was afraid it'd come to this. Bennett's reckless venture has cost us too many good men."

"Your Majesty," Valerie says, standing to face Oliver with a curtsy. "Could you please help us take Antoine's body out of this dreadful place? I'd like to see to it that he is prepared for burial."

"Of course, miss." Oliver orders one of his guards, "Bring us a stretcher."

"Yessir." The guard leaves.

I stand. "Prince Oliver, thank you for your help tonight. None of us would have survived if you hadn't sent the Paladins when you did."

Oliver smiles and places a hand on my shoulder. "Don't mention it, my friend. In fact, *I* should be the one thanking *you*. I've been meaning to apologize for my ignorance concerning the Königheim bombing. Your ragtag group of misfits may not seem like much, but you've all made significant contributions to the victory we can now celebrate, with Bennett behind bars and White Sand defeated for good. Cloud Summit will remember you as heroes, and rightfully so!"

I nearly blush at the prince's compliment. "Thank you, Your Majesty, I-I don't know what to say!"

"There's nothing to be said," Oliver says with a grand smile that reminds me of Eli. "We are in your debt, Connor the Seer."

Oliver's guard returns then, followed by two medics with a stretcher. The police and I hoist Antoine's body onto the stretcher and cover it with a white blanket provided by the medics. Oliver orders his guards to carry the stretcher so the medics can go treat more of the injured.

"Connor," Valerie says, eyeing me with a tearful smile. "Thank you for your words tonight. I would love to hear more about the Great King sometime."

I return her smile and nod. "Of course. After all this is over, I'll pay you a visit. Will I find you at the medicine guild?"

"Yes, just ask for me."

"I'll come too!" Yoko says to Valerie. "I have so many questions for you—about medic stuff, of course. Anything I can learn before we leave Cloud Summit would be really useful!"

Valerie chuckles. "Of course! I look forward to it."

59
Together
Summer, 1419 AIE

~Connor~

BY THE TIME my friends and I emerged from the White Sand hideout, it was late morning. Upon hearing we had no official place to stay, Prince Oliver sent a few of his noblemen with us to a hostel to make sure we were cared for. We had a meal that was both enormous and delicious, comfortable beds to sleep on, new clothes, and medics to treat and monitor our wounds. It's been two days since.

During that time, Celine told us about her illusion-battle with the Serpent, and how she finally chose allegiance to the Great King. We were in awe and encouraged to know the Great King and Prince Eli were fighting for Celine's life, even as we were fighting for her in the hideout.

She also mentioned the letter from Jaedis, which asked Shaama to destroy us. That knowledge, along with the others' accounts of the Glimmerbeast battle, was a sobering reminder that Jaedis is still our primary adversary and will stop at nothing to end our quest. It is to his kingdom in the north, the accursed land of Meiro, where we must journey next.

This morning, one of Prince Oliver's couriers came by with a formal invitation to attend a ceremony outside the Hall of Justice in the afternoon. He requested we all be present and prepared to be recognized for our efforts in the Battle of the Catacombs. We took

Chapter 59: Together

the opportunity to ask the courier for details about the aftermath of the battle and the fate of certain individuals.

All known Offspring of Sisera have been confirmed dead, except for Abdeel, who was arrested and imprisoned. In addition, fifteen White Sand insurgents were found alive and imprisoned.

A fair number of White Sand insurgents in the hideout were not Sunophsians at all, but Armavirans who volunteered to fight for White Sand against Chief Bennett. They, along with the police who helped load Königheim with explosives, were recruited over a period of several moons following the Purge. This explained how White Sand, supposedly few in number, had so many fighters in the catacombs. Dressed in White Sand garb, it was difficult to tell the Armavirans and Sunophsians apart in the heat of battle. Twenty Armaviran insurgents were captured and arrested.

All of the insurgents, along with Chief Bennett, were declared guilty in their respective trials and sentenced to life in prison.

Heiban, Ibara, and Kaze were convicted in their trial for meddling in the affairs of the Paladin Order, for conspiring with Chief Bennett, and for causing the shipyard fire in Bayside Harbor. They were given a two-year prison sentence, to be followed by permanent exile from Armavir.

A search is underway for Meiling and Heiban's soldiers in the coastal towns of Armavir, led by the Bayside Harbor division of the Paladin Order. But as of yet, no sightings have been reported.

What to do with the treasure in the hideout is a subject that will take some time to sort out. According to the courier, Oliver hopes to enact a distribution plan to stimulate economic growth in Armavir. However, the courier believes at least half of the treasure will be used to fund the reconstruction of Königheim Castle.

The Exotic Goods Hub has been tagged for shutdown by the Bureau of Commerce, but Kamau and Irena are negotiating with them for permission to legalize the shop and become the owners. Upon hearing this, we decided to write a letter to the Bureau of Commerce in support of Kamau, detailing his role in helping us discover White Sand's plot and outfitting us for the Battle of the Catacombs. The letter was signed by me, Jake, Tarento and Khai.

During the ceremony this afternoon, all of us stood onstage to receive medals of honor from King Alphonse V, cheered on by a crowd waving flags and banners. Along with us were Sylva, the survivors among Antoine's brave men, and the Paladins who fought against the Glimmerbeast.

We were given our medals by the king, a slender old man with a scraggly beard and a droopy face, clothed with a royal blue robe and a gold crown. Prince Oliver followed, face beaming, shaking our hands in congratulations.

Celine was the last person in line, and inevitably, she was singled out. The king refrained from giving her a medal. Instead, he placed a hand on her shoulder and said, "Step forward, young lady."

Celine looked at me with a glimmer of fear.

Oliver addressed the crowd, "Several days ago, as you may remember, this same woman was on this very stage, condemned to die for her crimes against the kingdom of Armavir. She has since renounced her White Sand affiliations and helped bring a favorable end to the Battle of the Catacombs. Nevertheless, the laws of Armavir must be upheld." He paused to look at the silent crowd. "I have decided to give the Illusionist a new sentence. Rather than death, she will be sent into exile."

Celine looked back at us with wide eyes.

"Prince Oliver!" I shouted, but he silenced me with a raised hand.

"She will be exiled from Cloud Summit, and furthermore, she is to be guarded at all times by the brave heroes you see beside me. Together, they will go on a perilous quest to the northern land of Meiro, where they will defeat a growing evil which threatens the security of the mainland." He then addressed Celine, "From this day onward, Celine, commit to using your abilities for the good of others. Convince us by your actions to see you as you are in the eyes of the Great King, not as the terror White Sand raised you to be. I'm confident you will impress us with your transition to goodness, so that in time, we may welcome you back to Cloud Summit with cheers of admiration and respect."

"Thank you," Celine said with a grateful smile.

With that, King Alphonse placed the medal around her neck. "For your bravery and your mercy in battle."

The crowd cheered.

Celine looked back at us, teary-eyed and beside herself with joy. She later told us she'd never felt so celebrated in her life.

The final segment of the ceremony was dedicated to those who had perished in the events of the last few days, most notably Captain Antoine. Oliver told the crowd of his bravery in the Battle of Königheim and the Battle of the Catacombs, the details of which were relayed to him by Tarento and others prior to the ceremony. Antoine was posthumously awarded a medal of honor, which was presented to Valerie. Finally, there was a moment of silence in memory of the fallen heroes.

Afterward, Prince Oliver delivered a riveting speech about rebuilding Armavir and rising from the afflictions of the past. He revealed his intention to take on the role of interim chief of police until another person was found or trained to inherit the position. In closing, he expressed his hope that he would be as great an example of valiance to the people of Armavir as Antoine was.

The crowd's roar of approval was deafening.

"That's a big responsibility for one man to take, don't you think?" Tarento whispered to me.

"I'd say. The Paladin Order alone must be difficult to manage. I hope he finds a new chief of police soon, or he'll be getting gray hairs quick."

Now, I stand on the balcony of our hostel room overlooking the nighttime cityscape of Cloud Summit. The moon shines in the cloudless sky, casting its glow upon the towers and spires of the city. A gentle breeze blows across my face. The dry chill it carries brings with it the first hint of autumn.

We've come a long way, my friends and I.

We've overcome hurdle after hurdle, obstacle after obstacle. It hasn't been easy, and we've lost many brave people along the way. Still, I know we're on the right track. I feel it deep within my heart. The Great King is proud of our progress and our faithfulness to him, and as we move forward, he'll continue to protect and provide for us.

It will be hard, yes. That is to be expected. The Great Serpent will not passively accept our advances, and he will try to stop us at every opportunity.

However, as chosen followers of the Great King, we will not stop. We will not give in. We will not let up, and we will not quit.

He is worth it all.

The Kingdom of Marindel is worth it all.

Melody is worth it all.

"Is everything all right?" Tarento asks, coming to stand beside me.

"I'm doing well. Just getting some air and collecting my thoughts."

"Do you mind if I join you?"

"Not at all, please do."

We stand together in silence, enjoying the cool breeze and gazing out at the city. After a few moments, Tarento says, "We should take another week to rest and recover. What do you think?"

"I don't see a problem with that. No one's after you anymore, and there isn't much Jaedis can do to get us while we're in the city. Once we leave, though, it'll be back to the grind. We should be ready when that happens."

"Indeed. Plus, I'd like to get to know Celine a bit before we go. Don't take this the wrong way, but it may be a while before I trust her with my life."

"I understand. I think we could all use a bit of team-bonding with our seventh member."

"Are you talking about me?" Celine asks, squeezing between us to lean against the banister.

"Yup," I say, moving aside to give her room. "All good things, I promise."

"Good," she says, her dark eyes glittering with the light of the stars as she looks out at the city.

"Celine," Tarento says, "I've been wanting to thank you for rescuing me from Heiban the other day."

"Not a problem. If anyone gives you trouble like that, you just let me know, all right?"

"Will do," Tarento says with a light smile, looking out at the city again.

"I uh…" Celine struggles for words, "I-I want to thank you both for…for believing in me."

I look at her. "Of course, Celine."

"No, I mean it," she meets my gaze, her eyes welling up. "I was hopelessly lost. I threw Jed in a garbage heap, I humiliated all of you at the restaurant, I *almost* left Scourge and Yoko behind as they were rescuing me, and I was *so* disrespectful when you invited me to dinner and told me the Great Story. I'm so sorry. I promise, I really am."

I place a hand on her back. "Yes, I know. I forgive you, Celine, and I hope you know the Great King does too."

"I know," she says, pulling me in for a hug.

I embrace her in return, having to fight against the feelings of excitement that come because Celine is hugging me. The fact that she pulls Tarento into it helps. This is a three-way friend-hug. Nothing more, nothing less.

Chapter 59: Together

After a moment, Celine says, "You guys are my brothers now. I don't think you can imagine how much that means to me."

Her statement is powerful.

Although I grew up without siblings, the Great King enables me to feel the weight of her words. She's lived her whole life in the footsteps of her older brothers, striving to please them and earn their affection. Now, having been deprived of them, she has no one to look to but us.

We're her family now.

We're siblings together with Prince Eli and Melody, in the royal family of the Great King. In time, I believe Celine will understand this truth more than Tarento and I ever will.

We stand on the balcony with our arms across each other's shoulders, beholding the view and relishing the breeze. I believe we are all, in our own ways, praising the Great King for his wise and loving leadership in our lives.

JAEDIS OPENS HIS eyes.

The interior of a simple wooden cottage greets him. He glances at the fireplace, which burns beneath a cauldron of stew. Then at the table across the room, set with plates and silverware for dinner. Then at the closed door, flanked on either side by windows covered with thick woolen drapes.

The sorcerer stands to his feet, holding his magic staff with a white-knuckle grip. He saw everything. Every detail of Shaama's defeat.

A simple task, failed by a dreadfully incompetent hag.

Jaedis steps toward the door. He glances aside, where a hallway leads to a couple of bedrooms. Three drops of blood lie at the entrance. Then he looks at the doormat in front of him and notes the presence of dusty hoof-prints.

How could a single Armaviran farm boy become such a nuisance? An absolute nobody! And yet, he assembled a team capable of defeating a monster as powerful as the Glimmerbeast. One of Typhon's most prized creations.

Jaedis opens the door and steps outside.

Everything around him glows green with the fire of the Nox Abyssae. Cottages, stables, carts, trees, and fields.

Everything.

Jaedis takes a deep breath, relishing the nighttime air laced with smoke.

It wasn't long ago when he received word that Melody was last seen in a village on the Armaviran shore of Solvys Lake. He immediately sent his elite champions to intercept her.

One of the Nox Abyssae trots up to greet its master. After rubbing against his legs, it yips and beckons with its tail for him to follow.

The creature leads Jaedis through the burning village toward the lakeshore, where a group has been gathered. The eerie firelight illuminates roughly a hundred people in kneeling positions, facing the lake, with their hands tied behind them. Typhon stands among them, along with a centaur, a faun, a gorgon, and the other two Nox Abyssae.

As Jaedis approaches he says, "Typhon, I'm afraid your friend has failed me."

Typhon blinks. "How unusual. She unleashed the Glimmerbeast, did she not?"

"The Glimmerbeast was destroyed. It appears as though a more *direct* approach will be required to deal with the rising threat in Armavir."

Typhon lowers his head. "I'm sorry to have disappointed you, my master."

"Hmph. Have you at least succeeded in finding the immortal queen?"

"Come and sssee for yourssself," the gorgon says, gesturing toward the people gathered on the shore. Her eyes and hair are hidden in the shadow of her cloak hood. "You know her faccce better than any of usss."

Jaedis walks to the front of the group and passes before them. The sapphire crowning his staff radiates with intense blue light to illuminate their faces. All of them are blond-haired women. Terrified, sniveling, pathetic, *mortal* blond women.

"She isn't here," Jaedis growls. "These prisoners are useless to me!"

"She's evaded us once again?" The centaur asks, voice husky. "Her newfound ability to teleport has proven to be quite a nuisance."

"Indeed," Jaedis agrees, scowling at the women.

"Master," Typhon says, "There is someone here who I believe you should speak with."

"Is that so?" Jaedis walks to the end of the group of prisoners, where Typhon stands behind the final captive. She's perhaps in her early thirties, blond like the rest of them. The tunic sleeve on her right arm has been torn off, and on her shoulder is a peculiar tattoo: small runic designs in the form of a crimson ring.

"There were two men in the village as well," Typhon says. "I kept their bodies here for you to see, rather than in the cottages with the others."

Jaedis glances at the two dead men beside the woman, both of whom have their right tunic sleeves ripped off to display identical crimson tattoos. His expression darkens. "Fellowship acolytes."

The captive woman speaks, her tone defiant, "That's right, sorcerer. You're not the *only* one who seeks the immortal queen."

"That's not unusual to me," Jaedis replies, kneeling down to her eye-level. "What irks me is that you got here first."

She spits in his face. "Of *course* we did. Our ranks swell with every passing season. There is no limit to our magical advancements. Soon, even *your* power will be made obsolete!"

Jaedis, expression unfazed, places the gem of his scepter under the woman's jaw. "Did you find her?"

"I'm not going to tell you anyth—"

The woman is decapitated by a blade of energy extending from the scepter.

The captives beside her shout in terror, inching away from the headless body that slumps on the ground beside them.

"This has been a waste of time," the faun says. "We're no closer to finding the immortal queen than when we first began!"

Jaedis stares at the ground beneath the Fellowship woman's body. His eyes twinkle.

"Master?" Typhon asks.

Jaedis moves the decapitated body aside to take a folded, brown-leather coat she had been kneeling on. He stands and unfurls it. The coat has a voluminous hood and extends down to the knees, perfect for getting caught in a downpour.

Melody's coat.

"It seems," Jaedis says, grinning at Typhon and the others, "this venture hasn't been a waste of time after all."

"Excellent," the centaur says with a smirk. "What are your orders, master?"

"My loyal, menacing champions," Jaedis addresses the centaur, the gorgon, and the faun, "see to it that our adversaries do not leave the central Armaviran mountains."

"Yes, master," the three say in unison. The gorgon transforms into a snake and wraps around the centaur's torso, and they depart, disappearing amongst the burning cottages with thundering hooves.

"Typhon, and my marvelous pets," Jaedis smiles at the Nox Abyssae, which gather around with eager yips and purrs. He drops the coat among them, and they bury their noses in it. "Find her, and bring her to me."

"Master," Typhon asks, "What of the captives?"

Jaedis glances briefly at the women on the lakeshore. "Leave them. They're not even worth the time it'd take to dispose of them."

The Nox Abyssae raise their heads, sniffing the air and waving their tendrils back and forth. One of them catches a scent on the wind, and with an excited howl, it takes off, running east along the lakeshore. The other two follow, howling in kind.

Jaedis looks at Typhon with eyes like daggers. "This task is far more important than the last. Do not disappoint me again."

"I will *not* fail," Typhon bows, disappearing amidst the shadows of the night.

Jaedis walks along the lakeshore, leaving the burning village and the miserable captives behind him. He says, "Here we are, at the crossroads of fate. The realm as we know it is about to change." He pauses to observe the reflection of the moon and stars on the surface of the lake. "Time is short. Time is very short, indeed."

"Have no fear, my faithful servant. Even with these setbacks, the stage is set for our greatest move yet. Tyrizah will be mine once again!"

Acknowledgments

FIRST AND FOREMOST, thank you to my amazing parents for believing in me. Not a day goes by when I'm not grateful to have a mom and dad who support me wholeheartedly in the dream that the Lord has given me. It really does mean the world to me.

Thank you to my friends and fellow writers at the San Diego Kingdom Writers Association, and especially to the directors, Brae, Jill, and Manna. Your instruction and guidance has proven invaluable in helping me write, edit, and publish my first epic fantasy novel. I look forward to partnering with you for many years to come!

To my beta readers—Jenny, Tyler, Jeff, Tiffany, Rikah, Jed, Sarah, Jan, and Rhonda—thank you for providing valuable insight and encouragement during beta-reads and professional edits, and for enduring my developmental info-dumps when I needed someone to share ideas with!

To everyone who gave to the professional editing fund, thank you for believing in me and this project enough to invest your hard-earned money during my time of need. The impending success and impact of *Chosen* will be as much your victory as it will be mine. I couldn't have done it without you!

To my editor, Zannie Carlson, thank you for challenging me to improve as a writer, and for bringing out more gold in *Chosen* than I even knew it had. I've learned so much in the months we spent working together.

To my housemates, past and present—Isaí, Pedro, Josh, Tyler, Andy, Bryton, Uriel, Greg, Tanner, Austin, Matt, and Jonathan—thank you for your patience and encouragement as I've worked many late nights and weekends to make this ambitious dream a reality. I appreciate you guys.

Finally, my highest thanks and praises go to my Lord Jesus Christ, the Great Prince, for whom and about whom this story has been written. Thank You for inviting me to write this inspiring, unique, and timely epic fantasy series about Your pursuit of Your Beloved. Despite the sacrifice of time, finances, and other opportunities, this has truly been the adventure of a lifetime, and I wouldn't trade it for anything else in the world. You are worthy of it all. May You be glorified, above all else, by the impact of *The Epic of Marindel*. Let's keep doing this thing, You and me!

About the Author

NATHAN KEYS IS an award-winning epic fantasy author based in southern California. It is his dream and vocation to write empowering stories that will not only captivate readers, but leave them with hope and purpose.

Nathan has been fascinated with storytelling from an early age. As a child, he invented worlds and creatures, played pretend, and told stories to anyone who would listen. He completed his first "novel," an 85,000-word fanfiction, at age 13. He spent high school summers creating plotlines for role-playing games on a forum site, where many concepts for characters, creatures, and kingdoms in *The Epic of Marindel* were first developed.

The Epic of Marindel: Chosen is his first published novel. The first of many.

In addition to writing, Nathan enjoys hiking, exercise, traveling, meeting random cats, and visiting coffee shops, breweries, and wineries with good friends.

Learn more about *The Epic of Marindel* by visiting www.nathankeys.com. You're also invited to follow Nathan's author journey on Facebook, Instagram, Goodreads, and Amazon. Onward and Upward!

Made in the USA
Middletown, DE
05 May 2024

53890165R00345